KT-389-711

RESERVE

ST. HELENS PUBLIC LIBRARIES

This book is due for return on or before the last date shown. Fines are
charged on overdue books. Renewal may be made by personal application,
post or telephone, quoting date, author, title and book number.

X37	– 3 FEB 2003	
28. APR 99	Bury	
13. MAY 98	SUBJECT TO EARLIER RECALL	
18. JUL	DSL 3/11/04	
29. SEP 00	19 OCT 2010	
22	ILL TAMESIDE	
02 OCT CL	Z495568	
28 JAN 2002	DUE 19.9.12	
18 FEB 2002		

TOLKIEN, J. R. R.

THE FELLOWSHIP OF THE RING

F95 160531

Community Services Library
01744 677898
communityservices@sthelens.gov.uk

ST. HELENS COMMUNITY LIBRARIES

3 8055 00343 5898

THE FELLOWSHIP OF THE RING

Other titles available in this series:

ISIS Clear Print

THE TWO TOWERS
THE RETURN OF THE KING

Windrush Large Print

THE HOBBIT

ISIS Audio

THE FELLOWSHIP OF THE RING
THE TWO TOWERS
THE RETURN OF THE KING

The Fellowship of the Ring

the Ring

Being the First Part of

THE LORD OF THE RINGS

J. R. R. TOLKIEN

ISIS
CLEAR TYPE
CLASSIC

ST. HELENS
COMMUNITY
LIBRARIES

ACC. No.
F95 160531

CLASS No.

Copyright © George Allen & Unwin (Publishers) Ltd, 1966

First published in Great Britain 1954 by George Allen & Unwin

Published in Large Print 1990 by Clio Press, 55 St Thomas' Street, Oxford, OX1 1JG, by arrangement with Unwin Hyman Ltd and Houghton Mifflin Co.

All rights reserved

British Library Cataloguing in Publication Data

Tolkien, J. R. R. (John Ronald Reuel) *1892-1973*
    The fellowship of the ring : being the first part of the Lord of the Rings.
    I. Title II. Series
    823.912 [F]

ISBN 1-85089-414-0

F ...

CLASS No.

Printed and bound by Hartnolls Ltd., Bodmin, Cornwall
Cover designed by CGS Studios, Cheltenham

THE LORD OF THE RINGS

Three Rings for the Elven-kings under the sky,
Seven for the Dwarf-lords in their halls of stone,
Nine for Mortal Men doomed to die,
One for the Dark Lord on his dark throne
In the Land of Mordor where the Shadows lie.
One Ring to rule them all, One Ring to find them,
One Ring to bring them all and in the darkness bind them
In the Land of Mordor where the Shadows lie.

FOREWORD

This tale grew in the telling, until it became a history of the Great War of the Ring and included many glimpses of the yet more ancient history that preceded it. It was begun soon after *The Hobbit* was written and before its publication in 1937; but I did not go on with this sequel, for I wished first to complete and set in order the mythology and legends of the Elder Days, which had then been taking shape for some years. I desired to do this for my own satisfaction, and I had little hope that other people would be interested in this work, especially since it was primarily linguistic in inspiration and was begun in order to provide the necessary background of "history" for Elvish tongues.

When those whose advice and opinion I sought corrected *little hope* to *no hope*, I went back to the sequel, encouraged by requests from readers for more information concerning hobbits and their adventures. But the story was drawn irresistibly towards the older world, and became an account, as it were, of its end and passing away before its beginning and middle had been told. The process had begun in the writing of *The Hobbit*, in which there were already some references to the older matter: Elrond, Gondolin, the High-elves, and the orcs, as well as glimpses that had arisen unbidden of things higher or deeper or darker than its surface: Durin, Moria, Gandalf, the Necromancer, the Ring. The discovery of the significance of these glimpses and of their relation to the ancient histories revealed the Third Age and its culmination in the War of the Ring.

Those who had asked for more information about hobbits eventually got it, but they had to wait a long time; for the composition of *The Lord of the Rings* went on at intervals during the years 1936 to 1949, a period in which I had many duties that I did not neglect, and many other interests as a learner and teacher that often absorbed me. The delay was, of course, also increased by the outbreak of war in 1939, by the end of which year the tale had not yet reached the end of Book I. In spite of the darkness of the next five years I found that the story could not now be wholly abandoned, and I plodded on, mostly by night, till I stood by Balin's tomb in Moria. There I halted for a long while. It was almost a year later when I went on and so came to Lothlórien and the Great River late in 1941. In the next year I wrote the first drafts of the matter that now stands as Book III, and the beginnings of Chapters 1 and 3 of Book V; and there as the beacons flared in Anórien and Théoden came to Harrowdale I stopped. Foresight had failed and there was no time for thought.

It was during 1944 that, leaving the loose ends and perplexities of a war which it was my task to conduct, or at least to report, I forced myself to tackle the journey of Frodo to Mordor. These chapters, eventually to become Book IV, were written and sent out as a serial to my son, Christopher, then in South Africa with the R.A.F. Nonetheless it took another five years before the tale was brought to its present end; in that time I changed my house, my chair, and my college, and the days though less dark were no less laborious. Then when the "end" had at last been reached the whole story had to be revised, and indeed largely re-written backwards. And it had to be typed, and re-typed: by me; the cost of professional typing by the ten-fingered was beyond my means.

The Lord of the Rings has been read by many people since it finally appeared in print; and I should like to say something here with reference to the many opinions or guesses that I have received or have read concerning the motives and meaning of the tale. The prime motive was the desire of a tale-teller to try his hand at a really long story that would hold the attention of readers, amuse them, delight them, and at times maybe excite them or deeply move them. As a guide I had only my own feelings for what is appealing or moving, and for many the guide was inevitably often at fault. Some who have read the book, or at any rate have reviewed it, have found it boring, absurd, or contemptible; and I have no cause to complain, since I have similar opinions of their works, or of the kinds of writing that they evidently prefer. But even from the points of view of many who have enjoyed my story there is much that fails to please. It is perhaps not possible in a long tale to please everybody at all points, nor to displease everybody at the same points; for I find from the letters that I have received that the passages or chapters that are to some a blemish are all by others specially approved. The most critical reader of all, myself, now finds many defects, minor and major, but being fortunately under no obligation either to review the book or to write it again, he will pass over these in silence, except one that has been noted by others: the book is too short.

As for any inner meaning or "message", it has in the intention of the author none. It is neither allegorical nor topical. As the story grew it put down roots (into the past) and threw out unexpected branches; but its main theme was settled from the outset by the inevitable choice of the Ring as the link between it and *The Hobbit*. The crucial chapter, "The Shadow of the Past", is one of the oldest parts of the tale. It was written long before the foreshadow of 1939 had yet become a threat of inevitable disaster, and from that point the story would have developed along essentially the same lines, if that disaster had been averted. Its sources are things long before in mind, or in some cases already written, and little or nothing in it was modified by the war that began in 1939 or its sequels.

The real war does not resemble the legendary war in its process or its conclusion. If it had inspired or directed the development of the legend, then certainly the Ring would have been seized and used against Sauron; he would not have been annihilated but enslaved, and Barad-dûr would not have been destroyed but occupied. Saruman, failing to get possession of the Ring, would in the confusion and treacheries of the time have found in Mordor the missing links in his own researches into Ring-lore, and before long he would have made a Great Ring of his own with which to challenge the self-styled Ruler of Middle-earth. In that conflict both sides would have held hobbits in hatred and contempt: they would not long have survived even as slaves.

Other arrangements could be devised according to the tastes or views of those who like allegory or topical reference. But I cordially dislike allegory in all its manifestations, and always have done so since I grew old and wary enough to detect its presence. I much prefer history, true or feigned, with its varied applicability to the thought and experience of readers. I think that many confuse "applicability" with "allegory"; but the one resides in the freedom of the reader, and the other in the purposed domination of the author.

An author cannot of course remain wholly unaffected by his experience, but the ways in which a story-germ uses the soil of experience are extremely complex, and attempts to define the process are at best guesses from evidence that is inadequate and ambiguous. It is also false, though naturally attractive, when the lives of an author and critic have overlapped, to suppose that the movements of thought or the events of times common to both were necessarily the most powerful influences. One has indeed personally to come under the shadow of war to feel fully its oppression; but as the years go by it seems now often forgotten that to be caught in youth by 1914 was no less hideous an experience than to be involved in 1939 and the following years. By 1918 all but one of my close friends were dead. Or to take a less grievous matter: it has been supposed by some that "The Scouring of the Shire" reflects the situation in England at the time when I was finishing my tale. It does not. It is an essential part of the plot, foreseen from the outset, though in the event modified by the character of Saruman as developed in the story without, need I say, any allegorical significance or contemporary political reference whatsoever. It has indeed some basis in experience, though slender (for the economic situation was entirely different), and much further back. The country in which I lived in childhood was being shabbily destroyed before I was ten, in days when motor-cars were rare objects (I had never seen one) and men were still building suburban railways. Recently I saw in a paper a picture of the last decrepitude of the once thriving corn-mill beside its pool that long ago seemed to me so important. I never liked the looks of the Young miller, but his father, the Old miller, had a black beard, and he was not named Sandyman.

The Lord of the Rings is now issued in a new edition, and the opportunity has been taken of revising it. A number of errors and inconsistencies that still remained in the text have been corrected, and an attempt has been made to provide information on a few points which attentive readers have raised. I have considered all their comments and enquiries, and if some seem to have been passed over that may be because I have failed to keep my notes in order; but many enquiries could only be answered by additional appendices, or indeed by the production of an accessory volume containing much of the material that I did not include in the original edition, in particular more detailed linguistic information. In the meantime this edition offers this Foreword, an addition to the Prologue, and some notes.

CONTENTS

Foreword
Prologue *Concerning Hobbits, and other matters*

BOOK ONE

BOOK TWO

PROLOGUE

I
Concerning Hobbits

This book is largely concerned with Hobbits, and from its pages a reader may discover much of their character and a little of their history. Further information will also be found in the selection from the Red Book of Westmarch that has already been published, under the title of *The Hobbit*. That story was derived from the earlier chapters of the Red Book, composed by Bilbo himself, the first Hobbit to become famous in the world at large, and called by him *There and Back Again*, since they told of his journey into the East and his return: an adventure which later involved all the Hobbits in the great events of that Age that are here related.

Many, however, may wish to know more about this remarkable people from the outset, while some may not possess the earlier book. For such readers a few notes on the more important points are here collected from Hobbit-lore, and the first adventure is briefly recalled.

Hobbits are an unobtrusive but very ancient people, more numerous formerly than they are today; for they love peace and quiet and good tilled earth: a well-ordered and well-farmed countryside was their favourite haunt. They do not and did not understand or like machines more complicated than a forge-bellows, a water-mill, or a hand-loom, though they were skilful with tools. Even in ancient days they were, as a rule, shy of "the Big Folk", as they call us, and now they avoid us with dismay and are becoming hard to find. They are quick of hearing and sharp-eyed, and though they are inclined to be fat and do not hurry unnecessarily, they are nonetheless nimble and deft in their movements. They possessed from the first the art of disappearing swiftly and silently, when large folk whom they do not wish to meet come blundering by; and this art they have developed until to Men it may seem magical. But Hobbits have never, in fact, studied magic of any kind, and their elusiveness is due solely to a professional skill that heredity and practice, and a close friendship with the earth, have rendered inimitable by bigger and clumsier races.

For they are a little people, smaller than Dwarves: less stout and stocky, that is, even when they are not actually much shorter. Their height is variable, ranging between two and four feet of our measure. They seldom now reach three feet; but they have dwindled, they say, and in ancient days they were taller. According to the Red Book, Bandobras Took (Bull-roarer), son of Isengrim the Second, was four foot five and able to ride a horse. He was surpassed in all Hobbit records only by two famous characters of old; but that curious matter is dealt with in this book.

As for the Hobbits of the Shire, with whom these tales are concerned, in the days of their peace and prosperity they were a merry folk. They dressed in bright colours, being notably fond of yellow and green; but they seldom wore shoes, since their feet had tough leathery soles and were clad in a thick curling hair, much like the hair of their heads, which was commonly brown. Thus, the only craft little practised among them was shoe-making; but they had long and skilful fingers and could make many other useful and comely things. Their faces were as a rule good-natured rather than beautiful, broad, bright-eyed, red-cheeked, with mouths apt to laughter, and to eating and drinking. And laugh they did, and eat, and drink, often and heartily, being fond of simple jests at all times, and of six meals a day (when they could get them). They were hospitable and delighted in parties, and in presents, which they gave away freely and eagerly accepted.

It is plain indeed that in spite of later estrangement Hobbits are relatives of ours: far nearer to us than Elves, or even than Dwarves. Of old they spoke the languages of Men, after their own fashion, and liked and disliked much the same things as Men did. But what exactly our relationship is can no longer be discovered. The beginning of Hobbits lies far back in the Elder Days that are now lost and forgotten. Only the Elves still preserve any records of that vanished time, and their traditions are concerned almost entirely with their own history, in which Men appear seldom and Hobbits are not mentioned at all. Yet it is clear that Hobbits had, in fact, lived quietly in Middle-earth for many long years before other folk became even aware of them. And the world being after all full of strange creatures beyond count, these little people seemed of very little importance. But in the days of Bilbo, and of Frodo his heir, they suddenly became, by no wish of their own, both important and renowned, and troubled the counsels of the Wise and the Great.

Those days, the Third Age of Middle-earth, are now long past, and the shape of all lands has been changed; but the regions in which Hobbits then lived were doubtless the same as those in which they still linger: the North-West of the Old World, east of the Sea. Of their original home the Hobbits in Bilbo's time preserved no knowledge. A love of learning (other than genealogical lore) was far from general among them, but there remained still a few in the older families who studied their own books, and even gathered reports of old times and distant lands from Elves, Dwarves, and Men. Their own records began only after the settlement of the Shire, and their most ancient legends hardly looked further back than their Wandering Days. It is clear, nonetheless, from these legends, and from the evidence of their peculiar words and customs, that like many other folk Hobbits had in the distant past moved westward. Their earliest tales seem to glimpse a time when they dwelt in the upper vales of Anduin, between the eaves of Greenwood the

Great and the Misty Mountains. Why they later undertook the hard and perilous crossing of the mountains into Eriador is no longer certain. Their own accounts speak of the multiplying of Men in the land, and of a shadow that fell on the forest, so that it became darkened and its new name was Mirkwood.

Before the crossing of the mountains the Hobbits had already become divided into three somewhat different breeds: Harfoots, Stoors, and Fallohides. The Harfoots were browner of skin, smaller, and shorter, and they were beardless and bootless; their hands and feet were neat and nimble; and they preferred highlands and hillsides. The Stoors were broader, heavier in build; their feet and hands were larger, and they preferred flat lands and riversides. The Fallohides were fairer of skin and also of hair, and they were taller and slimmer than the others; they were lovers of trees and of woodlands.

The Harfoots had much to do with Dwarves in ancient times, and long lived in the foothills of the mountains. They moved westward early, and roamed over Eriador as far as Weathertop while the others were still in Wilderland. They were the most normal and representative variety of Hobbit, and far the most numerous. They were the most inclined to settle in one place, and longest preserved their ancestral habit of living in tunnels and holes.

The Stoors lingered long by the banks of the Great River Anduin, and were less shy of Men. They came west after the Harfoots and followed the course of the Loudwater southwards; and there many of them long dwelt between Tharbad and the borders of Dunland before they moved north again.

The Fallohides, the least numerous, were a northerly branch. They were more friendly with Elves than the other Hobbits were, and had more skill in language and song than in handicrafts; and of old they preferred hunting to tilling. They crossed the mountains north of Rivendell and came down the River Hoarwell. In Eriador they soon mingled with the other kinds that had preceded them, but being somewhat bolder and more adventurous, they were often found as leaders or chieftains among clans of Harfoots or Stoors. Even in Bilbo's time the strong Fallohidish strain could still be noted among the greater families, such as the Tooks and the Masters of Buckland.

In the westlands of Eriador, between the Misty Mountains and the Mountains of Lune, the Hobbits found both Men and Elves. Indeed, a remnant still dwelt there of the Dúnedain, the kings of Men that came over the Sea out of Westernesse; but they were dwindling fast and the lands of their North Kingdom were falling far and wide into waste. There was room and to spare for incomers, and ere long the Hobbits began to settle in ordered communities. Most of their earlier settlements had long disappeared and been forgotten in Bilbo's time; but one of the first to become important still endured, though reduced in size; this was at Bree and in the Chetwood that lay round about, some forty miles east of the Shire.

It was in these early days, doubtless, that the Hobbits learned their letters and began to write after the manner of the Dúnedain, who had in their turn long before learned the art from the Elves. And in those days also they forgot whatever languages they had used before, and spoke ever after the Common Speech, the Westron as it was named, that was current through all the lands of the kings from Arnor to Gondor, and about all the coasts of the Sea from Belfalas to Lune. Yet they kept a few words of their own, as well as their own names of months and days, and a great store of personal names out of the past.

About this time legend among the Hobbits first becomes history with a reckoning of years. For it was in the one thousand six hundred and first year of the Third Age that the Fallohide brothers, Marcho and Blanco, set out from Bree; and having obtained permission from the high king at Fornost,* they crossed the brown river Baranduin with a great following

* As the records of Gondor relate this was Argeleb II, the twentieth of the Northern line, which came to an end with Arvedui three hundred years later.

of Hobbits. They passed over the Bridge of Stonebows, that had been built in the days of the power of the North Kingdom, and they took all the land beyond to dwell in, between the river and the Far Downs. All that was demanded of them was that they should keep the Great Bridge in repair, and all other bridges and roads, speed the king's messengers, and acknowledge his lordship.

Thus began the *Shire-reckoning*, for the year of the crossing of the Brandywine (as the Hobbits turned the name) became Year One of the Shire, and all later dates were reckoned from it.† At once the western Hobbits fell in love with their new land, and they remained there, and soon passed once more out of the history of Men and of Elves. While there was still a king they were in name his subjects, but they were, in fact, ruled by their own chieftains and meddled not at all with events in the world outside. To the last battle at Fornost with the Witch-lord of Angmar they sent some bowmen to the aid of the king, or so they maintained, though no tales of Men record it. But in that war the North Kingdom ended; and then the Hobbits took the land for their own, and they chose from their own chiefs a Thain to hold the authority of the king that was gone. There for a thousand years they were little troubled by wars, and they prospered and multiplied after the Dark Plague (S.R. 37) until the disaster of the Long Winter and the famine that followed it. Many thousands then perished, but the Days of Dearth (1158-60) were at the time of this tale long past and the Hobbits had again become accustomed to plenty. The land was rich and kindly, and though it had long been deserted when they entered it, it had before been well tilled, and there the king had once had many farms, cornlands, vineyards, and woods.

Forty leagues it stretched from the Far Downs to the Brandywine Bridge, and fifty from the northern moors to the marshes in the south. The Hobbits named it the Shire, as the

---

† Thus, the years of the Third Age in the reckoning of the Elves and the Dúnedain may be found by adding 1600 to the dates of Shire-reckoning.

region of the authority of their Thain, and a district of well-ordered business; and there in that pleasant corner of the world they plied their well-ordered business of living, and they heeded less and less the world outside where dark things moved, until they came to think that peace and plenty were the rule in Middle-earth and the right of all sensible folk. They forgot or ignored what little they had ever known of the Guardians, and of the labours of those that made possible the long peace of the Shire. They were, in fact, sheltered, but they had ceased to remember it.

At no time had Hobbits of any kind been warlike, and they had never fought among themselves. In olden days they had, of course, been often obliged to fight to maintain themselves in a hard world; but in Bilbo's time that was very ancient history. The last battle, before this story opens, and indeed the only one that had ever been fought within the borders of the Shire, was beyond living memory: the Battle of Greenfields, S.R. 1147, in which Bandobras Took routed an invasion of Orcs. Even the weathers had grown milder, and the wolves that had once come ravening out of the North in bitter white winters were now only a grandfather's tale. So, though there was still some store of weapons in the Shire, these were used mostly as trophies, hanging above hearths or on walls, or gathered into the museum at Michel Delving. The Mathom-house it was called; for anything that Hobbits had no immediate use for, but were unwilling to throw away, they called a *mathom*. Their dwellings were apt to become rather crowded with mathoms, and many of the presents that passed from hand to hand were of that sort.

Nonetheless, ease and peace had left this people still curiously tough. They were, if it came to it, difficult to daunt or to kill; and they were, perhaps, so unwearyingly fond of good things not least because they could, when put to it, do without them, and could survive rough handling by grief, foe, or weather in a way that astonished those who did not know them well and looked no further than their bellies and their well-fed faces. Though slow to quarrel, and for sport killing nothing that lived, they were doughty at bay, and at need could still handle arms. They shot well with the bow, for they were keen-eyed and sure at the mark. Not only with bows and arrows. If any Hobbit stooped for a stone, it was well to get quickly under cover, as all trespassing beasts knew very well.

All Hobbits had originally lived in holes in the ground, or so they believed, and in such dwellings they still felt most at home; but in the course of time they had been obliged to adopt other forms of abode. Actually in the Shire in Bilbo's days it was, as a rule, only the richest and the poorest Hobbits that maintained the old custom. The poorest went on living in burrows of the most primitive kind, mere holes indeed, with only one window or none; while the well-to-do still constructed more luxurious versions of the simple diggings of old. But suitable sites for these large and ramifying tunnels (or *smials* as they called them) were not everywhere to be found; and in the flats and the low-lying districts the Hobbits, as they multiplied, began to build above ground. Indeed, even in the hilly regions and the older villages, such as Hobbiton or Tuckborough, or in the chief township of the Shire, Michel Delving on the White Downs, there were now many houses of wood, brick, or stone. These were specially favoured by millers, smiths, ropers, and cartwrights, and others of that sort; for even when they had holes to live in, Hobbits had long been accustomed to build sheds and workshops.

The habit of building farm-houses and barns was said to have begun among the inhabitants of the Marish down by the Brandywine. The Hobbits of that quarter, the Eastfarthing, were rather large and heavy-legged, and they wore dwarf-boots in muddy weather. But they were well known to be Stoors in a large part of their blood, as indeed was shown by the down that many grew on their chins. No Harfoot or Fallohide had any trace of a beard. Indeed, the folk of the Marish, and of Buckland, east of the River, which they afterwards occupied, came for the most part later into the Shire up from south-away; and they still had many peculiar names and strange words not found elsewhere in the Shire.

It is probable that the craft of building, as many other crafts beside, was derived from the Dúnedain. But the Hobbits may have learned it direct from the Elves, the teachers of Men in their youth. For the Elves of the High Kindred had not yet forsaken Middle-earth, and they dwelt still at that time at the Grey Havens away to the west, and in other places within reach of the Shire. Three Elf-towers of immemorial age were still to be seen on the Tower Hills beyond the western marches. They shone far off in the moonlight. The tallest was furthest away, standing alone upon a green mound. The Hobbits of the Westfarthing said that one could see the Sea from the top of that tower; but no Hobbit had ever been known to climb it. Indeed, few Hobbits had ever seen or sailed upon the Sea, and fewer still had ever returned to report it. Most Hobbits regarded even rivers and small boats with deep misgivings, and not many of them could swim. And as the days of the Shire lengthened they spoke less and less with the Elves, and grew afraid of them, and distrustful of those that had dealings with them; and the Sea became a word of fear among them, and a token of death, and they turned their faces away from the hills in the west.

The craft of building may have come from Elves or Men, but the Hobbits used it in their own fashion. They did not go in for towers. Their houses were usually long, low, and comfortable. The oldest kind were, indeed, no more than built imitations of *smials*, thatched with dry grass or straw, or roofed with turves, and having walls somewhat bulged. That stage, however, belonged to the early days of the Shire, and hobbit-building had long since been altered, improved by devices, learned from Dwarves, or discovered by themselves. A preference for round windows, and even round doors, was the chief remaining peculiarity of hobbit-architecture.

The houses and the holes of Shire-hobbits were often large, and inhabited by large families. (Bilbo and Frodo Baggins were as bachelors very exceptional, as they were also in many other ways, such as their friendship with Elves.) Sometimes, as in the case of the Tooks of Great Smials, or the Brandybucks of Brandy Hall, many generations of relatives lived in (comparative) peace together in one ancestral and many-tunnelled mansion. All Hobbits were, in any case, clannish and reckoned up their relationships with great care. They drew long and elaborate family-trees with innumerable branches. In dealing with Hobbits it is important to remember who is related to whom, and in what degree. It would be impossible in this book to set out a family-tree that included even the more important members of the more important families at the time which these tales tell of. The genealogical trees at the end of the Red Book of Westmarch are a small book in themselves, and all but Hobbits would find them exceedingly dull. Hobbits delighted in such things, if they were accurate: they liked to have books filled with things that they already knew, set out fair and square with no contradictions.

2
Concerning Pipe-weed

There is another thing about the Hobbits of old that must be mentioned, an astonishing habit: they imbibed or inhaled, through pipes of clay or wood, the smoke of the burning leaves of a herb, which they called *pipe-weed* or *leaf*, a variety probably of *Nicotiana*. A great deal of mystery surrounds the origin of this peculiar custom, or "art" as the Hobbits preferred to call it. All that could be discovered about it in antiquity was put together by Meriadoc Brandybuck (later Master of Buckland), and since he and the tobacco of the Southfarthing play a part in the history that follows, his remarks in the introduction to his *Herblore of the Shire* may be quoted.

"This," he says, "is the one art that we can certainly claim to be our own invention. When Hobbits first began to smoke is not known, all the legends and family histories take it for granted; for ages folk in the Shire smoked various herbs, some fouler, some sweeter. But all accounts agree that Tobold

Hornblower of Longbottom in the Southfarthing first grew the true pipe-weed in his gardens in the days of Isengrim the Second, about the year 1070 of Shire-reckoning. The best home-grown still comes from that district, especially the varieties now known as Longbottom Leaf, Old Toby, and Southern Star.

"How Old Toby came by the plant is not recorded, for to his dying day he would not tell. He knew much about herbs, but he was no traveller. It is said that in his youth he went often to Bree, though he certainly never went further from the Shire than that. It is thus quite possible that he learned of this plant in Bree, where now, at any rate, it grows well on the south slopes of the hill. The Bree-hobbits claim to have been the first actual smokers of the pipe-weed. They claim, of course, to have done everything before the people of the Shire, whom they refer to as 'colonists'; but in this case their claim is, I think, likely to be true. And certainly it was from Bree that the art of smoking the genuine weed spread in the recent centuries among Dwarves and such other folk, Rangers, Wizards, or wanderers, as still passed to and fro through that ancient road-meeting. The home and centre of the art is thus to be found in the old inn of Bree, *The Prancing Pony*, that has been kept by the family of Butterbur from time beyond record.

"All the same, observations that I have made on my own many journeys south have convinced me that the weed itself is not native to our part of the world, but came northward from the lower Anduin, whither it was, I suspect, originally brought over Sea by the Men of Westernesse. It grows abundantly in Gondor, and there is richer and larger than in the North, where it is never found wild, and flourishes only in warm sheltered places like Longbottom. The Men of Gondor call it *sweet galenas*, and esteem it only for the fragrance of its flowers. From that land it must have been carried up the Greenway during the long centuries between the coming of Elendil and our own days. But even the Dúnedain of Gondor allow us this credit: Hobbits first put it into pipes. Not even the Wizards first thought of that before we did. Though one Wizard that I knew took up the art long ago, and became as skilful in it as in all other things that he put his mind to."

3
Of the Ordering of the Shire

The Shire was divided into four quarters, the Farthings already referred to, North, South, East, and West; and these again each into a number of folklands, which still bore the names of some of the old leading families, although by the time of this history these names were no longer found only in their proper folklands. Nearly all Tooks still lived in the Tookland, but that was not true of many other families, such as the Bagginses or the Boffins. Outside the Farthings were the East and West Marches: the Buckland (I 108); and the Westmarch added to the Shire in S.R. 1462.

The Shire at this time had hardly any "government". Families for the most part managed their own affairs. Growing food and eating it occupied most of their time. In other matters they were, as a rule, generous and not greedy, but contented and moderate, so that estates, farms, workshops, and small trades tended to remain unchanged for generations.

There remained, of course, the ancient tradition concerning the high king at Fornost, or Norbury as they called it, away north of the Shire. But there had been no king for nearly a thousand years, and even the ruins of Kings' Norbury were covered with grass. Yet the Hobbits still said of wild folk and wicked things (such as trolls) that they had not heard of the king. For they attributed to the king of old all their essential laws; and usually they kept the laws of free will, because they were The Rules (as they said), both ancient and just.

It is true that the Took family had long been pre-eminent; for the office of Thain had passed to them (from the Oldbucks) some centuries before, and the chief Took had borne that title ever since. The Thain was the master of the Shire-moot, and captain of the Shire-muster and the Hobbitry-in-arms, but as muster and moot were only held in times of emergency, which no longer occurred, the Thainship had ceased to be more than a nominal dignity. The Took family was still, indeed, accorded a special respect, for it remained both numerous and exceedingly wealthy, and was liable to produce in every generation strong characters of peculiar habits and even adventurous temperament. The latter qualities, however, were now rather tolerated (in the rich) than generally approved. The custom endured, nonetheless, of referring to the head of the family as The Took, and of adding to his name, if required, a number: such as Isengrim the Second, for instance.

The only real official in the Shire at this date was the Mayor of Michel Delving (or of the Shire), who was elected every seven years at the Free Fair on the White Downs at the Lithe, that is at Midsummer. As mayor almost his only duty was to preside at banquets, given on the Shire-holidays, which occurred at frequent intervals. But the offices of Postmaster and First Shirriff were attached to the mayoralty, so that he managed both the Messenger Service and the Watch. These were the only Shire-services, and the Messengers were the most numerous, and much the busier of the two. By no means all Hobbits were lettered, but those who were wrote constantly to all their friends (and a selection of their relations) who lived further off than an afternoon's walk.

The Shirriffs was the name that the Hobbits gave to their police, or the nearest equivalent that they possessed. They had, of course, no uniforms (such things being quite unknown), only a feather in their caps; and they were in practice rather haywards than policemen, more concerned with the strayings of beasts than of people. There were in all the Shire only twelve of them, three in each Farthing, for Inside Work. A rather larger body, varying at need, was employed to "beat the bounds", and to see that Outsiders of any kind, great or small, did not make themselves a nuisance.

At the time when this story begins the Bounders, as they were called, had been greatly increased. There were many reports and complaints of strange persons and creatures prowling about the borders, or over them: the first sign that all was not quite as it should be, and always had been except in tales and legends of long ago. Few heeded the sign, and not even Bilbo yet had any notion of what it portended. Sixty years had passed since he set out on his memorable journey, and he was old even for Hobbits, who reached a hundred as often as not; but much evidently still remained of the considerable wealth that he had brought back. How much or how little he revealed to no one, not even to Frodo his favourite "nephew". And he still kept secret the ring that he had found.

4

Of the Finding of the Ring

As is told in *The Hobbit*, there came one day to Bilbo's door the great Wizard, Gandalf the Grey, and thirteen dwarves with him: none other, indeed, than Thorin Oakenshield, descendant of kings, and his twelve companions in exile. With them he set out, to his own lasting astonishment, on a morning of April, it being then the year 1341 Shire-reckoning, on a quest of great treasure, the dwarf-hoards of the Kings under the Mountain, beneath Erebor in Dale, far off in the East. The quest was successful, and the Dragon that guarded the hoard was destroyed. Yet, though before all was won the Battle of Five Armies was fought, and Thorin was slain, and many deeds of renown were done, the matter would scarcely have concerned later history, or earned more than a note in the long annals of the Third Age, but for an "accident" by the way. The party was assailed by Orcs in a high pass of the Misty Mountains as they went towards Wilderland; and so it happened that Bilbo was lost for a while in the black orc-mines deep under the mountains, and there, as he groped in vain in the dark, he put his hand on a ring, lying on the floor of a tunnel. He put it in his pocket. It seemed then like mere luck.

Trying to find his way out, Bilbo went on down to the roots of the mountains, until he could go no further. At the bottom of the tunnel lay a cold lake far from the light, and on an island of rock in the water lived Gollum. He was a loathsome little creature: he paddled a small boat with his large flat feet, peering with pale luminous eyes and catching blind fish with long fingers, and eating them raw. He ate any living thing, even orc, if he could catch it and strangle it without a struggle. He possessed a secret treasure that had come to him long ages ago, when he lived still in the light: a ring of gold that made its wearer invisible. It was the one thing he loved, his "precious", and he talked to it, even when it was not with him. For he kept it hidden safe in a hole on his island, except when he was hunting or spying on the orcs of the mines.

Maybe he would have attacked Bilbo at once, if the ring had been on him when they met; but it was not, and the hobbit held in his hand an Elvish knife, which served him as a sword. So to gain time Gollum challenged Bilbo to the Riddle-game, saying that if he asked a riddle which Bilbo could not guess, then he would kill him and eat him; but if Bilbo defeated him, then he would do as Bilbo wished: he would lead him to a way out of the tunnels.

Since he was lost in the dark without hope, and could neither go on nor back, Bilbo accepted the challenge; and they asked one another many riddles. In the end Bilbo won the game, more by luck (as it seemed) than by wits; for he was stumped at last for a riddle to ask, and cried out, as his hand came upon the ring he had picked up and forgotten: *What have I got in my pocket?* This Gollum failed to answer, though he demanded three guesses.

The Authorities, it is true, differ whether this last question was a mere "question" and not a "riddle" according to the strict rules of the Game; but all agree that, after accepting it and trying to guess the answer, Gollum was bound by his promise. And Bilbo pressed him to keep his word; for the thought came to him that this slimy creature might prove false, even though such promises were held sacred, and of old all but the wickedest things feared to break them. But after ages alone in the dark Gollum's heart was black, and treachery was in it. He slipped away, and returned to his island, of which Bilbo knew nothing, not far off in the dark water. There, he thought, lay his ring. He was hungry now, and angry, and once his "precious" was with him he would not fear any weapon at all.

But the ring was not on the island; he had lost it, it was gone. His screech sent a shiver down Bilbo's back, though he did not yet understand what had happened. But Gollum had at last leaped to a guess, too late. *What has it got in its pocketses?* he cried. The light in his eyes was like a green flame as he sped back to murder the hobbit and recover his "precious". Just in time Bilbo saw his peril, and he fled blindly up the passage away from the water; and once more he was saved by his luck. For as he ran he put his hand in his pocket, and the ring slipped quietly on to his finger. So it was that Gollum passed him without seeing him, and went on to guard the way out, lest the "thief" should escape. Warily Bilbo followed him, as he went along, cursing, and talking to himself about his "precious"; from which talk at last even Bilbo guessed the truth, and hope came to him in the darkness: he himself had found the marvellous ring and a chance of escape from the orcs and from Gollum.

At length they came to a halt before an unseen opening that led to the lower gates of the mines, on the eastward side of the mountains. There Gollum crouched at bay, smelling and listening; and Bilbo was tempted to slay him with his sword. But pity stayed him, and though he kept the ring, in which his only hope lay, he would not use it to help him kill the wretched creature at a disadvantage. In the end, gathering his courage, he leaped over Gollum in the dark, and fled away down the passage, pursued by his enemy's cries of hate and despair: *Thief, thief! Baggins! We hates it for ever!*

Now it is a curious fact that this is not the story as Bilbo first told it to his companions. To them his account was that Gollum had promised to give him a *present*, if he won the game; but when Gollum went to fetch it from his island he found the treasure was gone: a magic ring, which had been given to him long ago on his birthday. Bilbo guessed that this was the very ring that he had found, and as he had won the game, it was already his by right. But being in a tight place, he said nothing about it, and made Gollum show him the way out, as a reward instead of a present. This account Bilbo set down in his memoirs, and he seems never to have altered it himself, not even after the Council of Elrond. Evidently it still appeared in the original Red Book, as it did in several of the copies and abstracts. But many copies contain the true account (as an alternative), derived no doubt from notes by Frodo or Samwise, both of whom learned the truth, though they seem to have been unwilling to delete anything actually written by the old hobbit himself.

Gandalf, however, disbelieved Bilbo's first story, as soon as he heard it, and he continued to be very curious about the ring. Eventually he got the true tale out of Bilbo after much questioning, which for a while strained their friendship; but the wizard seemed to think the truth important. Though he did not say so to Bilbo, he also thought it important, and disturbing, to find that the good hobbit had not told the truth from the first: quite contrary to his habit. The idea of a "present" was not mere hobbitlike invention, all the same. It was suggested to Bilbo, as he confessed, by Gollum's talk that he overheard; for Gollum did, in fact, call the ring his "birthday present", many times. That also Gandalf thought strange and suspicious; but he did not discover the truth in this point for many more years, as will be seen in this book.

Of Bilbo's later adventures little more need be said here. With the help of the ring he escaped from the orc-guards at the gate and rejoined his companions. He used the ring many times on his quest, chiefly for the help of his friends; but he kept it secret from them as long as he could. After his return to his home he never spoke of it again to anyone, save Gandalf and

Frodo; and no one else in the Shire knew of its existence, or so he believed. Only to Frodo did he show the account of his Journey that he was writing.

His sword, Sting, Bilbo hung over his fireplace, and his coat of marvellous mail, the gift of the Dwarves from the Dragon-hoard, he lent to a museum, to the Michel Delving Mathom-house in fact. But he kept in a drawer at Bag End the old cloak and hood that he had worn on his travels; and the ring, secured by a fine chain, remained in his pocket.

He returned to his home at Bag End on June the 22nd in his fifty-second year (S.R. 1342), and nothing very notable occurred in the Shire until Mr. Baggins began the preparations for the celebration of his hundred-and-eleventh birthday (S.R. 1401). At this point this History begins.

NOTE ON THE SHIRE RECORDS

At the end of the Third Age the part played by the Hobbits in the great events that led to the inclusion of the Shire in the Reunited Kingdom awakened among them a more widespread interest in their own history; and many of their traditions, up to that time still mainly oral, were collected and written down. The greater families were also concerned with events in the Kingdom at large, and many of their members studied its ancient histories and legends. By the end of the first century of the Fourth Age there were already to be found in the Shire several libraries that contained many historical books and records.

The largest of these collections were probably at Under-towers, at Great Smials, and at Brandy Hall. This account of the end of the Third Age is drawn mainly from the Red Book of Westmarch. That most important source for the history of the War of the Ring was so called because it was long preserved at Undertowers, the home of the Fairbairns, Wardens of the Westmarch.* It was in origin Bilbo's private diary, which he

* See Appendix B: annals *1451, 1462, 1482*; and note at end of Appendix C.

took with him to Rivendell. Frodo brought it back to the Shire, together with many loose leaves of notes, and during S.R. 1420-1 he nearly filled its pages with his account of the War. But annexed to it and preserved with it, probably in a single red case, were the three large volumes, bound in red leather, that Bilbo gave to him as a parting gift. To these four volumes there was added in Westmarch a fifth containing commentaries, genealogies, and various other matter concerning the hobbit members of the Fellowship.

The original Red Book has not been preserved, but many copies were made, especially of the first volume, for the use of the descendants of the children of Master Samwise. The most important copy, however, had a different history. It was kept at Great Smials, but it was written in Gondor, probably at the request of the great-grandson of Peregrin, and completed in S.R. 1592 (F.A. 172). Its southern scribe appended this note: Findegil, King's Writer, finished this work in IV 172. It is an exact copy in all details of the Thain's Book in Minas Tirith. That book was a copy, made at the request of King Elessar, of the Red Book of the Periannath, and was brought to him by the Thain Peregrin when he retired to Gondor in IV 64.

The Thain's book was thus the first copy made of the Red Book and contained much that was later omitted or lost. In Minas Tirith it received much annotation, and many corrections, especially of names, words, and quotations in the Elvish languages; and there was added to it an abbreviated version of those parts of *The Tale of Aragorn* and *Arwen* which lie outside the account of the War. The full tale is stated to have been written by Barahir, grandson of the Steward Faramir, some time after the passing of the King. But the chief importance of Findegil's copy is that it alone contains the whole of Bilbo's "Translations from the Elvish". These three volumes were found to be a work of great skill and learning in which, between 1403 and 1418, he had used all the sources available to him in Rivendell, both living and written. But since they were little used by Frodo, being almost entirely concerned with the Elder

Days, no more is said of them here.

Since Meriadoc and Peregrin became the heads of their great families, and at the same time kept up their connexions with Rohan and Gondor, the libraries at Bucklebury and Tuckborough contained much that did not appear in the Red Book. In Brandy Hall there were many works dealing with Eriador and the history of Rohan. Some of these were composed or begun by Meriadoc himself, though in the Shire he was chiefly remembered for his *Herblore of the Shire*, and for his *Reckoning of Years* in which he discussed the relation of the calendars of the Shire and Bree to those of Rivendell, Gondor, and Rohan. He also wrote a short treatise on *Old Words and Names in the Shire*, showing special interest in discovering the kinship with the language of the Rohirrim of such "shire-words" as *mathom* and old elements in place names.

At Great Smials the books were of less interest to Shire-folk, though more important for larger history. None of them was written by Peregrin, but he and his successors collected many manuscripts written by scribes of Gondor: mainly copies or summaries of histories or legends relating to Elendil and his heirs. Only here in the Shire were to be found extensive materials for the history of Númenor and the arising of Sauron. It was probably at Great Smials that *The Tale of Years** was put together, with the assistance of material collected by Meriadoc. Though the dates given are often conjectural, especially for the Second Age, they deserve attention. It is probable that Meriadoc obtained assistance and information from Rivendell, which he visited more than once. There, though Elrond had departed, his sons long remained, together with some of the High-elven folk. It is said that Celeborn went to dwell there after the departure of Galadriel; but there is no record of the day when at last he sought the Grey Havens, and with him went the last living memory of the Elder Days in Middle-earth.

* Represented in much reduced form in Appendix B as far as the end of the Third Age.

BOOK I

CHAPTER
ONE

A Long-Expected Party

When Mr. Bilbo Baggins of Bag End announced that he would shortly be celebrating his eleventy-first birthday with a party of special magnificence, there was much talk and excitement in Hobbiton.

Bilbo was very rich and very peculiar, and had been the wonder of the Shire for sixty years, ever since his remarkable disappearance and unexpected return. The riches he had brought back from his travels had now become a local legend, and it was popularly believed, whatever the old folk might say, that the Hill at Bag End was full of tunnels stuffed with treasure. And if that was not enough for fame, there was also his prolonged vigour to marvel at. Time wore on, but it seemed to have little effect on Mr. Baggins. At ninety he was much the same as at fifty. At ninety-nine they began to call him *well-preserved*; but *unchanged* would have been nearer the mark. There were some that shook their heads and thought this was too much of a good thing; it seemed unfair that anyone should possess (apparently) perpetual youth as well as (reputedly) inexhaustible wealth.

"It will have to be paid for," they said. "It isn't natural, and trouble will come of it!"

But so far trouble had not come; and as Mr. Baggins was generous with his money, most people were willing to forgive him his oddities and his good fortune. He remained on visiting terms with his relatives (except, of course, the Sackville-Bagginses), and he had many devoted admirers among the hobbits of poor and unimportant families. But he had no close friends, until some of his younger cousins began to grow up.

The eldest of these, and Bilbo's favourite, was young Frodo Baggins. When Bilbo was ninety-nine he adopted Frodo as his heir, and brought him to live at Bag End; and the hopes of the Sackville-Bagginses were finally dashed. Bilbo and Frodo happened to have the same birthday, September 22nd. "You had better come and live here, Frodo my lad," said Bilbo one day; "and then we can celebrate our birthday-parties comfortably together." At that time Frodo was still in his *tweens*, as the hobbits called the irresponsible twenties between childhood and coming of age at thirty-three.

Twelve more years passed. Each year the Bagginses had given very lively combined birthday-parties at Bag End; but now it was understood that something quite exceptional was being planned for that autumn. Bilbo was going to be *eleventy-one*, 111, a rather curious number, and a very respectable age for a hobbit (the Old Took himself had only reached 130); and Frodo was going to be *thirty-three*, 33, an important number: the date of his "coming of age".

Tongues began to wag in Hobbiton and Bywater; and rumour of the coming event travelled all over the Shire. The history and character of Mr. Bilbo Baggins became once again the chief topic of conversation; and the older folk suddenly found their reminiscences in welcome demand.

No one had a more attentive audience than old Ham Gamgee, commonly known as the Gaffer. He held forth at *The Ivy Bush*, a small inn on the Bywater road; and he spoke with some authority, for he had tended the garden at Bag End for forty years, and had helped old Holman in the same job before that.

Now that he was himself growing old and stiff in the joints, the job was mainly carried on by his youngest son, Sam Gamgee. Both father and son were on very friendly terms with Bilbo and Frodo. They lived on the Hill itself, in Number 3 Bagshot Row just below Bag End.

"A very nice well-spoken gentlehobbit is Mr. Bilbo, as I've always said," the Gaffer declared. With perfect truth: for Bilbo was very polite to him, calling him "Master Hamfast", and consulting him constantly upon the growing of vegetables — in the matter of "roots" especially potatoes, the Gaffer was recognized as the leading authority by all in the neighbourhood (including himself).

"But what about this Frodo that lives with him?" asked Old Noakes of Bywater. "Baggins is his name, but he's more than half a Brandybuck, they say. It beats me why any Baggins of Hobbiton should go looking for a wife away there in Buckland, where folks are so queer."

"And no wonder they're queer," put in Daddy Twofoot (the Gaffer's next-door neighbour), "if they live on the wrong side of the Brandywine River, and right agin the Old Forest. That's a dark bad place, if half the tales be true."

"You're right, Dad!" said the Gaffer. "Not that the Brandybucks of Buckland live *in* the Old Forest; but they're a queer breed, seemingly. They fool about with boats on that big river — and that isn't natural. Small wonder that trouble came of it, I say. But be that as it may, Mr. Frodo is as nice a young hobbit as you could wish to meet. Very much like Mr. Bilbo, and in more than looks. After all his father was a Baggins. A decent respectable hobbit was Mr. Drogo Baggins; there was never much to tell of him, till he was drownded."

"Drownded?" said several voices. They had heard this and other darker rumours before, of course; but hobbits have a passion for family history, and they were ready to hear it again.

"Well, so they say," said the Gaffer. "You see: Mr. Drogo, he married poor Miss Primula Brandybuck. She was our Mr. Bilbo's first cousin on the mother's side (her mother being the youngest of the Old Took's daughters); and Mr. Drogo was his second cousin. So Mr. Frodo is his first *and* second cousin, once removed either way, as the saying is, if you follow me. And Mr. Drogo was staying at Brandy Hall with his father-in-law, old Master Gorbadoc, as he often did after his marriage (him being partial to his vittles, and old Gorbadoc keeping a mighty generous table); and he went out *boating* on the Brandywine River; and he and his wife were drownded, and poor Mr. Frodo only a child and all."

"I've heard they went on the water after dinner in the moonlight," said Old Noakes; "and it was Drogo's weight as sunk the boat."

"And *I* heard she pushed him in, and he pulled her in after him," said Sandyman, the Hobbiton miller.

"You shouldn't listen to all you hear, Sandyman," said the Gaffer, who did not much like the miller. "There isn't no call to go talking of pushing and pulling. Boats are quite tricky enough for those that sit still without looking further for the cause of trouble. Anyway: there was this Mr. Frodo left an orphan and stranded, as you might say, among those queer Bucklanders, being brought up anyhow in Brandy Hall. A regular warren, by all accounts. Old Master Gorbadoc never had fewer than a couple of hundred relations in the place. Mr. Bilbo never did a kinder deed than when he brought the lad back to live among decent folk.

"But I reckon it was a nasty knock for those Sackville-Bagginses. They thought they were going to get Bag End, that time when he went off and was thought to be dead. And then he comes back and orders them off; and he goes on living and living, and never looking a day older, bless him! And suddenly he produces an heir, and has all the papers made out proper. The Sackville-Bagginses won't never see the inside of Bag End now, or it is to be hoped not."

"There's a tidy bit of money tucked away up there, I hear tell," said a stranger, a visitor on business from Michel Delving in the Westfarthing. "All the top of your hill is full of tunnels packed with chests of gold and silver, *and* jools, by what I've heard."

"Then you've heard more than I can speak to," answered the Gaffer. "I know nothing about *jools*. Mr. Bilbo is free with his money, and there seems no lack of it; but I know of no tunnel-making. I saw Mr. Bilbo when he came back, a matter of sixty years ago, when I was a lad. I'd not long come prentice to old Holman (him being my dad's cousin), but he had me up at Bag End helping him to keep folks from trampling and trapessing all over the garden while the sale was on. And in the middle of it all Mr. Bilbo comes up the Hill with a pony and some mighty big bags and a couple of chests. I don't doubt they were mostly full of treasure he had picked up in foreign parts, where there be mountains of gold, they say; but there wasn't enough to fill tunnels. But my lad Sam will know more about that. He's in and out of Bag End. Crazy about stories of the old days he is, and he listens to all Mr. Bilbo's tales. Mr. Bilbo has learned him his letters — meaning no harm, mark you, and I hope no harm will come of it.

"*Elves and Dragons!* I says to him. *Cabbages and potatoes are better for me and you. Don't go getting mixed up in the business of your betters, or you'll land in trouble too big for you,* I says to him. And I might say it to others," he added with a look at the stranger and the miller.

But the Gaffer did not convince his audience. The legend of Bilbo's wealth was now too firmly fixed in the minds of the younger generation of hobbits.

"Ah, but he has likely enough been adding to what he brought at first," argued the miller, voicing common opinion. "He's often away from home. And look at the outlandish folk that visit him: dwarves coming at night, and that old wandering conjuror, Gandalf, and all. You can say what you like, Gaffer, but Bag End's a queer place, and its folk are queerer."

"And you can say what *you* like, about what you know no more of than you do of boating, Mr. Sandyman," retorted the Gaffer, disliking the miller even more than usual. "If that's being queer, then we could do with a bit more queerness in these parts. There's some not far away that wouldn't offer a pint of beer to a friend, if they lived in a hole with golden walls. But they do things proper at Bag End. Our Sam says that *everyone's* going to be invited to the party, and there's going to be presents, mark you, presents for all — this very month as is."

That very month was September, and as fine as you could ask. A day or two later a rumour (probably started by the knowledgeable Sam) was spread about that there were going to be fireworks — fireworks, what is more, such as had not been seen in the Shire for nigh on a century, not indeed since the Old Took died.

Days passed and The Day drew nearer. An odd-looking waggon laden with odd-looking packages rolled into Hobbiton one evening and toiled up the Hill to Bag End. The startled hobbits peered out of lamplit doors to gape at it. It was driven by outlandish folk, singing strange songs: dwarves with long beards and deep hoods. A few of them remained at Bag End. At the end of the second week in September a cart came in through Bywater from the direction of Brandywine Bridge in broad daylight. An old man was driving it all alone. He wore a tall pointed blue hat, a long grey cloak, and a silver scarf. He had a long white beard and bushy eyebrows that stuck out beyond the brim of his hat. Small hobbit-children ran after the cart all through Hobbiton and right up the hill. It had a cargo of fireworks, as they rightly guessed. At Bilbo's front door the old man began to unload: there were great bundles of fireworks of all sorts and shapes, each labelled with a large red G ᚩ and the elf-rune, ᚹ.

That was Gandalf's mark, of course, and the old man was Gandalf the Wizard, whose fame in the Shire was due mainly to his skill with fires, smokes, and lights. His real business was far more difficult and dangerous, but the Shire-folk knew nothing about it. To them he was just one of the "attractions" at the

Party. Hence the excitement of the hobbit-children. "G for Grand!" they shouted, and the old man smiled. They knew him by sight, though he only appeared in Hobbiton occasionally and never stopped long; but neither they nor any but the oldest of their elders had seen one of his firework displays — they now belonged to a legendary past.

When the old man, helped by Bilbo and some dwarves, had finished unloading, Bilbo gave a few pennies away; but not a single squib or cracker was forthcoming, to the disappointment of the onlookers.

"Run away now!" said Gandalf. "You will get plenty when the time comes." Then he disappeared inside with Bilbo, and the door was shut. The young hobbits stared at the door in vain for a while, and then made off, feeling that the day of the party would never come.

Inside Bag End, Bilbo and Gandalf were sitting at the open window of a small room looking out west on to the garden. The late afternoon was bright and peaceful. The flowers glowed red and golden: snap-dragons and sunflowers, and nasturtians trailing all over the turf walls and peeping in at the round windows.

"How bright your garden looks!" said Gandalf.

"Yes," said Bilbo. "I am very fond indeed of it, and of all the dear old Shire; but I think I need a holiday."

"You mean to go on with your plan then?"

"I do. I made up my mind months ago, and I haven't changed it."

"Very well. It is no good saying any more. Stick to your plan — your whole plan, mind — and I hope it will turn out for the best, for you, and for all of us."

"I hope so. Anyway I mean to enjoy myself on Thursday, and have my little joke."

"Who will laugh, I wonder?" said Gandalf, shaking his head.

"We shall see," said Bilbo.

The next day more carts rolled up the Hill, and still more

carts. There might have been some grumbling about "dealing locally", but that very week orders began to pour out of Bag End for every kind of provision, commodity, or luxury that could be obtained in Hobbiton or Bywater or anywhere in the neighbourhood. People became enthusiastic; and they began to tick off the days on the calendar; and they watched eagerly for the postman, hoping for invitations.

Before long the invitations began pouring out, and the Hobbiton post-office was blocked, and the Bywater post-office was snowed under, and voluntary assistant postmen were called for. There was a constant stream of them going up the Hill, carrying hundreds of polite variations on *Thank you, I shall certainly come.*

A notice appeared on the gate at Bag End: NO ADMITTANCE EXCEPT ON PARTY BUSINESS. Even those who had, or pretended to have Party Business were seldom allowed inside. Bilbo was busy: writing invitations, ticking off answers, packing up presents, and making some private preparations of his own. From the time of Gandalf's arrival he remained hidden from view.

One morning the hobbits woke to find the large field, south of Bilbo's front door, covered with ropes and poles for tents and pavilions. A special entrance was cut into the bank leading to the road, and wide steps and a large white gate were built there. The three hobbit-families of Bagshot Row, adjoining the field, were intensely interested and generally envied. Old Gaffer Gamgee stopped even pretending to work in his garden.

The tents began to go up. There was a specially large pavilion, so big that the tree that grew in the field was right inside it, and stood proudly near one end, at the head of the chief table. Lanterns were hung on all its branches. More promising still (to the hobbits' mind): an enormous open-air kitchen was erected in the north corner of the field. A draught of cooks, from every inn and eating-house for miles around, arrived to supplement the dwarves and other odd folk that were quartered at Bag End. Excitement rose to its height.

Then the weather clouded over. That was on Wednesday the eve of the Party. Anxiety was intense. Then Thursday, September the 22nd, actually dawned. The sun got up, the clouds vanished, flags were unfurled and the fun began.

Bilbo Baggins called it a *party*, but it was really a variety of entertainments rolled into one. Practically everybody living near was invited. A very few were overlooked by accident, but as they turned up all the same, that did not matter. Many people from other parts of the Shire were also asked; and there were even a few from outside the borders. Bilbo met the guests (and additions) at the new white gate in person. He gave away presents to all and sundry — the latter were those who went out again by a back way and came in again by the gate. Hobbits give presents to other people on their own birthdays. Not very expensive ones, as a rule, and not so lavishly as on this occasion; but it was not a bad system. Actually in Hobbiton and Bywater every day in the year was somebody's birthday, so that every hobbit in those parts had a fair chance of at least one present at least once a week. But they never got tired of them.

On this occasion the presents were unusually good. The hobbit-children were so excited that for a while they almost forgot about eating. There were toys the like of which they had never seen before, all beautiful and some obviously magical. Many of them had indeed been ordered a year before, and had come all the way from the Mountain and from Dale, and were of real dwarf-make.

When every guest had been welcomed and was finally inside the gate, there were songs, dances, music, games, and, of course, food and drink. There were three official meals: lunch, tea, and dinner (or supper). But lunch and tea were marked chiefly by the fact that at those times all the guests were sitting down and eating together. At other times there were merely lots of people eating and drinking — continuously from elevenses until six-thirty, when the fireworks started.

The fireworks were by Gandalf: they were not only brought by him, but designed and made by him; and the special effects, set pieces, and flights of rockets were let off by him. But there was also a generous distribution of squibs, crackers, backarappers, sparklers, torches, dwarf-candles, elf-fountains, goblin-barkers and thunder-claps. They were all superb. The art of Gandalf improved with age.

There were rockets like a flight of scintillating birds singing with sweet voices. There were green trees with trunks of dark smoke: their leaves opened like a whole spring unfolding in a moment, and their shining branches dropped glowing flowers down upon the astonished hobbits, disappearing with a sweet scent just before they touched their upturned faces. There were fountains of butterflies that flew glittering into the trees; there were pillars of coloured fires that rose and turned into eagles, or sailing ships, or a phalanx of flying swans; there was a red thunderstorm and a shower of yellow rain; there was a forest of silver spears that sprang suddenly into the air with a yell like an embattled army, and came down again into the Water with a hiss like a hundred hot snakes. And there was also one last surprise, in honour of Bilbo, and it startled the hobbits exceedingly, as Gandalf intended. The lights went out. A great smoke went up. It shaped itself like a mountain seen in the distance, and began to glow at the summit. It spouted green and scarlet flames. Out flew a red-golden dragon — not life-size, but terribly life-like: fire came from his jaws, his eyes glared down; there was a roar, and he whizzed three times over the heads of the crowd. They all ducked, and many fell flat on their faces. The dragon passed like an express train, turned a somersault, and burst over Bywater with a deafening explosion.

"That is the signal for supper!" said Bilbo. The pain and alarm vanished at once, and the prostrate hobbits leaped to their feet. There was a splendid supper for everyone; for everyone, that is, except those invited to the special family dinner-party. This was held in the great pavilion with the tree. The invitations were limited to twelve dozen (a number also called by the hobbits one Gross, though the word was not considered proper to use of people); and the guests were selected from all the families to which Bilbo and Frodo were related, with the addition of a few special unrelated friends (such as Gandalf). Many young hobbits were included, and present by parental permission; for hobbits were easy-going with their children in the matter of sitting up late, especially when there was a chance of getting them a free meal. Bringing up young hobbits took a lot of provender.

There were many Bagginses and Boffins, and also many Tooks and Brandybucks; there were various Grubbs (relations of Bilbo Baggins' grandmother), and various Chubbs (connexions of his Took grandfather); and a selection of Burrowses, Bolgers, Bracegirdles, Brockhouses, Goodbodies, Hornblowers and Proudfoots. Some of these were only very distantly connected with Bilbo, and some had hardly ever been in Hobbiton before, as they lived in remote corners of the Shire. The Sackville-Bagginses were not forgotten. Otho and his wife Lobelia were present. They disliked Bilbo and detested Frodo, but so magnificent was the invitation card, written in golden ink, that they had felt it was impossible to refuse. Besides, their cousin, Bilbo, had been specializing in food for many years and his table had a high reputation.

All the one hundred and forty-four guests expected a pleasant feast; though they rather dreaded the after-dinner speech of their host (an inevitable item). He was liable to drag in bits of what he called poetry; and sometimes, after a glass or two, would allude to the absurd adventures of his mysterious journey. The guests were not disappointed: they had a *very* pleasant feast, in fact an engrossing entertainment: rich, abundant, varied, and prolonged. The purchase of provisions fell almost to nothing throughout the district in the ensuing weeks; but as Bilbo's catering had depleted the stocks of most of the stores, cellars and warehouses for miles around, that did not matter much.

After the feast (more or less) came the Speech. Most of the company were, however, now in a tolerant mood, at that delightful stage which they called "filling up the corners". They were sipping their favourite drinks, and nibbling at their favourite dainties, and their fears were forgotten. They were prepared to listen to anything, and to cheer at every full stop.

My dear People, began Bilbo, rising in his place. "Hear! Hear! Hear!" they shouted, and kept on repeating it in chorus, seeming reluctant to follow their own advice. Bilbo left his place and went and stood on a chair under the illuminated tree. The light of the lanterns fell on his beaming face; the golden buttons shone on his embroidered silk waistcoat. They could all see him standing, waving one hand in the air, the other was in his trouser-pocket.

My dear Bagginses and Boffins, he began again; *and my dear Tooks and Brandybucks, and Grubbs, and Chubbs, and Burrowses, and Hornblowers, and Bolgers, Bracegirdles, Goodbodies, Brockhouses and Proudfoots.* "ProudFEET!" shouted an elderly hobbit from the back of the pavilion. His name, of course, was Proudfoot, and well merited; his feet were large, exceptionally furry, and both were on the table.

Proudfoots, repeated Bilbo. *Also my good Sackville-Bagginses that I welcome back at last to Bag End. Today is my one hundred and eleventh birthday: I am eleventy-one today!* "Hurray! Hurray! Many Happy Returns!" they shouted, and they hammered joyously on the tables. Bilbo was doing splendidly. This was the sort of stuff they liked: short and obvious.

I hope you are all enjoying yourselves as much as I am. Deafening cheers. Cries of *Yes* (and *No*). Noises of trumpets and horns, pipes and flutes, and other musical instruments. There were, as has been said, many young hobbits present. Hundreds of musical crackers had been pulled. Most of them bore the mark DALE on them; which did not convey much to most of the hobbits, but they all agreed they were marvellous crackers. They contained instruments, small, but of perfect make and enchanting tones. Indeed, in one corner some of the young Tooks and Brandybucks, supposing Uncle Bilbo to have finished (since he had plainly said all that was necessary), now got up an impromptu orchestra, and began a merry dance-tune.

Master Everard Took and Miss Melilot Brandybuck got on a table and with bells in their hands began to dance the Springle-ring: a pretty dance, but rather vigorous.

But Bilbo had not finished. Seizing a horn from a youngster near by, he blew three loud hoots. The noise subsided. *I shall not keep you long*, he cried. Cheers from all the assembly. *I have called you all together for a Purpose.* Something in the way that he said this made an impression. There was almost silence, and one or two of the Tooks pricked up their ears.

Indeed, for Three Purposes! First of all, to tell you that I am immensely fond of you all, and that eleventy-one years is too short a time to live among such excellent and admirable hobbits. Tremendous outburst of approval.

I don't know half of you half as well as I should like; and I like less than half of you half as well as you deserve. This was unexpected and rather difficult. There was some scattered clapping, but most of them were trying to work it out and see if it came to a compliment.

Secondly, to celebrate my birthday. Cheers again. *I should say: OUR birthday. For it is, of course, also the birthday of my heir and nephew, Frodo. He comes of age and into his inheritance today.* Some perfunctory clapping by the elders; and some loud shouts of "Frodo! Frodo! Jolly old Frodo," from the juniors. The Sackville-Bagginses scowled, and wondered what was meant by "coming into his inheritance".

Together we score one hundred and forty-four. Your numbers were chosen to fit this remarkable total: One Gross, if I may use the expression. No cheers. This was ridiculous. Many of the guests, and especially the Sackville-Bagginses, were insulted, feeling sure they had only been asked to fill up the required number, like goods in a package. "One Gross, indeed! Vulgar expression."

It is also, if I may be allowed to refer to ancient history, the anniversary of my arrival by barrel at Esgaroth on the Long Lake; though the fact that it was my birthday slipped my memory on that occasion. I was only fifty-one then, and birthdays did not seem so important. *The banquet was very splendid, however, though I had a bad cold at the time, I remember, and could only say "thag you very buch".* I *now repeat it more correctly: Thank you very much for coming to my little party.* Obstinate silence. They all feared that a song or some poetry was now imminent; and they were getting bored. Why couldn't he stop talking and let them drink his health? But Bilbo did not sing or recite. He paused for a moment.

Thirdly and finally, he said, *I wish to make an ANNOUNCE-MENT.* He spoke this last word so loudly and suddenly that everyone sat up who still could. *I regret to announce that — though, as I said, eleventy-one years is far too short a time to spend among you — this is the END. I am going. I am leaving NOW. GOOD-BYE!*

He stepped down and vanished. There was a blinding flash of light, and the guests all blinked. When they opened their eyes Bilbo was nowhere to be seen. One hundred and forty-four flabbergasted hobbits sat back speechless. Old Odo Proudfoot removed his feet from the table and stamped. Then there was a dead silence, until suddenly, after several deep breaths, every Baggins, Boffin, Took, Brandybuck, Grubb, Chubb, Burrows, Bolger, Bracegirdle, Brockhouse, Goodbody, Hornblower, and Proudfoot began to talk at once.

It was generally agreed that the joke was in very bad taste, and more food and drink were needed to cure the guests of shock and annoyance. "He's mad. I always said so," was probably the most popular comment. Even the Tooks (with a few exceptions) thought Bilbo's behaviour was absurd. For the moment most of them took it for granted that his disappearance was nothing more than a ridiculous prank.

But old Rory Brandybuck was not so sure. Neither age nor an enormous dinner had clouded his wits, and he said to his daughter-in-law, Esmeralda: "There's something fishy in this, my dear! I believe that mad Baggins is off again. Silly old fool. But why worry? He hasn't taken the vittles with him." He called loudly to Frodo to send the wine round again.

Frodo was the only one present who had said nothing. For some time he had sat silent beside Bilbo's empty chair, and ignored all remarks and questions. He had enjoyed the joke, of course, even though he had been in the know. He had difficulty in keeping from laughter at the indignant surprise of the guests. But at the same time he felt deeply troubled: he realized suddenly that he loved the old hobbit dearly. Most of the guests went on eating and drinking and discussing Bilbo Baggins' oddities, past and present; but the Sackville-Bagginses had already departed in wrath. Frodo did not want to have any more to do with the party. He gave orders for more wine to be served; then he got up and drained his own glass silently to the health of Bilbo, and slipped out of the pavilion.

As for Bilbo Baggins, even while he was making his speech, he had been fingering the golden ring in his pocket: his magic ring that he had kept secret for so many years. As he stepped down he slipped it on his finger, and he was never seen by any hobbit in Hobbiton again.

He walked briskly back to his hole, and stood for a moment listening with a smile to the din in the pavilion and to the sounds of merrymaking in other parts of the field. Then he went in. He took off his party clothes, folded up and wrapped in tissue-paper his embroidered silk waistcoat, and put it away. Then he put on quickly some old untidy garments, and fastened round his waist a worn leather belt. On it he hung a short sword in a battered black-leather scabbard. From a locked drawer, smelling of moth-balls, he took out an old cloak and hood. They had been locked up as if they were very precious, but they were so patched and weatherstained that their original colour could hardly be guessed: it might have been dark green. They were rather too large for him. He then went into his study, and from a large strong-box took out a bundle wrapped in old cloths, and a leather-bound manuscript; and also a large bulky envelope. The book and bundle he stuffed into the top of a heavy bag that was standing there, already nearly full. Into the envelope he slipped his golden ring, and its fine chain, and then sealed it, and addressed it to Frodo. At first he put it on the mantelpiece, but suddenly he removed it and stuck it in his pocket. At that moment the door opened and Gandalf came quickly in.

"Hullo!" said Bilbo. "I wondered if you would turn up."

"I am glad to find you visible," replied the wizard, sitting down in a chair, "I wanted to catch you and have a few final words. I suppose you feel that everything has gone off splendidly and according to plan?"

"Yes, I do," said Bilbo. "Though that flash was surprising: it quite startled me, let alone the others. A little addition of your own, I suppose?"

"It was. You have wisely kept that ring secret all these years, and it seemed to me necessary to give your guests something else that would seem to explain your sudden vanishment.

"And would spoil my joke. You are an interfering old busybody," laughed Bilbo, "but I expect you know best, as usual."

"I do — when I know anything. But I don't feel too sure about this whole affair. It has now come to the final point. You have had your joke, and alarmed or offended most of your relations, and given the whole Shire something to talk about for nine days, or ninety-nine more likely. Are you going any further?"

"Yes, I am. I feel I need a holiday, a very long holiday, as I have told you before. Probably a permanent holiday: I don't expect I shall return. In fact, I don't mean to, and I have made all arrangements.

"I am old, Gandalf. I don't look it, but I am beginning to feel it in my heart of hearts. *Well-preserved* indeed!" he snorted. "Why, I feel all thin, sort of *stretched*, if you know what I mean: like butter that has been scraped over too much bread. That can't be right. I need a change, or something."

Gandalf looked curiously and closely at him. "No, it does not seem right," he said thoughtfully. "No, after all I believe your plan is probably the best."

"Well, I've made up my mind, anyway. I want to see mountains again, Gandalf — *mountains*; and then find somewhere where I can *rest*. In peace and quiet, without a lot of relatives prying around, and a string of confounded visitors hanging on the bell. I might find somewhere where I can finish my book. I have thought of a nice ending for it: *and he lived happily ever after to the end of his days*."

Gandalf laughed. "I hope he will. But nobody will read the book, however it ends."

"Oh, they may, in years to come. Frodo has read some already, as far as it has gone. You'll keep an eye on Frodo, won't you?"

"Yes, I will — two eyes, as often as I can spare them."

"He would come with me, of course, if I asked him. In fact he offered to once, just before the party. But he does not really want to, yet. I want to see the wild country again before I die, and the Mountains; but he is still in love with the Shire, with woods and fields and little rivers. He ought to be comfortable here. I am leaving everything to him, of course, except a few oddments. I hope he will be happy, when he gets used to being on his own. It's time he was his own master now."

"Everything?" said Gandalf. "The ring as well? You agreed to that, you remember."

"Well, er, yes, I suppose so," stammered Bilbo. "Where is it?"

"In an envelope, if you must know," said Bilbo impatiently. "There on the mantelpiece. Well no! Here it is in my pocket!" He hesitated. "Isn't that odd now?" he said softly to himself. "Yet after all, why not? Why shouldn't it stay there?"

Gandalf look again very hard at Bilbo, and there was a gleam in his eyes. "I think, Bilbo," he said quietly, "I should leave it behind. Don't you want to?"

"Well yes — and no. Now it comes to it, I don't like parting with it at all, I may say. And I don't really see why I should.

Why do you want me to?" he asked, and a curious change came over his voice. It was sharp with suspicion and annoyance. "You are always badgering me about my ring; but you have never bothered me about the other things that I got on my journey."

"No, but I had to badger you," said Gandalf. "I wanted the truth. It was important. Magic rings are — well, magical; and they are rare and curious. I was professionally interested in your ring, you may say; and I still am. I should like to know where it is, if you go wandering again. Also I think *you* have had it quite long enough. You won't need it any more, Bilbo, unless I am quite mistaken."

Bilbo flushed, and there was an angry light in his eyes. His kindly face grew hard. "Why not?" he cried. "And what business is it of yours, anyway, to know what I do with my own things? It is my own. I found it. It came to me."

"Yes, yes," said Gandalf. "But there is no need to get angry."

"If I am it is your fault," said Bilbo. "It is mine, I tell you. My own. My precious. Yes, my precious."

The wizard's face remained grave and attentive, and only a flicker in his deep eyes showed that he was startled and indeed alarmed. "It has been called that before," he said, "but not by you."

"But I say it now. And why not? Even if Gollum said the same once. It's not his now, but mine. And I shall keep it, I say."

Gandalf stood up. He spoke sternly. "You will be a fool if you do, Bilbo," he said. "You make that clearer with every word you say. It has got far too much hold on you. Let it go! And then you can go yourself, and be free."

"I'll do as I choose and go as I please," said Bilbo obstinately.

"Now, now, my dear hobbit!" said Gandalf. "All your long life we have been friends, and you owe me something. Come! Do as you promised: give it up!"

"Well, if you want my ring yourself, say so!" cried Bilbo. "But you won't get it. I won't give my precious away, I tell you." His hand strayed to the hilt of his small sword.

Gandalf's eyes flashed. "It will be my turn to get angry soon," he said. "If you say that again, I shall. Then you will see Gandalf the Grey uncloaked." He took a step towards the hobbit, and he seemed to grow tall and menacing; his shadow filled the little room.

Bilbo backed away to the wall, breathing hard, his hand clutching at his pocket. They stood for a while facing one another, and the air of the room tingled. Gandalf's eyes remained bent on the hobbit. Slowly his hands relaxed, and he began to tremble.

"I don't know what has come over you, Gandalf," he said. "You have never been like this before. What is it all about? It is mine isn't it? I found it, and Gollum would have killed me, if I hadn't kept it. I'm not a thief, whatever he said."

"I have never called you one," Gandalf answered. "And I am not one either. I am not trying to rob you, but to help you. I wish you would trust me, as you used." He turned away, and the shadow passed. He seemed to dwindle again to an old grey man, bent and troubled.

Bilbo drew his hand over his eyes. "I am sorry," he said. "But I felt so queer. And yet it would be a relief in a way not to be bothered with it any more. It has been so growing on my mind lately. Sometimes I have felt it was like an eye looking at me. And I am always wanting to put it on and disappear, don't you know; or wondering if it is safe, and pulling it out to make sure. I tried locking it up, but I found I couldn't rest without it in my pocket. I don't know why. And I don't seem able to make up my mind."

"Then trust mine," said Gandalf. "It is quite made up. Go away and leave it behind. Stop possessing it. Give it to Frodo, and I will look after him."

Bilbo stood for a moment tense and undecided. Presently he sighed. "All right," he said with an effort. "I will." Then he shrugged his shoulders, and smiled rather ruefully. "After all that's what this party business was all about, really: to give away lots of birthday presents, and somehow make it easier to give it away at the same time. It hasn't made it any easier in the end, but it would be a pity to waste all my preparations. It would quite spoil the joke."

"Indeed it would take away the only point I ever saw in the affair," said Gandalf.

"Very well," said Bilbo, "it goes to Frodo with all the rest." He drew a deep breath. "And now I really must be starting, or somebody else will catch me. I have said good-bye, and I couldn't bear to do it all over again." He picked up his bag and moved to the door.

"You have still got the ring in your pocket," said the wizard.

"Well, so I have!" cried Bilbo. "And my will and all the other documents too. You had better take it and deliver it for me. That will be safest."

"No, don't give the ring to me," said Gandalf. "Put it on the mantelpiece. It will be safe enough there, till Frodo comes. I shall wait for him."

Bilbo took out the envelope, but just as he was about to set it by the clock, his hand jerked back, and the packet fell on the floor. Before he could pick it up, the wizard stooped and seized it and set it in its place. A spasm of anger passed swiftly over the hobbit's face again. Suddenly it gave way to a look of relief and a laugh.

"Well, that's that," he said. "Now I'm off!"

They went out into the hall. Bilbo chose his favourite stick from the stand; then he whistled. Three dwarves came out of different rooms where they had been busy.

"Is everything ready?" asked Bilbo. "Everything packed and labelled?"

"Everything," they answered.

"Well, let's start then!" He stepped out of the front-door.

It was a fine night, and the black sky was dotted with stars. He looked up, sniffing the air. "What fun! What fun to be off again, off on the Road with dwarves! This is what I have really been longing for, for years! Good-bye!" he said, looking at his old home and bowing to the door. "Good-bye, Gandalf!"

"Good-bye, for the present, Bilbo. Take care of yourself! You are old enough, and perhaps wise enough."

"Take care! I don't care. Don't you worry about me! I am as happy now as I have ever been, and that is saying a great deal. But the time has come. I am being swept off my feet at last," he added, and then in a low voice, as if to himself, he sang softly in the dark:

> *The Road goes ever on and on*
> *Down from the door where it began.*
> *Now far ahead the Road has gone,*
> *And I must follow, if I can,*
> *Pursuing it with eager feet,*
> *Until it joins some larger way*
> *Where many paths and errands meet.*
> *And whither then? I cannot say.*

He paused, silent for a moment. Then without another word he turned away from the lights and voices in the fields and tents, and followed by his three companions went round into his garden, and trotted down the long sloping path. He jumped over a low place in the hedge at the bottom, and took to the meadows, passing into the night like a rustle of wind in the grass.

Gandalf remained for a while staring after him into the darkness. "Good-bye, my dear Bilbo — until our next meeting!" he said softly and went back indoors.

Frodo came in soon afterwards, and found him sitting in the dark, deep in thought. "Has he gone?" he asked.

"Yes," answered Gandalf, "he has gone at last."

"I wish — I mean, I hoped until this evening that it was only a joke," said Frodo. "But I knew in my heart that he really meant to go. He always used to joke about serious things. I wish I had come back sooner, just to see him off."

"I think really he preferred slipping off quietly in the end," said Gandalf. "Don't be too troubled. He'll be all right — now. He left a packet for you. There it is!"

Frodo took the envelope from the mantelpiece, and glanced at it, but did not open it.

"You'll find his will and all the other documents in there, I think," said the wizard. "You are the master of Bag End now. And also, I fancy, you'll find a golden ring."

"The ring!" exclaimed Frodo. "Has he left me that? I wonder why. Still, it may be useful."

"It may, and it may not," said Gandalf. "I should not make use of it, if I were you. But keep it secret, and keep it safe! Now I am going to bed."

As master of Bag End Frodo felt it his painful duty to say goodbye to the guests. Rumours of strange events had by now spread all over the field, but Frodo would only say *no doubt everything will be cleared up in the morning*. About midnight carriages came for the important folk. One by one they rolled away, filled with full but very unsatisfied hobbits. Gardeners came by arrangement, and removed in wheelbarrows those that had inadvertently remained behind.

Night slowly passed. The sun rose. The hobbits rose rather later. Morning went on. People came and began (by orders) to clear away the pavilions and the tables and the chairs, and the spoons and knives and bottles and plates, and the lanterns, and the flowering shrubs in boxes, and the crumbs and cracker-paper, the forgotten bags and gloves and handkerchiefs, and the uneaten food (a very small item). Then a number of other people came (without orders): Bagginses, and Boflins, and Bolgers, and Tooks, and other guests that lived or were staying near. By mid-day, when even the best-fed were out and about again, there was a large crowd at Bag End, uninvited but not unexpected.

Frodo was waiting on the step, smiling, but looking rather tired and worried. He welcomed all the callers, but he had not much more to say than before. His reply to all inquiries was simply this: "Mr. Bilbo Baggins has gone away; as far as I know, for good." Some of the visitors he invited to come inside, as Bilbo had left "messages" for them.

Inside in the hall there was piled a large assortment of packages and parcels and small articles of furniture. On every item there was a label tied. There were several labels of this sort:

For ADELARD TOOK, for his VERY OWN, from Bilbo; on an umbrella. Adelard had carried off many unlabelled ones.

For DORA BAGGINS in memory of a LONG correspondence, with love from Bilbo; on a large waste-paper basket. Dora was Drogo's sister and the eldest surviving female relative of Bilbo and Frodo; she was ninety-nine, and had written reams of good advice for more than half a century.

For MILO BURROWS, hoping it will be useful, from B.B.; on a gold pen and ink-bottle. Milo never answered letters.

For ANGELICA'S use, from Uncle Bilbo; on a round convex mirror. She was a young Baggins, and too obviously considered her face shapely.

For the collection of HUGO BRACEGIRDLE, from a contributor; on an (empty) book-case. Hugo was a great borrower of books, and worse than usual at returning them.

For LOBELIA SACKVILLE-BAGGINS, as a PRESENT; on a case of silver spoons. Bilbo believed that she had acquired a good many of his spoons, while he was away on his former journey. Lobelia knew that quite well. When she arrived later in the day, she took the point at once, but she also took the spoons.

This is only a small selection of the assembled presents. Bilbo's residence had got rather cluttered up with things in the course of his long life. It was a tendency of hobbit-holes to get cluttered up: for which the custom of giving so many birthday-presents was largely responsible. Not, of course, that the birthday-presents were always new; there were one or two old *mathoms* of forgotten uses that had circulated all round the district; but Bilbo had usually given new presents, and kept those that he received. The old hole was now being cleared a little.

Every one of the various parting gifts had labels, written out personally by Bilbo, and several had some point, or some joke. But, of course, most of the things were given where they would be wanted and welcome. The poorer hobbits, and especially those of Bagshot Row, did very well. Old Gaffer Gamgee got two sacks of potatoes, a new spade, a woollen waistcoat, and a bottle of ointment for creaking joints. Old Rory Brandybuck, in return for much hospitality, got a dozen bottles of Old Winyards: a strong red wine from the Southfarthing, and now quite mature, as it had been laid down by Bilbo's father. Rory quite forgave Bilbo, and voted him a capital fellow after the first bottle.

There was plenty of everything left for Frodo. And, of course, all the chief treasures, as well as the books, pictures, and more than enough furniture, were left in his possession. There was, however, no sign nor mention of money or jewellery: not a penny-piece or a glass bead was given away.

Frodo had a very trying time that afternoon. A false rumour that the whole household was being distributed free spread like wildfire; and before long the place was packed with people who had no business there, but could not be kept out. Labels got torn off and mixed, and quarrels broke out. Some people tried to do swaps and deals in the hall; and others tried to make off with minor items not addressed to them, or with anything that seemed unwanted or unwatched. The road to the gate was blocked with barrows and handcarts.

In the middle of the commotion the Sackville-Bagginses arrived. Frodo had retired for a while and left his friend Merry Brandybuck to keep an eye on things. When Otho loudly demanded to see Frodo, Merry bowed politely.

"He is indisposed," he said. "He is resting."

"Hiding, you mean," said Lobelia. "Anyway we want to see him and we mean to see him. Just go and tell him so!"

Merry left them a long while in the hall, and they had time to discover their parting gift of spoons. It did not improve their tempers. Eventually they were shown into the study. Frodo was sitting at a table with a lot of papers in front of him. He looked indisposed — to see Sackville-Bagginses at any rate; and he stood up, fidgeting with something in his pocket. But he spoke quite politely.

The Sackville-Bagginses were rather offensive. They began by offering him bad bargain-prices (as between friends) for various valuable and unlabelled things. When Frodo replied that only the things specially directed by Bilbo were being given away, they said the whole affair was very fishy.

"Only one thing is clear to me," said Otho, "and that is that you are doing exceedingly well out of it. I insist on seeing the will."

Otho would have been Bilbo's heir, but for the adoption of Frodo. He read the will carefully and snorted. It was, unfortunately, very clear and correct (according to the legal customs of hobbits, which demand among other things seven signatures of witnesses in red ink).

"Foiled again!" he said to his wife. "And after waiting *sixty* years. Spoons? Fiddlesticks!" He snapped his fingers under Frodo's nose and stumped off. But Lobelia was not so easily got rid of. A little later Frodo came out of the study to see how things were going on and found her still about the place, investigating nooks and corners and tapping the floors. He escorted her firmly off the premises, after he had relieved her of several small (but rather valuable) articles that had somehow fallen inside her umbrella. Her face looked as if she was in the throes of thinking out a really crushing parting remark; but all she found to say, turning round on the step, was: "You'll live to regret it, young fellow! Why didn't you go too? You don't belong here; you're no Baggins — you — you're a Brandy-buck!"

"Did you hear that, Merry? That was an insult, if you like," said Frodo as he shut the door on her.

"It was a compliment," said Merry Brandybuck, "and so, of course, not true."

Then they went round the hole, and evicted three young hobbits (two Boffins and a Bolger) who were knocking holes in the walls of one of the cellars. Frodo also had a tussle with young Sancho Proudfoot (old Odo Proudfoot's grandson), who had begun an excavation in the larger pantry, where he thought there was an echo. The legend of Bilbo's gold excited both curiosity and hope; for legendary gold (mysteriously obtained, if not positively ill-gotten) is, as every one knows, any one's for the finding — unless the search is interrupted.

When he had overcome Sancho and pushed him out, Frodo collapsed on a chair in the hall. "It's time to close the shop, Merry," he said. "Lock the door, and don't open it to anyone today, not even if they bring a battering-ram." Then he went to revive himself with a belated cup of tea.

He had hardly sat down, when there came a soft knock at the front-door. "Lobelia again most likely," he thought. "She must have thought of something really nasty, and have come back again to say it. It can wait."

He went on with his tea. The knock was repeated, much louder, but he took no notice. Suddenly the wizard's head appeared at the window.

"If you don't let me in, Frodo, I shall blow your door right down your hole and out through the hill," he said.

"My dear Gandalf! Half a minute!" cried Frodo, running out of the room to the door. "Come in! Come in! I thought it was Lobelia."

"Then I forgive you. But I saw her some time ago, driving a pony-trap towards Bywater with a face that would have curdled new milk."

"She had already nearly curdled me. Honestly, I nearly tried on Bilbo's ring. I longed to disappear."

"Don't do that!" said Gandalf, sitting down. "Do be careful of that ring, Frodo! In fact, it is partly about that that I have come to say a last word."

"Well, what about it?"

"What do you know already?"

"Only what Bilbo told me. I have heard his story: how he found it, and how he used it: on his journey, I mean."

"Which story, I wonder," said Gandalf.

"Oh, not what he told the dwarves and put in his book," said Frodo. "He told me the true story soon after I came to live here. He said you had pestered him till he told you, so I had better know too. 'No secrets between us, Frodo,' he said; 'but they are not to go any further. It's mine anyway.'"

"That's interesting," said Gandalf. "Well, what did you think of it all?"

"If you mean, inventing all that about a 'present', well, I thought the true story much more likely, and I couldn't see the point of altering it at all. It was very unlike Bilbo to do so, anyway; and I thought it rather odd."

"So did I. But odd things may happen to people that have such treasures — if they use them. Let it be a warning to you to be very careful with it. It may have other powers than just making you vanish when you wish to."

"I don't understand," said Frodo.

"Neither do I," answered the wizard. "I have merely begun to wonder about the ring, especially since last night. No need to worry. But if you take my advice you will use it very seldom, or not at all. At least I beg you not to use it in any way that will cause talk or rouse suspicion. I say again: keep it safe, and keep it secret!"

"You are very mysterious! What are you afraid of?"

"I am not certain, so I will say no more. I may be able to tell you something when I come back. I am going off at once: so this is good-bye for the present." He got up.

"At once!" cried Frodo. "Why, I thought you were staying on for at least a week. I was looking forward to your help."

"I did mean to — but I have had to change my mind. I may be away for a good while; but I'll come and see you again, as soon as I can. Expect me when you see me! I shall slip in quietly. I shan't often be visiting the Shire openly again. I find that I have become rather unpopular. They say I am a nuisance and a disturber of the peace. Some people are actually accusing me of spiriting Bilbo away, or worse. If you want to know, there is supposed to be a plot between you and me to get hold of his wealth."

"Some people!" exclaimed Frodo. "You mean Otho and Lobelia. How abominable! I would give them Bag End and everything else, if I could get Bilbo back and go off tramping in the country with him. I love the Shire. But I begin to wish, somehow, that I had gone too. I wonder if I shall ever see him again."

"So do I," said Gandalf. "And I wonder many other things. Good-bye now! Take care of yourself! Look out for me, especially at unlikely times! Good-bye!"

Frodo saw him to the door. He gave a final wave of his hand, and walked off at a surprising pace; but Frodo thought the old wizard looked unusually bent, almost as if he was carrying a great weight. The evening was closing in, and his cloaked figure quickly vanished into the twilight. Frodo did not see him again for a long time.

CHAPTER
TWO

The Shadow of
the Past

The talk did not die down in nine or even ninety-nine days. The second disappearance of Mr. Bilbo Baggins was discussed in Hobbiton, and indeed all over the Shire, for a year and a day, and was remembered much longer than that. It became a fireside-story for young hobbits; and eventually Mad Baggins, who used to vanish with a bang and a flash and reappear with bags of jewels and gold, became a favourite character of legend and lived on long after all the true events were forgotten.

But in the meantime, the general opinion in the neighbourhood was that Bilbo, who had always been rather cracked, had at last gone quite mad, and had run off into the Blue. There he had undoubtedly fallen into a pool or a river and come to a tragic, but hardly an untimely, end. The blame was mostly laid on Gandalf.

"If only that dratted wizard will leave young Frodo alone, perhaps he'll settle down and grow some hobbit-sense," they said. And to all appearance the wizard did leave Frodo alone, and he did settle down, but the growth of hobbit-sense was not very noticeable. Indeed, he at once began to carry on Bilbo's reputation for oddity. He refused to go into mourning; and the next year he gave a party in honour of Bilbo's hundred-and-twelfth birthday, which he called a Hundred-weight Feast. But that was short of the mark, for twenty guests were invited, and there were several meals at which it snowed food and rained drink, as hobbits say.

Some people were rather shocked; but Frodo kept up the custom of giving Bilbo's Birthday Party year after year until they got used to it. He said that he did not think Bilbo was dead. When they asked: "Where is he then?" he shrugged his shoulders.

He lived alone, as Bilbo had done; but he had a good many friends, especially among the younger hobbits (mostly descendants of the Old Took) who had as children been fond of Bilbo and often in and out of Bag End. Folco Boffin and Fredegar Bolger were two of these; but his closest friends were Peregrin Took (usually called Pippin), and Merry Brandybuck (his real name was Meriadoc, but that was seldom remembered). Frodo went tramping over the Shire with them; but more often he wandered by himself, and to the amazement of sensible folk he was sometimes seen far from home walking in the hills and woods under the starlight. Merry and Pippin suspected that he visited the Elves at times, as Bilbo had done.

As time went on, people began to notice that Frodo also showed signs of good "preservation": outwardly he retained the appearance of a robust and energetic hobbit just out of his tweens. "Some folk have all the luck," they said; but it was not until Frodo approached the usually more sober age of fifty that they began to think it queer.

Frodo himself, after the first shock, found that being his own master and *the* Mr. Baggins of Bag End was rather pleasant. For some years he was quite happy and did not worry much about the future. But half unknown to himself the regret that he had not gone with Bilbo was steadily growing. He found himself wondering at times, especially in the autumn, about the wild lands, and strange visions of mountains that he had never seen came into his dreams. He began to say to himself:

"Perhaps I shall cross the River myself one day." To which the other half of his mind always replied: "Not yet."

So it went on, until his forties were running out, and his fiftieth birthday was drawing near: fifty was a number that he felt was somehow significant (or ominous); it was at any rate at that age that adventure had suddenly befallen Bilbo. Frodo began to feel restless, and the old paths seemed too well-trodden. He looked at maps, and wondered what lay beyond their edges: maps made in the Shire showed mostly white spaces beyond its borders. He took to wandering further afield and more often by himself; and Merry and his other friends watched him anxiously. Often he was seen walking and talking with the strange wayfarers that began at this time to appear in the Shire.

There were rumours of strange things happening in the world outside; and as Gandalf had not at that time appeared or sent any message for several years, Frodo gathered all the news he could. Elves, who seldom walked in the Shire, could now be seen passing westward through the woods in the evening, passing and not returning; but they were leaving Middle-earth and were no longer concerned with its troubles. There were, however, dwarves on the road in unusual numbers. The ancient East-West Road ran through the Shire to its end at the Grey Havens, and dwarves had always used it on their way to their mines in the Blue Mountains. They were the hobbits' chief source of news from distant parts — if they wanted any: as a rule dwarves said little and hobbits asked no more. But now Frodo often met strange dwarves of far countries, seeking refuge in the West. They were troubled, and some spoke in whispers of the Enemy and of the Land of Mordor.

That name the hobbits only knew in legends of the dark past, like a shadow in the background of their memories; but it was ominous and disquieting. It seemed that the evil power in Mirkwood had been driven out by the White Council only to reappear in greater strength in the old strongholds of Mordor.

The Dark Tower had been rebuilt, it was said. From there the power was spreading far and wide, and away far east and south there were wars and growing fear. Orcs were multiplying again in the mountains. Trolls were abroad, no longer dull-witted, but cunning and armed with dreadful weapons. And there were murmured hints of creatures more terrible than all these, but they had no name.

Little of all this, of course, reached the ears of ordinary hobbits. But even the deafest and most stay-at-home began to hear queer tales; and those whose business took them to the borders saw strange things. The conversation in *The Green Dragon* at Bywater, one evening in the spring of Frodo's fiftieth year, showed that even in the comfortable heart of the Shire rumours had been heard, though most hobbits still laughed at them.

Sam Gamgee was sitting in one corner near the fire, and opposite him was Ted Sandyman, the miller's son; and there were various other rustic hobbits listening to their talk.

"Queer things you do hear these days, to be sure," said Sam.

"Ah," said Ted, "you do, if you listen. But I can hear fireside-tales and children's stories at home, if I want to."

"No doubt you can," retorted Sam, "and I daresay there's more truth in some of them than you reckon. Who invented the stories anyway? Take dragons now."

"No thank 'ee," said Ted, "I won't. I heard tell of them when I was a youngster, but there's no call to believe in them now. There's only one Dragon in Bywater, and that's Green," he said, getting a general laugh.

"All right," said Sam, laughing with the rest. "But what about these Tree-men, these giants, as you might call them? They do say that one bigger than a tree was seen up away beyond the North Moors not long back."

"Who's *they*?"

"My cousin Hal for one. He works for Mr. Boffin at Overhill and goes up to the Northfarthing for the hunting. He *saw* one.

"Says he did, perhaps. Your Hal's always saying that he's seen things; and maybe he sees things that ain't there."

"But this one was as big as an elm tree, and walking — walking seven yards to a stride, if it was an inch."

"Then I bet it wasn't an inch. What he saw *was* an elm tree, as like as not."

"But this one was *walking*, I tell you; and there ain't no elm tree on the North Moors."

"Then Hal can't have seen one," said Ted. There was some laughing and clapping: the audience seemed to think that Ted had scored a point.

"All the same," said Sam, "you can't deny that others besides our Halfast have seen queer folk crossing the Shire — crossing it, mind you: there are more that are turned back at the borders. The Bounders have never been so busy before.

"And I've heard tell that Elves are moving west. They do say they are going to the harbours, out away beyond the White Towers." Sam waved his arm vaguely: neither he nor any of them knew how far it was to the Sea, past the old towers beyond the western borders of the Shire. But it was an old tradition that away over there stood the Grey Havens, from which at times elven-ships set sail, never to return.

"They are sailing, sailing, sailing over the Sea, they are going into the West and leaving us," said Sam, half chanting the words, shaking his head sadly and solemnly. But Ted laughed.

"Well, that isn't anything new, if you believe the old tales. And I don't see what it matters to me or you. Let them sail! But I warrant you haven't seen them doing it; nor any one else in the Shire."

"Well, I don't know," said Sam thoughtfully. He believed he had once seen an Elf in the woods, and still hoped to see more one day. Of all the legends that he had heard in his early years such fragments of tales and half-remembered stories about the Elves as the hobbits knew, had always moved him most deeply. "There are some, even in these parts, as know the Fair Folk and get news of them," he said.

"There's Mr. Baggins now, that I work for. He told me that they were sailing, and he knows a bit about Elves. And old Mr. Bilbo knew more: many's the talk I had with him when I was a little lad."

"Oh, they're both cracked," said Ted. "Leastways old Bilbo *was* cracked, and Frodo's cracking. If that's where you get your news from, you'll never want for moonshine. Well, friends, I'm off home. Your good health!" He drained his mug and went out noisily.

Sam sat silent and said no more. He had a good deal to think about. For one thing, there was a lot to do up in the Bag End garden, and he would have a busy day tomorrow, if the weather cleared. The grass was growing fast. But Sam had more on his mind than gardening. After a while he sighed, and got up and went out.

It was early April and the sky was now clearing after heavy rain. The sun was down, and a cool pale evening was quietly fading into night. He walked home under the early stars through Hobbiton and up the Hill, whistling softly and thoughtfully.

It was just at this time that Gandalf reappeared after his long absence. For three years after the Party he had been away. Then he paid Frodo a brief visit, and after taking a good look at him he went off again. During the next year or two he had turned up fairly often, coming unexpectedly after dusk, and going off without warning before sunrise. He would not discuss his own business and journeys, and seemed chiefly interested in small news about Frodo's health and doings.

Then suddenly his visits had ceased. It was over nine years since Frodo had seen or heard of him, and he had begun to think that the wizard would never return and had given up all interest in hobbits. But that evening, as Sam was walking home and twilight was fading, there came the once familiar tap on the study window.

Frodo welcomed his old friend with surprise and great

delight. They looked hard at one another.

"All well eh?" said Gandalf. "You look the same as ever, Frodo!"

"So do you," Frodo replied; but secretly he thought that Gandalf looked older and more careworn. He pressed him for news of himself and of the wide world, and soon they were deep in talk, and they stayed up far into the night.

Next morning after a late breakfast, the wizard was sitting with Frodo by the open window of the study. A bright fire was on the hearth, but the sun was warm, and the wind was in the South. Everything looked fresh, and the new green of Spring was shimmering in the fields and on the tips of the trees' fingers.

Gandalf was thinking of a spring, nearly eighty years before, when Bilbo had run out of Bag End without a handkerchief. His hair was perhaps whiter than it had been then, and his beard and eyebrows were perhaps longer, and his face more lined with care and wisdom; but his eyes were as bright as ever, and he smoked and blew smoke-rings with the same vigour and delight.

He was smoking now in silence, for Frodo was sitting still, deep in thought. Even in the light of morning he felt the dark shadow of the tidings that Gandalf had brought. At last he broke. the silence.

"Last night you began to tell me strange things about my ring, Gandalf," he said. "And then you stopped, because you said that such matters were best left until daylight. Don't you think you had better finish now? You say the ring is dangerous, far more dangerous than I guess. In what way?"

"In many ways," answered the wizard. "It is far more powerful than I ever dared to think at first, so powerful that in the end it would utterly overcome anyone of mortal race who possessed it. It would possess him.

"In Eregion long ago many Elven-rings were made, magic rings as you call them, and they were, of course, of various kinds: some more potent and some less. The lesser rings were only essays in the craft before it was full-grown, and to the Elven-smiths they were but trifles — yet still to my mind dangerous for mortals. But the Great Rings, the Rings of Power, they were perilous.

"A mortal, Frodo, who keeps one of the Great Rings, does not die, but he does not grow or obtain more life, he merely continues, until at last every minute is a weariness. And if he often uses the Ring to make himself invisible, he *fades*: he becomes in the end invisible permanently, and walks in the twilight under the eye of the dark power that rules the Rings. Yes, sooner or later — later, if he is strong or well-meaning to begin with, but neither strength nor good purpose will last-sooner or later the dark power will devour him."

"How terrifying!" said Frodo. There was another long silence. The sound of Sam Gamgee cutting the lawn came in from the garden.

"How long have you known this?" asked Frodo at length. "And how much did Bilbo know?"

"Bilbo knew no more than he told you, I am sure," said Gandalf. "He would certainly never have passed on to you anything that he thought would be a danger, even though I promised to look after you. He thought the ring was very beautiful, and very useful at need; and if anything was wrong or queer, it was himself. He said that it was 'growing on his mind', and he was always worrying about it; but he did not suspect that the ring itself was to blame. Though he had found out that the thing needed looking after; it did not seem always of the same size or weight; it shrank or expanded in an odd way, and might suddenly slip off a finger where it had been tight."

"Yes, he warned me of that in his last letter," said Frodo, "so I have always kept it on its chain."

"Very wise," said Gandalf. "But as for his long life, Bilbo never connected it with the ring at all. He took all the credit for that to himself, and he was very proud of it. Though he was getting restless and uneasy. *Thin and stretched* he said. A sign that the ring was getting control."

"How long have you known all this?" asked Frodo again.

"Known?" said Gandalf. "I have known much that only the Wise know, Frodo. But if you mean "known about *this* ring", well, I still do not *know*, one might say. There is a last test to make. But I no longer doubt my guess.

"When did I first begin to guess?" he mused, searching back in memory. "Let me see — it was in the year that the White Council drove the dark power from Mirkwood, just before the Battle of Five Armies, that Bilbo found his ring. A shadow fell on my heart then, though I did not know yet what I feared. I wondered often how Gollum came by a Great Ring, as plainly it was — that at least was clear from the first. Then I heard Bilbo's strange story of how he had 'won' it, and I could not believe it. When I at last got the truth out of him, I saw at once that he had been trying to put his claim to the ring beyond doubt. Much like Gollum with his 'birthday present'. The lies were too much alike for my comfort. Clearly the ring had an unwholesome power that set to work on its keeper at once. That was the first real warning I had that all was not well. I told Bilbo often that such rings were better left unused; but he resented it, and soon got angry. There was little else that I could do. I could not take it from him without doing greater harm; and I had no right to do so anyway. I could only watch and wait. I might perhaps have consulted Saruman the White, but something always held me back."

"Who is he?" asked Frodo. "I have never heard of him before."

"Maybe not," answered Gandalf. "Hobbits are, or were, no concern of his. Yet he is great among the Wise. He is the chief of my order and the head of the Council. His knowledge is deep, but his pride has grown with it, and he takes ill any meddling. The lore of the Elven-rings, great and small, is his province. He has long studied it, seeking the lost secrets of their making; but when the Rings were debated in the Council, all that he would reveal to us of his ring-lore told against my fears. So my doubt slept — but uneasily. Still I watched and I waited.

"And all seemed well with Bilbo. And the years passed. Yes, they passed, and they seemed not to touch him. He showed no signs of age. The shadow fell on me again. But I said to myself: 'After all he comes of a long-lived family on his mother's side. There is time yet. Wait!'

"And I waited. Until that night when he left this house. He said and did things then that filled me with a fear that no words of Saruman could allay. I knew at last that something dark and deadly was at work. And I have spent most of the years since then in finding out the truth of it."

"There wasn't any permanent harm done, was there?" asked Frodo anxiously. "He would get all right in time, wouldn't he? Be able to rest in peace, I mean?"

"He felt better at once," said Gandalf. "But there is only one Power in this world that knows all about the Rings and their effects; and as far as I know there is no Power in the world that knows all about hobbits. Among the Wise I am the only one that goes in for hobbit-lore: an obscure branch of knowledge, but full of surprises. Soft as butter they can be, and yet sometimes as tough as old tree-roots. I think it likely that some would resist the Rings far longer than most of the Wise would believe. I don't think you need worry about Bilbo.

"Of course, he possessed the ring for many years, and used it, so it might take a long while for the influence to wear off — before it was safe for him to see it again, for instance. Otherwise, he might live on for years, quite happily: just stop as he was when he parted with it. For he gave it up in the end of his own accord: an important point No, I was not troubled about dear Bilbo any more, once he had let the thing go. It is for *you* that I feel responsible.

"Ever since Bilbo left I have been deeply concerned about you, and about all these charming, absurd, helpless hobbits. It would be a grievous blow to the world, if the Dark Power overcame the Shire; if all your kind, jolly, stupid Bolgers, Hornblowers, Boffins, Bracegirdles, and the rest, not to mention the ridiculous Bagginses, became enslaved."

Frodo shuddered. "But why should we be?" he asked. "And why should he want such slaves?"

"To tell you the truth," replied Gandalf, "I believe that hitherto — *hitherto*, mark you — he has entirely overlooked the existence of hobbits. You should be thankful. But your safety has passed. He does not need you — he has many more useful servants — but he won't forget you again. And hobbits as miserable slaves would please him far more than hobbits happy and free. There is such a thing as malice and revenge!"

"Revenge?" said Frodo. "Revenge for what? I still don't understand what all this has to do with Bilbo and myself, and our ring."

"It has everything to do with it," said Gandalf. "You do not know the real peril yet; but you shall. I was not sure of it myself when I was last here; but the time has come to speak. Give me the ring for a moment."

Frodo took it from his breeches-pocket, where it was clasped to a chain that hung from his belt. He unfastened it and handed it slowly to the wizard. It felt suddenly very heavy, as if either it or Frodo himself was in some way reluctant for Gandalf to touch it.

Gandalf held it up. It looked to be made of pure and solid gold. "Can you see any markings on it?" he asked.

"No," said Frodo. "There are none. It is quite plain, and it never shows a scratch or sign of wear."

"Well then, look!" To Frodo's astonishment and distress the wizard threw it suddenly into the middle of a glowing corner of the fire. Frodo gave a cry and groped for the tongs; but Gandalf held him back.

"Wait!" he said in a commanding voice, giving Frodo a quick look from under his bristling brows.

No apparent change came over the ring. After a while Gandalf got up, closed the shutters outside the window, and drew the curtains. The room became dark and silent, though the clack of Sam's shears, now nearer to the windows, could still be heard faintly from the garden. For a moment the wizard stood looking at the fire; then he stooped and removed the ring to the hearth with the tongs, and at once picked it up. Frodo gasped.

"It is quite cool," said Gandalf. "Take it!" Frodo received it on his shrinking palm: it seemed to have become thicker and heavier than ever.

"Hold it up!" said Gandau "And look closely!"

As Frodo did so he now saw fine lines, finer than the finest pen-strokes, running along the ring, outside and inside: lines of fire that seemed to form the letters of a flowing script. They shone piercingly bright, and yet remote, as if out of a great depth.

"I cannot read the fiery letters," said Frodo in a quavering voice. "No," said Gandalf, "but I can. The letters are Elvish, of an ancient mode, but the language is that of Mordor, which I will not utter here. But this in the Common Tongue is what is said, close enough:

> *One Ring to rule them all, One Ring to find them,*
> *One Ring to bring them all and in the darkness bind them.*

It is only two lines of a verse long known in Elven-lore:

> *Three Rings for the Elven-kings under the sky*
> *Seven for the Dwarf-lords in their halls of stone,*

Nine for Mortal Men doomed to die,
  One for the Dark Lord on his dark throne
In the Land of Mordor where the Shadows lie.
  One Ring to rule them all, One Ring to find them,
  One Ring to bring them all and in the darkness bind them
In the Land of Mordor where the Shadows lie."

He paused, and then said slowly in a deep voice: "This is the Master-ring, the One Ring to rule them all. This is the One Ring that he lost many ages ago, to the great weakening of his power. He greatly desires it — but he must *not* get it."

Frodo sat silent and motionless. Fear seemed to stretch out a vast hand, like a dark cloud rising in the East and looming up to engulf him. "This ring!" he stammered. "How, how on earth did it come to me?"

"Ah!" said Gandalf. "That is a very long story. The beginnings lie back in the Black Years, which only the lore-masters now remember. If I were to tell you all that tale, we should still be sitting here when Spring had passed into Winter.

"But last night I told you of Sauron the Great, the Dark Lord. The rumours that you have heard are true: he has indeed arisen again and left his hold in Mirkwood and returned to his ancient fastness in the Dark Tower of Mordor. That name even you hobbits have heard of, like a shadow on the borders of old stories. Always after a defeat and a respite, the Shadow takes another shape and grows again."

"I wish it need not have happened in my time," said Frodo.

"So do I," said Gandalf, "and so do all who live to see such times. But that is not for them to decide. All we have to decide is what to do with the time that is given us. And already, Frodo, our time is beginning to look black. The Enemy is fast becoming very strong. His plans are far from ripe, I think, but they are ripening. We shall be hard put to it. We should be very hard put to it, even if it were not for this dreadful chance.

"The Enemy still lacks one thing to give him strength and knowledge to beat down all resistance, break the last defences, and cover all the lands in a second darkness. He lacks the One Ring.

"The Three, fairest of all, the Elf-lords hid from him, and his hand never touched them or sullied them. Seven the Dwarf-kings possessed, but three he has recovered, and the others the dragons have consumed. Nine he gave to Mortal Men, proud and great, and so ensnared them. Long ago they fell under the dominion of the One, and they became Ringwraiths, shadows under his great Shadow, his most terrible servants. Long ago. It is many a year since the Nine walked abroad. Yet who knows? As the Shadow grows once more, they too may walk again. But come! We will not speak of such things even in the morning of the Shire.

"So it is now: the Nine he has gathered to himself; the Seven also, or else they are destroyed. The Three are hidden still. But that no longer troubles him. He only needs the One; for he made that Ring himself, it is his, and he let a great part of his own former power pass into it, so that he could rule all the others. If he recovers it, then he will command them all again, wherever they be, even the Three, and all that has been wrought with them will be laid bare, and he will be stronger than ever.

"And this is the dreadful chance, Frodo. He believed that the One had perished; that the Elves had destroyed it, as should have been done. But he knows now that it has *not* perished, that it has been found. So he is seeking it, seeking it, and all his thought is bent on it. It is his great hope and our great fear."

"Why, why wasn't it destroyed?" cried Frodo. "And how did the Enemy ever come to lose it, if he was so strong, and it was so precious to him?" He clutched the Ring in his hand, as if he saw already dark fingers stretching out to seize it.

"It was taken from him," said Gandalf. "The strength of the Elves to resist him was greater long ago; and not all Men were estranged from them. The Men of Westernesse came to their aid. That is a chapter of ancient history which it might be good to recall; for there was sorrow then too, and gathering dark, but great valour, and great deeds that were not wholly vain. One day, perhaps, I will tell you all the tale, or you shall hear it told in full by one who knows it best.

"But for the moment, since most of all you need to know how this thing came to you, and that will be tale enough, this is all that I will say. It was Gil-galad, Elven-king and Elendil of Westernesse who overthrew Sauron, though they themselves perished in the deed; and Isildur Elendil's son cut the Ring from Sauron's hand and took it for his own. Then Sauron was vanquished and his spirit fled and was hidden for long years, until his shadow took shape again in Mirkwood.

"But the Ring was lost. It fell into the Great River, Anduin, and vanished. For Isildur was marching north along the east banks of the River, and near the Gladden Fields he was waylaid by the Orcs of the Mountains, and almost all his folk were slain. He leaped into the waters, but the Ring slipped from his finger as he swam, and then the Orcs saw him and killed him with arrows."

Gandalf paused. "And there in the dark pools amid the Gladden Fields," he said, "the Ring passed out of knowledge and legend; and even so much of its history is known now only to a few, and the Council of the Wise could discover no more. But at last I can carry on the story, I think.

"Long after, but still very long ago, there lived by the banks of the Great River on the edge of Wilderland a clever-handed and quiet-footed little people. I guess they were of hobbit-kind; akin to the fathers of the fathers of the Stoors, for they loved the River, and often swam in it, or made little boats of reeds. There was among them a family of high repute, for it was large and wealthier than most, and it was ruled by a grandmother of the folk, stern and wise in old lore, such as they had. The most inquisitive and curious-minded of that family was called Sméagol. He was interested in roots and beginnings; he dived into deep pools; he burrowed under trees and growing plants; he tunnelled into green mounds; and he ceased to look up at the hill-tops, or the leaves on trees, or the flowers opening in the air: his head and his eyes were downward.

"He had a friend called Déagol, of similar sort, sharper-eyed but not so quick and strong. On a time they took a boat and went down to the Gladden Fields, where there were great beds of iris and flowering reeds. There Sméagol got out and went nosing about the banks but Déagol sat in the boat and fished. Suddenly a great fish took his hook, and before he knew where he was, he was dragged out and down into the water, to the bottom. Then he let go of his line, for he thought he saw something shining in the river-bed; and holding his breath he grabbed at it.

"Then up he came spluttering, with weeds in his hair and a handful of mud; and he swam to the bank. And behold! when he washed the mud away, there in his hand lay a beautiful golden ring; and it shone and glittered in the sun, so that his heart was glad. But Sméagol had been watching him from behind a tree, and as Déagol gloated over the ring, Sméagol came softly up behind.

"'Give us that, Déagol, my love,' said Sméagol, over his friend's shoulder.

"'Why?' said Déagol.

"'Because it's my birthday, my love, and I wants it,' said Sméagol.

"'I don't care,' said Déagol. 'I have given you a present already, more than I could afford. I found this, and I'm going to keep it.'

"'Oh, are you indeed, my love,' said Sméagol; and he caught Déagol by the throat and strangled him, because the gold looked so bright and beautiful. Then he put the ring on his finger.

"No one ever found out what had become of Déagol; he was murdered far from home, and his body was cunningly hidden. But Sméagol returned alone; and he found that none of his family could see him, when he was wearing the ring. He was very pleased with his discovery and he concealed it; and he used it to find out secrets, and he put his knowledge to crooked and malicious uses. He became sharp-eyed and keen-eared for all that was hurtful. The ring had given him power according to his stature. It is not to be wondered at that he became very unpopular and was shunned (when visible) by all his relations. They kicked him, and he bit their feet. He took to thieving, and going about muttering to himself, and gurgling in his throat. So they called him *Gollum*, and cursed him, and told him to go far away; and his grandmother, desiring peace, expelled him from the family and turned him out of her hole.

"He wandered in loneliness, weeping a little for the hardness of the world, and he journeyed up the River, till he came to a stream that flowed down from the mountains, and he went that way. He caught fish in deep pools with invisible fingers and ate them raw. One day it was very hot, and as he was bending over a pool, he felt a burning on the back of his head, and a dazzling light from the water pained his wet eyes. He wondered at it, for he had almost forgotten about the Sun. Then for the last time he looked up and shook his fist at her.

"But as he lowered his eyes, he saw far ahead the tops of the Misty Mountains out of which the stream came. And he thought suddenly: It would be cool and shady under those mountains. The Sun could not watch me there. The roots of those mountains must be roots indeed; there must be great secrets buried there which have not been discovered since the beginning.'

"So he journeyed by night up into the highlands, and he found a little cave out of which the dark stream ran; and he wormed his way like a maggot into the heart of the hills, and vanished out of all knowledge. The Ring went into the shadows with him, and even the maker, when his power had begun to grow again, could learn nothing of it."

"Gollum!" cried Frodo. "Gollum? Do you mean that this is

the very Gollum-creature that Bilbo met? How loathsome!"

"I think it is a sad story," said the wizard, "and it might have happened to others, even to some hobbits that I have known."

"I can't believe that Gollum was connected with hobbits, however distantly," said Frodo with some heat. "What an abominable notion!"

"It is true all the same," replied Gandalf. "About their origins, at any rate, I know more than hobbits do themselves. And even Bilbo's story suggests the kinship. There was a great deal in the background of their minds and memories that was very similar. They understood one another remarkably well, very much better than a hobbit would understand, say, a Dwarf, or an Orc, or even an Elf. Think of the riddles they both knew, for one thing."

"Yes," said Frodo. "Though other folk besides hobbits ask riddles, and of much the same sort. And hobbits don't cheat. Gollum meant to cheat all the time. He was just trying to put poor Bilbo off his guard. And I daresay it amused his wickedness to start a game which might end in providing him with an easy victim, but if he lost would not hurt him."

"Only too true, I fear," said Gandalf. "But there was something else in it, I think, which you don't see yet. Even Gollum was not wholly ruined. He had proved tougher than even one of the Wise would have guessed — as a hobbit might. There was a little corner of his mind that was still his own, and light came through it, as through a chink in the dark: light out of the past. It was actually pleasant, I think, to hear a kindly voice again, bringing up memories of wind, and trees, and sun on the grass, and such forgotten things.

"But that, of course, would only make the evil part of him angrier in the end — unless it could be conquered. Unless it could be cured." Gandalf sighed. "Alas! there is little hope of that for him. Yet not no hope. No, not though he possessed the Ring so long, almost as far back as he can remember. For it was long since he had worn it much: in the black darkness it was seldom needed. Certainly he had never 'faded'. He is thin and tough still. But the thing was eating up his mind, of course, and the torment had become almost unbearable.

"All the 'great secrets' under the mountains had turned out to be just empty night: there was nothing more to find out, nothing worth doing, only nasty furtive eating and resentful remembering. He was altogether wretched. He hated the dark, and he hated light more: he hated everything, and the Ring most of all."

"What do you mean?" said Frodo. "Surely the Ring was his precious and the only thing he cared for? But if he hated it, why didn't he get rid of it, or go away and leave it?"

"You ought to begin to understand, Frodo, after all you have heard," said Gandalf. "He hated it and loved it, as he hated and loved himself. He could not get rid of it. He had no will left in the matter.

"A Ring of Power looks after itself, Frodo. *It* may slip off treacherously, but its keeper never abandons it. At most he plays with the idea of handing it on to some one else's care — and that only at an early stage, when it first begins to grip. But as far as I know Bilbo alone in history has ever gone beyond playing, and really done it. He needed all my help, too. And even so he would never have just forsaken it, or cast it aside. It was not Gollum, Frodo, but the Ring itself that decided things. The Ring left *him*."

"What, just in time to meet Bilbo?" said Frodo. "Wouldn't an Orc have suited it better?"

"It is no laughing matter," said Gandalf. "Not for you. It was the strangest event in the whole history of the Ring so far: Bilbo's arrival just at that time, and putting his hand on it, blindly, in the dark.

"There was more than one power at work, Frodo. The Ring was trying to get back to its master. It had slipped from Isildur's hand and betrayed him; then when a chance came it caught poor Déagol, and he was murdered; and after that Gollum, and it had devoured him. It could make no further use of him: he was too small and mean; and as long as it stayed with him he would never leave his deep pool again. So now, when its master was awake once more and sending out his dark thought from Mirkwood, it abandoned Gollum. Only to be picked up by the most unlikely person imaginable: Bilbo from the Shire!

"Behind that there was something else at work, beyond any design of the Ring-maker. I can put it no plainer than by saying that Bilbo was *meant* to find the Ring, and *not* by its maker. In which case you also were *meant* to have it. And that may be an encouraging thought."

"It is not," said Frodo. "Though I am not sure that I understand you. But how have you learned all this about the Ring, and about Gollum? Do you really know it all, or are you just guessing still?"

Gandalf looked at Frodo, and his eyes glinted. "I knew much and I have learned much," he answered. "But I am not going to give an account of all my doings to *you*. The history of Elendil and Isildur and the One Ring is known to all the Wise. Your ring is shown to be that One Ring by the fire-writing alone, apart from any other evidence."

"And when did you discover that?" asked Frodo, interrupting.

"Just now in this room, of course," answered the wizard sharply. "But I expected to find it. I have come back from dark journeys and long search to make that final test. It is the last proof, and all is now only too clear. Making out Gollum's part, and fitting it into the gap in the history, required some thought. I may have started with guesses about Gollum, but I am not guessing now. I know. I have seen him."

"You have seen Gollum?" exclaimed Frodo in amazement.

"Yes. The obvious thing to do, of course, if one could. I tried long ago; but I have managed it at last."

"Then what happened after Bilbo escaped from him? Do you know that?"

"Not so clearly. What I have told you is what Gollum was willing to tell — though not, of course, in the way I have reported it. Gollum is a liar, and you have to sift his words. For

50

instance, he called the Ring his 'birthday present', and he stuck to that. He said it came from his grandmother, who had lots of beautiful things of that kind. A ridiculous story. I have no doubt that Sméagol's grandmother was a matriarch, a great person in her way, but to talk of her possessing many Elven-rings was absurd, and as for giving them away, it was a lie. But a lie with a grain of truth.

"The murder of Déagol haunted Gollum, and he had made up a defence, repeating it to his 'precious' over and over again, as he gnawed bones in the dark, until he almost believed it. It *was* his birthday. Déagol ought to have given the ring to him. It had obviously turned up just so as to be a present. It *was* his birthday present, and so on, and on.

"I endured him as long as I could, but the truth was desperately important, and in the end I had to be harsh. I put the fear of fire on him, and wrung the true story out of him, bit by bit, together with much snivelling and snarling. He thought he was misunderstood and ill-used. But when he had at last told me his history, as far as the end of the Riddle-game and Bilbo's escape, he would not say any more, except in dark hints. Some other fear was on him greater than mine. He muttered that he was going to get his own back. People would see if he would stand being kicked, and driven into a hole and then *robbed*. Gollum had good friends now, good friends and very strong. They would help him. Baggins would pay for it. That was his chief thought. He hated Bilbo and cursed his name. What is more, he knew where he came from."

"But how did he find that out?" asked Frodo,

"Well, as for the name, Bilbo very foolishly told Gollum himself; and after that it would not be difficult to discover his country, once Gollum came out. Oh yes, he came out. His longing for the Ring proved stronger than his fear of the Orcs, or even of the light. After a year or two he left the mountains. You see, though still bound by desire of it, the Ring was no longer devouring him; he began to revive a little. He felt old, terribly old, yet less timid, and he was mortally hungry.

"Light, light of Sun and Moon, he still feared and hated, and he always will, I think; but he was cunning. He found he could hide from daylight and moonshine, and make his way swiftly and softly by dead of night with his pale cold eyes, and catch small frightened or unwary things. He grew stronger and bolder with new food and new air. He found his way into Mirkwood, as one would expect."

"Is that where you found him?" asked Frodo.

"I saw him there," answered Gandalf, "but before that he had wandered far, following Bilbo's trail. It was difficult to learn anything from him for certain, for his talk was constantly interrupted by curses and threats. 'What had it got in its pocketses?' he said. 'I wouldn't say, no precious. Little cheat. Not a fair question. It cheated first, it did. It broke the rules. We ought to have squeezed it, yes precious. And we will, precious!'

"That is a sample of his talk. I don't suppose you want any more. I had weary days of it. But from hints dropped among the snarls I gathered that his padding feet had taken him at last to Esgaroth, and even to the streets of Dale, listening secretly and peering. Well, the news of the great events went far and wide in Wilderland, and many had heard Bilbo's name and knew where he came from. We had made no secret of our return journey to his home in the West. Gollum's sharp ears would soon learn what he wanted."

"Then why didn't he track Bilbo further?" asked Frodo. "Why didn't he come to the Shire?"

"Ah," said Gandalf, "now we come to it. I think Gollum tried to. He set out and came back westward, as far as the Great River. But then he turned aside. He was not daunted by the distance, I am sure. No, something else drew him away. So my friends think, those that hunted him for me.

"The Wood-elves tracked him first, an easy task for them, for his trail was still fresh then. Through Mirkwood and back again it led them, though they never caught him. The wood was full of the rumour of him, dreadful tales even among beasts and birds. The Woodmen said that there was some new terror abroad, a ghost that drank blood. It climbed trees to find nests; it crept into holes to find the young; it slipped through windows to find cradles.

"But at the western edge of Mirkwood the trail turned away. It wandered off southwards and passed out of the Wood-elves ken, and was lost. And then I made a great mistake. Yes, Frodo, and not the first; though I fear it may prove the worst. I let the matter be. I let him go; for I had much else to think of at that time, and I still trusted the lore of Saruman.

"Well, that was years ago. I have paid for it since with many dark and dangerous days. The trail was long cold when I took it up again, after Bilbo left here. And my search would have been in vain, but for the help that I had from a friend: Aragorn, the greatest traveller and huntsman of this age of the world. Together we sought for Gollum down the whole length of Wilderland, without hope, and without success. But at last, when I had given up the chase and turned to other parts, Gollum was found. My friend returned out of great perils bringing the miserable creature with him.

"What he had been doing he would not say. He only wept and called us cruel, with many a *gollum* in his throat; and when we pressed him he whined and cringed, and rubbed his long hands, licking his fingers as if they pained him, as if he remembered some old torture. But I am afraid there is no possible doubt: he had made his slow, sneaking way, step by step, mile by mile, south, down at last to the Land of Mordor."

A heavy silence fell in the room. Frodo could hear his heart beating. Even outside everything seemed still. No sound of Sam's shears could now be heard.

"Yes, to Mordor," said Gandalf. "Alas! Mordor draws all wicked things, and the Dark Power was bending all its will to gather them there. The Ring of the Enemy would leave its mark, too, leave him open to the summons. And all folk were whispering then of the new Shadow in the South, and its hatred of the West. There were his fine new friends, who would help him in his revenge!

"Wretched fool! In that land he would learn much, too much for his comfort. And sooner or later as he lurked and pried on the borders he would be caught, and taken — for examination. That was the way of it, I fear. When he was found he had already been there long, and was on his way back. On some errand of mischief. But that does not matter much now. His worst mischief was done.

"Yes, alas! through him the Enemy has learned that the One has been found again. He knows where Isildur fell. He knows where Gollum found his ring. He knows that it is a Great Ring, for it gave long life. He knows that it is not one of the Three, for they have never been lost, and they endure no evil. He knows that it is not one of the Seven, or the Nine, for they are accounted for. He knows that it is the One. And he has at last heard, I think, of *hobbits* and the *Shire*.

"The Shire — he may be seeking for it now, if he has not already found out where it lies. Indeed, Frodo, I fear that he may even think that the long-unnoticed name of *Baggins* has become important."

"But this is terrible!" cried Frodo. "Far worse than the worst that I imagined from your hints and warnings. O Gandalf, best of friends, what am I to do? For now I am really afraid. What am I to do? What a pity that Bilbo did not stab that vile creature, when he had a chance!"

"Pity? It was Pity that stayed his hand. Pity, and Mercy: not to strike without need. And he has been well rewarded, Frodo. Be sure that he took so little hurt from the evil, and escaped in the end, because he began his ownership of the Ring so. With Pity."

"I am sorry," said Frodo. "But I am frightened; and I do not feel any pity for Gollum."

"You have not seen him," Gandalf broke in.

"No, and I don't want to," said Frodo. "I can't understand you. Do you mean to say that you, and the Elves, have let him live on after all those horrible deeds? Now at any rate he is as bad as an Orc, and just an enemy. He deserves death."

"Deserves it! I daresay he does. Many that live deserve death. And some that die deserve life. Can you give it to them? Then do not be too eager to deal out death in judgement. For even the very wise cannot see all ends. I have not much hope that Gollum can be cured before he dies, but there is a chance of it. And he is bound up with the fate of the Ring. My heart tells me that he has some part to play yet, for good or ill, before the end; and when that comes, the pity of Bilbo may rule the fate of many — yours not least. In any case we did not kill him: he is very old and very wretched. The Wood-elves have him in prison, but they treat him with such kindness as they can find in their wise hearts."

"All the same," said Frodo, "even if Bilbo could not kill Gollum, I wish he had not kept the Ring. I wish he had never found it, and that I had not got it! Why did you let me keep it? Why didn't you make me throw it away, or, or destroy it?"

"Let you? Make you?" said the wizard. "Haven't you been listening to all that I have said? You are not thinking of what you are saying. But as for throwing it away, that was obviously wrong. These Rings have a way of being found. In evil hands it might have done great evil. Worst of all, it might have fallen into the hands of the Enemy. Indeed it certainly would; for this is the One, and he is exerting all his power to find it or draw it to himself.

"Of course, my dear Frodo, it was dangerous for you; and that has troubled me deeply. But there was so much at stake that I had to take some risk — though even when I was far away there has never been a day when the Shire has not been guarded by watchful eyes. As long as you never used it, I did not think that the Ring would have any lasting effect on you, not for evil, not at any rate for a very long time. And you must remember that nine years ago, when I last saw you, I still knew little for certain."

"But why not destroy it, as you say should have been done

long ago?" cried Frodo again. "If you had warned me, or even sent me a message, I would have done away with it."

"Would you? How would you do that? Have you ever tried?"

"No. But I suppose one could hammer it or melt it."

"Try!" said Gandalf. "Try now!"

Frodo drew the Ring out of his pocket again and looked at it. It now appeared plain and smooth, without mark or device that he could see. The gold looked very fair and pure, and Frodo thought how rich and beautiful was its colour, how perfect was its roundness. It was an admirable thing and altogether precious. When he took it out he had intended to fling it from him into the very hottest part of the fire. But he found now that he could not do so, not without a great struggle. He weighed the Ring in his hand, hesitating, and forcing himself to remember all that Gandalf had told him; and then with an effort of will he made a movement, as if to cast it away — he found that he had put it back in his pocket.

Gandalf laughed grimly. "You see? Already you too, Frodo, cannot easily let it go, nor will to damage it. And I could not 'make' you — except by force, which would break your mind. But as for breaking the Ring, force is useless. Even if you took it and struck it with a heavy sledgehammer, it would make no dint in it. It cannot be unmade by your hands, or by mine.

"Your small fire, of course, would not melt even ordinary gold. This Ring has already passed through it unscathed, and even unheated. But there is no smith's forge in this Shire that could change it at all. Not even the anvils and furnaces of the Dwarves could do that. It has been said that dragon-fire could melt and consume the Rings of Power, but there is not now any dragon left on earth in which the old fire is hot enough; nor was there ever any dragon, not even Ancalagon the Black, who could have harmed the One Ring, the Ruling Ring, for that was made by Sauron himself.

"There is only one way: to find the Cracks of Doom in the depths of Orodruin, the Fire-mountain, and cast the Ring in there, if you really wish to destroy it, to put it beyond the grasp of the Enemy for ever."

"I do really wish to destroy it!" cried Frodo. "Or, well, to have it destroyed. I am not made for perilous quests. I wish I had never seen the Ring! Why did it come to me? Why was I chosen?"

"Such questions cannot be answered," said Gandalf. "You may be sure that it was not for any merit that others do not possess: not for power or wisdom, at any rate. But you have been chosen, and you must therefore use such strength and heart and wits as you have."

"But I have so little of any of these things! You are wise and powerful. Will you not take the Ring?"

"No!" cried Gandalf, springing to his feet. "With that power I should have power too great and terrible. And over me the Ring would gain a power still greater and more deadly." His eyes flashed and his face was lit as by a fire within. "Do not tempt me! For I do not wish to become like the Dark Lord himself. Yet the way of the Ring to my heart is by pity, pity for weakness and the desire of strength to do good. Do not tempt me! I dare not take it, not even to keep it safe, unused. The wish to wield it would be too great for my strength. I shall have such need of it. Great perils lie before me."

He went to the window and drew aside the curtains and the shutters. Sunlight streamed back again into the room. Sam passed along the path outside whistling. "And now," said the wizard, turning back to Frodo, "the decision lies with you. But I will always help you." He laid his hand on Frodo's shoulder. "I will help you bear this burden, as long as it is yours to bear. But we must do something, soon. The Enemy is moving."

There was a long silence. Gandalf sat down again and puffed at his pipe, as if lost in thought. His eyes seemed closed, but under the lids he was watching Frodo intently. Frodo gazed fixedly at the red embers on the hearth, until they filled all his vision, and he seemed to be looking down into profound wells of fire. He was thinking of the fabled Cracks of Doom and the terror of the Fiery Mountain.

"Well!" said Gandalf at last. "What are you thinking about? Have you decided what to do?"

"No!" answered Frodo, coming back to himself out of darkness, and finding to his surprise that it was not dark, and that out of the window he could see the sunlit garden. "Or perhaps, yes. As far as I understand what you have said, I suppose I must keep the Ring and guard it, at least for the present, whatever it may do to me."

"Whatever it may do, it will be slow, slow to evil, if you keep it with that purpose," said Gandalf.

"I hope so," said Frodo. "But I hope that you may find some other better keeper soon. But in the meanwhile it seems that I am a danger, a danger to all that live near me. I cannot keep the Ring and stay here. I ought to leave Bag End, leave the Shire, leave everything and go away." He sighed.

"I should like to save the Shire, if I could — though there have been times when I thought the inhabitants too stupid and dull for words, and have felt that an earthquake or an invasion of dragons might be good for them. But I don't feel like that now. I feel that as long as the Shire lies behind, safe and comfortable, I shall find wandering more bearable: I shall know that somewhere there is a firm foothold, even if my feet cannot stand there again.

"Of course, I have sometimes thought of going away, but I imagined that as a kind of holiday, a series of adventures like Bilbo's or better, ending in peace. But this would mean exile, a flight from danger into danger, drawing it after me. And I suppose I must go alone, if I am to do that and save the Shire. But I feel very small, and very uprooted, and well — desperate. The Enemy is so strong and terrible."

He did not tell Gandalf, but as he was speaking a great desire to follow Bilbo flamed up in his heart — to follow Bilbo, and even perhaps to find him again. It was so strong that it overcame his fear: he could almost have run out there and then down the road without his hat, as Bilbo had done on a similar morning long ago.

"My dear Frodo!" exclaimed Gandalf. "Hobbits really are amazing creatures, as I have said before. You can learn all that there is to know about their ways in a month, and yet after a hundred years they can still surprise you at a pinch. I hardly expected to get such an answer, not even from you. But Bilbo made no mistake in choosing his heir, though he little thought how important it would prove. I am afraid you are right. The Ring will not be able to stay hidden in the Shire much longer; and for your own sake, as well as for others, you will have to go, and leave the name of Baggins behind you. That name will not be safe to have, outside the Shire or in the Wild. I will give you a travelling name now. When you go, go as Mr. Underhill.

"But I don't think you need go alone. Not if you know of anyone you can trust, and who would be willing to go by your side — and that you would be willing to take into unknown perils. But if you look for a companion, be careful in choosing! And be careful of what you say, even to your closest friends! The enemy has many spies and many ways of hearing."

Suddenly he stopped as if listening. Frodo became aware that all was very quiet, inside and outside. Gandalf crept to one side of the window. Then with a dart he sprang to the sill, and thrust a long arm out and downwards. There was a squawk, and up came Sam Gamgee's curly head hauled by one ear.

"Well, well, bless my beard!" said Gandalf. "Sam Gamgee is it? Now what may you be doing?"

"Lor bless you, Mr. Gandalf, sir!" said Sam. "Nothing! Leastways I was just trimming the grass-border under the window, if you follow me." He picked up his shears and exhibited them as evidence.

"I don't," said Gandalf grimly. "It is some time since I last heard the sound of your shears. How long have you been eavesdropping?"

"Eavesdropping, sir? I don't follow you, begging your pardon. There ain't no eaves at Bag End, and that's a fact."

"Don't be a fool! What have you heard, and why did you listen?" Gandalf's eyes flashed and his brows stuck out like bristles.

"Mr. Frodo, sir!" cried Sam quaking. "Don't let him hurt me, sir! Don't let him turn me into anything unnatural! My old dad would take on so. I meant no harm, on my honour, sir!"

"He won't hurt you," said Frodo, hardly able to keep from laughing, although he was himself startled and rather puzzled. "He knows, as well as I do, that you mean no harm. But just you up and answer his questions straight away!"

"Well, sir," said Sam dithering a little. "I heard a deal that I didn't rightly understand, about an enemy, and rings, and Mr. Bilbo, sir, and dragons, and a fiery mountain, and — and Elves, sir. I listened because I couldn't help myself, if you know what I mean. Lor bless me, sir, but I do love tales of that sort. And I believe them too, whatever Ted may say. Elves, sir! I would dearly love to see *them*. Couldn't you take me to see Elves, sir, when you go?"

Suddenly Gandalf laughed. "Come inside!" he shouted, and putting out both his arms he lifted the astonished Sam, shears, grass-clippings and all, right through the window and stood him on the floor. "Take you to see Elves, eh?" he said, eyeing Sam closely, but with a smile flickering on his face. "So you heard that Mr. Frodo is going away?"

"I did, sir. And that's why I choked: which you heard seemingly. I tried not to, sir, but it burst out of me: I was so upset."

"It can't be helped, Sam," said Frodo sadly. He had suddenly realized that flying from the Shire would mean more painful partings than merely saying farewell to the familiar comforts of Bag End. "I shall have to go. But — and here he looked hard at Sam — "if you really care about me, you will keep that *dead* secret. See? If you don't, if you even breathe a word of what you've heard here, then I hope Gandalf will turn you into a spotted toad and fill the garden full of grass-snakes."

Sam fell on his knees, trembling. "Get up, Sam!" said

Gandalf. "I have thought of something better than that. Something to shut your mouth, and punish you properly for listening. You shall go away with Mr. Frodo!"

"Me, sir!" cried Sam, springing up like a dog invited for a walk. "Me go and see Elves and all! Hooray!" he shouted, and then burst into tears.

CHAPTER
THREE

Three is Company

"You ought to go quietly, and you ought to go soon," said Gandalf. Two or three weeks had passed, and still Frodo made no sign of getting ready to go.

"I know. But it is difficult to do both," he objected. "If I just vanish like Bilbo, the tale will be all over the Shire in no time."

"Of course you mustn't vanish!" said Gandalf. "That wouldn't do at all! I said *soon, not instantly*. If you can think of any way of slipping out of the Shire without its being generally known, it will be worth a little delay. But you must not delay too long."

"What about the autumn, on or after Our Birthday?" asked Frodo. "I think I could probably make some arrangements by then."

To tell the truth, he was very reluctant to start, now that it had come to the point. Bag End seemed a more desirable residence than it had for years, and he wanted to savour as much as he could of his last summer in the Shire. When autumn came, he knew that part at least of his heart would think more kindly of journeying, as it always did at that season. He had indeed privately made up his mind to leave on this fiftieth birthday: Bilbo's one hundred and twenty-eighth. It seemed somehow the proper day on which to set out and follow him. Following Bilbo was uppermost in his mind, and the one thing that made the thought of leaving bearable. He thought as little as possible about the Ring, and where it might lead him in the end. But he did not tell all his thoughts to Gandalf. What the wizard guessed was always difficult to tell.

He looked at Frodo and smiled. "Very well," he said. "I think that will do — but it must not be any later. I am getting very anxious. In the meanwhile, do take care, and don't let out any hint of where you are going! And see that Sam Gamgee does not talk. If he does, I really shall turn him into a toad."

"As for *where* I am going," said Frodo, "it would be difficult to give that away, for I have no clear idea myself, yet."

"Don't be absurd!" said Gandalf. "I am not warning you against leaving an address at the post-office! But you are leaving the Shire — and that should not be known, until you are far away. And you must go, or at least set out, either North, South, West or East — and the direction should certainly not be known."

"I have been so taken up with the thoughts of leaving Bag End, and of saying farewell, that I have never even considered the direction," said Frodo. "For where am I to go? And by what shall I steer? What is to be my quest? Bilbo went to find a treasure, there and back again; but I go to lose one, and not return, as far as I can see."

"But you cannot see very far," said Gandalf. "Neither can I. It may be your task to find the Cracks of Doom; but that quest may be for others: I do not know. At any rate you are not ready for that long road yet."

"No indeed!" said Frodo. "But in the meantime what course am I to take?"

"Towards danger; but not too rashly, nor too straight," answered the wizard. "If you want my advice, make for Rivendell. That journey should not prove too perilous, though the Road is less easy than it was, and it will grow worse as the year fails."

"Rivendell!" said Frodo. "Very good: I will go east, and I will make for Rivendell. I will take Sam to visit the Elves; he will be delighted." He spoke lightly; but his heart was moved suddenly with a desire to see the house of Elrond Halfelven, and breathe the air of that deep valley where many of the Fair Folk still dwelt in peace.

One summer's evening an astonishing piece of news reached the *Ivy Bush* and *Green Dragon*. Giants and other portents on the borders of the Shire were forgotten for more important matters: Mr. Frodo was selling Bag End, indeed he had already sold it — to the Sackville-Bagginses!

"For a nice bit, too," said some. "At a bargain price," said others, "and that's more likely when Mistress Lobelia's the buyer." (Otho had died some years before, at the ripe but disappointed age of 102.)

Just why Mr. Frodo was selling his beautiful hole was even more debatable than the price. A few held the theory — supported by the nods and hints of Mr. Baggins himself — that Frodo's money was running out: he was going to leave Hobbiton and live in a quiet way on the proceeds of the sale down in Buckland among his Brandybuck relations. "As far from the Sackville-Bagginses as may be," some added. But so firmly fixed had the notion of the immeasurable wealth of the Bagginses of Bag End become that most found this hard to believe, harder than any other reason or unreason that their fancy could suggest: to most it suggested a dark and yet unrevealed plot by Gandalf. Though he kept himself very quiet and did not go about by day, it was well known that he was "hiding up in the Bag End". But however a removal might fit in with the designs of his wizardry, there was no doubt about the fact: Frodo Baggins was going back to Buckland.

"Yes, I shall be moving this autumn," he said. "Merry Brandybuck is looking out for a nice little hole for me, or perhaps a small house."

As a matter of fact with Merry's help he had already chosen and bought a little house at Crickhollow in the country beyond Bucklebury. To all but Sam he pretended he was going to settle down there permanently. The decision to set out eastwards had suggested the idea to him; for Buckland was on the eastern borders of the Shire, and as he had lived there in childhood his going back would at least seem credible.

Gandalf stayed in the Shire for over two months. Then one evening, at the end of June, soon after Frodo's plan had been finally arranged, he suddenly announced that he was going off again next morning. "Only for a short while, I hope," he said. "But I am going down beyond the southern borders to get some news, if I can. I have been idle longer than I should."

He spoke lightly, but it seemed to Frodo that he looked rather worried. "Has anything happened?" he asked.

"Well no; but I have heard something that has made me anxious and needs looking into. If I think it necessary after all for you to get off at once, I shall come back immediately, or at least send word. In the meanwhile stick to your plan; but be more careful than ever, especially of the Ring. Let me impress on you once more: *don't use it!*"

He went off at dawn. "I may be back any day," he said. "At the very latest I shall come back for the farewell party. I think after all you may need my company on the Road."

At first Frodo was a good deal disturbed, and wondered often what Gandalf could have heard; but his uneasiness wore off, and in the fine weather he forgot his troubles for a while. The Shire had seldom seen so fair a summer, or so rich an autumn: the trees were laden with apples, honey was dripping in the combs, and the corn was tall and full.

Autumn was well under way before Frodo began to worry about Gandalf again. September was passing and there was still no news of him. The Birthday, and the removal, drew nearer, and still he did not come, or send word. Bag End began to be busy. Some of Frodo's friends came to stay and help him with the packing: there was Fredegar Bolger and Folco Boffin, and of course his special friends Pippin Took and Merry Brandybuck.

Between them they turned the whole place upside-down.

On September 20th two covered carts went off laden to Buckland, conveying the furniture and goods that Frodo had not sold to his new home, by way of the Brandywine Bridge. The next day Frodo became really anxious, and kept a constant look-out for Gandalf. Thursday, his birthday morning, dawned as fair and clear as it had long ago for Bilbo's great party. Still Gandalf did not appear. In the evening Frodo gave his farewell feast: it was quite small, just a dinner for himself and his four helpers; but he was troubled and felt in no mood for it. The thought that he would so soon have to part with his young friends weighed on his heart. He wondered how he would break it to them.

The four younger hobbits were, however, in high spirits, and the party soon became very cheerful in spite of Gandalf's absence. The dining-room was bare except for a table and chairs, but the food was good, and there was good wine: Frodo's wine had not been included in the sale to the Sackville-Bagginses.

"Whatever happens to the rest of my stuff, when the S.-B.s get their claws on it, at any rate I have found a good home for this!" said Frodo, as he drained his glass. It was the last drop of Old Winyards.

When they had sung many songs, and talked of many things they had done together, they toasted Bilbo's birthday, and they drank his health and Frodo's together according to Frodo's custom. Then they went out for a sniff of air, and glimpse of the stars, and then they went to bed. Frodo's party was over, and Gandalf had not come.

The next morning they were busy packing another cart with the remainder of the luggage. Merry took charge of this, and drove off with Fatty (that is Fredegar Bolger). "Someone must get there and warm the house before you arrive," said Merry. "Well, see you later — the day after tomorrow, if you don't go to sleep on the way!"

Folco went home after lunch, but Pippin remained behind. Frodo was restless and anxious, listening in vain for a sound of Gandalf. He decided to wait until nightfall. After that, if Gandalf wanted him urgently, he would go to Crickhollow, and might even get there first. For Frodo was going on foot. His plan — for pleasure and a last look at the Shire as much as any other reason — was to walk from Hobbiton to Bucklebury Ferry, taking it fairly easy.

"I shall get myself a bit into training, too," he said, looking at himself in a dusty mirror in the half-empty hall. He had not done any strenuous walking for a long time, and the reflection looked rather flabby, he thought.

After lunch, the Sackville-Bagginses, Lobelia and her sandy-haired son, Lotho, turned up, much to Frodo's annoyance. "Ours at last!" said Lobelia, as she stepped inside. It was not polite; nor strictly true, for the sale of Bag End did not take effect until midnight. But Lobelia can perhaps be forgiven: she had been obliged to wait about seventy-seven years longer for Bag End than she once hoped, and she was now a hundred years old. Anyway, she had come to see that nothing she had paid for had been carried off; and she wanted the keys. It took a long while to satisfy her, as she had brought a complete inventory with her and went right through it. In the end she departed with Lotho and the spare key and the promise that the other key would be left at the Gamgees' in Bagshot Row. She snorted, and showed plainly that she thought the Gamgees capable of plundering the hole during the night. Frodo did not offer her any tea.

He took his own tea with Pippin and Sam Gamgee in the kitchen. It had been officially announced that Sam was coming to Buckland "to do for Mr. Frodo and look after his bit of garden": an arrangement that was approved by the Gaffer, though it did not console him for the prospect of having Lobelia as a neighbour.

"Our last meal at Bag End!" said Frodo, pushing back his chair. They left the washing up for Lobelia. Pippin and Sam strapped up their three packs and piled them in the porch. Pippin went out for a last stroll in the garden. Sam disappeared.

The sun went down. Bag End seemed sad and gloomy and dishevelled. Frodo wandered round the familiar rooms, and saw the light of the sunset fade on the walls, and shadows creep out of the corners. It grew slowly dark indoors. He went out and walked down to the gate at the bottom of the path, and then on a short way down the Hill Road. He half expected to see Gandalf come striding up through the dusk.

The sky was clear and the stars were growing bright. "It's going to be a fine night," he said aloud. "That's good for a beginning. I feel like walking. I can't bear any more hanging about. I am going to start, and Gandalf must follow me." He turned to go back, and then stopped, for he heard voices, just round the corner by the end of Bagshot Row. One voice was certainly the old Gaffer's; the other was strange, and somehow unpleasant. He could not make out what it said, but he heard the Gaffer's answers, which were rather shrill. The old man seemed put out.

"No, Mr. Baggins has gone away. Went this morning, and my Sam went with him: anyway all his stuff went. Yes, sold out and gone, I tell'ee. Why? Why's none of my business, or yours. Where to? That ain't no secret. He's moved to Bucklebury or some such place, away down yonder. Yes it is — a tidy way. I've never been so far myself; they're queer folks in Buckland. No, I can't give no message. Good night to you!"

Footsteps went away down the Hill. Frodo wondered vaguely why the fact that they did not come on up the Hill seemed a great relief. "I am sick of questions and curiosity about my doings, I suppose," he thought. "What an inquisitive lot they all are!" He had half a mind to go and ask the Gaffer who the inquirer was; but he thought better (or worse) of it, and turned and walked quickly back to Bag End.

Pippin was sitting on his pack in the porch. Sam was not

there. Frodo stepped inside the dark door. "Sam!" he called.
"Sam! Time!"

"Coming, sir!" came the answer from far within, followed
soon by Sam himself, wiping his mouth. He had been saying
farewell to the beer-barrel in the cellar.

"All aboard, Sam?" said Frodo.

"Yes, sir. I'll last for a bit now, sir."

Frodo shut and locked the round door, and gave the key to
Sam. "Run down with this to your home, Sam!" he said. "Then
cut along the Row and meet us as quick as you can at the gate
in the lane beyond the meadows. We are not going through the
village tonight. Too many ears pricking and eyes prying." Sam
ran off at full speed.

"Well, now we're off at last!" said Frodo. They shouldered
their packs and took up their sticks, and walked round the
corner to the west side of Bag End. "Good-bye!" said Frodo,
looking at the dark blank windows. He waved his hand, and
then turned and (following Bilbo, if he had known it) hurried
after Peregrin down the garden-path. They jumped over the
low place in the hedge at the bottom and took to the fields,
passing into the darkness like a rustle in the grasses.

At the bottom of the Hill on its western side they came to the
gate opening on to a narrow lane. There they halted and
adjusted the straps of their packs. Presently Sam appeared,
trotting quickly and breathing hard; his heavy pack was hoisted
high on his shoulders, and he had put on his head a tall
shapeless felt bag, which he called a hat. In the gloom he
looked very much like a dwarf.

"I am sure you have given me all the heaviest stuff," said Frodo.
"I pity snails, and all that carry their homes on their backs."

"I could take a lot more yet, sir. My packet is quite light,"
said Sam stoutly and untruthfully.

"No, you don't, Sam!" said Pippin. "It is good for him. He's got
nothing except what he ordered us to pack. He's been slack lately,
and he'll feel the weight less when he's walked off some of his own."

"Be kind to a poor old hobbit!" laughed Frodo. "I shall be as thin as a willow-wand, I'm sure, before I get to Buckland. But I was talking nonsense. I suspect you have taken more than your share, Sam, and I shall look into it at our next packing." He picked up his stick again. "Well, we all like walking in the dark," he said, "so let's put some miles behind us before bed."

For a short way they followed the lane westwards. Then leaving it they turned left and took quietly to the fields again. They went in single file along hedgerows and the borders of coppices, and night fell dark about them. In their dark cloaks they were as invisible as if they all had magic rings. Since they were all hobbits, and were trying to be silent, they made no noise that even hobbits would hear. Even the wild things in the fields and woods hardly noticed their passing.

After some time they crossed the Water, west of Hobbiton, by a narrow plank-bridge. The stream was there no more than a winding black ribbon, bordered with leaning alder-trees. A mile or two further south they hastily crossed the great road from the Brandywine Bridge; they were now in the Tookland and bending south-eastwards they made for the Green Hill Country. As they began to climb its first slopes they looked back and saw the lamps in Hobbiton far off twinkling in the gentle valley of the Water. Soon it disappeared in the folds of the darkened land, and was followed by Bywater beside its grey pool. When the light of the last farm was far behind, peeping among the trees, Frodo turned and waved a hand in farewell.

"I wonder if I shall ever look down into that valley again," he said quietly.

When they had walked for about three hours they rested. The night was clear, cool, and starry, but smoke-like wisps of mist were creeping up the hill-sides from the streams and deep meadows. Thin-clad birches, swaying in a light wind above their heads, made a black net against the pale sky. They ate a very frugal supper (for hobbits), and then went on again. Soon they struck a narrow road, that went rolling up and down, fading grey into the darkness ahead: the road to Woodhall and Stock, and the Bucklebury Ferry. It climbed away from the main road in the Water-valley, and wound over the skirts of the Green Hills towards Woody-End, a wild corner of the Eastfarthing.

After a while they plunged into a deeply cloven track between tall trees that rustled their dry leaves in the night. It was very dark. At first they talked, or hummed a tune softly together, being now far away from inquisitive ears. Then they marched on in silence, and Pippin began to lag behind. At last, as they began to climb a steep slope, he stopped and yawned.

"I am so sleepy," he said, "that soon I shall fall down on the road. Are you going to sleep on your legs? It is nearly midnight."

"I thought you liked walking in the dark," said Frodo. "But there is no great hurry. Merry expects us some time the day after tomorrow; but that leaves us nearly two days more. We'll halt at the first likely spot."

"The wind's in the West," said Sam. "If we get to the other side of this hill, we shall find a spot that is sheltered and snug enough, sir. There is a dry fir-wood just ahead, if I remember rightly." Sam knew the land well within twenty miles of Hobbiton, but that was the limit of his geography.

Just over the top of the hill they came on the patch of fir-wood. Leaving the road they went into the deep resin-scented darkness of the trees, and gathered dead sticks and cones to make a fire. Soon they had a merry crackle of flame at the foot of a large fir-tree and they sat round it for a while, until they began to nod. Then, each in an angle of the great tree's roots, they curled up in their cloaks and blankets, and were soon fast alseep. They set no watch; even Frodo feared no danger yet, for they were still in the heart of the Shire. A few creatures came and looked at them when the fire had died away. A fox passing through the wood on business of his own stopped several minutes and sniffed.

"Hobbits!" he thought. "Well, what next? I have heard of

strange doings in this land, but I have seldom heard of a hobbit sleeping out of doors under a tree. Three of them! There's something mighty queer behind this." He was quite right, but he never found out any more about it.

The morning came, pale and clammy. Frodo woke up first, and found that a tree-root had made a hole in his back, and that his neck was stiff. "Walking for pleasure! Why didn't I drive?" he thought, as he usually did at the beginning of an expedition. "And all my beautiful feather beds are sold to the Sackville-Bagginses! These tree-roots would do them good." He stretched. "Wake up, hobbits!" he cried. "It's a beautiful morning."

"What's beautiful about it?" said Pippin, peering over the edge of his blanket with one eye. "Sam! Get breakfast ready for half-past nine! Have you got the bath-water hot?"

Sam jumped up, looking rather bleary. "No, sir, I haven't, sir!" he said.

Frodo stripped the blankets from Pippin and rolled him over, and then walked off to the edge of the wood. Away eastward the sun was rising red out of the mists that lay thick on the world. Touched with gold and red the autumn trees seemed to be sailing rootless in a shadowy sea. A little below him to the left the road ran down steeply into a hollow and disappeared.

When he returned Sam and Pippin had got a good fire going. "Water!" shouted Pippin. "Where's the water?"

"I don't keep water in my pockets," said Frodo.

"We thought you had gone to find some," said Pippin, busy setting out the food, and cups. "You had better go now."

"You can come too," said Frodo, "and bring all the water-bottles." There was a stream at the foot of the hill. They filled their bottles and the small camping kettle at a little fall where the water fell a few feet over an outcrop of grey stone. It was icy cold; and they spluttered and puffed as they bathed their faces and hands.

When their breakfast was over, and their packs all trussed up again, it was after ten o'clock, and the day was beginning to turn fine and hot. They went down the slope, and across the stream where it dived under the road, and up the next slope, and up and down another shoulder of the hills; and by that time their cloaks, blankets, water, food, and other gear already seemed a heavy burden.

The day's march promised to be warm and tiring work. After some miles, however, the road ceased to roll up and down: it climbed to the top of a steep bank in a weary zig-zagging sort of way, and then prepared to go down for the last time. In front of them they saw the lower lands dotted with small clumps of trees that melted away in the distance to a brown woodland haze. They were looking across the Woody End towards the Brandywine River. The road wound away before them like a piece of string.

"The road goes on for ever," said Pippin; "but I can't without a rest. It is high time for lunch." He sat down on the bank at the side of the road and looked away east into the haze, beyond which lay the River, and the end of the Shire in which he had spent all his life. Sam stood by him. His round eyes were wide open — for he was looking across lands he had never seen to a new horizon.

"Do Elves live in those woods?" he asked.

"Not that I ever heard," said Pippin. Frodo was silent. He too was gazing eastward along the road, as if he had never seen it before. Suddenly he spoke, aloud but as if to himself, saying slowly:

> *The Road goes ever on and on*
> *Down from the door where it began.*
> *Now far ahead the Road has gone,*
> *And I must follow, if I can,*
> *Pursuing it with weary feet,*
> *Until it joins some larger way,*
> *Where many paths and errands meet.*
> *And whither then? I cannot say.*

"That sounds like a bit of old Bilbo's rhyming," said Pippin. "Or is it one of your imitations? It does not sound altogether encouraging."

"I don't know," said Frodo. "It came to me then, as if I was making it up; but I may have heard it long ago. Certainly it reminds me very much of Bilbo in the last years, before he went away. He used often to say there was only one Road; that it was like a great river: its springs were at every doorstep, and every path was its tributary. 'It's a dangerous business, Frodo, going out of your door.' he used to say. 'You step into the Road, and if you don't keep your feet, there is no knowing where you might be swept off to. Do you realize that this is the very path that goes through Mirkwood, and that if you let it, it might take you to the Lonely Mountain or even further and to worse places?' He used to say that on the path outside the front door at Bag End, especially after he had been out for a long walk."

"Well, the Road won't sweep me anywhere for an hour at least," said Pippin, unslinging his pack. The others followed his example, putting their packs against the bank and their legs out into the road. After a rest they had a good lunch, and then more rest.

The sun was beginning to get low and the light of afternoon was on the land as they went down the hill. So far they had not met a soul on the road. This way was not much used, being hardly fit for carts, and there was little traffic to the Woody End. They had been jogging along again for an hour or more when Sam stopped a moment as if listening. They were now on level ground, and the road after much winding lay straight ahead through grass-land sprinkled with tall trees, outliers of the approaching woods.

"I can hear a pony or a horse coming along the road behind," said Sam.

They looked back, but the turn of the road prevented them from seeing far. "I wonder if that is Gandalf coming after us," said Frodo; but even as he said it, he had a feeling that it was not so, and a sudden desire to hide from the view of the rider came over him.

"It may not matter much," he said apologetically, "but I would rather not be seen on the road — by anyone. I am sick of my doings being noticed and discussed. And if it is Gandalf," he added as an afterthought, "we can give him a little surprise, to pay him out for being so late. Let's get out of sight!"

The other two ran quickly to the left and down into a little hollow not far from the road. There they lay flat. Frodo hesitated for a second: curiosity or some other feeling was struggling with his desire to hide. The sound of hoofs drew nearer. Just in time he threw himself down in a patch of long grass behind a tree that over-shadowed the road. Then he lifted his head and peered cautiously above one of the great roots.

Round the corner came a black horse, no hobbit-pony but a full-sized horse; and on it sat a large man, who seemed to crouch in the saddle, wrapped in a great black cloak and hood, so that only his boots in the high stirrups showed below; his face was shadowed and invisible.

When it reached the tree and was level with Frodo the horse stopped. The riding figure sat quite still with its head bowed, as if listening. From inside the hood came a noise as of someone sniffing to catch an elusive scent; the head turned from side to side of the road.

A sudden unreasoning fear of discovery laid hold of Frodo, and he thought of his Ring. He hardly dared to breathe, and yet the desire to get it out of his pocket became so strong that he began slowly to move his hand. He felt that he had only to slip it on, and then he would be safe. The advice of Gandalf seemed absurd. Bilbo had used the Ring. "And I am still in the Shire," he thought, as his hand touched the chain on which it hung. At that moment the rider sat up, and shook the reins. The horse stepped forward, walking slowly at first, and then breaking into a quick trot.

Frodo crawled to the edge of the road and watched the rider, until he dwindled into the distance. He could not be quite sure, but it seemed to him that suddenly, before it passed out of sight, the horse turned aside and went into the trees on the right.

"Well, I call that very queer, and indeed disturbing," said Frodo to himself, as he walked towards his companions. Pippin and Sam had remained flat in the grass, and had seen nothing; so Frodo described the rider and his strange behaviour.

"I can't say why, but I felt certain he was looking or *smelling* for me; and also I felt certain that I did not want him to discover me. I've never seen or felt anything like it in the Shire before."

"But what has one of the Big People got to do with us?" said Pippin. "And what is he doing in this part of the world?"

"There are some Men about," said Frodo. "Down in the South-farthing they have had trouble with Big People, I believe. But I have never heard of anything like this rider. I wonder where he comes from."

"Begging your pardon," put in Sam suddenly, "I know where he comes from. It's from Hobbiton that this here black rider comes, unless there's more than one. And I know where he's going to."

"What do you mean?" said Frodo sharply, looking at him in astonishment. "Why didn't you speak up before?"

"I have only just remembered, sir. It was like this: when I got back to our hole yesterday evening with the key, my dad, he says to me: *Hallo, Sam!* he says. *I thoight you were away with Mr. Frodo this morning. There's been a strange customer asking for Mr. Baggins of Bag End, and he's only just gone. I've sent him on to Bucklebury. Not that I liked the sound of him. He seemed mighty put out, when I told him Mr. Baggins had left his old home for good. Hissed at me, he did. It gave me quite a shudder. What sort of a fellow was he? says I to the Gaffer. I don't know, says he; but he wasn't a hobbit. He was tall and black-like, and he stooped over me. I reckon it was one of the Big Folk from foreign parts. He spoke funny.*

"I couldn't stay to hear more, sir, since you were waiting;

and I didn't give much heed to it myself. The Gaffer is getting old, and more than a bit blind, and it must have been near dark when this fellow come up the Hill and found him taking the air at the end of our Row. I hope he hasn't done no harm, sir, nor me."

"The Gaffer can't be blamed anyway," said Frodo. "As a matter of fact I heard him talking to a stranger, who seemed to be inquiring for me, and I nearly went and asked him who it was. I wish I had, or you had told me about it before. I might have been more careful on the road."

"Still, there may be no connexion between this rider and the Gaffer's stranger," said Pippin. "We left Hobbiton secretly enough, and I don't see how he could have followed us."

"What about the *smelling*, sir?" said Sam. "And the Gaffer said he was a black chap."

"I wish I had waited for Gandalf," Frodo muttered. "But perhaps it would only have made matters worse."

"Then you know or guess something about this rider?" said Pippin, who had caught the muttered words.

"I don't know, and I would rather not guess," said Frodo.

"All right, cousin Frodo! You can keep your secret for the present, if you want to be mysterious. In the meanwhile what are we to do? I should like a bite and a sup, but somehow I think we had better move on from here. Your talk of sniffing riders with invisible noses bas unsettled me."

"Yes, I think we will move on now," said Frodo; "but not on the road — in case that rider comes back, or another follows him. We ought to do a good step more today. Buckland is still miles away."

The shadows of the trees were long and thin on the grass, as they started off again. They now kept a stone's throw to the left of the road, and kept out of sight of it as much as they could. But this hindered them; for the grass was thick and tussocky, and the ground uneven, and the trees began to draw together into thickets.

The sun had gone down red behind the hills at their backs, and evening was coming on before they came back to the road at the end of the long level over which it had run straight for some miles. At that point it bent left and went down into the lowlands of the Yale making for Stock; but a lane branched right, winding through a wood of ancient oak-trees on its way to Woodhall. "That is the way for us," said Frodo.

Not far from the road-meeting they came on the huge hulk of a tree: it was still alive and had leaves on the small branches that it had put out round the broken stumps of its long-fallen limbs; but it was hollow, and could be entered by a great crack on the side away from the road. The hobbits crept inside, and sat there upon a floor of old leaves and decayed wood. They rested and had a light meal, talking quietly and listening from time to time.

Twilight was about them as they crept back to the lane. The West wind was sighing in the branches. Leaves were whispering. Soon the road began to fall gently but steadily into the dusk. A star came out above the trees in the darkening East before them. They went abreast and in step, to keep up their spirits. After a time, as the stars grew thicker and brighter, the feeling of disquiet left them, and they no longer listened for the sound of hoofs. They began to hum softly, as hobbits have a way of doing as they walk along, especially when they are drawing near to home at night. With most hobbits it is a supper-song or a bed-song; but these hobbits hummed a walking-song (though not, of course, without any mention of supper and bed). Bilbo Baggins had made the words, to a tune that was as old as the hills, and taught it to Frodo as they walked in the lanes of the Water-valley and talked about Adventure.

> *Upon the hearth the fire is red,*
> *Beneath the roof there is a bed;*
> *But not yet weary are our feet,*
> *Still round the corner we may meet*

A sudden tree or standing stone
That none have seen but we alone.
Tree and flower and leaf and grass,
Let them pass! Let them pass!
Hill and water under sky,
Pass them by! Pass them by!

Still round the corner there may wait
A new road or a secret gate,
And though we pass them by today,
Tomorrow we may come this way
And take the hidden paths that run
Towards the Moon or to the Sun.
Apple, thorn, and nut and sloe,
Let them go! Let them go!
Sand and stone and pool and dell,
Fare you well! Fare you well!

Home is behind, the world ahead,
And there are many paths to tread
Through shadows to the edge of night,
Until the stars are all alight.
Then world behind and home ahead,
We'll wander back to home and bed.
Mist and twilight, cloud and shade,
Away shall fade! Away shall fade!
Fire and lamp, and meat and bread,
And then to bed! And then to bed!

The song ended. "And *now* to bed! And *now* to bed!" sang Pippin in a high voice.

"Hush!" said Frodo. "I think I hear hoofs again."

They stopped suddenly and stood as silent as tree-shadows, listening. There was a sound of hoofs in the lane, some way behind, but coming slow and clear down the wind. Quickly and quietly they slipped off the path, and ran into the deeper shade under the oak-trees.

"Don't let us go too far!" said Frodo. "I don't want to be seen, but I want to see if it is another Black Rider."

"Very well!" said Pippin. "But don't forget the sniffing!"

The hoofs drew nearer. They had no time to find any hiding-place better than the general darkness under the trees; Sam and Pippin crouched behind a large tree-bole, while Frodo crept back a few yards towards the lane. It showed grey and pale, a line of fading light through the wood. Above it the stars were thick in the dim sky, but there was no moon.

The sound of hoofs stopped. As Frodo watched he saw something dark pass across the lighter space between two trees, and then halt. It looked like the black shade of a horse led by a smaller black shadow. The black shadow stood close to the point where they had left the path, and it swayed from side to side. Frodo thought he heard the sound of snuffling. The shadow bent to the ground, and then began to crawl towards him.

Once more the desire to slip on the Ring came over Frodo; but this time it was stronger than before. So strong that, almost before he realized what he was doing, his hand was groping in his pocket. But at that moment there came a sound like mingled song and laughter. Clear voices rose and fell in the starlit air. The black shadow straightened up and retreated. It climbed on to the shadowy horse and seemed to vanish across the lane into the darkness on the other side. Frodo breathed again.

"Elves!" exclaimed Sam in a hoarse whisper. "Elves, sir!" He would have burst out of the trees and dashed off towards the voices, if they had not pulled him back.

"Yes, it is Elves," said Frodo. "One can meet them sometimes in the Woody End. They don't live in the Shire, but they wander into it in Spring and Autumn, out of their own lands away beyond the Tower Hills. I am thankful that they do! You did not see, but that Black Rider stopped just here and was actually crawling towards us when the song began. As soon as he heard the voices he slipped away."

"What about the Elves?" said Sam, too excited to trouble about the rider. "Can't we go and see them?"

"Listen! They are coming this way," said Frodo. "We have only to wait."

The singing drew nearer. One clear voice rose now above the others. It was singing in the fair elven-tongue, of which Frodo knew only a little, and the others knew nothing. Yet the sound blending with the melody seemed to shape itself in their thought into words which they only partly understood. This was the song as Frodo heard it:

> *Snow-white! Snow-white! O Lady clear!*
> *O Queen beyond the Western Seas!*
> *O Light to us that wander here*
> *Amid the world of woven trees!*
>
> *Gilthoniel! O Elbereth!*
> *Clear are thy eyes and bright thy breath!*
> *Snow-white! Snow-white! We sing to thee*
> *In a far land beyond the Sea.*
>
> *O stars that in the Sunless Year*
> *With shining hand by her were sown,*
> *In windy fields now bright and clear*
> *We see your silver blossom blown!*
>
> *O Elbereth! Gilthoniel!*
> *We still remember, we who dwell*
> *In this far land beneath the trees,*
> *Thy starlight on the Western Seas.*

The song ended. "These are High Elves! They spoke the name of Elbereth!" said Frodo in amazement. "Few of that fairest folk are ever seen in the Shire. Not many now remain in Middle-earth, east of the Great Sea. This is indeed a strange chance!"

The hobbits sat in shadow by the wayside. Before long the Elves came down the lane towards the valley. They passed slowly, and the hobbits could see the starlight glimmering on their hair and in their eyes. They bore no lights, yet as they walked a shimmer, like the light of the moon above the rim of the hills before it rises, seemed to fall about their feet. They were now silent, and as the last Elf passed he turned and looked towards the hobbits and laughed.

"Hail, Frodo!" he cried. "You are abroad late. Or are you perhaps lost?" Then he called aloud to the others, and all the company stopped and gathered round.

"This is indeed wonderful!" they said. "Three hobbits in a wood at night! We have not seen such a thing since Bilbo went away. What is the meaning of it?"

"The meaning of it, fair people," said Frodo, "is simply that we seem to be going the same way as you are. I like walking under the stars. But I would welcome your company.

"But we have no need of other company, and hobbits are so dull," they laughed. "And how do you know that we go the same way as you, for you do not know whither we are going?"

"And how do you know my name?" asked Frodo in return.

"We know many things," they said. "We have seen you often before with Bilbo, though you may not have seen us."

"Who are you, and who is your lord?" asked Frodo.

"I am Gildor," answered their leader, the Elf who had first hailed him. "Gildor Inglorion of the House of Finrod. We are Exiles, and most of our kindred have long ago departed and we too are now only tarrying here a while, ere we return over the Great Sea. But some of our kinsfolk dwell still in peace in Rivendell. Come now, Frodo, tell us what you are doing? For we see that there is some shadow of fear upon you."

"O Wise People!" interrupted Pippin eagerly. "Tell us about the Black Riders!"

"Black Riders?" they said in low voices. "Why do you ask about Black Riders?"

"Because two Black Riders have overtaken us today, or one has done so twice," said Pippin; "only a little while ago he slipped away as you drew near."

The Elves did not answer at once, but spoke together softly in their own tongue. At length Gildor turned to the hobbits. "We will not speak of this here," he said. "We think you had best come now with us. It is not our custom, but for this time we will take you on our road, and you shall lodge with us tonight, if you will."

"O Fair Folk! This is good fortune beyond my hope," said Pippin. Sam was speechless. "I thank you indeed, Gildor Inglorion," said Frodo bowing. "*Elen síla lúmenn' omentielvo*, a star shines on the hour of our meeting," he added in the high-elven speech.

"Be careful, friends!" cried Gildor laughing. "Speak no secrets! Here is a scholar in the Ancient Tongue. Bilbo was a good master. Hail, Elf-friend!" he said, bowing to Frodo. "Come now with your friends and join our company! You had best walk in the middle so that you may not stray. You may be weary before we halt."

"Why? Where are you going?" asked Frodo.

"For tonight we go to the woods on the hills above Woodhall. It is some miles, but you shall have rest at the end of it, and it will shorten your journey tomorrow.

They now marched on again in silence, and passed like shadows and faint lights: for Elves (even more than hobbits) could walk when they wished without sound or footfall. Pippin soon began to feel sleepy, and staggered once or twice; but each time a tall Elf at his side put out his arm and saved him from a fall. Sam walked along at Frodo's side, as if in a dream, with an expression on his face half of fear and half of astonished joy.

The woods on either side became denser; the trees were now younger and thicker; and as the lane went lower, running down into a fold of the hills, there were many deep brakes of hazel on the rising slopes at either hand. At last the Elves turned aside from the path. A green ride lay almost unseen through the thickets on the right; and this they followed as it wound away back up the wooded slopes on to the top of a shoulder of the hills that stood out into the lower land of the river-valley. Suddenly they came out of the shadow of the trees, and before them lay a wide space of grass, grey under the night. On three sides the woods pressed upon it; but eastward the ground fell steeply and the tops of the dark trees, growing at the bottom of the slope, were below their feet. Beyond, the low lands lay dim and flat under the stars. Nearer at hand a few lights twinkled in the village of Woodhall.

The Elves sat on the grass and spoke together in soft voices; they seemed to take no further notice of the hobbits. Frodo and his companions wrapped themselves in cloaks and blankets, and drowsiness stole over them. The night grew on, and the lights in the valley went out. Pippin fell asleep, pillowed on a green hillock.

Away high in the East swung Remmirath, the Netted Stars, and slowly above the mists red Borgil rose, glowing like a jewel of fire. Then by some shift of airs all the mist was drawn away like a veil, and there leaned up, as he climbed over the rim of the world, the Swordsman of the Sky, Menelvagor with his shining belt. The Elves all burst into song. Suddenly under the trees a fire sprang up with a red light.

"Come!" the Elves called to the hobbits. "Come! Now is the time for speech and merriment!"

Pippin sat up and rubbed his eyes. He shivered. "There is a fire in the hall, and food for hungry guests," said an Elf standing before him.

At the south end of the greensward there was an opening. There the green floor ran on into the wood, and formed a wide space like a hall, roofed by the boughs of trees. Their great trunks ran like pillars down each side. In the middle there was a wood-fire blazing, and upon the tree-pillars torches with lights of gold and silver were burning steadily. The Elves sat round the fire upon the grass or upon the sawn rings of old trunks. Some went to and fro bearing cups and pouring drink; others brought food on heaped plates and dishes.

"This is poor fare," they said to the hobbits; "for we are lodging in the greenwood far from our halls. If ever you are our guests at home, we will treat you better."

"It seems to me good enough for a birthday-party," said Frodo.

Pippin afterwards recalled little of either food or drink, for his mind was filled with the light upon the elf-faces, and the sound of voices so various and so beautiful that he felt in a waking dream. But he remembered that there was bread, surpassing the savour of a fair white loaf to one who is starving; and fruits sweet as wildberries and richer than the tended fruits of gardens; he drained a cup that was filled with a fragrant draught, cool as a clear fountain, golden as a summer afternoon.

Sam could never describe in words, nor picture clearly to himself, what he felt or thought that night, though it remained in his memory as one of the chief events of his life. The nearest he ever got was to say: "Well, sir, if I could grow apples like that, I would call myself a gardener. But it was the singing that went to my heart, if you know what I mean."

Frodo sat, eating, drinking, and talking with delight; but his mind was chiefly on the words spoken. He knew a little of the elf-speech and listened eagerly. Now and again he spoke to those that served him and thanked them in their own language. They smiled at him and said laughing: "Here is a Jewel among hobbits!"

After a while Pippin fell fast asleep, and was lifted up and borne away to a bower under the trees; there he was laid upon a soft bed and slept the rest of the night away. Sam refused to leave his master. When Pippin had gone, he came and sat curled up at Frodo's feet, where at last he nodded and closed his eyes. Frodo remained long awake, talking with Gildor.

They spoke of many things, old and new, and Frodo

questioned Gildor much about happenings in the wide world outside the Shire. The tidings were mostly sad and ominous: of gathering darkness, the wars of Men, and the flight of the Elves. At last Frodo asked the question that was nearest to his heart:

"Tell me, Gildor, have you ever seen Bilbo since he left us?"

Gildor smiled. "Yes," he answered. "Twice. He said farewell to us on this very spot. But I saw him once again, far from here." He would say no more about Bilbo, and Frodo fell silent.

"You do not ask me or tell me much that concerns yourself, Frodo," said Gildor. "But I already know a little, and I can read more in your face and in the thought behind your questions. You are leaving the Shire, and yet you doubt that you will find what you seek, or accomplish what you intend, or that you will ever return. Is not that so?"

"It is," said Frodo; "but I thought my going was a secret known only to Gandalf and my faithful Sam." He looked down at Sam, who was snoring gently.

"The secret will not reach the Enemy from us," said Gildor.

"The Enemy?" said Frodo. "Then you know why I am leaving the Shire?"

"I do not know for what reason the Enemy is pursuing you," answered Gildor; "but I perceive that he is — strange indeed though that seems to me. And I warn you that peril is now both before you and behind you, and upon either side."

"You mean the Riders? I feared that they were servants of the Enemy. What *are* the Black Riders?"

"Has Gandalf told you nothing?"

"Nothing about such creatures."

"Then I think it is not for me to say more — lest terror should keep you from your journey. For it seems to me that you have set out only just in time, if indeed you are in time. You must now make haste, and neither stay nor turn back; for the Shire is no longer any protection to you."

"I cannot imagine what information could be more terrifying

than your hints and warnings," exclaimed Frodo. "I knew that danger lay ahead, of course; but I did not expect to meet it in our own Shire. Can't a hobbit walk from the Water to the River in peace?"

"But it is not your own Shire," said Gildor. "Others dwelt here before hobbits were; and others will dwell here again when hobbits are no more. The wide world is all about you: you can fence yourselves in, but you cannot for ever fence it out."

"I know — and yet it has always seemed so safe and familiar. What can I do now? My plan was to leave the Shire secretly, and make my way to Rivendell; but now my footsteps are dogged, before ever I get to Buckland."

"I think you should still follow that plan," said Gildor. "I do not think the Road will prove too hard for your courage. But if you desire clearer counsel, you should ask Gandalf. I do not know the reason for your flight, and therefore I do not know by what means your pursuers will assail you. These things Gandalf must know. I suppose that you will see him before you leave the Shire?"

"I hope so. But that is another thing that makes me anxious. I have been expecting Gandalf for many days. He was to have come to Hobbiton at the latest two nights ago; but he has never appeared. Now I am wondering what can have happened. Should I wait for him?"

Gildor was silent for a moment. "I do not like this news," he said at last. "That Gandalf should be late, does not bode well. But it is said: *Do not meddle in the affairs of Wizards, for they are subtle and quick to anger.* The choice is yours: to go or wait."

"And it is also said," answered Frodo: "*Go not to the Elves for counsel, for they will say both no and yes.*"

"Is it indeed?" laughed Gildor. "Elves seldom give unguarded advice, for advice is a dangerous gift, even from the wise to the wise, and all courses may run ill. But what would you? You have not told me all concerning yourself; and how then shall I choose better than you? But if you demand advice, I will for friendship's sake give it. I think you should now go at once, without delay; and if Gandalf does not come before you set out, then I also advise this: do not go alone. Take such friends as are trusty and willing. Now you should be grateful, for I do not give this counsel gladly. The Elves have their own labours and their own sorrows, and they are little concerned with the ways of hobbits, or of any other creatures upon earth. Our paths cross theirs seldom, by chance or purpose. In this meeting there may be more than chance; but the purpose is not clear to me, and I fear to say too much."

"I am deeply grateful," said Frodo; "but I wish you would tell me plainly what the Black Riders are. If I take your advice I may not see Gandalf for a long while, and I ought to know what is the danger that pursues me."

"Is it not enough to know that they are servants of the Enemy?" answered Gildor. "Flee them! Speak no words to them! They are deadly. Ask no more of me! But my heart forbodes that, ere all is ended, you, Frodo son of Drogo, will know more of these fell things than Gildor Inglorion. May Elbereth protect you!"

"But where shall I find courage?" asked Frodo. "That is what I chiefly need."

"Courage is found in unlikely places," said Gildor. "Be of good hope! Sleep now! In the morning we shall have gone; but we will send our messages through the lands. The Wandering Companies shall know of your journey, and those that have power for good shall be on the watch. I name you Elf-friend; and may the stars shine upon the end of your road! Seldom have we had such delight in strangers, and it is fair to hear words of the Ancient Speech from the lips of other wanderers in the world."

Frodo felt sleep coming upon him, even as Gildor finished speaking. "I will sleep now," he said; and the Elf led him to a bower beside Pippin, and he threw himself upon a bed and fell at once into a dreamless slumber.

CHAPTER
FOUR

A Short Cut to Mushrooms

In the morning Frodo woke refreshed. He was lying in a bower made by a living tree with branches laced and drooping to the ground; his bed was of fern and grass, deep and soft and strangely fragrant. The sun was shining through the fluttering leaves, which were still green upon the tree. He jumped up and went out.

Sam was sitting on the grass near the edge of the wood. Pippin was standing studying the sky and weather. There was no sign of the Elves.

"They have left us fruit and drink, and bread," said Pippin. "Come and have your breakfast. The bread tastes almost as good as it did last night. I did not want to leave you any, but Sam insisted."

Frodo sat down beside Sam and began to eat. "What is the plan for today?" asked Pippin.

"To walk to Bucklebury as quickly as possible," answered Frodo, and gave his attention to the food.

"Do you think we shall see anything of those Riders?" asked Pippin cheerfully. Under the morning sun the prospect of seeing a whole troop of them did not seem very alarming to him.

"Yes, probably," said Frodo, not liking the reminder. "But I hope to get across the river without their seeing us."

"Did you find out anything about them from Gildor?"

"Not much — only hints and riddles," said Frodo evasively.

"Did you ask about the sniffing?"

"We didn't discuss it," said Frodo with his mouth full.

"You should have. I am sure it is very important."

"In that case I am sure Gildor would have refused to explain it," said Frodo sharply. "And now leave me in peace for a bit! I don't want to answer a string of questions while I am eating. I want to think!"

"Good heavens!" said Pippin. "At breakfast?" He walked away towards the edge of the green.

From Frodo's mind the bright morning — treacherously bright, he thought — had not banished the fear of pursuit; and he pondered the words of Gildor. The merry voice of Pippin came to him. He was running on the green turf and singing.

"No! I could not!" he said to himself. "It is one thing to take my young friends walking over the Shire with me, until we are hungry and weary, and food and bed are sweet. To take them into exile, where hunger and weariness may have no cure, is quite another — even if they are willing to come. The inheritance is mine alone. I don't think I ought even to take Sam." He looked at Sam Gamgee, and discovered that Sam was watching him.

"Well, Sam!" he said. "What about it? I am leaving the Shire as soon as ever I can — in fact I have made up my mind now not even to wait a day at Crickhollow, if it can be helped."

"Very good, sir!"

"You still mean to come with me?"

"I do."

"It is going to be very dangerous, Sam. It is already dangerous. Most likely neither of us will come back."

"If you don't come back, sir, then I shan't, that's certain," said Sam. "*Don't you leave him!* they said to me. *Leave him!* I said. *I never mean to. I am going with him, if he climbs to the Moon; and if any of those Black Riders try to stop him, they'll have*

Sam Gamgee to reckon with, I said. They laughed."

"Who are *they*, and what are you talking about?"

"The Elves, sir. We had some talk last night; and they seemed to know you were going away, so I didn't see the use of denying it. Wonderful folk, Elves, sir! Wonderful!"

"They are," said Frodo. "Do you like them still, now you have had a closer view?"

"They seem a bit above my likes and dislikes, so to speak," answered Sam slowly. "It don't seem to matter what I think about them. They are quite different from what I expected — so old and young, and so gay and sad, as it were."

Frodo looked at Sam rather startled, half expecting to see some outward sign of the odd change that seemed to have come over him. It did not sound like the voice of the old Sam Gamgee that he thought he knew. But it looked like the old Sam Gamgee sitting there, except that his face was unusually thoughtful.

"Do you feel any need to leave the Shire now — now that your wish to see them has come true already?" he asked.

"Yes, sir. I don't know how to say it, but after last night I feel different. I seem to see ahead, in a kind of way. I know we are going to take a very long road, into darkness; but I know I can't turn back. It isn't to see Elves now, nor dragons, nor mountains, that I want — I don't rightly know what I want: but I have something to do before the end, and it lies ahead, not in the Shire. I must see it through, sir, if you understand me."

"I don't altogether. But I understand that Gandalf chose me a good companion. I am content. We will go together."

Frodo finished his breakfast in silence. Then standing up he looked over the land ahead, and called to Pippin.

"All ready to start?" he said as Pippin ran up. "We must be getting off at once. We slept late; and there are a good many miles to go."

"*You* slept late, you mean," said Pippin. "I was up long before; and we are only waiting for you to finish eating and thinking."

"I have finished both now. And I am going to make for Bucklebury Ferry as quickly as possible. I am not going out of the way, back to the road we left last night: I am going to cut straight across country from here."

"Then you are going to fly," said Pippin. "You won't cut straight on foot anywhere in this country."

"We can cut straighter than the road anyway," answered Frodo. "The Ferry is east from Woodhall; but the hard road curves away to the left — you can see a bend of it away north over there. It goes round the north end of the Marish so as to strike the causeway from the Bridge above Stock. But that is miles out of the way. We could save a quarter of the distance if we made a line for the Ferry from where we stand."

"*Short cuts make long delays*," argued Pippin. "The country is rough round here, and there are bogs and all kinds of difficulties down in the Marish — I know the land in these parts. And if you are worrying about Black Riders, I can't see that it is any worse meeting them on a road than in a wood or a field."

"It is less easy to find people in the woods and fields," answered Frodo. "And if you are supposed to be on the road, there is some chance that you will be looked for on the road and not off it."

"All right!" said Pippin. "I will follow you into every bog and ditch. But it is hard! I had counted on passing the *Golden Perch* at Stock before sundown. The best beer in the Eastfarthing, or used to be: it is a long time since I tasted it."

"That settles it!" said Frodo. "Short cuts make delays, but inns make longer ones. At all costs we must keep you away from the *Golden Perch*. We want to get to Bucklebury before dark. What do you say, Sam?"

"I will go along with you, Mr. Frodo," said Sam (in spite of private misgiving and a deep regret for the best beer in the Eastfarthing).

"Then if we are going to toil through bog and briar, let's go now!" said Pippin.

It was already nearly as hot as it had been the day before; but clouds were beginning to come up from the West. It looked likely to turn to rain. The hobbits scrambled down a steep green bank and plunged into the thick trees below. Their course had been chosen to leave Woodhall to their left, and to cut slanting through the woods that clustered along the eastern side of the hill, until they reached the flats beyond. Then they could make straight for the Ferry over country that was open, except for a few ditches and fences. Frodo reckoned they had eighteen miles to go in a straight line.

He soon found that the thicket was closer and more tangled than it had appeared. There were no paths in the undergrowth, and they did not get on very fast. When they had struggled to the bottom of the bank, they found a stream running down from the hills behind in a deeply dug bed with steep slippery sides overhung with brambles. Most inconveniently it cut across the line they had chosen. They could not jump over it, nor indeed get across it at all without getting wet, scratched, and muddy. They halted, wondering what to do. "First check!" said Pippin, smiling grimly.

Sam Gamgee looked back. Through an opening in the trees he caught a glimpse of the top of the green bank from which they had climbed down.

"Look!" he said, clutching Frodo by the arm. They all looked, and on the edge high above them they saw against the sky a horse standing. Beside it stooped a black figure.

They at once gave up any idea of going back. Frodo led the way, and plunged quickly into the thick bushes beside the stream. "Whew!" he said to Pippin. "We were both right! The short cut has gone crooked already; but we got under cover only just in time. You've got sharp ears, Sam: can you hear anything coming?"

They stood still, almost holding their breath as they listened; but there was no sound of pursuit. "I don't fancy he would try bringing his horse down that bank," said Sam. "But I guess he knows we came down it. We had better be going on."

Going on was not altogether easy. They had packs to carry, and the bushes and brambles were reluctant to let them through. They were cut off from the wind by the ridge behind, and the air was still and stuffy. When they forced their way at last into more open ground, they were hot and tired and very scratched, and they were also no longer certain of the direction in which they were going. The banks of the stream sank, as it reached the levels and became broader and shallower, wandering off towards the Marish and the River.

"Why, this is the Stock-brook!" said Pippin. "If we are going to try and get back on to our course, we must cross at once and bear right."

They waded the stream, and hurried over a wide open space, rush-grown and treeless, on the further side. Beyond that they came again to a belt of trees: tall oaks, for the most part, with here and there an elm tree or an ash. The ground was fairly level, and there was little undergrowth; but the trees were too close for them to see far ahead. The leaves blew upwards in sudden gusts of wind, and spots of rain began to fall from the overcast sky. Then the wind died away and the rain came streaming down. They trudged along as fast as they could, over patches of grass, and through thick drifts of old leaves; and all about them the rain pattered and trickled. They did not talk, but kept glancing back, and from side to side.

After half an hour Pippin said: "I hope we have not turned too much towards the south, and are not walking longwise through this wood! It is not a very broad belt — I should have said no more than a mile at the widest — and we ought to have been through it by now."

"It is no good our starting to go in zig-zags," said Frodo. "That won't mend matters. Let us keep on as we are going! I am not sure that I want to come out into the open yet."

They went on for perhaps another couple of miles. Then the

sun gleamed out of ragged clouds again and the rain lessened. It was now past mid-day, and they felt it was high time for lunch. They halted under an elm tree: its leaves though fast turning yellow were still thick, and the ground at its feet was fairly dry and sheltered. When they came to make their meal, they found that the Elves had filled their bottles with a clear drink, pale golden in colour: it had the scent of a honey made of many flowers, and was wonderfully refreshing. Very soon they were laughing, and snapping their fingers at rain, and at Black Riders. The last few miles, they felt, would soon be behind them.

Frodo propped his back against the tree-trunk, and closed his eyes. Sam and Pippin sat near, and they began to hum, and then to sing softly:

> *Ho! Ho! Ho! to the bottle I go*
> *To heal my heart and drown my woe.*
> *Rain may fall and wind may blow,*
> *And many miles be still to go,*
> *But under a tall tree I will lie,*
> *And let the clouds go sailing by.*

Ho! Ho! Ho! they began again louder. They stopped short suddenly. Frodo sprang to his feet. A long-drawn wail came down the wind, like the cry of some evil and lonely creature. It rose and fell, and ended on a high piercing note. Even as they sat and stood, as if suddenly frozen, it was answered by another cry, fainter and further off, but no less chilling to the blood. There was then a silence, broken only by the sound of the wind in the leaves.

"And what do you think that was?" Pippin asked at last, trying to speak lightly, but quavering a little. "If it was a bird, it was one that I never heard in the Shire before."

"It was not bird or beast," said Frodo. "It was a call, or a signal — there were words in that cry, though I could not catch them. But no hobbit has such a voice."

No more was said about it. They were all thinking of the Riders, but no one spoke of them. They were now reluctant either to stay or go on; but sooner or later they had got to get across the open country to the Ferry, and it was best to go sooner and in daylight. In a few moments they had shouldered their packs again and were off.

Before long the wood came to a sudden end. Wide grass-lands stretched before them. They now saw that they had, in fact, turned too much to the south. Away over the flats they could glimpse the low hill of Bucklebury across the River, but it was now to their left. Creeping cautiously out from the edge of the trees, they set off across the open as quickly as they could.

At first they felt afraid, away from the shelter of the wood. Far back behind them stood the high place where they had breakfasted. Frodo half expected to see the small distant figure of a horseman on the ridge dark against the sky; but there was no sign of one. The escaping from the breaking clouds, as it sank towards the hills they had left, was now shining brightly again. Their fear left them, though they still felt uneasy. But the land became steadily more tame and well-ordered. Soon they came into well-tended fields and meadows: there were hedges and gates and dikes for drainage. Everything seemed quiet and peaceful, just an ordinary corner of the Shire. Their spirits rose with every step. The line of the River grew nearer; and the Black Riders began to seem like phantoms of the woods now left far behind.

They passed along the edge of a huge turnip-field, and came to a stout gate. Beyond it a rutted lane ran between low well-laid hedges towards a distant clump of trees. Pippin stopped.

"I know these fields and this gate!" he said. "This is Bamfurlong; old Farmer Maggot's land. That's his farm away there in the trees."

"One trouble after another!" said Frodo, looking nearly as much alarmed as if Pippin had declared the lane was the slot leading to a dragon's den. The others looked at him in surprise.

"What's wrong with old Maggot?" asked Pippin. "He's a good friend to all the Brandybucks. Of course he's a terror to trespassers, and keeps ferocious dogs — but after all, folk down here are near the border and have to be more on their guard."

"I know," said Frodo. "But all the same," he added with a shame-faced laugh, "I am terrified of him and his dogs. I have avoided his farm for years and years. He caught me several times trespassing after mushrooms, when I was a youngster at Brandy Hall. On the last occasion he beat me, and then took me and showed me to his dogs. 'See, lads,' he said, 'next time this young varmint sets foot on my land, you can eat him. Now see him off!' They chased me all the way to the Ferry. I have never got over the fright — though I daresay the beasts knew their business and would not really have touched me."

Pippin laughed. "Well, it's time you made it up. Especially if you are coming back to live in Buckland. Old Maggot is really a stout fellow — if you leave his mushrooms alone. Let's get into the lane and then we shan't be trespassing. If we meet him, I'll do the talking. He is a friend of Merry's, and I used to come here with him a good deal at one time."

They went along the lane, until they saw the thatched roofs of a large house and farm-buildings peeping out among the trees ahead. The Maggots, and the Puddifoots of Stock, and most of the inhabitants of the Marish, were house-dwellers; and his farm was stoutly built of brick and had a high wall all round it. There was a wide wooden gate opening out of the wall into the lane.

Suddenly as they drew nearer a terrific baying and barking broke out, and a loud voice was heard shouting: "Grip! Fang! Wolf! Come on, lads!"

Frodo and Sam stopped dead, but Pippin walked on a few paces. The gate opened and three huge dogs came pelting out into the lane, and dashed towards the travellers, barking fiercely. They took no notice of Pippin; but Sam shrank against the wall, while two wolvish-looking dogs sniffed at him suspiciously, and snarled if he moved. The largest and most ferocious of the three halted in front of Frodo, bristling and growling.

Through the gate there now appeared a broad thick-set hobbit with a round red face. "Hallo! Hallo! And who may you be, and what may you be wanting?" he asked.

"Good afternoon, Mr. Maggot!" said Pippin.

The farmer looked at him closely. "Well, if it isn't Master Pippin — Mr. Peregrin Took, I should say!" he cried, changing from a scowl to a grin. "It's a long time since I saw you round here. It's lucky for you that I know you. I was just going out to set my dogs on any strangers. There are some funny things going on today. Of course, we do get queer folk wandering in these parts at times. Too near the River," he said, shaking his head. "But this fellow was the most outlandish I have ever set eyes on. He won't cross my land without leave a second time, not if I can stop it."

"What fellow do you mean?" asked Pippin.

"Then you haven't seen him?" said the farmer. "He went up the lane towards the causeway not a long while back. He was a funny customer and asking funny questions. But perhaps you'll come along inside, and we'll pass the news more comfortable. I've a drop of good ale on tap, if you and your friends are willing, Mr. Took."

It seemed plain that the farmer would tell them more, if allowed to do it in his own time and fashion, so they all accepted the invitation. "What about the dogs?" asked Frodo anxiously.

The farmer laughed. "They won't harm you — not unless I tell 'em to. Here, Grip! Fang! Heel!" he cried. "Heel, Wolf!" To the relief of Frodo and Sam, the dogs walked away and let them go free.

Pippin introduced the other two to the farmer. "Mr. Frodo Baggins," he said. "You may not remember him, but he used to live at Brandy Hall." At the name Baggins the farmer started, and gave Frodo a sharp glance. For a moment Frodo thought that the memory of stolen mushrooms had been aroused, and that the dogs would be told to see him off. But Farmer Maggot took him by the arm.

"Well, if that isn't queerer than ever?" he exclaimed. "Mr. Baggins is it? Come inside! We must have a talk."

They went into the farmer's kitchen, and sat by the wide fireplace. Mrs. Maggot brought out beer in a huge jug, and filled four large mugs. It was a good brew, and Pippin found himself more than compensated for missing the *Golden Perch*. Sam sipped his beer suspiciously. He had a natural mistrust of the inhabitants of other parts of the Shire; and also he was not disposed to be quick friends with anyone who had beaten his master, however long ago.

After a few remarks about the weather and the agricultural prospects (which were no worse than usual), Farmer Maggot put down his mug and looked at them all in turn.

"Now, Mr. Peregrin," he said, "where might you be coming from, and where might you be going to? Were you coming to visit me? For, if so, you had gone past my gate without my seeing you."

"Well, no," answered Pippin. "To tell you the truth, since you have guessed it, we got into the lane from the other end: we had come over your fields. But that was quite by accident. We lost our way in the woods, back near Woodhall, trying to take a short cut to the Ferry."

"If you were in a hurry, the road would have served you better," said the farmer. "But I wasn't worrying about that. You have leave to walk over my land, if you have a mind, Mr. Peregrin. And you, Mr. Baggins — though I daresay you still like mushrooms." He laughed. "Ah yes, I recognized the name. I recollect the time when young Frodo Baggins was one of the worst young rascals of Buckland. But it wasn't mushrooms I was thinking of. I had just heard the name Baggins before you turned up. What do you think that funny customer asked me?"

They waited anxiously for him to go on. "Well," the farmer

continued, approaching his point with slow relish, "he came riding on a big black horse in at the gate, which happened to be open, and right up to my door. All black he was himself, too, and cloaked and hooded up, as if he did not want to be known. 'Now what in the Shire can he want?' I thought to myself. We don't see many of the Big Folk over the border; and anyway I had never heard of any like this black fellow.

"'Good-day to you!' I says, going out to him. 'This lane don't lead anywhere, and wherever you may be going, your quickest way will be back to the road.' I didn't like the looks of him; and when Grip came out, he took one sniff and let out a yelp as if he had been stung: he put down his tail and bolted off howling. The black fellow sat quite still.

"'I come from yonder,' he said, slow and stiff-like, pointing back west, over *my* fields, if you please. 'Have you seen *Baggins*?' he asked in a queer voice, and bent down towards me. I could not see any face, for his hood fell down so low; and I felt a sort of shiver down my back. But I did not see why he should come riding over my land so bold.

"'Be off!' I said. 'There are no Bagginses here. You're in the wrong part of the Shire. You had better go back west to Hobbiton — but you can go by road this time.'

"'Baggins has left,' he answered in a whisper. 'He is coming. He is not far away. I wish to find him. If he passes will you tell me? I will come back with gold.'

"'No you won't,' I said. 'You'll go back where you belong, double quick. I give you one minute before I call all my dogs.'

"He gave a sort of hiss. It might have been laughing, and it might not. Then he spurred his great horse right at me, and I jumped out of the way only just in time. I called the dogs, but he swung off, and rode through the gate and up the lane towards the causeway like a bolt of thunder. What do you think of that?"

Frodo sat for a moment looking at the fire, but his only thought was how on earth would they reach the Ferry. "I don't know what to think," he said at last.

"Then I'll tell you what to think," said Maggot. "You should never have gone mixing yourself up with Hobbiton folk, Mr. Frodo. Folk are queer up there." Sam stirred in his chair, and looked at the farmer with an unfriendly eye. "But you were always a reckless lad. When I heard you had left the Brandybucks and gone off to that old Mr. Bilbo, I said that you were going to find trouble. Mark my words, this all comes of those strange doings of Mr. Bilbo's. His money was got in some strange fashion in foreign parts, they say. Maybe there is some that want to know what has become of the gold and jewels that he buried in the hill of Hobbiton, as I hear?"

Frodo said nothing: the shrewd guesses of the farmer were rather disconcerting.

"Well, Mr. Frodo," Maggot went on, "I"m glad that you've had the sense to come back to Buckland. My advice is: stay there! And don't get mixed up with these outlandish folk. You'll have friends in these parts. If any of these black fellows come after you again, I'll deal with them. I'll say you're dead, or have left the Shire, or anything you like. And that might be true enough; for as like as not it is old Mr. Bilbo they want news of."

"Maybe you're right," said Frodo, avoiding the farmer's eye and staring at the fire.

Maggot looked at him thoughtfully. "Well, I see you have ideas of your own," he said. "It is as plain as my nose that no accident brought you and that rider here on the same afternoon; and maybe my news was no great news to you, after all. I am not asking you to tell me anything you have a mind to keep to yourself; but I see you are in some kind of trouble. Perhaps you are thinking it won't be too easy to get to the Ferry without being caught?"

"I was thinking so," said Frodo. "But we have got to try and get there; and it won't be done by sitting and thinking. So I am afraid we must be going. Thank you very much indeed for your kindness! I've been in terror of you and your dogs for over thirty years, Farmer Maggot, though you may laugh to hear it.

It's a pity: for I've missed a good friend. And now I'm sorry to leave so soon. But I'll come back, perhaps, one day — if I get a chance."

"You'll be welcome when you come," said Maggot. "But now I've a notion. It's near sundown already, and we are going to have our supper; for we mostly go to bed soon after the Sun. If you and Mr. Peregrin and all could stay and have a bite with us, we would be pleased!"

"And so should we!" said Frodo. "But we must be going at once, I'm afraid. Even now it will be dark before we can reach the Ferry."

"Ah! but wait a minute! I was going to say: after a bit of supper, I'll get out a small waggon, and I'll drive you all to the Ferry. That will save you a good step, and it might also save you trouble of another sort."

Frodo now accepted the invitation gratefully, to the relief of Pippin and Sam. The sun was already behind the western hills, and the light was failing. Two of Maggot's sons and his three daughters came in, and a generous supper was laid on the large table. The kitchen was lit with candles and the fire was mended. Mrs. Maggot bustled in and out. One or two other hobbits belonging to the farm-household came in. In a short while fourteen sat down to eat. There was beer in plenty, and a mighty dish of mushrooms and bacon, besides much other solid farmhouse fare. The dogs lay by the fire and gnawed rinds and cracked bones.

When they had finished, the farmer and his sons went out with a lantern and got the waggon ready. It was dark in the yard, when the guests came out. They threw their packs on board and climbed in. The farmer sat in the driving-seat, and whipped up his two stout ponies. His wife stood in the light of the open door.

"You be careful of yourself, Maggot!" she called. "Don't go arguing with any foreigners, and come straight back!"

"I will!" said he, and drove out of the gate. There was now no breath of wind stirring; the night was still and quiet, and a chill was in the air. They went without lights and took it slowly. After a mile or two the lane came to an end, crossing a deep dike, and climbing a short slope up on to the high-banked causeway.

Maggot got down and took a good look either way, north and south, but nothing could be seen in the darkness, and there was not a sound in the still air. Thin strands of river-mist were hanging above the dikes, and crawling over the fields.

"It's going to be thick," said Maggot; "but I'll not light my lanterns till I turn for home. We'll hear anything on the road long before we meet it tonight."

It was five miles or more from Maggot's lane to the Ferry. The hobbits wrapped themselves up, but their ears were strained for any sound above the creak of the wheels and the slow *clop* of the ponies' hoofs. The waggon seemed slower than a snail to Frodo. Beside him Pippin was nodding towards sleep; but Sam was staring forwards into the rising fog.

They reached the entrance to the Ferry lane at last. It was marked by two tall white posts that suddenly loomed up on their right. Farmer Maggot drew in his ponies and the waggon creaked to a halt. They were just beginning to scramble out, when suddenly they heard what they had all been dreading: hoofs on the road ahead. The sound was coming towards them.

Maggot jumped down and stood holding the ponies' heads, and peering forward into the gloom. *Clip-clop, clip-clop* came the approaching rider. The fall of the hoofs sounded loud in the still, foggy air.

"You'd better be hidden, Mr. Frodo," said Sam anxiously. "You get down in the waggon and cover up with blankets, and we'll send this rider to the rightabouts!" He climbed out and went to the farmer's side. Black Riders would have to ride over him to get near the waggon.

Clop-clop, clop-clop. The rider was nearly on them.

"Hallo there!" called Farmer Maggot. The advancing hoofs stopped short. They thought they could dimly guess a dark cloaked shape in the mist, a yard or two ahead.

"Now then!" said the farmer, throwing the reins to Sam and striding forward. "Don't you come a step nearer! What do you want, and where are you going?"

"I want Mr. Baggins. Have you seen him?" said a muffled voice — but the voice was the voice of Merry Brandybuck. A dark lantern was uncovered, and its light fell on the astonished face of the farmer.

"Mr. Merry!" he cried.

"Yes, of course! Who did you think it was?" said Merry coming forward. As he came out of the mist and their fears subsided, he seemed suddenly to diminish to ordinary hobbit-size. He was riding a pony, and a scarf was swathed round his neck and over his chin to keep out the fog.

Frodo sprang out of the waggon to greet him. "So there you are at last!" said Merry. "I was beginning to wonder if you would turn up at all today, and I was just going back to supper. When it grew foggy I came across and rode up towards Stock to see if you had fallen in any ditches. But I'm blest if I know which way you have come. Where did you find them, Mr. Maggot? In your duck-pond?"

"No, I caught 'em trespassing," said the farmer, "and nearly set my dogs on 'em; but they'll tell you all the story, I've no doubt. Now, if you'll excuse me, Mr. Merry and Mr. Frodo and all, I'd best be turning for home. Mrs. Maggot will be worriting with the night getting thick."

He backed the waggon into the lane and turned it. "Well, good night to you all," he said. "It's been a queer day, and no mistake. But all's well as ends well; though perhaps we should not say that until we reach our own doors. I'll not deny that I'll be glad now when I do." He lit his lanterns, and got up. Suddenly he produced a large basket from under the seat. "I was nearly forgetting," he said. "Mrs. Maggot put this up for Mr. Baggins, with her compliments." He handed it down and moved off, followed by a chorus of thanks and good-nights.

They watched the pale rings of light round his lanterns as

they dwindled into the foggy night. Suddenly Frodo laughed: from the covered basket he held, the scent of mushrooms was rising.

CHAPTER
FIVE

A Conspiracy
Unmasked

"Now we had better get home ourselves," said Merry. "There's something funny about all this, I see; but it must wait till we get in."

They turned down the Ferry lane, which was straight and well-kept and edged with large white-washed stones. In a hundred yards or so it brought them to the river-bank, where there was a broad wooden landing-stage. A large flat ferry-boat was moored beside it. The white bollards near the water's edge glimmered in the light of two lamps on high posts. Behind them the mists in the flat fields were now above the hedges; but the water before them was dark, with only a few curling wisps like steam among the reeds by the bank. There seemed to be less fog on the further side.

Merry led the pony over a gangway on to the ferry, and the others followed. Merry then pushed slowly off with a long pole. The Brandywine flowed slow and broad before them. On the other side the bank was steep, and up it a winding path climbed from the further landing. Lamps were twinkling there. Behind loomed up the Buck Hill; and out of it, through stray shrouds of mist, shone many round windows, yellow and red. They were the windows of Brandy Hall, the ancient home of the Brandybucks.

Long ago Gorhendad Oldbuck, head of the Oldbuck family, one of the oldest in the Marish or indeed in the Shire, had crossed the river, which was the original boundary of the land eastwards. He built (and excavated) Brandy Hall, changed his name to Brandybuck, and settled down to become master of what was virtually a small independent country. His family grew and grew, and after his days continued to grow, until Brandy Hall occupied the whole of the low hill, and had three large front-doors, many side-doors, and about a hundred windows. The Brandybucks and their numerous dependants then began to burrow, and later to build, all round about. That was the origin of Buckland, a thickly inhabited strip between the river and the Old Forest, a sort of colony from the Shire. Its chief village was Bucklebury, clustering in the banks and slopes behind Brandy Hall.

The people in the Marish were friendly with the Bucklanders, and the authority of the Master of the Hall (as the head of the Brandybuck family was called) was still acknowledged by the farmers between Stock and Rushey. But most of the folk of the old Shire regarded the Bucklanders as peculiar, half foreigners as it were. Though, as a matter of fact, they were not very different from the other hobbits of the Four Farthings. Except in one point: they were fond of boats, and some of them could swim.

Their land was originally unprotected from the East; but on that side they had built a hedge: the High Hay. It had been planted many generations ago, and was now thick and tall, for it was constantly tended. It ran all the way from Brandywine Bridge, in a big loop curving away from the river, to Haysend (where the Withywindle flowed out of the Forest into the Brandywine): well over twenty miles from end to end. But, of course, it was not a complete protection. The Forest drew close to the hedge in many places. The Bucklanders kept their doors locked after dark, and that also was not usual in the Shire.

The ferry-boat moved slowly across the water. The Buckland

shore drew nearer. Sam was the only member of the party who had not been over the river before. He had a strange feeling as the slow gurgling stream slipped by: his old life lay behind in the mists, dark adventure lay in front. He scratched his head, and for a moment had a passing wish that Mr. Frodo could have gone on living quietly at Bag End.

The four hobbits stepped off the ferry. Merry was tying it up, and Pippin was already leading the pony up the path, when Sam (who had been looking back, as if to take farewell of the Shire) said in a hoarse whisper:

"Look back, Mr. Frodo! Do you see anything?"

On the far stage, under the distant lamps, they could just make out a figure: it looked like a dark black bundle left behind. But as they looked it seemed to move and sway this way and that, as if searching the ground. It then crawled, or went crouching, back into the gloom beyond the lamps.

"What in the Shire is that?" exclaimed Merry.

"Something that is following us," said Frodo. "But don't ask any more now! Let's get away at once!" They hurried up the path to the top of the bank, but when they looked back the far shore was shrouded in mist, and nothing could be seen.

"Thank goodness you don't keep any boats on the west-bank!" said Frodo. "Can horses cross the river?"

"They can go twenty miles north to Brandywine Bridge — or they might swim," answered Merry. "Though I never heard of any horse swimming the Brandywine. But what have horses to do with it?"

"I'll tell you later. Let's get indoors and then we can talk."

"All right! You and Pippin know your way; so I'll just ride on and tell Fatty Bolger that you are coming. We'll see about supper and things."

"We had our supper early with Farmer Maggot," said Frodo; "but we could do with another."

"You shall have it! Give me that basket!" said Merry, and rode ahead into the darkness.

It was some distance from the Brandywine to Frodo's new house at Crickhollow. They passed Buck Hill and Brandy Hall on their left, and on the outskirts of Bucklebury struck the main road of Buckland that ran south from the Bridge. Half a mile northward along this they came to a lane opening on their right. This they followed for a couple of miles as it climbed up and down into the country.

At last they came to a narrow gate in a thick hedge. Nothing could be seen of the house in the dark: it stood back from the lane in the middle of a wide circle of lawn surrounded by a belt of low trees inside the outer hedge. Frodo had chosen it, because it stood in an out-of-the-way corner of the country, and there were no other dwellings close by. You could get in and out without being noticed. It had been built a long while before by the Brandybucks, for the use of guests, or members of the family that wished to escape from the crowded life of Brandy Hall for a time. It was an old-fashioned countrified house, as much like a hobbit-hole as possible: it was long and low, with no upper storey; and it had a roof of turf, round windows, and a large round door.

As they walked up the green path from the gate no light was visible; the windows were dark and shuttered. Frodo knocked on the door, and Fatty Bolger opened it. A friendly light streamed out. They slipped in quickly and shut themselves and the light inside. They were in a wide hall with doors on either side; in front of them a passage ran back down the middle of the house.

"Well, what do you think of it?" asked Merry coming up the passage. "We have done our best in a short time to make it look like home. After all Fatty and I only got here with the last cart-load yesterday."

Frodo looked round. It did look like home. Many of his own favourite things — or Bilbo's things (they reminded him sharply of him in their new setting) — were arranged as nearly as possible as they had been at Bag End. It was a pleasant, comfortable, welcoming place; and he found himself wishing that he was really coming here to settle down in quiet retirement. It seemed unfair to have put his friends to all this trouble; and he wondered again how he was going to break the news to them that he must leave them so soon, indeed at once. Yet that would have to be done that very night, before they all went to bed.

"It's delightful!" he said with an effort. "I hardly feel that I have moved at all."

The travellers hung up their cloaks, and piled their packs on the floor. Merry led them down the passage and threw open a door at the far end. Firelight came out, and a puff of steam.

"A bath!" cried Pippin. "O blessed Meriadoc!"

"Which order shall we go in?" said Frodo. "Eldest first, or quickest first? You'll be last either way, Master Peregrin."

"Trust me to arrange things better than that!" said Merry. "We can't begin life at Crickhollow with a quarrel over baths. In that room there are *three* tubs, and a copper full of boiling water. There are also towels, mats and soap. Get inside, and be quick!"

Merry and Fatty went into the kitchen on the other side of the passage, and busied themselves with the final preparations for a late supper. Snatches of competing songs came from the bathroom mixed with the sound of splashing and wallowing. The voice of Pippin was suddenly lifted up above the others in one of Bilbo's favourite bath-songs.

Sing hey! for the bath at close of day
that washes the weary mud away!
A loon is he that will not sing:
O! Water Hot is a noble thing!

O! Sweet is the sound of falling rain,
and the brook that leaps from hill to plain;
but better than rain or rippling streams
is Water Hot that smokes and steams.

O! Water cold we may pour at need
down a thirsty throat and be glad indeed;
but better is Beer, if drink we lack,
and Water Hot poured down the back.

O! Water is fair that leaps on high
in a fountain white beneath the sky;
but never did fountain sound so sweet
as splashing Hot Water with my feet!

There was a terrific splash, and a shout of *Whoa!* from Frodo. It appeared that a lot of Pippin's bath had imitated a fountain and leaped on high.

Merry went to the door: "What about supper and beer in the throat?" he called. Frodo came out drying his hair.

"There's so much water in the air that I'm coming into the kitchen to finish," he said.

"Lawks!" said Merry, looking in. The stone floor was swimming. "You ought to mop all that up before you get anything to eat, Peregrin," he said. "Hurry up, or we shan't wait for you."

They had supper in the kitchen on a table near the fire. "I suppose you three won't want mushrooms again?" said Fredegar without much hope.

"Yes we shall!" cried Pippin.

"They're mine!" said Frodo. "Given to *me* by Mrs. Maggot, a queen among farmer's wives. Take your greedy hands away, and I'll serve them."

Hobbits have a passion for mushrooms, surpassing even the greediest likings of Big People. A fact which partly explains young Frodo's long expeditions to the renowned fields of the Marish, and the wrath of the injured Maggot. On this occasion there was plenty for all, even according to hobbit standards. There were also many other things to follow, and when they had finished even Fatty Bolger heaved a sigh of content. They pushed back the table, and drew chairs round the fire.

"We'll clear up later," said Merry. "Now tell me all about it! I guess that you have been having adventures, which was not quite fair without me. I want a full account; and most of all I want to know what was the matter with old Maggot, and why he spoke to me like that. He sounded almost as if he was *scared*, if that is possible."

"We have all been scared," said Pippin after a pause, in which Frodo stared at the fire and did not speak. "You would have been, too, if you had been chased for two days by Black Riders."

"And what are they?"

"Black figures riding on black horses," answered Pippin. "If Frodo won't talk, I will tell you the whole tale from the beginning." He then gave a full account of their journey from the time when they left Hobbiton. Sam gave various supporting nods and exclamations. Frodo remained silent.

"I should think you were making it all up," said Merry, "if I had not seen that black shape on the landing-stage — and heard the queer sound in Maggot's voice. What do you make of it all, Frodo?"

"Cousin Frodo has been very close," said Pippin. "But the time has come for him to open out. So far we have been given nothing more to go on than Farmer Maggot's guess that it has something to do with old Bilbo's treasure."

"That was only a guess," said Frodo hastily. "Maggot does not *know* anything."

"Old Maggot is a shrewd fellow," said Merry. "A lot goes on behind his round face that does not come out in his talk. I've heard that he used to go into the Old Forest at one time, and he has the reputation of knowing a good many strange things. But you can at least tell us, Frodo, whether you think his guess good or bad."

"I *think*," answered Frodo slowly, "that it was a good guess, as far as it goes. There is a connexion with Bilbo's old adventures, and the Riders are looking, or perhaps one ought to say *searching*, for him or for me. I also fear, if you want to know, that it is no joke at all; and that I am not safe here or anywhere elsc." He looked round at the windows and walls, as if he was afraid they would suddenly give way. The others looked at him in silence, and exchanged meaning glances among themselves.

"It's coming out in a minute," whispered Pippin to Merry. Merry nodded.

"Well!" said Frodo at last, sitting up and straightening his back, as if he had made a decision. "I can't keep it dark any longer. I have got something to tell you all. But I don't know quite how to begin."

"I think I could help you," said Merry quietly, "by telling you some of it myself."

"What do you mean?" said Frodo, looking at him anxiously.

"Just this, my dear old Frodo: you are miserable, because you don't know how to say good-bye. You meant to leave the Shire, of course. But danger has come on you sooner than you expected, and now you are making up your mind to go at once. And you don't want to. We are very sorry for you."

Frodo opened his mouth and shut it again. His look of surprise was so comical that they laughed. "Dear old Frodo!" said Pippin. "Did you really think you had thrown dust in all our eyes? You have not been nearly careful or clever enough for that! You have obviously been planning to go and saying farewell to all your haunts all this year since April. We have constantly heard you muttering: 'Shall I ever look down into that valley again, I wonder', and things like that. And pretending that you had come to the end of your money, and actually selling your beloved Bag End to those Sackville-Bagginses! And all those close talks with Gandalf."

"Good heavens!" said Frodo. "I thought I had been both careful and clever. I don't know what Gandalf would say. Is all the Shire discussing my departure then?"

"Oh no!" said Merry. "Don't worry about that! The secret won't keep for long, of course; but at present it is, I think, only known to us conspirators. After all, you must remember that we know you well, and are often with you. We can usually guess what you are thinking. I knew Bilbo, too. To tell you the truth, I had been watching you rather closely ever since he left. I thought you would go after him sooner or later; indeed I expected you to go sooner, and lately we have been very anxious. We have been terrified that you might give us the slip, and go off suddenly, all on your own like he did. Ever since this spring we have kept our eyes open, and done a good deal of planning on our own account. You are not going to escape so easily!"

"But I must go," said Frodo. "It cannot be helped, dear friends. It is wretched for us all, but it is no use your trying to keep me. Since you have guessed so much, please help me and do not hinder me!"

"You do not understand!" said Pippin. "You must go — and therefore we must, too. Merry and I are coming with you. Sam is an excellent fellow, and would jump down a dragon's throat to save you, if he did not trip over his own feet; but you will need more than one companion in your dangerous adventure."

"My dear and most beloved hobbits!" said Frodo deeply moved. "But I could not allow it. I decided that long ago, too. You speak of danger, but you do not understand. This is no treasure-hunt, no there-and-back journey. I am flying from deadly peril into deadly peril."

"Of course we understand," said Merry firmly. "That is why we have decided to come. We know the Ring is no laughing-matter; but we are going to do our best to help you against the Enemy."

"The Ring!" said Frodo, now completely amazed.

"Yes, the Ring," said Merry. "My dear old hobbit, you don't allow for the inquisitiveness of friends. I have known about the existence of the Ring for years — before Bilbo went away, in fact; but since he obviously regarded it as secret, I kept the knowledge in my head, until we formed our conspiracy. I did not know Bilbo, of course, as well as I know you; I was too young, and he was also more careful — but he was not careful enough. If you want to know how I first found out, I will tell you."

"Go on!" said Frodo faintly.

"It was the Sackville-Bagginses that were his downfall, as you might expect. One day, a year before the Party, I happened to be walking along the road, when I saw Bilbo ahead. Suddenly in the distance. the S.-B.s appeared, coming towards us. Bilbo slowed down, and then hey presto! he vanished. I was so startled that I hardly had the wits to hide myself in a more ordinary fashion; but I got through the hedge and walked along the field inside. I was peeping through into the road, after the S.-B.s had passed, and was looking straight at Bilbo when he suddenly reappeared. I caught a glint of gold as he put something back in his trouser-pocket.

"After that I kept my eyes open. In fact, I confess that I spied. But you must admit that it was very intriguing, and I was only in my teens. I must be the only one in the Shire, besides you Frodo, that has ever seen the odd fellow's secret book."

"You have read his book!" cried Frodo. "Good heavens above! Is nothing safe?"

"Not too safe, I should say," said Merry. "But I have only had one rapid glance, and that was difficult to get. He never left the book about. I wonder what became of it. I should like another look. Have you got it, Frodo?"

"No. It was not at Bag End. He must have taken it away."

"Well, as I was saying," Merry proceeded, "I kept my knowledge to myself, till this Spring when things got serious. Then we formed our conspiracy; and as we were serious, too, and meant business, we have not been too scrupulous. You are not a very easy nut to crack, and Gandalf is worse. But if you want to be introduced to our chief investigator, I can produce him."

"Where is he?" said Frodo, looking round, as if he expected a masked and sinister figure to come out of a cupboard.

"Step forward, Sam!" said Merry; and Sam stood up with a face scarlet up to the ears. "Here's our collector of information! And he collected a lot, I can tell you, before he was finally caught. After which, I may say, he seemed to regard himself as on parole, and dried up."

"Sam!" cried Frodo, feeling that amazement could go no further, and quite unable to decide whether he felt angry, amused, relieved, or merely foolish.

"Yes, sir!" said Sam. "Begging your pardon, sir! But I meant no wrong to you, Mr. Frodo, nor to Mr. Gandalf for that matter. *He* has some sense, mind you; and when you said *go alone*, he said *no! take someone as you can trust*."

"But it does not seem that I can trust anyone," said Frodo.

Sam looked at him unhappily. "It all depends on what you want," put in Merry. "You can trust us to stick to you through thick and thin — to the bitter end. And you can trust us to keep any secret of yours — closer than you keep it yourself. But you cannot trust us to let you face trouble alone, and go off without a word. We are your friends, Frodo. Anyway: there it is. We know most of what Gandalf has told you. We know a good deal about the Ring. We are horribly afraid — but we are coming with you; or following you like hounds."

"And after all, sir," added Sam, "you did ought to take the Elves' advice. Gildor said you should take them as was willing, and you can't deny it."

"I don't deny it," said Frodo, looking at Sam, who was now grinning. "I don't deny it, but I'll never believe you are sleeping again, whether you snore or not. I shall kick you hard to make sure."

"You are a set of deceitful scoundrels!" he said, turning to the others. "But bless you!" he laughed, getting up and waving his arms, "I give in. I will take Gildor's advice. If the danger were not so dark, I should dance for joy. Even so, I cannot help feeling happy; happier than I have felt for a long time. I had dreaded this evening."

"Good! That's settled. Three cheers for Captain Frodo and

company!" they shouted; and they danced round him. Merry and Pippin began a song, which they had apparently got ready for the occasion.

It was made on the model of the dwarf-song that started Bilbo on his adventure long ago, and went to the same tune:

> *Farewell we call to hearth and hall!*
> *Though wind may blow and rain may fall,*
> *We must away ere break of day*
> *Far over wood and mountain tall.*
>
> *To Rivendell, where Elves yet dwell*
> *In glades beneath the misty fell,*
> *Through moor and waste we ride in haste,*
> *And whither then we cannot tell.*
>
> *With foes ahead, behind us dread,*
> *Beneath the sky shall be our bed,*
> *Until at last our toil be passed,*
> *Our journey done, our errand sped.*
>
> *We must away! We must away!*
> *We ride before the break of day!*

"Very good!" said Frodo. "But in that case there are a lot of things to do before we go to bed — under a roof, for tonight at any rate."

"Oh! That was poetry!" said Pippin. "Do you really mean to start before the break of day?"

"I don't know," answered Frodo. "I fear those Black Riders, and I am sure it is unsafe to stay in one place long, especially in a place to which it is known I was going. Also Gildor advised me not to wait. But I should very much like to see Gandalf. I could see that even Gildor was disturbed when he heard that Gandalf had never appeared. It really depends on two things. How soon could the Riders get to Bucklebury? And how soon could we get off? It will take a good deal of preparation."

"The answer to the second question," said Merry, "is that we could get off in an hour. I have prepared practically everything. There are six ponies in a stable across the fields; stores and tackle are all packed, except for a few extra clothes, and the perishable food."

"It seems to have been a very efficient conspiracy," said Frodo. "But what about the Black Riders? Would it be safe to wait one day for Gandalf?"

"That all depends on what you think the Riders would do, if they found you here," answered Merry. "They *could* have reached here by now, of course, if they were not stopped at the North-gate, where the Hedge runs down to the river-bank, just this side of the Bridge. The gate-guards would not let them through by night, though they might break through. Even in the daylight they would try to keep them out, I think, at any rate until they got a message through to the Master of the Hall — for they would not like the look of the Riders, and would certainly be frightened by them. But, of course, Buckland cannot resist a determined attack for long. And it is possible that in the morning even a Black Rider that rode up and asked for Mr. Baggins would be let through. It is pretty generally known that you are coming back to live at Crickhollow."

Frodo sat for a while in thought. "I have made up my mind," he said finally. "I am starting tomorrow, as soon as it is light. But I am not going by road: it would be safer to wait here than that. If I go through the North-gate my departure from Buckland will be known at once, instead of being secret for several days at least, as it might be. And what is more, the Bridge and the East Road near the borders will certainly be watched, whether any Rider gets into Buckland or not. We don't know how many there are; but there are at least two, and possibly more. The only thing to do is to go off in a quite unexpected direction."

"But that can only mean going into the Old Forest!" said

Fredegar horrified. "You can't be thinking of doing that. It is quite as dangerous as Black Riders."

"Not quite," said Merry. "It sounds very desperate, but I believe Frodo is right. It is the only way of getting off without being followed at once. With luck we might get a considerable start. "

"But you won't have any luck in the Old Forest," objected Fredegar. "No one ever has luck in there. You'll get lost. People don't go in there."

"Oh yes they do!" said Merry. "The Brandybucks go in — occasionally when the fit takes them. We have a private entrance. Frodo went in once, long ago. I have been in several times: usually in daylight, of course, when the trees are sleepy and fairly quiet."

"Well, do as you think best!" said Fredegar. "I am more afraid of the Old Forest than of anything I know about: the stories about it are a nightmare; but my vote hardly counts, as I am not going on the journey. Still, I am very glad someone is stopping behind, who can tell Gandalf what you have done, when he turns up, as I am sure he will before long."

Fond as he was of Frodo, Fatty Bolger had no desire to leave the Shire, nor to see what lay outside it. His family came from the Eastfarthing, from Budgeford in Bridgefields in fact, but he had never been over the Brandywine Bridge. His task, according to the original plans of the conspirators, was to stay behind and deal with inquisitive folk, and to keep up as long as possible the pretence that Mr. Baggins was still living at Crickhollow. He had even brought along some old clothes of Frodo's to help him in playing the part. They little thought how dangerous that part might prove.

"Excellent!" said Frodo, when he understood the plan. "We could not have left any message behind for Gandalf otherwise. I don't know whether these Riders can read or not, of course, but I should not have dared to risk a written message, in case they got in and searched the house. But if Fatty is willing to hold the fort, and I can be sure of Gandalf knowing the way we have gone, that decides me. I am going into the Old Forest first thing tomorrow."

"Well, that's that," said Pippin. "On the whole I would rather have. our job than Fatty's — waiting here till Black Riders come."

"You wait till you are well inside the Forest," said Fredegar. "You'll wish you were back here with me before this time tomorrow."

"It's no good arguing about it any more," said Merry. "We have still got to tidy up and put the finishing touches to the packing, before we get to bed. I shall call you all before the break of day."

When at last he had got to bed, Frodo could not sleep for some time. His legs ached. He was glad that he was riding in the morning. Eventually he fell into a vague dream, in which he seemed to be looking out of a high window over a dark sea of tangled trees. Down below among the roots there was the sound of creatures crawling and snuflling. He felt sure they would smell him out sooner or later.

Then he heard a noise in the distance. At first he thought it was a great wind coming over the leaves of the forest. Then he knew that it was not leaves, but the sound of the Sea far-off; a sound he had never heard in waking life, though it had often troubled his dreams. Suddenly he found he was out in the open. There were no trees after all. He was on a dark heath, and there was a strange salt smell in the air. Looking up he saw before him a tall white tower, standing alone on a high ridge. A great desire came over him to climb the tower and see the Sea. He started to struggle up the ridge towards the tower: but suddenly a light came in the sky, and there was a noise of thunder.

CHAPTER
SIX

The Old Forest

Frodo woke suddenly. It was still dark in the room. Merry was standing there with a candle in one hand, and banging on the door with the other. "All right! What is it?" said Frodo, still shaken and bewildered.

"What is it!" cried Merry. "It is time to get up. It is half past four and very foggy. Come on! Sam is already getting breakfast ready. Even Pippin is up. I am just going to saddle the ponies, and fetch the one that is to be the baggage-carrier. Wake that sluggard Fatty! At least he must get up and see us off."

Soon after six o'clock the five hobbits were ready to start. Fatty Bolger was still yawning. They stole quietly out of the house. Merry went in front leading a laden pony, and took his way along a path that went through a spinney behind the house, and then cut across several fields. The leaves of trees were glistening, and every twig was dripping; the grass was grey with cold dew. Everything was still, and far-away noises seemed near and clear: fowls chattering in a yard, someone closing a door of a distant house.

In their shed they found the ponies; sturdy little beasts of the kind loved by hobbits, not speedy, but good for a long day's work. They mounted, and soon they were riding off into the mist, which seemed to open reluctantly before them and close forbiddingly behind them. After riding for about an hour, slowly and without talking, they saw the Hedge looming suddenly ahead. It was tall and netted over with silver cobwebs.

"How are you going to get through this?" asked Fredegar.

"Follow me!" said Merry, "and you will see." He turned to the left along the Hedge, and soon they came to a point where it bent inwards, running along the lip of a hollow. A cutting had been made, at some distance from the Hedge, and went sloping gently down into the ground. It had walls of brick at the sides, which rose steadily, until suddenly they arched over and formed a tunnel that dived deep under the Hedge and came out in the hollow on the other side.

Here Fatty Bolger halted. "Good-bye, Frodo!" he said. "I wish you were not going into the Forest. I only hope you will not need rescuing before the day is out. But good luck to you — today and every day!"

"If there are no worse things ahead than the Old Forest, I shall be lucky," said Frodo. "Tell Gandalf to hurry along the East Road: we shall soon be back on it and going as fast as we can. Good-bye!" they cried, and rode down the slope and disappeared from Fredegar's sight into the tunnel.

It was dark and damp. At the far end it was closed by a gate of thick-set iron bars. Merry got down and unlocked the gate, and when they had all passed through he pushed it to again. It shut with a clang, and the lock clicked. The sound was ominous.

"There!" said Merry. "You have left the Shire, and are now outside, and on the edge of the Old Forest."

"Are the stories about it true?" asked Pippin.

"I don't know what stories you mean," Merry answered. "If you mean the old bogey-stories Fatty's nurses used to tell him, about goblins and wolves and things of that sort, I should say no. At any rate I don't believe them. But the Forest *is* queer. Everything in it is very much more alive, more aware of what is going on, so to speak, than things are in the Shire. And the trees do not like strangers. They watch you. They are usually content merely to watch you, as long as daylight lasts, and don't do much. Occasionally the most unfriendly ones may drop a branch, or stick a root out, or grasp at you with a long trailer. But at night things can be most alarming, or so I am told. I have only once or twice been in here after dark, and then only near the hedge. I thought all the trees were whispering to each other, passing news and plots along in an unintelligible language; and the branches swayed and groped without any wind. They do say the trees do actually move, and can surround strangers and hem them in. In fact long ago they attacked the Hedge: they came and planted themselves right by it, and leaned over it. But the hobbits came and cut down hundreds of trees, and made a great bonfire in the Forest, and burned all the ground in a long strip east of the Hedge. After that the trees gave up the attack, but they became very unfriendly. There is still a wide bare space not far inside where the bonfire was made."

"Is it only the trees that are dangerous?" asked Pippin.

"There are various queer things living deep in the Forest, and on the far side," said Merry, "or at least I have heard so; but I have never seen any of them. But something makes paths. Whenever one comes inside one finds open tracks; but they seem to shift and change from time to time in a queer fashion. Not far from this tunnel there is, or was for a long time, the beginning of quite a broad path leading to the Bonfire Glade, and then on more or less in our direction, east and a little north. That is the path I am going to try and find."

The hobbits now left the tunnel-gate and rode across the wide hollow. On the far side was a faint path leading up on to the floor of the Forest, a hundred yards and more beyond the Hedge; but it vanished as soon as it brought them under the trees. Looking back they could see the dark line of the Hedge through the stems of trees that were already thick about them. Looking ahead they could see only tree-trunks of innumerable sizes and shapes: straight or bent, twisted, leaning, squat or slender, smooth or gnarled and branched; and all the stems were green or grey with moss and slimy, shaggy growths.

Merry alone seemed fairly cheerful. "You had better lead on and find that path," Frodo said to him. "Don't let us lose one another, or forget which way the Hedge lies!"

They picked a way among the trees, and their ponies plodded along, carefully avoiding the many writhing and interlacing roots. There was no undergrowth. The ground was rising steadily, and as they went forward it seemed that the trees became taller, darker, and thicker. There was no sound, except an occasional drip of moisture falling through the still leaves. For the moment there was no whispering or movement among the branches; but they all got an uncomfortable feeling that they were being watched with disapproval, deepening to dislike and even enmity. The feeling steadily grew, until they found themselves looking up quickly, or glancing back over their shoulders, as if they expected a sudden blow.

There was not as yet any sign of a path, and the trees seemed constantly to bar their way. Pippin suddenly felt that he could not bear it any longer, and without warning let out a shout. "Oi! Oi!" he cried. "I am not going to do anything. Just let me pass through, will you!"

The others halted startled; but the cry fell as if muffled by a heavy curtain. There was no echo or answer though the wood seemed to become more crowded and more watchful than before.

"I should not shout, if I were you," said Merry. "It does more harm than good."

Frodo began to wonder if it were possible to find a way through, and if he had been right to make the others come into this abominable wood. Merry was looking from side to side, and seemed already uncertain which way to go. Pippin noticed it. "It has not taken you long to lose us," he said. But at that moment Merry gave a whistle of relief and pointed ahead.

"Well, well!" he said. "These trees *do* shift. There is the Bonfire Glade in front of us (or I hope so), but the path to it seems to have moved away!"

The light grew clearer as they went forward. Suddenly they came out of the trees and found themselves in a wide circular space. There was sky above them, blue and clear to their surprise, for down under the Forest-roof they had not been able to see the rising morning and the lifting of the mist. The sun was not, however, high enough yet to shine down into the clearing, though its light was on the tree-tops. The leaves were all thicker and greener about the edges of the glade, enclosing it with an almost solid wall. No tree grew there, only rough grass and many tall plants: stalky and faded hemlocks and wood-parsley, fire-weed seeding into fluffy ashes, and rampant nettles and thistles. A dreary place: but it seemed a charming and cheerful garden after the close Forest.

The hobbits felt encouraged, and looked up hopefully at the broadening daylight in the sky. At the far side of the glade there was a break in the wall of trees, and a clear path beyond it. They could see it running on into the wood, wide in places and open above, though every now and again the trees drew in and overshadowed it with their dark boughs. Up this path they rode. They were still climbing gently, but they now went much quicker, and with better heart; for it seemed to them that the Forest had relented, and was going to let them pass unhindered after all.

But after a while the air began to get hot and stuffy. The trees drew close again on either side, and they could no longer see far ahead. Now stronger than ever they felt again the ill will of the wood pressing on them. So silent was it that the fall of their ponies' hoofs, rustling on dead leaves and occasionally stumbling on hidden roots, seemed to thud in their ears. Frodo tried to sing a song to encourage them, but his voice sank to a murmur.

> *O! Wanderers in the shadowed land*
> *despair not! For though dark they stand,*
> *all woods there be must end at last,*
> *and see the open sun go past:*

> *the setting sun, the rising sun,*
> *the day's end, or the day begun.*
> *For east or west all woods must fail . . .*

Fail — even as he said the word his voice faded into silence. The air seemed heavy and the making of words wearisome. Just behind them a large branch fell from an old overhanging tree with a crash into the path. The trees seemed to close in before them.

"They do not like all that about ending and failing," said Merry. "I should not sing any more at present. Wait till we do get to the edge, and then we'll turn and give them a rousing chorus!"

He spoke cheerfully, and if he felt any great anxiety, he did not show it. The others did not answer. They were depressed. A heavy weight was settling steadily on Frodo's heart, and he regretted now with every step forward that he had ever thought of challenging the menace of the trees. He was, indeed, just about to stop and propose going back (if that was still possible), when things took a new turn. The path stopped climbing, and became for a while nearly level. The dark trees drew aside, and ahead they could see the path going almost straight forward. Before them, but some distance off, there stood a green hilltop, treeless, rising like a bald head out of the encircling wood. The path seemed to be making directly for it.

They now hurried forward again, delighted with the thought of climbing out for a while above the roof of the Forest. The path dipped, and then again began to climb upwards, leading them at last to the foot of the steep hillside. There it left the trees and faded into the turf. The wood stood all round the hill like thick hair that ended sharply in a circle round a shaven crown.

The hobbits led their ponies up, winding round and round until they reached the top. There they stood and gazed about them. The air was gleaming and sunlit, but hazy; and they could not see to any great distance. Near at hand the mist was now almost gone; though here and there it lay in hollows of the wood, and to the south of them, out of a deep fold cutting right across the Forest, the fog still rose like steam or wisps of white smoke.

"That," said Merry, pointing with his hand, 'that is the line of the Withywindle. It comes down out of the Downs and flows south-west through the midst of the Forest to join the Brandywine below Haysend. We don't want to go *that* way! The Withywindle valley is said to be the queerest part of the whole wood — the centre from which all the queerness comes, as it were."

The others looked in the direction that Merry pointed out, but they could see little but mists over the damp and deep-cut valley; and beyond it the southern half of the Forest faded from view.

The sun on the hill-top was now getting hot. It must have been about eleven o'clock; but the autumn haze still prevented them from seeing much in other directions. In the west they could not make out either the line of the Hedge or the valley of the Brandywine beyond it. Northward, where they looked most hopefully, they could see nothing that might be the line of the great East Road, for which they were making. They were on an island in a sea of trees, and the horizon was veiled.

On the south-eastern side the ground fell very steeply, as if the slopes of the hill were continued far down under the trees, like island-shores that really are the sides of a mountain rising out of deep waters. They sat on the green edge and looked out over the woods below them, while they ate their midday meal. As the sun rose and passed noon they glimpsed far off in the east the grey-green lines of the Downs that lay beyond the Old Forest on that side. That cheered them greatly; for it was good to see a sight of anything beyond the wood's borders, though they did not mean to go that way, if they could help it: the Barrow-downs had as sinister a reputation in hobbit-legend as the Forest itself.

At length they made up their minds to go on again. The path that had brought them to the hill reappeared on the northward side; but they had not followed it far before they became aware that it was bending steadily to the right. Soon it began to descend rapidly and they guessed that it must actually be heading towards the Withywindle valley: not at all the direction they wished to take. After some discussion they decided to leave this misleading path and strike northward; for although they had not been able to see it from the hill-top, the Road must lie that way, and it could not be many miles off. Also northward, and to the left of the path, the land seemed to be drier and more open, climbing up to slopes where the trees were thinner, and pines and firs replaced the oaks and ashes and other strange and nameless trees of the denser wood.

At first their choice seemed to be good: they got along at a fair speed, though whenever they got a glimpse of the sun in an open glade they seemed unaccountably to have veered eastwards. But after a time the trees began to close in again, just where they had appeared from a distance to be thinner and less tangled. Then deep folds in the ground were discovered unexpectedly, like the ruts of great giant-wheels or wide moats and sunken roads long disused and choked with brambles. These lay usually right across their line of march, and could only be crossed by scrambling down and out again, which was troublesome and difficult with their ponies. Each time they climbed down they found the hollow filled with thick bushes and matted undergrowth, which somehow would not yield to the left, but only gave way when they turned to the right; and they had to go some distance along the bottom before they could find a way up the further bank. Each time they clambered out, the trees seemed deeper and darker; and always to the left and upwards it was most difficult to find a way, and they were forced to the right and downwards.

After an hour or two they had lost all clear sense of direction, though they knew well enough that they had long ceased to go northward at all. They were being headed off, and were simply following a course chosen for them — eastwards and southwards, into the heart of the Forest and not out of it.

The afternoon was wearing away when they scrambled and stumbled into a fold that was wider and deeper than any they had yet met. It was so steep and overhung that it proved impossible to climb out of it again, either forwards or backwards, without leaving their ponies and their baggage behind. All they could do was to follow the fold — downwards. The ground grew soft, and in places boggy; springs appeared in the banks, and soon they found themselves following a brook that trickled and babbled through a weedy bed. Then the ground began to fall rapidly, and the brook growing strong and noisy, flowed and leaped swiftly downhill. They were in a deep dim-lit gully over-arched by trees high above them.

After stumbling along for some way along the stream, they came quite suddenly out of the gloom. As if through a gate they saw the sunlight before them. Coming to the opening they found that they had made their way down through a cleft in a high steep bank, almost a cliff. At its feet was a wide space of grass and reeds; and in the distance could be glimpsed another bank almost as steep. A golden afternoon of late sunshine lay warm and drowsy upon the hidden land between. In the midst of it there wound lazily a dark river of brown water, bordered with ancient willows, arched over with willows, blocked with fallen willows, and flecked with thousands of faded willow-leaves. The air was thick with them, fluttering yellow from the branches; for there was a warm and gentle breeze blowing softly in the valley, and the reeds were rustling, and the willow-boughs were creaking.

"Well, now I have at least some notion of where we are!" said Merry. "We have come almost in the opposite direction to which we intended. This is the River Withywindle! I will go on and explore."

He passed out into the sunshine and disappeared into the long grasses. After a while he reappeared, and reported that there was fairly solid ground between the cliff-foot and the river; in some places firm turf went down to the water's edge. "What's more," he said, "there seems to be something like a footpath winding along on this side of the river. If we turn left and follow it, we shall be bound to come out on the east side of the Forest eventually."

"I dare say!" said Pippin. "That is, if the track goes on so far, and does not simply lead us into a bog and leave us there. Who made the track, do you suppose, and why? I am sure it was not for our benefit. I am getting very suspicious of this Forest and everything in it, and I begin to believe all the stories about it. And have you any idea how far eastward we should have to go?"

"No," said Merry, "I haven't. I don't know in the least how far down the Withywindle we are, or who could possibly come here often enough to make a path along it. But there is no other way out that I can see or think of."

There being nothing else for it, they filed out, and Merry led them to the path that he had discovered. Everywhere the reeds and grasses were lush and tall, in places far above their heads; but once found, the path was easy to follow, as it turned and twisted, picking out the sounder ground among the bogs and pools. Here and there it passed over other rills, running down gullies into the Withywindle out of the higher forest-lands, and at these points there were tree-trunks or bundles of brushwood laid carefully across.

The hobbits began to feel very hot. There were armies of flies of all kinds buzzing round their ears, and the afternoon sun was burning on their backs. At last they came suddenly into a thin shade; great grey branches reached across the path. Each step forward became more reluctant than the last. Sleepiness seemed to be creeping out of the ground and up their legs, and falling softly out of the air upon their heads and eyes.

Frodo felt his chin go down and his head nod. Just in front of him Pippin fell forward on to his knees. Frodo halted. "It's no good," he heard Merry saying. "Can't go another step without rest. Must have nap. It's cool under the willows. Less flies!"

Frodo did not like the sound of this. "Come on!" he cried. "We can't have a nap yet. We must get clear of the Forest first." But the others were too far gone to care. Beside them Sam stood yawning and blinking stupidly.

Suddenly Frodo himself felt sleep overwhelming him. His head swam. There now seemed hardly a sound in the air. The flies had stopped buzzing. Only a gentle noise on the edge of hearing, a soft fluttering as of a song half whispered, seemed to stir in the boughs above. He lifted his heavy eyes and saw leaning over him a huge willow-tree, old and hoary. Enormous it looked, its sprawling branches going up like reaching arms with many long-fingered hands, its knotted and twisted trunk gaping in wide fissures that creaked faintly as the boughs moved. The leaves fluttering against the bright sky dazzled him, and he toppled over, lying where he fell upon the grass.

Merry and Pippin dragged themselves forward and lay down with their backs to the willow-trunk. Behind them the great cracks gaped wide to receive them as the tree swayed and creaked. They looked up at the grey and yellow leaves, moving softly against the light, and singing. They shut their eyes, and then it seemed that they could almost hear words, cool words, saying something about water and sleep. They gave themselves up to the spell and fell fast asleep at the foot of the great grey willow.

Frodo lay for a while fighting with the sleep that was overpowering him; then with an effort he struggled to his feet again. He felt a compelling desire for cool water. "Wait for me, Sam," he stammered. "Must bathe feet a minute."

Half in a dream he wandered forward to the riverward side of the tree, where great winding roots grew out into the stream, like gnarled dragonets straining down to drink. He straddled one of these, and paddled his hot feet in the cool brown water; and there he too suddenly fell asleep with his back against the tree.

Sam sat down and scratched his head, and yawned like a cavern. He was worried. The afternoon was getting late, and he thought this sudden sleepiness uncanny. "There's more behind this than sun and warm air," he muttered to himself. "I don't like this great big tree. I don't trust it. Hark at it singing about sleep now! This won't do at all!"

He pulled himself to his feet, and staggered off to see what had become of the ponies. He found that two had wandered on a good way along the path; and he had just caught them and brought them back towards the others, when he heard two noises; one loud, and the other soft but very clear. One was the splash of something heavy falling into the water; the other was a noise like the snick of a lock when a door quietly closes fast.

He rushed back to the bank. Frodo was in the water close to the edge, and a great tree-root seemed to be over him and holding him down, but he was not struggling. Sam gripped him by the jacket, and dragged him from under the root; and then with difficulty hauled him on to the bank. Almost at once he woke, and coughed and spluttered.

"Do you know, Sam," he said at length, "the beastly tree *threw* me in! I felt it. The big root just twisted round and tipped me in!"

"You were dreaming I expect, Mr. Frodo," said Sam. "You shouldn't sit in such a place, if you feel sleepy."

"What about the others?" Frodo asked. "I wonder what sort of dreams they are having."

They went round to the other side of the tree, and then Sam understood the click that he had heard. Pippin had vanished. The crack, by which he had laid himself, had closed together, so that not a chink could be seen. Merry was trapped: another crack had closed about his waist; his legs lay outside, but the rest of him was inside a dark opening, the edges of which gripped like a pair of pincers.

Frodo and Sam beat first upon the tree-trunk where Pippin had lain. They then struggled frantically to pull open the jaws of the crack that held poor Merry. It was quite useless.

132

"What a foul thing to happen!" cried Frodo wildly. "Why did we ever come into this dreadful Forest? I wish we were all back at Crickhollow!" He kicked the tree with all his strength, heedless of his own feet. A hardly perceptible shiver ran through the stem and up into the branches; the leaves rustled and whispered, but with a sound now of faint and far-off laughter.

"I suppose we haven't got an axe among our luggage, Mr. Frodo?" asked Sam.

"I brought a little hatchet for chopping firewood," said Frodo. "That wouldn't be much use."

"Wait a minute!" cried Sam, struck by an idea suggested by firewood. "We might do something with fire!"

"We might," said Frodo doubtfully. "We might succeed in roasting Pippin alive inside."

"We might try to hurt or frighten this tree to begin with," said Sam fiercely. "If it don't let them go, I'll have it down, if I have to gnaw it." He ran to the ponies and before long came back with two tinder-boxes and a hatchet.

Quickly they gathered dry grass and leaves, and bits of bark; and made a pile of broken twigs and chopped sticks. These they heaped against the trunk on the far side of the tree from the prisoners. As soon as Sam had struck a spark into the tinder, it kindled the dry grass and a flurry of flame and smoke went up. The twigs crackled. Little fingers of fire licked against the dry scored rind of the ancient tree and scorched it. A tremor ran through the whole willow. The leaves seemed to hiss above their heads with a sound of pain and anger. A loud scream came from Merry, and from far inside the tree they heard Pippin give a muffled yell.

"Put it out! Put it out!" cried Merry. "He'll squeeze me in two, if you don't. He says so!"

"Who? What?" shouted Frodo, rushing round to the other side of the tree.

"Put it out! Put it out!" begged Merry. The branches of the willow began to sway violently. There was a sound as of a wind rising and spreading outwards to the branches of all the other trees round about, as though they had dropped a stone into the quiet slumber of the river-valley and set up ripples of anger that ran out over the whole Forest. Sam kicked at the little fire and stamped out the sparks. But Frodo, without any clear idea of why he did so, or what he hoped for, ran along the path crying *help! help! help!* It seemed to him that he could hardly hear the sound of his own shrill voice: it was blown away from him by the willow-wind and drowned in a clamour of leaves, as soon as the words left his mouth. He felt desperate: lost and witless.

Suddenly he stopped. There was an answer, or so he thought; but it seemed to come from behind him, away down the path further back in the Forest. He turned round and listened, and soon there could be no doubt: someone was singing a song; a deep glad voice was singing carelessly and happily, but it was singing nonsense:

> *Hey dol! merry dol! ring a dong dillo!*
> *Ring a dong! hop along! fal lal the willow!*
> *Tom Bom, jolly Tom, Tom Bombadillo!*

Half hopeful and half afraid of some new danger, Frodo and Sam now both stood still. Suddenly out of a long string of nonsense-words (or so they seemed) the voice rose up loud and clear and burst into this song:

> *Hey! Come merry dol! derry dol! My darling!*
> *Light goes the weather-wind and the feathered starling.*
> *Down along under Hill, shining in the sunlight,*
> *Waiting on the doorstep for the cold starlight,*
> *There my pretty lady is, River-woman's daughter,*
> *Slender as the willow-wand, clearer than the water.*
> *Old Tom Bombadil water-lilies bringing*
> *Comes hopping home again. Can you hear him singing?*
> *Hey! Come merry dol! derry dol! and merry-o,*
> *Goldberry, Goldberry, merry yellow berry-o!*

Poor old Willow-man, you tuck your roots away!
Tom's in a hurry now. Evening will follow day.
Tom's going home again water-lilies bringing.
Hey! Come derry dol! Can you hear me singing?

Frodo and Sam stood as if enchanted. The wind puffed out. The leaves hung silently again on stiff branches. There was another burst of song, and then suddenly, hopping and dancing along the path, there appeared above the reeds an old battered hat with a tall crown and a long blue feather stuck in the band. With another hop and a bound there came into view a man, or so it seemed. At any rate he was too large and heavy for a hobbit, if not quite tall enough for one of the Big People, though he made noise enough for one, stumping along with great yellow boots on his thick legs, and charging through grass and rushes like a cow going down to drink. He had a blue coat and a long brown beard; his eyes were blue and bright, and his face was red as a ripe apple, but creased into a hundred wrinkles of laughter. In his hands he carried on a large leaf as on a tray a small pile of white water-lilies.

"Help!" cried Frodo and Sam running towards him with their hands stretched out.

"Whoa! Whoa! steady there!" cried the old man, holding up one hand, and they stopped short, as if they had been struck stiff. "Now, my little fellows, where be you a-going to, puffing like a bellows? What's the matter here then? Do you know who I am? I'm Tom Bombadil. Tell me what's your trouble! Tom's in a hurry now. Don't you crush my lilies!"

"My friends are caught in the willow-tree," cried Frodo breathlessly.

"Master Merry's being squeezed in a crack!" cried Sam.

"What?" shouted Tom Bombadil, leaping up in the air. "Old Man Willow? Naught worse than that, eh? That can soon be mended. I know the tune for him. Old grey Willow-man! I'll freeze his marrow cold, if he don't behave himself. I'll sing his roots off. I'll sing a wind up and blow leaf and branch away.

Old Man Willow!"

Setting down his lilies carefully on the grass, he ran to the tree. There he saw Merry's feet still sticking out — the rest had already been drawn further inside. Tom put his mouth to the crack and began singing into it in a low voice. They could not catch the words, but evidently Merry was aroused. His legs began to kick. Tom sprang away, and breaking off a hanging branch smote the side of the willow with it. "You let them out again, Old Man Willow!" he said. "What be you a-thinking of? You should not be waking. Eat earth! Dig deep! Drink water! Go to sleep! Bombadil is talking!" He then seized Merry's feet and drew him out of the suddenly widening crack.

There was a tearing creak and the other crack split open, and out of it Pippin sprang, as if he had been kicked. Then with a loud snap both cracks closed fast again. A shudder ran through the tree from root to tip, and complete silence fell.

"Thank you!" said the hobbits, one after the other.

Tom Bombadil burst out laughing. "Well, my little fellows!" said he, stooping so that he peered into their faces. "You shall come home with me! The table is all laden with yellow cream, honeycomb, and white bread and butter. Goldberry is waiting. Time enough for questions around the supper table. You follow after me as quick as you are able!" With that he picked up his lilies, and then with a beckoning wave of his hand went hopping and dancing along the path eastward, still singing loudly and nonsensically.

Too surprised and too relieved to talk, the hobbits followed after him as fast as they could. But that was not fast enough. Tom soon disappeared in front of them, and the noise of his singing got fainter and further away. Suddenly his voice came floating back to them in a loud halloo!

> *Hop along, my little friends, up the Withywindle!*
> *Tom's going on ahead candles for to kindle.*
> *Down west sinks the Sun: soon you will be groping.*
> *When the night-shadows fall, then the door will open,*

Out of the window-panes light will twinkle yellow.
Fear no alder black! Heed no hoary willow!
Fear neither root nor bough! Tom goes on before you.
Hey now! merry dol! We'll be waiting for you!

After that the hobbits heard no more. Almost at once the sun seemed to sink into the trees behind them. They thought of the slanting light of evening glittering on the Brandywine River, and the windows of Bucklebury beginning to gleam with hundreds of lights. Great shadows fell across them; trunks and branches of trees hung dark and threatening over the path. White mists began to rise and curl on the surface of the river and stray about the roots of the trees upon its borders. Out of the very ground at their feet a shadowy steam arose and mingled with the swiftly falling dusk.

It became difficult to follow the path, and they were very tired. Their legs seemed leaden. Strange furtive noises ran among the bushes and reeds on either side of them; and if they looked up to the pale sky, they caught sight of queer gnarled and knobbly faces that gloomed dark against the twilight, and leered down at them from the high bank and the edges of the wood. They began to feel that all this country was unreal, and that they were stumbling through an ominous dream that led to no awakening.

Just as they felt their feet slowing down to a standstill, they noticed that the ground was gently rising. The water began to murmur. In the darkness they caught the white glimmer of foam, where the river flowed over a short fall. Then suddenly the trees came to an end and the mists were left behind. They stepped out from the Forest, and found a wide sweep of grass welling up before them. The river, now small and swift, was leaping merrily down to meet them, glinting here and there in the light of the stars, which were already shining in the sky.

The grass under their feet was smooth and short, as if it had been mown or shaven. The eaves of the Forest behind were clipped, and trim as a hedge. The path was now plain before them, well-tended and bordered with stone. It wound up on to the top of a grassy knoll, now grey under the pale starry night; and there, still high above them on a further slope, they saw the twinkling lights of a house. Down again the path went, and then up again, up a long smooth hillside of turf, towards the light. Suddenly a wide yellow beam flowed out brightly from a door that was opened. There was Tom Bombadil's house before them, up, down, under hill. Behind it a steep shoulder of the land lay grey and bare, and beyond that the dark shapes of the Barrow-downs stalked away into the eastern night.

They all hurried forward, hobbits and ponies. Already half their weariness and all their fears had fallen from them. *Hey! Come merry dol!* rolled out the song to greet them.

> *Hey! Come derry dol! Hop along, my hearties!*
> *Hobbits! Ponies all! We are fond of parties.*
> *Now let the fun begin! Let us sing together!*

Then another clear voice, as young and as ancient as Spring, like the song of a glad water flowing down into the night from a bright morning in the hills, came falling like silver to meet them:

> *Now let the song begin! Let us sing together*
> *Of sun, stars, moon and mist, rain and cloudy weather,*
> *Light on the budding leaf, dew on the feather,*
> *Wind on the open hill, bells on the heather,*
> *Reeds by the shady pool, lilies on the water:*
> *Old Tom Bombadil and the River-daughter!*

And with that song the hobbits stood upon the threshold, and a golden light was all about them.

CHAPTER
SEVEN

In the House of Tom Bombadil

The four hobbits stepped over the wide stone threshold, and stood still, blinking. They were in a long low room, filled with the light of lamps swinging from the beams of the roof; and on the table of dark polished wood stood many candles, tall and yellow, burning brightly.

In a chair, at the far side of the room facing the outer door, sat a woman. Her long yellow hair rippled down her shoulders; her gown was green, green as young reeds, shot with silver like beads of dew; and her belt was of gold, shaped like a chain of flag-lilies set with the pale-blue eyes of forget-me-nots. About her feet in wide vessels of green and brown earthenware, white water-lilies were floating, so that she seemed to be enthroned in the midst of a pool.

"Enter, good guests!" she said, and as she spoke they knew that it was her clear voice they had heard singing. They came a few timid steps further into the room, and began to bow low, feeling strangely surprised and awkward, like folk that, knocking at a cottage door to beg for a drink of water, have been answered by a fair young elf-queen clad in living flowers. But before they could say anything, she sprang lightly up and over the lily-bowls, and ran laughing towards them; and as she ran her gown rustled softly like the wind in the flowering borders of a river.

"Come dear folk!" she said, taking Frodo by the hand. "Laugh and be merry! I am Goldberry, daughter of the River." Then lightly she passed them and closing the door she turned her back to it, with her white arms spread out across it. "Let us shut out the night!" she said. "For you are still afraid, perhaps, of mist and tree-shadows and deep water, and untame things. Fear nothing! For tonight you are under the roof of Tom Bombadil."

The hobbits looked at her in wonder; and she looked at each of them and smiled. "Fair lady Goldberry!" said Frodo at last, feeling his heart moved with a joy that he did not understand. He stood as he had at times stood enchanted by fair elven-voices; but the spell that was now laid upon him was different: less keen and lofty was the delight, but deeper and nearer to mortal heart; marvellous and yet not strange. "Fair lady Goldberry!" he said again. "Now the joy that was hidden in the songs we heard is made plain to me.

O slender as a willow-wand! O clearer than clear water!
O reed by the living pool! Fair River-daughter!
O spring-time and summer-time, and spring again after!
O wind on the waterfall, and the leaves' laughter!"

Suddenly he stopped and stammered, overcome with surprise to hear himself saying such things. But Goldberry laughed.

"Welcome!" she said. "I had not heard that folk of the Shire were so sweet-tongued. But I see you are an elf-friend; the light in your eyes and the ring in your voice tells it. This is a merry meeting! Sit now, and wait for the Master of the house! He will not be long. He is tending your tired beasts."

The hobbits sat down gladly in low rush-seated chairs, while Goldberry busied herself about the table; and their eyes followed her, for the slender grace of her movement filled them with quiet delight. From somewhere behind the house came the sound of singing. Every now and again they caught, among many a *derry dol* and a *merry dol* and a *ring a ding dillo* the repeated words:

> *Old Tom Bombadil is a merry fellow;*
> *Bright blue his jacket is, and his boots are yellow.*

"Fair lady!" said Frodo again after a while. "Tell me, if my asking does not seem foolish, who is Tom Bombadil?"

"He is," said Goldberry, staying her swift movements and smiling.

Frodo looked at her questioningly. "He is, as you have seen him," she said in answer to his look. "He is the Master of wood, water, and hill."

"Then all this strange land belongs to him?"

"No indeed!" she answered, and her smile faded. "That would indeed be a burden," she added in a low voice, as if to herself. "The trees and the grasses and all things growing or living in the land belong each to themselves. Tom Bombadil is the Master. No one has ever caught old Tom walking in the forest, wading in the water, leaping on the hill-tops under light and shadow. He has no fear. Tom Bombadil is master."

A door opened and in came Tom Bombadil. He had now no hat and his thick brown hair was crowned with autumn leaves. He laughed, and going to Goldberry, took her hand.

"Here's my pretty lady" he said, bowing to the hobbits. "Here's my Goldberry clothed all in silver-green with flowers in her girdle! Is the table laden? I see yellow cream and honeycomb, and white bread, and butter; milk, cheese, and green herbs and ripe berries gathered. Is that enough for us? Is the supper ready?"

"It is," said Goldberry; "but the guests perhaps are not?"

Tom clapped his hands and cried: "Tom, Tom! your guests are tired, and you had near forgotten! Come now, my merry friends, and Tom will refresh you! You shall clean grimy hands, and wash your weary faces; cast off your muddy cloaks and comb out your tangles!"

He opened the door, and they followed him down a short passage and round a sharp turn. They came to a low room with a sloping roof (a penthouse, it seemed, built on to the north end of the house). Its walls were of clean stone, but they were mostly covered with green hanging mats and yellow curtains. The floor was flagged, and strewn with fresh green rushes. There were four deep mattresses, each piled with white blankets, laid on the floor along one side. Against the opposite wall was a long bench laden with wide earthen-ware basins, and beside it stood brown ewers filled with water, some cold, some steaming hot. There were soft green slippers set ready beside each bed.

Before long, washed and refreshed, the hobbits were seated at the table, two on each side, while at either end sat Goldberry and the Master. It was a long and merry meal. Though the hobbits ate, as only famished hobbits can eat, there was no lack. The drink in their drinking-bowls seemed to be clear cold water, yet it went to their hearts like wine and set free their voices. The guests became suddenly aware that they were singing merrily, as if it was easier and more natural than talking.

At last Tom and Goldberry rose and cleared the table swiftly. The guests were commanded to sit quiet, and were set in chairs, each with a footstool to his tired feet. There was a fire in the wide hearth before them, and it was burning with a sweet smell, as if it were built of apple-wood. When everything was set in order, all the lights in the room were put out, except one lamp and a pair of candles at each end of the chimney-shelf. Then Goldberry came and stood before them, holding a candle; and she wished them each a good night and deep sleep.

"Have peace now," she said, "until the morning! Heed no nightly noises! For nothing passes door and window here save moonlight and starlight and the wind off the hill-top. Good night!" She passed out of the room with a glimmer and a rustle.

The sound of her footsteps was like a stream falling gently away downhill over cool stones in the quiet of night.

Tom sat on a while beside them in silence, while each of them tried to muster the courage to ask one of the many questions he had meant to ask at supper. Sleep gathered on their eyelids. At last Frodo spoke:

"Did you hear me calling, Master, or was it just chance that brought you at that moment?"

Tom stirred like a man shaken out of a pleasant dream. "Eh, what?" said he. "Did I hear you calling? Nay, I did not hear: I was busy singing. Just chance brought me then, if chance you call it. It was no plan of mine, though I was waiting for you. We heard news of you, and learned that you were wandering. We guessed you'd come ere long down to the water: all paths lead that way, down to Withywindle. Old grey Willow-man, he's a mighty singer; and it's hard for little folk to escape his cunning mazes. But Tom had an errand there, that he dared not hinder." Tom nodded as if sleep was taking him again; but he went on in a soft singing voice:

I had an errand there: gathering water-lilies,
green leaves and lilies white to please my pretty lady,
the last ere the year's end to keep them from the winter,
to flower by her pretty feet till the snows are melted.
Each year at summer's end I go to find them for her,
in a wide pool, deep and clear, far down Withywindle;
there they open first in spring and there they linger latest.
By that pool long ago I found the River-daughter,
fair young Goldberry sitting in the rushes.
Sweet was her singing then, and her heart was beating!

He opened his eyes and looked at them with a sudden glint of blue:

And that proved well for you — for now I shall no longer
go down deep again along the forest-water,

not while the year is old. Nor shall I be passing
Old Man Willow's house this side of spring-time,
not till the merry spring, when the River-daughter
dances down the withy-path to bathe in the water.

He fell silent again; but Frodo could not help asking one more question: the one he most desired to have answered. "Tell us, Master," he said, "about the Willow-man. What is he? I have never heard of him before."

"No, don't!" said Merry and Pippin together, sitting suddenly upright. "Not now! Not until the morning!"

"That is right!" said the old man. "Now is the time for resting. Some things are ill to hear when the world's in shadow. Sleep till the morning-light, rest on the pillow! Heed no nightly noise! Fear no grey willow!" And with that he took down the lamp and blew it out, and grasping a candle in either hand he led them out of the room.

Their mattresses and pillows were soft as down, and the blankets were of white wool. They had hardly laid themselves on the deep beds and drawn the light covers over them before they were asleep.

In the dead night, Frodo lay in a dream without light. Then he saw the young moon rising; under its thin light there loomed before him a black wall of rock, pierced by a dark arch like a great gate. It seemed to Frodo that he was lifted up, and passing over he saw that the rock-wall was a circle of hills, and that within it was a plain, and in the midst of the plain stood a pinnacle of stone, like a vast tower but not made by hands. On its top stood the figure of a man. The moon as it rose seemed to hang for a moment above his head and glistened in his white hair as the wind stirred it. Up from the dark plain below came the crying of fell voices, and the howling of many wolves. Suddenly a shadow, like the shape of great wings, passed across the moon. The figure lifted his arms and a light flashed from the staff that he wielded. A mighty eagle swept down and bore him away. The voices wailed and the wolves yammered. There was a noise like a strong wind blowing, and on it was borne the sound of hoofs, galloping, galloping, galloping from the East. "Black Riders!" thought Frodo as he wakened, with the sound of the hoofs still echoing in his mind. He wondered if he would ever again have the courage to leave the safety of these stone walls. He lay motionless, still listening; but all was now silent, and at last he turned and fell asleep again or wandered into some other unremembered dream.

At his side Pippin lay dreaming pleasantly; but a change came over his dreams and he turned and groaned. Suddenly he woke, or thought he had waked, and yet still heard in the darkness the sound that had disturbed his dream: *tip-tap, squeak*: the noise was like branches fretting in the wind, twig-fingers scraping wall and window: *creak, creak, creak*. He wondered if there were willow-trees close to the house; and then suddenly he had a dreadful feeling that he was not in an ordinary house at all, but inside the willow and listening to that horrible dry creaking voice laughing at him again. He sat up, and felt the soft pillows yield to his hands, and he lay down again relieved. He seemed to hear the echo of words in his ears: "Fear nothing! Have peace until the morning! Heed no nightly noises!" Then he went to sleep again.

It was the sound of water that Merry heard falling into his quiet sleep: water streaming down gently, and then spreading, spreading irresistibly all round the house into a dark shoreless pool. It gurgled under the walls, and was rising slowly but surely. "I shall be drowned!" he thought. "It will find its way in, and then I shall drown." He felt that he was lying in a soft slimy bog, and springing up he set his foot on the corner of a cold hard flagstone. Then he remembered where he was and lay down again. He seemed to hear or remember hearing: "Nothing passes doors or windows save moonlight and starlight and the wind off the hill-top." A little breath of sweet air moved the curtain. He breathed deep and fell asleep again.

As far as he could remember, Sam slept through the night in deep content, if logs are contented.

They woke up, all four at once, in the morning light. Tom was moving about the room whistling like a starling. When he heard them stir he clapped his hands, and cried: "Hey! Come merry dol! derry dol! My hearties!" He drew back the yellow curtains, and the hobbits saw that these had covered the windows, at either end of the room, one looking east and the other looking west.

They leapt up refreshed. Frodo ran to the eastern window, and found himself looking into a kitchen-garden grey with dew. He had half expected to see turf right up to the walls, turf all pocked with hoof-prints. Actually his view was screened by a tall line of beans on poles; but above and far beyond them the grey top of the hill loomed up against the sunrise. It was a pale morning: in the East, behind long clouds like lines of soiled wool stained red at the edges, lay glimmering deeps of yellow. The sky spoke of rain to come; but the light was broadening quickly, and the red flowers on the beans began to glow against the wet green leaves.

Pippin looked out of the western window, down into a pool of mist. The Forest was hidden under a fog. It was like looking down on to a sloping cloud-roof from above. There was a fold or channel where the mist was broken into many plumes and billows; the valley of the Withywindle. The stream ran down the hill on the left and vanished into the white shadows. Near at hand was a flower-garden and a clipped hedge silver-netted, and beyond that grey shaven grass pale with dew-drops. There was no willow-tree to be seen.

"Good morning, merry friends!" cried Tom, opening the eastern window wide. A cool air flowed in; it had a rainy smell. "Sun won't show her face much today, I'm thinking. I have been walking wide, leaping on the hill-tops, since the grey dawn began, nosing wind and weather, wet grass underfoot, wet sky above me. I wakened Goldberry singing under window; but nought wakes hobbit-folk in the early morning. In the night little folk wake up in the darkness, and sleep after light has come! Ring a ding dillo! Wake now, my merry friends! Forget the nightly noises! Ring a ding dillo del! derry del, my hearties! If you come soon you'll find breakfast on the table. If you come late you'll get grass and rain-water!"

Needless to say — not that Tom's threat sounded very serious — the hobbits came soon, and left the table late and only when it was beginning to look rather empty. Neither Tom nor Goldberry were there. Tom could be heard about the house, clattering in the kitchen, and up and down the stairs, and singing here and there outside. The room looked westward over the mist-clouded valley, and the window was open. Water dripped down from the thatched eaves above. Before they had finished breakfast the clouds had joined into an unbroken roof, and a straight grey rain came softly and steadily down. Behind its deep curtain the Forest was completely veiled.

As they looked out of the window there came falling gently as if it was flowing down the rain out of the sky, the clear voice of Goldberry singing up above them. They could hear few words, but it seemed plain to them that the song was a rain-song, as sweet as showers on dry hills, that told the tale of a river from the spring in the highlands to the Sea far below. The hobbits listened with delight; and Frodo was glad in his heart, and blessed the kindly weather, because it delayed them from departing. The thought of going had been heavy upon him from the moment he awoke; but he guessed now that they would not go further that day.

The upper wind settled in the West and deeper and wetter clouds rolled up to spill their laden rain on the bare heads of the Downs. Nothing could be seen all round the house but falling water. Frodo stood near the open door and watched the white chalky path turn into a little river of milk and go bubbling away down into the valley. Tom Bombadil came trotting round the corner of the house, waving his arms as if he was warding off the rain — and indeed when he sprang over the threshold he seemed quite dry, except for his boots. These he took off and put in the chimney-corner. Then he sat in the largest chair and called the hobbits to gather round him.

"This is Goldberry's washing day," he said, "and her autumn cleaning. Too wet for hobbit-folk — let them rest while they are able! It's a good day for long tales, for questions and for answers, so Tom will start the talking."

He then told them many remarkable stories, sometimes half as if speaking to himself, sometimes looking at them suddenly with a bright blue eye under his deep brows. Often his voice would turn to song, and he would get out of his chair and dance about. He told them tales of bees and flowers, the ways of trees, and the strange creatures of the Forest, about evil things and good things, things friendly and things unfriendly, cruel things and kind things, and secrets hidden under brambles.

As they listened, they began to understand the lives of the Forest, apart from themselves, indeed to feel themselves as the strangers where all other things were at home. Moving constantly in and out of his talk was Old Man Willow, and Frodo learned now enough to content him, indeed more than enough, for it was not comfortable lore. Tom's words laid bare the hearts of trees and their thoughts, which were often dark and strange, and filled with a hatred of things that go free upon the earth, gnawing, biting, breaking, hacking, burning: destroyers and usurpers. It was not called the Old Forest without reason, for it was indeed ancient, a survivor of vast forgotten woods; and in it there lived yet, ageing no quicker than the hills, the fathers of the fathers of trees, remembering times when they were lords. The countless years had filled them with pride and rooted wisdom, and with malice. But none were more dangerous than the Great Willow: his heart was rotten, but his strength was green; and he was cunning, and a master of winds, and his song and thought ran through the woods on both sides of the river. His grey thirsty spirit drew power out of the earth and spread like fine root-threads in the ground, and invisible twig-fingers in the air, till it had under its dominion nearly all the trees of the Forest from the Hedge to the Downs.

Suddenly Tom's talk left the woods and went leaping up the young stream, over bubbling waterfalls, over pebbles and worn rocks, and among small flowers in close grass and wet crannies, wandering at last up on to the Downs. They heard of the Great Barrows, and the green mounds, and the stone-rings upon the hills and in the hollows among the hills. Sheep were bleating in flocks. Green walls and white walls rose. There were fortresses on the heights. Kings of little kingdoms fought together, and the young Sun shone like fire on the red metal of their new and greedy swords. There was victory and defeat; and towers fell, fortresses were burned, and flames went up into the sky. Gold was piled on the biers of dead kings and queens; and mounds covered them, and the stone doors were shut; and the grass grew over all. Sheep walked for a while biting the grass, but soon the hills were empty again. A shadow came out of dark places far away, and the bones were stirred in the mounds. Barrow-wights walked in the hollow places with a clink of rings on cold fingers, and gold chains in the wind. Stone rings grinned out of the ground like broken teeth in the moonlight.

The hobbits shuddered. Even in the Shire the rumour of the Barrow-wights of the Barrow-downs beyond the Forest had been heard. But it was not a tale that any hobbit liked to listen to, even by a comfortable fireside far away. These four now suddenly remembered what the joy of this house had driven from their minds: the house of Tom Bombadil nestled under the very shoulder of those dreaded hills. They lost the thread of his tale and shifted uneasily, looking aside at one another.

When they caught his words again they found that he had now wandered into strange regions beyond their memory and beyond their waking thought, into times when the world was wider, and the seas flowed straight to the western Shore; and still on and back Tom went singing out into ancient starlight, when only the Elf-sires were awake. Then suddenly he stopped, and they saw that he nodded as if he was falling asleep. The hobbits sat still before him, enchanted; and it seemed as if under the spell of his words, the wind had gone, and the clouds had dried up, and the day had been withdrawn, and darkness had come from East and West, and all the sky was filled with the light of white stars.

Whether the morning and evening of one day or of many days had passed Frodo could not tell. He did not feel either hungry or tired, only filled with wonder. The stars shone through the window and the silence of the heavens seemed to be round him. He spoke at last out of his wonder and a sudden fear of that silence:

"Who are you, Master?" he asked.

"Eh, what?" said Tom sitting up, and his eyes glinting in the gloom. "Don't you know my name yet? That's the only answer. Tell me, who are you, alone, yourself and nameless? But you are young and I am old. Eldest, that's what I am. Mark my words, my friends: Tom was here before the river and the trees; Tom remembers the first raindrop and the first acorn. He made paths before the Big People, and saw the little People arriving. He was here before the Kings and the graves and the Barrow-wights. When the Elves passed westward, Tom was here already, before the seas were bent. He knew the dark under the stars when it was fearless — before the Dark Lord came from Outside."

A shadow seemed to pass by the window, and the hobbits glanced hastily through the panes. When they turned again, Goldberry stood in the door behind, framed in light. She held a candle, shielding its flame from the draught with her hand; and the light flowed through it, like sunlight through a white shell.

"The rain has ended," she said; "and new waters are running downhill, under the stars. Let us now laugh and be glad!"

"And let us have food and drink!" cried Tom. "Long tales are thirsty. And long listening's hungry work, morning, noon, and evening!" With that he jumped out of his chair, and with a bound took a candle from the chimney-shelf and lit it in the flame that Goldberry held; then he danced about the table.

Suddenly he hopped through the door and disappeared.

Quickly he returned, bearing a large and laden tray. Then Tom and Goldberry set the table; and the hobbits sat half in wonder and half in laughter: so fair was the grace of Goldberry and so merry and odd the caperings of Tom. Yet in some fashion they seemed to weave a single dance, neither hindering the other, in and out of the room, and round about the table; and with great speed food and vessels and lights were set in order. The boards blazed with candles, white and yellow. Tom bowed to his guests. "Supper is ready," said Goldberry; and now the hobbits saw that she was clothed all in silver with a white girdle, and her shoes were like fishes' mail. But Tom was all in clean blue, blue as rain-washed forget-me-nots, and he had green stockings.

It was a supper even better than before. The hobbits under the spell of Tom's words may have missed one meal or many, but when the food was before them it seemed at least a week since they had eaten. They did not sing or even speak much for a while, and paid close attention to business. But after a time their hearts and spirits rose high again, and their voices rang out in mirth and laughter.

After they had eaten, Goldberry sang many songs for them, songs that began merrily in the hills and fell softly down into silence; and in the silences they saw in their minds pools and waters wider than any they had known, and looking into them they saw the sky below them and the stars like jewels in the depths. Then once more she wished them each good night and left them by the fireside. But Tom now seemed wide awake and plied them with questions.

He appeared already to know much about them and all their families, and indeed to know much of all the history and doings of the Shire down from days hardly remembered among the hobbits themselves. It no longer surprised them; but he made no secret that he owed his recent knowledge largely to Farmer Maggot, whom he seemed to regard as a person of more importance than they had imagined. "There's earth under his old feet, and clay on his fingers; wisdom in his bones, and both his eyes are open," said Tom. It was also clear that Tom had dealings with the Elves, and it seemed that in some fashion, news had reached him from Gildor concerning the flight of Frodo.

Indeed so much did Tom know, and so cunning was his questioning, that Frodo found himself telling him more about Bilbo and his own hopes and fears than he had told before even to Gandalf. Tom wagged his head up and down, and there was a glint in his eyes when he heard of the Riders.

"Show me the precious Ring!" he said suddenly in the midst of the story: and Frodo, to his own astonishment, drew out the chain from his pocket, and unfastening the Ring handed it at once to Tom.

It seemed to grow larger as it lay for a moment on his big brown-skinned hand. Then suddenly he put it to his eye and laughed. For a second the hobbits had a vision, both comical and alarming, of his bright blue eye gleaming through a circle of gold. Then Tom put the Ring round the end of his little finger and held it up to the candle-light. For a moment the hobbits noticed nothing strange about this. Then they gasped. There was no sign of Tom disappearing!

Tom laughed again, and then he spun the Ring in the air — and it vanished with a flash. Frodo gave a cry — and Tom leaned forward and handed it back to him with a smile.

Frodo looked at it closely, and rather suspiciously (like one who has lent a trinket to a juggler). It was the same Ring, or looked the same and weighed the same: for that Ring had always seemed to Frodo to weigh strangely heavy in the hand. But something prompted him to make sure. He was perhaps a trifle annoyed with Tom for seeming to make so light of what even Gandalf thought so perilously important. He waited for an opportunity, when the talk was going again, and Tom was telling an absurd story about badgers and their queer ways — then he slipped the Ring on.

Merry turned towards him to say something and gave a start, and checked an exclamation. Frodo was delighted (in a way): it was his own ring all right, for Merry was staring blankly at his chair, and obviously could not see him. He got up and crept quietly away from the fireside towards the outer door.

"Hey there!" cried Tom, glancing towards him with a most seeing look in his shining eyes. "Hey! Come Frodo, there! Where be you a-going? Old Tom Bombadil's not as blind as that yet. Take off your golden ring! Your hand's more fair without it. Come back! Leave your game and sit down beside me! We must talk a while more, and think about the morning. Tom must teach the right road, and keep your feet from wandering."

Frodo laughed (trying to feel pleased), and taking off the Ring he came and sat down again. Tom now told them that he reckoned the Sun would shine tomorrow, and it would be a glad morning, and setting out would be hopeful. But they would do well to start early; for weather in that country was a thing that even Tom could not be sure of for long, and it would change sometimes quicker than he could change his jacket. "I am no weather-master," he said; "nor is aught that goes on two legs."

By his advice they decided to make nearly due North from his house, over the western and lower slopes of the Downs: they might hope in that way to strike the East Road in a day's journey, and avoid the Barrows. He told them not to be afraid — but to mind their own business.

"Keep to the green grass. Don't you go a-meddling with old stone or cold Wights or prying in their houses, unless you be strong folk with hearts that never falter!" He said this more than once; and he advised them to pass barrows by on the west-side, if they chanced to stray near one. Then he taught them a rhyme to sing, if they should by ill-luck fall into any danger or difficulty the next day.

Ho! Tom Bombadil, Tom Bombadillo!
By water, wood and hill, by the reed and willow,

By fire, sun and moon, harken now and hear us!
Come, Tom Bombadil, for our need is near us!

When they had sung this altogether after him, he clapped them each on the shoulder with a laugh, and taking candles led them back to their bedroom.

CHAPTER
EIGHT

Fog on the
Barrow-Downs

That night they heard no noises. But either in his dreams or out
of them, he could not tell which, Frodo heard a sweet singing
running in his mind: a song that seemed to come like a pale
light behind a grey rain-curtain, and growing stronger to turn
the veil all to glass and silver, until at last it was rolled back,
and a far green country opened before him under a swift
sunrise.

The vision melted into waking; and there was Tom whistling
like a tree-full of birds; and the sun was already slanting down
the hill and through the open window. Outside everything was
green and pale gold.

After breakfast, which they again ate alone, they made ready
to say farewell, as nearly heavy of heart as was possible on such
a morning: cool, bright, and clean under a washed autumn sky
of thin blue. The air came fresh from the North-west. Their
quiet ponies were almost frisky, sniffing and moving restlessly.
Tom came out of the house and waved his hat and danced upon
the doorstep, bidding the hobbits to get up and be off and go
with good speed.

They rode off along a path that wound away from behind the
house, and went slanting up towards the north end of the hill-

brow under which it sheltered. They had just dismounted to lead their ponies up the last steep slope, when suddenly Frodo stopped.

"Goldberry!" he cried. "My fair lady, clad all in silver green! We have never said farewell to her, nor seen her since the evening!" He was so distressed that he turned back; but at that moment a clear call came rippling down. There on the hill-brow she stood beckoning to them: her hair was flying loose, and as it caught the sun it shone and shimmered. A light like the glint of water on dewy grass flashed from under her feet as she danced.

They hastened up the last slope, and stood breathless beside her. They bowed, but with a wave of her arm she bade them look round; and they looked out from the hill-top over lands under the morning. It was now as clear and far-seen as it had been veiled and misty when they stood upon the knoll in the Forest, which could now be seen rising pale and green out of the dark trees in the West. In that direction the land rose in wooded ridges, green, yellow, russet under the sun, beyond which lay hidden the valley of the Brandywine. To the South, over the line of the Withywindle, there was a distant glint like pale glass where the Brandywine River made a great loop in the lowlands and flowed away out of the knowledge of the hobbits. Northward beyond the dwindling downs the land ran away in flats and swellings of grey and green and pale earth-colours, until it faded into a featureless and shadowy distance. Eastward the Barrow-downs rose, ridge behind ridge into the morning, and vanished out of eye-sight into a guess: it was no more than a guess of blue and a remote white glimmer blending with the hem of the sky, but it spoke to them, out of memory and old tales, of the high and distant mountains.

They took a deep draught of the air, and felt that a skip and a few stout strides would bear them wherever they wished. It seemed fainthearted to go jogging aside over the crumpled skirts of the downs towards the Road, when they should be leaping, as lusty as Tom, over the stepping stones of the hills straight towards the Mountains.

Goldberry spoke to them and recalled their eyes and thoughts. "Speed now, fair guests!" she said. "And hold to your purpose! North with the wind in the left eye and a blessing on your footsteps! Make haste while the Sun shines!" And to Frodo she said: "Farewell, Elf-friend, it was a merry meeting!"

But Frodo found no words to answer. He bowed low, and mounted his pony, and followed by his friends jogged slowly down the gentle slope behind the hill. Tom Bombadil's house and the valley, and the Forest were lost to view. The air grew warmer between the green walls of hillside and hillside, and the scent of turf rose strong and sweet as they breathed. Turning back, when they reached the bottom of the green hollow, they saw Goldberry, now small and slender like a sunlit flower against the sky: she was standing still watching them, and her hands were stretched out towards them. As they looked she gave a clear call, and lifting up her hand she turned and vanished behind the hill.

Their way wound along the floor of the hollow, and round the green feet of a steep hill into another deeper and broader valley, and then over the shoulder of further hills, and down their long limbs, and up their smooth sides again, up on to new hill-tops and down into new valleys. There was no tree nor any visible water: it was a country of grass and short springy turf, silent except for the whisper of the air over the edges of the land, and high lonely cries of strange birds. As they journeyed the sun mounted, and grew hot. Each time they climbed a ridge the breeze seemed to have grown less. When they caught a glimpse of the country westward the distant Forest seemed to be smoking, as if the fallen rain was steaming up again from leaf and root and mould. A shadow now lay round the edge of sight, a dark haze above which the upper sky was like a blue cap, hot and heavy.

About mid-day they came to a hill whose top was wide and flattened, like a shallow saucer with a green mounded rim.

Inside there was no air stirring, and the sky seemed near their heads. They rode across and looked northwards. Then their hearts rose, for it seemed plain that they had come further already than they had expected. Certainly the distances had now all become hazy and deceptive, but there could be no doubt that the Downs were coming to an end. A long valley lay below them winding away northwards, until it came to an opening between two steep shoulders. Beyond, there seemed to be no more hills. Due north they faintly glimpsed a long dark line. "That is a line of trees," said Merry, "and that must mark the Road. All along it for many leagues east of the Bridge there are trees growing. Some say they were planted in the old days."

"Splendid!" said Frodo. "If we make as good going this afternoon as we have done this morning, we shall have left the Downs before the Sun sets and be jogging on in search of a camping place." But even as he spoke he turned his glance eastwards, and he saw that on that side the hills were higher and looked down upon them; and all those hills were crowned with green mounds, and on some were standing stones, pointing upwards like jagged teeth out of green gums.

That view was somehow disquieting; so they turned from the sight and went down into the hollow circle. In the midst of it there stood a single stone, standing tall under the sun above, and at this hour casting no shadow. It was shapeless and yet significant: like a landmark, or a guarding finger, or more like a warning. But they were now hungry, and the sun was still at the fearless noon; so they set their backs against the east side of the stone. It was cool, as if the sun had had no power to warm it; but at that time this seemed pleasant. There they took food and drink, and made as good a noon-meal under the open sky as anyone could wish; for the food came from "down under Hill". Tom had provided them with plenty for the comfort of the day. Their ponies unburdened strayed upon the grass.

Riding over the hills, and eating their fill, the warm sun and the scent of turf, lying a little too long, stretching out their legs and looking at the sky above their noses: these things are, perhaps, enough to explain what happened. However, that may be: they woke suddenly and uncomfortably from a sleep they had never meant to take. The standing stone was cold, and it cast a long pale shadow that stretched eastward over them. The sun, a pale and watery yellow, was gleaming through the mist just above the west wall of the hollow in which they lay; north, south, and east, beyond the wall the fog was thick, cold and white. The air was silent, heavy and chill. Their ponies were standing crowded together with their heads down.

The hobbits sprang to their feet in alarm, and ran to the western rim. They found that they were upon an island in the fog. Even as they looked out in dismay towards the setting sun, it sank before their eyes into a white sea, and a cold grey shadow sprang up in the East behind. The fog rolled up to the walls and rose above them, and as it mounted it bent over their heads until it became a roof: they were shut in a hall of mist whose central pillar was the standing stone.

They felt as if a trap was closing about them; but they did not quite lose heart. They still remembered the hopeful view they had had of the line of the Road ahead, and they still knew in which direction it lay. In any case, they now had so great a dislike for that hollow place about the stone that no thought of remaining there was in their minds. They packed up as quickly as their chilled fingers would work.

Soon they were leading their ponies in single file over the rim and down the long northward slope of the hill, down into a foggy sea. As they went down the mist became colder and damper, and their hair hung lank and dripping on their foreheads. When they reached the bottom it was so cold that they halted and got out cloaks and hoods, which soon became bedewed with grey drops. Then, mounting their ponies, they went slowly on again, feeling their way by the rise and fall of the ground. They were steering, as well as they could guess, for the gate-like opening at the far northward end of the long valley which they had seen in the morning. Once they were through the gap, they had only to keep on in anything like a straight line and they were bound in the end to strike the Road. Their thoughts did not go beyond that, except for a vague hope that perhaps away beyond the Downs there might be no fog.

Their going was very slow. To prevent their getting separated and wandering in different directions they went in file, with Frodo leading. Sam was behind him, and after him came Pippin, and then Merry. The valley seemed to stretch on endlessly. Suddenly Frodo saw a hopeful sign. On either side ahead a darkness began to loom through the mist; and he guessed that they were at last approaching the gap in the hills, the north-gate of the Barrow-downs. If they could pass that, they would be free.

"Come on! Follow me!" he called back over his shoulder, and he hurried forward. But his hope soon changed to bewilderment and alarm. The dark patches grew darker, but they shrank; and suddenly he saw, towering ominous before him and leaning slightly towards one another like the pillars of a headless door, two huge standing stones. He could not remember having seen any sign of these in the valley, when he looked out from the hill in the morning. He had passed between them almost before he was aware: and even as he did so darkness seemed to fall round him. His pony reared and snorted, and he fell off. When he looked back he found that he was alone: the others had not followed him.

"Sam!" he called. "Pippin! Merry! Come along! Why don't you keep up?"

There was no answer. Fear took him, and he ran back past the stones shouting wildly: "Sam! Sam! Merry! Pippin!" The pony bolted into the mist and vanished. From some way off, or so it seemed, he thought he heard a cry: "Hoy! Frodo! Hoy!" It was away eastward, on his left as he stood under the great stones, staring and straining into the gloom. He plunged off in the direction of the call, and found himself going steeply uphill.

As he struggled on he called again, and kept on calling more and more frantically; but he heard no answer for some time, and then it seemed faint and far ahead and high above him. "Frodo! Hoy!" came the thin voices out of the mist: and then a cry that sounded like *help, help!* often repeated, ending with a last *help!* that trailed off into a long wail suddenly cut short. He stumbled forward with all the speed he could towards the cries; but the light was now gone, and clinging night had closed about him, so that it was impossible to be sure of any direction. He seemed all the time to be climbing up and up.

Only the change in the level of the ground at his feet told him when he at last came to the top of a ridge or hill. He was weary, sweating and yet chilled. It was wholly dark.

"Where are you?" he cried out miserably.

There was no reply. He stood listening. He was suddenly aware that it was getting very cold, and that up here a wind was beginning to blow, an icy wind. A change was coming in the weather. The mist was flowing past him now in shreds and tatters. His breath was smoking, and the darkness was less near and thick. He looked up and saw with surprise that faint stars were appearing overhead amid the strands of hurrying cloud and fog. The wind began to hiss over the grass.

He imagined suddenly that he caught a muffled cry, and he made towards it; and even as he went forward the mist was rolled up and thrust aside, and the starry sky was unveiled. A glance showed him that he was now facing southwards and was on a round hill-top, which he must have climbed from the north. Out of the east the biting wind was blowing. To his right there loomed against the westward stars a dark black shape. A great barrow stood there.

"Where are you?" he cried again, both angry and afraid.

"Here!" said a voice, deep and cold, that seemed to come out of the ground. "I am waiting for you!"

"No!" said Frodo; but he did not run away. His knees gave, and he fell on the ground. Nothing happened, and there was no sound. Trembling he looked up, in time to see a tall dark figure like a shadow against the stars. It leaned over him. He thought there were two eyes, very cold though lit with a pale light that seemed to come from some remote distance. Then a grip stronger and colder than iron seized him. The icy touch froze his bones, and he remembered no more.

When he came to himself again, for a moment he could recall nothing except a sense of dread. Then suddenly he knew that he was imprisoned, caught hopelessly; he was in a barrow. A Barrow-wight had taken him, and he was probably already under the dreadful spells of the Barrow-wights about which whispered tales spoke. He dared not move, but lay as he found himself: flat on his back upon a cold stone with his hands on his breast.

But though his fear was so great that it seemed to be part of the very darkness that was round him, he found himself as he lay thinking about Bilbo Baggins and his stories, of their jogging along together in the lanes of the Shire and talking about roads and adventures. There is a seed of courage hidden (often deeply, it is true) in the heart of the fattest and most timid hobbit, waiting for some final and desperate danger to make it grow. Frodo was neither very fat nor very timid; indeed, though he did not know it, Bilbo (and Gandalf) had thought him the best hobbit in the Shire. He thought he had come to the end of his adventure, and a terrible end, but the thought hardened him. He found himself stiffening, as if for a final spring; he no longer felt limp like a helpless prey.

As he lay there, thinking and getting a hold on himself, he noticed all at once that the darkness was slowly giving way: a pale greenish light was growing round him. It did not at first show him what kind of a place he was in, for the light seemed to be coming out of himself, and from the floor beside him, and had not yet reached the roof or wall. He turned, and there in the cold glow he saw lying beside him Sam, Pippin, and Merry. They were on their backs, and their faces looked deathly pale; and they were clad in white. About them lay many treasures, of gold maybe, though in that light they looked cold and unlovely. On their heads were circlets, gold chains were about their waists, and on their fingers were many rings. Swords lay by their sides, and shields were at their feet. But across their three necks lay one long naked sword.

Suddenly a song began: a cold murmur, rising and falling. The voice seemed far away and immeasurably dreary, sometimes high in the air and thin, sometimes like a low moan from the ground. Out of the formless stream of sad but horrible sounds, strings of words would now and again shape themselves: grim, hard, cold words, heartless and miserable. The night was railing against the morning of which it was bereaved, and the cold was cursing the warmth for which it hungered. Frodo was chilled to the marrow. After a while the song became clearer, and with dread in his heart he perceived that it had changed into an incantation:

> *Cold be hand and heart and bone,*
> *and cold be sleep under stone:*
> *never more to wake on stony bed,*
> *never, till the Sun fails and the Moon is dead.*
> *In the black wind the stars shall die,*
> *and still on gold here let them lie,*
> *till the dark lord lifts his hand*
> *over dead sea and withered land.*

He heard behind his head a creaking and scraping sound. Raising himself on one arm he looked, and saw now in the pale light that they were in a kind of passage which behind them turned a corner. Round the corner a long arm was groping, walking on its fingers towards Sam, who was lying nearest, and towards the hilt of the sword that lay upon him.

At first Frodo felt as if he had indeed been turned into stone by the incantation. Then a wild thought of escape came to him. He wondered if he put on the Ring, whether the Barrow-wight would miss him, and he might find some way out. He thought of himself running free over the grass, grieving for Merry, and Sam, and Pippin, but free and alive himself. Gandalf would admit that there had been nothing else he could do.

But the courage that had been awakened in him was now too strong: he could not leave his friends so easily. He wavered, groping in his pocket, and then fought with himself again; and as he did so the arm crept nearer. Suddenly resolve hardened in him, and he seized a short sword that lay beside him, and kneeling he stooped low over the bodies of his companions. With what strength he had he hewed at the crawling arm near the wrist, and the hand broke off; but at the same moment the sword splintered up to the hilt. There was a shriek and the light vanished. In the dark there was a snarling noise.

Frodo fell forward over Merry, and Merry's face felt cold. All at once back into his mind, from which it had disappeared with the first coming of the fog, came the memory of the house down under the Hill, and of Tom singing. He remembered the rhyme that Tom had taught them. In a small desperate voice he began: *Ho! Tom Bombadil!* and with that name his voice seemed to grow strong: it had a full and lively sound, and the dark chamber echoed as if to drum and trumpet.

> *Ho! Tom Bombadil, Tom Bombadillo!*
> *By water, wood and hill, by the reed and willow,*
> *By fire, sun and moon, harken now and hear us!*
> *Come, Tom Bombadil, for our need is near us!*

There was a sudden deep silence, in which Frodo could hear his heart beating. After a long slow moment he heard plain, but far away, as if it was coming down through the ground or through thick walls, an answering voice singing:

> *Old Tom Bombadil is a merry fellow,*
> *Bright blue his jacket is, and his boots are yellow.*

None has ever caught him yet, for Tom, he is the master:
His songs are stronger songs, and his feet are faster.

There was a loud rumbling sound, as of stones rolling and falling, and suddenly light streamed in, real light, the plain light of day. A low door-like opening appeared at the end of the chamber beyond Frodo's feet; and there was Tom's head (hat, feather, and all) framed against the light of the sun rising red behind him. The light fell upon the floor, and upon the faces of the three hobbits lying beside Frodo. They did not stir, but the sickly hue had left them. They looked now as if they were only very deeply asleep.

Tom stooped, removed his hat, and came into the dark chamber, singing:

Get out, you old Wight! Vanish in the sunlight!
Shrivel like the cold mist, like the winds go wailing,
Out into the barren lands far beyond the mountains!
Come never here again! Leave your barrow empty!
Lost and forgotten be, darker than the darkness,
Where gates stand for ever shut, till the world is mended.

At these words there was a cry and part of the inner end of the chamber fell in with a crash. Then there was a long trailing shriek, fading away into an unguessable distance; and after that silence.

"Come, friend Frodo!" said Tom. "Let us get out on to clean grass! You must help me bear them."

Together they carried out Merry, Pippin, and Sam. As Frodo left the barrow for the last time he thought he saw a severed hand wriggling still, like a wounded spider, in a heap of fallen earth. Tom went back in again, and there was a sound of much thumping and stamping. When he came out he was bearing in his arms a great load of treasure: things of gold, silver, copper, and bronze; many beads and chains and jewelled ornaments. He climbed the green barrow and laid them all on top in the sunshine.

There he stood, with his hat in his hand and the wind in his hair, and looked down upon the three hobbits, that had been laid on their backs upon the grass at the west side of the mound. Raising his right hand he said in a clear and commanding voice:

> *Wake now my merry lads! Wake and hear me calling!*
> *Warm now be heart and limb! The cold stone is fallen;*
> *Dark door is standing wide; dead hand is broken.*
> *Night under Night is flewn, and the Gate is open!*

To Frodo's great joy the hobbits stirred, stretched their arms, rubbed their eyes, and then suddenly sprang up. They looked about in amazement, first at Frodo, and then at Tom standing large as life on the barrow-top above them; and then at themselves in their thin white rags, crowned and belted with pale gold, and jingling with trinkets.

"What in the name of wonder?" began Merry, feeling the golden circlet that had slipped over one eye. Then he stopped, and a shadow came over his face, and he closed his eyes. "Of course, I remember!" he said. "The men of Carn Dûm came on us at night, and we were worsted. Ah! the spear in my heart!" He clutched at his breast. "No! No!" he said, opening his eyes. "What am I saying? I have been dreaming. Where did you get to, Frodo?"

"I thought that I was lost," said Frodo; "but I don't want to speak of it. Let us think of what we are to do now! Let us go on!"

"Dressed up like this, sir?" said Sam. "Where are my clothes?" He flung his circlet, belt, and rings on the grass, and looked round helplessly, as if he expected to find his cloak, jacket, and breeches, and other hobbit-garments lying somewhere to hand.

"You won't find your clothes again," said Tom, bounding down from the mound, and laughing as he danced round them in the sunlight. One would have thought that nothing dangerous or dreadful had happened; and indeed the horror faded out of their hearts as they looked at him, and saw the merry glint in his eyes.

"What do you mean?" asked Pippin, looking at him, half puzzled and half amused. "Why not?"

But Tom shook his head, saying: "You've found yourselves again, out of the deep water. Clothes are but little loss, if you escape from drowning. Be glad, my merry friends, and let the warm sunlight heat now heart and limb! Cast off these cold rags! Run naked on the grass, while Tom goes a-hunting!"

He sprang away down hill, whistling and calling. Looking down after him Frodo saw him running away southwards along the green hollow between their hill and the next, still whistling and crying:

> *Hey! now! Come hoy now! Whither do you wander?*
> *Up, down, near or far, here, there or yonder?*
> *Sharp-ears, Wise-nose, Swish-tail and Bumpkin,*
> *White-socks my little lad, and old Fatty Lumpkin!*

So he sang, running fast, tossing up his hat and catching it, until he was hidden by a fold of the ground: but for some time his *hey now! hoy now!* came floating back down the wind, which had shifted round towards the south.

The air was growing very warm again. The hobbits ran about for a while on the grass, as he told them. Then they lay basking in the sun with the delight of those that have been wafted suddenly from bitter winter to a friendly clime, or of people that, after being long ill and bedridden, wake one day to find that they are unexpectedly well and the day is again full of promise.

By the time that Tom returned they were feeling strong (and hungry). He reappeared, hat first, over the brow of the hill, and behind him came in an obedient line *six* ponies: their own five and one more. The last was plainly old Fatty Lumpkin: he was larger, stronger, fatter (and older) than their own ponies. Merry, to whom the others belonged, had not, in fact, given them any such names, but they answered to the new names that Tom had given them for the rest of their lives. Tom called them one by one and they climbed over the brow and stood in a line. Then Tom bowed to the hobbits.

"Here are your ponies, now" he said. "They've more sense (in some ways) than you wandering hobbits have — more sense in their noses. For they sniff danger ahead which you walk right into; and if they run to save themselves, then they run the right way. You must forgive them all; for though their hearts are faithful, to face fear of Barrow-wights is not what they were made for. See, here they come again, bringing all their burdens!"

Merry, Sam, and Pippin now clothed themselves in spare garments from their packs; and they soon felt too hot, for they were obliged to put on some of the thicker and warmer things that they had brought against the oncoming of winter.

"Where does that other old animal, that Fatty Lumpkin, come from?" asked Frodo.

"He's mine," said Tom. "My four-legged friend; though I seldom ride him, and he wanders often far, free upon the hillsides. When your ponies stayed with me, they got to know my Lumpkin; and they smelt him in the night, and quickly ran to meet him. I thought he"d look for them and with his words of wisdom take all their fear away. But now, my jolly Lumpkin, old Tom's going to ride. Hey! he's coming with you, just to set you on the road; so he needs a pony. For you cannot easily talk to hobbits that are riding, when you're on your own legs trying to trot beside them."

The hobbits were delighted to hear this, and thanked Tom many times; but he laughed, and said that they were so good at losing themselves that he would not feel happy till he had seen them safe over the borders of his land. "I've got things to do," he said: "my making and my singing, my talking and my walking, and my watching of the country. Tom can't be always near to open doors and willow-cracks. Tom has his house to mind, and Goldberry is waiting."

It was still fairly early by the sun, something between nine and ten, and the hobbits turned their minds to food. Their last meal had been lunch beside the standing stone the day before. They breakfasted now off the remainder of Tom's provisions, meant for their supper, with additions that Tom had brought with him. It was not a large meal (considering hobbits and the circumstances), but they felt much better for it. While they were eating Tom went up to the mound, and looked through the treasures. Most of these he made into a pile that glistened and sparkled on the grass. He bade them lie there "free to all finders, birds, beasts, Elves or Men, and all kindly creatures"; for so the spell of the mound should be broken and scattered and no Wight ever come back to it. He chose for himself from the pile a brooch set with blue stones, many-shaded like flax-flowers or the wings of blue butterflies. He looked long at it, as if stirred by some memory, shaking his head, and saying at last:

"Here is a pretty toy for Tom and for his lady! Fair was she who long ago wore this on her shoulder. Goldberry shall wear it now, and we will not forget her!"

For each of the hobbits he chose a dagger, long, leaf-shaped, and keen, of marvellous workmanship, damasked with serpent-forms in red and gold. They gleamed as he drew them from their black sheaths, wrought of some strange metal, light and strong, and set with many fiery stones. Whether by some virtue in these sheaths or because of the spell that lay on the mound, the blades seemed untouched by time, unrusted, sharp, glittering in the sun.

"Old knives are long enough as swords for hobbit-people," he said. "Sharp blades are good to have, if Shire-folk go walking, east, south, or far away into dark and danger." Then he told them that these blades were forged many long years ago by Men of Westernesse: they were foes of the Dark Lord, but they were overcome by the evil king of Carn Dûm in the Land of Angmar.

"Few now remember them," Tom murmured, "yet still some go wandering, sons of forgotten kings walking in loneliness, guarding from evil things folk that are heedless."

The hobbits did not understand his words, but as he spoke they had a vision as it were of a great expanse of years behind them, like a vast shadowy plain over which there strode shapes of Men, tall and grim with bright swords, and last came one with a star on his brow. Then the vision faded, and they were back in the sunlit world. It was time to start again. They made ready, packing their bags and lading their ponies. Their new weapons they hung on their leather belts under their jackets, feeling them very awkward, and wondering if they would be of any use. Fighting had not before occurred to any of them as one of the adventures in which their flight would land them.

At last they set off. They led their ponies down the hill; and then mounting they trotted quickly along the valley. They looked back and saw the top of the old mound on the hill, and from it the sunlight on the gold went up like a yellow flame. Then they turned a shoulder of the Downs and it was hidden from view.

Though Frodo looked about him on every side he saw no sign of the great stones standing like a gate, and before long they came to the northern gap and rode swiftly through, and the land fell away before them. It was a merry journey with Tom Bombadil trotting gaily beside them, or before them, on Fatty Lumpkin, who could move much faster than his girth promised. Tom sang most of the time, but it was chiefly nonsense, or else perhaps a strange language unknown to the hobbits, an ancient language whose words were mainly those of wonder and delight.

They went forward steadily, but they soon saw that the Road was further away than they had imagined. Even without a fog, their sleep at mid-day would have prevented them from reaching it until after nightfall on the day before. The dark line they had seen was not a line of trees, but a line of bushes growing on the edge of a deep dike with a steep wall on the further side. Tom said that it had once been the boundary of a kingdom, but a very long time ago. He seemed to remember something sad about it, and would not say much.

They climbed down and out of the dike and through a gap in the wall, and then Tom turned due north, for they had been bearing somewhat to the west. The land was now open and fairly level, and they quickened their pace, but the sun was already sinking low when at last they saw a line of tall trees ahead, and they knew that they had come back to the Road after many unexpected adventures. They galloped their ponies over the last furlongs, and halted under the long shadows of the trees. They were on the top of a sloping bank, and the Road, now dim as evening drew on, wound away below them. At this point it ran nearly from South-west to North-east, and on their right it fell quickly down into a wide hollow. It was rutted and bore many signs of the recent heavy rain; there were pools and potholes full of water.

They rode down the bank and looked up and down. There was nothing to be seen. "Well, here we are again at last!" said Frodo. "I suppose we haven't lost more than two days by my short cut through the Forest! But perhaps the delay will prove useful — it may have put them off our trail."

The others looked at him. The shadow of the fear of the Black Riders came suddenly over them again. Ever since they had entered the Forest they had thought chiefly of getting back to the Road; only now when it lay beneath their feet did they remember the danger which pursued them, and was more than likely to be lying in wait for them upon the Road itself. They looked anxiously back towards the setting sun, but the Road was brown and empty.

"Do you think," asked Pippin hesitatingly, "do you think we may be pursued, tonight?"

"No, I hope not tonight," answered Tom Bombadil; "nor perhaps the next day. But do not trust my guess; for I cannot tell for certain. Out east my knowledge fails. Tom is not master of Riders from the Black Land far beyond his country."

All the same the hobbits wished he was coming with them. They felt that he would know how to deal with Black Riders, if anyone did. They would soon now be going forward into lands wholly strange to them, and beyond all but the most vague and distant legends of the Shire, and in the gathering twilight they longed for home. A deep loneliness and sense of loss was on them. They stood silent, reluctant to make the final parting, and only slowly became aware that Tom was wishing them farewell, and telling them to have good heart and to ride on till dark without halting.

"Tom will give you good advice, till this day is over (after that your own luck must go with you and guide you): four miles along the Road you'll come upon a village, Bree under Bree-hill, with doors looking westward. There you'll find an old inn that is called *The Prancing Pony*. Barliman Butterbur is the worthy keeper. There you can stay the night, and afterwards the morning will speed you upon your way. Be bold, but wary! Keep up your merry hearts, and ride to meet your fortune!"

They begged him to come at least as far as the inn and drink once more with them; but he laughed and refused, saying:

> *Tom's country ends here: he will not pass the borders.*
> *Tom has his house to mind, and Goldberry is waiting!*

Then he turned, tossed up his hat, leaped on Lumpkin's back, and rode up over the bank and away singing into the dusk.

The hobbits climbed up and watched him until he was out of sight.

"I am sorry to take leave of Master Bombadil," said Sam. "He's a caution and no mistake. I reckon we may go a good deal further and see naught better, nor queerer. But I won't deny I'll be glad to see this *Prancing Pony* he spoke of. I hope it'll be like *The Green Dragon* away back home! What sort of folk are they in Bree?"

"There are hobbits in Bree," said Merry, "as well as Big Folk. I daresay it will be homelike enough. The Pony is a good inn by all accounts. My people ride out there now and again."

"It may be all we could wish," said Frodo; "but it is outside the Shire all the same. Don't make yourselves too much at home! Please remember — all of you — that the name of Baggins must NOT be mentioned. I am Mr. Underhill, if any name must be given."

They now mounted their ponies and rode off silently into the evening. Darkness came down quickly, as they plodded slowly downhill and up again, until at last they saw lights twinkling some distance ahead.

Before them rose Bree-hill barring the way, a dark mass against misty stars; and under its western flank nestled a large village. Towards it they now hurried desiring only to find a fire, and a door between them and the night.

CHAPTER
NINE

At the Sign of the Prancing Pony

Bree was the chief village of the Bree-land, a small inhabited region, like an island in the empty lands round about. Besides Bree itself, there was Staddle on the other side of the hill, Combe in a deep valley a little further eastward, and Archet on the edge of the Chetwood. Lying round Bree-hill and the villages was a small country of fields and tamed woodland only a few miles broad.

The Men of Bree were brown-haired, broad, and rather short, cheerful and independent: they belonged to nobody but themselves; but they were more friendly and familiar with Hobbits, Dwarves, Elves, and other inhabitants of the world about them than was (or is) usual with Big People. According to their own tales they were the original inhabitants and were the descendants of the first Men that ever wandered into the West of the middle-world. Few had survived the turmoils of the Elder Days; but when the Kings returned again over the Great Sea they had found the Bree-men still there, and they were still there now, when the memory of the old Kings had faded into the grass.

In those days no other Men had settled dwellings so far west, or within a hundred leagues of the Shire. But in the wild lands beyond Bree there were mysterious wanderers. The Bree-folk called them Rangers, and knew nothing of their origin. They were taller and darker than the Men of Bree and were believed to have strange powers of sight and hearing, and to understand the languages of beasts and birds. They roamed at will southwards, and eastwards even as far as the Misty Mountains; but they were now few and rarely seen. When they appeared they brought news from afar, and told strange forgotten tales which were eagerly listened to; but the Bree-folk did not make friends of them.

There were also many families of hobbits in the Bree-land and *they* claimed to be the oldest settlement of Hobbits in the world, one that was founded long before even the Brandywine was crossed and the Shire colonized. They lived mostly in Staddle though there were some in Bree itself, especially on the higher slopes of the hill, above the houses of the Men. The Big Folk and the Little Folk (as they called one another) were on friendly terms, minding their own affairs in their own ways, but both rightly regarding themselves as necessary parts of the Bree-folk. Nowhere else in the world was this peculiar (but excellent) arrangement to be found.

The Bree-folk, Big and Little, did not themselves travel much; and the affairs of the four villages were their chief concern. Occasionally the Hobbits of Bree went as far as Buckland, or the Eastfarthing; but though their little land was not much further than a day's riding east of the Brandywine Bridge, the Hobbits of the Shire now seldom visited it. An occasional Bucklander or adventurous Took would come out to the Inn for a night or two, but even that was becoming less and less usual. The Shire-hobbits referred to those of Bree, and to any others that lived beyond the borders, as Outsiders, and took very little interest in them, considering them dull and uncouth. There were probably many more Outsiders scattered about in the West of the World in those days than the people of the Shire imagined. Some, doubtless, were no better than tramps, ready to dig a hole in any bank and stay only as long as it suited them. But in the Bree-land, at any rate, the hobbits were decent and prosperous, and no more rustic than most of their distant relatives Inside. It was not yet forgotten that there had been a time when there was much coming and going between the Shire and Bree. There was Bree-blood in the Brandybucks by all accounts.

The village of Bree had some hundred stone houses of the Big Folk, mostly above the Road, nestling on the hillside with windows looking west. On that side, running in more than half a circle from the hill and back to it, there was a deep dike with a thick hedge on the inner side. Over this the Road crossed by a causeway; but where it pierced the hedge it was barred by a great gate. There was another gate in the southern corner where the Road ran out of the village. The gates were closed at nightfall; but just inside them were small lodges for the gatekeepers.

Down on the Road, where it swept to the right to go round the foot of the hill, there was a large inn. It had been built long ago when the traffic on the roads had been far greater. For Bree stood at an old meeting of ways; another ancient road crossed the East Road just outside the dike at the western end of the village, and in former days Men and other folk of various sorts had travelled much on it. *Strange as News from Bree* was still a saying in the Eastfarthing, descending from those days, when news from North, South, and East could be heard in the inn, and when the Shire-hobbits used to go more often to hear it. But the Northern Lands had long been desolate, and the North Road was now seldom used: it was grass-grown, and the Bree-folk called it the Greenway.

The Inn of Bree was still there, however, and the innkeeper was an important person. His house was a meeting place for the idle, talkative, and inquisitive among the inhabitants, large and small, of the four villages; and a resort of Rangers and other wanderers, and for such travellers (mostly dwarves) as still journeyed on the East Road, to and from the Mountains.

It was dark, and white stars were shining, when Frodo and his companions came at last to the Greenway-crossing and drew near the village. They came to the West-gate and found it shut, but at the door of the lodge beyond it, there was a man sitting. He jumped up and fetched a lantern and looked over the gate at them in surprise.

"What do you want, and where do you come from?" he asked gruffly.

"We are making for the inn here," answered Frodo. "We are journeying east and cannot go further tonight."

"Hobbits! Four hobbits! And what's more, out of the Shire by their talk," said the gatekeeper, softly as if speaking to himself. He stared at them darkly for a moment, and then slowly opened the gate and let them ride through.

"We don't often see Shire-folk riding on the Road at night," he went on, as they halted a moment by his door. "You'll pardon my wondering what business takes you away east of Bree! What may your names be, might I ask?"

"Our names and our business are our own, and this does not seem a good place to discuss them," said Frodo, not liking the look of the man or the tone of his voice.

"Your business is your own, no doubt," said the man; "but it's my business to ask questions after nightfall."

"We are hobbits from Buckland, and we have a fancy to travel and to stay at the inn here," put in Merry. "I am Mr. Brandybuck. Is that enough for you? The Bree-folk used to be fair-spoken to travellers, or so I had heard."

"All right, all right!" said the man. "I meant no offence. But you'll find maybe that more folk than old Harry at the gate will be asking you questions. There's queer folk about. If you go on to *The Pony*, you'll find you're not the only guests."

He wished them good night, and they said no more; but Frodo could see in the lantern-light that the man was still eyeing them curiously. He was glad to hear the gate clang to behind them, as they rode forward. He wondered why the man was so suspicious, and whether any one had been asking for

177

news of a party of hobbits. Could it have been Gandalf? He might have arrived, while they were delayed in the Forest and the Downs. But there was something in the look and the voice of the gatekeeper that made him uneasy.

The man stared after the hobbits for a moment, and then he went back to his house. As soon as his back was turned, a dark figure climbed quickly in over the gate and melted into the shadows of the village street.

The hobbits rode on up a gentle slope, passing a few detached houses, and drew up outside the inn. The houses looked large and strange to them. Sam stared up at the inn with its three storeys and many windows, and felt his heart sink. He had imagined himself meeting giants taller than trees, and other creatures even more terrifying, some time or other in the course of his journey; but at the moment he was finding his first sight of Men and their tall houses quite enough, indeed too much for the dark end of a tiring day. He pictured black horses standing all saddled in the shadows of the inn-yard, and Black Riders peering out of dark upper windows.

"We surely aren't going to stay here for the night, are we, sir?" he exclaimed. "If there are hobbit-folk in these parts, why don't we look for some that would be willing to take us in? It would be more homelike."

"What's wrong with the inn?" said Frodo. "Tom Bombadil recommended it. I expect it's homelike enough inside."

Even from the outside the inn looked a pleasant house to familiar eyes. It had a front on the Road, and two wings running back on land partly cut out of the lower slopes of the hill, so that at the rear the second-floor windows were level with the ground. There was a wide arch leading to a courtyard between the two wings, and on the left under the arch there was a large doorway reached by a few broad steps. The door was open and light streamed out of it. Above the arch there was a lamp, and beneath it swung a large signboard: a fat white pony reared up on its hind legs. Over the door was painted in white letters: THE PRANCING PONY by BARLIMAN BUTTERBUR. Many of the lower windows showed lights behind thick curtains.

As they hesitated outside in the gloom, someone began singing a merry song inside, and many cheerful voices joined loudly in the chorus. They listened to this encouraging sound for a moment and then got off their ponies. The song ended and there was a burst of laughter and clapping.

They led their ponies under the arch, and leaving them standing in the yard they climbed up the steps. Frodo went forward and nearly bumped into a short fat man with a bald head and a red face. He had a white apron on, and was bustling out of one door and in through another, carrying a tray laden with full mugs.

"Can we ——" began Frodo.

"Half a minute, if you please!" shouted the man over his shoulder, and vanished into a babel of voices and a cloud of smoke. In a moment he was out again, wiping his hands on his apron.

"Good evening, little master!" he said, bending down. "What may you be wanting?"

"Beds for four, and stabling for five ponies, if that can be managed. Are you Mr. Butterbur?"

"That's right! Barliman is my name. Barliman Butterbur at your service! You're from the Shire, eh?" he said, and then suddenly he clapped his hand to his forehead, as if trying to remember something. "Hobbits!" he cried. "Now what does that remind me of? Might I ask your names, sir?"

"Mr. Took and Mr. Brandybuck," said Frodo; "and this is Sam Gamgee. My name is Underhill."

"There now!" said Mr. Butterbur, snapping his fingers. "It's gone again! But it'll come back, when I have time to think. I'm run off my feet; but I'll see what I can do for you. We don't often get a party out of the Shire nowadays, and I should be sorry not to make you welcome. But there is such a crowd already in the house tonight as there hasn't been for long enough. It never rains but it pours, we say in Bree.

"Hi! Nob!" he shouted. "Where are you, you woolly-footed slow-coach? Nob!"

"Coming, sir! Coming!" A cheery-looking hobbit bobbed out of a door, and seeing the travellers, stopped short and stared at them with great interest.

"Where's Bob?" asked the landlord. "You don't know? Well find him! Double sharp! I haven't got six legs, nor six eyes neither! Tell Bob there's five ponies that have to be stabled. He must find room somehow." Nob trotted off with a grin and a wink.

"Well, now, what was I going to say?" said Mr. Butterbur, tapping his forehead. "One thing drives out another, so to speak. I'm that busy tonight, my head is going round. There's a party that came up the Greenway from down South last night — and that was strange enough to begin with. Then there's a travelling company of dwarves going West come in this evening. And now there's you. If you weren't hobbits, I doubt if we could house you. But we've got a room or two in the north wing that were made special for hobbits, when this place was built. On the ground floor as they usually prefer; round windows and all as they like it. I hope you'll be comfortable. You'll be wanting supper, I don't doubt. As soon as may be. This way now!"

He led them a short way down a passage, and opened a door. "Here is a nice little parlour!" he said. "I hope it will suit. Excuse me now. I'm that busy. No time for talking. I must be trotting. It's hard work for two legs, but I don't get thinner. I'll look in again later. If you want anything, ring the hand-bell, and Nob will come. If he don't come, ring and shout!"

Off he went at last, and left them feeling rather breathless. He seemed capable of an endless stream of talk, however busy he might be. They found themselves in a small and cosy room. There was a bit of bright fire burning on the hearth, and in front of it were some low and comfortable chairs. There was a round table, already spread with a white cloth, and on it was a large hand-bell. But Nob, the hobbit servant, came bustling in long before they thought of ringing. He brought candles and a tray full of plates.

"Will you be wanting anything to drink, masters?" he asked. "And shall I show you the bedrooms, while your supper is got ready?"

They were washed and in the middle of good deep mugs of beer when Mr. Butterbur and Nob came in again. In a twinkling the table was laid. There was hot soup, cold meats, a blackberry tart, new loaves, slabs of butter, and half a ripe cheese: good plain food, as good as the Shire could show, and homelike enough to dispel the last of Sam's misgivings (already much relieved by the excellence of the beer).

The landlord hovered round for a little, and then proposed to leave them. "I don't know whether you would care to join the company, when you have supped," he said, standing at the door. "Perhaps you would rather go to your beds. Still the company would be very pleased to welcome you, if you had a mind. We don't get Outsiders — travellers from the Shire, I should say, begging your pardon — often; and we like to hear a bit of news, or any story or song you may have in mind. But as you please! Ring the bell, if you lack anything!"

So refreshed and encouraged did they feel at the end of their supper (about three quarters of an hour's steady going, not hindered by unnecessary talk) that Frodo, Pippin, and Sam decided to join the company. Merry said it would be too stuffy. "I shall sit here quietly by the fire for a bit, and perhaps go out later for a sniff of the air. Mind your Ps and Qs, and don't forget that you are supposed to be escaping in secret, and are still on the high-road and not very far from the Shire!"

"All right!" said Pippin. "Mind yourself! Don't get lost, and don't forget that it is safer indoors!"

The company was in the big common-room of the inn. The gathering was large and mixed, as Frodo discovered, when his eyes got used to the light. This came chiefly from a blazing log-fire, for the three lamps hanging from the beams were dim, and half veiled in smoke. Barliman Butterbur was standing near the fire, talking to a couple of dwarves and one or two strange-looking men. On the benches were various folk: men of Bree, a collection of local hobbits (sitting chattering together), a few more dwarves, and other vague figures difficult to make out away in the shadows and corners.

As soon as the Shire-hobbits entered, there was a chorus of welcome from the Bree-landers. The strangers, especially those that had come up the Greenway, stared at them curiously. The landlord introduced the newcomers to the Bree-folk, so quickly that, though they caught many names, they were seldom sure who the names belonged to. The Men of Bree seemed all to have rather botanical (and to the Shire-folk rather odd) names, like Rushlight, Goatleaf, Heathertoes, Appledore, Thistlewool and Ferny (not to mention Butterbur). Some of the hobbits had similar names. The Mugworts, for instance, seemed numerous. But most of them had natural names, such as Banks, Brockhouse, Longholes, Sandheaver, and Tunnelly, many of which were used in the Shire. There were several Underhills from Staddle, and as they could not imagine sharing a name without being related, they took Frodo to their hearts as a long-lost cousin.

The Bree-hobbits were, in fact, friendly and inquisitive, and Frodo soon found that some explanation of what he was doing would have to be given. He gave out that he was interested in history and geography (at which there was much wagging of heads, although neither of these words were much used in the Bree-dialect). He said he was thinking of writing a book (at which there was silent astonishment), and that he and his friends wanted to collect information about hobbits living outside the Shire, especially in the eastern lands.

At this a chorus of voices broke out. If Frodo had really wanted to write a book, and had had many ears, he would have learned enough for several chapters in a few minutes. And if that was not enough, he was given a whole list of names, beginning with "Old Barliman here", to whom he could go for further information. But after a time, as Frodo did not show any sign of writing a book on the spot, the hobbits returned to their questions about doings in the Shire. Frodo did not prove very communicative, and he soon found himself sitting alone in a corner, listening and looking around.

The Men and Dwarves were mostly talking of distant events and telling news of a kind that was becoming only too familiar. There was trouble away in the South, and it seemed that the Men who had come up the Greenway were on the move, looking for lands where they could find some peace. The Bree-folk were sympathetic, but plainly not very ready to take a large number of strangers into their little land. One of the travellers, a squint-eyed ill-favoured fellow, was foretelling that more and more people would be coming north in the near future. "If room isn't found for them, they'll find it for themselves. They've a right to live, same as other folk," he said loudly. The local inhabitants did not look pleased at the prospect.

The hobbits did not pay much attention to all this, and it did not at the moment seem to concern hobbits. Big Folk could hardly beg for lodgings in hobbit-holes. They were more interested in Sam and Pippin, who were now feeling quite at home, and were chatting gaily about events in the Shire. Pippin roused a good deal of laughter with an account of the collapse of the roof of the Town Hole in Michel Delving: Will Whitfoot, the Mayor, and the fattest hobbit in the Westfarthing, had been buried in chalk, and came out like a floured dumpling. But there were several questions asked that made Frodo a little uneasy. One of the Bree-landers, who seemed to have been in the Shire several times, wanted to know where the Underhills lived and who they were related to.

Suddenly Frodo noticed that a strange-looking weather-beaten man, sitting in the shadows near the wall, was also listening intently to the hobbit-talk. He had a tall tankard in front of him, and was smoking a long-stemmed pipe curiously carved. His legs were stretched out before him, showing high boots of supple leather that fitted him well, but had seen much wear and were now caked with mud. A travel-stained cloak of heavy dark-green cloth was drawn close about him, and in spite of the heat of the room he wore a hood that overshadowed his face; but the gleam of his eyes could be seen as he watched the hobbits.

"Who is that?" Frodo asked, when he got a chance to whisper to Mr. Butterbur. "I don't think you introduced him?"

"Him?" said the landlord in an answering whisper, cocking an eye without turning his head. "I don't rightly know. He is one of the wandering folk — Rangers we call them. He seldom talks: not but what he can tell a rare tale when he has the mind. He disappears for a month, or a year, and then he pops up again. He was in and out pretty often last spring; but I haven't seen him about lately. What his right name is I've never heard: but he's known round here as Strider. Goes about at a great pace on his long shanks; though he don't tell nobody what cause he has to hurry. But there's no accounting for East and West, as we say in Bree, meaning the Rangers and the Shire-folk, begging your pardon. Funny you should ask about him." But at that moment Mr. Butterbur was called away by a demand for more ale and his last remark remained unexplained.

Frodo found that Strider was now looking at him, as if he had heard or guessed all that had been said. Presently, with a wave of his hand and a nod, he invited Frodo to come over and sit by him. As Frodo drew near he threw back his hood, showing a shaggy head of dark hair flecked with grey, and in a pale stern face a pair of keen grey eyes.

"I am called Strider," he said in a low voice. "I am very pleased to meet you, Master — Underhill, if old Butterbur got your name right."

"He did," said Frodo stiffly. He felt far from comfortable under the stare of those keen eyes.

"Well, Master Underhill," said Strider, "if I were you, I should stop your young friends from talking too much. Drink, fire, and chance-meeting are pleasant enough, but, well — this isn't the Shire. There are queer folk about. Though I say it as shouldn't, you may think," he added with a wry smile, seeing Frodo's glance. "And there have been even stranger travellers through Bree lately," he went on, watching Frodo's face.

Frodo returned his gaze but said nothing; and Strider made no further sign. His attention seemed suddenly to be fixed on Pippin. To his alarm Frodo became aware that the ridiculous young Took, encouraged by his success with the fat Mayor of Michel Delving, was now actually giving a comic account of Bilbo's farewell party. He was already giving an imitation of the Speech, and was drawing near to the astonishing Disappearance.

Frodo was annoyed. It was a harmless enough tale for most of the local hobbits, no doubt: just a funny story about those funny people away beyond the River; but some (old Butterbur, for instance) knew a thing or two, and had probably heard rumours long ago about Bilbo's vanishing. It would bring the name of Baggins to their minds, especially if there had been inquiries in Bree after that name.

Frodo fidgeted, wondering what to do. Pippin was evidently much enjoying the attention he was getting, and had become quite forgetful of their danger. Frodo had a sudden fear that in his present mood he might even mention the Ring; and that might well be disastrous.

"You had better do something quick!" whispered Strider in his ear.

Frodo jumped up and stood on a table, and began to talk. The attention of Pippin's audience was disturbed. Some of the hobbits looked at Frodo and laughed and clapped, thinking that Mr. Underhill had taken as much ale as was good for him.

Frodo suddenly felt very foolish, and found himself (as was his habit when making a speech) fingering the things in his pocket. He felt the Ring on its chain, and quite unaccountably the desire came over him to slip it on and vanish out of the silly situation. It seemed to him, somehow, as if the suggestion came to him from outside, from someone or something in the room. He resisted the temptation firmly, and clasped the Ring in his hand, as if to keep a hold on it and prevent it from escaping or doing any mischief. At any rate it gave him no inspiration. He spoke "a few suitable words", as they would have said in the Shire: *We are all very much gratified by the kindness of your reception, and I venture to hope that my brief visit will help to renew the old ties of friendship between the Shire and Bree;* and then he hesitated and coughed.

Everyone in the room was now looking at him. "A song!" shouted one of the hobbits. "A song! A song!" shouted all the others. "Come on now, master, sing us something that we haven't heard before!"

For a moment Frodo stood gaping. Then in desperation he began a ridiculous song that Bilbo had been rather fond of (and indeed rather proud of, for he had made up the words himself). It was about an inn; and that is probably why it came into Frodo's mind just then. Here it is in full. Only a few words of it are now, as a rule, remembered.

> *There is an inn, a merry old inn*
>   *beneath an old grey hill,*
> *And there they brew a beer so brown*
>   *That the Man in the Moon himself came down*
>   *one night to drink his fill.*

> *The ostler has a tipsy cat*
>   *that plays a five-stringed fiddle;*
> *And up and down he runs his bow,*
> *Now squeaking high, now purring low,*
>   *now sawing in the middle.*

> *The landlord keeps a little dog*
>   *that is mighty fond of jokes;*
> *When there's good cheer among the guests,*
> *He cocks an ear at all the jests*
>   *and laughs until he chokes.*

They also keep a hornéd cow
 as proud as any queen;
But music turns her head like ale,
And makes her wave her tufted tail
 and dance upon the green.

And O! the rows of silver dishes
 and the store of silver spoons!
For Sunday* there's a special pair,
And these they polish up with care
 on Saturday afternoons.

The Man in the Moon was drinking deep,
 and the cat began to wail;
A dish and a spoon on the table danced,
The cow in the garden madly pranced,
 and the little dog chased his tail.

The Man in the Moon took another mug,
 and then rolled beneath his chair;
And there he dozed and dreamed of ale,
Till in the sky the stars were pale,
 and dawn was in the air.

Then the ostler said to his tipsy cat:
 "The white horses of the Moon,
They neigh and champ their silver bits:
But their master's been and drowned his wits,
 and the Sun'll be rising soon!"

So the cat on his fiddle played hey-diddle-diddle,
 a jig that would wake the dead:

* See note, III 504

He squeaked and sawed and quickened the tune,
While the landlord shook the Man in the Moon:
    "It's after three!" he said.

They rolled the Man slowly up the hill
    and bundled him into the Moon,
While his horses galloped up in rear,
And the cow came capering like a deer,
    and a dish ran up with the spoon.

Now quicker the fiddle went deedle-dum-diddle;
    the dog began to roar,
The cow and the horses stood on their heads;
The guests all bounded from their beds
    and danced upon the floor.

With a ping and a pong the fiddle-strings broke!
    the cow jumped over the Moon,
And the little dog laughed to see such fun,
And the Saturday dish went off at a run
    with the silver Sunday spoon.

The round Moon rolled behind the hill,
    as the Sun raised up her head.
She⋆ hardly believed her fiery eyes;
For though it was day, to her surprise
    they all went back to bed!

There was loud and long applause. Frodo had a good voice, and the song tickled their fancy. "Where's old Barley?" they cried. "He ought to hear this. Bob ought to learn his cat the fiddle, and then we'd have a dance." They called for more ale,

⋆ Elves (and Hobbits) always refer to the Sun as She.

and began to shout: "Let's have it again, master! Come on now! Once more!"

They made Frodo have another drink, and then begin his song again, while many of them joined in; for the tune was well known, and they were quick at picking up words. It was now Frodo's turn to feel pleased with himself. He capered about on the table; and when he came a second time to *the cow jumped over the Moon*, he leaped in the air. Much too vigorously; for he came down, bang, into a tray full of mugs, and slipped, and rolled off the table with a crash, clatter, and bump! The audience all opened their mouths wide for laughter, and stopped short in gaping silence; for the singer disappeared. He simply vanished, as if he had gone slap through the floor without leaving a hole!

The local hobbits stared in amazement, and then sprang to their feet and shouted for Barliman. All the company drew away from Pippin and Sam, who found themselves left alone in a corner, and eyed darkly and doubtfully from a distance. It was plain that many people regarded them now as the companions of a travelling magician of unknown powers and purpose. But there was one swarthy Bree-lander, who stood looking at them with a knowing and half-mocking expression that made them feel very uncomfortable. Presently he slipped out of the door, followed by the squint-eyed southerner: the two had been whispering together a good deal during the evening. Harry the gatekeeper also went out just behind them.

Frodo felt a fool. Not knowing what else to do, he crawled away under the tables to the dark corner by Strider, who sat unmoved, giving no sign of his thoughts. Frodo leaned back against the wall and took off the Ring. How it came to be on his finger he could not tell. He could only suppose that he had been handling it in his pocket while he sang, and that somehow it had slipped on when he stuck out his hand with a jerk to save his fall. For a moment he wondered if the Ring itself had not played him a trick; perhaps it had tried to reveal itself in response to some wish or command that was felt in the room.

He did not like the looks of the men that had gone out.

"Well?" said Strider, when he reappeared. "Why did you do that? Worse than anything your friends could have said! You have put your foot in it! Or should I say your finger?"

"I don't know what you mean," said Frodo, annoyed and alarmed.

"Oh yes, you do," answered Strider; "but we had better wait until the uproar has died down. Then, if you please, Mr. *Baggins*, I should like a quiet word with you."

"What about?" asked Frodo, ignoring the sudden use of his proper name.

"A matter of some importance — to us both," answered Strider, looking Frodo in the eye. "You may hear something to your advantage."

"Very well," said Frodo, trying to appear unconcerned. "I'll talk to you later."

Meanwhile an argument was going on by the fireplace. Mr. Butterbur had come trotting in, and he was now trying to listen to several conflicting accounts of the event at the same time.

"I saw him, Mr. Butterbur," said a hobbit; "or leastways I didn't see him, if you take my meaning. He just vanished into thin air, in a manner of speaking."

"You don't say, Mr. Mugwort!" said the landlord, looking puzzled.

"Yes I do!" replied Mugwort. "And I mean what I say, what's more."

"There's some mistake somewhere," said Butterbur, shaking his head. "There was too much of that Mr. Underhill to go vanishing into thin air; or into thick air, as is more likely in this room."

"Well, where is he now?" cried several voices.

"How should I know? He's welcome to go where he will, so long as he pays in the morning. There's Mr. Took, now: he's not vanished."

"Well, I saw what I saw, and I saw what I didn't," said

Mugwort obstinately.

"And I say there's some mistake," repeated Butterbur, picking up the tray and gathering up the broken crockery.

"Of course there's a mistake!" said Frodo. "I haven't vanished. Here I am! I've just been having a few words with Strider in the corner."

He came forward into the firelight; but most of the company backed away, even more perturbed than before. They were not in the least satisfied by his explanation that he had crawled away quickly under the tables after he had fallen. Most of the Hobbits and the Men of Bree went off then and there in a huff, having no fancy for further entertainment that evening. One or two gave Frodo a black look and departed muttering among themselves. The Dwarves and the two or three strange Men that still remained got up and said good night to the landlord, but not to Frodo and his friends. Before long no one was left but Strider, who sat on, unnoticed, by the wall.

Mr. Butterbur did not seem much put out. He reckoned, very probably, that his house would be full again on many future nights, until the present mystery had been thoroughly discussed. "Now what have you been doing, Mr. Underhill?" he asked. "Frightening my customers and breaking up my crocks with your acrobatics!"

"I am very sorry to have caused any trouble," said Frodo. "It was quite unintentional, I assure you. A most unfortunate accident."

"All right, Mr. Underhill! But if you're going to do any more tumbling, or conjuring, or whatever it was, you'd best warn folk beforehand — and warn *me*. We're a bit suspicious round here of anything out of the way — uncanny, if you understand me; and we don't take to it all of a sudden."

"I shan't be doing anything of the sort again, Mr. Butterbur, I promise you. And now I think I'll be getting to bed. We shall be making an early start. Will you see that our ponies are ready by eight o'clock?"

"Very good! But before you go, I should like a word with you in private, Mr. Underhill. Something has just come back to my mind that I ought to tell you. I hope that you'll not take it amiss. When I've seen to a thing or two, I'll come along to your room, if you're willing."

"Certainly!" said Frodo; but his heart sank. He wondered how many private talks he would have before he got to bed, and what they would reveal. Were these people all in league against him? He began to suspect even old Butterbur's fat face of concealing dark designs.

CHAPTER
TEN

Strider

Frodo, Pippin, and Sam made their way back to the parlour. There was no light. Merry was not there, and the fire had burned low. It was not until they had puffed up the embers into a blaze and thrown on a couple of faggots that they discovered Strider had come with them. There he was calmly sitting in a chair by the door!

"Hallo!" said Pippin. "Who are you, and what do you want?"

"I am called Strider," he answered: "and though he may have forgotten it, your friend promised to have a quiet talk with me."

"You said I might hear something to my advantage, I believe," said Frodo. "What have you to say?"

"Several things," answered Strider. "But, of course, I have my price."

"What do you mean?" asked Frodo sharply.

"Don't be alarmed! I mean just this: I will tell you what I know, and give you some good advice — but I shall want a reward."

"And what will that be, pray?" said Frodo. He suspected now that he had fallen in with a rascal, and he thought uncomfortably that he had brought only a little money with him. All of it would hardly satisfy a rogue, and he could not spare any of it.

"No more than you can afford," answered Strider with a slow smile, as if he guessed Frodo's thoughts. "Just this: you must take me along with you, until I wish to leave you."

"Oh, indeed!" replied Frodo, surprised, but not much relieved. "Even if I wanted another companion, I should not agree to any such thing, until I knew a good deal more about you, and your business."

"Excellent!" exclaimed Strider, crossing his legs and sitting back comfortably. "You seem to be coming to your senses again, and that is all to the good. You have been much too careless so far. Very well! I will tell you what I know, and leave the reward to you. You may be glad to grant it, when you have heard me."

"Go on then!" said Frodo. "What do you know?"

"Too much; too many dark things," said Strider grimly. "But as for your business ——" He got up and went to the door, opened it quickly and looked out. Then he shut it quietly and sat down again. "I have quick ears," he went on, lowering his voice, "and though I cannot disappear, I have hunted many wild and wary things and I can usually avoid being seen, if I wish. Now, I was behind the hedge this evening on the Road west of Bree, when four hobbits came out of the Downlands. I need not repeat all that they said to old Bombadil or to one another, but one thing interested me. Please remember, said one of them, *that the name of Baggins must not be mentioned. I am Mr. Underhill, if any name must be given.* That interested me so much that I followed them here. I slipped over the gate just behind them. Maybe Mr. Baggins has an honest reason for leaving his name behind; but if so, I should advise him and his friends to be more careful."

"I don't see what interest my name has for any one in Bree," said Frodo angrily, "and I have still to learn why it interests you. Mr. Strider may have an honest reason for spying and eavesdropping; but if so, I should advise him to explain it."

"Well answered!" said Strider laughing. "But the explanation is simple: I was looking for a Hobbit called Frodo Baggins. I wanted to find him quickly. I had learned that he was carrying out of the Shire, well, a secret that concerned me and my friends.

"Now, don't mistake me!" he cried, as Frodo rose from his seat, and Sam jumped up with a scowl. "I shall take more care of the secret than you do. And care is needed!" He leaned forward and looked at them. "Watch every shadow!" he said in a low voice. "Black horsemen have passed through Bree. On Monday one came down the Greenway, they say; and another appeared later, coming up the Greenway from the south."

There was a silence. At last Frodo spoke to Pippin and Sam: "I ought to have guessed it from the way the gatekeeper greeted us," he said. "And the landlord seems to have heard something. Why did he press us to join the company? And why on earth did we behave so foolishly: we ought to have stayed quiet in here."

"It would have been better," said Strider. "I would have stopped your going into the common-room, if I could; but the innkeeper would not let me in to see you, or take a message."

"Do you think he ——" began Frodo.

"No, I don't think any harm of old Butterbur. Only he does not altogether like mysterious vagabonds of my sort." Frodo gave him a puzzled look. "Well, I have rather a rascally look, have I not?" said Strider with a curl of his lip and a queer gleam in his eye. "But I hope we shall get to know one another better. When we do, I hope you will explain what happened at the end of your song. For that little prank ——"

"It was sheer accident!" interrupted Frodo.

"I wonder," said Strider. "Accident, then. That accident has made your position dangerous."

"Hardly more than it was already," said Frodo. "I knew these horsemen were pursuing me; but now at any rate they seem to have missed me and to have gone away."

"You must not count on that!" said Strider sharply. "They will return. And more are coming. There are others. I know their number. I know these Riders." He paused, and his eyes were cold and hard. "And there are some folk in Bree who are not to be trusted," he went on. "Bill Ferny, for instance. He has an evil name in the Bree-land, and queer folk call at his house. You must have noticed him among the company: a swarthy sneering fellow. He was very close with one of the Southern strangers, and they slipped out together just after your 'accident'. Not all of those Southerners mean well; and as for Ferny, he would sell anything to anybody; or make mischief for amusement."

"What will Ferny sell, and what has my accident got to do with him?" said Frodo, still determined not to understand Strider's hints.

"News of you, of course," answered Strider. "An account of your performance would be very interesting to certain people. After that they would hardly need to be told your real name. It seems to me only too likely that they will hear of it before this night is over. Is that enough? You can do as you like about my reward: take me as a guide or not. But I may say that I know all the lands between the Shire and the Misty Mountains, for I have wandered over them for many years. I am older than I look. I might prove useful. You will have to leave the open road after tonight; for the horsemen will watch it night and day. You may escape from Bree, and be allowed to go forward while the Sun is up; but you won't go far. They will come on you in the wild, in some dark place where there is no help. Do you wish them to find you? They are terrible!"

The hobbits looked at him, and saw with surprise that his face was drawn as if with pain, and his hands clenched the arms of his chair. The room was very quiet and still, and the light seemed to have grown dim. For a while he sat with unseeing eyes as if walking in distant memory or listening to sounds in the Night far away.

"There!" he cried after a moment, drawing his hand across his brow. "Perhaps I know more about these pursuers than you do. You fear them, but you do not fear them enough, yet.

Tomorrow you will have to escape, if you can. Strider can take you by paths that are seldom trodden. Will you have him?"

There was a heavy silence. Frodo made no answer, his mind was confused with doubt and fear. Sam frowned, and looked at his master; and at last he broke out:

"With your leave, Mr. Frodo, I'd say *no*! This Strider here, he warns and he says take care; and I say *yes* to that, and let's begin with him. He comes out of the Wild, and I never heard no good of such folk. He knows something, that's plain, and more than I like; but it's no reason why we should let him go leading us out into some dark place far from help, as he puts it."

Pippin fidgeted and looked uncomfortable. Strider did not reply to Sam, but turned his keen eyes on Frodo. Frodo caught his glance and looked away. "No," he said slowly. "I don't agree. I think, I think you are not really as you choose to look. You began to talk to me like the Bree-folk, but your voice has changed. Still Sam seems right in this: I don't see why you should warn us to take care, and yet ask us to take you on trust. Why the disguise? Who are you? What do you really know about — about my business; and how do you know it?"

"The lesson in caution has been well learned," said Strider with a grim smile. "But caution is one thing and wavering is another. You will never get to Rivendell now on your own, and to trust me is your only chance. You must make up your mind. I will answer some of your questions, if that will help you to do so. But why should you believe my story, if you do not trust me already? Still here it is ——"

At that moment there came a knock at the door. Mr. Butterbur had arrived with candles, and behind him was Nob with cans of hot water. Strider withdrew into a dark corner.

"I've come to bid you good night," said the landlord, putting the candles on the table. "Nob! Take the water to the rooms!" He came in and shut the door.

"It's like this," he began, hesitating and looking troubled. "If

I've done any harm, I'm sorry indeed. But one thing drives out another, as you'll admit; and I'm a busy man. But first one thing and then another this week have jogged my memory, as the saying goes; and not too late I hope. You see, I was asked to look out for hobbits of the Shire, and for one by the name of Baggins in particular."

"And what has that got to do with me?" asked Frodo.

"Ah! you know best," said the landlord, knowingly. "I won't give you away; but I was told that this Baggins would be going by the name of Underhill, and I was given a description that fits you well enough, if I may say so."

"Indeed! Let's have it then!" said Frodo, unwisely interrupting.

"*A stout little fellow with red cheeks,*" said Mr. Butterbur solely. Pippin chuckled, but Sam looked indignant. "*That won't help you much; it goes for most hobbits, Barley,* he says to me," continued Mr. Butterbur with a glance at Pippin. "*But this one is taller than some and fairer than most, and he has a cleft in his chin: perky chap with a bright eye.* Begging your pardon, but he said it, not me."

"*He* said it? And who was he?" asked Frodo eagerly.

"Ah! That was Gandalf, if you know who I mean. A wizard they say he is, but he's a good friend of mine, whether or no. But now I don't know what he'll have to say to me, if I see him again: turn all my ale sour or me into a block of wood, I shouldn't wonder. He's a bit hasty. Still what's done can't be undone."

"Well, what have you done?" said Frodo, getting impatient with the slow unravelling of Butterbur's thoughts.

"Where was I?" said the landlord, pausing and snapping his fingers. "Ah, yes! Old Gandalf. Three months back he walked right into my room without a knock. *Barley,* he says, *I'm off in the morning. Will you do something for me?* You've only to name it, I said. *I'm in a hurry,* said he, *and I've no time myself, but I want a message took to the Shire. Have you anyone you can send, and trust to go?* I can find someone, I said, *tomorrow, maybe, or the day after. Make it tomorrow*, he says, and then he gave me a letter.

"It's addressed plain enough," said Mr. Butterbur, producing a letter from his pocket, and reading out the address slowly and proudly (he valued his reputation as a lettered man):

Mr. *FRODO BAGGINS, BAG END, HOBBITON in the SHIRE.*

"A letter for me from Gandalf!" cried Frodo.

"Ah!" said Mr. Butterbur. "Then your right name is Baggins?"

"It is," said Frodo, "and you had better give me that letter at once, and explain why you never sent it. That's what you came to tell me, I suppose, though you've taken a long time to come to the point."

Poor Mr. Butterbur looked troubled. "You're right, master," he said, "and I beg your pardon. And I'm mortal afraid of what Gandalf will say, if harm comes of it. But I didn't keep it back a-purpose. I put it by safe. Then I couldn't find nobody willing to go to the Shire next day, nor the day after, and none of my own folk were to spare; and then one thing after another drove it out of my mind. I'm a busy man. I'll do what I can to set matters right, and if there's any help I can give, you've only to name it.

"Leaving the letter aside, I promised Gandalf no less. *Barley,* he says to me, *this friend of mine from the Shire, he may be coming out this way before long, him and another. He'll be calling himself Underhill. Mind that! But you need ask no questions. And if I'm not with him, he may be in trouble, and he may need help. Do whatever you can for him, and I'll be grateful*, he says. And here you are, and trouble is not far off, seemingly."

"What do you mean?" asked Frodo.

"These black men," said the landlord lowering his voice. "They're looking for *Baggins*, and if they mean well, then I"m a hobbit. It was on Monday, and all the dogs were yammering and the geese screaming. Uncanny, I called it. Nob, he came and told me that two black men were at the door asking for a hobbit called Baggins. Nob's hair was all stood on end. I bid the black fellows be off, and slammed the door on them; but they've been asking the same question all the way to Archet, I hear. And that Ranger, Strider, he's been asking questions, too. Tried to get in here to see you, before you'd had bite or sup, he did."

"He did!" said Strider suddenly, coming forward into the light. "And much trouble would have been saved, if you had let him in, Barliman."

The landlord jumped with surprise. "You!" he cried. "You're always popping up. What do you want now?"

"He's here with my leave," said Frodo. "He came to offer me his help."

"Well, you know your own business, maybe," said Mr. Butterbur, looking suspiciously at Strider. "But if I was in your plight, I wouldn't take up with a Ranger."

"Then who would you take up with?" asked Strider. "A fat inn-keeper who only remembers his own name because people shout it at him all day? They cannot stay in *The Pony* for ever, and they cannot go home. They have a long road before them. Will you go with them and keep the black men off?"

"Me? Leave Bree! I wouldn't do that for any money," said Mr. Butterbur, looking really scared. "But why can't you stay here quiet for a bit, Mr. Underhill? What are all these queer goings on? What are these black men after, and where do they come from, I'd like to know?"

"I'm sorry I can't explain it all," answered Frodo. "I am tired and very worried, and it's a long tale. But if you mean to help me, I ought to warn you that you will be in danger as long as I am in your house. These Black Riders: I am not sure, but I think, I fear they come from ——"

"They come from Mordor," said Strider in a low voice. "From Mordor, Barliman, if that means anything to you."

"Save us!" cried Mr. Butterbur turning pale; the name

evidently was known to him. "That is the worst news that has come to Bree in my time."

"It is," said Frodo. "Are you still willing to help me?"

"I am," said Mr. Butterbur. "More than ever. Though I don't know what the likes of me can do against, against ——" he faltered.

"Against the Shadow in the East," said Strider quietly. "Not much, Barliman, but every little helps. You can let Mr. Underhill stay here tonight, as Mr. Underhill, and you can forget the name of Baggins, till he is far away."

"I'll do that," said Butterbur. "But they'll find out he's here without help from me, I'm afraid. Its a pity Mr. Baggins drew attention to himself this evening, to say no more. The story of that Mr. Bilbo's going off has been heard before tonight in Bree. Even our Nob has been doing some guessing in his slow pate; and there are others in Bree quicker in thc uptake than he is."

"Well, we can only hope the Riders won't come back yet," said Frodo.

"I hope not, indeed," said Butterbur. "But spooks or no spooks, they won't get in *The Pony* so easy. Don't you worry till the morning. Nob'll say no word. No black man shall pass my doors, while I can stand on my legs. Me and my folk'll keep watch tonight; but you had best get some sleep, if you can."

"In any case we must be called at dawn," said Frodo. "We must get off as early as possible. Breakfast at six-thirty, please."

"Right! I'll see to the orders," said the landlord. "Good night, Mr. Baggins — Underhill, I should say! Good night — now, bless me! Where's your Mr. Brandybuck?"

"I don't know," said Frodo with sudden anxiety. They had forgotten all about Merry, and it was getting late. "I am afraid he is out. He said something about going for a breath of air."

"Well, you do want looking after and no mistake: your party might be on a holiday!" said Butterbur. "I must go and bar the doors quick, but I'll see your friend is let in when he comes. I'd better send Nob to look for him. Good night to you all!" At last Mr. Butterbur went out, with another doubtful look at Strider and a shake of his head. His footsteps retreated down the passage.

"Well?" said Strider. "When are you going to open that letter?" Frodo looked carefully at the seal before he broke it. It seemed certainly to be Gandalf's. Inside, written in the wizard's strong but graceful script, was the following message:

THE PRANCING PONY, BREE. Midyear's Day, Shire Year, 1418.

Dear Frodo,
  Bad news has reached me here. I must go off at once. You had better leave Bag End soon, and get out of the Shire before the end of July at latest. I will return as soon as I can; and I will follow you, if I find that you are gone. Leave a message for me here, if you pass through Bree. You can trust the landlord (Butterbur). You may meet a friend of mine on the Road: a Man, lean, dark, tall, by some called Strider. He knows our business and will help you. Make for Rivendell. There I hope we may meet again. If I do not come,
                          Elrond will advise you. Yours in haste
                                    GANDALF. ℙ

  PS. Do NOT use It again, not for any reason whatever! Do not travel by night! ℙ
  PPS. Make sure that it is the real Strider. There are many strange men on the roads. His true name is Aragorn. ℙ

        All that is gold does not glitter,
            Not all those who wander are lost;
        The old that is strong does not wither,
            Deep roots are not reached by the frost.

From the ashes a fire shall be woken,
A light from the shadows shall spring;
Renewed shall be blade that was broken,
The crownless again shall be king.

PPPS.   I hope Butterbur sends this promptly. A worthy man,
but his memory is like a
lumber-room: thing wanted
always buried. If he
forgets, I shall roast him.
Fare Well!

Frodo read the letter to himself, and then passed it to Pippin and Sam. "Really old Butterbur has made a mess of things!" he said. "He deserves roasting. If I had got this at once, we might all have been safe in Rivendell by now. But what can have happened to Gandalf? He writes as if he was going into great danger."

"He has been doing that for many years," said Strider.

Frodo turned and looked at him thoughtfully, wondering about Gandalf's second postscript. "Why didn't you tell me that you were Gandalf's friend at once?" he asked. "It would have saved time."

"Would it? Would any of you have believed me till now?" said Strider. "I knew nothing of this letter. For all I knew I had to persuade you to trust me without proofs, if I was to help you. In any case, I did not intend to tell you all about myself at once. I had to study *you* first, and make sure of you. The Enemy has set traps for me before now. As soon as I had made up my mind, I was ready to tell you whatever you asked. But I must admit," he added with a queer laugh, "that I hoped you would take to me for my own sake. A hunted man sometimes wearies of distrust and longs for friendship. But there, I believe my looks are against me."

"They are — at first sight at any rate," laughed Pippin with sudden relief after reading Gandalf's letter. "But handsome is as handsome does, as we say in the Shire; and I daresay we shall all look much the same after lying for days in hedges and ditches."

"It would take more than a few days, or weeks, or years, of wandering in the Wild to make you look like Strider," he answered. "And you would die first, unless you are made of sterner stuff than you look to be."

Pippin subsided; but Sam was not daunted, and he still eyed Strider dubiously. "How do we know you are the Strider that Gandalf speaks about?" he demanded. "You never mentioned Gandalf, till this letter came out. You might be a play-acting spy, for all I can see, trying to get us to go with you. You might have done in the real Strider and took his clothes. What have you to say to that?"

"That you are a stout fellow," answered Strider; "but I am afraid my only answer to you, Sam Gamgee, is this. If I had killed the real Strider, I could *kill* you. And I should have killed you already without so much talk. If I was after the Ring, I could have it — NOW!"

He stood up, and seemed suddenly to grow taller. In his eyes gleamed a light, keen and commanding. Throwing back his cloak, he laid his hand on the hilt of a sword that had hung concealed by his side. They did not dare to move. Sam sat wide-mouthed staring at him dumbly.

"But I *am* the real Strider, fortunately," he said, looking down at them with his face softened by a sudden smile. "I am Aragorn son of Arathorn; and if by life or death I can save you, I will."

There was a long silence. At last Frodo spoke with hesitation. "I believed that you were a friend before the letter came," he said, "or at least I wished to. You have frightened me several times tonight, but never in the way that servants of the Enemy would, or so I imagine. I think one of his spies would — well, seem fairer and feel fouler, if you understand"

"I see," laughed Strider. "I look foul and feel fair. Is that it?

All that is gold does not glitter, not all those who wander are lost."

"Did the verses apply to you then?" asked Frodo. "I could not make out what they were about. But how did you know that they were in Gandalf's letter, if you have never seen it?"

"I did not know," he answered. "But I am Aragorn, and those verses go with that name." He drew out his sword, and they saw that the blade was indeed broken a foot below the hilt. "Not much use is it, Sam?" said Strider. "But the time is near when it shall be forged anew."

Sam said nothing.

"Well," said Strider, "with Sam's permission we will call that settled. Strider shall be your guide. We shall have a rough road tomorrow. Even if we are allowed to leave Bree unhindered, we can hardly hope now to leave it unnoticed. But I shall try to get lost as soon as possible. I know one or two ways out of Bree-land other than the main road. If once we shake off the pursuit, I shall make for Weathertop."

"Weathertop?" said Sam. "What's that?"

"It is a hill, just to the north of the Road, about half way from here to Rivendell. It commands a wide view all round; and there we shall have a chance to look about us. Gandalf will make for that point, if he follows us. After Weathertop our journey will become more difficult, and we shall have to choose between various dangers."

"When did you last see Gandalf?" asked Frodo. "Do you know where he is, or what he is doing?"

Strider looked grave. "I do not know," he said. "I came west with him in the spring. I have often kept watch on the borders of the Shire in the last few years, when he was busy elsewhere. He seldom left it unguarded. We last met on the first of May: at Sarn Ford down the Brandywine. He told me that his business with you had gone well, and that you would be starting for Rivendell in the last week of September. As I knew he was at your side, I went away on a journey of my own. And that has proved ill; for plainly some news reached him, and I was not at hand to help.

"I am troubled, for the first time since I have known him. We should have had messages, even if he could not come himself. When I returned, many days ago, I heard the ill news. The tidings had gone far and wide that Gandalf was missing and the horsemen had been seen. It was the Elven-folk of Gildor that told me this; and later they told me that you had left your home; but there was no news of your leaving Buckland. I have been watching the East Road anxiously."

"Do you think the Black Riders have anything to do with it — with Gandalf's absence, I mean?" asked Frodo.

"I do not know of anything else that could have hindered him, except the Enemy himself," said Strider. "But do not give up hope! Gandalf is greater than you Shire-folk know — as a rule you can only see his jokes and toys. But this business of ours will be his greatest task."

Pippin yawned. "I am sorry," he said, "but I am dead tired. In spite of all the danger and worry I must go to bed, or sleep where I sit. Where is that silly fellow, Merry? It would be the last straw, if we had to go out in the dark to look for him."

At that moment they heard a door slam; then feet came running along the passage. Merry came in with a rush followed by Nob. He shut the door hastily, and leaned against it. He was out of breath. They stared at him in alarm for a moment before he gasped: "I have seen them, Frodo! I have seen them! Black Riders!"

"Black Riders!" cried Frodo. "Where?"

"Here. In the village. I stayed indoors for an hour. Then as you did not come back, I went out for a stroll. I had come back again and was standing just outside the light of the lamp looking at the stars. Suddenly I shivered and felt that something horrible was creeping near: there was a sort of deeper shade among the shadows across the road, just beyond the edge of the lamplight. It slid away at once into the dark without a sound. There was no horse."

"Which way did it go?" asked Strider, suddenly and sharply.

Merry started, noticing the stranger for the first time. "Go on!" said Frodo. "This is a friend of Gandalf's. I will explain later."

"It seemed to make off up the Road, eastward," continued Merry. "I tried to follow. Of course, it vanished almost at once; but I went round the corner and on as far as the last house on the Road."

Strider looked at Merry with wonder. "You have a stout heart," he said; "but it was foolish."

"I don't know," said Merry. "Neither brave nor silly, I think. I could hardly help myself. I seemed to be drawn somehow. Anyway, I went, and suddenly I heard voices by the hedge. One was muttering; and the other was whispering, or hissing. I couldn't hear a word that was said. I did not creep any closer, because I began to tremble all over. Then I felt terrified, and I turned back, and was just going to bolt home, when something came behind me and I . . . I fell over."

"I found him, sir," put in Nob. "Mr. Butterbur sent me out with a lantern. I went down to West-gate, and then back up towards South-gate. Just nigh Bill Ferny's house I thought I could see something in the Road. I couldn't swear to it, but it looked to me as if two men was stooping over something, lifting it. I gave a shout, but when I got up to the spot there was no signs of them, and only Mr. Brandybuck lying by the roadside. He seemed to be asleep. 'I thought I had fallen into deep water,' he says to me, when I shook him. Very queer he was, and as soon as I had roused him, he got up and ran back here like a hare."

"I am afraid that's true," said Merry, "though I don't know what I said. I had an ugly dream, which I can't remember. I went to pieces. I don't know what came over me.

"I do," said Strider. "The Black Breath. The Riders must have left their horses outside, and passed back through the South-gate in secret. They will know all the news now, for they have visited Bill Ferny; and probably that Southerner was a spy as well. Something may happen in the night, before we leave Bree."

"What will happen?" said Merry. "Will they attack the inn?"

"No, I think not," said Strider. "They are not all here yet. And in any case that is not their way. In dark and loneliness they are strongest; they will not openly attack a house where there are lights and many people — not until they are desperate, not while all the long leagues of Eriador still lie before us. But their power is in terror, and already some in Bree are in their clutch. They will drive these wretches to some evil work: Ferny, and some of the strangers, and, maybe, the gatekeeper too. They had words with Harry at West-gate on Monday. I was watching them. He was white and shaking when they left him."

"We seem to have enemies all round," said Frodo. "What are we to do?"

"Stay here, and do not go to your rooms! They are sure to have found out which those are. The hobbit-rooms have windows looking north and close to the ground. We will all remain together and bar this window and the door. But first Nob and I will fetch your luggage."

While Strider was gone, Frodo gave Merry a rapid account of all that had happened since supper. Merry was still reading and pondering Gandalf's letter when Strider and Nob returned.

"Well Masters," said Nob, "I've ruffled up the clothes and put in a bolster down the middle of each bed. And I made a nice imitation of your head with a brown woollen mat, Mr. Bag — Underhill, sir," he added with a grin.

Pippin laughed. "Very life-like!" he said. "But what will happen when they have penetrated the disguise?"

"We shall see," said Strider. "Let us hope to hold the fort till morning."

"Good night to you," said Nob, and went off to take his part in the watch on the doors.

Their bags and gear they piled on the parlour-floor. They pushed a low chair against the door and shut the window. Peering out, Frodo saw that the night was still clear. The

Sickle★ was swinging bright above the shoulders of Bree-hill. He then closed and barred the heavy inside shutters and drew the curtains together. Strider built up the fire and blew out all the candles.

The hobbits lay down on their blankets with their feet towards the hearth; but Strider settled himself in the chair against the door. They talked for a little, for Merry still had several questions to ask.

"Jumped over the Moon!" chuckled Merry as he rolled himself in his blanket. "Very ridiculous of you, Frodo! But I wish I had been there to see. The worthies of Bree will be discussing it a hundred years hence."

"I hope so," said Strider. Then they all fell silent, and one by one the hobbits dropped off to sleep.

★ "The Hobbits" name for the Plough or Great Bear.

CHAPTER
ELEVEN

A Knife in the Dark

As they prepared for sleep in the inn at Bree, darkness lay on Buckland; a mist strayed in the dells and along the river-bank. The house at Crickhollow stood silent. Fatty Bolger opened the door cautiously and peered out. A feeling of fear had been growing on him all day, and he was unable to rest or go to bed: there was a brooding threat in the breathless night-air. As he stared out into the gloom, a black shadow moved under the trees; the gate seemed to open of its own accord and close again without a sound. Terror seized him. He shrank back, and for a moment he stood trembling in the hall. Then he shut and locked the door.

The night deepened. There came the soft sound of horses led with stealth along the lane. Outside the gate they stopped, and three black figures entered, like shades of night creeping across the ground. One went to the door, one to the corner of the house on either side; and there they stood, as still as the shadows of stones, while night went slowly on. The house and the quiet trees seemed to be waiting breathlessly.

There was a faint stir in the leaves, and a cock crowed far away. The cold hour before dawn was passing. The figure by the door moved. In the dark without moon or stars a drawn blade gleamed, as if a chill light had been unsheathed. There was a blow, soft but heavy, and the door shuddered.

210

"Open, in the name of Mordor!" said a voice thin and menacing.

At a second blow the door yielded and fell back, with timbers burst and lock broken. The black figures passed swiftly in.

At that moment, among the trees nearby, a horn rang out. It rent the night like fire on a hill-top.

AWAKE! FEAR! FIRE! FOES! AWAKE!

Fatty Bolger had not been idle. As soon as he saw the dark shapes creep from the garden, he knew that he must run for it, or perish. And run he did, out of the back door, through the garden, and over the fields. When he reached the nearest house, more than a mile away, he collapsed on the doorstep. "No, no, no!" he was crying. "No, not me! I haven't got it!" It was some time before anyone could make out what he was babbling about. At last they got the idea that enemies were in Buckland, some strange invasion from the Old Forest. And then they lost no more time.

FEAR! FIRE! FOES!

The Brandybucks were blowing the Horn-call of Buckland, that had not been sounded for a hundred years, not since the white wolves came in the Fell Winter, when the Brandywine was frozen over.

AWAKE! AWAKE!

Far-away answering horns were heard. The alarm was spreading.

The black figures fled from the house. One of them let fall a hobbit-cloak on the step, as he ran. In the lane the noise of hoofs broke out, and gathering to a gallop, went hammering away into the darkness. All about Crickhollow there was the sound of horns blowing, and voices crying and feet running.

But the Black Riders rode like a gale to the North-gate. Let the little people blow! Sauron would deal with them later. Meanwhile they had another errand: they knew now that the house was empty and the Ring had gone. They rode down the guards at the gate and vanished from the Shire.

In the early night Frodo woke from deep sleep, suddenly, as if some sound or presence had disturbed him. He saw that Strider was sitting alert in his chair: his eyes gleamed in the light of the fire, which had been tended and was burning brightly; but he made no sign or movement.

Frodo soon went to sleep again; but his dreams were again troubled with the noise of wind and of galloping hoofs. The wind seemed to be curling round the house and shaking it; and far off he heard a horn blowing wildly. He opened his eyes, and heard a cock crowing lustily in the inn-yard. Strider had drawn the curtains and pushed back the shutters with a clang. The first grey light of day was in the room, and a cold air was coming through the open window.

As soon as Strider had roused them all, he led the way to their bedrooms. When they saw them they were glad that they had taken his advice: the windows had been forced open and were swinging, and the curtains were flapping; the beds were tossed about, and the bolsters slashed and flung upon the floor; the brown mat was torn to pieces.

Strider immediately went to fetch the landlord. Poor Mr. Butterbur looked sleepy and frightened. He had hardly closed his eyes all night (so he said), but he had never heard a sound.

"Never has such a thing happened in my time!" he cried, raising his hands in horror. "Guests unable to sleep in their beds, and good bolsters ruined and all! What are we coming to?"

"Dark times," said Strider. "But for the present you may be left in peace, when you have got rid of us. We will leave at once. Never mind about breakfast: a drink and a bite standing will have to do. We shall be packed in a few minutes."

Mr. Butterbur hurried off to see that their ponies were got ready, and to fetch them a "bite". But very soon he came back in dismay. The ponies had vanished! The stable-doors had all been opened in the night, and they were gone: not only Merry's ponies, but every other horse and beast in the place.

Frodo was crushed by the news. How could they hope to reach Rivendell on foot, pursued by mounted enemies? They might as well set out for the Moon. Strider sat silent for a while, looking at the hobbits, as if he was weighing up their strength and courage.

"Ponies would not help us to escape horsemen," he said at last, thoughtfully, as if he guessed what Frodo had in mind. "We should not go much slower on foot, not on the roads that I mean to take. I was going to walk in any case. It is the food and stores that trouble me. We cannot count on getting anything to eat between here and Rivendell, except what we take with us; and we ought to take plenty to spare; for we may be delayed, or forced to go round-about, far out of the direct way. How much are you prepared to carry on your backs?"

"As much as we must," said Pippin with a sinking heart, but trying to show that he was tougher than he looked (or felt).

"I can carry enough for two," said Sam defiantly.

"Can't anything be done, Mr. Butterbur?" asked Frodo. "Can't we get a couple of ponies in the village, or even one just for the baggage? I don't suppose we could hire them, but we might be able to buy them," he added, doubtfully, wondering if he could afford it.

"I doubt it," said the landlord unhappily. "The two or three riding-ponies that there were in Bree were stabled in my yard, and they're gone. As for other animals, horses or ponies for draught or what not, there are very few of them in Bree, and they won't be for sale. But I'll do what I can. I'll rout out Bob and send him round as soon as may be."

"Yes," said Strider reluctantly, "you had better do that. I am afraid we shall have to try to get one pony at least. But so ends all hope of starting early, and slipping away quietly! We might as well have blown a horn to announce our departure. That was part of their plan, no doubt."

"There is one crumb of comfort," said Merry, "and more than a crumb, I hope: we can have breakfast while we wait — and sit down to it. Let's get hold of Nob!"

In the end there was more than three hours delay. Bob came back with the report that no horse or pony was to be got for love or money in the neighbourhood — except one: Bill Ferny had one that he might possibly sell. "A poor old half-starved creature it is," said Bob; "but he won't part with it for less than thrice its worth, seeing how you're placed, not if I knows Bill Ferny."

"Bill Ferny?" said Frodo. "Isn't there some trick? Wouldn't the beast bolt back to him with all our stuff, or help in tracking us, or something?"

"I wonder," said Strider. "But I cannot imagine any animal running home to him, once it got away. I fancy this is only an afterthought of kind Master Ferny's: just a way of increasing his profits from the affair. The chief danger is that the poor beast is probably at death's door. But there does not seem any choice. What does he want for it?"

Bill Ferny's price was twelve silver pennies; and that was indeed at least three times the pony's value in those parts. It proved to be a bony, underfed, and dispirited animal; but it did not look like dying just yet. Mr. Butterbur paid for it himself, and offered Merry another eighteen pence as some compensation for the lost animals. He was an honest man, and well-off as things were reckoned in Bree; but thirty silver pennies was a sore blow to him, and being cheated by Bill Ferny made it harder to bear.

As a matter of fact he came out on the right side in the end. It turned out later that only one horse had been actually stolen. The others had been driven off, or had bolted in terror, and were found wandering in different corners of the Bree-land. Merry's ponies had escaped altogether, and eventually (having a good deal of sense) they made their way to the Downs in search of Fatty Lumpkin. So they came under the care of Tom Bombadil for a while, and were well-off. But when news of the events at Bree came to Tom's ears, he sent them to Mr. Butterbur, who thus got five good beasts at a very fair price. They had to work harder in Bree, but Bob treated them well; so on the whole they were lucky: they missed a dark and dangerous journey. But they never came to Rivendell.

However, in the meanwhile for all Mr. Butterbur knew his money was gone for good, or for bad. And he had other troubles. For there was a great commotion as soon as the remaining guests were astir and heard news of the raid on the inn. The southern travellers had lost several horses and blamed the innkeeper loudly, until it became known that one of their own number had also disappeared in the night, none other than Bill Ferny's squint-eyed companion. Suspicion fell on him at once.

"If you pick up with a horse-thief, and bring him to my house," said Butterbur angrily, "you ought to pay for all the damage yourselves and not come shouting at me. Go and ask Ferny where your handsome friend is!" But it appeared that he was nobody's friend, and nobody could recollect when he had joined their party.

After their breakfast the hobbits had to re-pack, and get together further supplies for the longer journey they were now expecting. It was close on ten o'clock before they at last got off. By that time the whole of Bree was buzzing with excitement. Frodo's vanishing trick; the appearance of the black horsemen; the robbing of the stables; and not least the news that Strider the Ranger had joined the mysterious hobbits, made such a tale as would last for many uneventful years. Most of the inhabitants of Bree and Staddle, and many even from Combe and Archet, were crowded in the road to see the travellers start. The other guests in the inn were at the doors or hanging out of the windows.

Strider had changed his mind, and he decided to leave Bree by the main road. Any attempt to set off across country at once would only make matters worse: half the inhabitants would follow them, to see what they were up to, and to prevent them from trespassing.

They said farewell to Nob and Bob, and took leave of Mr. Butterbur with many thanks. "I hope we shall meet again some day, when things are merry once more," said Frodo. "I should like nothing better than to stay in your house in peace for a while."

They tramped off, anxious and downhearted, under the eyes of the crowd. Not all the faces were friendly, nor all the words that were shouted. But Strider seemed to be held in awe by most of the Breelanders, and those that he stared at shut their mouths and drew away. He walked in front with Frodo; next came Merry and Pippin; and last came Sam leading the pony, which was laden with as much of their baggage as they had the heart to give it; but already it looked less dejected, as if it approved of the change in its fortunes. Sam was chewing an apple thoughtfully. He had a pocket full of them: a parting present from Nob and Bob. "Apples for walking, and a pipe for sitting," he said. "But I reckon I'll miss them both before long."

The hobbits took no notice of the inquisitive heads that peeped out of doors, or popped over walls and fences, as they passed. But as they drew near to the further gate, Frodo saw a dark ill-kept house behind a thick hedge: the last house in the village. In one of the windows he caught a glimpse of a sallow face with sly, slanting eyes; but it vanished at once.

"So that's where that southerner is hiding!" he thought. "He looks more than half like a goblin."

Over the hedge another man was staring boldly. He had heavy black brows, and dark scornful eyes; his large mouth curled in a sneer. He was smoking a short black pipe. As they approached he took it out of his mouth and spat.

"Morning, Longshanks!" he said. "Off early? Found some

friends at last?" Strider nodded, but did not answer.

"Morning, my little friends!" he said to the others. "I suppose you know who you've taken up with? That's Stick-at-naught Strider, that is! Though I've heard other names not so pretty. Watch out tonight! And you, Sammie, don't go ill-treating my poor old pony! Pah!" He spat again.

Sam turned quickly. "And you, Ferny," he said, "put your ugly face out of sight, or it will get hurt." With a sudden flick, quick as lightning, an apple left his hand and hit Bill square on the nose. He ducked too late, and curses came from behind the hedge. "Waste of a good apple," said Sam regretfully, and strode on.

At last they left the village behind. The escort of children and stragglers that had followed them got tired and turned back at the South-gate. Passing through, they kept on along the Road for some miles. It bent to the left, curving back into its eastward line as it rounded the feet of Bree-hill, and then it began to run swiftly downwards into wooded country. To their left they could see some of the houses and hobbit-holes of Staddle on the gentler south-eastern slopes of the hill; down in a deep hollow away north of the Road there were wisps of rising smoke that showed where Combe lay; Archet was hidden in the trees beyond.

After the Road had run down some way, and had left Bree-hill standing tall and brown behind, they came on a narrow track that led off towards the North. "This is where we leave the open and take to cover," said Strider.

"Not a 'short cut', I hope," said Pippin. "Our last short cut through woods nearly ended in disaster."

"Ah, but you had not got me with you then," laughed Strider. "My cuts, short or long, don't go wrong." He took a look up and down the Road. No one was in sight; and he led the way quickly down towards the wooded valley.

His plan, as far as they could understand it without knowing the country, was to go towards Archet at first, but to bear right and pass it on the east, and then to steer as straight as he could over the wild lands to Weathertop Hill. In that way they would, if all went well, cut off a great loop of the Road, which further on bent southwards to avoid the Midgewater Marshes. But, of course, they would have to pass through the marshes themselves, and Strider's description of them was not encouraging.

However, in the meanwhile, walking was not unpleasant. Indeed, if it had not been for the disturbing events of the night before, they would have enjoyed this part of the journey better than any up to that time. The sun was shining, clear but not too hot. The woods in the valley were still leafy and full of colour, and seemed peaceful and wholesome. Strider guided them confidently among the many crossing paths, although left to themselves they would soon have been at a loss. He was taking a wandering course with many turns and doublings, to put off any pursuit.

"Bill Ferny will have watched where we left the Road, for certain," he said; 'though I don't think he will follow us himself. He knows the land round here well enough, but he knows he is not a match for me in a wood. It is what he may tell others that I am afraid of. I don't suppose they are far away. If they think we have made for Archet, so much the better."

Whether because of Strider's skill or for some other reason, they saw no sign and heard no sound of any other living thing all that day: neither two-footed, except birds; nor four-footed, except one fox and a few squirrels. The next day they began to steer a steady course eastwards; and still all was quiet and peaceful. On the third day out from Bree they came out of the Chetwood. The land had been falling steadily, ever since they turned aside from the Road, and they now entered a wide flat expanse of country, much more difficult to manage. They were far beyond the borders of the Bree-land, out in the pathless wilderness, and drawing near to the Midgewater Marshes.

The ground now became damp, and in places boggy and here

and there they came upon pools, and wide stretches of reeds and rushes filled with the warbling of little hidden birds. They had to pick their way carefully to keep both dry-footed and on their proper course. At first they made fair progress, but as they went on, their passage became slower and more dangerous. The marshes were bewildering and treacherous, and there was no permanent trail even for Rangers to find through their shifting quagmires. The flies began to torment them, and the air was full of clouds of tiny midges that crept up their sleeves and breeches and into their hair.

"I am being eaten alive!" cried Pippin. "Midgewater! There are more midges than water!"

"What do they live on when they can't get hobbit?" asked Sam, scratching his neck.

They spent a miserable day in this lonely and unpleasant country. Their camping-place was damp, cold, and uncomfortable; and the biting insects would not let them sleep. There were also abominable creatures haunting the reeds and tussocks that from the sound of them were evil relatives of the cricket. There were thousands of them, and they squeaked all round, *neek-breek*, *breek-neek*, unceasingly all the night, until the hobbits were nearly frantic.

The next day, the fourth, was little better, and the night almost as comfortless. Though the Neekerbreekers (as Sam called them) had been left behind, the midges still pursued them.

As Frodo lay, tired but unable to close his eyes, it seemed to him that far away there came a light in the eastern sky: it flashed and faded many times. It was not the dawn, for that was still some hours off.

"What is the light?" he said to Strider, who had risen, and was standing, gazing ahead into the night.

"I do not know," Strider answered. "It is too distant to make out. It is like lightning that leaps up from the hill-tops."

Frodo lay down again, but for a long while he could still see the white flashes, and against them the tall dark figure of

Strider, standing silent and watchful. At last he passed into uneasy sleep.

They had not gone far on the fifth day when they left the last straggling pools and reed-beds of the marshes behind them. The land before them began steadily to rise again. Away in the distance eastward they could now see a line of hills. The highest of them was at the right of the line and a little separated from the others. It had a conical top, slightly flattened at the summit.

"That is Weathertop," said Strider. "The Old Road, which we have left far away on our right, runs to the south of it and passes not far from its foot. We might reach it by noon tomorrow, if we go straight towards it. I suppose we had better do so."

"What do you mean?" asked Frodo.

"I mean: when we do get there, it is not certain what we shall find. It is close to the Road."

"But surely we were hoping to find Gandalf there?"

"Yes; but the hope is faint. If he comes this way at all, he may not pass through Bree, and so he may not know what we are doing. And anyway, unless by luck we arrive almost together, we shall miss one another; it will not be safe for him or for us to wait there long. If the Riders fail to find us in the wilderness, they are likely to make for Weathertop themselves. It commands a wide view all round. Indeed, there are many birds and beasts in this country that could see us, as we stand here, from that hill-top. Not all the birds are to be trusted, and there are other spies more evil than they are."

The hobbits looked anxiously at the distant hills. Sam looked up into the pale sky, fearing to see hawks or eagles hovering over them with bright unfriendly eyes. "You do make me feel uncomfortable and lonesome, Strider!" he said.

"What do you advise us to do?" asked Frodo.

"I think," answered Strider slowly, as if he was not quite sure, "I think the best thing is to go as straight eastward from here as we can, to make for the line of hills, not for

Weathertop. There we can strike a path I know that runs at their feet; it will bring us to Weathertop from the north and less openly. Then we shall see what we shall see."

All that day they plodded along, until the cold and early evening came down. The land became drier and more barren; but mists and vapours lay behind them on the marshes. A few melancholy birds were piping and wailing, until the round red sun sank slowly into the western shadows; then an empty silence fell. The hobbits thought of the soft light of sunset glancing through the cheerful windows of Bag End far away.

At the day's end they came to a stream that wandered down from the hills to lose itself in the stagnant marshland, and they went up along its banks while the light lasted. It was already night when at last they halted and made their camp under some stunted alder-trees by the shores of the stream. Ahead there loomed now against the dusky sky the bleak and treeless backs of the hills. That night they set a watch, and Strider, it seemed, did not sleep at all. The moon was waxing, and in the early night-hours a cold grey light lay on the land.

Next morning they set out again soon after sunrise. There was a frost in the air, and the sky was a pale clear blue. The hobbits felt refreshed, as if they had had a night of unbroken sleep. Already they were getting used to much walking on short commons — shorter at any rate than what in the Shire they would have thought barely enough to keep them on their legs. Pippin declared that Frodo was looking twice the hobbit that he had been.

"Very odd," said Frodo, tightening his belt, "considering that there is actually a good deal less of me. I hope the thinning process will not go on indefinitely, or I shall become a wraith."

"Do not speak of such things!" said Strider quickly, and with surprising earnestness.

The hills drew nearer. They made an undulating ridge, often rising almost to a thousand feet, and here and there falling again to low clefts or passes leading into the eastern land beyond. Along the crest of the ridge the hobbits could see what looked to be the remains of green-grown walls and dikes, and in the clefts there still stood the ruins of old works of stone. By night they had reached the feet of the westward slopes, and there they camped. It was the night of the fifth of October, and they were six days out from Bree.

In the morning they found, for the first time since they had left the Chetwood, a track plain to see. They turned right and followed it southwards. It ran cunningly, taking a line that seemed chosen so as to keep as much hidden as possible from the view, both of the hill-tops above and of the flats to the west. It dived into dells, and hugged steep banks; and where it passed over flatter and more open ground on either side of it there were lines of large boulders and hewn stones that screened the travellers almost like a hedge.

"I wonder who made this path, and what for," said Merry, as they walked along one of these avenues, where the stones were unusually large and closely set. "I am not sure that I like it: it has a — well, rather a barrow-wightish look. Is there any barrow on Weathertop?"

"No. There is no barrow on Weathertop, nor on any of these hills," answered Strider. "The Men of the West did not live here; though in their latter days they defended the hills for a while against the evil that came out of Angmar. This path was made to serve the forts along the walls. But long before, in the first days of the North Kingdom, they built a great watch-tower on Weathertop, Arnon Sûl they called it. It was burned and broken, and nothing remains of it now but a tumbled ring, like a rough crown on the old hill's head. Yet once it was tall and fair. It is told that Elendil stood there watching for the coming of Gil-galad out of the West, in the days of the Last Alliance."

The hobbits gazed at Strider. It seemed that he was learned in old lore, as well as in the ways of the wild. "Who was Gil-galad?" asked Merry; but Strider did not answer, and seemed to be lost in thought. Suddenly a low voice murmured:

Gil-galad was an Elven-king.
Of him the harpers sadly sing:
the last whose realm was fair and free
between the Mountains and the Sea.

His sword was long, his lance was keen,
his shining helm afar was seen;
the countless stars of heaven's field
were mirrored in his silver shield.

But long ago he rode away,
and where he dwelleth none can say;
for into darkness fell his star
in Mordor where the shadows are.

The others turned in amazement, for the voice was Sam's. "Don't stop!" said Merry.

"That's all I know," stammered Sam, blushing. "I learned it from Mr. Bilbo when I was a lad. He used to tell me tales like that, knowing how I was always one for hearing about Elves. It was Mr. Bilbo as taught me my letters. He was mighty book-learned was dear old Mr. Bilbo. And he wrote *poetry*. He wrote what I have just said."

"He did not make it up," said Strider. "It is part of the lay that is called *The Fall of Gil-galad*, which is in an ancient tongue. Bilbo must have translated it. I never knew that."

"There was a lot more," said Sam, "all about Mordor. I didn't learn that part, it gave me the shivers. I never thought I should be going that way myself!"

"Going to Mordor!" cried Pippin. "I hope it won't come to that!"

"Do not speak that name so loudly!" said Strider.

It was already mid-day when they drew near the southern end of the path, and saw before them, in the pale clear light of the October sun, a grey-green bank, leading up like a bridge on to the northward slope of the hill. They decided to make for the top at once, while the daylight was broad. Concealment was no longer possible, and they could only hope that no enemy or spy was observing them. Nothing was to be seen moving on the hill. If Gandalf was anywhere about, there was no sign of him.

On the western flank of Weathertop they found a sheltered hollow, at the bottom of which there was a bowl-shaped dell with grassy sides. There they left Sam and Pippin with the pony and their packs and luggage. The other three went on. After half an hour's plodding climb Strider reached the crown of the hill; Frodo and Merry followed, tired and breathless. The last slope had been steep and rocky.

On the top they found, as Strider had said, a wide ring of ancient stone-work, now crumbling or covered with age-long grass. But in the centre a cairn of broken stones had been piled. They were blackened as if with fire. About them the turf was burned to the roots and all within the ring the grass was scorched and shrivelled, as if flames had swept the hill-top; but there was no sign of any living thing.

Standing upon the rim of the ruined circle, they saw all round below them a wide prospect, for the most part of lands empty and featureless, except for patches of woodland away to the south, beyond which they caught here and there the glint of distant water. Beneath them on this southern side there ran like a ribbon the Old Road, coming out of the West and winding up and down, until it faded behind a ridge of dark land to the east. Nothing was moving on it. Following its line eastward with their eyes they saw the Mountains: the nearer foothills were brown and sombre; behind them stood taller shapes of grey, and behind those again were high white peaks glimmering among the clouds.

"Well, here we are!" said Merry. "And very cheerless and uninviting it looks! There is no water and no shelter. And no sign of Gandalf. But I don't blame him for not waiting — if he ever came here."

"I wonder," said Strider, looking round thoughtfully. "Even

if he was a day or two behind us at Bree, he could have arrived here first. He can ride very swiftly when need presses." Suddenly he stooped and looked at the stone on the top of the cairn; it was flatter than the others, and whiter, as if it had escaped the fire. He picked it up and examined it, turning it in his fingers. "This has been handled recently," he said. "What do you think of these marks?"

On the flat under-side Frodo saw some scratches:WW "There seems to be a stroke, a dot, and three more strokes," he said.

"The stroke on the left might be a G-rune with thin branches," said Strider. "It might be a sign left by Gandalf, though one cannot be sure. The scratches are fine, and they certainly look fresh. But the marks might mean something quite different, and have nothing do with us. Rangers use runes, and they come here sometimes."

"What could they mean, even if Gandalf made them?" asked Merry.

"I should say," answered Strider, "that they stood for G3, and were a sign that Gandalf was here on October the third: that is three days ago now. It would also show that he was in a hurry and danger was at hand, so that he had no time or did not dare to write anything longer or plainer. If that is so, we must be wary."

"I wish we could feel sure that he made the marks, whatever they may mean," said Frodo. "It would be a great comfort to know that he was on the way, in front of us or behind us."

"Perhaps," said Strider. "For myself, I believe that he was here, and was in danger. There have been scorching flames here; and now the light that we saw three nights ago in the eastern sky comes back to my mind. I guess that he was attacked on this hill-top, but with what result I cannot tell. He is here no longer, and we must now look after ourselves and make our own way to Rivendell, as best we can."

"How far is Rivendell?" asked Merry, gazing round wearily. The world looked wild and wide from Weathertop.

"I don't know if the Road has ever been measured in miles beyond the *Forsaken Inn*, a day's journey east of Bree," answered Strider. "Some say it is so far, and some say otherwise. It is a strange road, and folk are glad to reach their journey's end, whether the time is long or short. But I know how long it would take me on my own feet, with fair weather and no ill fortune: twelve days from here to the Ford of Bruinen, where the Road crosses the Loudwater that runs out of Rivendell. We have at least a fortnight's journey before us, for I do not think we shall be able to use the Road."

"A fortnight!" said Frodo. "A lot may happen in that time."

"It may," said Strider.

They stood for a while silent on the hill-top, near its southward edge. In that lonely place Frodo for the first time fully realized his homelessness and danger. He wished bitterly that his fortune had left him in the quiet and beloved Shire. He stared down at the hateful Road, leading back westward — to his home. Suddenly he was aware that two black specks were moving slowly along it, going westward; and looking again he saw that three others were creeping eastward to meet them. He gave a cry and clutched Strider's arm.

"Look," he said, pointing downwards.

At once Strider flung himself on the ground behind the ruined circle, pulling Frodo down beside him. Merry threw himself alongside.

"What is it?" he whispered.

"I do not know, but I fear the worst," answered Strider.

Slowly they crawled up to the edge of the ring again, and peered through a cleft between two jagged stones. The light was no longer bright, for the clear morning had faded, and clouds creeping out of the East had now overtaken the sun, as it began to go down. They could all see the black specks, but neither Frodo nor Merry could make out their shapes for certain; yet something told them that there, far below, were Black Riders assembling on the Road beyond the foot of the hill.

"Yes," said Strider, whose keener sight left him in no doubt. "The enemy is here!"

Hastily they crept away and slipped down the north side of the hill to find their companions.

Sam and Peregrin had not been idle. They had explored the small dell and the surrounding slopes. Not far away they found a spring of clear water in the hillside, and near it footprints not more than a day or two old. In the dell itself they found recent traces of a fire, and other signs of a hasty camp. There were some fallen rocks on the edge of the dell nearest to the hill. Behind them Sam came upon a small store of firewood neatly stacked.

"I wonder if old Gandalf has been here," he said to Pippin. "Whoever it was put this stuff here meant to come back it seems."

Strider was greatly interested in these discoveries. "I wish I had waited and explored the ground down here myself," he said, hurrying off to the spring to examine the footprints.

"It is just as I feared," he said, when he came back. "Sam and Pippin have trampled the soft ground, and the marks are spoilt or confused. Rangers have been here lately. It is they who left the firewood behind. But there are also several newer tracks that were not made by Rangers. At least one set was made, only a day or two ago, by heavy boots. At least one. I cannot now be certain, but I think there were many booted feet." He paused and stood in anxious thought.

Each of the hobbits saw in his mind a vision of the cloaked and booted Riders. If the horsemen had already found the dell, the sooner Strider led them somewhere else the better. Sam viewed the hollow with great dislike, now that he had heard news of their enemies on the Road, only a few miles away.

"Hadn't we better clear out quick, Mr. Strider?" he asked impatiently. "It is getting late, and I don't like this hole: it makes my heart sink somehow."

"Yes, we certainly must decide what to do at once," answered Strider, looking up and considering the time and the weather. "Well, Sam," he said at last, "I do not like this place either; but I cannot think of anywhere better that we could reach before nightfall. At least we are out of sight for the moment, and if we moved we should be much more likely to be seen by spies. All we could do would be to go right out of our way back north on this side of the line of hills, where the land is all much the same as it is here. The Road is watched, but we should have to cross it, if we tried to take cover in the thickets away to the south. On the north side of the Road beyond the hills the country is bare and flat for miles."

"Can the Riders *see?*" asked Merry. "I mean, they seem usually to have used their noses rather than their eyes, smelling for us, if smelling is the right word, at least in the daylight. But you made us lie down flat when you saw them down below; and now you talk of being seen, if we move."

"I was too careless on the hill-top," answered Strider. "I was very anxious to find some sign of Gandalf; but it was a mistake for three of us to go up and stand there so long. For the black horses can see, and the Riders can use men and other creatures as spies, as we found at Bree. They themselves do not see the world of light as we do, but our shapes cast shadows in their minds, which only the noon sun destroys; and in the dark they perceive many signs and forms that are hidden from us: then they are most to be feared. And at all times they smell the blood of living things, desiring and hating it. Senses, too, there are other than sight or smell. We can feel their presence — it troubled our hearts, as soon as we came here, and before we saw them; they feel ours more keenly. Also," he added, and his voice sank to a whisper, "the Ring draws them."

"Is there no escape then?" said Frodo, looking round wildly. "If I move I shall be seen and hunted! If I stay, I shall draw them to me!"

Strider laid his hand on his shoulder. "There is still hope," he said. "You are not alone. Let us take this wood that is set ready for the fire as a sign. There is little shelter or defence here, but fire shall serve for both. Sauron can put fire to his evil uses, as he can all things, but these Riders do not love it, and fear those who wield it. Fire is our friend in the wilderness."

"Maybe," muttered Sam. "It is also as good a way of saying 'here we are' as I can think of, bar shouting."

Down in the lowest and most sheltered corner of the dell they lit a fire, and prepared a meal. The shades of evening began to fall, and it grew cold. They were suddenly aware of great hunger, for they had not eaten anything since breakfast; but they dared not make more than a frugal supper. The lands ahead were empty of all save birds and beasts, unfriendly places deserted by all the races of the world. Rangers passed at times beyond the hills, but they were few and did not stay. Other wanderers were rare, and of evil sort: trolls might stray down at times out of the northern valleys of the Misty Mountains. Only on the Road would travellers be found, most often dwarves, hurrying along on business of their own, and with no help and few words to spare for strangers.

"I don't see how our food can be made to last," said Frodo. "We have been careful enough in the last few days, and this supper is no feast; but we have used more than we ought, if we have two weeks still to go, and perhaps more."

"There is food in the wild," said Strider; "berry, root, and herb; and I have some skill as a hunter at need. You need not be afraid of starving before winter comes. But gathering and catching food is long and weary work, and we need haste. So tighten your belts, and think with hope of the tables of Elrond's house!"

The cold increased as darkness came on. Peering out from the edge of the dell they could see nothing but a grey land now vanishing quickly into shadow. The sky above had cleared again and was slowly filled with twinkling stars. Frodo and his companions huddled round the fire, wrapped in every garment and blanket they possessed; but Strider was content with a single cloak, and sat a little apart, drawing thoughtfully at his pipe.

As night fell and the light of the fire began to shine out brightly he began to tell them tales to keep their minds from fear. He knew many histories and legends of long ago, of Elves and Men and the good and evil deeds of the Elder Days. They wondered how old he was, and where he had learned all this lore.

"Tell us of Gil-galad," said Merry suddenly, when he paused at the end of a story of the Elf-Kingdoms. "Do you know any more of that old lay that you spoke of?"

"I do indeed," answered Strider. "So also does Frodo, for it concerns us closely." Merry and Pippin looked at Frodo, who was staring into the fire.

"I know only the little that Gandalf has told me," said Frodo slowly. "Gil-galad was the last of the great Elf-kings of Middle-earth. Gil-galad is *Starlight* in their tongue. With Elendil, the Elf-friend, he went to the land of ——"

"No!" said Strider interrupting, "I do not think that tale should be told now with the servants of the Enemy at hand. If we win through to the house of Elrond, you may hear it there, told in full."

"Then tell us some other tale of the old days," begged Sam; "a tale about the Elves before the fading time. I would dearly like to hear more about Elves; the dark seems to press round so close."

"I will tell you the tale of Tinúviel," said Strider, "in brief — for it is a long tale of which the end is not known; and there are none now, except Elrond, that remember it aright as it was told of old. It is a fair tale, though it is sad, as are all the tales of Middle-earth, and yet it may lift up your hearts." He was silent for some time, and then he began not to speak but to chant softly:

> *The leaves were long, the grass was green,*
> *The hemlock-umbels tall and fair,*
> *And in the glade a light was seen*
> *Of stars in shadow shimmering.*

Tinúviel was dancing there
To music of a pipe unseen,
And light of stars was in her hair,
And in her raiment glimmering.

There Beren came from mountains cold,
And lost he wandered under leaves,
And where the Elven-river rolled
He walked alone and sorrowing.
He peered between the hemlock-leaves
And saw in wonder flowers of gold
Upon her mantle and her sleeves,
And her hair like shadow following.

Enchantment healed his weary feet
That over hills were doomed to roam;
And forth he hastened, strong and fleet,
And grasped at moonbeams glistening.
Through woven woods in Elvenhome
She lightly fled on dancing feet,
And left him lonely still to roam
In the silent forest listening.

He heard there oft the flying sound
Of feet as light as linden-leaves,
Or music welling underground,
In hidden hollows quavering.
Now withered lay the hemlock-sheaves,
And one by one with sighing sound
Whispering fell the beechen leaves
In the wintry woodland wavering.

He sought her ever, wandering far
Where leaves of years were thickly strewn,
By light of moon and ray of star
In frosty heavens shivering.

231

Her mantle glinted in the moon,
  As on a hill-top high and far
She danced, and at her feet was strewn
  A mist of silver quivering.

When winter passed, she came again,
  And her song released the sudden spring,
Like rising lark, and falling rain,
  And melting water bubbling.
He saw the elven-flowers spring
  About her feet, and healed again
He longed by her to dance and sing
  Upon the grass untroubling.

Again she fled, but swift he came.
  Tinúviel! Tinúviel!
He called her by her elvish name;
  And there she halted listening.
One moment stood she, and a spell
  His voice laid on her: Beren came,
And doom fell on Tinúviel
  That in his arms lay glistening.

As Beren looked into her eyes
  Within the shadows of her hair,
The trembling starlight of the skies
  He saw there mirrored shimmering.
Tinúviel the elven-fair,
  Immortal maiden elven-wise,
About him cast her shadowy hair
  And arms like silver glimmering.

Long was the way that fate them bore,
  O'er stony mountains cold and grey,
Through halls of iron and darkling door,
  And woods of nightshade morrowless.

The Sundering Seas between them
And yet at last they met once more,
And long ago they passed away
In the forest singing sorrowless.

Strider sighed and paused before he spoke again. "That is a song," he said, "in the mode that is called *ann-thennath* among the Elves, but is hard to render in our Common Speech, and this is but a rough echo of it. It tells of the meeting of Beren son of Barahir and Lúthien Tinúviel. Beren was a mortal man, but Lúthien was the daughter of Thingol, a King of Elves upon Middle-earth when the world was young; and she was the fairest maiden that has ever been among all the children of this world. As the stars above the mists of the Northern lands was her loveliness, and in her face was a shining light. In those days the Great Enemy, of whom Sauron of Mordor was but a servant, dwelt in Angband in the North, and the Elves of the West coming back to Middle-earth made war upon him to regain the Silmarils which he had stolen; and the fathers of Men aided the Elves. But the Enemy was victorious and Barahir was slain, and Beren escaping through great peril came over the Mountains of Terror into the hidden Kingdom of Thingol in the forest of Neldoreth. There he beheld Lúthien singing and dancing in a glade beside the enchanted river Esgalduin; and he named her Tinúviel, that is Nightingale in the language of old. Many sorrows befell them afterwards, and they were parted long. Tinúviel rescued Beren from the dungeons of Sauron, and together they passed through great dangers, and cast down even the Great Enemy from his throne, and took from his iron crown one of the three Silmarils, brightest of all jewels, to be the bride-price of Lúthien to Thingol her father. Yet at the last Beren was slain by the Wolf that came from the gates of Angband, and he died in the arms of Tinúviel. But she chose mortality, and to die from the world, so that she might follow him; and it is sung that they met again beyond the Sundering Seas, and after a brief time walking alive once more in the green woods, together they passed, long ago, beyond the confines of this world. So it is that Lúthien Tinúviel alone of the Elf-kindred has died indeed and left the world, and they have lost her whom they most loved. But from her the lineage of the Elf-lords of old descended among Men. There live still those of whom Lúthien was the foremother, and it is said that her line shall never fail. Elrond of Rivendell is of that Kin. For of Beren and Lúthien was born Dior Thingol's heir; and of him Elwing the White whom Eärendil wedded, he that sailed his ship out of the mists of the world into the seas of heaven with the Silmaril upon his brow. And of Eärendil came the Kings of Númenor, that is Westernesse."

As Strider was speaking they watched his strange eager face, dimly lit in the red glow of the wood-fire. His eyes shone, and his voice was rich and deep. Above him was a black starry sky. Suddenly a pale light appeared over the crown of Weathertop behind him. The waxing moon was climbing slowly above the hill that overshadowed them, and the stars above the hill-top faded.

The story ended. The hobbits moved and stretched. "Look!" said Merry. "The Moon is rising: it must be getting late."

The others looked up. Even as they did so, they saw on the top of the hill something small and dark against the glimmer of the moonrise. It was perhaps only a large stone or jutting rock shown up by the pale light.

Sam and Merry got up and walked away from the fire. Frodo and Pippin remained seated in silence. Strider was watching the moonlight on the hill intently. All seemed quiet and still, but Frodo felt a cold dread creeping over his heart, now that Strider was no longer speaking. He huddled closer to the fire. At that moment Sam came running back from the edge of the dell.

"I don't know what it is," he said, "but I suddenly felt afraid. I durstn't go outside this dell for any money; I felt that something was creeping up the slope."

"Did you *see* anything?" asked Frodo, springing to his feet.

"No, sir. I saw nothing, but I didn't stop to look."

"I saw something," said Merry; "or I thought I did — away westwards where the moonlight was falling on the flats beyond the shadow of the hill-tops, I *thought* there were two or three black shapes. They seemed to be moving this way."

"Keep close to the fire, with your faces outward!" cried Strider. "Get some of the longer sticks ready in your hands!"

For a breathless time they sat there, silent and alert, with their backs turned to the wood-fire, each gazing into the shadows that encircled them. Nothing happened. There was no sound or movement in the night. Frodo stirred, feeling that he must break the silence: he longed to shout out aloud.

"Hush!" whispered Strider. "What's that?" gasped Pippin at the same moment.

Over the lip of the little dell, on the side away from the hill, they felt, rather than saw, a shadow rise, one shadow or more than one. They strained their eyes, and the shadows seemed to grow. Soon there could be no doubt: three or four tall black figures were standing there on the slope, looking down on them. So black were they that they seemed like black holes in the deep shade behind them. Frodo thought that he heard a faint hiss as of venomous breath and felt a thin piercing chill. Then the shapes slowly advanced.

Terror overcame Pippin and Merry, and they threw themselves flat on the ground. Sam shrank to Frodo's side. Frodo was hardly less terrified than his companions; he was quaking as if he was bitter cold, but his terror was swallowed up in a sudden temptation to put on the Ring. The desire to do this laid hold of him, and he could think of nothing else. He did not forget the Barrow, nor the message of Gandalf; but something seemed to be compelling him to disregard all warnings, and he longed to yield. Not with the hope of escape, or of doing anything, either good or bad: he simply felt that he must take the Ring and put it on his finger. He could not speak. He felt Sam looking at him, as if he knew that his master was in some great trouble, but he could not turn towards him. He shut his eyes and struggled for a while; but resistance became unbearable, and at last he slowly drew out the chain, and slipped the Ring on the forefinger of his left hand.

Immediately, though everything else remained as before, dim and dark, the shapes became terribly clear. He was able to see beneath their black wrappings. There were five tall figures: two standing on the lip of the dell, three advancing. In their white faces burned keen and merciless eyes; under their mantles were long grey robes; upon their grey hairs were helms of silver; in their haggard hands were swords of steel. Their eyes fell on him and pierced him, as they rushed towards him. Desperate, he drew his own sword, and it seemed to him that it flickered red, as if it was a firebrand. Two of the figures halted. The third was taller than the others: his hair was long and gleaming and on his helm was a crown. In one hand he held a long sword, and in the other a knife; both the knife and the hand that held it glowed with a pale light. He sprang forward and bore down on Frodo.

At that moment Frodo threw himself forward on the ground, and he heard himself crying aloud: *O Elbereth! Gilthoniel!* At the same time he struck at the feet of his enemy. A shrill cry rang out in the night; and he felt a pain like a dart of poisoned ice pierce his left shoulder. Even as he swooned he caught, as through a swirling mist, a glimpse of Strider leaping out of the darkness with a flaming brand of wood in either hand. With a last effort Frodo, dropping his sword, slipped the Ring from his finger and closed his right hand tight upon it.

CHAPTER
TWELVE

Flight to the Ford

When Frodo came to himself he was still clutching the Ring desperately. He was lying by the fire, which was now piled high and burning brightly. His three companions were bending over him.

"What has happened? Where is the pale king?" he asked wildly.

They were too overjoyed to hear him speak to answer for a while; nor did they understand his question. At length he gathered from Sam that they had seen nothing but the vague shadowy shapes coming towards them. Suddenly to his horror Sam found that his master had vanished; and at that moment a black shadow rushed past him, and he fell. He heard Frodo's voice, but it seemed to come from a great distance, or from under the earth, crying out strange words. They saw nothing more, until they stumbled over the body of Frodo, lying as if dead, face downwards on the grass with his sword beneath him. Strider ordered them to pick him up and lay him near the fire, and then he disappeared. That was now a good while ago.

Sam plainly was beginning to have doubts again about Strider; but while they were talking he returned, appearing suddenly out of the shadows. They started, and Sam drew his sword and stood over Frodo; but Strider knelt down swiftly at his side.

"I am not a Black Rider, Sam," he said gently, "nor in league with them. I have been trying to discover something of their movements; but I have found nothing. I cannot think why they have gone and do not attack again. But there is no feeling of their presence anywhere at hand."

When he heard what Frodo had to tell, he became full of concern, and shook his head and sighed. Then he ordered Pippin and Merry to heat as much water as they could in their small kettles, and to bathe the wound with it. "Keep the fire going well, and keep Frodo warm!" he said. Then he got up and walked away, and called Sam to him. "I think I understand things better now," he said in a low voice. "There seem only to have been five of the enemy. Why they were not all here, I don't know; but I don't think they expected to be resisted. They have drawn off for the time being. But not far, I fear. They will come again another night, if we cannot escape. They are only waiting, because they think that their purpose is almost accomplished, and that the Ring cannot fly much further. I fear, Sam, that they believe your master has a deadly wound that will subdue him to their will. We shall see!"

Sam choked with tears. "Don't despair!" said Strider. "You must trust me now. Your Frodo is made of sterner stuff than I had guessed, though Gandalf hinted that it might prove so. He is not slain, and I think he will resist the evil power of the wound longer than his enemies expect. I will do all I can to help and heal him. Guard him well, while I am away!" He hurried off and disappeared again into the darkness.

Frodo dozed, though the pain of his wound was slowly growing, and a deadly chill was spreading from his shoulder to his arm and side. His friends watched over him, warming him, and bathing his wound. The night passed slowly and wearily. Dawn was growing in the sky, and the dell was filling with grey light, when Strider at last returned.

"Look!" he cried; and stooping he lifted from the ground a black cloak that had lain there hidden by the darkness. A foot above the lower hem there was a slash. "This was the stroke of Frodo's sword," he said. "The only hurt that it did to his enemy, I fear; for it is unharmed but all blades perish that pierce that dreadful King. More deadly to him was the name of Elbereth."

"And more deadly to Frodo was this!" He stooped again and lifted up a long thin knife. There was a cold gleam in it. As Strider raised it they saw that near the end its edge was notched and the point was broken off. But even as he held it up in the growing light, they gazed in astonishment, for the blade seemed to melt, and vanished like a smoke in the air, leaving only the hilt in Strider's hand. "Alas!" he cried. "It was this accursed knife that gave the wound. Few now have the skill in healing to match such evil weapons. But I will do what I can."

He sat down on the ground, and taking the dagger-hilt laid it on his knees, and he sang over it a slow song in a strange tongue. Then setting it aside, he turned to Frodo and in a soft tone spoke words the others could not catch. From the pouch at his belt he drew out the long leaves of a plant.

"These leaves," he said, "I have walked far to find; for this plant does not grow in the bare hills; but in the thickets away south of the Road I found it in the dark by the scent of its leaves." He crushed a leaf in his fingers, and it gave out a sweet and pungent fragrance. "It is fortunate that I could find it, for it is a healing plant that the Men of the West brought to Middle-earth. *Athelas* they named it, and it grows now sparsely and only near places where they dwelt or camped of old; and it is not known in the North, except to some of those who wander in the Wild. It has great virtues, but over such a wound as this its healing powers may be small."

He threw the leaves into boiling water and bathed Frodo's shoulder. The fragrance of the steam was refreshing, and those that were unhurt felt their minds calmed and cleared. The herb had also some power over the wound, for Frodo felt the pain and also the sense of frozen cold lessen in his side; but the life did not return to his arm, and he could not raise or use his hand. He bitterly regretted his foolishness, and reproached himself for weakness of will; for he now perceived that in putting on the Ring he obeyed not his own desire but the commanding wish of his enemies. He wondered if he would remain maimed for life, and how they would now manage to continue their journey. He felt too weak to stand.

The others were discussing this very question. They quickly decided to leave Weathertop as soon as possible. "I think now," said Strider, "that the enemy has been watching this place for some days. If Gandalf ever came here, then he must have been forced to ride away, and he will not return. In any case we are in great peril here after dark, since the attack of last night, and we can hardly meet greater danger wherever we go."

As soon as the daylight was full, they had some hurried food and packed. It was impossible for Frodo to walk, so they divided the greater part of their baggage among the four of them, and put Frodo on the pony. In the last few days the poor beast had improved wonderfully; it already seemed fatter and stronger, and had begun to show an affection for its new masters, especially for Sam. Bill Ferny's treatment must have been very hard for the journey in the wild to seem so much better than its former life.

They started off in a southerly direction. This would mean crossing the Road, but it was the quickest way to more wooded country. And they needed fuel; for Strider said that Frodo must be kept warm, especially at night, while fire would be some protection for them all. It was also his plan to shorten their journey by cutting across another great loop of the Road: east beyond Weathertop it changed its course and took a wide bend northwards.

They made their way slowly and cautiously round the south-western slopes of the hill, and came in a little while to the edge of the Road. There was no sign of the Riders. But even as they were hurrying across they heard far away two cries: a cold voice calling and a cold voice answering. Trembling they sprang forward, and made for the thickets that lay ahead. The land before them sloped away southwards, but it was wild and pathless; bushes and stunted trees grew in dense patches with wide barren spaces in between. The grass was scanty, coarse, and grey; and the leaves in the thickets were faded and falling. It was a cheerless land, and their journey was slow and gloomy. They spoke little as they trudged along. Frodo's heart was grieved as he watched them walking beside him with their heads down, and their backs bowed under their burdens. Even Strider seemed tired and heavy-hearted.

Before the first day's march was over Frodo's pain began to grow again, but he did not speak of it for a long time. Four days passed, without the ground or the scene changing much, except that behind them Weathertop slowly sank, and before them the distant mountains loomed a little nearer. Yet since that far cry they had seen and heard no sign that the enemy had marked their flight or followed them. They dreaded the dark hours, and kept watch in pairs by night, expecting at any time to see black shapes stalking in the grey night, dimly lit by the cloud-veiled moon; but they saw nothing, and heard no sound but the sigh of withered leaves and grass. Not once did they feel the sense of present evil that had assailed them before the attack in the dell. It seemed too much to hope that the Riders had already lost their trail again. Perhaps they were waiting to make some ambush in a narrow place?

At the end of the fifth day the ground began once more to rise slowly out of the wide shallow valley into which they had descended. Strider now turned their course again north-eastwards, and on the sixth day they reached the top of a long slow-climbing slope, and saw far ahead a huddle of wooded hills. Away below them they could see the Road sweeping round the feet of the hills; and to their right a grey river gleamed pale in the thin sunshine. In the distance they glimpsed yet another river in a stony valley half-veiled in mist.

"I am afraid we must go back to the Road here for a while,"

said Strider. "We have now come to the River Hoarwell, that the Elves call Mitheithel. It flows down out of the Ettenmoors, the troll-fells north of Rivendell, and joins the Loudwater away in the South. Some call it the Greyflood after that. It is a great water before it finds the Sea. There is no way over it below its sources in the Ettenmoors, except by the Last Bridge on which the Road crosses."

"What is that other river we can see far away there?" asked Merry.

"That is Loudwater, the Bruinen of Rivendell," answered Strider. "The Road runs along the edge of the hills for many miles from the Bridge to the Ford of Bruinen. But I have not yet thought how we shall cross that water. One river at a time! We shall be fortunate indeed if we do not find the Last Bridge held against us."

Next day, early in the morning, they came down again to the borders of the Road. Sam and Strider went forward, but they found no sign of any travellers or riders. Here under the shadow of the hills there had been some rain. Strider judged that it had fallen two days before, and had washed away all footprints. No horseman had passed since then, as far as he could see.

They hurried along with all the speed they could make, and after a mile or two they saw the Last Bridge ahead, at the bottom of a short steep slope. They dreaded to see black figures waiting there, but they saw none. Strider made them take cover in a thicket at the side of the Road, while he went forward to explore.

Before long he came hurrying back. "I can see no sign of the enemy," he said, "and I wonder very much what that means. But I have found something very strange."

He held out his hand, and showed a single pale-green jewel. "I found it in the mud in the middle of the Bridge," he said. "It is a beryl, an elf-stone. Whether it was set there, or let fall by chance, I cannot say; but it brings hope to me. I will take it as a sign that we may pass the Bridge; but beyond that I dare not keep to the Road, without some clearer token."

At once they went on again. They crossed the Bridge in safety, hearing no sound but the water swirling against its three great arches. A mile further on they came to a narrow ravine that led away northwards through the steep lands on the left of the Road. Here Strider turned aside, and soon they were lost in a sombre country of dark trees winding among the feet of sullen hills.

The hobbits were glad to leave the cheerless lands and the perilous Road behind them; but this new country seemed threatening and unfriendly. As they went forward the hills about them steadily rose. Here and there upon heights and ridges they caught glimpses of ancient walls of stone, and the ruins of towers: they had an ominous look. Frodo, who was not walking, had time to gaze ahead and to think. He recalled Bilbo's account of his journey and the threatening towers on the hills north of the Road, in the country near the Troll's wood where his first serious adventure had happened. Frodo guessed that they were now in the same region, and wondered if by chance they would pass near the spot.

"Who lives in this land?" he asked. "And who built these towers? Is this troll-country?"

"No!" said Strider. "Trolls do not build. No one lives in this land. Men once dwelt here, ages ago; but none remain now. They became an evil people, as legends tell, for they fell under the shadow of Angmar. But all were destroyed in the war that brought the North Kingdom to its end. But that is now so long ago that the hills have forgotten them, though a shadow still lies on the land."

"Where did you learn such tales, if all the land is empty and forgetful?" asked Peregrin. "The birds and beasts do not tell tales of that sort."

"The heirs of Elendil do not forget all things past," said Strider; "and many more things than I can tell are remembered in Rivendell."

"Have you often been to Rivendell?" said Frodo.

"I have," said Strider. "I dwelt there once, and still I return when I may. There my heart is; but it is not my fate to sit in peace, even in the fair house of Elrond."

The hills now began to shut them in. The Road behind held on its way to the River Bruinen, but both were now hidden from view. The travellers came into a long valley; narrow, deeply cloven, dark and silent. Trees with old and twisted roots hung over cliffs, and piled up behind into mounting slopes of pine-wood.

The hobbits grew very weary. They advanced slowly, for they had to pick their way through a pathless country, encumbered by fallen trees and tumbled rocks. As long as they could they avoided climbing for Frodo's sake, and because it was in fact difficult to find any way up out of the narrow dales. They had been two days in this country when the weather turned wet. The wind began to blow steadily out of the West and pour the water of the distant seas on the dark heads of the hills in fine drenching rain. By nightfall they were all soaked, and their camp was cheerless, for they could not get any fire to burn. The next day the hills rose still higher and steeper before them, and they were forced to turn away northwards out of their course. Strider seemed to be getting anxious: they were nearly ten days out from Weathertop, and their stock of provisions was beginning to run low. It went on raining.

That night they camped on a stony shelf with a rock-wall behind them, in which there was a shallow cave, a mere scoop in the cliff. Frodo was restless. The cold and wet had made his wound more painful than ever, and the ache and sense of deadly chill took away all sleep. He lay tossing and turning and listening fearfully to the stealthy night-noises: wind in chinks of rock, water dripping, a crack, the sudden rattling fall of a loosened stone. He felt that black shapes were advancing to smother him; but when he sat up he saw nothing but the back of Strider sitting hunched up, smoking his pipe, and watching.

He lay down again and passed into an uneasy dream, in which he walked on the grass in his garden in the Shire, but it seemed faint and dim, less clear than the tall black shadows that stood looking over the hedge.

In the morning he woke to find that the rain had stopped. The clouds were still thick, but they were breaking, and pale strips of blue appeared between them. The wind was shifting again. They did not start early. Immediately after their cold and comfortless breakfast Strider went off alone, telling the others to remain under the shelter of the cliff, until he came back. He was going to climb up, if he could, and get a look at the lie of the land.

When he returned he was not reassuring. "We have come too far to the north," he said, "and we must find some way to turn back southwards again. If we keep on as we are going we shall get up into the Ettendales far north of Rivendell. That is troll-country, and little known to me. We could perhaps find our way through and come round to Rivendell from the north; but it would take too long, for I do not know the way, and our food would not last. So somehow or other we must find the Ford of Bruinen."

The rest of that day they spent scrambling over rocky ground. They found a passage between two hills that led them into a valley running south-east, the direction that they wished to take; but towards the end of the day they found their road again barred by a ridge of high land; its dark edge against the sky was broken into many bare points like teeth of a blunted saw. They had a choice between going back or climbing over it.

They decided to attempt the climb, but it proved very difficult. Before long Frodo was obliged to dismount and struggle along on foot. Even so they often despaired of getting their pony up, or indeed of finding a path for themselves, burdened as they were. The light was nearly gone, and they were all exhausted, when at last they reached the top. They had climbed on to a narrow saddle between two higher points, and the land fell steeply away again, only a short distance ahead. Frodo threw himself down, and lay on the ground shivering. His left arm was lifeless, and his side and shoulder felt as if icy claws were laid upon them. The trees and rocks about him seemed shadowy and dim.

"We cannot go any further," said Merry to Strider. "I am afraid this has been too much for Frodo. I am dreadfully anxious about him. What are we to do? Do you think they will be able to cure him in Rivendell, if we ever get there?"

"We shall see," answered Strider. "There is nothing more that I can do in the wilderness; and it is chiefly because of his wound that I am so anxious to press on. But I agree that we can go no further tonight."

"What is the matter with my master?" asked Sam in a low voice, looking appealingly at Strider. "His wound was small, and it is already closed. There's nothing to be seen but a cold white mark on his shoulder."

"Frodo has been touched by the weapons of the Enemy," said Strider, "and there is some poison or evil at work that is beyond my skill to drive out. But do not give up hope, Sam!"

Night was cold up on the high ridge. They lit a small fire down under the gnarled roots of an old pine, that hung over a shallow pit: it looked as if stone had once been quarried there. They sat huddled together. The wind blew chill through the pass, and they heard the tree-tops lower down moaning and sighing. Frodo lay half in a dream, imagining that endless dark wings were sweeping by above him, and that on the wings rode pursuers that sought him in all the hollows of the hills.

The morning dawned bright and fair; the air was clean, and the light pale and clear in a rain-washed sky. Their hearts were encouraged, but they longed for the sun to warm their cold stiff limbs. As soon as it was light, Strider took Merry with him and went to survey the country from the height to the east of the pass. The sun had risen and was shining brightly when he returned with more comforting news. They were now going more or less in the right direction. If they went on, down the further side of the ridge, they would have the Mountains on their left. Some way ahead Strider had caught a glimpse of the Loudwater again, and he knew that, though it was hidden from view, the Road to the Ford was not far from the River and lay on the side nearest to them.

"We must make for the Road again," he said. "We cannot hope to find a path through these hills. Whatever danger may beset it, the Road is our only way to the Ford."

As soon as they had eaten they set out again. They climbed slowly down the southern side of the ridge; but the way was much easier than they had expected, for the slope was far less steep on this side, and before long Frodo was able to ride again. Bill Ferny's poor old pony was developing an unexpected talent for picking out a path, and for sparing its rider as many jolts as possible. The spirits of the party rose again. Even Frodo felt better in the morning light, but every now and again a mist seemed to obscure his sight, and he passed his hands over his eyes.

Pippin was a little ahead of the others. Suddenly he turned round and called to them. "There is a path here!" he cried.

When they came up with him, they saw that he had made no mistake: there were clearly the beginnings of a path, that climbed with many windings out of the woods below and faded away on the hill-top behind. In places it was now faint and overgrown, or choked with fallen stones and trees; but at one time it seemed to have been much used. It was a path made by strong arms and heavy feet. Here and there old trees had been cut or broken down, and large rocks cloven or heaved aside to make a way.

They followed the track for some while, for it offered much the easiest way down, but they went cautiously, and their anxiety increased as they came into the dark woods, and the path grew plainer and broader. Suddenly coming out of a belt of fir-trees it ran steeply down a slope, and turned sharply to the left round the corner of a rocky shoulder of the hill. When they came to the corner they looked round and saw that the path ran on over a level strip under the face of a low cliff overhung with trees. In the stony wall there was a door hanging crookedly ajar upon one great hinge.

Outside the door they all halted. There was a cave or rock-chamber behind, but in the gloom inside nothing could be seen. Strider, Sam, and Merry pushing with all their strength managed to open the door a little wider, and then Strider and Merry went in. They did not go far, for on the floor lay many old bones, and nothing else was to be seen near the entrance except some great empty jars and broken pots.

"Surely this is a troll-hole, if ever there was one!" said Pippin. "Come out, you two, and let us get away. Now we know who made the path — and we had better get off it quick."

"There is no need, I think," said Strider, coming out. "It is certainly a troll-hole, but it seems to have been long forsaken. I don't think we need be afraid. But let us go on down warily, and we shall see."

The path went on again from the door, and turning to the right again across the level space plunged down a thick wooded slope. Pippin, not liking to show Strider that he was still afraid, went on ahead with Merry. Sam and Strider came behind, one on each side of Frodo's pony, for the path was now broad enough for four or five hobbits to walk abreast. But they had not gone very far before Pippin came running back, followed by Merry. They both looked terrified.

"There *are* trolls!" Pippin panted. "Down in a clearing in the woods not far below. We got a sight of them through the tree-trunks. They are very large!"

"We will come and look at them," said Strider, picking up a stick. Frodo said nothing, but Sam looked scared.

The sun was now high, and it shone down through the half-stripped branches of the trees, and lit the clearing with bright patches of light. They halted suddenly on the edge, and peered through the tree-trunks, holding their breath. There stood the trolls: three large trolls. One was stooping, and the other two stood staring at him.

Strider walked forward unconcernedly. "Get up, old stone!" he said, and broke his stick upon the stooping troll.

Nothing happened. There was a gasp of astonishment from the hobbits, and then even Frodo laughed. "Well!" he said. "We are forgetting our family history! These must be the very three that were caught by Gandalf, quarrelling over the right way to cook thirteen dwarves and one hobbit."

"I had no idea we were anywhere near the place!" said Pippin. He knew the story well. Bilbo and Frodo had told it often; but as a matter of fact he had never more than half believed it. Even now he looked at the stone trolls with suspicion, wondering if some magic might not suddenly bring them to life again.

"You are forgetting not only your family history, but all you ever knew about trolls," said Strider. "It is broad daylight with a bright sun, and yet you come back trying to scare me with a tale of live trolls waiting for us in this glade! In any case you might have noticed that one of them has an old bird's nest behind his ear. That would be a most unusual ornament for a live troll!"

They all laughed. Frodo felt his spirits reviving: the reminder of Bilbo's first successful adventure was heartening. The sun, too, was warm and comforting, and the mist before his eyes seemed to be lifting a little. They rested for some time in the glade, and took their mid-day meal right under the shadow of the trolls' large legs.

"Won't somebody give us a bit of a song, while the sun is high?" said Merry, when they had finished. "We haven't had a song or a tale for days."

"Not since Weathertop," said Frodo. The others looked at him. "Don't worry about me!" he added. "I feel much better, but I don't think I could sing. Perhaps Sam could dig something out of his memory."

"Come on, Sam!" said Merry. "There's more stored in your head than you let on about."

"I don't know about that," said Sam. "But how would this suit? It ain't what I call proper poetry, if you understand me: just a bit of nonsense. But these old images here brought it to my mind." Standing up, with his hands behind his back, as if he was at school, he began to sing to an old tune.

> *Troll sat alone on his seat of stone,*
> *And munched and mumbled a bare old bone;*
> *For many a year he had gnawed it near,*
> *For meat was hard to come by.*
> *Done by! Gum by!*
> *In a cave in the hills he dwelt alone,*
> *And meat was hard to come by.*
>
> *Up came Tom with his big boots on.*
> *Said he to Troll: "Pray, what is yon?*
> *For it looks like the shin o' my nuncle Tim,*
> *As should be a-lyin' in graveyard.*
> *Caveyard! Paveyard!*
> *This many a year has Tim been gone,*
> *And I thought he were lyin' in graveyard."*
>
> *"My lad," said Troll, "this bone I stole.*
> *But what be bones that lie in a hole?*
> *Thy nuncle was dead as a lump o' lead,*
> *Afore I found his shinbone.*
> *Tinbone! Thinbone!*
> *He can spare a share for a poor old troll,*
> *For he don't need his shinbone."*
>
> *Said Tom: "I don't see why the likes o' thee*
> *Without axin' leave should go makin' free*
> *With the shank or the shin o' my father's kin;*

So hand the old bone over!
  Rover! Trover!
Though dead he be, it belongs to he;
  So hand the old bone over!"

"For a couple o' pins," says Troll, and grins,
"I'll eat thee too, and gnaw thy shins.
  A bit o' fresh meat will go down sweet!
    I'll try my teeth on thee now.
      Hee now! See now!
  I'm tired o' gnawing old bones and skins,
    I've a mind to dine on thee now."

But just as he thought his dinner was caught,
He found his hands had hold of naught.
  Before he could mind, Tom slipped behind
    And gave him the boot to larn him.
      Warn him! Darn him!
  A bump o' the boot on the seat, Tom thought,
    Would be the way to larn him.

But harder than stone is the flesh and bone
Of a troll that sits in the hills alone.
  As well set your boot to the mountain's root,
    For the seat of a troll don't feel it.
      Peel it! Heal it!
  Old Troll laughed, when he heard Tom groan,
    And he knew his toes could feel it.

Tom's leg is game, since home he came,
And his bootless foot is lasting lame;
  But Troll don't care, and he's still there
    With the bone he boned from its owner.
      Doner! Boner!
  Troll's old seat is still the same,
    And the bone he boned from its owner!

"Well, that's a warning to us all!" laughed Merry. "It is as well you used a stick, and not your hand, Strider!"

"Where did you come by that, Sam?" asked Pippin. "I've never heard those words before."

Sam muttered something inaudible. "It's out of his own head, of course," said Frodo. "I am learning a lot about Sam Gamgee on this journey. First he was a conspirator, now he's a jester. He'll end up by becoming a wizard — or a warrior!"

"I hope not," said Sam. "I don't want to be neither!"

In the afternooon they went on down the woods. They were probably following the very track that Gandalf, Bilbo, and the dwarves had used many years before. After a few miles they came out on the top of a high bank above the Road. At this point the Road had left the Hoarwell far behind in its narrow valley, and now clung close to the feet of the hills, rolling and winding eastward among woods and heather-covered slopes towards the Ford and the Mountains. Not far down the bank Strider pointed out a stone in the grass. On it roughly cut and now much weathered could still be seen dwarf-runes and secret marks.

"There!" said Merry. "That must be the stone that marked the place where the trolls' gold was hidden. How much is left of Bilbo's share, I wonder, Frodo?"

Frodo looked at the stone, and wished that Bilbo had brought home no treasure more perilous, nor less easy to part with. "None at all," he said. "Bilbo gave it all away. He told me he did not feel it was really his, as it came from robbers."

The Road lay quiet under the long shadows of early evening. There was no sign of any other travellers to be seen. As there was now no other possible course for them to take, they climbed down the bank, and turning left went off as fast as they could. Soon a shoulder of the hills cut off the light of the fast westering sun. A cold wind flowed down to meet them from the mountains ahead.

They were beginning to look out for a place off the Road, where they could camp for the night, when they heard a sound that brought sudden fear back into their hearts: the noise of hoofs behind them. They looked back, but they could not see far because of the many windings and rollings of the Road. As quickly as they could they scrambled off the beaten way and up into the deep heather and bilberry brushwood on the slopes above, until they came to a small patch of thick-growing hazels. As they peered out from among the bushes, they could see the Road, faint and grey in the failing light, some thirty feet below them. The sound of hoofs drew nearer. They were going fast, with a light *clippety-clippety-clip*. Then faintly, as if it was blown away from them by the breeze, they seemed to catch a dim ringing, as of small bells tinkling.

"That does not sound like a Black Rider's horse!" said Frodo, listening intently. The other hobbits agreed hopefully that it did not, but they all remained full of suspicion. They had been in fear of pursuit for so long that any sound from behind seemed ominous and unfriendly. But Strider was now leaning forward, stooped to the ground, with a hand to his ear, and a look of joy on his face.

The light faded, and the leaves on the bushes rustled softly. Clearer and nearer now the bells jingled, and *clippety-clip* came the quick trotting feet. Suddenly into view below came a white horse, gleaming in the shadows, running swiftly. In the dusk its headstall flickered and flashed, as if it were studded with gems like living stars. The rider's cloak streamed behind him, and his hood was thrown back; his golden hair flowed shimmering in the wind of his speed. To Frodo it appeared that a white light was shining through the form and raiment of the rider, as if through a thin veil.

Strider sprang from hiding and dashed down towards the Road, leaping with a cry through the heather; but even before he had moved or called, the rider had reined in his horse and halted, looking up towards the thicket where they stood. When he saw Strider, he dismounted and ran to meet him calling out:

Ai na vedui Dúnadan! Mae govannen! His speech and clear ringing voice left no doubt in their hearts: the rider was of the Elven-folk. No others that dwelt in the wide world had voices so fair to hear. But there seemed to be a note of haste or fear in his call, and they saw that he was now speaking quickly and urgently to Strider.

Soon Strider beckoned to them, and the hobbits left the bushes and hurried down to the Road. "This is Glorfindel, who dwells in the house of Elrond," said Strider.

"Hail, and well met at last!" said the Elf-lord to Frodo. "I was sent from Rivendell to look for you. We feared that you were in danger upon the road."

"Then Gandalf has reached Rivendell?" cried Frodo joyfully.

"No. He had not when I departed; but that was nine days ago," answered Glorfindel. "Elrond received news that troubled him. Some of my kindred, journeying in your land beyond the Baranduin,* learned that things were amiss, and sent messages as swiftly as they could. They said that the Nine were abroad, and that you were astray bearing a great burden without guidance, for Gandalf had not returned. There are few even in Rivendell that can ride openly against the Nine; but such as there were, Elrond sent out north, west, and south. It was thought that you might turn far aside to avoid pursuit, and become lost in the Wilderness.

"It was my lot to take the Road, and I came to the Bridge of Mitheithel, and left a token there, nigh on seven days ago. Three of the servants of Sauron were upon the Bridge, but they withdrew and I pursued them westward. I came also upon two others, but they turned away southward. Since then I have searched for your trail. Two days ago I found it, and followed it over the Bridge; and today I marked where you descended from the hills again. But come! There is no time for further news. Since you are here we must risk the peril of the Road and go.

* The Brandywine River.

There are five behind us, and when they find your trail upon the Road they will ride after us like the wind. And they are not all. Where the other four may be, I do not know. I fear that we may find the Ford is already held against us."

While Glorfindel was speaking the shades of evening deepened. Frodo felt a great weariness come over him. Ever since the sun began to sink the mist before his eyes had darkened, and he felt that a shadow was coming between him and the faces of his friends. Now pain assailed him, and he felt cold. He swayed, clutching at Sam's arm.

"My master is sick and wounded," said Sam angrily. "He can't go on riding after nightfall. He needs rest."

Glorfindel caught Frodo as he sank to the ground, and taking him gently in his arms he looked in his face with grave anxiety.

Briefly Strider told of the attack on their camp under Weathertop, and of the deadly knife. He drew out the hilt, which he had kept, and handed it to the Elf. Glorfindel shuddered as he took it, but he looked intently at it.

"There are evil things written on this hilt," he said; 'though maybe your eyes cannot see them. Keep it, Aragorn, till we reach the house of Elrond! But be wary, and handle it as little as you may! Alas! the wounds of this weapon are beyond my skill to heal. I will do what I can — but all the more do I urge you now to go on without rest."

He searched the wound on Frodo's shoulder with his fingers, and his face grew graver, as if what he learned disquieted him. But Frodo felt the chill lessen in his side and arm; a little warmth crept down from his shoulder to his hand, and the pain grew easier. The dusk of evening seemed to grow lighter about him, as if a cloud had been withdrawn. He saw his friends' faces more clearly again, and a measure of new hope and strength returned.

"You shall ride my horse," said Glorfindel. "I will shorten the stirrups up to the saddle-skirts, and you must sit as tight as you can. But you need not fear: my horse will not let any rider fall that I command him to bear. His pace is light and smooth;

and if danger presses too near, he will bear you away with a speed that even the black steeds of the enemy cannot rival."

"No, he will not!" said Frodo. "I shall not ride him, if I am to be carried off to Rivendell or anywhere else, leaving my friends behind in danger."

Glorfindel smiled. "I doubt very much," he said, "if your friends would be in danger if you were not with them! The pursuit would follow you and leave us in peace, I think. It is you, Frodo, and that which you bear that brings us all in peril."

To that Frodo had no answer, and he was persuaded to mount Glorfindel's white horse. The pony was laden instead with a great part of the others' burdens, so that they now marched lighter, and for a time made good speed; but the hobbits began to find it hard to keep up with the swift tireless feet of the Elf. On he led them, into the mouth of darkness, and still on under the deep clouded night. There was neither star nor moon. Not until the grey of dawn did he allow them to halt. Pippin, Merry, and Sam were by that time nearly asleep on their stumbling legs; and even Strider seemed by the sag of his shoulders to be weary. Frodo sat upon the horse in a dark dream.

They cast themselves down in the heather a few yards from the road-side, and fell asleep immediately. They seemed hardly to have closed their eyes when Glorfindel, who had set himself to watch while they slept, awoke them again. The sun had now climbed far into the morning, and the clouds and mists of the night were gone.

"Drink this!" said Glorfindel to them, pouring for each in turn a little liquor from his silver-studded flask of leather. It was clear as spring water and had no taste, and it did not feel either cool or warm in the mouth; but strength and vigour seemed to flow into all their limbs as they drank it. Eaten after that draught the stale bread and dried fruit (which was now all that they had left) seemed to satisfy their hunger better than many a good breakfast in the Shire had done.

They had rested rather less than five hours when they took to the Road again. Glorfindel still urged them on, and only allowed two brief halts during the day's march. In this way they covered almost twenty miles before nightfall, and came to a point where the Road bent right and ran down towards the bottom of the valley, now making straight for the Bruinen. So far there had been no sign or sound of pursuit that the hobbits could see or hear; but often Glorfindel would halt and listen for a moment, if they lagged behind, and a look of anxiety clouded his face. Once or twice he spoke to Strider in the elf-tongue.

But however anxious their guides might be, it was plain that the hobbits could go no further that night. They were stumbling along dizzy with weariness, and unable to think of anything but their feet and legs. Frodo's pain had redoubled, and during the day things about him faded to shadows of ghostly grey. He almost welcomed the coming of night, for then the world seemed less pale and empty.

The hobbits were still weary, when they set out again early next morning. There were many miles yet to go between them and the Ford, and they hobbled forward at the best pace they could manage.

"Our peril will be greatest just ere we reach the river," said Glorfindel; "for my heart warns me that the pursuit is now swift behind us, and other danger may be waiting by the Ford."

The Road was still running steadily downhill, and there was now in places much grass at either side, in which the hobbits walked when they could, to ease their tired feet. In the late afternoon they came to a place where the Road went suddenly under the dark shadow of tall pine-trees, and then plunged into a deep cutting with steep moist walls of red stone. Echoes ran along as they hurried forward; and there seemed to be a sound of many footfalls following their own. All at once, as if through a gate of light, the Road ran out again from the end of the tunnel into the open. There at the bottom of a sharp incline they saw before them a long flat mile, and beyond that the Ford of Rivendell. On the further side was a steep brown bank, threaded by a winding path; and behind that the tall mountains climbed, shoulder above shoulder, and peak beyond peak, into the fading sky.

There was still an echo as of following feet in the cutting behind them; a rushing noise as if a wind were rising and pouring through the branches of the pines. One moment Glorfindel turned and listened, then he sprang forward with a loud cry.

"Fly!" he called. "Fly! The enemy is upon us!"

The white horse leaped forward. The hobbits ran down the slope. Glorfindel and Strider followed as rear-guard. They were only half way across the flat, when suddenly there was a noise of horses galloping. Out of the gate in the trees that they had just left rode a Black Rider. He reined his horse in, and halted, swaying in his saddle. Another followed him, and then another; then again two more.

"Ride forward! Ride!" cried Glorfindel to Frodo.

He did not obey at once, for a strange reluctance seized him. Checking the horse to a walk, he turned and looked back. The Riders seemed to sit upon their great steeds like threatening statues upon a hill, dark and solid, while all the woods and land about them receded as if into a mist. Suddenly he knew in his heart that they were silently commanding him to wait. Then at once fear and hatred awoke in him. His hand left the bridle and gripped the hilt of his sword, and with a red flash he drew it.

"Ride on! Ride on!" cried Glorfindel, and then loud and clear he called to the horse in the elf-tongue: *noro lim, noro lim, Asfaloth!*

At once the white horse sprang away and sped like the wind along the last lap of the Road. At the same moment the black horses leaped down the hill in pursuit, and from the Riders came a terrible cry, such as Frodo had heard filling the woods with horror in the Eastfarthing far away. It was answered; and to the dismay of Frodo and his friends out from the trees and rocks away on the left four other Riders came flying. Two rode towards Frodo: two galloped madly towards the Ford to cut off his escape. They seemed to him to run like the wind and to grow swiftly larger and darker, as their courses converged with his.

Frodo looked back for a moment over his shoulder. He could no longer see his friends. The Riders behind were falling back: even their great steeds were no match in speed for the white elf-horse of Glorfindel. He looked forward again, and hope faded. There seemed no chance of reaching the Ford before he was cut off by the others that had lain in ambush. He could see them clearly now: they appeared to have cast aside their hoods and black cloaks, and they were robed in white and grey. Swords were naked in their pale hands; helms were on their heads. Their cold eyes glittered, and they called to him with fell voices.

Fear now filled all Frodo's mind. He thought no longer of his sword. No cry came from him. He shut his eyes and clung to the horse's mane. The wind whistled in his ears, and the bells upon the harness rang wild and shrill. A breath of deadly cold pierced him like a spear, as with a last spurt, like a flash of white fire, the elf-horse speeding as if on wings, passed right before the face of the foremost Rider.

Frodo heard the splash of water. It foamed about his feet. He felt the quick heave and surge as the horse left the river and struggled up the stony path. He was climbing the steep bank. He was across the Ford.

But the pursuers were close behind. At the top of the bank the horse halted and turned about neighing fiercely. There were Nine Riders at the water's edge below, and Frodo's spirit quailed before the threat of their uplifted faces. He knew of nothing that would prevent them from crossing as easily as he had done; and he felt that it was useless to try to escape over the long uncertain path from the Ford to the edge of Rivendell, if once the Riders crossed. In any case he felt that he was commanded urgently to halt. Hatred again stirred in him, but he had no longer the strength to refuse.

Suddenly the foremost Rider spurred his horse forward. It checked at the water and reared up. With a great effort Frodo sat upright and brandished his sword.

"Go back!" he cried. "Go back to the Land of Mordor, and follow me no more!" His voice sounded thin and shrill in his own ears. The Riders halted, but Frodo had not the power of Bombadil. His enemies laughed at him with a harsh and chilling laughter. "Come back! Come back!" they called. "To Mordor we will take you!"

"Go back!" he whispered.

"The Ring! The Ring!" they cried with deadly voices; and immediately their leader urged his horse forward into the water, followed closely by two others.

"By Elbereth and Lúthien the Fair," said Frodo with a last effort, lifting up his sword, "you shall have neither the Ring nor me!"

Then the leader, who was now half across to Ford, stood up menacing in his stirrups, and raised up his hand. Frodo was stricken dumb. He felt his tongue cleave to his mouth, and his heart labouring. His sword broke and fell out of his shaking hand. The elf-horse reared and snorted. The foremost of the black horses had almost set foot upon the shore.

At that moment there came a roaring and a rushing: a noise of loud waters rolling many stones. Dimly Frodo saw the river below him rise, and down along its course there came a plumed cavalry of waves. White flames seemed to Frodo to flicker on their crests and he half fancied that he saw amid the water white riders upon white horses with frothing manes. The three Riders that were still in the midst of the Ford were overwhelmed: they disappeared, buried suddenly under angry foam. Those that were behind drew back in dismay.

With his last failing senses Frodo heard cries, and it seemed to him that he saw, beyond the Riders that hesitated on the shore, a shining figure of white light; and behind it ran small shadowy forms waving flames, that flared red in the grey mist that was falling over the world.

The black horses were filled with madness, and leaping forward in terror they bore their riders into the rushing flood. Their piercing cries were drowned in the roaring of the river as it carried them away. Then Frodo felt himself falling, and the roaring and confusion seemed to rise and engulf him together with his enemies. He heard and saw no more.

BOOK II

CHAPTER
ONE

Many Meetings

Frodo woke and found himself lying in bed. At first he thought that he had slept late, after a long unpleasant dream that still hovered on the edge of memory. Or perhaps he had been ill? But the ceiling looked strange; it was flat, and it had dark beams richly carved. He lay a little while longer looking at patches of sunlight on the wall, and listening to the sound of a waterfall.

"Where am I, and what is the time?" he said aloud to the ceiling.

"In the House of Elrond, and it is ten o'clock in the morning," said a voice. "It is the morning of October the twenty-fourth, if you want to know."

"Gandalf!" cried Frodo, sitting up. There was the old wizard, sitting in a chair by the open window.

"Yes," he said, "I am here. And you are lucky to be here, too, after all the absurd things you have done since you left home."

Frodo lay down again. He felt too comfortable and peaceful to argue, and in any case he did not think he would get the better of an argument. He was fully awake now, and the memory of his journey was returning: the disastrous "short cut" through the Old Forest; the "accident" at *The Prancing Pony*; and his madness in putting on the Ring in the dell under

Weathertop. While he was thinking of all these things and trying in vain to bring his memory down to his arriving in Rivendell, there was a long silence, broken only by the soft puffs of Gandalf's pipe, as he blew white smoke-rings out of the window.

"Where's Sam?" Frodo asked at length. "And are the others all right?"

"Yes, they are all safe and sound," answered Gandalf. "Sam was here until I sent him off to get some rest, about half an hour ago."

"What happened at the Ford?" said Frodo. "It all seemed so dim, somehow; and it still does."

"Yes, it would. You were beginning to fade," answered Gandalf. "The wound was overcoming you at last. A few more hours and you would have been beyond our aid. But you have some strength in you, my dear hobbit! As you showed in the Barrow. That was touch and go: perhaps the most dangerous moment of all. I wish you could have held out at Weathertop."

"You seem to know a great deal already," said Frodo. "I have not spoken to the others about the Barrow. At first it was too horrible, and afterwards there were other things to think about. How do you know about it?"

"You have talked long in your sleep, Frodo," said Gandalf gently, "and it has not been hard for me to read your mind and memory. Do not worry! Though I said 'absurd' just now, I did not mean it. I think well of you — and of the others. It is no small feat to have come so far, and through such dangers, still bearing the Ring."

"We should never have done it without Strider," said Frodo. "But we needed you. I did not know what to do without you."

"I was delayed," said Gandalf, "and that nearly proved our ruin. And yet I am not sure: it may have been better so."

"I wish you would tell me what happened!"

"All in good time! You are not supposed to talk or worry about anything today, by Elrond's orders."

"But talking would stop me thinking and wondering, which

are quite as tiring," said Frodo. "I am wide awake now, and I remember so many things that want explaining. Why were you delayed? You ought to tell me that at least."

"You will soon hear all you wish to know," said Gandalf. "We shall have a Council, as soon as you are well enough. At the moment I will only say that I was held captive."

"You?" cried Frodo.

"Yes, I, Gandalf the Grey," said the wizard solemnly. "There are many powers in the world, for good or for evil. Some are greater than I am. Against some I have not yet been measured. But my time is coming. The Morgul-lord and his Black Riders have come forth. War is preparing!"

"Then you knew of the Riders already — before I met them?"

"Yes, I knew of them. Indeed I spoke of them once to you; for the Black Riders are the Ringwraiths, the Nine Servants of the Lord of the Rings. But I did not know that they had arisen again or I should have fled with you at once. I heard news of them only after I left you in June; but that story must wait. For the moment we have been saved from disaster, by Aragorn."

"Yes," said Frodo, "it was Strider that saved us. Yet I was afraid of him at first. Sam never quite trusted him, I think, not at any rate until we met Glorfindel."

Gandalf smiled. "I have heard all about Sam," he said. "He has no more doubts now."

"I am glad," said Frodo. "For I have become very fond of Strider. Well, *fond* is not the right word. I mean he is dear to me; though he is strange, and grim at times. In fact, he reminds me often of you. I didn't know that any of the Big People were like that. I thought, well, that they were just big, and rather stupid: kind and stupid like Butterbur; or stupid and wicked like Bill Ferny. But then we don't know much about Men in the Shire, except perhaps the Breelanders."

"You don't know much even about them, if you think old Barliman is stupid," said Gandalf. "He is wise enough on his own ground. He thinks less than he talks, and slower; yet he can see through a brick wall in time (as they say in Bree). But there are few left in Middle-earth like Aragorn son of Arathorn. The race of the Kings from over the Sea is nearly at an end. It may be that this War of the Ring will be their last adventure."

"Do you really mean that Strider is one of the people of the old Kings?" said Frodo in wonder. "I thought they had all vanished long ago. I thought he was only a Ranger."

"Only a Ranger!" cried Gandalf "My dear Frodo, that is just what the Rangers are: the last remnant in the North of the great people, the Men of the West. They have helped me before; and I shall need their help in the days to come; for we have reached Rivendell, but the Ring is not yet at rest."

"I suppose not," said Frodo. "But so far my only thought has been to get here; and I hope I shan't have to go any further. It is very pleasant just to rest. I have had a month of exile and adventure, and I find that has been as much as I want."

He fell silent and shut his eyes. After a while he spoke again. "I have been reckoning," he said, "and I can't bring the total up to October the twenty-fourth. It ought to be the twenty-first. We must have reached the Ford by the twentieth."

"You have talked and reckoned more than is good for you," said Gandalf. "How do the side and shoulder feel now?"

"I don't know," Frodo answered. "They don't feel at all: which is an improvement, but" — he made an effort — "I can move my arm again a little. Yes, it is coming back to life. It is not cold," he added, touching his left hand with his right.

"Good!" said Gandalf. "It is mending fast. You will soon be sound again. Elrond has cured you: he has tended you for days, ever since you were brought in.

"Days?" said Frodo.

"Well, four nights and three days, to be exact. The Elves brought you from the Ford on the night of the twentieth, and that is where you lost count. We have been terribly anxious, and Sam has hardly left your side, day or night, except to run messages. Elrond is a master of healing, but the weapons of our Enemy are deadly. To tell you the truth, I had very little hope;

for I suspected that there was some fragment of the blade still in the closed wound. But it could not be found until last night. Then Elrond removed a splinter. It was deeply buried, and it was working inwards."

Frodo shuddered, remembering the cruel knife with notched blade that had vanished in Strider's hands. "Don't be alarmed!" said Gandalf. "It is gone now. It has been melted. And it seems that Hobbits fade very reluctantly. I have known strong warriors of the Big People who would quickly have been overcome by that splinter, which you bore for seventeen days."

"What would they have done to me?" asked Frodo. "What were the Riders trying to do?"

"They tried to pierce your heart with a Morgul-knife which remains in the wound. If they had succeeded, you would have become like they are, only weaker and under their command. You would have become a wraith under the dominion of the Dark Lord; and he would have tormented you for trying to keep his Ring, if any greater torment were possible than being robbed of it and seeing it on his hand."

"Thank goodness I did not realize the horrible danger!" said Frodo faintly. "I was mortally afraid, of course; but if I had known more, I should not have dared even to move. It is a marvel that I escaped!"

"Yes, fortune or fate have helped you," said Gandalf, "not to mention courage. For your heart was not touched, and only your shoulder was pierced; and that was because you resisted to the last. But it was a terribly narrow shave, so to speak. You were in gravest peril while you wore the Ring, for then you were half in the wraith-world yourself, and they might have seized you. You could see them, and they could see you."

"I know," said Frodo. "They were terrible to behold! But why could we all see their horses?"

"Because they are real horses; just as the black robes are real robes that they wear to give shape to their nothingness when they have dealings with the living."

"Then why do these black horses endure such riders? All

other animals are terrified when they draw near, even the elf-horse of Glorfindel. The dogs howl and the geese scream at them."

"Because these horses are born and bred to the service of the Dark Lord in Mordor. Not all his servants and chattels are wraiths! There are orcs and trolls, there are wargs and werewolves; and there have been and still are many Men, warriors and kings, that walk alive under the Sun, and yet are under his sway. And their number is growing daily."

"What about Rivendell and the Elves? Is Rivendell safe?"

"Yes, at present, until all else is conquered. The Elves may fear the Dark Lord, and they may fly before him, but never again will they listen to him or serve him. And here in Rivendell there live still some of his chief foes: the Elven-wise, lords of the Eldar from beyond the furthest seas. They do not fear the Ringwraiths, for those who have dwelt in the Blessed Realm live at once in both worlds, and against both the Seen and the Unseen they have great power."

"I thought that I saw a white figure that shone and did not grow dim like the others. Was that Glorfindel then?"

"Yes, you saw him for a moment as he is upon the other side: one of the mighty of the Firstborn. He is an Elf-lord of a house of princes. Indeed there is a power in Rivendell to withstand the might of Mordor, for a while: and elsewhere other powers still dwell. There is power, too, of another kind in the Shire. But all such places will soon become islands under siege, if things go on as they are going. The Dark Lord is putting forth all his strength.

"Still," he said, standing suddenly up and sticking out his chin, while his beard went stiff and straight like bristling wire, "we must keep up our courage. You will soon be well, if I do not talk you to death. You are in Rivendell, and you need not worry about anything for the present."

"I haven't any courage to keep up," said Frodo, "but I am not worried at the moment. Just give me news of my friends, and tell me the end of the affair at the Ford, as I keep on asking, and I shall be content for the present. After that I shall have another sleep, I think; but I shan't be able to close my eyes until you have finished the story for me."

Gandalf moved his chair to the bedside, and took a good look at Frodo. The colour had come back to his face, and his eyes were clear, and fully awake and aware. He was smiling, and there seemed to be little wrong with him. But to the wizard's eye there was a faint change, just a hint as it were of transparency, about him, and especially about the left hand that lay outside upon the coverlet.

"Still that must be expected," said Gandalf to himself. "He is not half through yet, and to what he will come in the end not even Elrond can foretell. Not to evil, I think. He may become like a glass filled with a clear light for eyes to see that can."

"You look splendid," he said aloud. "I will risk a brief tale without consulting Elrond. But quite brief, mind you, and then you must sleep again. This is what happened, as far as I can gather. The Riders made straight for you, as soon as you fled. They did not need the guidance of their horses any longer: you had become visible to them, being already on the threshold of their world. And also the Ring drew them. Your friends sprang aside, off the road, or they would have been ridden down. They knew that nothing could save you, if the white horse could not. The Riders were too swift to overtake, and too many to oppose. On foot even Glorfindel and Aragorn together could not withstand all the Nine at once.

"When the Ringwraiths swept by, your friends ran up behind. Close to the Ford there is a small hollow beside the road masked by a few stunted trees. There they hastily kindled fire; for Glorfindel knew that a flood would come down, if the Riders tried to cross, and then he would have to deal with any that were left on his side of the river. The moment the flood appeared, he rushed out, followed by Aragorn and the others with flaming brands. Caught between fire and water, and seeing an Elf-lord revealed in his wrath, they were dismayed, and their horses were stricken with madness. Three were carried away by the first assault of the flood; the others were now hurled into the water by their horses and overwhelmed."

"And is that the end of the Black Riders?" asked Frodo.

"No," said Gandalf. "Their horses must have perished, and without them they are crippled. But the Ringwraiths themselves cannot be so easily destroyed. However, there is nothing more to fear from them at present. Your friends crossed after the flood had passed; and they found you lying on your face at the top of the bank, with a broken sword under you. The horse was standing guard beside you. You were pale and cold, and they feared that you were dead, or worse. Elrond's folk met them, carrying you slowly towards Rivendell."

"Who made the flood?" asked Frodo.

"Elrond commanded it," answered Gandalf. "The river of this valley is under his power, and it will rise in anger when he has great need to bar the Ford. As soon as the captain of the Ringwraiths rode into the water the flood was released. If I may say so, I added a few touches of my own: you may not have noticed, but some of the waves took the form of great white horses with shining white riders; and there were many rolling and grinding boulders. For a moment I was afraid that we had let loose too fierce a wrath, and the flood would get out of hand and wash you all away. There is great vigour in the waters that come down from the snows of the Misty Mountains."

"Yes, it all comes back to me now," said Frodo: "the tremendous roaring. I thought I was drowning, with my friends and enemies and all. But now we are safe!"

Gandalf looked quickly at Frodo, but he had shut his eyes. "Yes, you are all safe for the present. Soon there will be feasting and merrymaking to celebrate the victory at the Ford of Bruinen, and you will all be there in places of honour."

"Splendid!" said Frodo. "It is wonderful that Elrond, and Glorfindel and such great lords, not to mention Strider, should take so much trouble and show me so much kindness."

"Well, there are many reasons why they should," said Gandalf, smiling. "I am one good reason. The Ring is another:

you are the Ring-bearer. And you are the heir of Bilbo, the Ring-finder."

"Dear Bilbo!" said Frodo sleepily. "I wonder where he is. I wish he was here and could hear all about it. It would have made him laugh. The cow jumped over the Moon! And the poor old troll!" With that he fell fast asleep.

Frodo was now safe in the Last Homely House east of the Sea. That house was, as Bilbo had long ago reported, "a perfect house, whether you like food or sleep or story-telling or singing, or just sitting and thinking best, or a pleasant mixture of them all". Merely to be there was a cure for weariness, fear, and sadness.

As the evening drew on, Frodo woke up again, and he found that he no longer felt in need of rest or sleep, but had a mind for food and drink, and probably for singing and story-telling afterwards. He got out of bed and discovered that his arm was already nearly as useful again as it ever had been. He found laid ready clean garments of green cloth that fitted him excellently. Looking in a mirror he was startled to see a much thinner reflection of himself than he remembered: it looked remarkably like the young nephew of Bilbo who used to go tramping with his uncle in the Shire; but the eyes looked out at him thoughtfully.

"Yes, you have seen a thing or two since you last peeped out of a looking-glass," he said to his reflection. "But now for a merry meeting!" He stretched out his arms and whistled a tune.

At that moment there was a knock on the door, and Sam came in. He ran to Frodo and took his left hand, awkwardly and shyly. He stroked it gently and then he blushed and turned hastily away.

"Hullo, Sam!" said Frodo.

"It's warm!" said Sam. "Meaning your hand, Mr. Frodo. It has felt so cold through the long nights. But glory and trumpets!" he cried, turning round again with shining eyes and dancing on the floor. "It's fine to see you up and yourself again, sir! Gandalf asked me to come and see if you were ready to come down, and I thought he was joking."

"I am ready," said Frodo. "Let's go and look for the rest of the party!"

"I can take you to them, sir," said Sam. "It's a big house this, and very peculiar. Always a bit more to discover, and no knowing what you'll find round a corner. And Elves, sir! Elves here, and Elves there! Some like kings, terrible and splendid; and some as merry as children. And the music and the singing — not that I have had the time or the heart for much listening since we got here. But I'm getting to know some of the ways of the place."

"I know what you have been doing, Sam," said Frodo, taking his arm. "but you shall be merry tonight, and listen to your heart's content. Come on, guide me round the corners!"

Sam led him along several passages and down many steps and out into a high garden above the steep bank of the river. He found his friends sitting in a porch on the side of the house looking east. Shadows had fallen in the valley below, but there was still a light on the faces of the mountains far above. The air was warm. The sound of running and falling water was loud, and the evening was filled with a faint scent of trees and flowers, as if summer still lingered in Elrond's gardens.

"Hurray!" cried Pippin, springing up. "Here is our noble cousin! Make way for Frodo, Lord of the Ring!"

"Hush!" said Gandalf from the shadows at the back of the porch. "Evil things do not come into this valley; but all the same we should not name them. The Lord of the Ring is not Frodo, but the master of the Dark Tower of Mordor, whose power is again stretching out over the world! We are sitting in a fortress. Outside it is getting dark."

"Gandalf has been saying many cheerful things like that," said Pippin. "He thinks I need keeping in order. But it seems impossible, somehow, to feel gloomy or depressed in this place. I feel I could sing, if I knew the right song for the occasion."

"I feel like singing myself," laughed Frodo. "Though at the

moment I feel more like eating and drinking!"

"That will soon be cured," said Pippin. "You have shown your usual cunning in getting up just in time for a meal."

"More than meal! A feast!" said Merry. "As soon as Gandalf reported that you were recovered, the preparations began." He had hardly finished speaking when they were summoned to the hall by the ringing of many bells.

The hall of Elrond's house was filled with folk: Elves for the most part, though there were a few guests of other sorts. Elrond, as was his custom, sat in a great chair at the end of the long table upon the dais; and next to him on the one side sat Glorfindel, on the other side sat Gandalf.

Frodo looked at them in wonder, for he had never before seen Elrond, of whom so many tales spoke; and as they sat upon his right hand and his left, Glorfindel, and even Gandalf, whom he thought he knew so well, were revealed as lords of dignity and power.

Gandalf was shorter in stature than the other two; but his long white hair, his sweeping silver beard, and his broad shoulders, made him look like some wise king of ancient legend. In his aged face under great snowy brows his dark eyes were set like coals that could leap suddenly into fire.

Glorfindel was tall and straight; his hair was of shining gold, his face fair and young and fearless and full of joy; his eyes were bright and keen, and his voice like music; on his brow sat wisdom, and in his hand was strength.

The face of Elrond was ageless, neither old nor young, though in it was written the memory of many things both glad and sorrowful. His hair was dark as the shadows of twilight, and upon it was set a circlet of silver; his eyes were grey as a clear evening, and in them was a light like the light of stars. Venerable he seemed as a king crowned with many winters, and yet hale as a tried warrior in the fulness of his strength. He was the Lord of Rivendell and mighty among both Elves and Men.

In the middle of the table, against the woven cloths upon the wall, there was a chair under a canopy, and there sat a lady fair to look upon, and so like was she in form of womanhood to Elrond that Frodo guessed that she was one of his close kindred. Young she was and yet not so. The braids of her dark hair were touched by no frost, her white arms and clear face were flawless and smooth, and the light of stars was in her bright eyes, grey as a cloudless night; yet queenly she looked, and thought and knowledge were in her glance, as of one who has known many things that the years bring. Above her brow her head was covered with a cap of silver lace netted with small gems, glittering white; but her soft grey raiment had no ornament save a girdle of leaves wrought in silver.

So it was that Frodo saw her whom few mortals had yet seen; Arwen, daughter of Elrond, in whom it was said that the likeness of Lúthien had come on earth again; and she was called Undómiel, for she was the Evenstar of her people. Long she had been in the land of her mother's kin, in Lórien beyond the mountains, and was but lately returned to Rivendell to her father's house. But her brothers, Elladan and Elrohir, were out upon errantry: for they rode often far afield with the Rangers of the North, forgetting never their mother's torment in the dens of the orcs.

Such loveliness in living thing Frodo had never seen before nor imagined in his mind; and he was both surprised and abashed to find that he had a seat at Elrond's table among all these folk so high and fair. Though he had a suitable chair, and was raised upon several cushions, he felt very small, and rather out of place; but that feeling quickly passed. The feast was merry and the food all that his hunger could desire. It was some time before he looked about him again or even turned to his neighbours.

He looked first for his friends. Sam had begged to be allowed to wait on his master, but had been told that for this time he was a guest of honour. Frodo could see him now, sitting with Pippin and Merry at the upper end of one of the side-tables close to the dais. He could see no sign of Strider.

Next to Frodo on his right sat a dwarf of important appearance, richly dressed. His beard, very long and forked, was white, nearly as white as the snow-white cloth of his garments. He wore a silver belt, and round his neck hung a chain of silver and diamonds. Frodo stopped eating to look at him.

"Welcome and well met!" said the dwarf, turning towards him. Then he actually rose from his seat and bowed. "Glóin at your service," he said, and bowed still lower.

"Frodo Baggins at your service and your family's," said Frodo correctly, rising in surprise and scattering his cushions. "Am I right in guessing that you are *the* Glóin, one of the twelve companions of the great Thorin Oakenshield?"

"Quite right," answered the dwarf, gathering up the cushions and courteously assisting Frodo back into his seat. "And I do not ask, for I have already been told that you are the kinsman and adopted heir of our friend Bilbo the renowned. Allow me to congratulate you on your recovery."

"Thank you very much," said Frodo.

"You have had some very strange adventures, I hear," said Glóin. "I wonder greatly what brings *four* hobbits on so long a journey. Nothing like it has happened since Bilbo came with us. But perhaps I should not inquire too closely, since Elrond and Gandalf do not seem disposed to talk of this?"

"I think we will not speak of it, at least not yet," said Frodo politely. He guessed that even in Elrond's house the matter of the Ring was not one for casual talk; and in any case he wished to forget his troubles for a time. "But I am equally curious," he added, "to learn what brings so important a dwarf so far from the Lonely Mountain."

Glóin looked at him. "If you have not heard, I think we will not speak yet of that either. Master Elrond will summon us all ere long, I believe, and then we shall all hear many things. But there is much else that may be told."

Throughout the rest of the meal they talked together, but Frodo listened more than he spoke; for the news of the Shire, apart from the Ring, seemed small and far-away and unimportant, while Glóin had much to tell of events in the northern regions of Wilderland. Frodo learned that Grimbeorn the Old, son of Beorn, was now the lord of many sturdy men, and to their land between the Mountains and Mirkwood neither orc nor wolf dared to go.

"Indeed," said Glóin, "if it were not for the Beornings, the passage from Dale to Rivendell would long ago have become impossible. They are valiant men and keep open the High Pass and the Ford of Carrock. But their tolls are high," he added with a shake of his head; "and like Beorn of old they are not over fond of dwarves. Still, they are trusty, and that is much in these days. Nowhere are there any men so friendly to us as the Men of Dale. They are good folk, the Bardings. The grandson of Bard the Bowman rules them, Brand son of Bain son of Bard. He is a strong king, and his realm now reaches far south and east of Esgaroth."

"And what of your own people?" asked Frodo.

"There is much to tell, good and bad," said Glóin; "yet it is mostly good: we have so far been fortunate, though we do not escape the shadow of these times. If you really wish to hear of us, I will tell you tidings gladly. But stop me when you are weary! Dwarves' tongues run on when speaking of their handiwork, they say."

And with that Glóin embarked on a long account of the doings of the Dwarf-kingdom. He was delighted to have found so polite a listener; for Frodo showed no sign of weariness and made no attempt to change the subject, though actually he soon got rather lost among the strange names of people and places that he had never heard of before. He was interested, however, to hear that Dáin was still King under the Mountain, and was now old (having passed his two hundred and fiftieth year), venerable, and fabulously rich. Of the ten companions who had survived the Battle of Five Armies seven were still with him: Dwalin, Glóin, Dori, Nori, Bifur, Bofur, and Bombur. Bombur was now so fat that he could not move himself from his couch to his chair at table, and it took six young dwarves to lift him.

"And what has become of Balin and Ori and Óin?" asked Frodo.

A shadow passed over Glóin's face. "We do not know," he answered. "It is largely on account of Balin that I have come to ask the advice of those that dwell in Rivendell. But tonight let us speak of merrier things!"

Glóin began then to talk of the works of his people, telling Frodo about their great labours in Dale and under the Mountain. "We have done well," he said. "But in metal-work we cannot rival our fathers, many of those secrets are lost. We make good armour and keen swords, but we cannot again make mail or blade to match those that were made before the dragon came. Only in mining and building have we surpassed the old days. You should see the waterways of Dale, Frodo, and the mountains, and the pools! You should see the stone-paved roads of many colours! And the halls and cavernous streets under the earth with arches carved like trees; and the terraces and towers upon the Mountain's sides! Then you would see that we have not been idle."

"I will come and see them, if ever I can," said Frodo. "How surprised Bilbo would have been to see all the changes in the Desolation of Smaug!"

Glóin looked at Frodo and smiled. "You were very fond of Bilbo were you not?" he asked.

"Yes," answered Frodo. "I would rather see him than all the towers and palaces in the world."

At length the feast came to an end. Elrond and Arwen rose and went down the hall, and the company followed them in due order. The doors were thrown open, and they went across a wide passage and through other doors, and came into a further hall. In it were no tables, but a bright fire was burning in a great hearth between the carven pillars upon either side.

Frodo found himself walking with Gandalf. "This is the Hall of Fire," said the wizard. "Here you will hear many songs and tales — if you can keep awake. But except on high days it usually stands empty and quiet, and people come here who wish for peace, and thought. There is always a fire here, all the year round, but there is little other light."

As Elrond entered and went towards the seat prepared for him, elvish minstrels began to make sweet music. Slowly the hall filled, and Frodo looked with delight upon the many fair faces that were gathered together; the golden firelight played upon them and shimmered in their hair. Suddenly he noticed, not far from the further end of the fire, a small dark figure seated on a stool with his back propped against a pillar. Beside him on the ground was a drinking-cup and some bread. Frodo wondered whether he was ill (if people were ever ill in Rivendell), and had been unable to come to the feast. His head seemed sunk in sleep on his breast, and a fold of his dark cloak was drawn over his face.

Elrond went forward and stood beside the silent figure. "Awake, little master!" he said, with a smile. Then, turning to Frodo, he beckoned to him. "Now at last the hour has come that you have wished for, Frodo," he said. "Here is a friend that you have long missed."

The dark figure raised its head and uncovered its face.

"Bilbo!" cried Frodo with sudden recognition, and he sprang forward.

"Hullo, Frodo my lad!" said Bilbo. "So you have got here at last. I hoped you would manage it. Well, well! So all this feasting is in your honour, I hear. I hope you enjoyed yourself?"

"Why weren't you there?" cried Frodo. "And why haven't I been allowed to see you before?"

"Because you were asleep. I have seen a good deal of *you*. I have sat by your side with Sam each day. But as for the feast, I don't go in for such things much now. And I had something else to do."

"What were you doing?"

"Why, sitting and thinking. I do a lot of that nowadays, and this is the best place to do it in, as a rule. Wake up, indeed!" he said, cocking an eye at Elrond. There was a bright twinkle in it and no sign of sleepiness that Frodo could see. "Wake up! I was not asleep, Master Elrond. If you want to know, you have all come out from your feast too soon, and you have disturbed me — in the middle of making up a song. I was stuck over a line or two, and was thinking about them; but now I don't suppose I shall ever get them right. There will be such a deal of singing that the ideas will be driven clean out of my head. I shall have to get my friend the Dúnadan to help me. Where is he?"

Elrond laughed. "He shall be found," he said. "Then you two shall go into a corner and finish your task, and we will hear it and judge it before we end our merrymaking." Messengers were sent to find Bilbo's friend, though none knew where he was, or why he had not been present at the feast.

In the meanwhile Frodo and Bilbo sat side by side, and Sam came quickly and placed himself near them. They talked together in soft voices, oblivious of the mirth and music in the hall about them. Bilbo had not much to say of himself. When he had left Hobbiton he had wandered off aimlessly, along the Road or in the country on either side; but somehow he had steered all the time towards Rivendell.

"I got here without much adventure," he said, "and after a rest I went on with the dwarves to Dale: my last journey. I shan't travel again. Old Balin had gone away. Then I came back here, and here I have been. I have done this and that. I have written some more of my book. And, of course, I make up a few songs. They sing them occasionally: just to please me, I think; for, of course, they aren't really good enough for Rivendell. And I listen and I think. Time doesn't seem to pass here: it just is. A remarkable place altogether.

"I hear all kinds of news, from over the Mountains, and out of the South, but hardly anything from the Shire. I heard about the Ring, of course. Gandalf has been here often. Not that he has told me a great deal, he has become closer than ever these last few years. The Dúnadan has told me more. Fancy that ring of mine causing such a disturbance! It is a pity that Gandalf did not find out more sooner. I could have brought the thing here myself long ago without so much trouble. I have thought several times of going back to Hobbiton for it; but I am getting old, and they would not let me: Gandalf and Elrond, I mean. They seemed to think that the Enemy was looking high and low for me, and would make mincemeat of me, if he caught me tottering about in the Wild.

"And Gandalf said: 'The Ring has passed on, Bilbo. It would do no good to you or to others, if you tried to meddle with it again.' Odd sort of remark, just like Gandalf. But he said he was looking after you, so I let things be. I am frightfully glad to see you safe and sound." He paused and looked at Frodo doubtfully.

"Have you got it here?" he asked in a whisper. "I can't help feeling curious, you know, after all I've heard. I should very much like just to peep at it again."

"Yes, I've got it," answered Frodo, feeling a strange reluctance. "It looks just the same as ever it did."

"Well, I should just like to see it for a moment," said Bilbo.

When he had dressed, Frodo found that while he slept the Ring had been hung about his neck on a new chain, light but strong. Slowly he drew it out. Bilbo put out his hand. But Frodo quickly drew back the Ring. To his distress and amazement he found that he was no longer looking at Bilbo; a shadow seemed to have fallen between them, and through it he found himself eyeing a little wrinkled creature with a hungry face and bony groping hands. He felt a desire to strike him.

The music and singing round them seemed to falter, and a silence fell. Bilbo looked quickly at Frodo's face and passed his hand across his eyes. "I understand now," he said. "Put it away! I am sorry: sorry you have come in for this burden: sorry about everything. Don't adventures ever have an end? I suppose not. Someone else always has to carry on the story. Well, it can't be helped. I wonder if it's any good trying to finish my book? But don't let's worry about it now — let's have some real News! Tell me all about the Shire!"

Frodo hid the Ring away, and the shadow passed leaving hardly a shred of memory. The light and music of Rivendell was about him again. Bilbo smiled and laughed happily. Every item of news from the Shire that Frodo could tell — aided and corrected now and again by Sam — was of the greatest interest to him, from the felling of the least tree to the pranks of the smallest child in Hobbiton. They were so deep in the doings of the Four Farthings that they did not notice the arrival of a man clad in dark green cloth. For many minutes he stood looking down at them with a smile.

Suddenly Bilbo looked up. "Ah, there you are at last, Dúnadan!" he cried.

"Strider!" said Frodo. "You seem to have a lot of names."

"Well, *Strider* is one that I haven't heard before, anyway," said Bilbo. "What do you call him that for?"

"They call me that in Bree," said Strider laughing, "and that is how I was introduced to him."

"And why do you call him Dúnadan?" asked Frodo.

"*The* Dúnadan," said Bilbo. "He is often called that here. But I thought you knew enough Elvish at least to know *dún-adan*: Man of the West, Númenorean. But this is not the time for lessons!" He turned to Strider. "Where have you been, my friend? Why weren't you at the feast? The Lady Arwen was there."

Strider looked down at Bilbo gravely. "I know," he said. "But often I must put mirth aside. Elladan and Elrohir have returned out of the Wild unlooked-for, and they had tidings that I wished to hear at once."

"Well, my dear fellow," said Bilbo, "now you've heard the news, can't you spare me a moment? I want your help in something urgent. Elrond says this song of mine is to be finished before the end of the evening, and I am stuck. Let's go off into a corner and polish it up!"

Strider smiled. "Come then!" he said. "Let me hear it!"

Frodo was left to himself for a while, for Sam had fallen asleep. He was alone and felt rather forlorn, although all about him the folk of Rivendell were gathered. But those near him were silent, intent upon the music of the voices and the instruments, and they gave no heed to anything else. Frodo began to listen.

At first the beauty of the melodies and of the interwoven words in elven-tongues, even though he understood them little, held him in a spell, as soon as he began to attend to them. Almost it seemed that the words took shape, and visions of far lands and bright things that he had never yet imagined opened out before him; and the firelit hall became like a golden mist above seas of foam that sighed upon the margins of the world. Then the enchantment became more and more dreamlike, until he felt that an endless river of swelling gold and silver was flowing over him, too multitudinous for its pattern to be comprehended; it became part of the throbbing air about him, and it drenched and drowned him. Swiftly he sank under its shining weight into a deep realm of sleep.

There he wandered long in a dream of music that turned into running water, and then suddenly into a voice. It seemed to be the voice of Bilbo chanting verses. Faint at first and then clearer ran the words.

> *Eärendil was a mariner*
> *that tarried in Arvernien;*
> *he built a boat of timber felled*
> *in Nimbrethil to journey in;*
> *her sails he wove of silver fair,*
> *of silver were her lanterns made,*
> *her prow was fashioned like a swan,*
> *and light upon her banners laid.*
>
> *In panoply of ancient kings,*
> *in chained rings he armoured him;*

his shining shield was scored with runes
to ward all wounds and harm from him;
his bow was made of dragon-horn,
his arrows shorn of ebony,
of silver was his habergeon,
his scabbard of chalcedony;
his sword of steel was valiant,
of adamant his helmet tall,
an eagle-plume upon his crest,
upon his breast an emerald.

Beneath the Moon and under star
he wandered far from northern strands,
bewildered on enchanted ways
beyond the days of mortal lands.
From gnashing of the Narrow Ice
where shadow lies on frozen hills,
from nether heats and burning waste
he turned in haste, and roving still
on starless waters far astray
at last he came to Night of Naught,
and passed, and never sight he saw
of shining shore nor light he sought.
The winds of wrath came driving him,
and blindly in the foam he fled
from west to east and errandless,
unheralded he homeward sped.

There flying Elwing came to him,
and flame was in the darkness lit;
more bright than light of diamond
the fire upon her carcanet.
The Silmaril she bound on him
and crowned him with the living light
and dauntless then with burning brow
he turned his prow; and in the night

from Otherworld beyond the Sea
there strong and free a storm arose,
a wind of power in Tarmenel;
by paths that seldom mortal goes
his boat it bore with biting breath
as might of death across the grey
and long-forsaken seas distressed:
from east to west he passed away.

Through Evernight he back was borne
on black and roaring waves that ran
o'er leagues unlit and foundered shores
that drowned before the Days began,
until he heard on strands of pearl
where ends the world the music long,
where ever-foaming billows roll
the yellow gold and jewels wan.
He saw the Mountain silent rise
where twilight lies upon the knees
of Valinor, and Eldamar
beheld afar beyond the seas.
A wanderer escaped from night
to haven white he came at last,
to Elvenhome the green and fair
where keen the air, where pale as glass
beneath the Hill of Ilmarin
a-glimmer in a valley sheer
the lamp lit towers of Tirion
are mirrored on the Shadowmere.

He tarried there from errantry,
and melodies they taught to him,
and sages old him marvels told,
and harps of gold they brought to him.
They clothed him then in elven-white,
  and seven lights before him sent,

as through the Calacirian
to hidden land forlorn he went.
He came unto the timeless halls
where shining fall the countless years,
and endless reigns the Elder King
in Ilmarin on Mountain sheer;
and words unheard were spoken then
of folk of Men and Elven-kin,
beyond the world were visions showed
forbid to those that dwell therein.

A ship then new they built for him
of mithril and of elven-glass
with shining prow; no shaven oar
nor sail she bore on silver mast:
the Silmaril as lantern light
and banner bright with living flame
to gleam thereon by Elbereth
herself was set, who thither came
and wings immortal made for him,
and laid on him undying doom,
to sail the shoreless skies and come
behind the Sun and light of Moon.

From Evereven's lofty hills
where softly silver fountains fall
his wings him bore, a wandering light,
beyond the mighty Mountain Wall.
From World's End then he turned away,
and yearned again to find afar
his home through shadows journeying,
and burning as an island star
on high above the mists he came,
a distant flame before the Sun,
a wonder ere the waking dawn
where grey the Norland waters run.

> *And over Middle-earth he passed*
> *and heard at last the weeping sore*
> *of women and of elven-maids*
> *in Elder Days, in years of yore.*
> *But on him mighty doom was laid,*
> *till Moon should fade, an orbéd star*
> *to pass, and tarry never more*
> *on Hither Shores where mortals are;*
> *for ever still a herald on*
> *an errand that should never rest*
> *to bear his shining lamp afar,*
> *the Flammifer of Westernesse.*

The chanting ceased. Frodo opened his eyes and saw that Bilbo was seated on his stool in a circle of listeners, who were smiling and applauding.

"Now we had better have it again," said an Elf.

Bilbo got up and bowed. "I am flattered, Lindir," he said. "But it would be too tiring to repeat it all."

"Not too tiring for you," the Elves answered laughing. "You know you are never tired of reciting your own verses. But really we cannot answer your question at one hearing!"

"What!" cried Bilbo. "You can't tell which parts were mine, and which were the Dúnadan's?"

"It is not easy for us to tell the difference between two mortals," said the Elf.

"Nonsense, Lindir," snorted Bilbo. "If you can't distinguish between a Man and a Hobbit, your judgement is poorer than I imagined. They're as different as peas and apples."

"Maybe. To sheep other sheep no doubt appear different," laughed Lindir. "Or to shepherds. But Mortals have not been our study. We have other business."

"I won't argue with you," said Bilbo. "I am sleepy after so much music and singing. I'll leave you to guess, if you want to."

He got up and came towards Frodo. "Well, that's over," he

said in a low voice. "It went off better than I expected. I don't often get asked for a second hearing. What did you think of it?"

"I am not going to try and guess," said Frodo smiling.

"You needn't," said Bilbo. "As a matter of fact it was all mine. Except that Aragorn insisted on my putting in a green stone. He seemed to think it important. I don't know why. Otherwise he obviously thought the whole thing rather above my head, and he said that if I had the cheek to make verses about Eärendil in the house of Elrond, it was my affair. I suppose he was right."

"I don't know," said Frodo. "It seemed to me to fit somehow, though I can't explain. I was half asleep when you began, and it seemed to follow on from something that I was dreaming about. I didn't understand that it was really you speaking until near the end."

"It *is* difficult to keep awake here, until you get used to it," said Bilbo. "Not that hobbits would ever acquire quite the elvish appetite for music and poetry and tales. They seem to like them as much as food, or more. They will be going on for a long time yet. What do you say to slipping off for some more quiet talk?"

"Can we?" said Frodo.

"Of course. This is merrymaking not business. Come and go as you like, as long as you don't make a noise."

They got up and withdrew quietly into the shadows, and made for the doors. Sam they left behind, fast asleep still with a smile on his face. In spite of his delight in Bilbo's company Frodo felt a tug of regret as they passed out of the Hall of Fire. Even as they stepped over the threshold a single clear voice rose in song.

> *A Elbereth Gilthoniel,*
> *silivren penna míriel*
> *o menel aglar elenath!*
> *Na-chaered palan-díriel*

> *o galadhremmin ennorath,*
> *Fanuilos, le linnathon*
> *nef aear, sí nef aearon!*

Frodo halted for a moment, looking back. Elrond was in his chair and the fire was on his face like summer-light upon the trees. Near him sat the Lady Arwen. To his surprise Frodo saw that Aragorn stood beside her; his dark cloak was thrown back, and he seemed to be clad in elven-mail, and a star shone on his breast. They spoke together, and then suddenly it seemed to Frodo that Arwen turned towards him, and the light of her eyes fell on him from afar and pierced his heart.

He stood still enchanted, while the sweet syllables of the elvish song fell like clear jewels of blended word and melody. "It is a song to Elbereth," said Bilbo. "They will sing that, and other songs of the Blessed Realm, many times tonight. Come on!"

He led Frodo back to his own little room. It opened on to the gardens and looked south across the ravine of the Bruinen. There they sat for some while, looking through the window at the bright stars above the steep-climbing woods, and talking softly. They spoke no more of the small news of the Shire far away, nor of the dark shadows and perils that encompassed them, but of the fair things they had seen in the world together, of the Elves, of the stars, of trees, and the gentle fall of the bright year in the woods.

At last there came a knock on the door. "Begging your pardon," said Sam, putting in his head, "but I was just wondering if you would be wanting anything."

"And begging yours, Sam Gamgee," replied Bilbo. "I guess you mean that it is time your master went to bed."

"Well, sir, there is a Council early tomorrow, I hear, and he only got up today for the first time."

"Quite right, Sam," laughed Bilbo. "You can trot off and tell Gandalf that he has gone to bed. Good night, Frodo! Bless me, but it has been good to see you again! There are no folk like hobbits after all for a real good talk. I am getting very old, and I began to wonder if I should ever live to see your chapters of our story. Good night! I'll take a walk, I think, and look at the stars of Elbereth in the garden. Sleep well!"

CHAPTER
TWO

The Council of Elrond

Next day Frodo woke early, feeling refreshed and well. He walked along the terraces above the loud-flowing Bruinen and watched the pale, cool sun rise above the far mountains, and shine down, slanting through the thin silver mist; the dew upon the yellow leaves was glimmering, and the woven nets of gossamer twinkled on every bush. Sam walked beside him, saying nothing, but sniffing the air, and looking every now and again with wonder in his eyes at the great heights in the East. The snow was white upon their peaks.

On a seat cut in the stone beside a turn in the path they came upon Gandalf and Bilbo deep in talk. "Hullo! Good morning!" said Bilbo. "Feel ready for the great council?"

"I feel ready for anything," answered Frodo. "But most of all I should like to go walking today and explore the valley. I should like to get into those pine-woods up there." He pointed away far up the side of Rivendell to the north.

"You may have a chance later," said Gandalf. "But we cannot make any plans yet. There is much to hear and decide today."

Suddenly as they were talking a single clear bell rang out. "That is the warning bell for the Council of Elrond," cried

Gandalf. "Come along now! Both you and Bilbo are wanted."

Frodo and Bilbo followed the wizard quickly along the winding path back to the house; behind them, uninvited and for the moment forgotten, trotted Sam.

Gandalf led them to the porch where Frodo had found his friends the evening before. The light of the clear autumn morning was now glowing in the valley. The noise of bubbling waters came up from the foaming river-bed. Birds were singing, and a wholesome peace lay on the land. To Frodo his dangerous flight, and the rumours of the darkness growing in the world outside, already seemed only the memories of a troubled dream; but the faces that were turned to meet them as they entered were grave.

Elrond was there, and several others were seated in silence about him. Frodo saw Glorfindel and Glóin; and in a corner alone Strider was sitting, clad in his old travel-worn clothes again. Elrond drew Frodo to a seat by his side, and presented him to the company, saying:

"Here, my friends, is the hobbit, Frodo son of Drogo. Few have ever come hither through greater peril or on an errand more urgent."

He then pointed out and named those whom Frodo had not met before. There was a younger dwarf at Glóin's side: his son Gimli. Beside Glorfindel there were several other counsellors of Elrond's household, of whom Erestor was the chief; and with him was Galdor, an Elf from the Grey Havens who had come on an errand from Círdan the Shipwright. There was also a strange Elf clad in green and brown, Legolas, a messenger from his father, Thranduil, the King of the Elves of Northern Mirkwood. And seated a little apart was a tall man with a fair and noble face, dark-haired and grey-eyed, proud and stern of glance.

He was cloaked and booted as if for a journey on horseback; and indeed though his garments were rich, and his cloak was lined with fur, they were stained with long travel. He had a collar of silver in which a single white stone was set; his locks were shorn about his shoulders. On a baldric he wore a great horn tipped with silver that now was laid upon his knees. He gazed at Frodo and Bilbo with sudden wonder.

"Here," said Elrond, turning to Gandalf, "is Boromir, a man from the South. He arrived in the grey morning, and seeks for counsel. I have bidden him to be present, for here his questions will be answered."

Not all that was spoken and debated in the Council need now be told. Much was said of events in the world outside, especially in the South, and in the wide lands east of the Mountains. Of these things Frodo had already heard many rumours; but the tale of Glóin was new to him, and when the dwarf spoke he listened attentively. It appeared that amid the splendour of their works of hand the hearts of the Dwarves of the Lonely Mountain were troubled.

"It is now many years ago," said Glóin, "that a shadow of disquiet fell upon our people. Whence it came we did not at first perceive. Words began to be whispered in secret: it was said that we were hemmed in a narrow place, and that greater wealth and splendour would be found in a wider world. Some spoke of Moria: the mighty works of our fathers that are called in our own tongue Khazad-dûm; and they declared that now at last we had the power and numbers to return."

Glóin sighed. "Moria! Moria! Wonder of the Northern world! Too deep we delved there, and woke the nameless fear. Long have its vast mansions lain empty since the children of Durin fled. But now we spoke of it again with longing, and yet with dread; for no dwarf has dared to pass the doors of Khazad-dûm for many lives of kings, save Thrór only, and he perished. At last, however, Balin listened to the whispers, and resolved to go; and though Dáin did not give leave willingly, he took with him Ori and Óin and many of our folk, and they went away south.

"That was nigh on thirty years ago. For a while we had news and it seemed good: messages reported that Moria had been entered and a great work begun there. Then there was silence, and no word has ever come from Moria since.

"Then about a year ago a messenger came to Dáin, but not from Moria — from Mordor: a horseman in the night, who called Dáin to his gate. The Lord Sauron the Great, so he said, wished for our friendship. Kings he would give for it, such as he gave of old. And he asked urgently concerning *hobbits*, of what kind they were, and where they dwelt. 'For Sauron knows,' said he, 'that one of these was known to you on a time.'

"At this we were greatly troubled, and we gave no answer. And then his fell voice was lowered, and he would have sweetened it if he could. 'As a small token only of your friendship Sauron asks this,' he said: 'that you should find this thief,' such was his word, 'and get from him, willing or no, a little ring, the least of rings, that once he stole. It is but a trifle that Sauron fancies, and an earnest of your good will. Find it, and three rings that the Dwarf-sires possessed of old shall be returned to you, and the realm of Moria shall be yours for ever. Find only news of the thief, whether he still lives and where, and you shall have great reward and lasting friendship from the Lord. Refuse, and things will not seem so well. Do you refuse?'

"At that his breath came like the hiss of snakes, and all who stood by shuddered, but Dáin said: 'I say neither yea nor nay. I must consider this message and what it means under its fair cloak.'

"'Consider well, but not too long,' said he.

"'The time of my thought is my own to spend,' answered Dáin,

"'For the present,' said he, and rode into the darkness.

"Heavy have the hearts of our chieftains been since that night. We needed not the fell voice of the messenger to warn us that his words held both menace and deceit; for we knew already that the power that has re-entered Mordor has not changed, and ever it betrayed us of old. Twice the messenger has returned, and has gone unanswered. The third and last time, so he says, is soon to come, before the ending of the year.

"And so I have been sent at last by Dáin to warn Bilbo that he is sought by the Enemy, and to learn, if may be, why he desires this ring, this least of rings. Also we crave the advice of Elrond. For the Shadow grows and draws nearer. We discover that messengers have come also to King Brand in Dale, and that he is afraid. We fear that he may yield. Already war is gathering on his eastern borders. If we make no answer, the Enemy may move Men of his rule to assail King Brand, and Dáin also."

"You have done well to come," said Elrond. "You will hear today all that you need in order to understand the purposes of the Enemy. There is naught that you can do, other than to resist, with hope or without it. But you do not stand alone. You will learn that your trouble is but part of the trouble of all the western world. The Ring! What shall we do with the Ring, the least of rings, the trifle that Sauron fancies? That is the doom that we must deem.

"That is the purpose for which you are called hither. Called, I say, though I have not called you to me, strangers from distant lands. You have come and are here met, in this very nick of time, by chance as it may seem. Yet it is not so. Believe rather that it is so ordered that we, who sit here, and none others, must now find counsel for the peril of the world.

"Now, therefore, things shall be openly spoken that have been hidden from all but a few until this day. And first, so that all may understand what is the peril, the Tale of the Ring shall be told from the beginning even to this present. And I will begin that tale, though others shall end it."

Then all listened while Elrond in his clear voice spoke of Sauron and the Kings of Power, and their forging in the Second Age of the world long ago. A part of his tale was known to some there, but the full tale to none, and many eyes were turned to Elrond in fear and wonder as he told of the Elven-smiths of Eregion and their friendship with Moria, and their eagerness for knowledge, by which Sauron ensnared them. For in that time he was not yet evil to behold, and they received his aid and grew mighty in craft, whereas he learned all their secrets, and betrayed them, and forged secretly in the Mountain of Fire the One Ring to be their master. But Celebrimbor was aware of him, and hid the Three which he had made; and there was war, and the land was laid waste, and the gate of Moria was shut.

Then through all the years that followed he traced the Ring; but since that history is elsewhere recounted, even as Elrond himself set it down in his books of lore, it is not here recalled. For it is a long tale, full of deeds great and terrible, and briefly though Elrond spoke, the sun rode up the sky, and the morning was passing ere he ceased.

Of Númenor he spoke, its glory and its fall, and the return of the Kings of Men to Middle-earth out of the deeps of the Sea, borne upon the wings of storm. Then Elendil the Tall and his mighty sons, Isildur and Anárion, became great lords; and the North-realm they made in Arnor, and the South-realm in Gondor above the mouths of Anduin. But Sauron of Mordor assailed them, and they made the Last Alliance of Elves and Men, and the hosts of Gil-galad and Elendil were mustered in Arnor.

Thereupon Elrond paused a while and sighed. "I remember well the splendour of their banners," he said. "It recalled to me the glory of the Elder Days and the hosts of Beleriand, so many great princes and captains were assembled. And yet not so many, nor so fair, as when Thangorodrim was broken, and the Elves deemed that evil was ended for ever, and it was not so."

"You remember?" said Frodo, speaking his thought aloud in his astonishment. "But I thought," he stammered as Elrond turned towards him, "I thought that the fall of Gil-galad was a long age ago."

"So it was indeed," answered Elrond gravely. "But my memory reaches back even to the Elder Days. Eärendil was my sire, who was born in Gondolin before its fall; and my mother was Elwing, daughter of Dior, son of Luthien of Doriath. I have seen three ages in the West of the world, and many defeats, and many fruitless victories.

"I was the herald of Gil-galad and marched with his host. I was at the Battle of Dagorlad before the Black Gate of Mordor, where we had the mastery: for the Spear of Gil-galad and the Sword of Elendil, Aiglos and Narsil, none could withstand. I beheld the last combat on the slopes of Orodruin, where Gil-galad died, and Elendil fell, and Narsil broke beneath him; but Sauron himself was overthrown, and Isildur cut the Ring from his hand with the hilt-shard of his father's sword, and took it for his own."

At this the stranger, Boromir, broke in. "So that is what became of the Ring!" he cried. "If ever such a tale was told in the South, it has long been forgotten. I have heard of the Great Ring of him that we do not name; but we believed that it perished from the world in the ruin of his first realm. Isildur took it! That is tidings indeed."

"Alas! yes," said Elrond. "Isildur took it, as should not have been. It should have been cast then into Orodruin's fire nigh at hand where it was made. But few marked what Isildur did. He alone stood by his father in that last mortal contest; and by Gil-galad only Círdan stood, and I. But Isildur would not listen to our counsel.

"'This I will have as weregild for my father, and my brother,' he said; and therefore whether we would or no, he took it to treasure it. But soon he was betrayed by it to his death; and so it is named in the North Isildur's Bane. Yet death maybe was better than what else might have befallen him.

"Only to the North did these tidings come, and only to a few. Small wonder it is that you have not heard them, Boromir. From the ruin of the Gladden Fields, where Isildur perished, three men only came ever back over the mountains after long wandering. One of these was Ohtar, the esquire of Isildur, who bore the shards of the sword of Elendil; and he brought them to Valandil, the heir of Isildur, who being but a child had remained here in Rivendell. But Narsil was broken and its light extinguished, and it has not yet been forged again.

"Fruitless did I call the victory of the Last Alliance? Not wholly so, yet it did not achieve its end. Sauron was diminished, but not destroyed. His Ring was lost but not unmade. The Dark Tower was broken, but its foundations were not removed; for they were made with the power of the Ring, and while it remains they will endure. Many Elves and many mighty Men, and many of their friends, had perished in the war. Anárion was slain, and Isildur was slain; and Gil-galad and Elendil were no more. Never again shall there be any such league of Elves and Men; for Men multiply and the Firstborn decrease, and the two kindreds are estranged. And ever since that day the race of Númenor has decayed, and the span of their years has lessened.

"In the North after the war and the slaughter of the Gladden Fields the Men of Westernesse were diminished, and their city of Annúminas beside Lake Evendim fell into ruin; and the heirs of Valandil removed and dwelt at Fornost on the high North Downs, and that now too is desolate. Men call it Deadmen's Dike, and they fear to tread there. For the folk of Arnor dwindled, and their foes devoured them, and their lordship passed, leaving only green mounds in the grassy hills.

"In the South the realm of Gondor long endured; and for a while its splendour grew, recalling somewhat of the might of Númenor, ere it fell. High towers that people built, and strong places, and havens of many ships; and the winged crown of the Kings of Men was held in awe by folk of many tongues. Their chief city was Osgiliath, Citadel of the Stars, through the midst of which the River flowed. And Minas Ithil they built, Tower of the Rising Moon, eastward upon a shoulder of the Mountains of Shadow; and westward at the feet of the White Mountains Minas Anor they made, Tower of the Setting Sun. There in the courts of the King grew a white tree, from the seed of that tree which Isildur brought over the deep waters, and the seed of that tree before came from Eressëa, and before that out of the Uttermost West in the Day before days when the world was young.

"But in the wearing of the swift years of Middle-earth the line of Meneldil son of Anárion failed, and the Tree withered, and the blood of the Númenoreans became mingled with that of lesser men. Then the watch upon the walls of Mordor slept, and dark things crept back to Gorgoroth. And on a time evil things came forth, and they took Minas Ithil and abode in it, and they made it into a place of dread; and it is called Minas Morgul, the Tower of Sorcery. Then Minas Anor was named anew Minas Tirith, the Tower of Guard; and these two cities were ever at war, but Osgiliath which lay between was deserted and in its ruins shadows walked.

"So it has been for many lives of men. But the Lords of Minas Tirith still fight on, defying our enemies, keeping the passage of the River from Argonath to the Sea. And now that part of the tale that I shall tell is drawn to its close. For in the days of Isildur the Ruling Ring passed out of all knowledge, and the Three were released from its dominion. But now in this latter day they are in peril once more, for to our sorrow the One has been found. Others shall speak of its finding, for in that I played small part."

He ceased, but at once Boromir stood up, tall and proud, before them. "Give me leave, Master Elrond," said he, "first to say more of Gondor; for verily from the land of Gondor I am come. And it would be well for all to know what passes there. For few, I deem, know of our deeds, and therefore guess little of their peril, if we should fail at last.

"Believe not that in the land of Gondor the blood of Númenor is spent, nor all its pride and dignity forgotten. By our valour the wild folk of the East are still restrained, and the terror of Morgul kept at bay; and thus alone are peace and freedom maintained in the lands behind us, bulwark of the West. But if the passages of the River should be won, what then?

"Yet that hour, maybe, is not now far away. The Nameless Enemy has arisen again. Smoke rises once more from Orodruin that we call Mount Doom. The power of the Black Land grows and we are hard beset. When the Enemy returned our folk were driven from Ithilien, our fair domain east of the River, though we kept a foothold there and strength of arms. But this very year, in the days of June, sudden war came upon us out of Mordor, and we were swept away. We were outnumbered, for Mordor has allied itself with the Easterlings and the cruel Haradrim; but it was not by numbers that we were defeated. A power was there that we have not felt before.

"Some said that it could be seen, like a great black horseman, a dark shadow under the moon. Wherever he came a madness filled our foes, but fear fell on our boldest, so that horse and man gave way and fled. Only a remnant of our eastern force came back, destroying the last bridge that still stood amid the ruins of Osgiliath.

"I was in the company that held the bridge, until it was cast down behind us. Four only were saved by swimming: my brother and myself and two others. But still we fight on, holding all the west shores of Anduin; and those who shelter behind us give us praise, if ever they hear our name: much praise but little help. Only from Rohan now will any men ride to us when we call.

"In this evil hour I have come on an errand over many dangerous leagues to Elrond: a hundred and ten days I have journeyed all alone. But I do not seek allies in war. The might of Elrond is in wisdom not in weapons, it is said. I come to ask for counsel and the unravelling of hard words. For on the eve of the sudden assault a dream came to my brother in a troubled sleep; and afterwards a like dream came oft to him again, and once to me.

"In that dream I thought the eastern sky grew dark and there was a growing thunder, but in the West a pale light lingered, and out of it I heard a voice, remote but clear, crying:

> Seek for the Sword that was broken:
> In Imladris it dwells;

> *There shall be counsels taken*
> *Stronger than Morgul-spells.*
> *There shall be shown a token*
> *That Doom is near at hand,*
> *For Isildur's Bane shall waken,*
> *And the Halfling forth shall stand.*

Of these words we could understand little, and we spoke to our father, Denethor, Lord of Minas Tirith, wise in the lore of Gondor. This only would he say, that Imladris was of old the name among the Elves of a far northern dale, where Elrond the Halfelven dwelt, greatest of lore-masters. Therefore my brother, seeing how desperate was our need, was eager to heed the dream and seek for Imladris; but since the way was full of doubt and danger, I took the journey upon myself. Loth was my father to give me leave, and long have I wandered by roads forgotten, seeking the house of Elrond, of which many had heard, but few knew where it lay."

"And here in the house of Elrond more shall be made clear to you," said Aragorn, standing up. He cast his sword upon the table that stood before Elrond, and the blade was in two pieces. "Here is the Sword that was Broken!" he said.

"And who are you, and what have you to do with Minas Tirith?" asked Boromir, looking in wonder at the lean face of the Ranger and his weather-stained cloak.

"He is Aragorn son of Arathorn," said Elrond; "and he is descended through many fathers from Isildur Elendil's son of Minas Ithil. He is the Chief of the Dúnedain in the North, and few are now left of that folk."

"Then it belongs to you, and not to me at all!" cried Frodo in amazement, springing to his feet, as if he expected the Ring to be demanded at once.

"It does not belong to either of us," said Aragorn; "but it has been ordained that you should hold it for a while."

"Bring out the Ring, Frodo!" said Gandalf solemnly. "The time has come. Hold it up, and then Boromir will understand the remainder of his riddle."

There was a hush, and all turned their eyes on Frodo. He was shaken by a sudden shame and fear; and he felt a great reluctance to reveal the Ring, and a loathing of its touch. He wished he was far away. The Ring gleamed and flickered as he held it up before them in his trembling hand.

"Behold Isildur's Bane!" said Elrond.

Boromir's eyes glinted as he gazed at the golden thing. "The Halfling!" he muttered. "Is then the doom of Minas Tirith come at last? But why then should we seek a broken sword?"

"The words were not *the doom of Minas Tirith*," said Aragorn. "But doom and great deeds are indeed at hand. For the Sword that was Broken is the Sword of Elendil that broke beneath him when he fell. It has been treasured by his heirs when all other heirlooms were lost; for it was spoken of old among us that it should be made again when the Ring, Isildur's Bane, was found. Now you have seen the sword that you have sought, what would you ask? Do you wish for the House of Elendil to return to the Land of Gondor?"

"I was not sent to beg any boon, but to seek only the meaning of a riddle," answered Boromir proudly. "Yet we are hard pressed, and the Sword of Elendil would be a help beyond our hope — if such a thing could indeed return out of the shadows of the past." He looked again at Aragorn, and doubt was in his eyes.

Frodo felt Bilbo stir impatiently at his side. Evidently he was annoyed on his friend's behalf. Standing suddenly up he burst out:

> All that is gold does not glitter,
>   Not all those who wander are lost;
> The old that is strong does not wither,
>   Deep roots are not reached by the frost,

> *From the ashes a fire shall be woken,*
> *A light from the shadows shall spring;*
> *Renewed shall be blade that was broken:*
> *The crownless again shall be king.*

"Not very good perhaps, but to the point — if you need more beyond the word of Elrond. If that was worth a journey of a hundred and ten days to hear, you had best listen to it." He sat down with a snort.

"I made that up myself," he whispered to Frodo, "for the Dúnadan, a long time ago when he first told me about himself. I almost wish that my adventures were not over, and that I could go with him when his day comes."

Aragorn smiled at him; then he turned to Boromir again. "For my part I forgive your doubt," he said. "Little do I resemble the figures of Elendil and Isildur as they stand carven in their majesty in the halls of Denethor. I am but the heir of Isildur, not Isildur himself. I have had a hard life and a long; and the leagues that lie between here and Gondor are a small part in the count of my journeys. I have crossed many mountains and many rivers, and trodden many plains, even into the far countries of Rhûn and Harad where the stars are strange.

"But my home, such as I have, is in the North. For here the heirs of Valandil have ever dwelt in long line unbroken from father unto son for many generations. Our days have darkened, and we have dwindled; but ever the Sword has passed to a new keeper. And this I will say to you, Boromir, ere I end. Lonely men are we, Rangers of the wild, hunters — but hunters ever of the servants of the Enemy; for they are found in many places, not in Mordor only.

"If Gondor, Boromir, has been a stalwart tower, we have played another part. Many evil things there are that your strong walls and bright swords do not stay. You know little of the lands beyond your bounds. Peace and freedom, do you say? The North would have known them little but for us. Fear would have destroyed them. But when dark things come from the houseless hills, or creep from sunless woods, they fly from us. What roads would any dare to tread, what safety would there be in quiet lands, or in the homes of simple men at night, if the Dúnedain were asleep, or were all gone into the grave?

"And yet less thanks have we than you. Travellers scowl at us, and countrymen give us scornful names. 'Strider' I am to one fat man who lives within a day's march of foes that would freeze his heart, or lay his little town in ruin, if he were not guarded ceaselessly. Yet we would not have it otherwise. If simple folk are free from care and fear, simple they will be, and we must be secret to keep them so. That has been the task of my kindred, while the years have lengthened and the grass has grown.

"But now the world is changing once again. A new hour comes. Isildur's Bane is found. Battle is at hand. The Sword shall be reforged. I will come to Minas Tirith."

"Isildur's Bane is found, you say," said Boromir. "I have seen a bright ring in the Halfling's hand; but Isildur perished ere this age of the world began, they say. How do the Wise know that this ring is his? And how has it passed down the years, until it is brought hither by so strange a messenger?"

"That shall be told," said Elrond.

"But not yet, I beg, Master!" said Bilbo. "Already the Sun is climbing to noon, and I feel the need of something to strengthen me."

"I had not named you," said Elrond smiling. "But I do so now. Come! Tell us your tale. And if you have not yet cast your story into verse, you may tell it in plain words. The briefer, the sooner shall you be refreshed."

"Very well," said Bilbo. "I will do as you bid. But I will now tell the true story, and if some here have heard me tell it otherwise" — he looked sidelong at Glóin — "I ask them to forget it and forgive me. I only wished to claim the treasure as my very own in those days, and to be rid of the name of thief that was put on me. But perhaps I understand things a little better now. Anyway, this is what happened."

To some there Bilbo's tale was wholly new, and they listened with amazement while the old hobbit, actually not at all displeased, recounted his adventure with Gollum, at full length. He did not omit a single riddle. He would have given also an account of his party and disappearance from the Shire, if he had been allowed; but Elrond raised his hand.

"Well told, my friend," he said, "but that is enough at this time. For the moment it suffices to know that the King passed to Frodo, your heir. Let him now speak!"

Then, less willingly than Bilbo, Frodo told of all his dealings with the Ring from the day that it passed into his keeping. Every step of his journey from Hobbiton to the Ford of Bruinen was questioned and considered, and everything that he could recall concerning the Black Riders was examined. At last he sat down again.

"Not bad," Bilbo said to him. "You would have made a good story of it, if they hadn't kept on interrupting. I tried to make a few notes, but we shall have to go over it all again together some time, if I am to write it up. There are whole chapters of stuff before you ever got here!"

"Yes, it made quite a long tale," answered Frodo. "But the story still does not seem complete to me. I still want to know a good deal, especially about Gandalf."

Galdor of the Havens, who sat near by, overheard him. "You speak for me also," he cried, and turning to Elrond he said: "The Wise may have good reason to believe that the halfling's trove is indeed the Great Ring of long debate, unlikely though that may seem to those who know less. But may we not hear the proofs? And I would ask this also. What of Saruman? He is learned in the lore of the Rings, yet he is not among us. What is his counsel — if he knows the things that we have heard?"

"The questions that you ask, Galdor, are bound together,"

said Elrond. "I had not overlooked them, and they shall be answered. But these things it is the part of Gandalf to make clear; and I call upon him last, for it is the place of honour, and in all this matter he has been the chief."

"Some, Galdor," said Gandalf, "would think the tidings of Glóin, and the pursuit of Frodo, proof enough that the halfling's trove is a thing of great worth to the Enemy. Yet it is a ring. What then? The Nine the Nazgûl keep. The Seven are taken or destroyed," At this Glóin stirred, but did not speak. "The Three we know of. What then is this one that he desires so much?

"There is indeed a wide waste of time between the River and the Mountain, between the loss and the finding. But the gap in the knowledge of the Wise has been filled at last. Yet too slowly. For the Enemy has been close behind, closer even than I feared. And well is it that not until this year, this very summer, as it seems, did he learn the full truth.

"Some here will remember that many years ago I myself dared to pass the doors of the Necromancer in Dol Guldur, and secretly explored his ways, and found thus that our fears were true: he was none other than Sauron, our Enemy of old, at length taking shape and power again. Some, too, will remember also that Saruman dissuaded us from open deeds against him, and for long we watched him only. Yet at last, as his shadow grew, Saruman yielded, and the Council put forth its strength and drove the evil out of Mirkwood — and that was in the very year of the finding of this Ring: a strange chance, if chance it was.

"But we were too late, as Elrond foresaw. Sauron also had watched us, and had long prepared against our stroke, governing Mordor from afar through Minas Morgul, where his Nine servants dwelt, until all was ready. Then he gave way before us, but only feigned to flee, and soon after came to the Dark Tower and openly declared himself. Then for the last time the Council met; for now we learned that he was seeking ever more eagerly for the One. We feared then that he had some news of it that we knew nothing of. But Saruman said nay, and repeated what he had said to us before: that the One would never again be found in Middle-earth.

"'At the worst,' said he, 'our Enemy knows that we have it not, and that it still is lost. But what was lost may yet be found, he thinks. Fear not! His hope will cheat him. Have I not earnestly studied this matter? Into Anduin the Great it fell; and long ago, while Sauron slept, it was rolled down the River to the Sea. There let it lie until the End.'"

Gandalf fell silent, gazing eastward from the porch to the far peaks of the Misty Mountains, at whose great roots the peril of the world had so long lain hidden. He sighed.

"There I was at fault," he said. "I was lulled by the words of Saruman the Wise; but I should have sought for the truth sooner, and our peril would now be less."

"We were all at fault," said Elrond, "and but for your vigilance the Darkness, maybe, would already be upon us. But say on!"

"From the first my heart misgave me, against all reason that I knew," said Gandalf, "and I desired to know how this thing came to Gollum, and how long he had possessed it. So I set a watch for him, guessing that he would ere long come forth from his darkness to seek for his treasure. He came, but he escaped and was not found. And then alas! I let the matter rest, watching and waiting only, as we have too often done.

"Time passed with many cares, until my doubts were awakened again to sudden fear. Whence came the hobbit's ring? What, if my fear was true, should be done with it? Those things I must decide. But I spoke yet of my dread to none, knowing the peril of an untimely whisper, if it went astray. In all the long wars with the Dark Tower treason has ever been our greatest foe.

"That was seventeen years ago. Soon I became aware that spies of many sorts, even beasts and birds, were gathered round the Shire, and my fear grew. I called for the help of the Dúnedain, and their watch was doubled; and I opened my heart to Aragorn, the heir of Isildur."

"And I," said Aragorn, "counselled that we should hunt for Gollum, too late though it may seem. And since it seemed fit that Isildur's heir should labour to repair Isildur's fault, I went with Gandalf on the long and hopeless search."

Then Gandalf told how they had explored the whole length of Wilderland, down even to the Mountains of Shadow and the fences of Mordor. "There we had rumour of him, and we guess that he dwelt there long in the dark hills; but we never found him, and at last I despaired. And then in my despair I thought again of a test that might make the finding of Gollum unneeded. The ring itself might tell if it were the One. The memory of words at the Council came back to me: words of Saruman, half-heeded at the time. I heard them now clearly in my heart.

"'The Nine, the Seven, and the Three,' he said, 'had each their proper gem. Not so the One. It was round and unadorned, as it were one of the lesser rings; but its maker set marks upon it that the skilled, maybe, could still see and read.'

"What those marks were he had not said. Who now would know? The maker. And Saruman? But great though his lore may be, it must have a source. What hand save Sauron's ever held this thing, ere it was lost? The hand of Isildur alone.

"With that thought, I forsook the chase, and passed swiftly to Gondor. In former days the members of my order had been well received there, but Saruman most of all. Often he had been for long the guest of the Lords of the City. Less welcome did the Lord Denethor show me then than of old, and grudgingly he permitted me to search among his hoarded scrolls and books.

"'If indeed you look only, as you say, for records of ancient days, and the beginnings of the City, read on!' he said. 'For to me what was is less dark than what is to come, and that is my care. But unless you have more skill even than Saruman, who has studied here long, you will find naught that is not well known to me, who am master of the lore of this City.'

"So said Denethor. And yet there lie in his hoards many records that few now can read, even of the lore-masters, for their scripts and tongues have become dark to later men. And Boromir, there lies in Minas Tirith still, unread, I guess, by any save Saruman and myself since the kings failed, a scroll that Isildur made himself. For Isildur did not march away straight from the war in Mordor, as some have told the tale."

"Some in the North, maybe," Boromir broke in. "All know in Gondor that he went first to Minas Anor and dwelt a while with his nephew Meneldil, instructing him, before he committed to him the rule of the South Kingdom. In that time he planted there the last sapling of the White Tree in memory of his brother."

"But in that time also he made this scroll," said Gandalf; "and that is not remembered in Gondor, it would seem. For this scroll concerns the Ring, and thus wrote Isildur therein:

The Great Ring shall go now to be an heirloom of the North Kingdom but records of it shall be left in Gondor, where also dwell the heirs of Elendil, lest a time come when the memory of these great matters shall grow dim.

"And after these words Isildur described the Ring, such as he found it.

It was hot when I first took it, hot as a glede, and my hand was scorched, so that I doubt if ever again I shall be free of the pain of it. Yet even as I write it is cooled, and it seemeth to shrink, though it loseth neither its beauty nor its shape. Already the writing upon it, which at first was as clear as red flame, fadeth and is now only barely to be read. It is fashioned in an elven-script of Eregion, for they have no letters in Mordor for such subtle work; but the language is unknown to me. I deem it to be a tongue of the Black Land, since it is foul and uncouth. What evil it saith I do not know; but I trace here a copy of it, lest it fade beyond recall. The Ring misseth, maybe, the heat of Sauron's hand, which was black and yet burned like fire, and so Gil-galad was destroyed; and maybe were the gold made hot again, the writing would be refreshed. But for my part I will risk no hurt to this thing: of all the works of Sauron the only fair. It is precious to me, though I buy it with great pain.

"When I read these words, my quest was ended. For the traced writing was indeed as Isildur guessed, in the tongue of Mordor and the servants of the Tower. And what was said therein was already known. For in the day that Sauron first put on the One, Celebrimbor, maker of the Three, was aware of him, and from afar he heard him speak these words, and so his evil purposes were revealed.

"At once I took my leave of Denethor, but even as I went northwards, messages came to me out of Lórien that Aragorn had passed that way, and that he had found the creature called Gollum. Therefore I went first to meet him and hear his tale. Into what deadly perils he had gone alone I dared not guess."

"There is little need to tell of them," said Aragorn. "If a man must needs walk in sight of the Black Gate, or tread the deadly flowers of Morgul Vale, then perils he will have. I, too, despaired at last, and I began my homeward journey. And then, by fortune, I came suddenly on what I sought: the marks of soft feet beside a muddy pool. But now the trail was fresh and swift, and it led not to Mordor but away. Along the skirts of the Dead Marshes I followed it, and then I had him. Lurking by a stagnant mere, peering in the water as the dark eve fell, I caught him, Gollum. He was covered with green slime. He will never love me, I fear; for he bit me, and I was not gentle. Nothing more did I ever get from his mouth than the marks of his teeth. I deemed it the worst part of all my journey, the road back, watching him day and night, making him walk before me with a halter on his neck, gagged, until he was tamed by lack of drink and food, driving him ever towards Mirkwood. I brought him there at last and gave him to the Elves, for we had agreed that this should be done; and I was glad to be rid of his company, for he stank. For my part I hope never to look upon him again; but Gandalf came and endured long speech with him."

"Yes, long and weary," said Gandalf, "but not without profit. For one thing, the tale he told of his loss agreed with that which Bilbo has now told openly for the first time; but that mattered little, since I had already guessed it. But I learned then first that Gollum's ring came out of the Great River nigh to the Gladden Fields. And I learned also that he had possessed it long. Many lives of his small kind. The power of the ring had lengthened his years far beyond their span; but that power only the Great Rings wield.

"And if that is not proof enough, Galdor, there is the other test that I spoke of. Upon this very ring which you have here seen held aloft, round and unadorned, the letters that Isildur reported may still be read, if one has the strength of will to set the golden thing in the fire a while. That I have done, and this I have read:

Ash nazg durbatulûk, ash nazg gimbatul, ash nazg thrakatulûk agh burzum-ishi krimpatul."

The change in the wizard's voice was astounding. Suddenly it became menacing, powerful, harsh as stone. A shadow seemed to pass over the high sun, and the porch for a moment grew dark. All trembled, and the Elves stopped their ears.

"Never before has any voice dared to utter words of that tongue in Imladris, Gandalf the Grey," said Elrond, as the shadow passed and the company breathed once more.

"And let us hope that none will ever speak it here again," answered Gandalf. "Nonetheless I do not ask your pardon, Master Elrond. For if that tongue is not soon to be heard in every corner of the West, then let all put doubt aside that this thing is indeed what the Wise have declared: the treasure of the Enemy, fraught with all his malice; and in it lies a great part of his strength of old. Out of the Black Years come the words that the Smiths of Eregion heard, and knew that they had been betrayed:

One Ring to rule the all, One Ring to find them, One Ring to bring them all and in the Darkness bind them.

"Know also, my friends, that I learned more yet from Gollum. He was loth to speak and his tale was unclear, but it is beyond all doubt that he went to Mordor, and there all that he knew was forced from him. Thus the Enemy knows now that the One is found, that it was long in the Shire; and since his servants have pursued it almost to our door, he soon will know, already he may know, even as I speak, that we have it here."

All sat silent for a while, until at length Boromir spoke. "He is a small thing, you say, this Gollum? Small, but great in mischief. What became of him? To what doom did you put him?"

"He is in prison, but no worse," said Aragorn. "He had suffered much. There is no doubt that he was tormented, and the fear of Sauron lies black on his heart. Still I for one am glad that he is safely kept by the watchful Elves of Mirkwood. His malice is great and gives him a strength hardly to be believed in one so lean and withered. He could work much mischief still, if he were free. And I do not doubt that he was allowed to leave Mordor on some evil errand."

"Alas! alas!" cried Legolas, and in his fair elvish face there was great distress. "The tidings that I was sent to bring must now be told. They are not good, but only here have I learned how evil they may seem to this company. Sméagol, who is now called Gollum, has escaped."

"Escaped?" cried Aragorn. "That is ill news indeed. We shall all rue it bitterly, I fear. How came the folk of Thranduil to fail in their trust?"

"Not through lack of watchfulness," said Legolas; "but

perhaps through over-kindliness. And we fear that the prisoner had aid from others, and that more is known of our doings than we could wish. We guarded this creature day and night, at Gandalf's bidding, much though we wearied of the task. But Gandalf bade us hope still for his cure, and we had not the heart to keep him ever in dungeons under the earth, where he would fall back into his old black thoughts."

"You were less tender to me," said Glóin with a flash of his eyes, as old memories were stirred of his imprisonment in the deep places of the Elven-king's halls.

"Now come!" said Gandalf. "Pray do not interrupt, my good Glóin. That was a regrettable misunderstanding, long set right. If all the grievances that stand between Elves and Dwarves are to be brought up here, we may as well abandon this Council."

Glóin rose and bowed, and Legolas continued. "In the days of fair weather we led Gollum through the woods; and there was a high tree standing alone far from the others which he liked to climb. Often we let him mount up to the highest branches, until he felt the free wind; but we set a guard at the tree's foot. One day he refused to come down, and the guards had no mind to climb after him: he had learned the trick of clinging to boughs with his feet as well as with his hands; so they sat by the tree far into the night.

"It was that very night of summer, yet moonless and starless, that Orcs came on us at unawares. We drove them off after some time; they were many and fierce, but they came from over the mountains, and were unused to the woods. When the battle was over, we found that Gollum was gone, and his guards were slain or taken. It then seemed plain to us that the attack had been made for his rescue, and that he knew of it beforehand. How that was contrived we cannot guess; but Gollum is cunning, and the spies of the Enemy are many. The dark things that were driven out in the year of the Dragon's fall have returned in greater numbers, and Mirkwood is again an evil place, save where our realm is maintained.

"We have failed to recapture Gollum. We came on his trail

among those of many Orcs, and it plunged deep into the Forest, going south. But ere long it escaped our skill, and we dared not continue the hunt; for we were drawing nigh to Dol Guldur, and that is still a very evil place; we do not go that way."

"Well, well, he is gone," said Gandalf. "we have no time to seek for him again. He must do what he will. But he may play a part yet that neither he nor Sauron have foreseen.

"And now I will answer Galdor's other questions. What of Saruman? What are his counsels to us in this need? This tale I must tell in full, for only Elrond has heard it yet, and that in brief; but it will bear on all that we must resolve. It is the last chapter in the Tale of the Ring, so far as it has yet gone.

"At the end of June I was in the Shire, but a cloud of anxiety was on my mind, and I rode to the southern borders of the little land; for I had a foreboding of some danger, still hidden from me but drawing near. There messages reached me telling me of war and defeat in Gondor, and when I heard of the Black Shadow a chill smote my heart. But I found nothing save a few fugitives from the South; yet it seemed to me that on them sat a fear of which they would not speak. I turned then east and north and journeyed along the Greenway; and not far from Bree I came upon a traveller sitting on a bank beside the road with his grazing horse beside him. It was Radagast the Brown, who at one time dwelt at Rhosgobel, near the borders of Mirkwood. He is one of my order, but I had not seen him for many a year.

"'Gandalf!' he cried. 'I was seeking you. But I am a stranger in these parts. All I knew was that you might be found in a wild region with the uncouth name of Shire.'

"'Your information was correct,' I said. 'But do not put it that way, if you meet any of the inhabitants. You are near the borders of the Shire now. And what do you want with me? It must be pressing. You were never a traveller, unless driven by great need.'

"'I have an urgent errand,' he said. 'My news is evil.' Then he looked about him, as if the hedges might have ears. 'Nazgûl,' he whispered. 'The Nine are abroad again. They have crossed the River secretly and are moving westward. They have taken the guise of riders in black.'

"I knew then what I had dreaded without knowing it.

"'The Enemy must have some great need or purpose,' said Radagast; 'but what it is that makes him look to these distant and desolate parts, I cannot guess.'

"'What do you mean?' said I.

"'I have been told that wherever they go the Riders ask for news of a land called Shire.'

"'*The* Shire,' I said; but my heart sank. For even the Wise might fear to withstand the Nine, when they are gathered together under their fell chieftain. A great king and sorcerer he was of old, and now he wields a deadly fear. 'Who told you, and who sent you.' I asked.

"'Saruman the White,' answered Radagast. 'And he told me to say that if you feel the need, he will help; but you must seek his aid at once, or it will be too late.'

"And that message brought me hope. For Saruman the White is the greatest of my order. Radagast is, of course, a worthy Wizard, a master of shapes and changes of hue; and he has much lore of herbs and beasts, and birds are especially his friends. But Saruman has long studied the arts of the Enemy himself, and thus we have often been able to forestall him. It was by the devices of Saruman that we drove him from Dol Guldur. It might be that he had found some weapons that would drive back the Nine.

"'I will go to Saruman,' I said.

"'Then you must go *now*,' said Radagast; 'for I have wasted time in looking for you, and the days are running short. I was told to find you before Midsummer, and that is now here. Even if you set out from this spot, you will hardly reach him before the Nine discover the land that they seek. I myself shall turn back at once.' And with that he mounted and would have ridden straight off.

"'Stay a moment!' I said. 'We shall need your help, and the help of all things that will give it. Send out messages to all the beasts and birds that are your friends. Tell them to bring news of anything that bears on this matter to Saruman and Gandalf. Let messages be sent to Orthanc.'

"'I will do that,' he said, and rode off as if the Nine were after him.

"I could not follow him then and there. I had ridden very far already that day, and I was as weary as my horse; and I needed to consider matters. I stayed the night in Bree, and decided that I had no time to return to the Shire. Never did I make a greater mistake!

"However, I wrote a message to Frodo, and trusted to my friend the innkeeper to send it to him. I rode away at dawn; and I came at long last to the dwelling of Saruman. That is far south in Isengard, in the end of the Misty Mountains, not far from the Gap of Rohan. And Boromir will tell you that that is a great open vale that lies between the Misty Mountains and the northmost foothills of Ered Nimrais, the White Mountains of his home. But Isengard is a circle of sheer rocks that enclose a valley as with a wall, and in the midst of that valley is a tower of stone called Orthanc. It was not made by Saruman, but by the Men of Númenor long ago; and it is very tall and has many secrets; yet it looks not to be a work of craft. It cannot be reached save by passing the circle of Isengard; and in that circle there is only one gate.

"Late one evening I came to the gate, like a great arch in the wall of rock; and it was strongly guarded. But the keepers of the gate were on the watch for me and told me that Saruman awaited me. I rode under the arch, and the gate closed silently behind me, and suddenly I was afraid, though I knew no reason for it.

"But I rode to the foot of Orthanc, and came to the stair of Saruman; and there he met me and led me up to his high chamber. He wore a ring on his finger.

"'So you have come, Gandalf,' he said to me gravely; but in his eyes there seemed to be a white light, as if a cold laughter was in his heart.

"'Yes, I have come,' I said. 'I have come for your aid, Saruman the White.' And that title seemed to anger him.

"'Have you indeed, Gandalf the *Grey*!' he scoffed. 'For aid? It has seldom been heard of that Gandalf the Grey sought for aid, one so cunning and so wise, wandering about the lands, and concerning himself in every business, whether it belongs to him or not.'

"I looked at him and wondered. 'But if I am not deceived,' said I, 'things are now moving which will require the union of all our strength.'

"'That may be so,' he said, 'but the thought is late in coming to you. How long, I wonder, have you concealed from me, the head of the Council, a matter of greatest import? What brings you now from your lurking-place in the Shire?'

"'The Nine have come forth again,' I answered. 'They have crossed the River. So Radagast said to me.'

"'Radagast the Brown!' laughed Saruman, and he no longer concealed his scorn. 'Radagast the Bird-tamer! Radagast the Simple! Radagast the Fool! Yet he had just the wit to play the part that I set him. For you have come, and that was all the purpose of my message. And here you will stay, Gandalf the Grey, and rest from journeys. For I am Saruman the Wise, Saruman Ring-maker, Saruman of Many Colours!'

"I looked then and saw that his robes, which had seemed white, were not so, but were woven of all colours, and if he moved they shimmered and changed hue so that the eye was bewildered.

"'I liked white better,' I said.

"'White!' he sneered. 'It serves as a beginning. White cloth may be dyed. The white page can be overwritten; and the white light can be broken.'

"'In which case it is no longer white,' said I. 'And he that breaks a thing to find out what it is has left the path of wisdom.'

"'You need not speak to me as to one of the fools that you take for friends,' said he. 'I have not brought you hither to be instructed by you, but to give you a choice.'

"He drew himself up then and began to declaim, as if he were making a speech long rehearsed. 'The Elder Days are gone. The Middle Days are passing. The Younger Days are beginning. The time of the Elves is over, but our time is at hand: the world of Men, which we must rule. But we must have power, power to order all things as we will, for that good which only the Wise can see.

"'And listen, Gandalf, my old friend and helper!' he said, coming near and speaking now in a softer voice. 'I said *we*, for *we* it may be, if you will join with me. A new Power is rising. Against it the old allies and policies will not avail us at all. There is no hope left in Elves or dying Númenor. This then is one choice before you, before us. We may join with that Power. It would be wise, Gandalf. There is hope that way. Its victory is at hand; and there will be rich reward for those that aided it. As the Power grows, its proved friends will also grow; and the Wise, such as you and I, may with patience come at last to direct its courses, to control it. We can bide our time, we can keep our thoughts in our hearts, deploring maybe evils done by the way, but approving the high and ultimate purpose: Knowledge, Rule, Order; all the things that we have so far striven in vain to accomplish, hindered rather than helped by our weak or idle friends. There need not be, there would not be, any real change in our designs, only in our means.'

"'Saruman,' I said, 'I have heard speeches of this kind before, but only in the mouths of emissaries sent from Mordor to deceive the ignorant. I cannot think that you brought me so far only to weary my ears.'

"He looked at me sidelong, and paused a while considering. 'Well, I see that this wise course does not commend itself to you,' he said. 'Not yet? Not if some better way can be contrived?'

"He came and laid his long hand on my arm. 'And why not, Gandalf?' he whispered. 'Why not? The Ruling Ring? If we could command that, then the Power would pass to *us*. That is in truth why I brought you here. For I have many eyes in my service, and I believe that you know where this precious thing now lies. Is it not so? Or why do the Nine ask for the Shire, and what is your business there?' As he said this a lust which he could not conceal shone suddenly in his eyes.

"'Saruman,' I said, standing away from him, 'only one hand at a time can wield the One, and you know that well, so do not trouble to say *we*! But I would not give it, nay, I would not give even news of it to you, now that I learn your mind. You were head of the Council, but you have unmasked yourself at last. Well, the choices are, it seems, to submit to Sauron, or to yourself. I will take neither. Have you others to offer?'

"He was cold now and perilous. 'Yes,' he said. 'I did not expect you to show wisdom, even in your own behalf; but I gave you the chance of aiding me willingly, and so saving yourself much trouble and pain. The third choice is to stay here, until the end.'

"'Until what end?'

"'Until you reveal to me where the One may be found. I may find means to persuade you. Or until it is found in your despite, and the Ruler has time to turn to lighter matters: to devise, say, a fitting reward for the hindrance and insolence of Gandalf the Grey.'

"'That may not prove to be one of the lighter matters,' said I. He laughed at me, for my words were empty, and he knew it.

"They took me and they set me alone on the pinnacle of Orthanc, in the place where Saruman was accustomed to watch the stars. There is no descent save by a narrow stair of many thousand steps, and the valley below seems far away. I looked on it and saw that, whereas it had once been green and fair, it was now filled with pits and forges. Wolves and orcs were housed in Isengard, for Saruman was mustering a great force on his own account, in rivalry of Sauron and not in his service yet. Over all his works a dark smoke hung and wrapped itself about the sides of Orthanc. I stood alone on an island in the clouds; and I had no chance of escape, and my days were bitter. I was pierced with cold, and I had but little room in which to pace to and fro, brooding on the coming of the Riders to the North.

"That the Nine had indeed arisen I felt assured, apart from the words of Saruman which might be lies. Long ere I came to Isengard I had heard tidings by the way that could not be mistaken. Fear was ever in my heart for my friends in the Shire; but still I had some hope. I hoped that Frodo had set forth at once, as my letter had urged, and that he had reached Rivendell before the deadly pursuit began. And both my fear and my hope proved ill-founded. For my hope was founded on a fat man in Bree; and my fear was founded on the cunning of Sauron. But fat men who sell ale have many calls to answer; and the power of Sauron is still less than fear makes it. But in the circle of Isengard, trapped and alone, it was not easy to think that the hunters before whom all have fled or fallen would falter in the Shire far away."

"I saw you!" cried Frodo. "You were walking backwards and forwards. The moon shone in your hair."

Gandalf paused astonished and looked at him. "It was only a dream," said Frodo, "but it suddenly came back to me. I had quite forgotten it. It came some time ago; after I left the Shire, I think."

"Then it was late in coming," said Gandalf, "as you will see. I was in an evil plight. And those who know me will agree that I have seldom been in such need, and do not bear such misfortune well. Gandalf the Grey caught like a fly in a spider's treacherous web! Yet even the most subtle spiders may leave a weak thread.

"At first I feared, as Saruman no doubt intended, that Radagast had also fallen. Yet I had caught no hint of anything wrong in his voice or in his eye at our meeting. If I had, I should never have gone to Isengard, or I should have gone more warily. So Saruman guessed, and he had concealed his mind and deceived his messenger. It would have been useless in any case to try and win over the honest Radagast to treachery. He sought me in good faith, and so persuaded me.

"That was the undoing of Saruman's plot. For Radagast knew no reason why he should not do as I asked; and he rode away towards Mirkwood where he had many friends of old. And the Eagles of the Mountains went far and wide, and they saw many things: the gathering of wolves and the mustering of Orcs; and the Nine Riders going hither and thither in the lands; and they heard news of the escape of Gollum. And they sent a messenger to bring these tidings to me.

"So it was that when summer waned, there came a night of moon, and Gwaihir the Windlord, swiftest of the Great Eagles, came unlooked-for to Orthanc; and he found me standing on the pinnacle. Then I spoke to him and he bore me away, before Saruman was aware. I was far from Isengard, ere the wolves and orcs issued from the gate to pursue me.

"'How far can you bear me?' I said to Gwaihir.

"'Many leagues,' said he, 'but not to the ends of the earth. I was sent to bear tidings not burdens.'

"'Then I must have a steed on land,' I said, 'and a steed surpassingly swift, for I have never had such need of haste before.'

"'Then I will bear you to Edoras, where the Lord of Rohan sits in his halls,' he said; 'for that is not very far off.' And I was glad, for in the Riddermark of Rohan the Rohirrim, the Horse-lords, dwell, and there are no horses like those that are bred in that great vale between the Misty Mountains and the White.

"'Are the Men of Rohan still to be trusted, do you think?' I said to Gwaihir, for the treason of Saruman had shaken my faith.

"'They pay a tribute of horses,' he answered, 'and send many yearly to Mordor, or so it is said; but they are not yet under the yoke. But if Saruman has become evil, as you say, then their doom cannot be long delayed.'

"He set me down in the land of Rohan ere dawn; and now I have lengthened my tale over long. The rest must be more brief. In Rohan I found evil already at work: the lies of Saruman; and the king of the land would not listen to my warnings. He bade me take a horse and be gone; and I chose one much to my liking, but little to his. I took the best horse in his land, and I have never seen the like of him."

"Then he must be a noble beast indeed," said Aragorn; "and it grieves me more than many tidings that might seem worse to learn that Sauron levies such tribute. It was not so when last I was in that land."

"Nor is it now, I will swear," said Boromir. "It is a lie that comes from the Enemy. I know the Men of Rohan, true and valiant, our allies, dwelling still in the lands that we gave them long ago.

"The shadow of Mordor lies on distant lands," answered Aragorn. "Saruman has fallen under it. Rohan is beset. Who knows what you will find there, if ever you return?"

"Not this at least," said Boromir, "that they will buy their lives with horses. They love their horses next to their kin. And not without reason, for the horses of the Riddermark come from the fields of the North, far from the Shadow, and their race, as that of their masters, is descended from the free days of old."

"True indeed!" said Gandalf. "And there is one among them that might have been foaled in the morning of the world. The horses of the Nine cannot vie with him; tireless, swift as the flowing wind. Shadowfax they called him. By day his coat glistens like silver; and by night it is like a shade, and he passes unseen. Light is his footfall! Never before had any man mounted him, but I took him and I tamed him, and so speedily he bore me that I reached the Shire when Frodo was on the Barrow-downs, though I set out from Rohan only when he set out from Hobbiton.

"But fear grew in me as I rode. Ever as I came north I heard tidings of the Riders, and though I gained on them day by day,

they were ever before me. They had divided their forces, I
learned: some remained on the eastern borders, not far from the
Greenway, and some invaded the Shire from the south. I came
to Hobbiton and Frodo had gone; but I had words with old
Gamgee. Many words and few to the point. He had much to say
about the shortcomings of the new owners of Bag End.

"'I can't abide changes,' said he, 'not at my time of life, and
least of all changes for the worst.' 'Changes for the worst,' he
repeated many times.

"'Worst is a bad word,' I said to him, 'and I hope you do not
live to see it.' But amidst his talk I gathered at last that Frodo
had left Hobbiton less than a week before, and that a black
horseman had come to the Hill the same evening. Then I rode
on in fear. I came to Buckland and found it in uproar, as busy
as a hive of ants that has been stirred with a stick. I came to the
house at Crickhollow, and it was broken open and empty; but
on the threshold there lay a cloak that had been Frodo's. Then
for a while hope left me, and I did not wait to gather news, or I
might have been comforted; but I rode on the trail of the
Riders. It was hard to follow, for it went many ways, and I was
at a loss. But it seemed to me that one or two had ridden
towards Bree; and that way I went, for I thought of words that
might be said to the innkeeper.

"'Butterbur they call him,' thought I. 'If this delay was his
fault, I will melt all the butter in him. I will roast the old fool
over a slow fire.' He expected no less, and when he saw my face
he fell down flat and began to melt on the spot."

"What did you do to him?" cried Frodo in alarm. "He was
really very kind to us and did all that he could."

Gandalf laughed. "Don't be afraid!" he said. "I did not bite,
and I barked very little. So overjoyed was I by the news that I
got out of him, when he stopped quaking, that I embraced the
old fellow. How it happened I could not then guess, but I
learned that you had been in Bree the night before, and had
gone off that morning with Strider.

"'Strider!' I cried, shouting for joy.

"'Yes, sir, I am afraid so, sir,' said Butterbur, mistaking me. 'He got at them, in spite of all that I could do, and they took up with him. They behaved very queer all the time they were here: wilful, you might say.'

"'Ass! Fool! Thrice worthy and beloved Barliman!' said I. 'It's the best news I have had since midsummer: it's worth a gold piece at the least. May your beer be laid under an enchantment of surpassing excellence for seven years!' said I. 'Now I can take a night's rest, the first since I have forgotten when.'

"So I stayed there that night, wondering much what had become of the Riders; for only of two had there yet been any news in Bree, it seemed. But in the night we heard more. Five at least came from the west, and they threw down the gates and passed through Bree like a howling wind; and the Bree-folk are still shivering and expecting the end of the world. I got up before dawn and went after them.

"I do not know, but it seems clear to me that this is what happened. Their Captain remained in secret away south of Bree, while two rode ahead through the village, and four more invaded the Shire. But when these were foiled in Bree and at Crickhollow, they returned to their Captain with tidings, and so left the Road unguarded for a while, except by their spies. The Captain then sent some eastward straight across country, and he himself with the rest rode along the Road in great wrath.

"I galloped to Weathertop like a gale, and I reached it before sundown on my second day from Bree — and they were there before me. They drew away from me, for they felt the coming of my anger and they dared not face it while the Sun was in the sky. But they closed round at night, and I was besieged on the hill-top, in the old ring of Amon Sûl. I was hard put to it indeed: such light and flame cannot have been seen on Weathertop since the war-beacons of old.

"At sunrise I escaped and fled towards the north. I could not hope to do more. It was impossible to find you, Frodo, in the wilderness, and it would have been folly to try with all the Nine at my heels. So I had to trust to Aragorn. But I hoped to draw some of them off, and yet reach Rivendell ahead of you and send out help. Four Riders did indeed follow me, but they turned back after a while and made for the Ford, it seems. That helped a little, for there were only five, not nine, when your camp was attacked.

"I reached here at last by a long hard road, up the Hoarwell and through the Ettenmoors, and down from the north. It took me nearly fourteen days from Weathertop, for I could not ride among the rocks of the troll-fells, and Shadowfax departed. I sent him back to his master; but a great friendship has grown between us, and if I have need he will come at my call. But so it was that I came to Rivendell only three days before the Ring, and news of its peril had already been brought here — which proved well indeed.

"And that, Frodo, is the end of my account. May Elrond and the others forgive the length of it. But such a thing has not happened before, that Gandalf broke tryst and did not come when he promised. An account to the Ring-bearer of so strange an event was required, I think.

"Well, the Tale is now told, from first to last. Here we all are, and here is the Ring. But we have not yet come any nearer to our purpose. What shall we do with it?"

There was a silence. At last Elrond spoke again.

"This is grievous news concerning Saruman," he said; "for we trusted him and he is deep in all our counsels. It is perilous to study too deeply the arts of the Enemy, for good or for ill. But such falls and betrayals, alas, have happened before. Of the tales that we have heard this day the tale of Frodo was most strange to me. I have known few hobbits, save Bilbo here; and it seems to me that he is perhaps not so alone and singular as I had thought him. The world has changed much since I last was on the westward roads.

"The Barrow-wights we know by many names; and of the

Old Forest many tales have been told: all that now remains is but an outlier of its northern march. Time was when a squirrel could go from tree to tree from what is now the Shire to Dunland west of Isengard. In those lands I journeyed once, and many things wild and strange I knew. But I had forgotten Bombadil, if indeed this is still the same that walked the woods and hills long ago, and even then was older than the old. That was not then his name. Iarwain Ben-adar we called him, oldest and fatherless. But many another name he has since been given by other folk: Forn by the Dwarves, Orald by Northern Men, and other names beside. He is a strange creature, but maybe I should have summoned him to our Council."

"He would not have come," said Gandalf.

"Could we not still send messages to him and obtain his help?" asked Erestor. "It seems that he has a power even over the King."

"No, I should not put it so," said Gandalf. "Say rather that the Ring has no power over him. He is his own master. But he cannot alter the Ring itself, nor break its power over others. And now he is withdrawn into a little land, within bounds that he has set, though none can see them, waiting perhaps for a change of days, and he will not step beyond them."

"But within those bounds nothing seems to dismay him," said Erestor. "Would he not take the Ring and keep it there, for ever harmless?"

"No," said Gandalf, "not willingly. He might do so, if all the free folk of the world begged him, but he would not understand the need. And if he were given the Ring, he would soon forget it, or most likely throw it away. Such things have no hold on his mind. He would be a most unsafe guardian; and that alone is answer enough."

"But in any case," said Glorfindel, "to send the Ring to him would only postpone the day of evil. He is far away. We could not now take it back to him, unguessed, unmarked by any spy. And even if we could, soon or late the Lord of the Rings would learn of its hiding place and would bend all his power towards it. Could that power be defied by Bombadil alone? I think not. I think that in the end, if all else is conquered, Bombadil will fall, Last as he was First; and then Night will come."

"I know little of Iarwain save the name," said Galdor; "but Glorfindel, I think, is right. Power to defy our Enemy is not in him, unless such power is in the earth itself. And yet we see that Sauron can torture and destroy the very hills. What power still remains lies with us, here in Imladris, or with Círdan at the Havens, or in Lórien. But have they the strength, have we here the strength to withstand the Enemy, the coming of Sauron at the last, when all else is overthrown?"

"I have not the strength," said Elrond; "neither have they."

"Then if the Ring cannot be kept from him for ever by strength," said Glorfindel, "two things only remain for us to attempt: to send it over the Sea, or to destroy it."

"But Gandalf has revealed to us that we cannot destroy it by any craft that we here possess," said Elrond. "And they who dwell beyond the Sea would not receive it: for good or ill it belongs to Middle-earth; it is for us who still dwell here to deal with it."

"Then," said Glorfindel, "let us cast it into the deeps, and so make the lies of Saruman come true. For it is clear now that even at the Council his feet were already on a crooked path. He knew that the Ring was not lost for ever, but wished us to think so; for he began to lust for it for himself. Yet oft in lies truth is hidden: in the Sea it would be safe."

"Not safe for ever," said Gandalf. "There are many things in the deep waters; and seas and lands may change. And it is not our part here to take thought only for a season, or for a few lives of Men, or for a passing age of the world. We should seek a final end of this menace, even if we do not hope to make one."

"And that we shall not find on the roads to the Sea," said Caldor. "If the return to Iarwain be thought too dangerous, then flight to the Sea is now fraught with gravest peril. My heart tells me that Sauron will expect us to take the western way, when he learns what has befallen. He soon will. The Nine have been unhorsed indeed but that is but a respite, ere they find new steeds and swifter. Only the waning might of Gondor stands now between him and a march in power along the coasts into the North; and if he comes, assailing the White Towers and the Havens, hereafter the Elves may have no escape from the lengthening shadows of Middle-earth."

"Long yet will that march be delayed," said Boromir. "Gondor wanes, you say. But Gondor stands, and even the end of its strength is still very strong."

"And yet its vigilance can no longer keep back the Nine," said Galdor. "And other roads he may find that Gondor does not guard."

"Then," said Erestor, 'there are but two courses, as Glorfindel already has declared: to hide the Ring for ever; or to unmake it. But both are beyond our power. Who will read this riddle for us?"

"None here can do so," said Elrond gravely. "At least none can foretell what will come to pass, if we take this road or that. But it seems to me now clear which is the road that we must take. The westward road seems easiest. Therefore it must be shunned. It will be watched. Too often the Elves have fled that way. Now at this last we must take a hard road, a road unforeseen. There lies our hope, if hope it be. To walk into peril — to Mordor. We must send the Ring to the Fire."

Silence fell again. Frodo, even in that fair house, looking out upon a sunlit valley filled with the noise of clear waters, felt a dead darkness in his heart. Boromir stirred, and Frodo looked at him. He was fingering his great horn and frowning. At length he spoke.

"I do not understand all this," he said. "Saruman is a traitor, but did he not have a glimpse of wisdom? Why do you speak ever of hiding and destroying? Why should we not think that the Great King has come into our hands to serve us in the very hour of need? Wielding it the Free Lords of the Free may surely defeat the Enemy. That is what he most fears, I deem.

"The Men of Gondor are valiant, and they will never submit; but they may be beaten down. Valour needs first strength, and then a weapon. Let the Ring be your weapon, if it has such power as you say. Take it and go forth to victory!"

"Alas, no," said Elrond. "We cannot use the Ruling Ring. That we now know too well. It belongs to Sauron and was made by him alone, and is altogether evil. Its strength, Boromir, is too great for anyone to wield at will, save only those who have already a great power of their own. But for them it holds an even deadlier peril. The very desire of it corrupts the heart. Consider Saruman. If any of the Wise should with this King overthrow the Lord of Mordor, using his own arts, he would then set himself on Sauron's throne, and yet another Dark Lord would appear. And that is another reason why the Ring should be destroyed: as long as it is in the world it will be a danger even to the Wise. For nothing is evil in the beginning. Even Sauron was not so. I fear to take the King to hide it. I will not take the Ring to wield it."

"Nor I," said Gandalf.

Boromir looked at them doubtfully, but he bowed his head. "So be it," he said. "Then in Gondor we must trust to such weapons as we have. And at the least, while the Wise ones guard this Ring, we will fight on. Mayhap the Sword-that-was-Broken may still stem the tide — if the hand that wields it has inherited not an heirloom only, but the sinews of the Kings of Men."

"Who can tell?" said Aragorn. "But we will put it to the test one day."

"May the day not be too long delayed," said Boromir. "For though I do not ask for aid, we need it. It would comfort us to know that others fought also with all the means that they have."

"Then be comforted," said Elrond. "For there are other powers and realms that you know not, and they are hidden from you. Anduin the Great flows past many shores, ere it comes to Argonath and the Gates of Gondor."

"Still it might be well for all," said Glóin the Dwarf, "if all these strengths were joined, and the powers of each were used in league. Other rings there may be, less treacherous, that might be used in our need. The Seven are lost to us — if Balin has not found the ring of Thrór, which was the last; naught has been heard of it since Thrór perished in Moria. Indeed I may now reveal that it was partly in hope to find that ring that Balin went away."

"Balin will find no ring in Moria," said Gandalf. "Thrór gave it to Thráin his son, but not Thráin to Thorin. It was taken with torment from Thráin in the dungeons of Dol Guldur. I came too late."

"Ah, alas!" cried Glóin. "When will the day come of our revenge? But still there are the Three. What of the Three Kings of the Elves? Very mighty Rings, it is said. Do not the Elf-lords keep them? Yet they too were made by the Dark Lord long ago. Are they idle? I see Elf-lords here. Will they not say?"

The Elves returned no answer. "Did you not hear me, Glóin?" said Elrond. "The Three were not made by Sauron, nor did he ever touch them. But of them it is not permitted to speak. So much only in this hour of doubt I may now say. They are not idle. But they were not made as weapons of war or conquest: that is not their power. Those who made them did not desire strength or domination or hoarded wealth, but understanding, making, and healing, to preserve all things unstained. These things the Elves of Middle-earth have in some measure gained, though with sorrow. But all that has been wrought by those who wield the Three will turn to their undoing, and their minds and hearts will become revealed to Sauron, if he regains the One. It would be better if the Three had never been. That is his purpose."

"But what then would happen, if the Ruling King were destroyed, as you counsel?" asked Glóin.

"We know not for certain," answered Elrond sadly. "Some hope that the Three Rings, which Sauron has never touched, would then become free, and their rulers might heal the hurts of the world that he has wrought. But maybe when the One has gone, the Three will fail, and many fair things will fade and be forgotten. That is my belief."

"Yet all the Elves are willing to endure this chance," said Glorfindel, "if by it the power of Sauron may be broken, and the fear of his dominion be taken away for ever."

"Thus we return once more to the destroying of the Ring," said Erestor, "and yet we come no nearer. What strength have we for the finding of the Fire in which it was made? That is the path of despair. Of folly I would say, if the long wisdom of Elrond did not forbid me."

"Despair, or folly?" said Gandalf. "It is not despair, for despair is only for those who see the end beyond all doubt. We do not. It is wisdom to recognize necessity, when all other courses have been weighed, though as folly it may appear to those who cling to false hope. Well, let folly be our cloak, a veil before the eyes of the Enemy! For he is very wise, and weighs all things to a nicety in the scales of his malice. But the only measure that he knows is desire, desire for power; and so he judges all hearts. Into his heart the thought will not enter that any will refuse it, that having the Ring we may seek to destroy it. If we seek this, we shall put him out of reckoning."

"At least for a while," said Elrond. "The road must be trod, but it will be very hard. And neither strength nor wisdom will carry us far upon it. This quest may be attempted by the weak with as much hope as the strong. Yet such is oft the course of deeds that move the wheels of the world: small hands do them because they must, while the eyes of the great are elsewhere."

"Very well, very well, Master Elrond!" said Bilbo suddenly. "Say no more! It is plain enough what you are pointing at. Bilbo the silly hobbit started this affair, and Bilbo had better finish it, or himself. I was very comfortable here, and getting on with my book. If you want to know, I am just writing an ending for it. I had thought of putting: *and he lived happily ever afterwards to the end of his days*. It is a good ending, and none the worse for having been used before. Now I shall have to alter that: it does not look like coming true; and anyway there will evidently have to be several more chapters, if I live to write them. It is a frightful nuisance. When ought I to start?"

Boromir looked in surprise at Bilbo, but the laughter died on his lips when he saw that all the others regarded the old hobbit with grave respect. Ohly Glóin smiled, but his smile came from old memories.

"Of course, my dear Bilbo," said Gandalf. "If you had really started this affair, you might be expected to finish it. But you know well enough now that *starting* is too great a claim for any, and that only a small part is played in great deeds by any hero. You need not bow! Though the word was meant, and we do not doubt that under jest you are making a valiant offer. But one beyond your strength, Bilbo. You cannot take this thing back. It has passed on. If you need my advice any longer, I should say that your part is ended, unless as a recorder. Finish your book, and leave the ending unaltered! There is still hope for it. But get ready to write a sequel, when they come back."

Bilbo laughed. "I have never known you give me pleasant advice before," he said. "As all your unpleasant advice has been good, I wonder if this advice is not bad. Still, I don't suppose I have the strength or luck left to deal with the Ring. It has grown, and I have not. But tell me: what do you mean by *they*?"

"The messengers who are sent with the Ring."

"Exactly! And who are they to be? That seems to me what this Council has to decide, and all that it has to decide. Elves may thrive on speech alone, and Dwarves endure great weariness; but I am only an old hobbit, and I miss my meal at noon. Can't you think of some names now? Or put it off till after dinner?"

No one answered. The noon-bell rang. Still no one spoke. Frodo glanced at all the faces, but they were not turned to him. All the Council sat with downcast eyes, as if in deep thought. A

great dread fell on him, as if he was awaiting the pronounce-
ment of some doom that he had long foreseen and vainly hoped
might after all never be spoken. An overwhelming longing to
rest and remain at peace by Bilbo's side in Rivendell filled all
his heart. At last with an effort he spoke, and wondered to hear
his own words, as if some other will was using his small voice.

"I will take the Ring," he said, "though I do not know the
way."

Elrond raised his eyes and looked at him, and Frodo felt his
heart pierced by the sudden keenness of the glance. "If I
understand aright all that I have heard," he said, "I think that
this task is appointed for you, Frodo; and that if you do not
find a way, no one will. This is the hour of the Shire-folk, when
they arise from their quiet fields to shake the towers and
counsels of the Great. Who of all the Wise could have foreseen
it? Or, if they are wise, why should they expect to know it,
until the hour has struck?

"But it is a heavy burden. So heavy that none could lay it on
another. I do not lay it on you. But if you take it freely, I will
say that your choice is right; and though all the mighty elf-
friends of old, Hador, and Húrin, and Túrin, and Beren
himself were assembled together, your seat should be among
them."

"But you won't send him off alone surely, Master?" cried
Sam, unable to contain himself any longer, and jumping up
from the corner where he had been quietly sitting on the floor.

"No indeed!" said Elrond, turning towards him with a smile.
"You at least shall go with him. It is hardly possible to separate
you from him, even when he is summoned to a secret council
and you are not."

Sam sat down, blushing and muttering. "A nice pickle we
have landed ourselves in, Mr. Frodo!" he said, shaking his
head.

CHAPTER
THREE

The Ring Goes South

Later that day the hobbits held a meeting of their own in Bilbo's room. Merry and Pippin were indignant when they heard that Sam had crept into the Council, and had been chosen as Frodo's companion.

"It's most unfair," said Pippin. "Instead of throwing him out, and clapping him in chains, Elrond goes and *rewards* him for his cheek!"

"Rewards!" said Frodo. "I can't imagine a more severe punishment. You are not thinking what you are saying: condemned to go on this hopeless journey, a reward? Yesterday I dreamed that my task was done, and I could rest here, a long while, perhaps for good."

"I don't wonder," said Merry, "and I wish you could. But we are envying Sam, not you. If you have to go, then it will be a punishment for any of us to be left behind, even in Rivendell. We have come a long way with you and been through some stiff times. We want to go on."

"That's what I meant," said Pippin. "We hobbits ought to stick together, and we will. I shall go, unless they chain me up. There must be someone with intelligence in the party."

"Then you certainly will not be chosen, Peregrin Took!" said Gandalf, looking in through the window, which was near the ground. "But you are all worrying yourselves unnecessarily. Nothing is decided yet."

"Nothing decided!" cried Pippin. "Then what were you all doing? You were shut up for hours."

"Talking," said Bilbo. "There was a deal of talk, and everyone had an eye-opener. Even old Gandalf. I think Legolas's bit of news about Gollum caught even him on the hop, though he passed it off."

"You were wrong," said Gandalf. "You were inattentive. I had already heard of it from Gwaihir. If you want to know, the only real eye-openers, as you put it, were you and Frodo; and I was the only one that was not surprised."

"Well, anyway," said Bilbo, "nothing was decided beyond choosing poor Frodo and Sam. I was afraid all the time that it might come to that, if I was let off. But if you ask me, Elrond will send out a fair number, when the reports come in. Have they started yet, Gandalf?"

"Yes," said the wizard. "Some of the scouts have been sent out already. More will go tomorrow. Elrond is sending Elves, and they will get in touch with the Rangers, and maybe with Thranduil's folk in Mirkwood. And Aragorn has gone with Elrond's sons. We shall have to scour the lands all round for many long leagues before any move is made. So cheer up, Frodo! You will probably make quite a long stay here."

"Ah!" said Sam gloomily. "We'll just wait long enough for winter to come."

"That can't be helped," said Bilbo. "It's your fault partly, Frodo my lad: insisting on waiting for my birthday. A funny way of honouring it, I can't help thinking. Not the day I should have chosen for letting the S.-B.s into Bag End. But there it is: you can't wait now till spring; and you can't go till the reports come back.

> *When winter first begins to bite*
> *and stones crack in the frosty night,*
> *when pools are black and trees are bare,*
> *'tis evil in the Wild to fare.*

But that I am afraid will be just your luck."

"I am afraid it will," said Gandalf. "We can't start until we have found out about the Riders."

"I thought they were all destroyed in the flood," said Merry.

"You cannot destroy Ringwraiths like that," said Gandalf. "The power of their master is in them, and they stand or fall by him. We hope that they were all unhorsed and unmasked, and so made for a while less dangerous; but we must find out for certain. In the meantime you should try and forget your troubles, Frodo. I do not know if I can do anything to help you; but I will whisper this in your ears. Someone said that intelligence would be needed in the party. He was right. I think I shall come with you."

So great was Frodo's delight at this announcement that Gandalf left the window-sill, where he had been sitting, and took off his hat and bowed. "I only said *I think I shall come*. Do not count on anything yet. In this matter Elrond will have much to say, and your friend the Strider. Which reminds me, I want to see Elrond. I must be off."

"How long do you think I shall have here?" said Frodo to Bilbo when Gandalf had gone.

"Oh, I don't know. I can't count days in Rivendell," said Bilbo. "But quite long, I should think. We can have many a good talk. What about helping me with my book, and making a start on the next? Have you thought of an ending?"

"Yes, several, and all are dark and unpleasant," said Frodo.

"Oh, that won't do!" said Bilbo. "Books ought to have good endings. How would this do: *and they all setted down and lived together happily ever after?*"

"It will do well, if it ever comes to that," said Frodo.

"Ah!" said Sam. "And where will they live? That's what I often wonder."

For a while the hobbits continued to talk and think of the past journey and of the perils that lay ahead; but such was the virtue of the land of Rivendell that soon all fear and anxiety was lifted from their minds. The future, good or ill, was not forgotten, but ceased to have any power over the present. Health and hope grew strong in them, and they were content with each good day as it came, taking pleasure in every meal, and in every word and song.

So the days slipped away, as each morning dawned bright and fair, and each evening followed cool and clear. But autumn was waning fast; slowly the golden light faded to pale silver, and the lingering leaves fell from the naked trees. A wind began to blow chill from the Misty Mountains to the east. The Hunter's Moon waxed round in the night sky, and put to flight all the lesser stars. But low in the South one star shone red. Every night, as the Moon waned again, it shone brighter and brighter. Frodo could see it from his window, deep in the heavens, burning like a watchful eye that glared above the trees on the brink of the valley.

The hobbits had been nearly two months in the House of Elrond, and November had gone by with the last shreds of autumn, and December was passing, when the scouts began to return. Some had gone north beyond the springs of the Hoarwell into the Ettenmoors; and others had gone west, and with the help of Aragorn and the Rangers had searched the lands far down the Greyflood, as far as Tharbad, where the old North Road crossed the river by a ruined town. Many had gone east and south; and some of these had crossed the Mountains and entered Mirkwood, while others had climbed the pass at the source of the Gladden River, and had come down into Wilderland and over the Gladden Fields and so at length had reached the old home of Radagast at Rhosgobel. Radagast was not there; and they had returned over the high pass that was called the Dimrill Stair. The sons of Elrond, Elladan and Elrohir, were the last to return; they had made a great journey, passing down the Silverlode into a strange country, but of their errand they would not speak to any save to Elrond.

In no region had the messengers discovered any signs or

tidings of the Riders or other servants of the Enemy. Even from the Eagles of the Misty Mountains they had learned no fresh news. Nothing had been seen or heard of Gollum; but the wild wolves were still gathering, and were hunting again far up the Great River. Three of the black horses had been found at once drowned in the flooded Ford. On the rock of the rapids below it searchers discovered the bodies of five more, and also a long black cloak, slashed and tattered. Of the Black Riders no other trace was to be seen, and nowhere was their presence to be felt. It seemed that they had vanished from the North.

"Eight out of the Nine are accounted for at least," said Gandalf. "It is rash to be too sure, yet I think that we may hope now that the Ringwraiths were scattered, and have been obliged to return as best they could to their Master in Mordor, empty and shapeless.

"If that is so, it will be some time before they can begin the hunt again. Of course the Enemy has other servants, but they will have to journey all the way to the borders of Rivendell before they can pick up our trail. And if we are careful that will be hard to find. But we must delay no longer."

Elrond summoned the hobbits to him. He looked gravely at Frodo. "The time has come," he said. "If the Ring is to set out, it must go soon. But those who go with it must not count on their errand being aided by war or force. They must pass into the domain of the Enemy far from aid. Do you still hold to your word, Frodo, that you will be the Ring-bearer?"

"I do," said Frodo. "I will go with Sam."

"Then I cannot help you much, not even with counsel," said Elrond. "I can foresee very little of your road; and how your task is to be achieved I do not know. The Shadow has crept now to the feet of the Mountains, and draws nigh even to the borders of the Greyflood; and under the Shadow all is dark to me. You will meet many foes, some open, and some disguised; and you may find friends upon your way when you least look for it. I will send out messages, such as I can contrive, to those whom I know in the wide world; but so perilous are the lands now become that some may well miscarry, or come no quicker than you yourself.

"And I will choose you companions to go with you, as far as they will or fortune allows. The number must be few, since your hope is in speed and secrecy. Had I a host of Elves in armour of the Elder Days, it would avail little, save to arouse the power of Mordor.

"The Company of the Ring shall be Nine; and the Nine Walkers shall he set against the Nine Riders that are evil. With you and your faithful servant, Gandalf will go; for this shall be his great task, and maybe the end of his labours.

"For the rest, they shall represent the other Free Peoples of the World: Elves, Dwarves, and Men. Legolas shall be for the Elves; and Gimli son of Glóin for the Dwarves. They are willing to go at least to the passes of the Mountains, and maybe beyond. For men you shall have Aragorn son of Arathorn, for the Ring of Isildur concerns him closely."

"Strider!" cried Frodo.

"Yes," he said with a smile. "I ask leave once again to be your companion, Frodo."

"I would have begged you to come," said Frodo, "only I thought you were going to Minas Tirith with Boromir."

"I am," said Aragorn. "And the Sword-that-was-Broken shall be re-forged ere I set out to war. But your road and our road lie together for many hundreds of miles. Therefore Boromir will also be in the Company. He is a valiant man."

"There remain two more to be found," said Elrond. "These I will consider. Of my household I may find some that it seems good to me to send.

"But that will leave no place for us!" cried Pippin in dismay. "We don't want to be left behind. We want to go with Frodo."

"That is because you do not understand and cannot imagine what lies ahead," said Elrond.

"Neither does Frodo," said Gandalf, unexpectedly supporting Pippin. "Nor do any of us see clearly. It is true that if these hobbits understood the danger, they would not dare to go. But they would still wish to go, or wish that they dared, and be shamed and unhappy. I think, Elrond, that in this matter it would be well to trust rather to their friendship than to great wisdom. Even if you chose for us an elf-lord, such as Glorfindel, he could not storm the Dark Tower, nor open the road to the Fire by the power that is in him."

"You speak gravely," said Elrond, "but I am in doubt. The Shire, I forebode, is not free now from peril; and these two I had thought to send back there as messengers, to do what they could, according to the fashion of their country, to warn the people of their danger. In any case, I judge that the younger of these two, Peregrin Took, should remain. My heart is against his going."

"Then, Master Elrond, you will have to lock me in prison, or send me home tied in a sack," said Pippin. "For otherwise I shall follow the Company."

"Let it be so then. You shall go," said Elrond, and he sighed. "Now the tale of Nine is filled. In seven days the Company must depart."

The Sword of Elendil was forged anew by Elvish smiths, and on its blade was traced a device of seven stars set between the crescent Moon and the rayed Sun, and about them was written many runes; for Aragorn son of Arathorn was going to war upon the marches of Mordor. Very bright was that sword when it was made whole again; the light of the sun shone redly in it, and the light of the moon shone cold, and its edge was hard and keen. And Aragorn gave it a new name and called it Andúril, Flame of the West.

Aragorn and Gandalf walked together or sat speaking of their road and the perils they would meet; and they pondered the storied and figured maps and books of lore that were in the house of Elrond. Sometimes Frodo was with them; but he was content to lean on their guidance, and he spent as much time as he could with Bilbo.

In those last days the hobbits sat together in the evening in the Hall of Fire, and there among many tales they heard told in full the lay of Beren and Lúthien and the winning of the Great Jewel; but in the day, while Merry and Pippin were out and about, Frodo and Sam were to be found with Bilbo in his own small room. Then Bilbo would read passages from his book (which still seemed very incomplete), or scraps of his verses, or would take notes of Frodo's adventures.

On the morning of the last day Frodo was alone with Bilbo, and the old hobbit pulled out from under his bed a wooden box. He lifted the lid and fumbled inside.

"Here is your sword," he said. "But it was broken, you know. I took it to keep it safe but I've forgotten to ask if the smiths could mend it. No time now. So I thought, perhaps, you would care to have this, don't you know?"

He took from the box a small sword in an old shabby leathern scabbard. Then he drew it, and its polished and well-tended blade glittered suddenly, cold and bright. "This is Sting," he said, and thrust it with little effort deep into a wooden beam. "Take it, if you like. I shan't want it again, I expect."

Frodo accepted it gratefully.

"Also there is this!" said Bilbo, bringing out a parcel which seemed to be rather heavy for its size. He unwound several folds of old cloth, and held up a small shirt of mail. It was close-woven of many rings, as supple almost as linen, cold as ice, and harder than steel. It shone like moonlit silver, and was studded with white gems. With it was a belt of pearl and crystal.

"It's a pretty thing, isn't it?" said Bilbo, moving it in the light. "And useful. It is my dwarf-mail that Thorin gave me. I got it back from Michel Delving before I started, and packed it with my luggage. I brought all the mementoes of my Journey away with me, except the Ring. But I did not expect to use this, and I don't need it now, except to look at sometimes. You hardly feel any weight when you put it on."

"I should look — well, I don't think I should look right in it," said Frodo.

"Just what I said myself," said Bilbo. "But never mind about looks. You can wear it under your outer clothes. Come on! You must share this secret with me. Don't tell anybody else! But I should feel happier if I knew you were wearing it. I have a fancy it would turn even the knives of the Black Riders," he ended in a low voice.

"Very well, I will take it," said Frodo. Bilbo put it on him, and fastened Sting upon the glittering belt; and then Frodo put over the top his old weather-stained breeches, tunic, and jacket.

"Just a plain hobbit you look," said Bilbo. "But there is more about you now than appears on the surface. Good luck to you!" He turned away and looked out of the window, trying to hum a tune.

"I cannot thank you as I should, Bilbo, for this, and for all your past kindnesses," said Frodo.

"Don't try!" said the old hobbit, turning round and slapping him on the back. "Ow!" he cried. "You are too hard now to slap! But there you are: Hobbits must stick together, and especially Bagginses. All I ask in return is: take as much care of yourself as you can, and bring back all the news you can, and any old songs and tales you can come by. I'll do my best to finish my book before you return. I should like to write the second book, if I am spared." He broke off and turned to the window again, singing softly.

> *I sit beside the fire and think*
> *of all that I have seen,*
> *of meadow-flowers and butterflies*
> *in summers that have been;*
>
> *Of yellow leaves and gossamer*
> *in autumns that there were,*
> *with morning mist and silver sun*
> *and wind upon my hair.*

> *I sit beside the fire and think*
> *of how the world will be*
> *when winter comes without a spring*
> *that I shall ever see.*
>
> *For still there are so many things*
> *that I have never seen:*
> *in every wood in every spring*
> *there is a different green.*
>
> *I sit beside the fire and think*
> *of people long ago,*
> *and people who will see a world*
> *that I shall never know.*
>
> *But all the while I sit and think*
> *of times there were before,*
> *I listen for returning feet*
> *and voices at the door.*

It was a cold grey day near the end of December. The East Wind was streaming through the bare branches of the trees, and seething in the dark pines on the hills. Ragged clouds were hurrying overhead, dark and low. As the cheerless shadows of the early evening began to fall the Company made ready to set out. They were to start at dusk, for Elrond counselled them to journey under cover of night as often as they could, until they were far from Rivendell.

"You should fear the many eyes of the servants of Sauron," he said. "I do not doubt that news of the discomfiture of the Riders has already reached him, and he will be filled with wrath. Soon now his spies on foot and wing will be abroad in the northern lands. Even of the sky above you must beware as you go on your way."

The Company took little gear of war, for their hope was in

secrecy not in battle. Aragorn had Andúril but no other weapon, and he went forth clad only in rusty green and brown, as a Ranger of the wilderness Boromir had a long sword, in fashion like Andúril but of less lineage, and he bore also a shield and his war-horn.

"Loud and clear it sounds in the valleys of the hills," he said, "and then let all the foes of Gondor flee!" Putting it to his lips he blew a blast, and the echoes leapt from rock to rock, and all that heard that voice in Rivendell sprang to their feet.

"Slow should you be to wind that horn again, Boromir," said Elrond, "until you stand once more on the borders of your land, and dire need is on you."

"Maybe," said Boromir. "But always I have let my horn cry at setting forth, and though thereafter we may walk in the shadows, I will not go forth as a thief in the night."

Gimli the dwarf alone wore openly a short shirt of steel-rings, for dwarves make light of burdens; and in his belt was a broad-bladed axe. Legolas had a bow and a quiver, and at his belt a long white knife. The younger hobbits wore the swords that they had taken from the barrow; but Frodo took only Sting; and his mail-coat, as Bilbo wished, remained hidden. Gandalf bore his staff, but girt at his side was the elven-sword Glamdring, the mate of Orcrist that lay now upon the breast of Thorin under the Lonely Mountain.

All were well furnished by Elrond with thick warm clothes, and they had jackets and cloaks lined with fur. Spare food and clothes and blankets and other needs were laden on a pony, none other than the poor beast that they had brought from Bree.

The stay in Rivendell had worked a great wonder of change on him: he was glossy and seemed to have the vigour of youth. It was Sam who had insisted on choosing him, declaring that Bill (as he called him) would pine, if he did not come.

"That animal can nearly talk," he said, "and would talk, if he stayed here much longer. He gave me a look as plain as Mr. Pippin could speak it: if you don't let me go with you, Sam, I'll follow on my own." So Bill was going as the beast of burden, yet he was the only member of the Company that did not seem depressed.

Their farewells had been said in the great hall by the fire, and they were only waiting now for Gandalf, who had not yet come out of the house. A gleam of firelight came from the open doors, and soft lights were glowing in many windows. Bilbo huddled in a cloak stood silent on the doorstep beside Frodo. Aragorn sat with his head bowed to his knees; only Elrond knew fully what this hour meant to him. The others could be seen as grey shapes in the darkness.

Sam was standing by the pony, sucking his teeth, and staring moodily into the gloom where the river roared stonily below; his desire for adventure was at its lowest ebb.

"Bill, my lad," he said, "you oughtn't to have took up with us. You could have stayed here and et the best hay till the new grass comes." Bill swished his tail and said nothing.

Sam eased the pack on his shoulders, and went over anxiously in his mind all the things that he had stowed in it, wondering if he had forgotten anything: his chief treasure, his cooking gear; and the little box of salt that he always carried and refilled when he could; a good supply of pipe-weed (but not near enough, I'll warrant); flint and tinder; woollen hose; linen; various small belongings of his master's that Frodo had forgotten and Sam had stowed to bring them out in triumph when they were called for. He went through them all.

"Rope!" he muttered. "No rope! And only last night you said to yourself: 'Sam, what about a bit of rope? You'll want it, if you haven't got it.' Well, I'll want it. I can't get it now."

At that moment Elrond came out with Gandalf, and he called the Company to him. "This is my last word," he said in a low voice. "The Ring-bearer is setting out on the Quest of Mount Doom. On him alone is any charge laid: neither to cast away the Ring, nor to deliver it to any servant of the Enemy nor indeed to let any handle it, save members of the Company and the Council, and only then in gravest need. The others go with him as free companions, to help him on his way. You may tarry, or come back, or turn aside into other paths, as chance allows. The further you go, the less easy will it be to withdraw; yet no oath or bond is laid on you to go further than you will. For you do not yet know the strength of your hearts, and you cannot foresee what each may meet upon the road."

"Faithless is he that says farewell when the road darkens," said Gimli.

"Maybe," said Elrond, "but let him not vow to walk in the dark, who has not seen the nightfall."

"Yet sworn word may strengthen quaking heart," said Gimli.

"Or break it," said Elrond. "Look not too far ahead! But go now with good hearts! Farewell, and may the blessing of Elves and Men and all Free Folk go with you. May the stars shine upon your faces!"

"Good . . . good luck!" cried Bilbo, stuttering with the cold. "I don't suppose you will be able to keep a diary, Frodo my lad, but I shall expect a full account when you get back. And don't be too long! Farewell!"

Many others of Elrond's household stood in the shadows and watched them go, bidding them farewell with soft voices. There was no laughter, and no song or music. At last they turned away and faded silently into the dusk.

They crossed the bridge and wound slowly up the long steep paths that led out of the cloven vale of Rivendell; and they came at length to the high moor where the wind hissed through the heather. Then with one glance at the Last Homely House twinkling below them they strode away far into the night.

At the Ford of Bruinen they left the Road and turning southwards went on by narrow paths among the folded lands. Their purpose was to hold this course west of the Mountains for many miles and days. The country was much rougher and more barren than in the green vale of the Great River in Wilderland on the other side of the range, and their going would be slow; but they hoped in this way to escape the notice of unfriendly eyes. The spies of Sauron had hitherto seldom been seen in this empty country, and the paths were little known except to the people of Rivendell.

Gandalf walked in front, and with him went Aragorn, who knew this land even in the dark. The others were in file behind, and Legolas whose eyes were keen was the rearguard. The first part of their journey was hard and dreary, and Frodo remembered little of it, save the wind. For many sunless days an icy blast came from the Mountains in the east, and no garment seemed able to keep out its searching fingers. Though the Company was well clad, they seldom felt warm, either moving or at rest. They slept uneasily during the middle of the day, in some hollow of the land, or hidden under the tangled thorn-bushes that grew in thickets in many places. In the late afternoon they were roused by the watch, and took their chief meal: cold and cheerless as a rule, for they could seldom risk the lighting of a fire. In the evening they went on again, always as nearly southward as they could find a way.

At first it seemed to the hobbits that although they walked and stumbled until they were weary, they were creeping forward like snails, and getting nowhere. Each day the land looked much the same as it had the day before. Yet steadily the mountains were drawing nearer. South of Rivendell they rose ever higher, and bent westwards; and about the feet of the main range there was tumbled an ever wider land of bleak hills, and deep valleys filled with turbulent waters. Paths were few and winding, and led them often only to the edge of some sheer fall, or down into treacherous swamps.

They had been a fortnight on the way when the weather changed. The wind suddenly fell and then veered round to the south. The swift-flowing clouds lifted and melted away, and the sun came out, pale and bright. There came a cold clear dawn at the end of a long stumbling night-march. The travellers reached a low ridge crowned with ancient holly-trees whose grey-green trunks seemed to have been built out of the very stone of the hills. Their dark leaves shone and their berries glowed red in the light of the rising sun.

Away in the south Frodo could see the dim shapes of lofty mountains that seemed now to stand across the path that the Company was taking. At the left of this high range rose three peaks; the tallest and nearest stood up like a tooth tipped with snow; its great, bare, northern precipice was still largely in the shadow, but where the sunlight slanted upon it, it glowed red.

Gandalf stood at Frodo's side and looked out under his hand. "We have done well," he said. "We have reached the borders of the country that Men call Hollin; many Elves lived here in happier days, when Eregion was its name. Five-and-forty leagues as the crow flies we have come, though many long miles further our feet have walked. The land and the weather will be milder now, but perhaps all the more dangerous."

"Dangerous or not, a real sunrise is mighty welcome," said Frodo, throwing back his hood and letting the morning light fall on his face.

"But the mountains are ahead of us," said Pippin. "We must have turned eastwards in the night."

"No," said Gandalf. "But you see further ahead in the clear light. Beyond those peaks the range bends round south-west. There are many maps in Elrond's house, but I suppose you never thought to look at them?"

"Yes I did, sometimes," said Pippin, "but I don't remember them. Frodo has a better head for that sort of thing."

"I need no map," said Gimli, who had come up with Legolas, and was gazing out before him with a strange light in his deep eyes. "There is the land where our fathers worked of old, and we have wrought the image of those mountains into many works of metal and of stone, and into many songs and tales. They stand tall in our dreams: Baraz, Zirak, Shathûr.

"Only once before have I seen them from afar in waking life, but I know them and their names, for under them lies Khazad-dûm, the Dwarrowdelf, that is now called the Black Pit, Moria in the Elvish tongue. Yonder stands Barazinbar, the Redhorn, cruel Caradhras; and beyond him are Silvertine and Cloudyhead: Celebdil the White, and Fanuidhol the Grey, that we call Zirakzigil and Bundushathûr.

"There the Misty Mountains divide, and between their arms lies the deep-shadowed valley which we cannot forget: Azanulbizar, the Dimrill Dale, which the Elves call Nanduhirion."

"It is for the Dimrill Dale that we are making," said Gandalf. "If we climb the pass that is called the Redhorn Gate, under the far side of Caradhras, we shall come down by the Dimrill Stair into the deep vale of the Dwarves. There lies the Mirrormere, and there the River Silverlode rises in its icy springs."

"Dark is the water of Kheled-zâram," said Gimli, "and cold are the springs of Kibil-nâla. My heart trembles at the thought that I may see them soon."

"May you have joy of the sight, my good dwarf!" said Gandalf "But whatever you may do, we at least cannot stay in that valley. We must go down the Silverlode into the secret woods, and so to the Great River, and then——"

He paused.

"Yes, and where then?" asked Merry.

"To the end of the journey — in the end," said Gandalf. "We cannot look too far ahead. Let us be glad that the first stage is safely over. I think we will rest here, not only today but tonight as well. There is a wholesome air about Hollin. Much evil must befall a country before it wholly forgets the Elves, if once they dwelt there."

"That is true," said Legolas. "But the Elves of this land were of a race strange to us of the silvan folk, and the trees and the grass do not now remember them. Only I hear the stones lament them: *deep they delved us, fair they wrought us, high they builded us; but they are gone.* They are gone. They sought the Havens long ago."

That morning they lit a fire in a deep hollow shrouded by great bushes of holly, and their supper-breakfast was merrier than it had been since they set out. They did not hurry to bed afterwards, for they expected to have all the night to sleep in, and they did not mean to go on again until the evening of the next day. Only Aragorn was silent and restless. After a while he left the Company and wandered on to the ridge; there he stood in the shadow of a tree, looking out southwards and westwards, with his head posed as if he was listening. Then he returned to the brink of the dell and looked down at the others laughing and talking.

"What is the matter, Strider?" Merry called up. "What are you looking for? Do you miss the East Wind?"

"No indeed," he answered. "But I miss something. I have been in the country of Hollin in many seasons. No folk dwell here now, but many other creatures live here at all times, especially birds. Yet now all things but you are silent. I can feel it. There is no sound for miles about us, and your voices seem to make the ground echo. I do not understand it."

Gandalf looked up with sudden interest. "But what do you guess is the reason?" he asked. "Is there more in it than surprise at seeing four hobbits, not to mention the rest of us, where people are so seldom seen or heard?"

"I hope that is it," answered Aragorn. "But I have a sense of watchfulness, and of fear, that I have never had here before."

"Then we must be more careful," said Gandalf. "If you bring a Ranger with you, it is well to pay attention to him, especially if the Ranger is Aragorn. We must stop talking aloud, rest quietly, and set the watch."

It was Sam's turn that day to take the first watch, but Aragorn joined him. The others fell asleep. Then the silence grew until even Sam felt it. The breathing of the sleepers could be plainly heard. The swish of the pony's tail and the occasional movements of his feet became loud noises. Sam could hear his own joints creaking, if he stirred. Dead silence was around him, and over all hung a clear blue sky, as the Sun rode up from the East. Away in the South a dark patch appeared, and grew, and drove north like flying smoke in the wind.

"What's that, Strider? It don't look like a cloud," said Sam in a whisper to Aragorn. He made no answer, he was gazing intently at the sky; but before long Sam could see for himself what was approaching. Flocks of birds, flying at great speed, were wheeling and circling, and traversing all the land as if they were searching for something; and they were steadily drawing nearer.

"Lie flat and still!" hissed Aragorn, pulling Sam down into the shade of a holly-bush; for a whole regiment of birds had broken away suddenly from the main host, and came, flying low, straight towards the ridge. Sam thought they were a kind of crow of large size. As they passed overhead, in so dense a throng that their shadow followed them darkly over the ground below, one harsh croak was heard.

Not until they had dwindled into the distance, north and west, and the sky was again clear would Aragorn rise. Then he sprang up and went and wakened Gandalf.

"Regiments of black crows are flying over all the land between the Mountains and the Greyflood," he said, "and they have passed over Hollin. They are not natives here; they are *crebain* out of Fangorn and Dunland. I do not know what they are about: possibly there is some trouble away south from which they are fleeing; but I think they are spying out the land. I have also glimpsed hawks flying high up in the sky. I think we ought to move again this evening. Hollin is no longer wholesome for us: it is being watched."

"And in that case so is the Redhorn Gate," said Gandalf; "and how we can get over that without being seen, I cannot imagine. But we will think of that when we must. As for moving as soon as it is dark, I am afraid that you are right."

"Luckily our fire made little smoke, and had burned low before the *crebain* came," said Aragorn. "It must be put out and not lit again."

"Well if that isn't a plague and a nuisance!" said Pippin. The news: no fire, and a move again by night, had been broken to him, as soon as he woke in the late afternoon. "All because of a pack of crows! I had looked forward to a real good meal tonight: something hot."

"Well, you can go on looking forward," said Gandalf. "There may be many unexpected feasts ahead for you. For myself I should like a pipe to smoke in comfort, and warmer feet. However, we are certain of one thing at any rate: it will get warmer as we get south."

"Too warm, I shouldn't wonder," muttered Sam to Frodo. "But I'm beginning to think it's time we got a sight of that Fiery Mountain, and saw the end of the Road, so to speak. I thought at first that this here Redhorn, or whatever its name is, might be it, till Gimli spoke his piece. A fair jaw-cracker dwarf-language must be!" Maps conveyed nothing to Sam's mind, and all distances in these strange lands seemed so vast that he was quite out of his reckoning.

All that day the Company remained in hiding. The dark birds passed over now and again; but as the westering Sun grew red they disappeared southwards. At dusk the Company set out, and turning now half east they steered their course towards Caradhras, which far away still glowed faintly red in the last light of the vanished Sun. One by one white stars sprang forth as the sky faded.

Guided by Aragorn they struck a good path. It looked to Frodo like the remains of an ancient road, that had once been broad and well planned, from Hollin to the mountain-pass. The Moon, now at the full, rose over the mountains, and cast a pale light in which the shadows of stones were black. Many of them looked to have been worked by hands, though now they lay tumbled and ruinous in a bleak, barren land.

It was the cold chill hour before the first stir of dawn, and the moon was low. Frodo looked up at the sky. Suddenly he saw or felt a shadow pass over the high stars, as if for a moment they faded and then flashed out again. He shivered.

"Did you see anything pass over?" he whispered to Gandalf, who was just ahead.

"No, but I felt it, whatever it was," he answered. "It may be nothing, only a wisp of thin cloud."

"It was moving fast then," muttered Aragorn, "and not with the wind."

Nothing further happened that night. The next morning dawned even brighter than before. But the air was chill again; already the wind was turning back towards the east. For two more nights they marched on, climbing steadily but ever more slowly as their road wound up into the hills, and the mountains towered up, nearer and nearer. On the third morning Caradhras rose before them, a mighty peak, tipped with snow like silver, but with sheer naked sides, dull red as if stained with blood.

There was a black look in the sky, and the sun was wan. The wind had gone now round to the north-east. Gandalf snuffed the air and looked back.

"Winter deepens behind us," he said quietly to Aragorn. "The heights away north are whiter than they were; snow is lying far down their shoulders. Tonight we shall be on our way high up towards the Redhorn Gate. We may well be seen by watchers on that narrow path, and waylaid by some evil; but the weather may prove a more deadly enemy than any. What do you think of your course now, Aragorn?"

Frodo overheard these words, and understood that Gandalf and Aragorn were continuing some debate that had begun long before. He listened anxiously.

"I think no good of our course from beginning to end, as you know well, Gandalf," answered Aragorn. "And perils known and unknown will grow as we go on. But we must go on; and it is no good our delaying the passage of the mountains. Further south there are no passes, till one comes to the Gap of Rohan. I do not trust that way since your news of Saruman. Who knows which side now the marshals of the Horse-lords serve?"

"Who knows indeed!" said Gandalf. "But there is another

way, and not by the pass of Caradhras: the dark and secret way that we have spoken of."

"But let us not speak of it again! Not yet. Say nothing to the others, I beg, not until it is plain that there is no other way."

"We must decide before we go further," answered Gandalf.

"Then let us weigh the matter in our minds, while the others rest and sleep," said Aragorn.

In the late afternoon, while the others were finishing their breakfast, Gandalf and Aragorn went aside together and stood looking at Caradhras. Its sides were now dark and sullen, and its head was in grey cloud. Frodo watched them, wondering which way the debate would go. When they returned to the Company Gandalf spoke, and then he knew that it had been decided to face the weather and the high pass. He was relieved. He could not guess what was the other dark and secret way, but the very mention of it had seemed to fill Aragorn with dismay, and Frodo was glad that it had been abandoned.

"From signs that we have seen lately," said Gandalf, "I fear that the Redhorn Gate may be watched; and also I have doubts of the weather that is coming up behind. Snow may come. We must go with all the speed that we can. Even so it will take us more than two marches before we reach the top of the pass. Dark will come early this evening. We must leave as soon as you can get ready."

"I will add a word of advice, if I may," said Boromir. "I was born under the shadow of the White Mountains and know something of journeys in the high places. We shall meet bitter cold, if no worse, before we come down on the other side. It will not help us to keep so secret that we are frozen to death. When we leave here, where there are still a few trees and bushes, each of us should carry a faggot of wood, as large as he can bear."

"And Bill could take a bit more, couldn't you, lad?" said Sam. The pony looked at him mournfully.

"Very well," said Gandalf. "But we must not use the wood — not unless it is a choice between fire and death."

The Company set out again, with good speed at first; but soon their way became steep and difficult. The twisting and climbing road had in many places almost disappeared, and was blocked with many fallen stones. The night grew deadly dark under great clouds. A bitter wind swirled among the rocks. By midnight they had climbed to the knees of the great mountains. The narrow path now wound under a sheer wall of cliffs to the left, above which the grim flanks of Caradhras towered up invisible in the gloom; on the right was a gulf of darkness where the land fell suddenly into a deep ravine.

Laboriously they climbed a sharp slope and halted for a moment at the top. Frodo felt a soft touch on his face. He put out his arm and saw the dim white flakes of snow settling on his sleeve.

They went on. But before long the snow was falling fast, filling all the air, and swirling into Frodo's eyes. The dark bent shapes of Gandalf and Aragorn only a pace or two ahead could hardly be seen.

"I don't like this at all," panted Sam just behind. "Snow's all right on a fine morning, but I like to be in bed while it's falling. I wish this lot would go off to Hobbiton! Folk might welcome it there." Except on the high moors of the Northfarthing a heavy fall was rare in the Shire, and was regarded as a pleasant event and a chance for fun. No living hobbit (save Bilbo) could remember the Fell Winter of 1311, when white wolves invaded the Shire over the frozen Brandywine.

Gandalf halted. Snow was thick on his hood and shoulders; it was already ankle-deep about his boots.

"This is what I feared," he said. "What do you say now, Aragorn?"

"That I feared it too," Aragorn answered, "but less than other things. I knew the risk of snow, though it seldom falls heavily so far south, save high up in the mountains. But we are not high yet; we are still far down, where the paths are usually open all the winter."

"I wonder if this is a contrivance of the Enemy," said Boromir. "They say in my land that he can govern the storms in the Mountains of Shadow that stand upon the borders of Mordor. He has strange powers and many allies."

"His arm has grown long indeed," said Gimli, "if he can draw snow down from the North to trouble us here three hundred leagues away."

"His arm has grown long," said Gandalf.

While they were halted, the wind died down, and the snow slackened until it almost ceased. They tramped on again. But they had not gone more than a furlong when the storm returned with fresh fury. The wind whistled and the snow became a blinding blizzard. Soon even Boromir found it hard to keep going. The hobbits, bent nearly double, toiled along behind the taller folk, but it was plain that they could not go much further, if the snow continued. Frodo's feet felt like lead. Pippin was dragging behind. Even Gimli, as stout as any dwarf could be, was grumbling as he trudged.

The Company halted suddenly, as if they had come to an agreement without any words being spoken. They heard eerie noises in the darkness round them. It may have been only a trick of the wind in the cracks and gullies of the rocky wall, but the sounds were those of shrill cries, and wild howls of laughter. Stones began to fall from the mountain-side, whistling over their heads, or crashing on the path beside them. Every now and again they heard a dull rumble, as a great boulder rolled down from hidden heights above.

"We cannot go further tonight," said Boromir. "Let those call it the wind who will; there are fell voices on the air; and these stones are aimed at us."

"I do call it the wind," said Aragorn. "But that does not make what you say untrue. There are many evil and unfriendly things in the world that have little love for those that go on two legs, and yet are not in league with Sauron, but have purposes of their own. Some have been in this world longer than he."

"Caradhras was called the Cruel, and had an ill name," said Gimli, "long years ago, when rumour of Sauron had not been heard in these lands."

"It matters little who is the enemy, if we cannot beat off his attack," said Gandalf.

"But what can we do?" cried Pippin miserably. He was leaning on Merry and Frodo, and he was shivering.

"Either stop where we are, or go back," said Gandalf. "It is no good going on. Only a little higher, if I remember rightly, this path leaves the cliff and runs into a wide shallow trough at the bottom of a long hard slope. We should have no shelter there from snow, or stones — or anything else."

"And it is no good going back while the storm holds," said Aragorn. "We have passed no place on the way up that offered more shelter than this cliff-wall we are under now."

"Shelter!" muttered Sam. "If this is shelter, then one wall and no roof make a house."

The Company now gathered together as close to the cliff as they could. It faced southwards, and near the bottom it leaned out a little, so that they hoped it would give them some protection from the northerly wind and from the falling stones. But eddying blasts swirled round them from every side, and the snow flowed down in ever denser clouds.

They huddled together with their backs to the wall. Bill the pony stood patiently but dejectedly in front of the hobbits, and screened them a little; but before long the drifting snow was above his hocks, and it went on mounting. If they had had no larger companions the hobbits would soon have been entirely buried.

A great sleepiness came over Frodo; he felt himself sinking fast into a warm and hazy dream. He thought a fire was heating his toes, and out of the shadows on the other side of the hearth he heard Bilbo's voice speaking. *I don't think much of your diary*, he said. *Snowstorms on January the twelfth: there was no need to come back to report that!*

But I wanted rest and sleep, Bilbo, Frodo answered with an effort, when he felt himself shaken, and he came back painfully to wakefulness. Boromir had lifted him off the ground out of a nest of snow.

"This will be the death of the halflings, Gandalf," said Boromir. "It is useless to sit here until the snow goes over our heads. We must do something to save ourselves."

"Give them this," said Gandalf, searching in his pack and drawing out a leathern flask. "Just a mouthful each — for all of us. It is very precious. It is *miruvor,* the cordial of Imladris. Elrond gave it to me at our parting. Pass it round!"

As soon as Frodo had swallowed a little of the warm and fragrant liquor he felt a new strength of heart, and the heavy drowsiness left his limbs. The others also revived and found fresh hope and vigour. But the snow did not relent. It whirled about them thicker than ever, and the wind blew louder.

"What do you say to fire?" asked Boromir suddenly. "The choice seems near now between fire and death, Gandalf. Doubtless we shall be hidden from all unfriendly eyes when the snow has covered us, but that will not help us."

"You may make a fire, if you can," answered Gandalf. "If there are any watchers that can endure this storm, then they can see us, fire or no."

But though they had brought wood and kindlings by the advice of Boromir, it passed the skill of Elf or even Dwarf to strike a flame that would hold amid the swirling wind or catch in the wet fuel. At last reluctantly Gandalf himself took a hand. Picking up a faggot he held it aloft for a moment, and then with a word of command, *naur an edraith ammen!* he thrust the end of his staff into the midst of it. At once a great spout of green and blue flame sprang out, and the wood flared and sputtered.

"If there are any to see, then I at least am revealed to them," he said. "I have written *Gandalf is here* in signs that all can read from Rivendell to the mouths of Anduin."

But the Company cared no longer for watchers or unfriendly

eyes. Their hearts were rejoiced to see the light of the fire. The wood burned merrily; and though all round it the snow hissed, and pools of slush crept under their feet, they warmed their hands gladly at the blaze. There they stood, stooping in a circle round the little dancing and blowing flames. A red light was on their tired and anxious faces; behind them the night was like a black wall.

But the wood was burning fast, and the snow still fell.

The fire burned low, and the last faggot was thrown on.

"The night is getting old," said Aragorn. "The dawn is not far off."

"If any dawn can pierce these clouds," said Gimli.

Boromir stepped out of the circle and stared up into the blackness. "The snow is growing less," he said, "and the wind is quieter."

Frodo gazed wearily at the flakes still falling out of the dark to be revealed white for a moment in the light of the dying fire; but for a long time he could see no sign of their slackening. Then suddenly, as sleep was beginning to creep over him again, he was aware that the wind had indeed fallen, and the flakes were becoming larger and fewer. Very slowly a dim light began to grow. At last the snow stopped altogether.

As the light grew stronger it showed a silent shrouded world. Below their refuge were white humps and domes and shapeless deeps beneath which the path that they had trodden was altogether lost; but the heights above were hidden in great clouds still heavy with the threat of snow.

Gimli looked up and shook his head. "Caradhras has not forgiven us," he said. "He has more snow yet to fling at us, if we go on. The sooner we go back and down the better."

To this all agreed, but their retreat was now difficult. It might well prove impossible. Only a few paces from the ashes of their fire the snow lay many feet deep, higher than the heads of the hobbits; in places it had been scooped and piled by the wind into great drifts against the cliff.

"If Gandalf would go before us with a bright flame, he might melt a path for you," said Legolas. The storm had troubled him little, and he alone of the Company remained still light of heart.

"If Elves could fly over mountains, they might fetch the Sun to save us," answered Gandalf. "But I must have something to work on. I cannot burn snow."

"Well," said Boromir, "when heads are at a loss bodies must serve, as we say in my country. The strongest of us must seek a way. See! Though all is now snow-clad; our path, as we came up, turned about that shoulder of rock down yonder. It was there that the snow first began to burden us. If we could reach that point, maybe it would prove easier beyond. It is no more than a furlong off, I guess."

"Then let us force a path thither, you and I!" said Aragorn.

Aragorn was the tallest of the Company, but Boromir, little less in height, was broader and heavier in build. He led the way, and Aragorn followed him. Slowly they moved off, and were soon toiling heavily. In places the snow was breast-high, and often Boromir seemed to be swimming or burrowing with his great arms rather than walking.

Legolas watched them for a while with a smile upon his lips, and then he turned to the others. "The strongest must seek a way, say you? But I say: let a ploughman plough, but choose an otter for swimming, and for running light over grass and leaf, or over snow — an Elf."

With that he sprang forth nimbly, and then Frodo noticed as if for the first time, though he had long known it, that the Elf had no boots, but wore only light shoes, as he always did, and his feet made little imprint in the snow.

"Farewell!" he said to Gandalf. "I go to find the Sun!" Then swift as a runner over firm sand he shot away, and quickly overtaking the toiling men, with a wave of his hand he passed them, and sped into the distance, and vanished round the rocky turn.

The others waited huddled together, watching until Boromir

and Aragorn dwindled into black specks in the whiteness. At length they too passed from sight. The time dragged on. The clouds lowered, and now a few flakes of snow came curling down again.

An hour, maybe, went by, though it seemed far longer, and then at last they saw Legolas coming back. At the same time Boromir and Aragorn reappeared round the bend far behind him and came labouring up the slope.

"Well," cried Legolas as he ran up, "I have not brought the Sun. She is walking in the blue fields of the South, and a little wreath of snow on this Redhorn hillock troubles her not at all. But I have brought back a gleam of good hope for those who are doomed to go on feet. There is the greatest wind-drift of all just beyond the turn, and there our Strong Men were almost buried. They despaired, until I returned and told them that the drift was little wider than a wall. And on the other side the snow suddenly grows less, while further down it is no more than a white coverlet to cool a hobbit's toes."

"Ah, it is as I said," growled Gimli. "It was no ordinary storm. It is the ill will of Caradhras. He does not love Elves and Dwarves, and that drift was laid to cut off our escape."

"But happily your Caradhras has forgotten that you have Men with you," said Boromir, who came up at that moment. "And doughty Men too, if I may say it; though lesser men with spades might have served you better. Still, we have thrust a lane through the drift; and for that all here may be grateful who cannot run as light as Elves."

"But how are we to get down there, even if you have cut through the drift?" said Pippin, voicing the thought of all the hobbits.

"Have hope!" said Boromir. "I am weary, but I still have some strength left, and Aragorn too. We will bear the little folk. The others no doubt will make shift to tread the path behind us. Come, Master Peregrin! I will begin with you."

He lifted up the hobbit. "Cling to my back! I shall need my arms," he said and strode forward. Aragorn with Merry came behind. Pippin marvelled at his strength, seeing the passage that he had already forced with no other tool than his great limbs. Even now, burdened as he was, he was widening the track for those who followed, thrusting the snow aside as he went.

They came at length to the great drift. It was flung across the mountain-path like a sheer and sudden wall, and its crest, sharp as if shaped with knives, reared up more than twice the height of Boromir; but through the middle a passage had been beaten, rising and falling like a bridge. On the far side Merry and Pippin were set down, and there they waited with Legolas for the rest of the Company to arrive.

After a while Boromir returned carrying Sam. Behind in the narrow but now well-trodden track came Gandalf, leading Bill with Gimli perched among the baggage. Last came Aragorn carrying Frodo. They passed through the lane; but hardly had Frodo touched the ground when with a deep rumble there rolled down a fall of stones and slithering snow. The spray cf it half blinded the Company as they crouched against the cliff, and when the air cleared again they saw that the path was blocked behind them.

"Enough, enough!" cried Gimli. "We are departing as quickly as we may!" And indeed with that last stroke the malice of the mountain seemed to be expended, as if Caradhras was satisfied that the invaders had been beaten off and would not dare to return. The threat of snow lifted; the clouds began to break and the light grew broader.

As Legolas had reported, they found that the snow became steadily more shallow as they went down, so that even the hobbits could trudge along. Soon they all stood once more on the flat shelf at the head of the steep slope where they had felt the first flakes of snow the night before.

Thc morning was now far advanced. From thc high place they looked back westwards over the lower lands. Far away in the tumble of country that lay at the foot of the mountain was the dell from which they had started to climb the pass.

Frodo's legs ached. He was chilled to the bone and hungry; and his head was dizzy as he thought of the long and painful march downhill. Black specks swam before his eyes. He rubbed them, but the black specks remained. In the distance below him, but still high above the lower foothills, dark dots were circling in the air.

"The birds again!" said Aragorn, pointing down.

"That cannot be helped now," said Gandalf. "Whether they are good or evil, or have nothing to do with us at all, we must go down at once. Not even on the knees of Caradhras will we wait for another night-fall!"

A cold wind flowed down behind them, as they turned their backs on the Redhorn Gate, and stumbled wearily down the slope. Caradhras had defeated them.

CHAPTER
FOUR

A Journey in the Dark

It was evening, and the grey light was again waning fast, when they halted for the night. They were very weary. The mountains were veiled in deepening dusk, and the wind was cold. Gandalf spared them one more mouthful each of the *miruvor* of Rivendell. When they had eaten some food he called a council.

"We cannot, of course, go on again tonight," he said. "The attack on the Redhorn Gate has tired us out, and we must rest here for a while."

"And then where are we to go?" asked Frodo.

"We still have our journey and our errand before us," answered Gandalf. "We have no choice but to go on, or to return to Rivendell."

Pippin's face brightened visibly at the mere mention of return to Rivendell; Merry and Sam looked up hopefully. But Aragorn and Boromir made no sign. Frodo looked troubled.

"I wish I was back there," he said. "But how can I return without shame — unless there is indeed no other way, and we are already defeated?"

"You are right, Frodo," said Gandalf: "to go back is to admit defeat, and face worse defeat to come. If we go back now, then the Ring must remain there: we shall not be able to set out again. Then sooner or later Rivendell will be besieged, and after a brief and bitter time it will be destroyed. The Ringwraiths are deadly enemies, but they are only shadows yet of the power and terror they would possess if the Ruling Ring was on their master's hand again."

"Then we must go on, if there is a way," said Frodo with a sigh. Sam sank back into gloom.

"There is a way that we may attempt," said Gandalf. "I thought from the beginning, when first I considered this journey, that we should try it. But it is not a pleasant way, and I have not spoken of it to the Company before. Aragorn was against it, until the pass over the mountains had at least been tried."

"If it is a worse road than the Redhorn Gate, then it must be evil indeed," said Merry. "But you had better tell us about it, and let us know the worst at once."

"The road that I speak of leads to the Mines of Moria," said Gandalf. Only Gimli lifted up his head; a smouldering fire was in his eyes. On all the others a dread fell at the mention of that name. Even to the hobbits it was a legend of vague fear.

"The road may lead to Moria, but how can we hope that it will lead through Moria?" said Aragorn darkly.

"It is a name of ill omen," said Boromir. "Nor do I see the need to go there. If we cannot cross the mountains, let us journey southwards, until we come to the Gap of Rohan, where men are friendly to my people, taking the road that I followed on my way hither. Or we might pass by and cross the Isen into Langstrand and Lebennin, and so come to Gondor from the regions nigh to the sea."

"Things have changed since you came north, Boromir," answered Gandalf. "Did you not hear what I told you of Saruman? With him I may have business of my own ere all is over. But the Ring must not come near Isengard, if that can by any means be prevented. The Gap of Rohan is closed to us while we go with the Bearer.

"As for the longer road: we cannot afford the time. We might spend a year in such a journey, and we should pass through many lands that are empty and harbourless. Yet they would not be safe. The watchful eyes both of Saruman and of the Enemy are on them. When you came north, Boromir, you were in the Enemy's eyes only one stray wanderer from the South and a matter of small concern to him: his mind was busy with the pursuit of the Ring. But you return now as a member of the Ring's Company, and you are in peril as long as you remain with us. The danger will increase with every league that we go south under the naked sky.

"Since our open attempt on the mountain-pass our plight has become more desperate, I fear. I see now little hope, if we do not soon vanish from sight for a while, and cover our trail. Therefore I advise that we should go neither over the mountains, nor round them, but under them. That is a road at any rate that the Enemy will least expect us to take."

"We do not know what he expects," said Boromir. "He may watch all roads, likely and unlikely. In that case to enter Moria would be to walk into a trap, hardly better than knocking at the gates of the Dark Tower itself. The name of Moria is black."

"You speak of what you do not know, when you liken Moria to the stronghold of Sauron," answered Gandalf. "I alone of you have ever been in the dungeons of the Dark Lord, and only in his older and lesser dwelling in Dol Guldur. Those who pass the gates of Barad-dûr do not return. But I would not lead you into Moria if there were no hope of coming out again. If there are Orcs there, it may prove ill for us, that is true. But most of the Orcs of the Misty Mountains were scattered or destroyed in the Battle of Five Armies. The Eagles report that Orcs are gathering again from afar; but there is a hope that Moria is still free.

"There is even a chance that Dwarves are there, and that in some deep hall of his fathers, Balin son of Fundin may be found. However it may prove, one must tread the path that need chooses!"

"I will tread the path with you, Gandalf!" said Gimli. "I will go and look on the halls of Durin, whatever may wait there — if you can find the doors that are shut."

"Good, Gimli!" said Gandalf. "You encourage me. We will seek the hidden doors together. And we will come through. In the ruins of the Dwarves, a dwarf's head will be less easy to bewilder than Elves or Men or Hobbits. Yet it will not be the first time that I have been to Moria. I sought there long for Thráin son of Thrór after he was lost. I passed through, and I came out again alive!"

"I too once passed the Dimrill Gate," said Aragorn quietly; "but though I also came out again, the memory is very evil. I do not wish to enter Moria a second time."

"And I don't wish to enter it even once," said Pippin.

"Nor me," muttered Sam.

"Of course not!" said Gandalf. "Who would? But the question is: who will follow me, if I lead you there?"

"I will," said Gimli eagerly.

"I will," said Aragorn heavily. "You followed my lead almost to disaster in the snow, and have said no word of blame. I will follow your lead now — if this last warning does not move you. It is not of the Ring, nor of us others that I am thinking now, but of you, Gandalf. And I say to you: if you pass the doors of Moria, beware!"

"I will *not* go," said Boromir; "not unless the vote of the whole company is against me. What do Legolas and the little folk say? The Ring-bearer's voice surely should be heard?"

"I do not wish to go to Moria," said Legolas.

The hobbits said nothing. Sam looked at Frodo. At last Frodo spoke. "I do not wish to go," he said; "but neither do I wish to refuse the advice of Gandalf. I beg that there should be no vote, until we have slept on it. Gandalf will get votes easier in the light of the morning than in this cold gloom. How the wind howls!"

At these words all fell into silent thought. They heard the wind hissing among the rocks and trees, and there was a howling and wailing round them in the empty spaces of the night.

Suddenly Aragorn leapt to his feet. "How the wind howls!" he cried. "It is howling with wolf-voices. The Wargs have come west of the Mountains!"

"Need we wait until morning then?" said Gandalf. "It is as I said. The hunt is up! Even if we live to see the dawn, who now will wish to journey south by night with the wild wolves on his trail?"

"How far is Moria?" asked Boromir.

"There was a door south-west of Caradhras, some fifteen miles as the crow flies, and maybe twenty as the wolf runs," answered Gandalf grimly.

"Then let us start as soon as it is light tomorrow, if we can," said Boromir. "The wolf that one hears is worse than the orc that one fears."

"True!" said Aragorn, loosening his sword in its sheath. "But where the warg howls, there also the orc prowls."

"I wish I had taken Elrond's advice," muttered Pippin to Sam. "I am no good after all. There is not enough of the breed of Bandobras the Bullroarer in me: these howls freeze my blood. I don't ever remember feeling so wretched."

"My heart's right down in my toes, Mr. Pippin," said Sam. "But we aren't etten yet, and there are some stout folk here with us. Whatever may be in store for old Gandalf, I'll wager it isn't a wolf's belly."

For their defence in the night the Company climbed to the top of the small hill under which they had been sheltering. It was crowned with a knot of old and twisted trees, about which lay a broken circle of boulder-stones. In the midst of this they lit a fire, for there was no hope that darkness and silence would keep their trail from discovery by the hunting packs.

Round the fire they sat, and those that were not on guard dozed uneasily. Poor Bill the pony trembled and sweated where he stood. The howling of the wolves was now all round them, sometimes nearer and sometimes further off. In the dead of night many shining eyes were seen peering over the brow of the hill. Some advanced almost to the ring of stones. At a gap in the circle a great dark wolf-shape could be seen halted, gazing at them. A shuddering howl broke from him, as if he were a captain summoning his pack to the assault.

Gandalf stood up and strode forward, holding his staff aloft. "Listen, Hound of Sauron!" he cried. "Gandalf is here. Fly, if you value your foul skin! I will shrivel you from tail to snout, if you come within this ring."

The wolf snarled and sprang towards them with a great leap. At that moment there was a sharp twang. Legolas had loosed his bow. There was a hideous yell, and the leaping shape thudded to the ground; the elvish arrow had pierced its throat. The watching eyes were suddenly extinguished. Gandalf and Aragorn strode forward, but the hill was deserted; the hunting packs had fled. All about them the darkness grew silent, and no cry came on the sighing wind.

The night was old, and westward the waning moon was setting, gleaming fitfully through the breaking clouds. Suddenly Frodo started from sleep. Without warning a storm of howls broke out fierce and wild all about the camp. A great host of Wargs had gathered silently and was now attacking them from every side at once.

"Fling fuel on the fire!" cried Gandalf to the hobbits. "Draw your blades, and stand back to back!"

In the leaping light, as the fresh wood blazed up, Frodo saw many grey shapes spring over the ring of stones. More and more followed. Through the throat of one huge leader Aragorn passed his sword with a thrust; with a great sweep Boromir hewed the head off another. Beside them Gimli stood with his stout legs apart, wielding his dwarf-axe. The bow of Legolas was singing.

In the wavering firelight Gandalf seemed suddenly to grow:

he rose up, a great menacing shape like the monument of some ancient king of stone set upon a hill. Stooping like a cloud, he lifted a burning branch and strode to meet the wolves. They gave back before him. High in the air he tossed the blazing brand. It flared with a sudden white radiance like lightning; and his voice rolled like thunder.

"*Naur an edraith ammen! Naur dan i ngaurhoth!*" he cried.

There was a roar and a crackle, and the tree above him burst into a leaf and bloom of blinding flame. The fire leapt from tree-top to tree-top. The whole hill was crowned with dazzling light. The swords and knives of the defenders shone and flickered. The last arrow of Legolas kindled in the air as it flew, and plunged burning into the heart of a great wolf-chieftain. All the others fled.

Slowly the fire died till nothing was left but falling ash and sparks; a bitter smoke curled above the burned tree-stumps, and blew darkly from the hill, as the first light of dawn came dimly in the sky. Their enemies were routed and did not return.

"What did I tell you, Mr. Pippin?" said Sam, sheathing his sword. "Wolves won't get him. That was an eye-opener, and no mistake! Nearly singed the hair off my head!"

When the full light of the morning came no signs of the wolves were to be found, and they looked in vain for the bodies of the dead. No trace of the fight remained but the charred trees and the arrows of Legolas lying on the hill-top. All were undamaged save one of which only the point was left.

"It is as I feared," said Gandalf. "These were no ordinary wolves hunting for food in the wilderness. Let us eat quickly and go!"

That day the weather changed again, almost as if it was at the command of some power that had no longer any use for snow, since they had retreated from the pass, a power that wished now to have a clear light in which things that moved in the wild could be seen from far away. The wind had been turning through north to north-west during the night, and now it failed. The clouds vanished southwards and the sky was opened, high and blue. As they stood upon the hill-side, ready to depart, a pale sunlight gleamed over the mountain-tops.

"We must reach the doors before sunset," said Gandalf, "or I fear we shall not reach them at all. It is not far, but our path may be winding, for here Aragorn cannot guide us; he has seldom walked in this country, and only once have I been under the west wall of Moria, and that was long ago.

"There it lies," he said, pointing away south-eastwards to where the mountains' sides fell sheer into the shadows at their feet. In the distance could be dimly seen a line of bare cliffs, and in their midst, taller than the rest, one great grey wall. "When we left the pass I led you southwards, and not back to our starting point, as some of you may have noticed. It is well that I did so, for now we have several miles less to cross, and haste is needed. Let us go!"

"I do not know which to hope," said Boromir grimly: "that Gandalf will find what he seeks, or that coming to the cliff we shall find the gates lost for ever. All choices seem ill, and to be caught between wolves and the wall the likeliest chance. Lead on!"

Gimli now walked ahead by the wizard's side, so eager was he to come to Moria. Together they led the Company back towards the mountains. The only road of old to Moria from the west had lain along the course of a stream, the Sirannon, that ran out from the feet of the cliffs near where the doors had stood. But either Gandalf was astray, or else the land had changed in recent years; for he did not strike the stream where he looked to find it, only a few miles southwards from their start.

The morning was passing towards noon, and still the Company wandered and scrambled in a barren country of red stones. Nowhere could they see any gleam of water or hear any sound of it. All was bleak and dry. Their hearts sank. They saw no living thing, and not a bird was in the sky; but what the night would bring, if it caught them in that lost land, none of them cared to think.

Suddenly Gimli, who had pressed on ahead, called back to them. He was standing on a knoll and pointing to the right. Hurrying up they saw below them a deep and narrow channel. It was empty and silent, and hardly a trickle of water flowed among the brown and red-stained stones of its bed; but on the near side there was a path, much broken and decayed, that wound its way among the ruined walls and paving-stones of an ancient highroad.

"Ah! Here it is at last!" said Gandalf. "This is where the stream ran: Sirannon, the Gate-stream, they used to call it. But what has happened to the water, I cannot guess; it used to be swift and noisy. Come! We must hurry on. We are late."

The Company were footsore and tired; but they trudged doggedly along the rough and winding track for many miles. The sun turned from the noon and began to go west. After a brief halt and a hasty meal they went on again. Before them the mountains frowned, but their path lay in a deep trough of land and they could see only the higher shoulders and the far eastward peaks.

At length they came to a sharp bend. There the road, which had been veering southwards between the brink of the channel and a steep fall of the land to the left, turned and went due east again. Rounding the corner they saw before them a low cliff, some five fathoms high, with a broken and jagged top. Over it a trickling water dripped, through a wide cleft that seemed to have been carved out by a fall that had once been strong and full.

"Indeed things have changed!" said Gandalf. "But there is no mistaking the place. There is all that remains of the Stair Falls. If I remember right, there was a flight of steps cut in the rock at their side, but the main road wound away left and climbed with several loops up to the level ground at the top. There used to be a shallow valley beyond the falls right up to the Walls of Moria, and the Sirannon flowed through it with the road beside it. Let us go and see what things are like now!"

They found the stone steps without difficulty, and Gimli sprang swiftly up them, followed by Gandalf and Frodo. When they reached the top they saw that they could go no further that way, and the reason for the drying up of the Gate-stream was revealed. Behind them the sinking Sun filled the cool western sky with glimmering gold. Before them stretched a dark still lake. Neither sky nor sunset was reflected on its sullen surface. The Sirannon had been dammed and had filled all the valley. Beyond the ominous water were reared vast cliffs, their stern faces pallid in the fading light: final and impassable. No sign of gate or entrance, not a fissure or crack could Frodo see in the frowning stone.

"There are the Walls of Moria," said Gandalf, pointing across the water. "And there the Gate stood once upon a time, the Elven Door at the end of the road from Hollin by which we have come. But this way is blocked. None of the Company, I guess, will wish to swim this gloomy water at the end of the day. It has an unwholesome look."

"We must find a way round the northern edge," said Gimli. "The first thing for the Company to do is to climb up by the main path and see where that will lead us. Even if there were no lake, we could not get our baggage-pony up this stair."

"But in any case we cannot take the poor beast into the Mines," said Gandalf. "The road under the mountains is a dark road, and there are places narrow and steep which he cannot tread, even if we can."

"Poor old Bill!" said Frodo. "I had not thought of that. And poor Sam! I wonder what he will say?"

"I am sorry," said Gandalf. "Poor Bill has been a useful companion, and it goes to my heart to turn him adrift now. I would have travelled lighter and brought no animal, least of all this one that Sam is fond of, if I had had my way. I feared all along that we should be obliged to take this road."

The day was drawing to its end, and cold stars were glinting in the sky high above the sunset, when the Company, with all the speed they could, climbed up the slopes and reached the side of the lake. In breadth it looked to be no more than two or three furlongs at the widest point. How far it stretched away southward they could not see in the failing light; but its northern end was no more than half a mile from where they stood, and between the stony ridges that enclosed the valley and the water's edge there was a rim of open ground. They hurried forward, for they had still a mile or two to go before they could reach the point on the far shore that Gandalf was making for; and then he had still to find the doors.

When they came to the northernmost corner of the lake they found a narrow creek that barred their way. It was green and stagnant, thrust out like a slimy arm towards the enclosing hills. Gimli strode forward undeterred, and found that the water was shallow, no more than ankle-deep at the edge. Behind him they walked in file, threading their way with care, for under the weedy pools were sliding and greasy stones, and footing was treacherous. Frodo shuddered with disgust at the touch of the dark unclean water on his feet.

As Sam, the last of the Company, led Bill up on to the dry ground on the far side, there came a soft sound: a swish, followed by a plop, as if a fish had disturbed the still surface of the water. Turning quickly they saw ripples, black-edged with shadow in the waning light: great rings were widening outwards from a point far out in the lake. There was a bubbling noise, and then silence. The dusk deepened, and the last gleams of the sunset were veiled in cloud.

Gandalf now pressed on at a great pace, and the others followed as quickly as they could. They reached the strip of dry land between the lake and the cliffs: it was narrow, often hardly a dozen yards across, and encumbered with fallen rock and stones; but they found a way, hugging the cliff, and keeping as far from the dark water as they might. A mile southwards along the shore they came upon holly trees. Stumps and dead boughs were rotting in the shallows, the remains it seemed of old thickets, or of a hedge that had once lined the road across the drowned valley. But close under the cliff there stood, still strong and living, two tall trees, larger than any trees of holly that Frodo had ever seen or imagined. Their great roots spread from the wall to the water. Under the looming cliffs they had looked like mere bushes, when seen far off from the top of the Stair; but now they towered overhead, stiff, dark, and silent, throwing deep night-shadows about their feet, standing like sentinel pillars at the end of the road.

"Well, here we are at last!" said Gandalf. "Here the Elven-way from Hollin ended. Holly was the token of the people of that land, and they planted it here to mark the end of their domain; for the West-door was made chiefly for their use in their traffic with the Lords of Moria. Those were happier days, when there was still close friendship at times between folk of different race, even between Dwarves and Elves."

"It was not the fault of the Dwarves that the friendship waned," said Gimli.

"I have not heard that it was the fault of the Elves," said Legolas.

"I have heard both," said Gandalf; "and I will not give judgement now. But I beg you two, Legolas and Gimli, at least to be friends, and to help me. I need you both. The doors are shut and hidden, and the sooner we find them the better. Night is at hand!"

Turning to the others he said: "While I am searching, will you each make ready to enter the Mines? For here I fear we must say farewell to our good beast of burden. You must lay aside much of the stuff that we brought against bitter weather: you will not need it inside, nor, I hope, when we come through and journey on down into the South. Instead each of us must take a share of what the pony carried, especially the food and the water-skins."

"But you can't leave poor old Bill behind in this forsaken place, Mr. Gandalf!" cried Sam, angry and distressed. "I won't have it, and that's flat. After he has come so far and all!"

"I am sorry, Sam," said the wizard. "But when the Door opens I do not think you will be able to drag your Bill inside, into the long dark of Moria. You will have to choose between Bill and your master."

"He'd follow Mr. Frodo into a dragon's den, if I led him," protested Sam. "It'd be nothing short of murder to turn him loose with all these wolves about."

"It will be short of murder, I hope," said Gandalf. He laid his hand on the pony's head, and spoke in a low voice. "Go with words of guard and guiding on you," he said. "You are a wise beast, and have learned much in Rivendell. Make your ways to places where you can find grass, and so come in time to Elrond's house, or wherever you wish to go.

"There, Sam! He will have quite as much chance of escaping wolves and getting home as we have."

Sam stood sullenly by the pony and returned no answer. Bill, seeming to understand well what was going on, nuzzled up to him, putting his nose to Sam's ear. Sam burst into tears, and fumbled with the straps, unlading all the pony's packs and throwing them on the ground. The others sorted out the goods, making a pile of all that could be left behind, and dividing up the rest.

When this was done they turned to watch Gandalf. He appeared to have done nothing. He was standing between the two trees gazing at the blank wall of the cliff, as if he would bore a hole into it with his eyes. Gimli was wandering about, tapping the stone here and there with his axe. Legolas was pressed against the rock, as if listening.

"Well, here we are and all ready," said Merry; "but where are the Doors? I can't see any sign of them"

"Dwarf-doors are not made to be seen when shut," said Gimli. "They are invisible, and their own masters cannot find them or open them, if their secret is forgotten."

"But this Door was not made to be a secret known only to Dwarves," said Gandalf, coming suddenly to life and turning round. "Unless things are altogether changed, eyes that know what to look for may discover the signs."

He walked forward to the wall. Right between the shadow of the trees there was a smooth space, and over this he passed his hands to and fro, muttering words under his breath. Then he stepped back.

"Look!" he said. "Can you see anything now?"

The Moon now shone upon the grey face of the rock; but they could see nothing else for a while. Then slowly on the surface, where the wizard's hands had passed, faint lines appeared, like slender veins of silver running in the stone. At first they were no more than pale gossamer-threads, so fine that they only twinkled fitfully where the Moon caught them, but steadily they grew broader and clearer, until their design could be guessed.

At the top, as high as Gandalf could reach, was an arch of interlacing letters in an Elvish character. Below, though the threads were in places blurred or broken, the outline could be seen of an anvil and a hammer surmounted by a crown with seven stars. Beneath these again were two trees, each bearing crescent moons. More clearly than all else there shone forth in the middle of the door a single star with many rays.

"There are the emblems of Durin!" cried Gimli.

"And there is the Tree of the High Elves!" said Legolas.

"And the Star of the House of Fëanor," said Gandalf. "They are wrought of *ithildin* that mirrors only starlight and moonlight, and sleeps until it is touched by one who speaks words now long forgotten in Middle-earth. It is long since I heard them, and I thought deeply before I could recall them to my mind."

"What does the writing say?" asked Frodo, who was trying to decipher the inscription on the arch. "I thought I knew the elf-letters, but I cannot read these."

"The words are in the elven-tongue of the West of Middle-earth in the Elder Days," answered Gandalf. "But they do not say anything of importance to us. They say only: *The Doors of*

Durin, Lord Moria. Speak, friend, and enter. And underneath small and faint is written: *I, Narvi, made them. Celebrimbor of Hollin drew these signs.*"

"What does it mean by speak, friend, and enter?" asked Merry.

"That is plain enough," said Gimli. "If you are a friend, speak the password, and the doors will open, and you can enter."

"Yes," said Gandalf, 'these doors are probably governed by words. Some dwarf-gates will open only at special times, or for particular persons; and some have locks and keys that are still needed when all necessary times and words are known. These doors have no key. In the days of Durin they were not secret. They usually stood open and doorwards sat here. But if they were shut, any who knew the opening word could speak it and pass in. At least so it is recorded, is it not, Gimli?"

"It is," said the dwarf. "But what the word was is not remembered. Narvi and his craft and all his kindred have vanished from the earth."

"But do not *you* know the word, Gandalf?" asked Boromir in surprise.

"No!" said the wizard.

The others looked dismayed; only Aragorn, who knew Gandalf well, remained silent and unmoved.

"Then what was the use of bringing us to this accursed spot?" cried Boromir, glancing back with a shudder at the dark water. "You told us that you had once passed through the Mines. How could that be, if you did not know how to enter?"

"The answer to your first question, Boromir," said the wizard, "is that I do not know the word — yet. But we shall soon see. And," he added, with a glint in his eyes under their bristling brows, "you may ask what is the use of my deeds when they are proved useless. As for your other question: do you doubt my tale? Or have you no wits left? I did not enter this way. I came from the East.

"If you wish to know, I will tell you that these doors open

Here is written in the Feänorian characters according to the mode of Beleriand: Ennyn Durin Aran Moria: pedo mellon a minno. Im Narvi hain echant: Celebrimbor o Eregion teithant i thiw hin.

outwards. From the inside you may thrust them open with your hands. From the outside nothing will move them save the spell of command. They cannot be forced inwards."

"What are you going to do then?" asked Pippin, undaunted by the wizard's bristling brows.

"Knock on the doors with your head, Peregrin Took," said Gandalf. "But if that does not shatter them, and I am allowed a little peace from foolish questions, I will seek for the opening words.

"I once knew every spell in all the tongues of Elves or Men or Orcs, that was ever used for such a purpose. I can still remember ten score of them without searching in my mind. But only a few trials, I think, will be needed; and I shall not have to call on Gimli for words of the secret dwarf-tongue that they teach to none. The opening words were Elvish, like the writing on the arch: that seems certain."

He stepped up to the rock again, and lightly touched with his staff the silver star in the middle beneath the sign of the anvil.

Annon edhellen, edro hi ammen!
Fennas nogothrim, lasto beth lummen!

he said in a commanding voice. The silver lines faded, but the blank grey stone did not stir.

Many times he repeated these words in different order, or varied them. Then he tried other spells, one after another, speaking now faster and louder, now soft and slow. Then he spoke many single words of Elvish speech. Nothing happened. The cliff towered into the night, the countless stars were kindled, the wind blew cold, and the doors stood fast.

Again Gandalf approached the wall, and lifting up his arms he spoke in tones of command and rising wrath. *Edro, edro!* he cried, and struck the rock with his staff. *Open, open!* he shouted, and followed it with the same command in every language that had ever been spoken in the West of Middle-earth. Then he threw his staff on the ground, and sat down in silence.

At that moment from far off the wind bore to their listening ears the howling of wolves. Bill the pony started in fear, and Sam sprang to his side and whispered softly to him.

"Do not let him run away!" said Boromir. "It seems that we shall need him still, if the wolves do not find us. How I hate this foul pool!" He stooped and picking up a large stone he cast it far into the dark water.

The stone vanished with a soft slap; but at the same instant there was a swish and a bubble. Great rippling rings formed on the surface out beyond where the stone had fallen, and they moved slowly towards the foot of the cliff.

"Why did you do that, Boromir?" said Frodo. "I hate this place, too, and I am afraid. I don't know of what: not of wolves, or the dark behind the doors, but of something else. I am afraid of the pool. Don't disturb it!"

"I wish we could get away!" said Merry.

"Why doesn't Gandalf do something quick?" said Pippin.

Gandalf took no notice of them. He sat with his head bowed, either in despair or in anxious thought. The mournful howling of the wolves was heard again. The ripples on the water grew and came closer; some were already lapping on the shore.

With a suddenness that startled them all the wizard sprang to his feet. He was laughing! "I have it!" he cried. "Of course, of course! Absurdly simple, like most riddles when you see the answer."

Picking up his staff he stood before the rock and said in a clear voice: *Mellon!*

The star shone out briefly and faded again. Then silently a great doorway was outlined, though not a crack or joint had been visible before. Slowly it divided in the middle and swung outwards inch by inch, until both doors lay back against the wall. Through the opening a shadowy stair could be seen climbing steeply up; but beyond the lower steps the darkness was deeper than the night. The Company stared in wonder.

"I was wrong after all," said Gandalf, "and Gimli too. Merry, of all people, was on the right track. The opening word was inscribed on the archway all the time! The translation should have been: *Say 'Friend' and enter.* I had only to speak the Elvish word for *friend* and the doors opened. Quite simple. Too simple for a learned loremaster in these suspicious days. Those were happier times. Now let us go!"

He strode forward and set his foot on the lowest step. But at that moment several things happened. Frodo felt something seize him by the ankle, and he fell with a cry. Bill the pony gave a wild neigh of fear, and turned tail and dashed away along the lakeside into the darkness. Sam leaped after him, and then hearing Frodo's cry he ran back again, weeping and cursing. The others swung round and saw the waters of the lake seething, as if a host of snakes were swimming up from the southern end.

Out from the water a long sinuous tentacle had crawled; it was pale-green and luminous and wet. Its fingered end had hold of Frodo's foot, and was dragging him into the water. Sam on his knees was now slashing at it with a knife.

The arm let go of Frodo, and Sam pulled him away, crying out for help. Twenty other arms came rippling out. The dark water boiled, and there was a hideous stench.

"Into the gateway! Up the stairs! Quick!" shouted Gandalf leaping back. Rousing them from the horror that seemed to have rooted all but Sam to the ground where they stood, he drove them forward.

They were just in time. Sam and Frodo were only a few steps up, and Gandalf had just begun to climb, when the groping tentacles writhed across the narrow shore and fingered the cliff-wall and the doors. One came wriggling over the threshold, glistening in the starlight. Gandalf turned and paused. If he was considering what word would close the gate again from within, there was no need. Many coiling arms seized the doors on either side, and with horrible strength, swung them round. With a shattering echo they slammed, and all light was lost. A noise of rending and crashing came dully through the ponderous stone.

Sam, clinging to Frodo's arm, collapsed on a step in the black darkness. "Poor old Bill!" he said in a choking voice. "Poor old Bill! Wolves and snakes! But the snakes were too much for him. I had to choose, Mr. Frodo. I had to come with you."

They heard Gandalf go back down the steps and thrust his staff against the doors. There was a quiver in the stone and the stairs trembled, but the doors did not open.

"Well, well!" said the wizard. "The passage is blocked behind us now, and there is only one way out — on the other side of the mountains. I fear from the sounds that boulders have been piled up, and the trees uprooted and thrown across the gate. I am sorry; for the trees were beautiful, and had stood so long."

"I felt that something horrible was near from the moment that my foot first touched the water," said Frodo. "What was the thing, or were there many of them?"

"I do not know," answered Gandalf; "but the arms were all guided by one purpose. Something has crept, or has been driven out of dark waters under the mountains. There are older and fouler things than Orcs in the deep places of the world." He did not speak aloud his thought that whatever it was that dwelt in the lake, it had seized on Frodo first among all the Company.

Boromir muttered under his breath, but the echoing stone magnified the sound to a hoarse whisper that all could hear: "In the deep places of the world! And thither we are going against my wish. Who will lead us now in this deadly dark?"

"I will," said Gandalf, "and Gimli shall walk with me. Follow my staff!"

As the wizard passed on ahead up the great steps, he held his staff aloft, and from its tip there came a faint radiance. The wide stairway was sound and undamaged. Two hundred steps they counted, broad and shallow; and at the top they found an arched passage with a level floor leading on into the dark.

"Let us sit and rest and have something to eat, here on the landing, since we can't find a dining-room!" said Frodo. He had begun to shake off the terror of the clutching arm, and suddenly he felt extremely hungry.

The proposal was welcomed by all; and they sat down on the upper steps, dim figures in the gloom. After they had eaten, Gandalf gave them each a third sip of the *miruvor* of Rivendell.

"It will not last much longer, I am afraid," he said; "but I think we need it after that horror at the gate. And unless we have great luck, we shall need all that is left before we see the other side! Go carefully with the water, too! There are many streams and wells in the Mines, but they should not be touched. We may not have a chance of filling our skins and bottles till we come down into Dimrill Dale."

"How long is that going to take us?" asked Frodo.

"I cannot say," answered Gandalf. "It depends on many chances. But going straight, without mishap or losing our way, we shall take three or four marches, I expect. It cannot be less than forty miles from West-door to East-gate in a direct line, and the road may wind much."

After only a brief rest they started on their way again. All were eager to get the journey over as quickly as possible, and were willing, tired as they were, to go on marching still for several hours. Gandalf walked in front as before. In his left hand he held up his glimmering staff, the light of which just showed the ground before his feet; in his right he held his sword Glamdring. Behind him came Gimli, his eyes glinting in the dim light as he turned his head from side to side. Behind the dwarf walked Frodo, and he had drawn the short sword, Sting. No gleam came from the blades of Sting or of Glamdring; and that was some comfort, for being the work of

Elvish smiths in the Elder Days these swords shone with a cold light, if any Orcs were near at hand. Behind Frodo went Sam, and after him Legolas, and the young hobbits, and Boromir. In the dark at the rear, grim and silent, walked Aragorn.

The passage twisted round a few turns, and then began to descend. It went steadily down for a long while before it became level once again. The air grew hot and stifling, but it was not foul, and at times they felt currents of cooler air upon their faces, issuing from half-guessed openings in the walls. There were many of these. In the pale ray of the wizard's staff, Frodo caught glimpses of stairs and arches, and of other passages and tunnels, sloping up, or running steeply down, or opening blankly dark on either side. It was bewildering beyond hope of remembering.

Gimli aided Gandalf very little, except by his stout courage. At least he was not, as were most of the others, troubled by the mere darkness in itself. Often the wizard consulted him at points where the choice of way was doubtful; but it was always Gandalf who had the final word. The Mines of Moria were vast and intricate beyond the imagination of Gimli, Glóin's son, dwarf of the mountain-race though he was. To Gandalf the far-off memories of a journey long before were now of little help, but even in the gloom and despite all windings of the road he knew whither he wished to go, and he did not falter, as long as there was a path that led towards his goal.

"Do not be afraid!" said Aragorn. There was a pause longer than usual, and Gandalf and Gimli were whispering together; the others were crowded behind, waiting anxiously. "Do not be afraid! I have been with him on many a journey, if never on one so dark; and there are tales of Rivendell of greater deeds of his than any that I have seen. He will not go astray — if there is any path to find. He has led us in here against our fears, but he will lead us out again, at whatever cost to himself. He is surer of finding the way home in a blind night than the cats of Queen Berúthiel."

It was well for the Company that they had such a guide. They had no fuel nor any means of making torches; in the desperate scramble at the doors many things had been left behind. But without any light they would soon have come to grief. There were not only many roads to choose from, there were also in many places holes and pitfalls, and dark wells beside the path in which their passing feet echoed. There were fissures and chasms in the walls and floor, and every now and then a crack would open right before their feet. The widest was more than seven feet across, and it was long before Pippin could summon enough courage to leap over the dreadful gap. The noise of churning water came up from far below, as if some great mill-wheel was turning in the depths.

"Rope!" muttered Sam. "I knew I'd want it, if I hadn't got it!"

As these dangers became more frequent their march became slower. Already they seemed to have been tramping on, on, endlessly to the mountains' roots. They were more than weary, and yet there seemed no comfort in the thought of halting anywhere. Frodo's spirits had risen for a while after his escape, and after food and a draught of the cordial; but now a deep uneasiness, growing to dread, crept over him again. Though he had been healed in Rivendell of the knife-stroke, that grim wound had not been without effect. His senses were sharper and more aware of things that could not be seen. One sign of change that he soon had noticed was that he could see more in the dark than any of his companions, save perhaps Gandalf. And he was in any case the bearer of the Ring: it hung upon its chain against his breast, and at whiles it seemed a heavy weight. He felt the certainty of evil ahead and of evil following; but he said nothing. He gripped tighter on the hilt of his sword and went on doggedly.

The Company behind him spoke seldom, and then only in hurried whispers. There was no sound but the sound of their own feet; the dull stump of Gimli's dwarfboots; the heavy tread of Boromir; the light step of Legolas; the soft, scarce-heard patter of hobbit-feet; and in the rear the slow firm footfalls of Aragorn with his long stride. When they halted for a moment they heard nothing at all, unless it were occasionally a faint trickle and drip of unseen water. Yet Frodo began to hear, or to imagine that he heard, something else: like the faint fall of soft bare feet. It was never loud enough, or near enough, for him to feel certain that he heard it; but once it had started it never stopped, while the Company was moving. But it was not an echo, for when they halted it pattered on for a little all by itself, and then grew still.

It was after nightfall when they had entered the Mines. They had been going for several hours with only brief halts, when Gandalf came to his first serious check. Before him stood a wide dark arch opening into three passages: all led in the same general direction, eastwards; but the left-hand passage plunged down, while the right-hand climbed up, and the middle way seemed to run on, smooth and level but very narrow.

"I have no memory of this place at all!" said Gandalf, standing uncertainly under the arch. He held up his staff in the hope of finding some marks or inscription that might help his choice; but nothing of the kind was to be seen. "I am too weary to decide," he said, shaking his head. "And I expect that you are all as weary as I am, or wearier. We had better halt here for what is left of the night. You know what I mean! In here it is ever dark; but outside the late Moon is riding westward and the middle-night has passed."

"Poor old Bill!" said Sam. "I wonder where he is. I hope those wolves haven't got him yet."

To the left of the great arch they found a stone door: it was half closed, but swung back easily to a gentle thrust. Beyond there seemed to lie a wide chamber cut in the rock.

"Steady! Steady!" cried Gandalf as Merry and Pippin pushed forward, glad to find a place where they could rest with at least more feeling of shelter than in the open passage. "Steady! You do not know what is inside yet. I will go first."

He went in cautiously, and the others filed behind. "There!" he said, pointing with his staff to the middle of the floor. Before his feet they saw a large round hole like the mouth of a well. Broken and rusty chains lay at the edge and trailed down into the black pit. Fragments of stone lay near.

"One of you might have fallen in and still be wondering when you were going to strike the bottom," said Aragorn to Merry. "Let the guide go first while you have one."

"This seems to have been a guardroom, made for the watching of the three passages," said Gimli. "That hole was plainly a well for the guards' use, covered with a stone lid. But the lid is broken, and we must all take care in the dark."

Pippin felt curiously attracted by the well. While the others were unrolling blankets and making beds against the walls of the chamber, as far as possible from the hole in the floor, he crept to the edge and peered over. A chill air seemed to strike his face, rising from invisible depths. Moved by a sudden impulse he groped for a loose stone, and let it drop. He felt his heart beat many times before there was any sound. Then far below, as if the stone had fallen into deep water in some cavernous place, there came a *plunk*, very distant, but magnified and repeated in the hollow shaft.

"What's that?" cried Gandalf. He was relieved when Pippin confessed what he had done; but he was angry, and Pippin could see his eye glinting. "Fool of a Took!" he growled. "This is a serious journey, not a hobbit walking-party. Throw yourself in next time, and then you will be no further nuisance. Now be quiet!"

Nothing more was heard for several minutes; but then there came out of the depths faint knocks: *tom-tap, tap-tom*. They stopped, and when the echoes had died away, they were repeated: *tap-tom, tom-tap, tap-tap, tom*. They sounded disquietingly like signals of some sort; but after a while the knocking died away and was not heard again.

"That was the sound of a hammer, or I have never heard one," said Gimli.

"Yes," said Gandalf, "and I do not like it. It may have nothing to do with Peregrin's foolish stone; but probably something has been disturbed that would have been better left quiet. Pray, do nothing of the kind again! Let us hope we shall get some rest without further trouble. You, Pippin, can go on the first watch, as a reward," he growled, as he rolled himself in a blanket.

Pippin sat miserably by the door in the pitch dark; but he kept on turning round, fearing that some unknown thing would crawl up out of the well. He wished he could cover the hole, if only with a blanket, but he dared not move or go near it, even though Gandalf seemed to be asleep.

Actually Gandalf was awake, though lying still and silent. He was deep in thought, trying to recall every memory of his former journey in the Mines, and considering anxiously the next course that he should take; a false turn now might be disastrous. After an hour he rose up and came over to Pippin.

"Get into a corner and have a sleep, my lad," he said in a kindly tone. "You want to sleep, I expect. I cannot get a wink, so I may as well do the watching."

"I know what is the matter with me," he muttered, as he sat down by the door. "I need smoke! I have not tasted it since the morning before the snowstorm."

The last thing that Pippin saw, as sleep took him, was a dark glimpse of the old wizard huddled on the floor, shielding a glowing chip in his gnarled hands between his knees. The flicker for a moment showed his sharp nose, and the puff of smoke.

It was Gandalf who roused them all from sleep. He had sat and watched all alone for about six hours, and had let the others rest. "And in the watches I have made up my mind," he said. "I do not like the feel of the middle way; and I do not like the smell of the left-hand way: there is foul air down there, or I am no guide. I shall take the right-hand passage. It is time we began to climb up again."

For eight dark hours, not counting two brief halts, they marched on; and they met no danger, and heard nothing, and saw nothing but the faint gleam of the wizard's light, bobbing like a will-o'-the-wisp in front of them. The passage they had chosen wound steadily upwards. As far as they could judge it went in great mounting curves, and as it rose it grew loftier and wider. There were now no openings to other galleries or tunnels on either side, and the floor was level and sound, without pits or cracks. Evidently they had struck what once had been an important road; and they went forward quicker than they had done on their first march.

In this way they advanced some fifteen miles, measured in a direct line east, though they must have actually walked twenty miles or more. As the road climbed upwards, Frodo's spirits rose a little; but he still felt oppressed, and still at times he heard, or thought he heard, away behind the Company and beyond the fall and patter of their feet, a following footstep that was not an echo.

They had marched as far as the hobbits could endure without a rest, and all were thinking of a place where they could sleep, when suddenly the walls to right and left vanished. They seemed to have passed through some arched doorway into a black and empty space. There was a great draught of warmer air behind them, and before them the darkness was cold on their faces. They halted and crowded anxiously together.

Gandalf seemed pleased. "I chose the right way," he said. "At last we are coming to the habitable parts, and I guess that we are not far now from the eastern side. But we are high up, a good deal higher than the Dimrill Gate, unless I am mistaken. From the feeling of the air we must be in a wide hall. I will now risk a little real light."

He raised his staff, and for a brief instant there was blaze like a flash of lightning. Great shadows sprang up and fled, and for a second they saw a vast roof far above their heads upheld by many mighty pillars hewn of stone. Before them and on either side stretched a huge empty hall; its black walls, polished and smooth as glass, flashed and glittered. Three other entrances they saw, dark black arches: one straight before them eastwards, and one on either side. Then the light went out.

"That is all that I shall venture on for the present," said Gandalf. "There used to be great windows on the mountain-side, and shafts leading out to the light in the upper reaches of the Mines. I think we have reached them now, but it is night outside again, and we cannot tell until morning. If I am right, tomorrow we may actually see the morning peeping in. But in the meanwhile we had better go no further. Let us rest, if we can. Things have gone well so far, and the greater part of the dark road is over. But we are not through yet, and it is a long way down to the Gates that open on the world."

The Company spent that night in the great cavernous hall, huddled close together in a corner to escape the draught: there seemed to be a steady inflow of chill air through the eastern archway. All about them as they lay hung the darkness, hollow and immense, and they were oppressed by the loneliness and vastness of the dolven halls and endlessly branching stairs and passages. The wildest imaginings that dark rumour had ever suggested to the hobbits fell altogether short of the actual dread and wonder of Moria.

"There must have been a mighty crowd of dwarves here at one time," said Sam; "and every one of them busier than badgers for five hundred years to make all this, and most in hard rock too! What did they do it all for? They didn't live in these darksome holes surely?"

"These are not holes," said Gimli. "This is the great realm and city of the Dwarrowdelf. And of old it was not darksome, but full of light and splendour, as is still remembered in our songs."

He rose and standing in the dark he began to chant in a deep voice, while the echoes ran away into the roof.

The world was young, the mountains green,
No stain yet on the Moon was seen,
No words were laid on stream or stone
When Durin woke and walked alone.
He named the nameless hills and dells;
He drank from yet untasted wells;
He stooped and looked in Mirrormere,
And saw a crown of stars appear,
As gems upon a silver thread,
Above the shadow of his head.

The world was fair, the mountains tall,
In Elder Days before the fall
Of mighty kings in Nargothrond
And Gondolin, who now beyond
The Western Seas have passed away:
The world was fair in Durin's Day.

A king he was on carven throne
In many-pillared halls of stone
With golden roof and silver floor,
And runes of power upon the door.
The light of sun and star and moon
In shining lamps of crystal hewn
Undimmed by cloud or shade of night
There shone for ever fair and bright.

There hammer on the anvil smote,
There chisel clove, and graver wrote;
There forged was blade, and bound was hilt;
The delver mined, the mason built.
There beryl, pearl, and opal pale,
And metal wrought like fishes' mail,
Buckler and corslet, axe and sword,
And shining spears were laid in hoard.

> *Unwearied then were Durin's folk;*
> *Beneath the mountains music woke:*
> *The harpers harped, the minstrels sang,*
> *And at the gates the trumpets rang.*
>
> *The world is grey, the mountains old,*
> *The forge's fire is ashen-cold;*
> *No harp is wrung, no hammer falls:*
> *The darkness dwells in Durin's halls;*
> *The shadow lies upon his tomb*
> *In Moria, in Khazad-dûm.*
> *But still the sunken stars appear*
> *In dark and windless Mirrormere;*
> *There lies his crown in water deep,*
> *Till Durin wakes again from sleep.*

"I like that!" said Sam. "I should like to learn it. *In Moria, in Khazad-dûm!* But it makes the darkness seem heavier, thinking of all those lamps. Are there piles of jewels and gold lying about here still?"

Gimli was silent. Having sung his song he would say no more.

"Piles of jewels?" said Gandalf. "No. The Orcs have often plundered Moria; there is nothing left in the upper halls. And since the dwarves fled, no one dares to seek the shafts and treasuries down in the deep places: they are drowned in water — or in a shadow of fear."

"Then what do the dwarves want to come back for?" asked Sam.

"For *mithril*," answered Gandalf. "The wealth of Moria was not in gold and jewels, the toys of the Dwarves; nor in iron, their servant. Such things they found here, it is true, especially iron; but they did not need to delve for them: all things that they desired they could obtain in traffic. For here alone in the world was found Moria-silver, or true-silver as some have called it: *mithril* is the Elvish name. The Dwarves have a name which they do not tell. Its worth was ten times that of gold, and now it is beyond price; for little is left above ground, and even the Orcs dare not delve here for it. The lodes lead away north towards Caradhras, and down to darkness. The Dwarves tell no tale; but even as *mithril* was the foundation of their wealth, so also it was their destruction: they delved too greedily and too deep, and disturbed that from which they fled, Durin's Bane. Of what they brought to light the Orcs have gathered nearly all, and given it in tribute to Sauron, who covets it.

"*Mithril!* All folk desired it. It could be beaten like copper, and polished like glass; and the Dwarves could make of it a metal, light and yet harder than tempered steel. Its beauty was like to that of common silver, but the beauty of *mithril* did not tarnish or grow dim. The Elves dearly loved it, and among many uses they made of it *ithildin*, starmoon, which you saw upon the doors. Bilbo had a corslet of mithril-rings that Thorin gave him. I wonder what has become of it? Gathering dust still in Michel Delving Mathom-house, I suppose."

"What?" cried Gimli, startled out of his silence. "A corslet of Moria-silver? That was a kingly gift!"

"Yes," said Gandalf. "I never told him, but its worth was greater than the value of the whole Shire and everything in it."

Frodo said nothing, but he put his hand under his tunic and touched the rings of his mail-shirt. He felt staggered to think that he had been walking about with the price of the Shire under his jacket. Had Bilbo known? He felt no doubt that Bilbo knew quite well. It was indeed a kingly gift. But now his thoughts had been carried away from the dark Mines, to Rivendell, to Bilbo, and to Bag End in the days while Bilbo was still there. He wished with all his heart that he was back there, and in those days, mowing the lawn, or pottering among the flowers, and that he had never heard of Moria, or *mithril* — or the Ring.

A deep silence fell. One by one the others fell asleep. Frodo was on guard. As if it were a breath that came in through unseen doors out of deep places, dread came over him. His hands were cold and his brow damp. He listened. All his mind was given to listening and nothing else for two slow hours; but he heard no sound, not even the imagined echo of a footfall.

His watch was nearly over, when, far off where he guessed that the western archway stood, he fancied that he could see two pale points of light, almost like luminous eyes. He started. His head had nodded. "I must have nearly fallen asleep on guard," he thought. "I was on the edge of a dream." He stood up and rubbed his eyes, and remained standing, peering into the dark, until he was relieved by Legolas.

When he lay down he quickly went to sleep, but it seemed to him that the dream went on: he heard whispers, and saw the two pale points of light approaching, slowly. He woke and found that the others were speaking softly near him, and that a dim light was falling on his face. High up above the eastern archway through a shaft near the roof came a long pale gleam; and across the hall through the northern arch light also glimmered faint and distantly.

Frodo sat up. "Good morning!" said Gandalf. "For morning it is again at last. I was right, you see. We are high up on the east side of Moria. Before today is over we ought to find the Great Gates and see the waters of Mirrormere lying in the Dimrill Dale before us."

"I shall be glad," said Gimli. "I have looked on Moria, and it is very great, but it has become dark and dreadful; and we have found no sign of my kindred. I doubt now that Balin ever came here."

After they had breakfasted Gandalf decided to go on again at once. "We are tired, but we shall rest better when we are outside," he said. "I think that none of us will wish to spend another night in Moria."

"No indeed!" said Boromir. "Which way shall we take? Yonder eastward arch?"

"Maybe," said Gandalf. "But I do not know yet exactly

where we are. Unless I am quite astray, I guess that we are above and to the north of the Great Gates; and it may not be easy to find the right road down to them. The eastern arch will probably prove to be the way that we must take; but before we make up our minds we ought to look about us. Let us go towards that light in the north door. If we could find a window it would help, but I fear that the light comes only down deep shafts."

Following his lead the Company passed under the northern arch. They found themselves in a wide corridor. As they went along it the glimmer grew stronger, and they saw that it came through a doorway on their right. It was high and flat-topped, and the stone door was still upon its hinges, standing half open. Beyond it was a large square chamber. It was dimly lit, but to their eyes, after so long a time in the dark, it seemed dazzlingly bright, and they blinked as they entered.

Their feet disturbed a deep dust upon the floor, and stumbled among things lying in the doorway whose shapes they could not at first make out. The chamber was lit by a wide shaft high in the further eastern wall; it slanted upwards and, far above, a small square patch of blue sky could be seen. The light

of the shaft fell directly on a table in the middle of the room: a single oblong block, about two feet high, upon which was laid a great slab of white stone.

"It looks like a tomb," muttered Frodo, and bent forwards with a curious sense of foreboding, to look more closely at it. Gandalf came quickly to his side. On the slab runes were deeply graven:

"These are Daeron's Runes, such as were used of old in Moria," said Gandalf. "Here is written in the tongues of Men and Dwarves:

BALIN SON OF FUNDIN
LORD OF MORIA

"He is dead then," said Frodo. "I feared it was so." Gimli cast his hood over his face.

CHAPTER
FIVE

The Bridge of Khazad-dûm

The Company of the Ring stood silent beside the tomb of Balin. Frodo thought of Bilbo and his long friendship with the dwarf, and of Balin's visit to the Shire long ago. In that dusty chamber in the mountains it seemed a thousand years ago and on the other side of the world.

At length they stirred and looked up, and began to search for anything that would give them tidings of Balin's fate, or show what had become of his folk. There was another smaller door on the other side of the chamber, under the shaft. By both the doors they could now see that many bones were lying, and among them were broken swords and axe-heads, and cloven shields and helms. Some of the swords were crooked: orc-scimitars with blackened blades.

There were many recesses cut in the rock of the walls, and in them were large iron-bound chests of wood. All had been broken and plundered; but beside the shattered lid of one there lay the remains of a book. It had been slashed and stabbed and partly burned, and it was so stained with black and other dark marks like old blood that little of it could be read. Gandalf lifted it carefully, but the leaves crackled and broke as he laid it on the slab. He pored over it for some time without speaking.

Frodo and Gimli standing at his side could see, as he gingerly turned the leaves, that they were written by many different hands, in runes, both of Moria and of Dale, and here and there in Elvish script.

At last Gandalf looked up. "It seems to be a record of the fortunes of Balin's folk," he said. "I guess that it began with their coming to Dimrill Dale nigh on thirty years ago: the pages seem to have numbers referring to the years after their arrival. The top page is marked *one — three*, so at least two are missing from the beginning. Listen to this!

"*We drove out orcs from the great gate and guard* — I think; the next word is blurred and burned: probably *room — we slew many in the bright* — I think — *sun in the dale. Flói was killed by an arrow. He slew the great.* Then there is a blur followed by *Flói under grass near Mirror mere.* The next line or two I cannot read. Then comes *We have taken the twentyfirst hall of North end to dwell in. There is* I cannot read what. A *shaft* is mentioned. Then *Balin has set up his seat in the Chamber of Mazarbul.*"

"The Chamber of Records," said Gimli. "I guess that is where we now stand."

"Well, I can read no more for a long way," said Gandalf, "except the word *gold*, and *Durin's Axe* and something *helm*. Then *Balin is now lord of Moria.* That seems to end a chapter. After some stars another hand begins, and I can see *we found truesilver*, and later the word *wellforged*, and then something, I have it! *mithril*; and the last two lines *Óin to seek for the upper armouries of Third Deep*, something *go westwards*, a blur, *to Hollin gate.*"

Gandalf paused and set a few leaves aside. "There are several pages of the same sort, rather hastily written and much damaged," he said; "but I can make little of them in this light. Now there must be a number of leaves missing, because they begin to be numbered *five*, the fifth year of the colony, I suppose. Let me see! No, they are too cut and stained; I cannot read them. We might do better in the sunlight. Wait! Here is something: a large bold hand using an Elvish script."

"That would be Ori's hand," said Gimli, looking over the wizard's arm. "He could write well and speedily, and often used the Elvish characters."

"I fear he had ill tidings to record in a fair hand," said Gandalf. "The first clear word is *sorrow*, but the rest of the line is lost, unless it ends in *estre*. Yes, it must be *yestre* followed by *day being the tenth of novembre Balin lord of Moria fell in Dimrill Date. He went alone to look in Mirror mere. an orc shot him from behind a stone. we slew the orc, but many more . . . up from east up the Silverlode.* The remainder of the page is so blurred that I can hardly make anything out, but I think I can read *we have barred the gates*, and then *can hold them long if*, and then perhaps *horrible* and *suffer*. Poor Balin! He seems to have kept the title that he took for less than five years. I wonder what happened afterwards; but there is no time to puzzle out the last few pages. Here is the last page of all." He paused and sighed.

"It is grim reading," he said. "I fear their end was cruel. Listen! *We cannot get out. We cannot get out. They have taken the Bridge and second hall. Frár and Lóni and Náli fell there.* Then there are four lines smeared so that I can only read *went 5 days ago*. The last lines run *the pool is up to the wall at Westgate. The Watcher in the Water took Óin. We cannot get out. The end comes*, and then *drums, drums in the deep*. I wonder what that means. The last thing written is in a trailing scrawl of elf-letters: *they are coming*. There is nothing more." Gandalf paused and stood in silent thought.

A sudden dread and a horror of the chamber fell on the Company. "*We cannot get out*," muttered Gimli. "It was well for us that the pool had sunk a little, and that the Watcher was sleeping down at the southern end."

Gandalf raised his head and looked round. "They seem to have made a last stand by both doors," he said; "but there were not many left by that time. So ended the attempt to retake Moria! It was valiant but foolish. The time is not come yet. Now, I fear, we must say farewell to Balin son of Fundin. Here he must lie in the halls of his fathers. We will take this book, the Book of Mazarbul, and look at it more closely later. You had better keep it, Gimli, and take it back to Dáin, if you get a chance. It will interest him, though it will grieve him deeply. Come, let us go! The morning is passing."

"Which way shall we go?" asked Boromir.

"Back to the hall," answered Gandalf. "But our visit to this room has not been in vain. I now know where we are. This must be, as Gimli says, the Chamber of Mazarbul; and the hall must be the twenty-first of the North-end. Therefore we should leave by the eastern arch of the hall, and bear right and south, and go downwards. The Twenty-first Hall should be on the Seventh Level, that is six above the level of the Gates. Come now! Back to the hall!"

Gandalf had hardly spoken these words, when there came a great noise: a rolling *Boom* that seemed to come from depths far below, and to tremble in the stone at their feet. They sprang towards the door in alarm. *Doom, doom* it rolled again, as if huge hands were turning the very caverns of Moria into a vast drum. Then there came an echoing blast: a great horn was blown in the hall, and answering horns and harsh cries were heard further off. There was a hurrying sound of many feet.

"They are coming!" cried Legolas.

"We cannot get out," said Gimli.

"Trapped!" cried Gandalf. "Why did I delay? Here we are, caught, just as they were before. But I was not here then. We will see what——"

Doom, doom came the drum-beat and the walls shook.

"Slam the doors and wedge them!" shouted Aragorn. "And keep your packs on as long as you can: we may get a chance to cut our way out yet."

"No!" said Gandalf. "We must not get shut in. Keep the east door ajar! We will go that way, if we get a chance."

Another harsh horn-call and shrill cries rang out. Feet were coming down the corridor. There was a ring and clatter as the

Company drew their swords. Glamdring shone with a pale light, and Sting glinted at the edges. Boromir set his shoulder against the western door.

"Wait a moment! Do not close it yet!" said Gandalf. He sprang forward to Boromir's side and drew himself up to his full height.

"Who comes hither to disturb the rest of Balin Lord of Moria?" he cried in a loud voice.

There was a rush of hoarse laughter, like the fall of sliding stones into a pit; amid the clamour a deep voice was raised in command. *Doom, boom, doom* went the drums in the deep.

With a quick movement Gandalf stepped before the narrow opening of the door and thrust forward his staff. There was a dazzling flash that lit the chamber and the passage outside. For an instant the wizard looked out. Arrows whined and whistled down the corridor as he sprang back.

"There are Orcs, very many of them," he said. "And some are large and evil: black Uruks of Mordor. For the moment they are hanging back, but there is something else there. A great cave-troll, I think, or more than one. There is no hope of escape that way."

"And no hope at all, if they come at the other door as well," said Boromir.

"There is no sound outside here yet," said Aragorn, who was standing by the eastern door listening. "The passage on this side plunges straight down a stair: it plainly does not lead back towards the hall. But it is no good flying blindly this way with the pursuit just behind. We cannot block the door. Its key is gone and the lock is broken, and it opens inwards. We must do something to delay the enemy first. We will make them fear the Chamber of Mazarbul!" he said grimly, feeling the edge of his sword, Andúril.

Heavy feet were heard in the corridor. Boromir flung himself against the door and heaved it to; then he wedged it with broken sword-blades and splinters of wood. The Company retreated to the other side of the chamber. But they had no chance to fly yet. There was a blow on the door that made it quiver; and then it began to grind slowly open, driving back the wedges. A huge arm and shoulder, with a dark skin of greenish scales, was thrust through the widening gap. Then a great, flat, toeless foot was forced through below. There was a dead silence outside.

Boromir leaped forward and hewed at the arm with all his might; but his sword rang, glanced aside, and fell from his shaken hand, The blade was notched.

Suddenly, and to his own surprise, Frodo felt a hot wrath blaze up in his heart. "The Shire!" he cried, and springing beside Boromir, he stooped, and stabbed with Sting at the hideous foot. There was a bellow, and the foot jerked back, nearly wrenching Sting from Frodo's arm. Black drops dripped from the blade and smoked on the floor. Boromir hurled himself against the door and slammed it again.

"One for the Shire!" cried Aragorn. "The hobbit's bite is deep! You have a good blade, Frodo son of Drogo!"

There was a crash on the door, followed by crash after crash. Rams and hammers were beating against it. It cracked and staggered back, and the opening grew suddenly wide. Arrows came whistling in, but struck the northern wall, and fell harmlessly to the floor. There was a horn-blast and a rush of feet, and orcs one after another leaped into the chamber.

How many there were the Company could not count. The affray was sharp, but the orcs were dismayed by the fierceness of the defence. Legolas shot two through the throat. Gimli hewed the legs from under another that had sprung up on Balin's tomb. Boromir and Aragorn slew many. When thirteen had fallen the rest fled shrieking, leaving the defenders unharmed, except for Sam who had a scratch along the scalp. A quick duck had saved him; and he had felled his orc: a sturdy thrust with his Barrow-blade. A fire was smouldering in his brown eyes that would have made Ted Sandyman step backwards, if he had seen it.

"Now is the time!" cried Gandalf. "Let us go, before the troll returns!"

But even as they retreated, and before Pippin and Merry had reached the stair outside, a huge orc-chieftain, almost man-high, clad in black mail from head to foot, leaped into the chamber; behind him his followers clustered in the doorway. His broad flat face was swart, his eyes were like coals, and his tongue was red; he wielded a great spear. With a thrust of his huge hide shield he turned Boromir's sword and bore him backwards, throwing him to the ground. Diving under Aragorn's blow with the speed of a striking snake he charged into the Company and thrust with his spear straight at Frodo. The blow caught him on the right side, and Frodo was hurled against the wall and pinned. Sam, with a cry, hacked at the spear-shaft, and it broke. But even as the orc flung down the truncheon and swept out his scimitar, Andúril came down upon his helm. There was a flash like flame and the helm burst asunder. The orc fell with cloven head. His followers fled howling, as Boromir and Aragorn sprang at them.

Doom, doom went the drums in the deep. The great voice rolled out again.

"Now!" shouted Gandalf. "Now is the last chance. Run for it!"

Aragorn picked up Frodo where he lay by the wall and made for the stair, pushing Merry and Pippin in front of him. The others followed; but Gimli had to be dragged away by Legolas: in spite of the peril he lingered by Balin's tomb with his head bowed. Boromir hauled the eastern door to, grinding upon its hinges: it had great iron rings on either side, but could not be fastened.

"I am all right," gasped Frodo. "I can walk. Put me down!"

Aragorn nearly dropped him in his amazement. "I thought you were dead!" he cried.

"Not yet!" said Gandalf. "But there is no time for wonder. Off you go, all of you, down the stairs! Wait a few minutes for me at the bottom, but if I do not come soon, go on! Go quickly and choose paths leading right and downwards.”

“We cannot leave you to hold the door alone!” said Aragorn.

“Do as I say!” said Gandalf fiercely. “Swords are no more use here. Go!”

The passage was lit by no shaft and was utterly dark. They groped their way down a long flight of steps, and then looked back; but they could see nothing, except high above them the faint glimmer of the wizard’s staff. He seemed to be still standing on guard by the closed door. Frodo breathed heavily and leaned against Sam, who put his arms about him. They stood peering up the stairs into the darkness. Frodo thought he could hear the voice of Gandalf above, muttering words that ran down the sloping roof with a sighing echo. He could not catch what was said. The walls seemed to be trembling. Every now and again the drum-beats throbbed and rolled: *doom, doom.*

Suddenly at the top of the stair there was a stab of white light. Then there was a dull rumble and a heavy thud, The drum-beats broke out wildly: *doom-boom, doom-boom*, and then stopped. Gandalf came flying down the steps and fell to the ground in the midst of the Company.

“Well, well! That’s over!” said the wizard struggling to his feet. “I have done all that I could. But I have met my match, and have nearly been destroyed. But don’t stand here! Go on! You will have to do without light for a while: I am rather shaken. Go on! Go on! Where are you, Gimli? Come ahead with me! Keep close behind, all of you!”

They stumbled after him wondering what had happened. *Doom, doom* went the drum-beats again: they now sounded muffled and far away, but they were following. There was no other sound of pursuit, neither tramp of feet, nor any voice. Gandalf took no turns, right or left, for the passage seemed to be going in the direction that he desired. Every now and again it descended a flight of steps, fifty or more, to a lower level. At the moment that was their chief danger; for in the dark they could not see a descent, until they came on it and put their feet out into emptiness. Gandalf felt the ground with his staff like a blind man.

At the end of an hour they had gone a mile, or maybe a little more, and had descended many flights of stairs. There was still no sound of pursuit. Almost they began to hope that they would escape. At the bottom of the seventh flight Gandalf halted.

"It is getting hot!" he gasped. "We ought to be down at least to the level of the Gates now. Soon I think we should look for a left-hand turn to take us east. I hope it is not far. I am very weary. I must rest here a moment, even if all the orcs ever spawned are after us."

Gimli took his arm and helped him down to a seat on the step. "What happened away up there at the door?" he asked. "Did you meet the beater of the drums?"

"I do not know," answered Gandalf. "But I found myself suddenly faced by something that I have not met before. I could think of nothing to do but to try and put a shutting-spell on the door. I know many; but to do things of that kind rightly requires time, and even then the door can be broken by strength.

"As I stood there I could hear orc-voices on the other side: at any moment I thought they would burst it open. I could not hear what was said; they seemed to be talking in their own hideous language. All I caught was *ghâsh*: that is 'fire'. Then something came into the chamber — I felt it through the door, and the orcs themselves were afraid and fell silent. It laid hold of the iron ring, and then it perceived me and my spell.

"What it was I cannot guess, but I have never felt such a challenge. The counter-spell was terrible. It nearly broke me. For an instant the door left my control and began to open! I had to speak a word of Command. That proved too great a strain. The door burst in pieces. Something dark as a cloud was blocking out all the light inside, and I was thrown backwards down the stairs. All the wall gave way, and the roof of the chamber as well, I think.

"I am afraid Balin is buried deep, and maybe something else is buried there too. I cannot say. But at least the passage behind us was completely blocked. Ah! I have never felt so spent, but it is passing. And now what about you, Frodo? There was not time to say so, but I have never been more delighted in my life than when you spoke. I feared that it was a brave but dead hobbit that Aragorn was carrying."

"What about me?" said Frodo. "I am alive, and whole I think. I am bruised and in pain, but it is not too bad."

"Well," said Aragorn, "I can only say that hobbits are made of a stuff so tough that I have never met the like of it. Had I known, I would have spoken softer in the Inn at Bree! That spear-thrust would have skewered a wild boar!"

"Well, it did not skewer me, I am glad to say," said Frodo; "though I feel as if I had been caught between a hammer and an anvil." He said no more. He found breathing painful.

"You take after Bilbo," said Gandalf. "There is more about you than meets the eye, as I said of him long ago." Frodo wondered if the remark meant more than it said.

They now went on again. Before long Gimli spoke. He had keen eyes in the dark. "I think," he said, "that there is a light ahead. But it is not daylight. It is red. What can it be?"

"*Ghâsh!*" muttered Gandalf. "I wonder if that is what they meant: that the lower levels are on fire? Still, we can only go on."

Soon the light became unmistakable, and could be seen by all. It was flickering and glowing on the walls away down the passage before them. They could now see their way: in front the road sloped down swiftly, and some way ahead there stood a low archway; through it the growing light came. The air became very hot.

When they came to the arch Gandalf went through, signing to them to wait. As he stood just beyond the opening they saw his face lit by a red glow. Quickly he stepped back.

"There is some new devilry here," he said, "devised for our welcome, no doubt. But I know now where we are: we have reached the First Deep, the level immediately below the Gates. This is the Second Hall of Old Moria; and the Gates are near: away beyond the eastern end, on the left, not more than a quarter of a mile. Across the Bridge, up a broad stair, along a wide road, through the First Hall, and out! But come and look!"

They peered out. Before them was another cavernous hall. It was loftier and far longer than the one in which they had slept. They were near its eastern end; westward it ran away into darkness. Down the centre stalked a double line of towering pillars. They were carved like boles of mighty trees whose boughs upheld the roof with a branching tracery of stone. Their stems were smooth and black, but a red glow was darkly mirrored in their sides. Right across the floor, close to the feet of two huge pillars a great fissure had opened. Out of it a fierce red light came, and now and again flames licked at the brink and curled about the bases of the columns. Wisps of dark smoke wavered in the hot air.

"If we had come by the main road down from the upper halls, we should have been trapped here," said Gandalf. "Let us hope that the fire now lies between us and pursuit. Come! There is no time to lose."

Even as he spoke they heard again the pursuing drum-beat: *Doom, doom, doom.* Away beyond the shadows at the western end of the hall there came cries and horn-calls. *Doom, doom:* the pillars seemed to tremble and the flames to quiver.

"Now for the last race!" said Gandalf. "If the sun is shining outside, we may still escape. After me!"

He turned left and sped across the smooth floor of the hall. The distance was greater than it had looked. As they ran they heard the beat and echo of many hurrying feet behind. A shrill yell went up: they had been seen. There was a ring and clash of steel. An arrow whistled over Frodo's head.

Boromir laughed. "They did not expect this," he said. "The fire has cut them off. We are on the wrong side!"

"Look ahead!" called Gandalf "The Bridge is near. It is dangerous and narrow."

Suddenly Frodo saw before him a black chasm. At the end of the hall the floor vanished and fell to an unknown depth. The outer door could only be reached by a slender bridge of stone, without kerb or rail, that spanned the chasm with one curving spring of fifty feet. It was an ancient defence of the Dwarves against any enemy that might capture the First Hall and the outer passages. They could only pass across it in single file. At the brink Gandalf halted and the others came up in a pack behind.

"Lead the way, Gimli!" he said. "Pippin and Merry next. Straight on, and up the stair beyond the door!"

Arrows fell among them. One struck Frodo and sprang back. Another pierced Gandalf's hat and stuck there like a black feather. Frodo looked behind. Beyond the fire he saw swarming black figures: there seemed to be hundreds of orcs. They brandished spears and scimitars which shone red as blood in the firelight. *Doom, doom* rolled the drum-beats, growing louder and louder, *doom, doom.*

Legolas turned and set an arrow to the string, though it was a long shot for his small bow. He drew, but his hand fell, and the arrow slipped to the ground. He gave a cry of dismay and fear. Two great trolls appeared; they bore great slabs of stone, and flung them down to serve as gangways over the fire. But it was not the trolls that had filled the Elf with terror. The ranks of the orcs had opened, and they crowded away, as if they themselves were afraid. Something was coming up behind them. What it was could not be seen: it was like a great shadow, in the middle of which was a dark form, of man-shape maybe, yet greater; and a power and terror seemed to be in it and to go before it.

It came to the edge of the fire and the light faded as if a cloud had bent over it. Then with a rush it leaped across the fissure.

The flames roared up to greet it, and wreathed about it; and a black smoke swirled in the air. Its streaming mane kindled, and blazed behind it. In its right hand was a blade like a stabbing tongue of fire; in its left it held a whip of many thongs.

"Ai! ai!" wailed Legolas. "A Balrog! A Balrog is come!"

Gimli stared with wide eyes. "Durin's Bane!" he cried, and letting his axe fall he covered his face.

"A Balrog," muttered Gandalf. "Now I understand." He faltered and leaned heavily on his staff. "What an evil fortune! And I am already weary."

The dark figure streaming with fire raced towards them. The orcs yelled and poured over the stone gangways. Then Boromir raised his horn and blew. Loud the challenge rang and bellowed, like the shout of many throats under the cavernous roof. For a moment the orcs quailed and the fiery shadow halted. Then the echoes died as suddenly as a flame blown out by a dark wind, and the enemy advanced again.

"Over the bridge!" cried Gandalf, recalling his strength. "Fly! This is a foe beyond any of you. I must hold the narrow way. Fly!" Aragorn and Boromir did not heed the command, but still held their ground, side by side, behind Gandalf at the far end of the bridge. The others halted just within the doorway at the hall's end, and turned, unable to leave their leader to face the enemy alone.

The Balrog reached the bridge. Gandalf stood in the middle of the span, leaning on the staff in his left hand, but in his other hand Glamdring gleamed, cold and white. His enemy halted again, facing him, and the shadow about it reached out like two vast wings. It raised the whip, and the thongs whined and cracked. Fire came from its nostrils. But Gandalf stood firm.

"You cannot pass," he said. The orcs stood still, and a dead silence fell. "I am a servant of the Secret Fire, wielder of the flame of Anor. You cannot pass. The dark fire will not avail you, flame of Udûn. Go back to the Shadow! You cannot pass."

The Balrog made no answer. The fire in it seemed to die, but

411

the darkness grew. It stepped forward slowly on to the bridge, and suddenly it drew itself up to a great height, and its wings were spread from wall to wall; but still Gandalf could be seen, glimmering in the gloom; he seemed small, and altogether alone: grey and bent, like a wizened tree before the onset of a storm.

From out of the shadow a red sword leaped flaming.

Glamdring glittered white in answer.

There was a ringing clash and a stab of white fire. The Balrog fell back and its sword flew up in molten fragments. The wizard swayed on the bridge, stepped back a pace, and then again stood still.

"You cannot pass!" he said.

With a bound the Balrog leaped full upon the bridge. Its whip whirled and hissed.

"He cannot stand alone!" cried Aragorn suddenly and ran back along the bridge. *"Elendil!"* he shouted. "I am with you, Gandalf!"

"Gondor!" cried Boromir and leaped after him.

At that moment Gandalf lifted his staff, and crying aloud he smote the bridge before him. The staff broke asunder and fell from his hand. A blinding sheet of white flame sprang up. The bridge cracked. Right at the Balrog's feet it broke, and the stone upon which it stood crashed into the gulf, while the rest remained, poised, quivering like a tongue of rock thrust out into emptiness.

With a terrible cry the Balrog fell forward, and its shadow plunged down and vanished. But even as it fell it swung its whip, and the thongs lashed and curled about the wizard's knees, dragging him to the brink. He staggered and fell, grasped vainly at the stone, and slid into the abyss. "Fly, you fools!" he cried, and was gone.

The fires went out, and blank darkness fell. The Company stood rooted with horror staring into the pit. Even as Aragorn and Boromir came flying back, the rest of the bridge cracked and fell. With a cry Aragorn roused them.

"Come! I will lead you now!" he called. "We must obey his last command. Follow me!"

They stumbled wildly up the great stairs beyond the door. Aragorn leading, Boromir at the rear. At the top was a wide echoing passage. Along this they fled. Frodo heard Sam at his side weeping, and then he found that he himself was weeping as he ran. *Doom, doom, doom* the drum-beats rolled behind, mournful now and slow; *doom!*

They ran on. The light grew before them; great shafts pierced the roof. They ran swifter. They passed into a hall, bright with daylight from its high windows in the east. They fled across it. Through its huge broken doors they passed, and suddenly before them the Great Gates opened, an arch of blazing light.

There was a guard of orcs crouching in the shadows behind the great door-posts towering on either side, but the gates were shattered and cast down. Aragorn smote to the ground the captain that stood in his path, and the rest fled in terror of his wrath. The Company swept past them and took no heed of them. Out of the Gates they ran and sprang down the huge and age-worn steps, the threshold of Moria.

Thus, at last, they came beyond hope under the sky and felt the wind on their faces.

They did not halt until they were out of bowshot from the walls. Dimrill Dale lay about them. The shadow of the Misty Mountains lay upon it, but eastwards there was a golden light on the land. It was but one hour after noon. The sun was shining; the clouds were white and high.

They looked back. Dark yawned the archway of the Gates under the mountain-shadow. Faint and far beneath the earth rolled the slow drum-beats: *doom*. A thin black smoke trailed out. Nothing else was to be seen; the dale all around was empty. *Doom*. Grief at last wholly overcame them, and they wept long: some standing and silent, some cast upon the ground. *Doom, doom*. The drum-beats faded.

CHAPTER
SIX

Lothlórien

"Alas! I fear we cannot stay here longer," said Aragorn. He looked towards the mountains and held up his sword. "Farewell, Gandalf!" he cried. "Did I not say to you: *if you pass the doors of Moria, beware*? Alas that I spoke true! What hope have we without you?"

He turned to the Company. "We must do without hope," he said. "At least we may yet be avenged. Let us gird ourselves and weep no more! Come! We have a long road, and much to do."

They rose and looked about them. Northward the dale ran up into a glen of shadows between two great arms of the mountains, above which three white peaks were shining: Celebdil, Fanuidhol, Caradhras, the Mountains of Moria. At the head of the glen a torrent flowed like a white lace over an endless ladder of short falls, and a mist of foam hung in the air about the mountains' feet.

"Yonder is the Dimrill Stair," said Aragorn, pointing to the falls. "Down the deep-cloven way that climbs beside the torrent we should have come, if fortune had been kinder."

"Or Caradhras less cruel," said Gimli. "There he stands smiling in the sun!" He shook his fist at the furthest of the snow-capped peaks and turned away.

To the east the outflung arm of the mountains marched to a

414

sudden end, and far lands could be descried beyond them, wide and vague. To the south the Misty Mountains receded endlessly as far as sight could reach. Less than a mile away, and a little below them, for they still stood high up on the west side of the dale, there lay a mere. It was long and oval, shaped like a great spear-head thrust deep into the northern glen; but its southern end was beyond the shadows under the sunlit sky. Yet its waters were dark: a deep blue like clear evening sky seen from a lamp-lit room. Its face was still and unruffled. About it lay a smooth sward, shelving down on all sides to its bare unbroken rim.

"There lies the Mirrormere, deep Kheled-zâram!" said Gimli sadly. "I remember that he said: 'May you have joy of the sight! But we cannot linger there.' Now long shall I journey ere I have joy again. It is I that must hasten away, and he that must remain."

The Company now went down the road from the Gates. It was rough and broken, fading to a winding track between heather and whin that thrust amid the cracking stones. But still it could be seen that once long ago a great paved way had wound upwards from the lowlands of the Dwarf-kingdom. In places there were ruined works of stone beside the path, and mounds of green topped with slender birches, or fir-trees sighing in the wind. An eastward bend led them hard by the sward of Mirrormere, and there not far from the roadside stood a single column broken at the top.

"That is Durin's Stone!" cried Gimli. "I cannot pass without turning aside for a moment to look at the wonder of the dale!"

"Be swift then!" said Aragorn, looking back towards the Gates. "The Sun sinks early. The Orcs will not, maybe, come out till after dusk, but we must be far away before nightfall. The Moon is almost spent, and it will be dark tonight."

"Come with me, Frodo!" cried the dwarf, springing from the road. "I would not have you go without seeing Kheled-zâram." He ran down the long green slope. Frodo followed slowly, drawn by the still blue water in spite of hurt and weariness; Sam came up behind.

Beside the standing stone Gimli halted and looked up. It was cracked and weather-worn, and the faint runes upon its side could not be read. "This pillar marks the spot where Durin first looked in the Mirrormere," said the dwarf. "Let us look ourselves once, ere we go!"

They stooped over the dark water. At first they could see nothing. Then slowly they saw the forms of the encircling mountains mirrored in a profound blue, and the peaks were like plumes of white flame above them; beyond there was a space of sky. There like jewels sunk in the deep shone glinting stars, though sunlight was in the sky above. Of their own stooping forms no shadow could be seen.

"O Kheled-zâram fair and wonderful!" said Gimli. "There lies the crown of Durin till he wakes. Farewell!" He bowed, and turned away, and hastened back up the green-sward to the road again.

"What did you see?" said Pippin to Sam, but Sam was too deep in thought to answer.

The road now turned south and went quickly downwards, running out from between the arms of the dale. Some way below the mere they came on a deep well of water, clear as crystal, from which a freshet fell over a stone lip and ran glistening and gurgling down a steep rocky channel.

"Here is the spring from which the Silverlode rises," said Gimli. "Do not drink of it! It is icy cold."

"Soon it becomes a swift river, and it gathers water from many other mountain-streams," said Aragorn. "Our road leads beside it for many miles. For I shall take you by the road that Gandalf chose, and first I hope to come to the woods where the Silverlode flows into the Great River — out yonder." They looked as he pointed, and before them they could see the stream leaping down to the trough of the valley, and then running on and away into the lower lands, until it was lost in a golden haze.

"There lie the woods of Lothlórien!" said Legolas. "That is the fairest of all the dwellings of my people. There are no trees like the trees of that land. For in the autumn their leaves fall not, but turn to gold. Not till the spring comes and the new green opens do they fall, and then the boughs are laden with yellow flowers; and the floor of the wood is golden, and golden is the roof, and its pillars are of silver, for the bark of the trees is smooth and grey. So still our songs in Mirkwood say. My heart would be glad if I were beneath the eaves of that wood, and it were springtime!"

"My heart will be glad, even in the winter," said Aragorn. "But it lies many miles away. Let us hasten!"

For some time Frodo and Sam managed to keep up with the others; but Aragorn was leading them at a great pace, and after a while they lagged behind. They had eaten nothing since the early morning. Sam's cut was burning like fire, and his head felt light. In spite of the shining sun the wind seemed chill after the warm darkness of Moria. He shivered. Frodo felt every step more painful and he gasped for breath.

At last Legolas turned, and seeing them now far behind, he spoke to Aragorn. The others halted, and Aragorn ran back, calling to Boromir to come with him.

"I am sorry, Frodo!" he cried, full of concern. "So much has happened this day and we have such need of haste, that I have forgotten that you were hurt; and Sam too. You should have spoken. We have done nothing to ease you, as we ought, though all the orcs of Moria were after us. Come now! A little further on there is a place where we can rest for a little. There I will do what I can for you. Come, Boromir! We will carry them."

Soon afterwards they came upon another stream that ran down from the west, and joined its bubbling water with the hurrying Silverlode. Together they plunged over a fall of green-hued stone, and foamed down into a dell. About it stood fir-trees, short and bent, and its sides were steep and clothed with harts-tongue and shrubs of whortle-berry. At the bottom there was a level space through which the stream flowed noisily over shining pebbles. Here they rested. It was now nearly three hours after noon, and they had come only a few miles from the Gates. Already the sun was westering.

While Gimli and the two younger hobbits kindled a fire of brush- and fir-wood, and drew water, Aragorn tended Sam and Frodo. Sam's wound was not deep, but it looked ugly, and Aragorn's face was grave as he examined it. After a moment he looked up with relief.

"Good luck, Sam!" he said. "Many have received worse than this in payment for the slaying of their first orc. The cut is not poisoned, as the wounds of orc-blades too often are. It should heal well when I have tended it. Bathe it when Gimli has heated water."

He opened his pouch and drew out some withered leaves. "They are dry, and some of their virtue has gone," he said, "but here I have still some of the leaves of *athelas* that I gathered near Weathertop. Crush one in the water, and wash the wound clean, and I will bind it. Now it is your turn, Frodo!"

"I am all right," said Frodo, reluctant to have his garments touched. "All I needed was some food and a little rest."

"No!" said Aragorn. "We must have a look and see what the hammer and the anvil have done to you. I still marvel that you are alive at all." Gently he stripped off Frodo's old jacket and worn tunic, and gave a gasp of wonder. Then he laughed. The silver corslet shimmered before his eyes like the light upon a rippling sea. Carefully he took it off and held it up, and the gems on it glittered like stars, and the sound of the shaken rings was like the tinkle of rain in a pool.

"Look, my friends!" he called. "Here's a pretty hobbit-skin to wrap an elven-princeling in! If it were known that hobbits had such hides, all the hunters of Middle-earth would be riding to the Shire."

"And all the arrows of all the hunters in the world would be in vain," said Gimli, gazing at the mail in wonder. "It is a mithril-coat. Mithril! I have never seen or heard tell of one so fair. Is this the coat that Gandalf spoke of? Then he undervalued it. But it was well given!"

"I have often wondered what you and Bilbo were doing, so close in his little room," said Merry. "Bless the old hobbit! I love him more than ever. I hope we get a chance of telling him about it!"

There was a dark and blackened bruise on Frodo's right side and breast. Under the mail there was a shirt of soft leather, but at one point the rings had been driven through it into the flesh. Frodo's left side also was scored and bruised where he had been hurled against the wall. While the others set the food ready, Aragorn bathed the hurts with water in which *athelas* was steeped. The pungent fragrance filled the dell, and all those who stooped over the steaming water felt refreshed and strengthened. Soon Frodo felt the pain leave him, and his breath grew easy: though he was stiff and sore to the touch for many days. Aragorn bound some soft pads of cloth at his side.

"The mail is marvellously light," he said. "Put it on again, if you can bear it. My heart is glad to know that you have such a coat. Do not lay it aside, even in sleep, unless fortune brings you where you are safe for a while; and that will seldom chance while your quest lasts."

When they had eaten, the Company got ready to go on. They put out the fire and hid all traces of it. Then climbing out of the dell they took to the road again. They had not gone far before the sun sank behind the westward heights and great shadows crept down the mountain-sides. Dusk veiled their feet, and mist rose in the hollows. Away in the east the evening light lay pale upon the dim lands of distant plain and wood. Sam and Frodo now feeling eased and greatly refreshed were able to go at a fair pace, and with only one brief halt Aragorn led the Company on for nearly three more hours.

It was dark. Deep night had fallen. There were many clear stars, but the fast-waning moon would not be seen till late. Gimli and Frodo were at the rear, walking softly and not speaking, listening for any sound upon the road behind. At length Gimli broke the silence.

"Not a sound but the wind," he said. "There are no goblins near, or my ears are made of wood. It is to be hoped that the Orcs will be content with driving us from Moria. And maybe that was all their purpose, and they had nothing else to do with us — with the Ring. Though Orcs will often pursue foes for many leagues into the plain, if they have a fallen captain to avenge."

Frodo did not answer. He looked at Sting, and the blade was dull. Yet he had heard something, or thought he had. As soon as the shadows had fallen about them and the road behind was dim, he had heard again the quick patter of feet. Even now he heard it. He turned swiftly. There were two tiny gleams of light behind, or for a moment he thought he saw them, but at once they slipped aside and vanished.

"What is it?" said the dwarf.

"I don't know," answered Frodo. "I thought I heard feet, and I thought I saw a light — like eyes. I have thought so often, since we first entered Moria."

Gimli halted and stooped to the ground. "I hear nothing but the night-speech of plant and stone," he said. "Come! Let us hurry! The others are out of sight."

The night-wind blew chill up the valley to meet them. Before them a wide grey shadow loomed, and they heard an endless rustle of leaves like poplars in the breeze.

"Lothlórien!" cried Legolas. "Lothlórien! We have come to the eaves of the Golden Wood. Alas that it is winter!"

Under the night the trees stood tall before them, arched over the road and stream that ran suddenly beneath their spreading boughs. In the dim light of the stars their stems were grey, and their quivering leaves a hint of fallow gold.

"Lothlórien!" said Aragorn. "Glad I am to hear again the wind in the trees! We are still little more than five leagues from the Gates, but we can go no further. Here let us hope that the virtue of the Elves will keep us tonight from the peril that comes behind."

"If Elves indeed still dwell here in the darkening world," said Gimli.

"It is long since any of my own folk journeyed hither back to the land whence we wandered in ages long ago," said Legolas, "but we hear that Lórien is not yet deserted, for there is a secret power here that holds evil from the land. Nevertheless its folk are seldom seen, and maybe they dwell now deep in the woods and far from the northern border."

"Indeed deep in the wood they dwell," said Aragorn, and sighed as if some memory stirred in him. "We must fend for ourselves tonight. We will go forward a short way, until the trees are all about us, and then we will turn aside from the path and seek a place to rest in."

He stepped forward; but Boromir stood irresolute and did not follow. "Is there no other way?" he said.

"What other fairer way would you desire?" said Aragorn.

"A plain road, though it led through a hedge of swords," said Boromir. "By strange paths has this Company been led, and so far to evil fortune. Against my will we passed under the shades of Moria, to our loss. And now we must enter the Golden Wood, you say. But of that perilous land we have heard in Gondor, and it is said that few come out who once go in; and of that few none have escaped unscathed."

"Say not *unscathed*, but if you say *unchanged*, then maybe you will speak the truth," said Aragorn. "But lore wanes in Gondor, Boromir, if in the city of those who once were wise they now speak evil of Lothlórien. Believe what you will, there is no other way for us — unless you would go back to Moria-gate, or scale the pathless mountains, or swim the Great River all alone."

"Then lead on!" said Boromir. "But it is perilous."

"Perilous indeed," said Aragorn, "fair and perilous; but only evil need fear it, or those who bring some evil with them. Follow me!"

They had gone little more than a mile into the forest when they came upon another stream, flowing down swiftly from the tree-clad slopes that climbed back westward towards the mountains. They heard it splashing over a fall away among the shadows on their right. Its dark hurrying waters ran across the path before them, and joined the Silverlode in a swirl of dim pools among the roots of trees.

"Here is Nimrodel!" said Legolas. "Of this stream the Silvan Elves made many songs long ago, and still we sing them in the North, remembering the rainbow on its falls, and the golden flowers that floated in its foam. All is dark now and the Bridge of Nimrodel is broken down. I will bathe my feet, for it is said that the water is healing to the weary." He went forward and climbed down the deep-cloven bank and stepped into the stream.

"Follow me!" he cried. "The water is not deep. Let us wade across! On the further bank we can rest, and the sound of the falling water may bring us sleep and forgetfulness of grief."

One by one they climbed down and followed Legolas. For a moment Frodo stood near the brink and let the water flow over his tired feet. It was cold but its touch was clean, and as he went on and it mounted to his knees, he felt that the stain of travel and all weariness was washed from his limbs.

When all the Company had crossed, they sat and rested and ate a little food; and Legolas told them tales of Lothlórien that the Elves of Mirkwood still kept in their hearts, of sunlight and starlight upon the meadows by the Great River before the world was grey.

At length a silence fell, and they heard the music of the waterfall running sweetly in the shadows. Almost Frodo fancied that he could hear a voice singing, mingled with the sound of the water.

"Do you hear the voice of Nimrodel?" asked Legolas. "I will sing you a song of the maiden Nimrodel, who bore the same name as the stream beside which she lived long ago. It is a fair song in our woodland tongue; but this is how it runs in the Westron Speech, as some in Rivendell now sing it." In a soft voice hardly to be heard amid the rustle of the leaves above them he began:

> An Elven-maid there was of old,
>   A shining star by day:
> Her mantle white was hemmed with gold,
>   Her shoes of silver-grey.
>
> A star was bound upon her brows,
>   A light was on her hair
> As sun upon the golden boughs
>   In Lórien the fair.
>
> Her hair was long, her limbs were white,
>   And fair she was and free;
> And in the wind she went as light
>   As leaf of linden-tree.
>
> Beside the falls of Nimrodel,
>   By water clear and cool,
> Her voice as falling silver fell
>   Into the shining pool.
>
> Where now she wanders none can tell,
>   In sunlight or in shade;
> For lost of yore was Nimrodel
>   And in the mountains strayed.

The elven-ship in haven grey
Beneath the mountain-lee
Awaited her for many a day
Beside the roaring sea.

A wind by night in Northern lands
Arose, and loud it cried,
And drove the ship from elven-strands
Across the streaming tide.

When dawn came dim the land was lost,
The mountains sinking grey
Beyond the heaving waves that tossed
Their plumes of blinding spray.

Amroth beheld the fading shore
Now low beyond the swell,
And cursed the faithless ship that bore
Him far from Nimrodel.

Of old he was an Elven-king,
A lord of tree and glen,
When golden were the boughs in spring
In fair Lothlórien.

From helm to sea they saw him leap,
As arrow from the string,
And dive into the water deep,
As mew upon the wing.

The wind was in his flowing hair,
The foam about him shone;
Afar they saw him strong and fair
Go riding like a swan.

But from the West has come no word,
And on the Hither Shore
No tidings Elven-folk have heard
Of Amroth evermore.

The voice of Legolas faltered, and the song ceased. "I cannot sing any more," he said. "That is but a part, for I have forgotten much. It is long and sad, for it tells how sorrow came upon Lothlórien, Lórien of the Blossom, when the Dwarves awakened evil in the mountains."

"But the Dwarves did not make the evil," said Gimli.

"I said not so; yet evil came," answered Legolas sadly. "Then many of the Elves of Nimrodel's kindred left their dwellings and departed, and she was lost far in the South, in the passes of the White Mountains; and she came not to the ship where Amroth her lover waited for her. But in the spring when the wind is in the new leaves the echo of her voice may still be heard by the falls that bear her name. And when the wind is in the South the voice of Amroth comes up from the sea; for Nimrodel flows into Silverlode, that Elves call Celebrant, and Celebrant into Anduin the Great, and Anduin flows into the Bay of Belfalas whence the Elves of Lórien set sail. But neither Nimrodel nor Amroth ever came back.

"It is told that she had a house built in the branches of a tree that grew near the falls; for that was the custom of the Elves of Lórien, to dwell in the trees, and maybe it is so still. Therefore they were called the Galadhrim, the Tree-people. Deep in their forest the trees are very great. The people of the woods did not delve in the ground like Dwarves, nor build strong places of stone before the Shadow came."

"And even in these latter days dwelling in the trees might be thought safer than sitting on the ground," said Gimli. He looked across the stream to the road that led back to Dimrill Dale, and then up into the roof of dark boughs above.

"Your words bring good counsel, Gimli," said Aragorn. "We

cannot build a house, but tonight we will do as the Galadhrim and seek refuge in the tree-tops, if we can. We have sat here beside the road already longer than was wise."

The Company now turned aside from the path, and went into the shadow of the deeper woods, westward along the mountain-stream away from Silverlode. Not far from the falls of Nimrodel they found a cluster of trees, some of which overhung the stream. Their great grey trunks were of mighty girth, but their height could not be guessed.

"I will climb up," said Legolas. "I am at home among trees, by root or bough, though these trees are of a kind strange to me, save as a name in song. *Mellyrn* they are called, and are those that bear the yellow blossom, but I have never climbed in a one. I will see now what is their shape and way of growth."

"Whatever it may be," said Pippin, "they will be marvellous trees indeed if they can offer any rest at night, except to birds. I cannot sleep on a perch!"

"Then dig a hole in the ground," said Legolas, "if that is more after the fashion of your kind. But you must dig swift and deep, if you wish to hide from Orcs." He sprang lightly up from the ground and caught a branch that grew from the trunk high above his head. But even as he swung there for a moment, a voice spoke suddenly from the tree-shadows above him.

"*Daro!*" it said in commanding tone, and Legolas dropped back to earth in surprise and fear. He shrank against the bole of the tree.

"Stand still!" he whispered to the others. "Do not move or speak!"

There was a sound of soft laughter over their heads, and then another clear voice spoke in an elven-tongue. Frodo could understand little of what was said, for the speech that the Silvan folk east of the mountains used among themselves was unlike that of the West. Legolas looked up and answered in the same language.★

"Who are they, and what do they say?" asked Merry.

"They're Elves," said Sam. "Can't you hear their voices?"

"Yes, they are Elves," said Legolas; "and they say that you breathe so loud that they could shoot you in the dark." Sam hastily put his hand over his mouth. "But they say also that you need have no fear. They have been aware of us for a long while. They heard my voice across the Nimrodel, and knew that I was one of their Northern kindred, and therefore they did not hinder our crossing; and afterwards they heard my song. Now they bid me climb up with Frodo; for they seem to have had some tidings of him and of our journey. The others they ask to wait, a little, and to keep watch at the foot of the tree, until they have decided what is to be done."

Out of the shadows a ladder was let down: it was made of rope, silver-grey and glimmering in the dark, and though it looked slender it proved strong enough to bear many men. Legolas ran lightly up, and Frodo followed slowly; behind came Sam trying not to breathe loudly. The branches of the mallorn-tree grew out nearly straight from the trunk, and then swept upward; but near the top the main stem divided into a crown of many boughs, and among these they found that there had been built a wooden platform, or *flet* as such things were called in those days: the Elves called it a *talan*. It was reached by a round hole in the centre through which the ladder passed.

When Frodo came at last up on to the flet he found Legolas seated with three other Elves. They were clad in shadowy-grey, and could not be seen among the tree-stems, unless they moved suddenly. They stood up, and one of them uncovered a small lamp that gave out a slender silver beam. He held it up, looking at Frodo's face, and Sam's. Then he shut off the light again, and spoke words of welcome in his elven-tongue. Frodo spoke haltingly in return.

★ See note in Appendix F: *Of the Elves.*

"Welcome!" the Elf then said again in the Common Language, speaking slowly. "We seldom use any tongue but our own; for we dwell now in the heart of the forest, and do not willingly have dealings with any other folk. Even our own kindred in the North are sundered from us. But there are some of us still who go abroad for the gathering of news and the watching of our enemies, and they speak the languages of other lands. I am one. Haldir is my name. My brothers, Rúmil and Orophin, speak little of your tongue.

"But we have heard rumours of your coming, for the messengers of Elrond passed by Lórien on their way home up the Dimrill Stair. We had not heard of — hobbits, of halflings, for many a long year, and did not know that any yet dwelt in Middle-earth. You do not look evil! And since you come with an Elf of our kindred, we are willing to befriend you, as Elrond asked; though it is not our custom to lead strangers through our land. But you must stay here tonight. How many are you?"

"Eight," said Legolas. "Myself, four hobbits; and two men, one of whom, Aragorn, is an Elf-friend of the folk of Westernesse."

"The name of Aragorn son of Arathorn is known in Lórien," said Haldir, "and he has the favour of the Lady. All then is well. But you have yet spoken only of seven."

"The eighth is a dwarf," said Legolas.

"A dwarf!" said Haldir. "That is not well. We have not had dealings with the Dwarves since the Dark Days. They are not permitted in our land. I cannot allow him to pass."

"But he is from the Lonely Mountain, one of Dain's trusty people, and friendly to Elrond," said Frodo. "Elrond himself chose him to be one of our companions, and he has been brave and faithful."

The Elves spoke together in soft voices, and questioned Legolas in their own tongue. "Very good," said Haldir at last. "We will do this, though it is against our liking. If Aragorn and Legolas will guard him, and answer for him, he shall pass; but he must go blindfold through Lothlórien.

"But now we must debate no longer. Your folk must not remain on the ground. We have been keeping watch on the rivers, ever since we saw a great troop of Orcs going north toward Moria, along the skirts of the mountains, many days ago. Wolves are howling on the wood's borders. If you have indeed come from Moria, the peril cannot be far behind. Tomorrow early you must go on.

"The four hobbits shall climb up here and stay with us — we do not fear them! There is another *talan* in the next tree. There the others must take refuge. You, Legolas, must answer to us for them. Call us, if anything is amiss! And have an eye on that dwarf!"

Legolas at once went down the ladder to take Haldir's message; and soon afterwards Merry and Pippin clambered up on to the high flet. They were out of breath and seemed rather scared.

"There!" said Merry panting. "We have lugged up your blankets as well as our own. Strider has hidden all the rest of our baggage in a deep drift of leaves."

"You had no need of your burdens," said Haldir. "It is cold in the tree-tops in winter, though the wind tonight is in the South; but we have food and drink to give you that will drive away the night-chill, and we have skins and cloaks to spare."

The hobbits accepted this second (and far better) supper very gladly. Then they wrapped themselves warmly, not only in the fur-cloaks of the Elves, but in their own blankets as well, and tried to go to sleep. But weary as they were only Sam found that easy to do. Hobbits do not like heights, and do not sleep upstairs, even when they have any stairs. The flet was not at all to their liking as a bedroom. It had no walls, not even a rail; only on one side was there a light plaited screen, which could be moved and fixed in different places according to the wind.

Pippin went on talking for a while. "I hope, if I do go to sleep in this bed-loft, that I shan't roll off," he said.

"Once I do get to sleep," said Sam, "I shall go on sleeping, whether I roll off or no. And the less said, the sooner I'll drop off, if you take my meaning."

Frodo lay for some time awake, and looked up at the stars glinting through the pale roof of quivering leaves. Sam was snoring at his side long before he himself closed his eyes. He could dimly see the grey forms of two elves sitting motionless with their arms about their knees, speaking in whispers. The other had gone down to take up his watch on one of the lower branches. At last lulled by the wind in the boughs above, and the sweet murmur of the falls of Nimrodel below, Frodo fell asleep with the song of Legolas running in his mind.

Late in the night he awoke. The other hobbits were asleep. The Elves were gone. The sickle Moon was gleaming dimly among the leaves. The wind was still. A little way off he heard a harsh laugh and the tread of many feet on the ground below. There was a ring of metal. The sounds died slowly away, and seemed to go southward, on into the wood.

A head appeared suddenly through the hole in the flet. Frodo sat up in alarm and saw that it was a grey-hooded Elf. He looked towards the hobbits.

"What is it?" said Frodo.

"*Yrch!*" said the Elf in a hissing whisper, and cast on to the flet the rope-ladder rolled up.

"Orcs!" said Frodo. "What are they doing?" But the Elf had gone.

There were no more sounds. Even the leaves were silent, and the very falls seemed to be hushed. Frodo sat and shivered in his wraps. He was thankful that they had not been caught on the ground; but he felt that the trees offered little protection, except concealment. Orcs were as keen as hounds on a scent, it was said, but they could also climb. He drew out Sting: it flashed and glittered like a blue flame; and then slowly faded again and grew dull. In spite of the fading of his sword the feeling of immediate danger did not leave Frodo, rather it grew stronger. He got up and crawled to the opening and peered down. He was almost certain that he could hear stealthy movements at the tree's foot far below.

Not Elves; for the woodland folk were altogether noiseless in their movements. Then he heard faintly a sound like sniffing; and something seemed to be scrabbling on the bark of the tree-trunk. He stared down into the dark, holding his breath.

Something was now climbing slowly, and its breath came like a soft hissing through closed teeth. Then coming up, close to the stem, Frodo saw two pale eyes. They stopped and gazed upward unwinking. Suddenly they turned away, and a shadowy figure slipped round the trunk of the tree and vanished.

Immediately afterwards Haldir came climbing swiftly up through the branches. "There was something in this tree that I have never seen before," he said. "It was not an orc. It fled as soon as I touched the tree-stem. It seemed to be wary, and to have some skill in trees, or I might have thought that it was one of you hobbits.

"I did not shoot, for I dared not arouse any cries: we cannot risk battle. A strong company of Orcs has passed. They crossed the Nimrodel — curse their foul feet in its clean water — and went on down the old road beside the river. They seemed to pick up some scent, and they searched the ground for a while near the place where you halted. The three of us could not challenge a hundred, so we went ahead and spoke with feigned voices, leading them on into the wood.

"Orophin has now gone in haste back to our dwellings to warn our people. None of the Orcs will ever return out of Lórien. And there will be many Elves hidden on the northern border before another night falls. But you must take the road south as soon as it is fully light."

Day came pale from the East. As the light grew it filtered through the yellow leaves of the mallorn, and it seemed to the hobbits that the early sun of a cool summer's morning was shining. Pale-blue sky peeped among the moving branches.

Looking through an opening on the south side of the flet Frodo saw all the valley of the Silverlode lying like a sea of fallow gold tossing gently in the breeze.

The morning was still young and cold when the Company set out again, guided now by Haldir and his brother Rumil. "Farewell, sweet Nimrodel!" cried Legolas. Frodo looked back and caught a gleam of white foam among the grey tree-stems. "Farewell," he said. It seemed to him that he would never hear again a running water so beautiful, for ever blending its innumerable notes in an endless changeful music.

They went back to the path that still went on along the west side of the Silverlode, and for some way they followed it southward. There were the prints of orc-feet in the earth. But soon Haldir turned aside into the trees and halted on the bank of the river under their shadows.

"There is one of my people yonder across the stream," he said, "though you may not see him." He gave a call like the low whistle of a bird, and out of a thicket of young trees an Elf stepped, clad in grey, but with his hood thrown back; his hair glinted like gold in the morning sun. Haldir skilfully cast over the stream a coil of grey rope, and he caught it and bound the end about a tree near the bank

"Celebrant is already a strong stream here, as you see," said Haldir, "and it runs both swift and deep, and is very cold. We do not set foot in it so far north, unless we must. But in these days of watchfulness we do not make bridges. This is how we cross! Follow me!" He made his end of the rope fast about another tree, and then ran lightly along it, over the river and back again, as if he were on a road.

"I can walk this path," said Legolas; "but the others have not this skill. Must they swim?"

"No!" said Haldir. "We have two more ropes. We will fasten them above the other, one shoulder-high, and another half-high, and holding these the strangers should be able to cross with care."

When this slender bridge had been made, the Company

passed over, some cautiously and slowly, others more easily. Of the hobbits Pippin proved the best for he was sure-footed, and he walked over quickly, holding only with one hand; but he kept his eyes on the bank ahead and did not look down. Sam shuffled along, clutching hard, and looking down into the pale eddying water as if it was a chasm in the mountains.

He breathed with relief when he was safely across. "Live and learn! as my gaffer used to say. Though he was thinking of gardening, not of roosting like a bird, nor of trying to walk like a spider. Not even my uncle Andy ever did a trick like that!"

When at length all the Company was gathered on the east bank of the Silverlode, the Elves untied the ropes and coiled two of them. Rúmil, who had remained on the other side, drew back the last one, slung it on his shoulder, and with a wave of his hand went away, back to Nimrodel to keep watch.

"Now, friends," said Haldir, "you have entered the Naith of Lórien, or the Gore, as you would say, for it is the land that lies like a spear-head between the arms of Silverlode and Anduin the Great. We allow no strangers to spy out the secrets of the Naith. Few indeed are permitted even to set foot there.

"As was agreed, I shall here blindfold the eyes of Gimli the Dwarf. The others may walk free for a while, until we come nearer to our dwellings, down in Egladil, in the Angle between the waters."

This was not at all to the liking of Gimli. "The agreement was made without my consent," he said. "I will not walk blindfold, like a beggar or a prisoner. And I am no spy. My folk have never had dealings with any of the servants of the Enemy. Neither have we done harm to the Elves. I am no more likely to betray you than Legolas, or any other of my companions."

"I do not doubt you," said Haldir. "Yet this is our law. I am not the master of the law, and cannot set it aside. I have done much in letting you set foot over Celebrant."

Gimli was obstinate. He planted his feet firmly apart, and laid his hand upon the haft of his axe. "I will go forward free," he said, "or I will go back and seek my own land, where I am known to be true of word, though I perish alone in the wilderness."

"You cannot go back," said Haldir sternly. "Now you have come thus far, you must be brought before the Lord and the Lady. They shall judge you, to hold you or to give you leave, as they will. You cannot cross the rivers again, and behind you there are now secret sentinels that you cannot pass. You would be slain before you saw them."

Gimli drew his axe from his belt. Haldir and his companion bent their bows. "A plague on Dwarves and their stiff necks!" said Legolas.

"Come!" said Aragorn. "If I am still to lead this Company, you must do as I bid. It is hard upon the Dwarf to be thus singled out. We will all be blindfold, even Legolas. That will be best, though it will make the journey slow and dull."

Gimli laughed suddenly. "A merry troop of fools we shall look! Will Haldir lead us all on a string, like many blind beggars with one dog? But I will be content, if only Legolas here shares my blindness."

"I am an Elf and a kinsman here," said Legolas, becoming angry in his turn.

"Now let us cry: 'a plague on the stiff necks of Elves!'" said Aragorn. "But the Company shall all fare alike. Come, bind our eyes, Haldir!"

"I shall claim full amends for every fall and stubbed toe, if you do not lead us well," said Gimli as they bound a cloth about his eyes.

"You will have no claim," said Haldir. "I shall lead you well, and the paths are smooth and straight."

"Alas for the folly of these days!" said Legolas. "Here all are enemies of the one Enemy, and yet I must walk blind, while the sun is merry in the woodland under leaves of gold!"

"Folly it may seem," said Haldir. "Indeed in nothing is the power of the Dark Lord more clearly shown than in the estrangement that divides all those who still oppose him. Yet so little faith and trust do we find now in the world beyond Lothlórien, unless maybe in Rivendell, that we dare not by our own trust endanger our land. We live now upon an island amid many perils, and our hands are more often upon the bowstring than upon the harp.

"The rivers long defended us, but they are a sure guard no more; for the Shadow has crept northward all about us. Some speak of departing, yet for that it already seems too late. The mountains to the west are growing evil; to the east the lands are waste, and full of Sauron's creatures; and it is rumoured that we cannot now safely pass southward through Rohan, and the mouths of the Great River are watched by the Enemy. Even if we could come to the shores of the Sea, we should find no longer any shelter there. It is said that there are still havens of the High Elves, but they are far north and west, beyond the land of the Halflings. But where that may be, though the Lord and Lady may know, I do not."

"You ought at least to guess, since you have seen us," said Merry. "There are Elf-havens west of my land, the Shire, where Hobbits live."

"Happy folk are Hobbits to dwell near the shores of the sea!" said Haldir. "It is long indeed. since any of my folk have looked on it, yet still we remember it in song. Tell me of these havens as we walk."

"I cannot," said Merry. "I have never seen them. I have never been out of my own land before. And if I had known what the world outside was like, I don't think I should have had the heart to leave it."

"Not even to see fair Lothlórien?" said Haldir. "The world is indeed full of peril, and in it there are many dark places; but still there is much that is fair, and though in all lands love is now mingled with grief, it grows perhaps the greater.

"Some there are among us who sing that the Shadow will draw back, and peace shall come again. Yet I do not believe that the world about us will ever again be as it was of old, or the light of the Sun as it was aforetime. For the Elves, I fear, it will prove at best a truce, in which they may pass to the Sea unhindered and leave the Middle-earth for ever. Alas for Lothlórien that I love! It would be a poor life in a land where no mallorn grew. But if there are mallorn-trees beyond the Great Sea, none have reported it."

As they spoke thus, the Company filed slowly along the paths in the wood, led by Haldir, while the other Elf walked behind. They felt the ground beneath their feet smooth and soft, and after a while they walked more freely, without fear of hurt or fall. Being deprived of sight, Frodo found his hearing and other senses sharpened. He could smell the trees and the trodden grass. He could hear many different notes in the rustle of the leaves overhead, the river murmuring away on his right, and the thin clear voices of birds in the sky. He felt the sun upon his face and hands when they passed through an open glade.

As soon as he set foot upon the far bank of Silverlode a strange feeling had come upon him, and it deepened as he walked on into the Naith: it seemed to him that he had stepped over a bridge of time into a corner of the Elder Days, and was now walking in a world that was no more. In Rivendell there was memory of ancient things; in Lórien the ancient things still lived on in the waking world. Evil had been seen and heard there, sorrow had been known; the Elves feared and distrusted the world outside: wolves were howling on the wood's borders: but on the land of Lórien no shadow lay.

All that day the Company marched on, until they felt the cool evening come and heard the early night-wind whispering among many leaves. Then they rested and slept without fear upon the ground; for their guides would not permit them to unbind their eyes, and they could not climb. In the morning they went on again, walking without haste. At noon they halted, and Frodo was aware that they had passed out under the shining Sun. Suddenly he heard the sound of many voices all around him.

A marching host of Elves had come up silently: they were hastening toward the northern borders to guard against any attack from Moria; and they brought news, some of which Haldir reported. The marauding orcs had been waylaid and almost all destroyed; the remnant had fled westward towards the mountains, and were being pursued. A strange creature also had been seen, running with bent back and with hands near the ground, like a beast and yet not of beast-shape. It had eluded capture, and they had not shot it, not knowing whether it was good or ill, and it had vanished down the Silverlode southward.

"Also," said Haldir, "they bring me a message from the Lord and Lady of the Galadhrim. You are all to walk free, even the dwarf Gimli. It seems that the Lady knows who and what is each member of your Company. New messages have come from Rivendell perhaps."

He removed the bandage first from Gimli's eyes. "Your pardon!" he said, bowing low. "Look on us now with friendly eyes! Look and be glad, for you are the first dwarf to behold the trees of the Naith of Lórien since Durin's Day!"

When his eyes were in turn uncovered, Frodo looked up and caught his breath. They were standing in an open space. To the left stood a great mound, covered with a sward of grass as green as Spring-time in the Elder Days. Upon it, as a double crown, grew two circles of trees: the outer had bark of snowy white, and were leafless but beautiful in their shapely nakedness; the inner were mallorn-trees of great height, still arrayed in pale gold. High amid the branches of a towering tree that stood in the centre of all there gleamed a white flet. At the feet of the trees, and all about the green hillsides the grass was studded with small golden flowers shaped like stars. Among them, nodding on slender stalks, were other flowers, white and palest green: they glimmered as a mist amid the rich hue of the grass. Over all the sky was blue, and the sun of afternoon glowed upon the hill and cast long green shadows beneath the trees.

"Behold! You are come to Cerin Amroth," said Haldir. "For this is the heart of the ancient realm as it was long ago, and here is the mound of Amroth, where in happier days his high house was built. Here ever bloom the winter flowers in the unfading grass: the yellow *elanor*, and the pale *niphredil*. Here we will stay awhile, and come to the city of the Galadhrim at dusk."

The others cast themselves down upon the fragrant grass, but Frodo stood awhile still lost in wonder. It seemed to him that he had stepped through a high window that looked on a vanished world. A light was upon it for which his language had no name. All that he saw was shapely, but the shapes seemed at once clear cut, as if they had been first conceived and drawn at the uncovering of his eyes, and ancient as if they had endured for ever. He saw no colour but those he knew, gold and white and blue and green, but they were fresh and poignant, as if he had at that moment first perceived them and made for them names new and wonderful. In winter here no heart could mourn for summer or for spring. No blemish or sickness or deformity could be seen in anything that grew upon the earth. On the land of Lórien there was no stain.

He turned and saw that Sam was now standing beside him, looking round with a puzzled expression, and rubbing his eyes as if he was not sure that he was awake. "It's sunlight and bright day, right enough," he said. "I thought that Elves were all for moon and stars: but this is more elvish than anything I ever heard tell of. I feel as if I was *inside* a song, if you take my meaning."

Haldir looked at them, and he seemed indeed to take the meaning of both thought and word. He smiled. "You feel the power of the Lady of the Galadhrim," he said. "Would it please you to climb with me up Cerin Amroth?"

They followed him as he stepped lightly up the grass-clad slopes. Though he walked and breathed, and about him living leaves and flowers were stirred by the same cool wind as fanned his face, Frodo felt that he was in a timeless land that did not fade or change or fall into forgetfulness. When he had gone and passed again into the outer world, still Frodo the wanderer from the Shire would walk there, upon the grass among *elanor* and *niphredil* in fair Lothlórien.

They entered the circle of white trees. As they did so the South Wind blew upon Cerin Amroth and sighed among the branches. Frodo stood still, hearing far off great seas upon beaches that had long ago been washed away, and sea-birds crying whose race had perished from the earth.

Haldir had gone on and was now climbing to the high flet. As Frodo prepared to follow him, he laid his hand upon the tree beside the ladder: never before had he been so suddenly and so keenly aware of the feel and texture of a tree's skin and of the life within it. He felt a delight in wood and the touch of it, neither as forester nor as carpenter; it was the delight of the living tree itself.

As he stepped out at last upon the lofty platform, Haldir took his hand and turned him toward the South. "Look this way first!" he said.

Frodo looked and saw, still at some distance, a hill of many mighty trees, or a city of green towers: which it was he could not tell. Out of it, it seemed to him that the power and light came that held all the land in sway. He longed suddenly to fly like a bird to rest in the green city. Then he looked eastward and saw all the land of Lórien running down to the pale gleam of Anduin, the Great River. He lifted his eyes across the river and all the light went out, and he was back again in the world he knew. Beyond the river the land appeared flat and empty, formless and vague, until far away it rose again like a wall, dark and drear. The sun that lay on Lothlórien had no power to enlighten the shadow of that distant height.

"There lies the fastness of Southern Mirkwood," said Haldir. "It is clad in a forest of dark fir, where the trees strive one against another and their branches rot and wither. In the midst upon a stony height stands Dol Guldur, where long the hidden Enemy had his dwelling. We fear that now it is inhabited again, and with power sevenfold. A black cloud lies often over it of late. In this high place you may see the two powers that are opposed one to another; and ever they strive now in thought, but whereas the light perceives the very heart of the darkness, its own secret has not been discovered. Not yet." He turned and climbed swiftly down, and they followed him.

At the hill's foot Frodo found Aragorn, standing still and silent as a tree; but in his hand was a small golden bloom of *elanor*, and a light was in his eyes. He was wrapped in some fair memory: and as Frodo looked at him he knew that he beheld things as they once had been in this same place. For the grim years were removed from the face of Aragorn, and he seemed clothed in white, a young lord tall and fair; and he spoke words in the Elvish tongue to one whom Frodo could not see. *Arwen vanimelda, namarië!* he said, and then he drew a breath, and returning out of his thought he looked at Frodo and smiled.

"Here is the heart of Elvendom on earth," he said, "and here my heart dwells ever, unless there be a light beyond the dark roads that we still must tread, you and I. Come with me!" And taking Frodo's hand in his, he left the hill of Cerin Amroth and came there never again as living man.

CHAPTER
SEVEN

The Mirror of
Galadriel

The sun was sinking behind the mountains, and the shadows were deepening in the woods, when they went on again. Their paths now went into thickets where the dusk had already gathered. Night came beneath the trees as they walked, and the Elves uncovered their silver lamps.

Suddenly they came out into the open again and found themselves under a pale evening sky pricked by a few early stars. There was a wide treeless space before them, running in a great circle and bending away on either hand. Beyond it was a deep fosse lost in soft shadow, but the grass upon its brink was green, as if it glowed still in memory of the sun that had gone. Upon the further side there rose to a great height a green wall encircling a green hill thronged with mallorn-trees taller than any they had yet seen in all the land. Their height could not be guessed, but they stood up in the twilight like living towers. In their many-tiered branches and amid their ever-moving leaves countless lights were gleaming, green and gold and silver. Haldir turned towards the Company.

"Welcome to Caras Galadhon!" he said. "Here is the city of the Galadhrim where dwell the Lord Celeborn and Galadriel the Lady of Lórien. But we cannot enter here, for the gates do not look northward. We must go round to the southern side, and the way is not short for the city is great."

There was a road paved with white stone running on the outer brink of the fosse. Along this they went westward, with the city ever climbing up like a green cloud upon their left; and as the night deepened more lights sprang forth, until all the hill seemed afire with stars. They came at last to a white bridge, and crossing found the great gates of the city: they faced southwest, set between the ends of the encircling wall that here overlapped, and they were tall and strong, and hung with many lamps.

Haldir knocked and spoke, and the gates opened soundlessly; but of guards Frodo could see no sign. The travellers passed within, and the gates shut behind them. They were in a deep lane between the ends of the wall, and passing quickly through it they entered the City of the Trees. No folk could they see, nor hear any feet upon the paths; but there were many voices, about them, and in the air above. Far away up on the hill they could hear the sound of singing falling from on high like soft rain upon leaves.

They went along many paths and climbed many stairs, until they came to the high places and saw before them amid a wide lawn a fountain shimmering. It was lit by silver lamps that swung from the boughs of trees, and it fell into a basin of silver, from which a white stream spilled. Upon the south side of the lawn there stood the mightiest of all the trees; its great smooth bole gleamed like grey silk, and up it towered, until its first branches, far above, opened their huge limbs under shadowy clouds of leaves. Beside it a broad white ladder stood, and at its foot three Elves were seated. They sprang up as the travellers approached, and Frodo saw that they were tall and clad in grey mail, and from their shoulders hung long white cloaks.

"Here dwell Celeborn and Galadriel," said Haldir. "It is their wish that you should ascend and speak with them."

One of the Elf-wardens then blew a clear note on a small

horn, and it was answered three times from far above. "I will go first," said Haldir. "Let Frodo come next and with him Legolas. The others may follow as they wish. It is a long climb for those that are not accustomed to such stairs, but you may rest upon the way."

As he climbed slowly up Frodo passed many flets: some on one side, some on another, and some set about the bole of the tree, so that the ladder passed through them. At a great height above the ground he came to a wide *talan*, like the deck of a great ship. On it was built a house, so large that almost it would have served for a hall of Men upon the earth. He entered behind Haldir, and found that he was in a chamber of oval shape, in the midst of which grew the trunk of the great mallorn, now tapering towards its crown, and yet making still a pillar of wide girth.

The chamber was filled with a soft light; its walls were green and silver and its roof of gold. Many Elves were seated there. On two chairs beneath the bole of the tree and canopied by a living bough there sat, side by side, Celeborn and Galadriel. They stood up to greet their guests, after the manner of Elves, even those who were accounted mighty kings. Very tall they were, and the Lady no less tall than the Lord; and they were grave and beautiful. They were clad wholly in white; and the hair of the Lady was of deep gold, and the hair of the Lord Celeborn was of silver long and bright; but no sign of age was upon them, unless it were in the depths of their eyes; for these were keen as lances in the starlight, and yet profound, the wells of deep memory.

Haldir led Frodo before them, and the Lord welcomed him in his own tongue. The Lady Galadriel said no word but looked long upon his face.

"Sit now beside my chair, Frodo of the Shire!" said Celeborn. "When all have come we will speak together."

Each of the companions he greeted courteously by name as they entered. "Welcome Aragorn son of Arathorn!" he said. "It is eight and thirty years of the world outside since you came to this land; and those years lie heavy on you. But the end is near, for good or ill. Here lay aside your burden for a while!"

"Welcome son of Thranduil! Too seldom do my kindred journey hither from the North."

"Welcome Gimli son of Glóin! It is long indeed since we saw one of Durin's folk in Caras Galadhon. But today we have broken our long law. May it be a sign that though the world is now dark better days are at hand, and that friendship shall be renewed between our peoples." Gimli bowed low.

When all the guests were seated before his chair the Lord looked at them again. "Here there are eight," he said. "Nine were to set out: so said the messages. But maybe there has been some change of counsel that we have not heard. Elrond is far away, and darkness gathers between us, and all this year the shadows have grown longer."

"Nay, there was no change of counsel," said the Lady Galadriel, speaking for the first time. Her voice was clear and musical, but deeper than woman's wont. "Gandalf the Grey set out with the Company, but he did not pass the borders of this land. Now tell us where he is; for I much desired to speak with him again. But I cannot see him from afar, unless he comes within the fences of Lothlórien: a grey mist is about him, and the ways of his feet and of his mind are hidden from me."

"Alas!" said Aragorn. "Gandalf the Grey fell into shadow. He remained in Moria and did not escape."

At these words all the Elves in the hall cried aloud in grief and amazement. "These are evil tidings," said Celeborn, "the most evil that have been spoken here in long years full of grievous deeds." He turned to Haldir. "Why has nothing of this been told to me before?" he asked in the Elven-tongue.

"We have not spoken to Haldir of our deeds or our purpose," said Legolas. "At first we were weary and danger was too close behind; and afterwards we almost forgot our grief for a time, as we walked in gladness on the fair paths of Lórien."

"Yet our grief is great and our loss cannot be mended," said Frodo. "Gandalf was our guide, and he led us through Moria; and when our escape seemed beyond hope he saved us, and he fell."

"Tell us now the full tale!" said Celeborn.

Then Aragorn recounted all that had happened upon the pass of Caradhras, and in the days that followed; and he spoke of Balin and his book, and the fight in the Chamber of Mazarbul, and the fire, and the narrow bridge, and the coming of the Terror. "An evil of the Ancient World it seemed, such as I have never seen before," said Aragorn. "It was both a shadow and a flame, strong and terrible."

"It was a Balrog of Morgoth," said Legolas; "of all elf-banes the most deadly, save the One who sits in the Dark Tower."

"Indeed I saw upon the bridge that which haunts our darkest dreams, I saw Durin's Bane," said Gimli in a low voice, and dread was in his eyes.

"Alas!" said Celeborn. "We long have feared that under Caradhras a terror slept. But had I known that the Dwarves had stirred up this evil in Moria again, I would have forbidden you to pass the northern borders, you and all that went with you. And if it were possible, one would say that at the last Gandalf fell from wisdom into folly, going needlessly into the net of Moria."

"He would be rash indeed that said that thing," said Galadriel gravely. "Needless were none of the deeds of Gandalf in life. Those that followed him knew not his mind and cannot report his full purpose. But however it may be with the guide, the followers are blameless. Do not repent of your welcome to the Dwarf. If our folk had been exiled long and far from Lothlórien, who of the Galadhrim, even Celeborn the Wise, would pass nigh and would not wish to look upon their ancient home, though it had become an abode of dragons?

"Dark is the water of Kheled-zâram, and cold are the springs of Kibil-nâla, and fair were the many-pillared halls of Khazad-dûm in Elder Days before the fall of mighty kings beneath the stone." She looked upon Gimli, who sat glowering and sad, and she smiled. And the Dwarf, hearing the names given in his own ancient tongue, looked up and met her eyes; and it seemed to him that he looked suddenly into the heart of an enemy and saw there love and understanding. Wonder came into his face, and then he smiled in answer.

He rose clumsily and bowed in dwarf-fashion, saying: "Yet more fair is the living land of Lórien, and the Lady Galadriel is above all the jewels that lie beneath the earth!"

There was a silence. At length Celeborn spoke again. "I did not know that your plight was so evil," he said. "Let Gimli forget my harsh words: I spoke in the trouble of my heart. I will do what I can to aid you, each according to his wish and need, but especially that one of the little folk who bears the burden."

"Your quest is known to us," said Galadriel, looking at Frodo. "But we will not here speak of it more openly. Yet not in vain will it prove, maybe, that you came to this land seeking aid, as Gandalf himself plainly purposed. For the Lord of the Caladhrim is accounted the wisest of the Elves of Middle-earth, and a giver of gifts beyond the power of kings. He has dwelt in the West since the days of dawn, and I have dwelt with him years uncounted; for ere the fall of Nargothrond or Gondolin I passed over the mountains, and together through ages of the world we have fought the long defeat.

"I it was who first summoned the White Council. And if my designs had not gone amiss, it would have been governed by Gandalf the Grey, and then mayhap things would have gone otherwise. But even now there is hope left. I will not give you counsel, saying do this, or do that. For not in doing or contriving, nor in choosing between this course and another, can I avail; but only in knowing what was and is, and in part also what shall be. But this I will say to you: your Quest stands upon the edge of a knife. Stray but a little and it will fail, to the ruin of all. Yet hope remains while all the Company is true."

And with that word she held them with her eyes, and in silence looked searchingly at each of them in turn. None save Legolas and Aragorn could long endure her glance. Sam quickly blushed and hung his head.

At length the Lady Galadriel released them from her eyes, and she smiled. "Do not let your hearts be troubled," she said. "Tonight you shall sleep in peace." Then they sighed and felt suddenly weary, as those who have been questioned long and deeply, though no words had been spoken openly.

"Go now!" said Celeborn. "You are worn with sorrow and much toil. Even if your Quest did not concern us closely, you should have refuge in this City, until you were healed and refreshed. Now you shall rest, and we will not speak of your further road for a while."

That night the Company slept upon the ground, much to the satisfaction of the hobbits. The Elves spread for them a pavilion among the trees near the fountain, and in it they laid soft couches; then speaking words of peace with fair elvish voices they left them. For a little while the travellers talked of their night before in the tree-tops, and of their day's journey, and of the Lord and Lady; for they had not yet the heart to look further back.

"What did you blush for, Sam?" said Pippin. "You soon broke down. Anyone would have thought you had a guilty conscience. I hope it was nothing worse than a wicked plot to steal one of my blankets."

"I never thought no such thing," answered Sam, in no mood for jest. "If you want to know, I felt as if I hadn't got nothing on, and I didn't like it. She seemed to be looking inside me and asking me what I would do if she gave me the chance of flying back home to the Shire to a nice little hole with — with a bit of garden of my own."

"That's funny," said Merry. "Almost exactly what I felt myself; only, only well, I don't think I'll say any more," he ended lamely.

All of them, it seemed, had fared alike: each had felt that he was offered a choice between a shadow full of fear that lay ahead, and something that he greatly desired: clear before his mind it lay, and to get it he had only to turn aside from the road and leave the Quest and the war against Sauron to others.

"And it seemed to me, too," said Gimli, "that my choice would remain secret and known only to myself."

"To me it seemed exceedingly strange," said Boromir. "Maybe it was only a test, and she thought to read our thoughts for her own good purpose; but almost I should have said that she was tempting us, and offering what she pretended to have the power to give. It need not be said that I refused to listen. The Men of Minas Tirith are true to their word." But what he thought that the Lady had offered him Boromir did not tell.

And as for Frodo, he would not speak, though Boromir pressed him with questions. "She held you long in her gaze, Ring-bearer," he said.

"Yes," said Frodo; "but whatever came into my mind then I will keep there."

"Well, have a care!" said Boromir. "I do not feel too sure of this Elvish Lady and her purposes."

"Speak no evil of the Lady Galadriel!" said Aragorn sternly. "You know not what you say. There is in her and in this land no evil, unless a man bring it hither himself. Then let him beware! But tonight I shall sleep without fear for the first time since I left Rivendell. And may I sleep deep, and forget for a while my grief! I am weary in body and in heart." He cast himself down upon his couch and fell at once into a long sleep.

The others soon did the same, and no sound or dream disturbed their slumber. When they woke they found that the light of day was broad upon the lawn before the pavilion, and the fountain rose and fell glittering in the sun.

They remained some days in Lothlórien, so far as they could tell or remember. All the while that they dwelt there the sun shone clear, save for a gentle rain that fell at times, and passed away leaving all things fresh and clean. The air was cool and soft, as if it were early spring, yet they felt about them the deep and thoughtful quiet of winter. It seemed to them that they did little but eat and drink and rest, and walk among the trees; and it was enough.

They had not seen the Lord and Lady again, and they had little speech with the Elven-folk; for few of these knew or would use the Westron tongue. Haldir had bidden them farewell and gone back again to the fences of the North, where great watch was now kept since the tidings of Moria that the Company had brought. Legolas was away much among the Galadhrim, and after the first night he did not sleep with the other companions, though he returned to eat and talk with them. Often he took Gimli with him when he went abroad in the land, and the others wondered at this change.

Now as the companions sat or walked together they spoke of Gandalf, and all that each had known and seen of him came clear before their minds. As they were healed of hurt and weariness of body the grief of their loss grew more keen. Often they heard nearby Elvish voices singing, and knew that they were making songs of lamentation for his fall, for they caught his name among the sweet sad words that they could not understand.

Mithrandir, Mithrandir sang the Elves, *O Pilgrim Grey!* For so they loved to call him. But if Legolas was with the Company, he would not interpret the songs for them, saying that he had not the skill, and that for him the grief was still too near, a matter for tears and not yet for song.

It was Frodo who first put something of his sorrow into halting words. He was seldom moved to make song or rhyme; even in Rivendell he had listened and had not sung himself, though his memory was stored with many things that others had made before him. But now as he sat beside the fountain in Lórien and heard about him the voices of the Elves, his thought took shape in a song that seemed fair to

him; yet when he tried to repeat it to Sam only snatches
remained, faded as a handful of withered leaves.

> *When evening in the Shire was grey*
> *his footsteps on the Hill were heard;*
> *before the dawn he went away*
> *on journey long without a word.*
>
> *From Wilderland to Western shore,*
> *from northern waste to southern hill,*
> *through dragon-lair and hidden door*
> *and darkling woods he walked at will.*
>
> *With Dwarf and Hobbit, Elves and Men,*
> *with mortal and immortal folk,*
> *with bird on bough and beast in den,*
> *in their own secret tongues he spoke.*
>
> *A deadly sword, a healing hand,*
> *a back that bent beneath its load;*
> *a trumpet-voice, a burning brand,*
> *a weary pilgrim on the road.*
>
> *A lord of wisdom throned he sat,*
> *swift in anger, quick to laugh;*
> *an old man in a battered hat*
> *who leaned upon a thorny staff.*
>
> *He stood upon the bridge alone*
> *and Fire and Shadow both defied;*
> *his staff was broken on the stone,*
> *in Khazad-dûm his wisdom died.*

"Why, you'll be beating Mr. Bilbo next!" said Sam.

"No, I am afraid not," said Frodo. "But that is the best I can
do yet.

"Well, Mr. Frodo, if you do have another go, I hope you'll say a word about his fireworks," said Sam. "Something like this:

> *The finest rockets ever seen:*
> *they burst in stars of blue and green,*
> *or after thunder golden showers*
> *came falling like a rain of flowers.*

Though that doesn't do them justice by a long road."

"No, I'll leave that to you, Sam. Or perhaps to Bilbo. But — well, I can't talk of it any more. I can't bear to think of bringing the news to him."

One evening Frodo and Sam were walking together in the cool twilight. Both of them felt restless again. On Frodo suddenly the shadow of parting had fallen: he knew somehow that the time was very near when he must leave Lothlórien.

"What do you think of Elves now, Sam?" he said. "I asked you the same question once before — it seems a very long while ago; but you have seen more of them since then."

"I have indeed!" said Sam. "And I reckon there's Elves and Elves. They're all elvish enough, but they're not all the same. Now these folk aren't wanderers or homeless, and seem a bit nearer to the likes of us: they seem to belong here, more even than Hobbits do in the Shire. Whether they've made the land, or the land's made them, it's hard to say, if you take my meaning. It's wonderfully quiet here. Nothing seems to be going on, and nobody seems to want it to. If there's any magic about, it's right down deep, where I can't lay my hands on it, in a manner of speaking."

"You can see and feel it everywhere," said Frodo.

"Well," said Sam, "you can't see nobody working it. No fireworks like poor old Gandalf used to show. I wonder we don't see nothing of the Lord and Lady in all these days. I fancy now that *she* could do some wonderful things, if she had a mind. I'd dearly love to see some Elf-magic, Mr. Frodo!"

"I wouldn't," said Frodo. "I am content. And I don't miss Gandalf's fireworks, but his bushy eyebrows, and his quick temper, and his voice."

"You're right," said Sam. "And don't think I'm finding fault. I've often wanted to see a bit of magic like what it tells of in old tales, but I've never heard of a better land than this. It's like being at home and on a holiday at the same time, if you understand me. I don't want to leave. All the same, I'm beginning to feel that if we've got to go on, then we'd best get it over.

"*It's the job that's never started as takes longest to finish*, as my old gaffer used to say. And I don't reckon that these folk can do much more to help us, magic or no. It's when we leave this land that we shall miss Gandalf worse, I'm thinking."

"I am afraid that's only too true, Sam," said Frodo. "Yet I hope very much that before we leave we shall see the Lady of the Elves again."

Even as he spoke, they saw, as if she came in answer to their words, the Lady Galadriel approaching. Tall and white and fair she walked beneath the trees. She spoke no word, but beckoned to them.

Turning aside, she led them toward the southern slopes of the hill of Caras Galadhon, and passing through a high green hedge they came into an enclosed garden. No trees grew there, and it lay open to the sky. The evening star had risen and was shining with white fire above the western woods. Down a long flight of steps the Lady went into a deep green hollow, through which ran murmuring the silver stream that issued from the fountain on the hill. At the bottom, upon a low pedestal carved like a branching tree, stood a basin of silver, wide and shallow, and beside it stood a silver ewer.

With water from the stream Galadriel filled the basin to the brim, and breathed on it, and when the water was still again she spoke. "Here is the Mirror of Galadriel," she said. "I have brought you here so that you may look in it, if you will."

The air was very still, and the dell was dark, and the Elf-lady beside him was tall and pale. "What shall we look for, and what shall we see?" asked Frodo, filled with awe.

"Many things I can command the Mirror to reveal," she answered, "and to some I can show what they desire to see. But the Mirror will also show things unbidden, and those are often stranger and more profitable than things which we wish to behold. What you will see, if you leave the Mirror free to work, I cannot tell. For it shows things that were, and things that are, and things that yet may be. But which it is that he sees, even the wisest cannot always tell. Do you wish to look?"

Frodo did not answer.

"And you?" she said, turning to Sam. "For this is what your folk would call magic, I believe; though I do not understand clearly what they mean; and they seem also to use the same word of the deceits of the Enemy. But this, if you will, is the magic of Galadriel. Did you not say that you wished to see Elf-magic?"

"I did," said Sam, trembling a little between fear and curiosity. "I'll have a peep, Lady, if you're willing."

"And I'd not mind a glimpse of what's going on at home," he said in an aside to Frodo. "It seems a terrible long time that I've been away. But there, like as not I'll only see the stars, or something that I won't understand."

"Like as not," said the Lady with a gentle laugh. "But come, you shall look and see what you may. Do not touch the water!"

Sam climbed up on the foot of the pedestal and leaned over the basin. The water looked hard and dark. Stars were reflected in it.

"There's only stars, as I thought," he said. Then he gave a low gasp, for the stars went out. As if a dark veil had been withdrawn, the Mirror grew grey, and then clear. There was sun shining, and the branches of trees were waving and tossing in the wind. But before Sam could make up his mind what it was that he saw, the light faded; and now he thought he saw Frodo with a pale face lying fast asleep under a great dark cliff. Then he seemed to see himself going along a dim passage, and climbing an endless winding stair. It came to him suddenly that he was looking urgently for something, but what it was he did not know. Like a dream the vision shifted and went back, and he saw the trees again. But this time they were not so close, and he could see what was going on: they were not waving in the wind, they were falling, crashing to the ground.

"Hi!" cried Sam in an outraged voice. "There's that Ted Sandyman a-cutting down trees as he shouldn't. They didn't ought to be felled: it's that avenue beyond the Mill that shades the road to Bywater. I wish I could get at Ted, and I'd fell *him!*"

But now Sam noticed that the Old Mill had vanished, and a large red-brick building was being put up where it had stood. Lots of folk were busily at work. There was a tall red chimney nearby. Black smoke seemed to cloud the surface of the Mirror.

"There's some devilry at work in the Shire," he said. "Elrond knew what he was about when he wanted to send Mr. Merry back." Then suddenly Sam gave a cry and sprang away. "I can't stay here," he said wildly. "I must go home. They've dug up Bagshot Row, and there's the poor old gaffer going down the Hill with his bits of things on a barrow. I must go home!"

"You cannot go home alone," said the Lady. "You did not wish to go home without your master before you looked in the Mirror, and yet you knew that evil things might well be happening in the Shire. Remember that the Mirror shows many things, and not all have yet come to pass. Some never come to be, unless those that behold the visions turn aside from their path to prevent them. The Mirror is dangerous as a guide of deeds."

Sam sat on the ground and put his head in his hands. "I wish I had never come here, and I don't want to see no more magic," he said and fell silent. After a moment he spoke again thickly, as if struggling with tears. "No, I'll go home by the long road with Mr. Frodo or not at all," he said. "But I hope I do get back some day. If what I've seen turns out true, somebody's going to catch it hot!"

"Do you now wish to look, Frodo?" said the Lady Galadriel. "You did not wish to see Elf-magic and were content."

"Do you advise me to look?" asked Frodo.

"No," she said. "I do not counsel you one way or the other. I am not a counsellor. You may learn something, and whether what you see be fair or evil, that may be profitable, and yet it may not. Seeing is both good and perilous. Yet I think, Frodo, that you have courage and wisdom enough for the venture, or I would not have brought you here. Do as you will!"

"I will look," said Frodo, and he climbed on the pedestal and bent over the dark water. At once the Mirror cleared and he saw a twilit land. Mountains loomed dark in the distance against a pale sky. A long grey road wound back out of sight. Far away a figure came slowly down the road, faint and small at first, but growing larger and clearer as it approached. Suddenly Frodo realized that it reminded him of Gandalf. He almost called aloud the wizard's name, and then he saw that the figure was clothed not in grey but in white, in a white that shone faintly in the dusk; and in its hand there was a white staff. The head was so bowed that he could see no face, and presently the figure turned aside round a bend in the road and went out of the Mirror's view. Doubt came into Frodo's mind: was this a vision of Gandalf on one of his many lonely journeys long ago, or was it Saruman?

The vision now changed. Brief and small but very vivid he caught a glimpse of Bilbo walking restlessly about his room. The table was littered with disordered papers; rain was beating on the windows.

Then there was a pause, and after it many swift scenes followed that Frodo in some way knew to be parts of a great history in which he had become involved. The mist cleared and he saw a sight which he had never seen before but knew at once: the Sea. Darkness fell. The sea rose and raged in a great storm. Then he saw against the Sun, sinking blood-red into a wrack of clouds, the black outline of a tall ship with torn sails riding up out of the West. Then a wide river flowing through a populous city. Then a white fortress with seven towers. And then again a ship with black sails, but now it was morning again, and the water rippled with light, and a banner bearing the emblem of a white tree shone in the sun. A smoke as of fire and battle arose, and again the sun went down in a burning red that faded into a grey mist; and into the mist a small ship passed away, twinkling with lights. It vanished, and Frodo sighed and prepared to draw away.

But suddenly the Mirror went altogether dark, as dark as if a hole had opened in the world of sight, and Frodo looked into emptiness. In the black abyss there appeared a single Eye that slowly grew, until it filled nearly all the Mirror. So terrible was it that Frodo stood rooted, unable to cry out or to withdraw his gaze. The Eye was rimmed with fire, but was itself glazed, yellow as a cat's, watchful and intent, and the black slit of its pupil opened on a pit, a window into nothing.

Then the Eye began to rove, searching this way and that; and Frodo knew with certainty and horror that among the many things that it sought he himself was one. But he also knew that it could not see him — not yet, not unless he willed it. The Ring that hung upon its chain about his neck grew heavy, heavier than a great stone, and his head was dragged downwards. The Mirror seemed to be growing hot and curls of steam were rising from the water. He was slipping forward.

"Do not touch the water!" said the Lady Galadriel softly. The vision faded, and Frodo found that he was looking at the cool stars twinkling in the silver basin. He stepped back shaking all over and looked at the Lady.

"I know what it was that you last saw," she said; "for that is also in my mind. Do not be afraid! But do not think that only by singing amid the trees, nor even by the slender arrows of elven-bows, is this land of Lothlórien maintained and defended against its Enemy. I say to you, Frodo, that even as I speak to you, I perceive the Dark Lord and know his mind, or all of his mind that concerns the Elves. And he gropes ever to see me and my thought. But still the door is closed!"

She lifted up her white arms, and spread out her hands towards the East in a gesture of rejection and denial. Eärendil, the Evening Star, most beloved of the Elves, shone clear above. So bright was it that the figure of the Elven-lady cast a dim shadow on the ground. Its rays glanced upon a ring about her finger; it glittered like polished gold overlaid with silver light, and a white stone in it twinkled as if the Even-star had come down to rest upon her hand. Frodo gazed at the ring with awe; for suddenly it seemed to him that he understood.

"Yes," she said, divining his thought, "it is not permitted to speak of it, and Elrond could not do so. But it cannot be hidden from the King-bearer, and one who has seen the Eye. Verily it is in the land of Lórien upon the finger of Galadriel that one of the Three remains. This is Nenya, the Ring of Adamant, and I am its keeper.

"He suspects, but he does not know — not yet. Do you not see now wherefore your coming is to us as the footstep of Doom? For if you fail, then we are laid bare to the Enemy. Yet if you succeed, then our power is diminished, and Lothlórien will fade, and the tides of Time will sweep it away. We must depart into the West, or dwindle to a rustic folk of dell and cave, slowly to forget and to be forgotten."

Frodo bent his head. "And what do you wish?" he said at last.

"That what should be shall be," she answered. "The love of the Elves for their land and their works is deeper than the deeps of the Sea, and their regret is undying and cannot ever wholly be assuaged. Yet they will cast all away rather than submit to Sauron: for they know him now. For the fate of Lothlórien you are not answerable, but only for the doing of your own task. Yet I could wish, were it of any avail, that the One Ring had never been wrought, or had remained for ever lost."

"You are wise and fearless and fair, Lady Galadriel," said Frodo. "I will give you the One Ring, if you ask for it. It is too great a matter for me."

Galadriel laughed with a sudden clear laugh. "Wise the Lady

Galadriel may be," she said, "yet here she has met her match in courtesy. Gently are you revenged for my testing of your heart at our first meeting. You begin to see with a keen eye. I do not deny that my heart has greatly desired to ask what you offer. For many long years I had pondered what I might do, should the Great Ring come into my hands, and behold! it was brought within my grasp. The evil that was devised long ago works on in many ways, whether Sauron himself stands or falls. Would not that have been a noble deed to set to the credit of his Ring, if I had taken it by force or fear from my guest?

"And now at last it comes. You will give me the Ring freely! In place of the Dark Lord you will set up a Queen. And I shall not be dark, but beautiful and terrible as the Morning and the Night! Fair as the Sea and the Sun and the Snow upon the Mountain! Dreadful as the Storm and the Lightning! Stronger than the foundations of the earth. All shall love me and despair!"

She lifted up her hand and from the ring that she wore there issued a great light that illumined her alone and left all else dark. She stood before Frodo seeming now tall beyond measurement, and beautiful beyond enduring, terrible and worshipful. Then she let her hand fall, and the light faded, and suddenly she laughed again, and lo! she was shrunken: a slender elf-woman, clad in simple white, whose gentle voice was soft and sad.

"I pass the test," she said. "I will diminish, and go into the West, and remain Galadriel."

They stood for a long while in silence. At length the Lady spoke again. "Let us return!" she said. "In the morning you must depart, for now we have chosen, and the tides of fate are flowing."

"I would ask one thing before we go," said Frodo, "a thing which I often meant to ask Gandalf in Rivendell. I am permitted to wear the One Ring: why cannot I see all the others and know the thoughts of those that wear them?"

"You have not tried," she said. "Only thrice have you set the Ring upon your finger since you knew what you possessed. Do not try! It would destroy you. Did not Gandalf tell you that the rings give power according to the measure of each possessor? Before you could use that power you would need to become far stronger, and to train your will to the domination of others. Yet even so, as Ring-bearer and as one that has borne it on finger and seen that which is hidden, your sight is grown keener. You have perceived my thought more clearly than many that are accounted wise. You saw the Eye of him that holds the Seven and the Nine. And did you not see and recognize the ring upon my finger? Did you see my ring?" she asked turning again to Sam.

"No, Lady," he answered. "To tell you the truth, I wondered what you were talking about. I saw a star through your finger. But if you'll pardon my speaking out, I think my master was right. I wish you'd take his Ring. You'd put things to rights. You'd stop them digging up the gaffer and turning him adrift. You'd make some folk pay for their dirty work."

"I would," she said. "That is how it would begin. But it would not stop with that, alas! We will not speak more of it. Let us go!"

CHAPTER
EIGHT

Farewell to Lórien

That night the Company was again summoned to the chamber of Celeborn, and there the Lord and Lady greeted them with fair words. At length Celeborn spoke of their departure.

"Now is the time," he said, "when those who wish to continue the Quest must harden their hearts to leave this land. Those who no longer wish to go forward may remain here, for a while. But whether they stay or go, none can be sure of peace. For we are come now to the edge of doom. Here those who wish may await the oncoming of the hour till either the ways of the world lie open again, or we summon them to the last need of Lórien. Then they may return to their own lands, or else go to the long home of those that fall in battle."

There was a silence. "They all resolved to go forward," said Galadriel looking in their eyes.

"As for me," said Boromir, "my way home lies onward and not back."

"That is true," said Celeborn, "but is all this Company going with you to Minas Tirith?"

"We have not decided our course," said Aragorn. "Beyond Lothlórien I do not know what Gandalf intended to do. Indeed I do not think that even he had any clear purpose."

"Maybe not," said Celeborn: "yet when you leave this land, you can no longer forget the Great River. As some of you know well, it cannot be crossed by travellers with baggage between Lórien and Gondor, save by boat. And are not the bridges of Osgiliath broken down and all the landings held now by the Enemy?

"On which side will you journey? The way to Minas Tirith lies upon this side, upon the west; but the straight road of the Quest lies east of the River, upon the darker shore. Which shore will you now take?"

"If my advice is heeded, it will be the western shore, and the way to Minas Tirith," answered Boromir. "But I am not the leader of the Company." The others said nothing, and Aragorn looked doubtful and troubled.

"I see that you do not yet know what to do," said Celeborn. "It is not my part to choose for you; but I will help you as I may. There are some among you who can handle boats: Legolas, whose folk know the swift Forest River; and Boromir of Gondor; and Aragorn the traveller."

"And one Hobbit!" cried Merry. "Not all of us look on boats as wild horses. My people live by the banks of the Brandywine."

"That is well," said Celeborn. "Then I will furnish your Company with boats. They must be small and light, for if you go far by water, there are places where you will be forced to carry them. You will come to the rapids of Sarn Gebir, and maybe at last to the great falls of Rauros where the River thunders down from Nen Hithoel; and there are other perils. Boats may make your journey less toilsome for a while. Yet they will not give you counsel: in the end you must leave them and the River, and turn west — or east."

Aragorn thanked Celeborn many times. The gift of boats comforted him much, not least because there would now be no need to decide his course for some days. The others, too, looked more hopeful. Whatever perils lay ahead, it seemed better to float down the broad tide of Anduin to meet them than to plod forward with bent backs. Only Sam was doubtful: he at any rate still thought boats as bad as wild horses, or worse, and not all the dangers that he had survived made him think better of them.

"All shall be prepared for you and await you at the haven before noon tomorrow," said Celeborn. "I will send my people to you in the morning to help you make ready for the journey. Now we will wish you all a fair night and untroubled sleep."

"Good night, my friends!" said Galadriel. "Sleep in peace! Do not trouble your hearts overmuch with thought of the road tonight. Maybe the paths that you each shall tread are already laid before your feet, though you do not see them. Good night!"

The Company now took their leave and returned to their pavilion. Legolas went with them, for this was to be their last night in Lothlórien, and in spite of the words of Galadriel they wished to take counsel together.

For a long time they debated what they should do, and how it would be best to attempt the fulfilling of their purpose with the Ring; but they came to no decision. It was plain that most of them desired to go first to Minas Tirith, and to escape at least for a while from the terror of the Enemy. They would have been willing to follow a leader over the River and into the shadow of Mordor; but Frodo spoke no word, and Aragorn was still divided in his mind.

His own plan, while Gandalf remained with them, had been to go with Boromir, and with his sword help to deliver Gondor. For he believed that the message of the dreams was a summons, and that the hour had come at last when the heir of Elendil should come forth and strive with Sauron for the mastery. But in Moria the burden of Gandalf had been laid on him; and he knew that he could not now forsake the Ring, if Frodo refused in the end to go with Boromir. And yet what help could he or any of the Company give to Frodo, save to walk blindly with him into the darkness?

"I shall go to Minas Tirith, alone if need be, for it is my duty," said Boromir; and after that he was silent for a while, sitting with his eyes fixed on Frodo, as if he was trying to read the Halfling's thoughts. At length he spoke again, softly, as if he was debating with himself. "If you wish only to destroy the Ring," he said, "then there is little use in war and weapons; and the Men of Minas Tirith cannot help. But if you wish to destroy the armed might of the Dark Lord, then it is folly to go without force into his domain; and folly to throw away." He paused suddenly, as if he had become aware that he was speaking his thoughts aloud. "It would be folly to throw lives away, I mean," he ended. "It is a choice between defending a strong place and walking openly into the arms of death. At least, that is how I see it."

Frodo caught something new and strange in Boromir's glance, and he looked hard at him. Plainly Boromir's thought was different from his final words. It would be folly to throw away: what? The Ring of Power? He had said something like this at the Council, but then he had accepted the correction of Elrond. Frodo looked at Aragorn, but he seemed deep in his own thought and made no sign that he had heeded Boromir's words. And so their debate ended. Merry and Pippin were already asleep, and Sam was nodding. The night was growing old.

In the morning, as they were beginning to pack their slender goods, Elves that could speak their tongue came to them and brought them many gifts of food and clothing for the journey. The food was mostly in the form of very thin cakes, made of a meal that was baked a light brown on the outside, and inside was the colour of cream. Gimli took up one of the cakes and looked at it with a doubtful eye.

"*Cram*," he said under his breath, as he broke off a crisp corner and nibbled at it. His expression quickly changed, and he ate all the rest of the cake with relish.

"No more, no more." cried the Elves laughing. "You have eaten enough already for a long day's march."

"I thought it was only a kind of *cram*, such as the Dale-men make for journeys in the wild," said the Dwarf.

"So it is," they answered. "But we call it *lembas* or waybread, and it is more strengthening than any food made by Men, and it is more pleasant than *cram*, by all accounts."

"Indeed it is," said Gimli. "Why, it is better than the honeycakes of the Beornings, and that is great praise, for the Beornings are the best bakers that I know of; but they are none too willing to deal out their cakes to travellers in these days. You are kindly hosts!"

"All the same, we bid you spare the food," they said. "Eat little at a time, and only at need. For these things are given to serve you when all else fails. The cakes will keep sweet for many many days, if they are unbroken and left in their leaf-wrappings, as we have brought them. One will keep a traveller on his feet for a day of long labour, even if he be one of the tall Men of Minas Tirith."

The Elves next unwrapped and gave to each of the Company the clothes they had brought. For each they had provided a hood and cloak, made according to his size, of the light but warm silken stuff that the Galadhrim wove. It was hard to say of what colour they were: grey with the hue of twilight under the trees they seemed to be; and yet if they were moved, or set in another light, they were green as shadowed leaves, or brown as fallow fields by night, dusk-silver as water under the stars. Each cloak was fastened about the neck with a brooch like a green leaf veined with silver.

"Are these magic cloaks?" asked Pippin, looking at them with wonder.

"I do not know what you mean by that," answered the leader of the Elves. "They are fair garments, and the web is good, for it was made in this land. They are elvish robes certainly, if that is what you mean. Leaf and branch, water and stone: they have the hue and beauty of all these things under the twilight of Lórien that we love; for we put the thought of all that we love into all that we make. Yet they are garments, not armour, and they will not turn shaft or blade. But they should serve you well: they are light to wear, and warm enough or cool enough at need. And you will find them a great aid in keeping out of the sight of unfriendly eyes, whether you walk among the stones or the trees. You are indeed high in the favour of the Lady! For she herself and her maidens wove this stuff; and never before have we clad strangers in the garb of our own people."

After their morning meal the Company said farewell to the lawn by the fountain. Their hearts were heavy; for it was a fair place, and it had become like home to them, though they could not count the days and nights that they had passed there. As they stood for a moment looking at the white water in the sunlight, Haldir came walking towards them over the green grass of the glade. Frodo greeted him with delight.

"I have returned from the Northern Fences," said the Elf, "and I am sent now to be your guide again. The Dimrill Dale is full of vapour and clouds of smoke, and the mountains are troubled. There are noises in the deeps of the earth. If any of you had thought of returning northwards to your homes, you would not have been able to pass that way. But come! Your path now goes south."

As they walked through Caras Galadhon the green ways were empty; but in the trees above them many voices were murmuring and singing. They themselves went silently. At last Haldir led them down the southward slopes of the hill, and they came again to the great gate hung with lamps, and to the white bridge; and so they passed out and left the city of the Elves. Then they turned away from the paved road and took a path that went off into a deep thicket of mallorn-trees, and passed on, winding through rolling woodlands of silver shadow, leading them ever down, southwards and eastwards, towards the shores of the River.

They had gone some ten miles and noon was at hand when they came on a high green wall. Passing through an opening they came suddenly out of the trees. Before them lay a long lawn of shining grass, studded with golden *elanor* that glinted in the sun. The lawn ran out into a narrow tongue between bright margins: on the right and west the Silverlode flowed glittering; on the left and east the Great River rolled its broad waters, deep and dark. On the further shores the woodlands still marched on southwards as far as the eye could see, but all the banks were bleak and bare. No mallorn lifted its gold-hung boughs beyond the Land of Lórien.

On the bank of the Silverlode, at some distance up from the meeting of the streams, there was a hythe of white stones and white wood. By it were moored many boats and barges. Some were brightly painted, and shone with silver and gold and green, but most were either white or grey. Three small grey boats had been made ready for the travellers, and in these the Elves stowed their goods. And they added also coils of rope, three to each boat. Slender they looked, but strong, silken to the touch, grey of hue like the elven-cloaks.

"What are these?" asked Sam, handling one that lay upon the green-sward.

"Ropes indeed!" answered an Elf from the boats. "Never travel far without a rope! And one that is long and strong and light. Such are these. They may be a help in many needs."

"You don't need to tell me that!" said Sam. "I came without any, and I've been worried ever since. But I was wondering what these were made of, knowing a bit about rope-making: it's in the family as you might say."

"They are made of *hithlain*," said the Elf, "but there is no time now to instruct you in the art of their making. Had we known that this craft delighted you, we could have taught you much. But now alas! unless you should at some time return hither, you must be content with our gift. May it serve you well!"

"Come!" said Haldir. "All is now ready for you. Enter the boats! But take care at first!"

"Heed the words!" said the other Elves. "These boats are light-built, and they are crafty and unlike the boats of other folk. They will not sink, lade them as you will; but they are wayward if mishandled. It would be wise if you accustomed yourselves to stepping in and out, here where there is a landing-place, before you set off downstream."

The Company was arranged in this way: Aragorn, Frodo, and Sam were in one boat; Boromir, Merry, and Pippin in another; and in the third were Legolas and Gimli, who had now become fast friends. In this last boat most of the goods and packs were stowed. The boats were moved and steered with short-handled paddles that had broad leaf-shaped blades. When all was ready Aragorn led them on a trial up the Silverlode. The current was swift and they went forward slowly. Sam sat in the bows, clutching the sides, and looking back wistfully to the shore. The sunlight glittering on the water dazzled his eyes. As they passed beyond the green field of the Tongue, the trees drew down to the river's brink. Here and there golden leaves tossed and floated on the rippling stream. The air was very bright and still, and there was a silence, except for the high distant song of larks.

They turned a sharp bend in the river, and there, sailing proudly down the stream toward theme they saw a swan of great size. The water rippled on either side of the white breast beneath its curving neck. Its beak shone like burnished gold, and its eyes glinted like jet set in yellow stones; its huge white wings were half lifted. A music came down the river as it drew nearer; and suddenly they perceived that it was a ship, wrought and carved with elven-skill in the likeness of a bird. Two elves clad in white steered it with black paddles. In the midst of the vessel sat Celeborn, and behind him stood Galadriel, tall and white; a circlet of golden flowers was in her hair, and in her hand she held a harp, and she sang. Sad and sweet was the sound of her voice in the cool clear air:

I sang of leaves, of leaves of gold, and leaves of gold there grew:
Of wind I sang, a wind there came and in the branches blew.
Beyond the Sun, beyond the Moon, the foam was on the Sea,
And by the strand of Ilmarin there grew a golden Tree.

Beneath the stars of Ever-eve in Eldamar it shone,
In Eldamar beside the walls of Elven Tirion.
There long the golden leaves have grown upon the branching years,
While here beyond the Sundering Seas now fall the Elven-tears.
O Lórien! The Winter comes, the bare and leafless Day;
The leaves are falling in the stream, the River flows away.
O Lórien! Too long I have dwelt upon this Hither Shore
And in a fading crown have twined the golden elanor.
But if of ships I now should sing, what ship would come to me,
What ship would bear me ever back across so wide a Sea?

Aragorn stayed his boat as the Swan-ship drew alongside. The Lady ended her song and greeted them. "We have come to bid you our last farewell, she said, "and to speed you with blessings from our land."

"Though you have been our guests," said Celeborn, "you have not yet eaten with us, and we bid you, therefore, to a parting feast, here between the flowing waters that will bear you far from Lórien."

The Swan passed on slowly to the hythe, and they turned their boats and followed it. There in the last end of Egladil upon the green grass the parting feast was held; but Frodo ate and drank little, heeding only the beauty of the Lady and her voice. She seemed no longer perilous or terrible, nor filled with hidden power. Already she seemed to him, as by men of later days Elves still at times are seen: present and yet remote, a living vision of that which has already been left far behind by the flowing streams of Time.

After they had eaten and drunk, sitting upon the grass, Celeborn spoke to them again of their journey, and lifting his hand he pointed south to the woods beyond the Tongue.

"As you go down the water," he said, "you will find that the trees will fail, and you will come to a barren country. There the River flows in stony vales amid high moors, until at last after many leagues it comes to the tall island of the Tindrock, that we call Tol Brandir. There it casts its arms about the steep shores of the isle, and falls then with a great noise and smoke over the cataracts of Rauros down into the Nindalf, the Wetwang as it is called in your tongue. That is a wide region of sluggish fen where the stream becomes tortuous and much divided. There the Entwash flows in by many mouths from the Forest of Fangorn in the west. About that stream, on this side of the Great River, lies Rohan. On the further side are the bleak hills of the Emyn Muil. The wind blows from the East there, for they look out over the Dead Marshes and the Noman-lands to Cirith Gorgor and the black gates of Mordor.

"Boromir, and any that go with him seeking Minas Tirith, will do well to leave the Great River above Rauros and cross the Entwash before it finds the marshes. Yet they should not go too far up that stream, nor risk becoming entangled in the Forest of Fangorn. That is a strange land, and is now little known. But Boromir and Aragorn doubtless do not need this warning."

"Indeed we have heard of Fangorn in Minas Tirith," said Boromir. "But what I have heard seems to me for the most part old wives' tales, such as we tell to our children. All that lies north of Rohan is now to us so far away that fancy can wander freely there. Of old Fangorn lay upon the borders of our realm; but it is now many lives of men since any of us visited it, to prove or disprove the legends that have come down from distant years.

"I have myself been at whiles in Rohan, but I have never crossed it northwards. When I was sent out as a messenger, I passed through the Gap by the skirts of the White Mountains, and crossed the Isen and the Greyflood into Northerland. A long and wearisome journey. Four hundred leagues I reckoned it, and it took me many months; for I lost my horse at Tharbad, at the fording of the Greyflood. After that journey, and the road I have trodden with this Company, I do not much doubt that I shall find a way through Rohan, and Fangorn too, if need be."

"Then I need say no more," said Celeborn. "But do not despise the lore that has come down from distant years; for oft it may chance that old wives keep in memory word of things that once were needful for the wise to know."

Now Galadriel rose from the grass, and taking a cup from one of her maidens she filled it with white mead and gave it to Celeborn.

"Now it is time to drink the cup of farewell," she said. "Drink, Lord of the Galadhrim! And let not your heart be sad, though night must follow noon, and already our evening draweth nigh."

Then she brought the cup to each of the Company, and bade them drink and farewell. But when they had drunk she commanded them to sit again on the grass, and chairs were set for her and for Celeborn. Her maidens stood silent about her, and a while she looked upon her guests. At last she spoke again.

"We have drunk the cup of parting," she said, "and the shadows fall between us. But before you go, I have brought in my ship gifts which the Lord and Lady of the Galadhrim now offer you in memory of Lothlórien." Then she called to each in turn.

"Here is the gift of Celeborn and Galadriel to the leader of your Company," she said to Aragorn, and she gave him a sheath that had been made to fit his sword. It was overlaid with a tracery of flowers and leaves wrought of silver and gold, and on it were set in elven-runes formed of many gems the name Andúril and the lineage of the sword.

"The blade that is drawn from this sheath shall not be stained or broken even in defeat," she said. "But is there aught else that you desire of me at our parting? For darkness will flow between us, and it may be that we shall not meet again, unless it be far hence upon a road that has no returning."

And Aragorn answered: "Lady, you know all my desire, and long held in keeping the only treasure that I seek. Yet it is not yours to give me, even if you would; and only through darkness shall I come to it."

"Yet maybe this will lighten your heart," said Galadriel; "for it was left in my care to be given to you, should you pass through this land." Then she lifted from her lap a great stone of a clear green, set in a silver brooch that was wrought in the likeness of an eagle with outspread wings; and as she held it up the gem flashed like the sun shining through the leaves of spring. "This stone I gave to Celebrían my daughter, and she to hers; and now it comes to you as a token of hope. In this hour take the name that was foretold for you, Elessar, the Elfstone of the house of Elendil!"

Then Aragorn took the stone and pinned the brooch upon his breast, and those who saw him wondered; for they had not marked before how tall and kingly he stood, and it seemed to them that many years of toil had fallen from his shoulders. "For the gifts that you have given me I thank you," he said, "O Lady of Lórien of whom were sprung Celebrían and Arwen Evenstar. What praise could I say more?"

The Lady bowed her head, and she turned then to Boromir, and to him she gave a belt of gold; and to Merry and Pippin she gave small silver belts, each with a clasp wrought like a golden flower. To Legolas she gave a bow such as the Galadhrim used, longer and stouter than the bows of Mirkwood, and strung with a string of elf-hair. With it went a quiver of arrows.

"For you little gardener and lover of trees," she said to Sam, "I have only a small gift." She put into his hand a little box of plain grey wood, unadorned save for a single silver rune upon the lid. "Here is set G for Galadriel," she said; "but also it may stand for garden in your tongue. In this box there is earth from my orchard, and such blessing as Galadriel has still to bestow is upon it. It will not keep you on your road, nor defend you against any peril; but if you keep it and see your home again at last, then perhaps it may reward you. Though you should find all barren and laid waste, there will be few gardens in Middle-earth that will bloom like your garden, if you sprinkle this earth there. Then you may remember Galadriel, and catch a glimpse far off of Lórien, that you have seen only in our winter. For our spring and our summer are gone by, and they will never be seen on earth again save in memory."

Sam went red to the ears and muttered something inaudible, as he clutched the box and bowed as well as he could.

"And what gift would a Dwarf ask of the Elves?" said Galadriel, turning to Gimli.

"None, Lady," answered Gimli. "It is enough for me to have seen the Lady of the Galadhrim, and to have heard her gentle words."

"Hear all ye Elves!" she cried to those about her. "Let none say again that Dwarves are grasping and ungracious! Yet surely, Gimli son of Glóin, you desire something that I could give? Name it, I bid you! You shall not be the only guest without a gift."

"There is nothing, Lady Galadriel," said Gimli, bowing low and stammering. "Nothing, unless it might be — unless it is permitted to ask, nay, to name a single strand of your hair, which surpasses the gold of the earth as the stars surpass the gems of the mine. I do not ask for such a gift. But you commanded me to name my desire."

The Elves stirred and murmured with astonishment, and Celeborn gazed at the Dwarf in wonder, but the Lady smiled. "It is said that the skill of the Dwarves is in their hands rather than in their tongues," she said; "yet that is not true of Gimli. For none have ever made to me a request so bold and yet so courteous. And how shall I refuse, since I commanded him to speak? But tell me, what would you do with such a gift?"

"Treasure it, Lady," he answered, "in memory of your words to me at our first meeting. And if ever I return to the smithies of my home, it shall be set in imperishable crystal to be an heirloom of my house, and a pledge of good will between the Mountain and the Wood until the end of days."

Then the Lady unbraided one of her long tresses, and cut off three golden hairs, and laid them in Gimli's hand. "These words shall go with the gift," she said. "I do not foretell, for all foretelling is now vain: on the one hand lies darkness, and on the other only hope. But if hope should not fail, then I say to you, Gimli son of Glóin, that your hands shall flow with gold, and yet over you gold shall have no dominion.

"And you, Ring-bearer," she said, turning to Frodo. "I come to you last who are not last in my thoughts. For you I have prepared this." She held up a small crystal phial: it glittered as she moved it, and rays of white light sprang from her hand. "In this phial," she said, "is caught the light of Eärendil's star, set amid the waters of my fountain. It will shine still brighter when night is about you. May it be a light to you in dark places, when all other lights go out. Remember Galadriel and her Mirror!"

Frodo took the phial, and for a moment as it shone between them, he saw her again standing like a queen, great and beautiful, but no longer terrible. He bowed, but found no words to say.

Now the Lady arose, and Celeborn led them back to the hythe. A yellow noon lay on the green land of the Tongue, and the water glittered with silver. All at last was made ready. The Company took their places in the boats as before. Crying farewell, the Elves of Lórien with long grey poles thrust them out into the flowing stream, and the rippling waters bore them slowly away. The travellers sat still without moving or speaking. On the green bank near to the very point of the Tongue the Lady Galadriel stood alone and silent. As they passed her they turned and their eyes watched her slowly floating away from them. For so it seemed to them: Lórien was slipping backward, like a bright ship masted with enchanted trees, sailing on to forgotten shores, while they sat helpless upon the margin of the grey and leafless world.

Even as they gazed, the Silverlode passed out into the currents of the Great River, and their boats turned and began to speed southward. Soon the white form of the Lady was small and distant. She shone like a window of glass upon a far hill in the westering sun, or as a remote lake seen from a mountain: a crystal fallen in the lap of the land. Then it seemed to Frodo that she lifted her arms in a final farewell, and far but piercing-clear on the following wind came the sound of her voice singing. But now she sang in the ancient tongue of the Elves beyond the Sea, and he did not understand the words: fair was the music, but it did not comfort him.

Yet as is the way of Elvish words, they remained graven in his memory, and long afterwards he interpreted them, as well as he could: the language was that of Elven-song and spoke of things little known on Middle-earth.

> *Ai! laurië lantar lassi súrinen,*
> *Yéni únótimë ve rámar aldaron!*
> *Yéni ve lintë yuldar avánier*
> *mi oromardi lisse-miruvóreva*
> *Andúnë pella, Vardo tellumar*
> *nu luini yassen tintilar i eleni*
> *ómaryo airetári-lírinen.*
>
> *Sí man i yulma nin enquantuva?*
>
> *An sí Tintallë Varda Oiolossëo*
> *ve fanyar máryat Elentári ortanë*
> *ar ilyë tier undulávë lumbulë;*
> *ar sindanóriello caita mornië*
> *i falmalinnar imbë met, or hísië*
> *untúpo Calaciryo míri oialë.*
> *Sí vanwa ná, Rómello vanwa, Valimar!*
>
> *Namárië! Nai hiruvalyë Valimar.*
> *Nai elyë hiruva. Namárië!*

"Ah! like gold fall the leaves in the wind, long years numberless as the wings of trees! The long years have passed like swift draughts of the sweet mead in lofty halls beyond the West, beneath the blue vaults of Varda wherein the stars tremble in the song of her voice, holy and queenly. Who now shall refill the cup for me? For now the Kindler, Varda, the Queen of the Stars, from Mount Everwhite has uplifted her hands like clouds, and all paths are drowned deep in shadow; and out of a grey country darkness lies on the foaming waves between us, and mist covers the jewels of Calacirya for ever. Now lost, lost to those from the East is Valimar! Farewell! Maybe thou shalt find Valimar. Maybe even thou shalt find it. Farewell!" Varda is the name of that Lady whom the Elves in these lands of exile name Elbereth.

Suddenly the River swept round a bend, and the banks rose upon either side, and the light of Lórien was hidden. To that fair land Frodo never came again.

The travellers now turned their faces to the journey; the sun was before them, and their eyes were dazzled, for all were filled with tears. Gimli wept openly.

"I have looked the last upon that which was fairest," he said to Legolas his companion. "Henceforward I will call nothing fair, unless it be her gift." He put his hand to his breast.

"Tell me, Legolas, why did I come on this Quest? Little did I know where the chief peril lay! Truly Elrond spoke, saying that we could not foresee what we might meet upon our road. Torment in the dark was the danger that I feared, and it did not hold me back. But I would not have come, had I known the danger of light and joy. Now I have taken my worst wound in this parting, even if I were to go this night straight to the Dark Lord. Alas for Gimli son of Glóin!"

"Nay!" said Legolas. "Alas for us all! And for all that walk the world in these after-days. For such is the way of it: to find and lose, as it seems to those whose boat is on the running stream. But I count you blessed, Gimli son of Glóin: for your loss you suffer of your own free will, and you might have chosen otherwise. But you have not forsaken your companions, and the least reward that you shall have is that the memory of Lothlórien shall remain ever clear and unstained in your heart, and shall neither fade nor grow stale."

"Maybe," said Gimli; "and I thank you for your words. True words doubtless; yet all such comfort is cold. Memory is not what the heart desires. That is only a mirror, be it clear as Kheled-zâram. Or so says the heart of Gimli the Dwarf Elves may see things otherwise. Indeed I have heard that for them memory is more like to the waking world than to a dream. Not so for Dwarves.

"But let us talk no more of it. Look to the boat! She is too low in the water with all this baggage, and the Great River is swift. I do not wish to drown my grief in cold water." He took up a paddle, and steered towards the western bank, following Aragorn's boat ahead, which had already moved out of the middle stream.

So the Company went on their long way, down the wide hurrying waters, borne ever southwards. Bare woods stalked along either bank, and they could not see any glimpse of the lands behind. The breeze died away and the River flowed without a sound. No voice of bird broke the silence. The sun grew misty as the day grew old, until it gleamed in a pale sky like a high white pearl. Then it faded into the West, and dusk came early, followed by a grey and starless night. Far into the dark quiet hours they floated on, guiding their boats under the overhanging shadows of the western woods. Great trees passed by like ghosts, thrusting their twisted thirsty roots through the mist down into the water. It was dreary and cold. Frodo sat and listened to the faint lap and gurgle of the River fretting among the tree-roots and driftwood near the shore, until his head nodded and he fell into an uneasy sleep.

CHAPTER
NINE

The Great River

Frodo was roused by Sam. He found that he was lying, well wrapped, under tall grey-skinned trees in a quiet corner of the woodlands on the west bank of the Great River, Anduin. He had slept the night away, and the grey of morning was dim among the bare branches. Gimli was busy with a small fire near at hand.

They started again before the day was broad. Not that most of the Company were eager to hurry southwards: they were content that the decision, which they must make at latest when they came to Rauros and the Tindrock Isle, still lay some days ahead; and they let the River bear them on at its own pace, having no desire to hasten towards the perils that lay beyond, whichever course they took in the end. Aragorn let them drift with the stream as they wished, husbanding their strength against weariness to come. But he insisted that at least they should start early each day and journey on far into the evening; for he felt in his heart that time was pressing, and he feared that the Dark Lord had not been idle while they lingered in Lórien.

Nonetheless they saw no sign of an enemy that day, nor the next. The dull grey hours passed without event. As the third day of their voyage wore on the lands changed slowly: the trees thinned and then failed altogether. On the eastern bank to their left they saw long formless slopes stretching up and away toward the sky; brown and withered they looked, as if fire had passed over them, leaving no living blade of green: an unfriendly waste without even a broken tree or a bold stone to relieve the emptiness. They had come to the Brown Lands that lay, vast and desolate, between Southern Mirkwood and the hills of the Emyn Muil. What pestilence or war or evil deed of the Enemy had so blasted all that region even Aragorn could not tell.

Upon the west to their right the land was treeless also, but it was flat, and in many places green with wide plains of grass. On this side of the River they passed forests of great reeds, so tall that they shut out all view to the west, as the little boats went rustling by along their fluttering borders. Their dark withered plumes bent and tossed in the light cold airs, hissing softly and sadly. Here and there through openings Frodo could catch sudden glimpses of rolling meads, and far beyond them hills in the sunset, and away on the edge of sight a dark line, where marched the southernmost ranks of the Misty Mountains.

There was no sign of living moving things, save birds. Of these there were many: small fowl whistling and piping in the reeds, but they were seldom seen. Once or twice the travellers heard the rush and whine of swan-wings, and looking up they saw a great phalanx streaming along the sky.

"Swans!" said Sam. "And mighty big ones too!"

"Yes," said Aragorn, "and they are black swans."

"How wide and empty and mournful all this country looks!" said Frodo. "I always imagined that as one journeyed south it got warmer and merrier, until winter was left behind for ever."

"But we have not journeyed far south yet," answered Aragorn. "It is still winter, and we are far from the sea. Here the world is cold until the sudden spring, and we may yet have snow again. Far away down in the Bay of Belfalas, to which Anduin runs, it is warm and merry, maybe, or would be but for the Enemy. But here we are not above sixty leagues, I guess, south of the Southfarthing away in your Shire, hundreds of long miles yonder. You are looking now south-west across the north plains of the Riddermark, Rohan the land of the Horse-lords. Ere long we shall come to the mouth of the Limlight that runs down from Fangorn to join the Great River. That is the north boundary of Rohan; and of old all that lay between Limlight and the White Mountains belonged to the Rohirrim. It is a rich and pleasant land, and its grass has no rival; but in these evil days folk do not dwell by the River or ride often to its shores. Anduin is wide, yet the orcs can shoot their arrows far across the stream; and of late, it is said, they have dared to cross the water and raid the herds and studs of Rohan."

Sam looked from bank to bank uneasily. The trees had seemed hostile before, as if they harboured secret eyes and lurking dangers; now he wished that the trees were still there. He felt that the Company was too naked, afloat in little open boats in the midst of shelterless lands, and on a river that was the frontier of war.

In the next day or two, as they went on, borne steadily southwards, this feeling of insecurity grew on all the Company. For a whole day they took to their paddles and hastened forward. The banks slid by. Soon the River broadened and grew more shallow; long stony beaches lay upon the east, and there were gravel-shoals in the water, so that careful steering was needed. The Brown Lands rose into bleak wolds, over which flowed a chill air from the East. On the other side the meads had become rolling downs of withered grass amidst a land of fen and tussock. Frodo shivered, thinking of the lawns and fountains, the clear sun and gentle rains of Lothlórien. There was little speech and no laughter in any of the boats. Each member of the Company was busy with his own thoughts.

The heart of Legolas was running under the stars of a summer night in some northern glade amid the beech-woods; Gimli was fingering gold in his mind, and wondering if it were fit to be wrought into the housing of the Lady's gift. Merry and Pippin in the middle boat were ill at ease, for Boromir sat muttering to himself, sometimes biting his nails, as if some restlessness or doubt consumed him, sometimes seizing a paddle and driving the boat close behind Aragorn's. Then Pippin, who sat in the bow looking back, caught a queer gleam in his eye, as he peered forward gazing at Frodo. Sam had long ago made up his mind that, though boats were maybe not as dangerous as he had been brought up to believe, they were far more uncomfortable than even he had imagined. He was cramped and miserable, having nothing to do but stare at the winter-lands crawling by and the grey water on either side of him. Even when the paddles were in use they did not trust Sam with one.

As dusk drew down on the fourth day, he was looking back over the bowed heads of Frodo and Aragorn and the following boats; he was drowsy and longed for camp and the feel of earth under his toes. Suddenly something caught his sight: at first he stared at it listlessly, then he sat up and rubbed his eyes; but when he looked again he could not see it any more.

That night they camped on a small eyot close to the western bank. Sam lay rolled in blankets beside Frodo. "I had a funny dream an hour or two before we stopped, Mr. Frodo," he said. "Or maybe it wasn't a dream. Funny it was anyway."

"Well, what was it?" said Frodo, knowing that Sam would not settle down until he had told his tale, whatever it was. "I haven't seen or thought of anything to make me smile since we left Lothlórien."

"It wasn't funny that way, Mr. Frodo. It was queer. All wrong, if it wasn't a dream. And you had best hear it. It was like this: I saw a log with eyes!"

"The log's all right," said Frodo. "There are many in the River. But leave out the eyes!"

"That I won't," said Sam. "'Twas the eyes as made me sit up, so to speak. I saw what I took to be a log floating along in the half-light behind Gimli's boat; but I didn't give much heed to it. Then it seemed as if the log was slowly catching us up. And that was peculiar, as you might say, seeing as we were all floating on the stream together. Just then I saw the eyes: two pale sort of points, shiny-like, on a hump at the near end of the log. What's more, it wasn't a log, for it had paddle-feet, like a swan's almost, only they seemed bigger, and kept dipping in and out of the water.

"That's when I sat right up and rubbed my eyes, meaning to give a shout, if it was still there when I had rubbed the drowse out of my head. For the whatever-it-was was coming along fast now and getting close behind Gimli. But whether those two lamps spotted me moving and staring, or whether I came to my senses, I don't know. When I looked again, it wasn't there. Yet I think I caught a glimpse, with the tail of my eye, as the saying is, of something dark shooting under the shadow of the bank. I couldn't see no more eyes, though.

"I said to myself: 'dreaming again, Sam Gamgee,' I said, and I said no more just then. But I've been thinking since, and now I'm not so sure. What do you make of it, Mr. Frodo?"

"I should make nothing of it but a log and the dusk and sleep in your eyes, Sam," said Frodo, "if this was the first time that those eyes had been seen. But it isn't. I saw them away back north before we reached Lórien. And I saw a strange creature with eyes climbing to the flet that night. Haldir saw it too. And do you remember the report of the Elves that went after the orc-band?"

"Ah," said Sam, "I do; and I remember more too. I don't like my thoughts; but thinking of one thing and another, and Mr. Bilbo's stories and all, I fancy I could put a name on the creature, at a guess. A nasty name. Gollum, maybe?"

"Yes, that is what I have feared for some time," said Frodo. "Ever since the night on the flet. I suppose he was lurking in Moria, and picked up our trail then; but I hoped that our stay in Lórien would throw him off the scent again. The miserable creature must have been hiding in the woods by the Silverlode, watching us start off!"

"That's about it," said Sam. "And we'd better be a bit more watchful ourselves, or we'll feel some nasty fingers round our necks one of these nights, if we ever wake up to feel anything.

And that's what I was leading up to. No need to trouble Strider or the others tonight. I'll keep watch. I can sleep tomorrow, being no more than luggage in a boat, as you might say."

"I might," said Frodo, "and I might say 'luggage with eyes'. You shall watch; but only if you promise to wake me half-way towards morning, if nothing happens before then."

In the dead hours Frodo came out of a deep dark sleep to find Sam shaking him. "It's a shame to wake you," whispered Sam, "but that's what you said. There's nothing to tell, or not much. I thought I heard some soft plashing and a sniffing noise, a while back; but you hear a lot of such queer sounds by a river at night."

He lay down, and Frodo sat up, huddled in his blankets, and fought off his sleep. Minutes or hours passed slowly, and nothing happened. Frodo was just yielding to the temptation to lie down again when a dark shape, hardly visible, floated close to one of the moored boats. A long whitish hand could be dimly seen as it shot out and grabbed the gunwale; two pale lamplike eyes shone coldly as they peered inside, and then they lifted and gazed up at Frodo on the eyot. They were not more than a yard or two away, and Frodo heard the soft hiss of intaken breath. He stood up, drawing Sting from its sheath, and faced the eyes. Immediately their light was shut off. There was another hiss and a splash, and the dark log-shape shot away down-stream into the night. Aragorn stirred in his sleep, turned over, and sat up.

"What is it?" he whispered, springing up and coming to Frodo. "I felt something in my sleep. Why have you drawn your sword?"

"Gollum," answered Frodo. "Or at least, so I guess."

"Ah!" said Aragorn. "So you know about our little footpad, do you? He padded after us all through Moria and right down to Nimrodel. Since we took to boats, he has been lying on a log and paddling with hands and feet. I have tried to catch him once or twice at night; but he is slier than a fox, and as slippery as a fish. I hoped the river-voyage would beat him, but he is too clever a waterman.

"We shall have to try going faster tomorrow. You lie down now, and I will keep watch for what is left of the night. I wish I could lay my hands on the wretch. We might make him useful. But if I cannot, we shall have to try and lose him. He is very dangerous. Quite apart from murder by night on his own account, he may put any enemy that is about on our track."

The night passed without Gollum showing so much as a shadow again. After that the Company kept a sharp look-out, but they saw no more of Gollum while the voyage lasted. If he was still following, he was very wary and cunning. At Aragorn's bidding they paddled now for long spells, and the banks went swiftly by. But they saw little of the country, for they journeyed mostly by night and twilight, resting by day, and lying as hidden as the land allowed. In this way the time passed without event until the seventh day.

The weather was still grey and overcast, with wind from the East, but as evening drew into night the sky away westward cleared, and pools of faint light, yellow and pale green, opened under the grey shores of cloud. There the white rind of the new Moon could be seen glimmering in the remote lakes. Sam looked at it and puckered his brows.

The next day the country on either side began to change rapidly. The banks began to rise and grow stony. Soon they were passing through a hilly rocky land, and on both shores there were steep slopes buried in deep brakes of thorn and sloe, tangled with brambles and creepers. Behind them stood low crumbling cliffs, and chimneys of grey weathered stone dark with ivy; and beyond these again there rose high ridges crowned with wind-writhen firs. They were drawing near to the grey hill-country of the Emyn Muil, the southern march of Wilderland.

There were many birds about the cliffs and the rock-chimneys, and all day high in the air flocks of birds had been circling, black against the pale sky. As they lay in their camp that day Aragorn watched the flights doubtfully, wondering if Gollum had been doing some mischief and the news of their voyage was now moving in the wilderness. Later as the sun was setting, and the Company was stirring and getting ready to start again, he descried a dark spot against the fading light: a great bird high and far off, now wheeling, now flying on slowly southwards.

"What is that, Legolas?" he asked, pointing to the northern sky. "Is it, as I think, an eagle?"

"Yes," said Legolas. "It is an eagle, a hunting eagle. I wonder what that forebodes. It is far from the mountains."

"We will not start until it is fully dark," said Aragorn.

The eighth night of their journey came. It was silent and windless; the grey east wind had passed away. The thin crescent of the Moon had fallen early into the pale sunset, but the sky was clear above, and though far away in the South there were great ranges of cloud that still shone faintly, in the West stars glinted bright.

"Come!" said Aragorn. "We will venture one more journey by night. We are coming to reaches of the River that I do not know well; for I have never journeyed by water in these parts before, not between here and the rapids of Sarn Gebir. But if I am right in my reckoning, those are still many miles ahead. Still there are dangerous places even before we come there: rocks and stony eyots in the stream. We must keep a sharp watch and not try to paddle swiftly."

To Sam in the leading boat was given the task of watchman. He lay forward peering into the gloom. The night grew dark, but the stars above were strangely bright, and there was a glimmer on the face of the River. It was close on midnight, and they had been drifting for some while, hardly using the paddles, when suddenly Sam cried out. Only a few yards ahead dark shapes loomed up in the stream and he heard the swirl of racing water. There was a swift current which swung left, towards the eastern shore where the channel was clear. As they were swept aside the travellers could see, now very close, the pale foam of the River lashing against sharp rocks that were thrust out far into the stream like a ridge of teeth. The boats were all huddled together.

"Hoy there, Aragorn!" shouted Boromir, as his boat bumped into the leader. "This is madness! We cannot dare the Rapids by night! But no boat can live in Sarn Gebir, be it night or day."

"Back, back!" cried Aragorn. "Turn! Turn if you can!" He drove his paddle into the water, trying to hold the boat and bring it round.

"I am out of my reckoning," he said to Frodo. "I did not know that we had come so far: Anduin flows faster than I thought. Sarn Gebir must be close at hand already."

With great efforts they checked the boats and slowly brought them about; but at first they could make only small headway against the current, and all the time they were carried nearer and nearer to the eastern bank. Now dark and ominous it loomed up in the night.

"All together, paddle!" shouted Boromir. "Paddle! Or we shall be driven on the shoals." Even as he spoke Frodo felt the keel beneath him grate upon stone.

At that moment there was a twang of bowstrings: several arrows whistled over them, and some fell among them. One smote Frodo between the shoulders and he lurched forward with a cry, letting go his paddle: but the arrow fell back, foiled by his hidden coat of mail. Another passed through Aragorn's hood; and a third stood fast in the gunwale of the second boat, close by Merry's hand. Sam thought he could glimpse black figures running to and fro upon the long shingle-banks that lay under the eastern shore. They seemed very near.

"*Yrch!*" said Legolas, falling into his own tongue.

"Orcs!" cried Gimli.

"Gollum's doing, I'll be bound," said Sam to Frodo. "And a

nice place to choose, too. The River seems set on taking us right into their arms!"

They all leaned forward straining at the paddles: even Sam took a hand. Every moment they expected to feel the bite of black-feathered arrows. Many whined overhead or struck the water nearby; but there were no more hits. It was dark, but not too dark for the night-eyes of Orcs, and in the star-glimmer they must have offered their cunning foes some mark, unless it was that the grey cloaks of Lórien and the grey timber of the elf-wrought boats defeated the malice of the archers of Mordor.

Stroke by stroke they laboured on. In the darkness it was hard to be sure that they were indeed moving at all; but slowly the swirl of the water grew less, and the shadow of the eastern bank faded back into the night. At last, as far as they could judge, they had reached the middle of the stream again and had driven their boats back some distance above the jutting rocks. Then half turning they thrust them with all their strength towards the western shore. Under the shadow of bushes leaning out over the water they halted and drew breath.

Legolas laid down his paddle and took up the bow that he had brought from Lórien. Then he sprang ashore and climbed a few paces up the bank. Stringing the bow and fitting an arrow he turned, peering back over the River into the darkness. Across the water there were shrill cries, but nothing could be seen.

Frodo looked up at the Elf standing tall above him, as he gazed into the night, seeking a mark to shoot at. His head was dark, crowned with sharp white stars that glittered in the black pools of the sky behind. But now rising and sailing up from the South the great clouds advanced, sending out dark outriders into the starry fields. A sudden dread fell on the Company.

"*Elberth Gilthoniel!*" sighed Legolas as he looked up. Even as he did so, a dark shape, like a cloud and yet not a cloud, for it moved far more swiftly, came out of the blackness in the South, and sped towards the Company, blotting out all light as it approached. Soon it appeared as a great winged creature, blacker than the pits in the night. Fierce voices rose up to greet it from across the water. Frodo felt a sudden chill running through him and clutching at his heart; there was a deadly cold, like the memory of an old wound, in his shoulder. He crouched down, as if to hide.

Suddenly the great bow of Lórien sang. Shrill went the arrow from the elven-string. Frodo looked up. Almost above him the winged shape swerved. There was a harsh croaking scream, as it fell out of the air, vanishing down into the gloom of the eastern shore. The sky was clean again. There was a tumult of many voices far away, cursing and wailing in the darkness, and then silence. Neither shaft nor cry came again from the east that night.

After a while Aragorn led the boats back upstream. They felt their way along the water's edge for some distance, until they found a small shallow bay. A few low trees grew there close to the water, and behind them rose a steep rocky bank. Here the Company decided to stay and await the dawn: it was useless to attempt to move further by night. They made no camp and lit no fire, but lay huddled in the boats, moored close together.

"Praised be the bow of Galadriel, and the hand and eye of Legolas!" said Gimli, as he munched a wafer of *lembas*. "That was a mighty shot in the dark, my friend!"

"But who can say what it hit?" said Legolas.

"I cannot," said Gimli. "But I am glad that the shadow came no nearer. I liked it not at all. Too much it reminded me of the shadow in Moria — the shadow of the Balrog," he ended in a whisper.

"It was not a Balrog," said Frodo, still shivering with the chill that had come upon him. "It was something colder. I think it was ——" Then he paused and fell silent.

"What do you think?" asked Boromir eagerly, leaning from his boat, as if he was trying to catch a glimpse of Frodo's face.

"I think — No, I will not say," answered Frodo. "Whatever it was, its fall has dismayed our enemies."

"So it seems," said Aragorn. "Yet where they are, and how many, and what they will do next, we do not know. This night we must all be sleepless! Dark hides us now. But what the day will show who can tell? Have your weapons close to hand!"

Sam sat tapping the hilt of his sword as if he were counting on his fingers, and looking up at the sky. "It's very strange," he murmured. "The Moon's the same in the Shire and in Wilderland, or it ought to be. But either it's out of its running, or I'm all wrong in my reckoning. You'll remember, Mr. Frodo, the Moon was waning as we lay on the flet up in that tree: a week from the full, I reckon. And we'd been a week on the way last night, when up pops a New Moon as thin as a nail-paring, as if we had never stayed no time in the Elvish country.

"Well, I can remember three nights there for certain, and I seem to remember several more, but I would take my oath it was never a whole month. Anyone would think that time did not count in there!"

"And perhaps that was the way of it," said Frodo. "In that land, maybe, we were in a time that has elsewhere long gone by. It was not, I think, until Silverlode bore us back to Anduin that we returned to the time that flows through mortal lands to the Great Sea. And I don't remember any moon, either new or old, in Caras Galadon: only stars by night and sun by day."

Legolas stirred in his boat. "Nay, time does not tarry ever," he said; "but change and growth is not in all things and places alike. For the Elves the world moves, and it moves both very swift and very slow. Swift, because they themselves change little, and all else fleets by: it is a grief to them. Slow, because they do not count the running years, not for themselves. The passing seasons are but ripples ever repeated in the long long stream. Yet beneath the Sun all things must wear to an end at last."

"But the wearing is slow in Lórien," said Frodo. "The power of the Lady is on it. Rich are the hours, though short they seem, in Caras Galadon, where Galadriel wields the Elven-ring."

"That should not have been said outside Lórien, not even to me, said Aragorn. "Speak no more of it! But so it is, Sam: in that land you lost your count. There time flowed swiftly by us, as for the Elves. The old moon passed, and a new moon waxed and waned in the world outside, while we tarried there. And yestereve a new moon came again. Winter is nearly gone. Time flows on to a spring of little hope."

The night passed silently. No voice or call was heard again across the water. The travellers huddled in their boats felt the changing of the weather. The air grew warm and very still under the great moist clouds that had floated up from the South and the distant seas. The rushing of the River over the rocks of the rapids seemed to grow louder and closer. The twigs of the trees above them began to drip.

When the day came the mood of the world about them had become soft and sad. Slowly the dawn grew to a pale light, diffused and shadowless. There was mist on the River, and white fog swathed the shore; the far bank could not be seen.

"I can't abide fog," said Sam; "but this seems to be a lucky one. Now perhaps we can get away without those cursed goblins seeing us."

"Perhaps so," said Aragorn. "But it will be hard to find the path unless the fog lifts a little later on. And we must find the path, if we are to pass Sarn Gebir and come to the Emyn Muil."

"I do not see why we should pass the Rapids or follow the River any further," said Boromir. "If the Emyn Muil lie before us, then we can abandon these cockle-boats, and strike westward and southward, until we come to the Entwash and cross into my own land."

"We can, if we are making for Minas Tirith," said Aragorn, "but that is not yet agreed. And such a course may be more perilous than it sounds. The vale of Entwash is flat and fenny, and fog is a deadly peril there for those on foot and laden. I would not abandon our boats until we must. The River is at least a path that cannot be missed."

"But the Enemy holds the eastern bank," objected Boromir. "And even if you pass the Gates of Argonath and come unmolested to the Tindrock, what will you do then? Leap down the Falls and land in the marshes?"

"No!" answered Aragorn. "Say rather that we will bear our boats by the ancient way to Rauros-foot, and there take to the water again. Do you not know, Boromir, or do you choose to forget the North Stair, and the high seat upon Amon Hen, that were made in the days of the great kings? I at least have a mind to stand in that high place again, before I decide my further course. There, maybe, we shall see some sign that will guide us."

Boromir held out long against this choice; but when it became plain that Frodo would follow Aragorn, wherever he went, he gave in. "It is not the way of the Men of Minas Tirith to desert their friends at need," he said, "and you will need my strength, if ever you are to reach the Tindrock. To the tall isle I will go, but no further. There I shall turn to my home, alone if my help has not earned the reward of any companionship."

The day was now growing, and the fog had lifted a little. It was decided that Aragorn and Legolas should at once go forward along the shore, while the others remained by the boats. Aragorn hoped to find some way by which they could carry both their boats and their baggage to the smoother water beyond the Rapids.

"Boats of the Elves would not sink, maybe," he said, "but that does not say that we should come through Sarn Gebir alive. None have ever done so yet. No road was made by the Men of Gondor in this region, for even in their great days their realm did not reach up Anduin beyond the Emyn Muil; but there is a portage-way somewhere on the western shore, if I can find it. It cannot yet have perished; for light boats used to journey out of Wilderland down to Osgiliath, and still did so until a few years ago, when the Orcs of Mordor began to multiply."

"Seldom in my life has any boat come out of the North, and the Orcs prowl on the east-shore," said Boromir. "If you go forward, peril will grow with every mile, even if you find a path."

"Peril lies ahead on every southward road," answered Aragorn. "Wait for us one day. If we do not return in that time, you will know that evil has indeed befallen us. Then you must take a new leader and follow him as best you can."

It was with a heavy heart that Frodo saw Aragorn and Legolas climb the steep bank and vanish into the mists; but his fears proved groundless. Only two or three hours had passed, and it was barely mid-day, when the shadowy shapes of the explorers appeared again.

"All is well," said Aragorn, as he clambered down the bank. "There is a track, and it leads to a good landing that is still serviceable. The distance is not great: the head of the Rapids is but half a mile below us, and they are little more than a mile long. Not far beyond them the stream becomes clear and smooth again, though it runs swiftly. Our hardest task will be to get our boats and baggage to the old portage-way. We have found it, but it lies well back from the water-side here, and runs under the lee of a rock-wall, a furlong or more from the shore. We did not find where the northward landing lies. If it still remains, we must have passed it yesterday night. We might labour far upstream and yet miss it in the fog. I fear we must leave the River now, and make for the portage-way as best we can from here."

"That would not be easy, even if we were all Men," said Boromir.

"Yet such as we are we will try it," said Aragorn.

"Aye, we will," said Gimli. "The legs of Men will lag on a rough road, while a Dwarf goes on, be the burden twice his own weight, Master Boromir!"

The task proved hard indeed, yet in the end it was done. The goods were taken out of the boats and brought to the top of the bank, where there was a level space. Then the boats were drawn out of the water and carried up. They were far less heavy than any had expected. Of what tree growing in the elvish country they were made not even Legolas knew; but the wood was tough and yet strangely light. Merry and Pippin alone could carry their boat with ease along the flat. Nonetheless it needed the strength of the two Men to lift and haul them over the ground that the Company now had to cross. It sloped up away from the River, a tumbled waste of grey limestone-boulders, with many hidden holes shrouded with weeds and bushes; there were thickets of brambles, and sheer dells; and here and there boggy pools fed by waters trickling from the terraces further inland.

One by one Boromir and Aragorn carried the boats, while the others toiled and scrambled after them with the baggage. At last all was removed and laid on the portage-way. Then with little further hindrance, save from sprawling briars and many fallen stones, they moved forward all together. Fog still hung in veils upon the crumbling rock-wall, and to their left mist shrouded the River: they could hear it rushing and foaming over the sharp shelves and stony teeth of Sarn Gebir, but they could not see it. Twice they made the journey, before all was brought safe to the southern landing.

There the portage-way, turning back to the water-side, ran gently down to the shallow edge of a little pool. It seemed to have been scooped in the river-side, not by hand, but by the water swirling down from Sarn Gebir against a low pier of rock that jutted out some way into the stream. Beyond it the shore rose sheer into a grey cliff, and there was no further passage for those on foot.

Already the short afternoon was past, and a dim cloudy dusk was closing in. They sat beside the water listening to the confused rush and roar of the Rapids hidden in the mist; they were tired and sleepy, and their hearts were as gloomy as the dying day.

"Well, here we are, and here we must pass another night,"

said Boromir. "We need sleep, and even if Aragorn had a mind to pass the Gates of Argonath by night, we are all too tired — except, no doubt, our sturdy dwarf."

Gimli made no reply: he was nodding as he sat.

"Let us rest as much as we can now," said Aragorn. "Tomorrow we must journey by day again. Unless the weather changes once more and cheats us, we shall have a good chance of slipping through, unseen by any eyes on the eastern shore. But tonight two must watch together in turns: three hours off and one on guard."

Nothing happened that night worse than a brief drizzle of rain an hour before dawn. As soon as it was fully light they started. Already the fog was thinning. They kept as close as they could to the western side, and they could see the dim shapes of the low cliffs rising ever higher, shadowy walls with their feet in the hurrying river. In the mid-morning the clouds drew down lower, and it began to rain heavily. They drew the skin-covers over their boats to prevent them from being flooded, and drifted on; little could be seen before them or about them through the grey falling curtains.

The rain, however, did not last long. Slowly the sky above grew lighter, and then suddenly the clouds broke, and their draggled fringes trailed away northward up the River. The fogs and mists were gone. Before the travellers lay a wide ravine, with great rocky sides to which clung, upon shelves and in narrow crevices, a few thrawn trees. The channel grew narrower and the River swifter. Now they were speeding along with little hope of stopping or turning, whatever they might meet ahead. Over them was a lane of pale-blue sky, around them the dark overshadowed River, and before them black, shutting out the sun, the hills of Emyn Muil, in which no opening could be seen.

Frodo peering forward saw in the distance two great rocks approaching: like great pinnacles or pillars of stone they seemed. Tall and sheer and ominous they stood upon either side of the stream. A narrow gap appeared between them, and the River swept the boats towards it.

"Behold the Argonath, the Pillars of the Kings!" cried Aragorn. "We shall pass them soon. Keep the boats in line, and as far apart as you can! Hold the middle of the stream!"

As Frodo was borne towards them the great pillars rose like towers to meet him. Giants they seemed to him, vast grey figures silent but threatening. Then he saw that they were indeed shaped and fashioned: the craft and power of old had wrought upon them, and still they preserved through the suns and rains of forgotten years the mighty likenesses in which they had been hewn. Upon great pedestals founded in the deep waters stood two great kings of stone: still with blurred eyes and crannied brows they frowned upon the North. The left hand of each was raised palm outwards in gesture of warning; in each right hand there was an axe; upon each head there was a crumbling helm and crown. Great power and majesty they still wore, the silent wardens of a long-vanished kingdom. Awe and fear fell upon Frodo, and he cowered down, shutting his eyes and not daring to look up as the boat drew near. Even Boromir bowed his head as the boats whirled by, frail and fleeting as little leaves, under the enduring shadow of the sentinels of Numenor. So they passed into the dark chasm of the Gates.

Sheer rose the dreadful cliffs to unguessed heights on either side. Far off was the dim sky. The black waters roared and echoed, and a wind screamed over them. Frodo crouching over his knees heard Sam in front muttering and groaning: "What a place! What a horrible place! Just let me get out of this boat, and I'll never wet my toes in a puddle again, let alone a river!"

"Fear not!" said a strange voice behind him. Frodo turned and saw Strider, and yet not Strider; for the weatherworn Ranger was no longer there. In the stern sat Aragorn son of Arathorn, proud and erect, guiding the boat with skilful strokes; his hood was cast back, and his dark hair was blowing in the wind, a light was in his eyes: a king returning from exile to his own land.

"Fear not!" he said. "Long have I desired to look upon the likenesses of Isildur and Anárion, my sires of old. Under their shadow Elessar, the Elfstone son of Arathorn of the House of Valandil Isildur's son, heir of Elendil, has nought to dread!"

Then the light of his eyes faded, and he spoke to himself: "Would that Gandalf were here! How my heart yearns for Minas Anor and the walls of my own city! But whither now shall I go?"

The chasm was long and dark, and filled with the noise of wind and rushing water and echoing stone. It bent somewhat towards the west so that at first all was dark ahead; but soon Frodo saw a tall gap of light before him, ever growing. Swiftly it drew near, and suddenly the boats shot through, out into a wide clear light.

The sun, already long fallen from the noon, was shining in a windy sky. The pent waters spread out into a long oval lake, pale Nen Hithoel, fenced by steep grey hills whose sides were clad with trees, but their heads were bare, cold-gleaming in the sunlight. At the far southern end rose three peaks. The midmost stood somewhat forward from the others and sundered from them, an island in the waters, about which the flowing River flung pale shimmering arms. Distant but deep there came up on the wind a roaring sound like the roll of thunder heard far away.

"Behold Tol Brandir!" said Aragorn, pointing south to the tall peak. "Upon the left stands Amon Lhaw, and upon the right is Amon Hen, the Hills of Hearing and of Sight. In the days of the great kings there were high seats upon them, and watch was kept there. But it is said that no foot of man or beast has ever been set upon Tol Brandir. Ere the shade of night falls we shall come to them. I hear the endless voice of Rauros calling."

The Company rested now for a while, drifting south on the current that flowed through the middle of the lake. They ate some food, and then they took to their paddles and hastened on their way. The sides of the westward hills fell into shadow, and the Sun grew round and red. Here and there a misty star peered out. The three peaks loomed before them, darkling in the twilight. Rauros was roaring with a great voice. Already night was laid on the flowing waters when the travellers came at last under the shadow of the hills.

The tenth day of their journey was over. Wilderland was behind them. They could go no further without choice between the east-way and the west. The last stage of the Quest was before them.

CHAPTER
TEN

The Breaking of the Fellowship

Aragorn led them to the right arm of the River. Here upon its western side under the shadow of Tol Brandir a green lawn ran down to the water from the feet of Amon Hen. Behind it rose the first gentle slopes of the hill clad with trees, and trees marched away westward along the curving shores of the lake. A little spring fell tumbling down and fed the grass.

"Here we will rest tonight," said Aragorn. "This is the lawn of Parth Galen: a fair place in the summer days of old. Let us hope that no evil has yet come here."

They drew up their boats on the green banks, and beside them they made their camp. They set a watch, but had no sight nor sound of their enemies. If Gollum had contrived to follow them, he remained unseen and unheard. Nonetheless as the night wore on Aragorn grew uneasy, tossing often in his sleep and waking. In the small hours he got up and came to Frodo, whose turn it was to watch.

"Why are you waking?" asked Frodo. "It is not your watch."

"I do not know," answered Aragorn; "but a shadow and a threat has been growing in my sleep. It would be well to draw your sword."

"Why?" said Frodo. "Are enemies at hand?"

"Let us see what Sting may show," answered Aragorn.

Frodo then drew the elf-blade from its sheath. To his dismay the edges gleamed dimly in the night. "Orcs!" he said. "Not very near, and yet too near, it seems."

"I feared as much," said Aragorn. "But maybe they are not on this side of the River. The light of Sting is faint, and it may point to no more than spies of Mordor roaming on the slopes of Amon Lhaw. I have never heard before of Orcs upon Amon Hen. Yet who knows what may happen in these evil days, now that Minas Tirith no longer holds secure the passages of Anduin. We must go warily tomorrow. "

The day came like fire and smoke. Low in the East there were black bars of cloud like the fumes of a great burning. The rising sun lit them from beneath with flames of murky red; but soon it climbed above them into a clear sky. The summit of Tol Brandir was tipped with gold. Frodo looked out eastward and gazed at the tall island. Its sides sprang sheer out of the running water. High up above the tall cliffs were steep slopes upon which trees climbed, mounting one head above another; and above them again were grey faces of inaccessible rock, crowned by a great spire of stone. Many birds were circling about it, but no sign of other living things could be seen.

When they had eaten, Aragorn called the Company together. "The day has come at last," he said: "the day of choice which we have long delayed. What shall now become of our Company that has travelled so far in fellowship? Shall we turn west with Boromir and go to the wars of Gondor; or turn east to the Fear and Shadow; or shall we break our fellowship and go this way and that as each may choose? Whatever we do must be done soon. We cannot long halt here. The enemy is on the eastern shore, we know; but I fear that the Orcs may already be on this side of the water. "

There was a long silence in which no one spoke or moved.

"Well, Frodo," said Aragorn at last. "I fear that the burden is laid upon you. You are the Bearer appointed by the Council.

Your own way you alone can choose. In this matter I cannot advise you. I am not Gandalf, and though I have tried to bear his part, I do not know what design or hope he had for this hour, if indeed he had any. Most likely it seems that if he were here now the choice would still wait on you. Such is your fate."

Frodo did not answer at once. Then he spoke slowly. "I know that haste is needed, yet I cannot choose. The burden is heavy. Give me an hour longer, and I will speak. Let me be alone!"

Aragorn looked at him with kindly pity. "Very well, Frodo son of Drogo," he said. "You shall have an hour, and you shall be alone. We will stay here for a while. But do not stray far or out of call."

Frodo sat for a moment with his head bowed. Sam, who had been watching his master with great concern, shook his head and muttered: "Plain as a pikestaff it is, but it's no good Sam Gamgee putting in his spoke just now."

Presently Frodo got up and walked away; and Sam saw that while the others restrained themselves and did not stare at him, the eyes of Boromir followed Frodo intently, until he passed out of sight in the trees at the foot of Amon Hen.

Wandering aimlessly at first in the wood, Frodo found that his feet were leading him up towards the slopes of the hill. He came to a path, the dwindling ruins of a road of long ago. In steep places stairs of stone had been hewn, but now they were cracked and worn, and split by the roots of trees. For some while he climbed, not caring which way he went, until he came to a grassy place. Rowan-trees grew about it, and in the midst was a wide flat stone. The little upland lawn was open upon the East and was filled now with the early sunlight. Frodo halted and looked out over the River, far below him, to Tol Brandir and the birds wheeling in the great gulf of air between him and the untrodden isle. The voice of Rauros was a mighty roaring mingled with a deep throbbing boom.

He sat down upon the stone and cupped his chin in his

hands, staring eastwards but seeing little with his eyes. All that had happened since Bilbo left the Shire was passing through his mind, and he recalled and pondered everything that he could remember of Gandalf's words. Time went on, and still he was no nearer to a choice.

Suddenly he awoke from his thoughts: a strange feeling came to him that something was behind him, that unfriendly eyes were upon him. He sprang up and turned; but all that he saw to his surprise was Boromir, and his face was smiling and kind.

"I was afraid for you, Frodo," he said, coming forward. "If Aragorn is right and Orcs are near, then none of us should wander alone, and you least of all: so much depends on you. And my heart too is heavy. May I stay now and talk for a while, since I have found you? It would comfort me. Where there are so many, all speech becomes a debate without end. But two together may perhaps find wisdom."

"You are kind," answered Frodo. "But I do not think that any speech will help me. For I know what I should do, but I am afraid of doing it, Boromir: afraid."

Boromir stood silent. Rauros roared endlessly on. The wind murmured in the branches of the trees. Frodo shivered.

Suddenly Boromir came and sat beside him. "Are you sure that you do not suffer needlessly?" he said. "I wish to help you. You need counsel in your hard choice. Will you not take mine?"

"I think I know already what counsel you would give, Boromir," said Frodo. "And it would seem like wisdom but for the warning of my heart."

"Warning? Warning against what?" said Boromir sharply.

"Against delay. Against the way that seems easier. Against refusal of the burden that is laid on me. Against — well, if it must be said, against trust in the strength and truth of Men."

"Yet that strength has long protected you far away in your little country, though you knew it not."

"I do not doubt the valour of your people. But the world is changing. The walls of Minas Tirith may be strong, but they are not strong enough. If they fail, what then?"

"We shall fall in battle valiantly. Yet there is still hope that they will not fail."

"No hope while the Ring lasts," said Frodo.

"Ah! The Ring!" said Boromir, his eyes lighting. "The Ring! Is it not a strange fate that we should suffer so much fear and doubt for so small a thing? So small a thing! And I have seen it only for an instant in the House of Elrond. Could I not have a sight of it again?"

Frodo looked up. His heart went suddenly cold. He caught the strange gleam in Boromir's eyes, yet his face was still kind and friendly. "It is best that it should lie hidden," he answered.

"As you wish. I care not," said Boromir. "Yet may I not even speak of it? For you seem ever to think only of its power in the hands of the Enemy: of its evil uses not of its good. The world is changing, you say. Minas Tirith will fall, if the Ring lasts. But why? Certainly, if the Ring were with the Enemy. But why, if it were with us?"

"Were you not at the Council?" answered Frodo. "Because we cannot use it, and what is done with it turns to evil."

Boromir got up and walked about impatiently. "So you go on," he cried. "Gandalf, Elrond — all these folk have taught you to say so. For themselves they may be right. These elves and half-elves and wizards, they would come to grief perhaps. Yet often I doubt if they are wise and not merely timid. But each to his own kind. True-hearted Men, they will not be corrupted. We of Minas Tirith have been staunch through long years of trial. We do not desire the power of wizard-lords, only strength to defend ourselves, strength in a just cause. And behold! in our need chance brings to light the Ring of Power. It is a gift, I say; a gift to the foes of Mordor. It is mad not to use it, to use the power of the Enemy against him. The fearless, the ruthless, these alone will achieve victory. What could not a warrior do in this hour, a great leader? What could not Aragorn do? Or if he refuses, why not Boromir? The Ring would give me power of Command. How I would drive the hosts of

Mordor, and all men would flock to my banner!"

Boromir strode up and down, speaking ever more loudly. Almost he seemed to have forgotten Frodo, while his talk dwelt on walls and weapons, and the mustering of men; and he drew plans for great alliances and glorious victories to be; and he cast down Mordor, and became himself a mighty king, benevolent and wise. Suddenly he stopped and waved his arms.

"And they tell us to throw it away!" he cried. "I do not say *destroy* it. That might be well, if reason could show any hope of doing so. It does not. The only plan that is proposed to us is that a halfling should walk blindly into Mordor and offer the Enemy every chance of recapturing it for himself. Folly!

"Surely you see it, my friend?" he said, turning now suddenly to Frodo again. "You say that you are afraid. If it is so, the boldest should pardon you. But is it not really your good sense that revolts?"

"No, I am afraid," said Frodo. "Simply afraid. But I am glad to have heard you speak so fully. My mind is clearer now."

"Then you will come to Minas Tirith?" cried Boromir. His eyes were shining and his face eager.

"You misunderstand me," said Frodo.

"But you will come, at least for a while?" Boromir persisted. "My city is not far now; and it is little further from there to Mordor than from here. We have been long in the wilderness, and you need news of what the Enemy is doing before you make a move. Come with me, Frodo," he said. "You need rest before your venture, if go you must." He laid his hand on the hobbit's shoulder in friendly fashion; but Frodo felt the hand trembling with suppressed excitement. He stepped quickly away, and eyed with alarm the tall Man, nearly twice his height and many times his match in strength.

"Why are you so unfriendly?" said Boromir. "I am a true man, neither thief nor tracker. I need your Ring: that you know now; but I give you my word that I do not desire to keep it. Will you not at least let me make trial of my plan? Lend me the Ring!"

"No! no!" cried Frodo. "The Council laid it upon me to bear it."

"It is by our own folly that the Enemy will defeat us," cried Boromir. "How it angers me! Fool! Obstinate fool! Running wilfully to death and ruining our cause. If any mortals have claim to the Ring, it is the men of Númenor, and not Halflings. It is not yours save by unhappy chance. It might have been mine. It should be mine. Give it to me!"

Frodo did not answer, but moved away till the great flat stone stood between them. "Come, come, my friend!" said Boromir in a softer voice. "Why not get rid of it? Why not be free of your doubt and fear? You can lay the blame on me, if you will. You can say that I was too strong and took it by force. For I am too strong for you, halfling," he cried; and suddenly he sprang over the stone and leaped at Frodo. His fair and pleasant face was hideously changed; a raging fire was in his eyes.

Frodo dodged aside and again put the stone between them. There was only one thing he could do: trembling he pulled out the Ring upon its chain and quickly slipped it on his finger, even as Boromir sprang at him again. The Man gasped, stared for a moment amazed, and then ran wildly about, seeking here and there among the rocks and trees.

"Miserable trickster!" he shouted. "Let me get my hands on you! Now I see your mind. You will take the Ring to Sauron and sell us all. You have only waited your chance to leave us in the lurch. Curse you and all halflings to death and darkness!" Then, catching his foot on a stone, he fell sprawling and lay upon his face. For a while he was as still as if his own curse had struck him down; then suddenly he wept.

He rose and passed his hand over his eyes, dashing away the tears. "What have I said?" he cried. "What have I done? Frodo, Frodo!" he called. "Come back! A madness took me, but it has passed. Come back!"

There was no answer. Frodo did not even hear his cries. He

was already far away, leaping blindly up the path to the hill-top. Terror and grief shook him, seeing in his thought the mad fierce face of Boromir, and his burning eyes.

Soon he came out alone on the summit of Amon Hen, and halted, gasping for breath. He saw as through a mist a wide flat circle, paved with mighty flags, and surrounded with a crumbling battlement; and in the middle, set upon four carven pillars, was a high seat, reached by a stair of many steps. Up he went and sat upon the ancient chair, feeling like a lost child that had clambered upon the throne of mountain-kings.

At first he could see little. He seemed to be in a world of mist in which there were only shadows: the Ring was upon him. Then here and there the mist gave way and he saw many visions: small and clear as if they were under his eyes upon a table, and yet remote. There was no sound, only bright living images. The world seemed to have shrunk and fallen silent. He was sitting upon the Seat of Seeing, on Amon Hen, the Hill of the Eye of the Men of Númenor. Eastward he looked into wide uncharted lands, nameless plains, and forests unexplored. Northward he looked, and the Great River lay like a ribbon beneath him, and the Misty Mountains stood small and hard as broken teeth. Westward he looked and saw the broad pastures of Rohan; and Orthanc, the pinnacle of Isengard, like a black spike. Southward he looked, and below his very feet the Great River curled like a toppling wave and plunged over the falls of Rauros into a foaming pit; a glimmering rainbow played upon the fume. And Ethir Anduin he saw, the mighty delta of the River, and myriads of sea-birds whirling like a white dust in the sun, and beneath them a green and silver sea, rippling in endless lines.

But everywhere he looked he saw the signs of war. The Misty Mountains were crawling like anthills: orcs were issuing out of a thousand holes. Under the boughs of Mirkwood there was deadly strife of Elves and Men and fell beasts. The land of the Beornings was aflame; a cloud was over Moria; smoke rose on the borders of Lórien.

Horsemen were galloping on the grass of Rohan; wolves poured from Isengard. From the havens of Harad ships of war put out to sea; and out of the East Men were moving endlessly: swordsmen, spearmen, bowmen upon horses, chariots of chieftains and laden wains. All the power of the Dark Lord was in motion. Then turning south again he beheld Minas Tirith. Far away it seemed, and beautiful: white-walled, many-towered, proud and fair upon its mountain-seat; its battlements glittered with steel, and its turrets were bright with many banners. Hope leaped his heart. But against Minas Tirith was set another fortress, greater and more strong. Thither, eastward, unwilling his eye was drawn. It passed the ruined bridges of Osgiliath, the grinning gates of Minas Morgul, and the haunted Mountains, and it looked upon Gorgoroth, the valley of terror in the Land of Mordor. Darkness lay there under the Sun. Fire glowed amid the smoke. Mount Doom was burning, and a great reek rising. Then at last his gaze was held: wall upon wall, battlement upon battlement, black, im-measurably strong, mountain of iron, gate of steel, tower of adamant, he saw it: Barad-dûr, Fortress of Sauron. All hope left him.

And suddenly he felt the Eye. There was an eye in the Dark Tower that did not sleep. He knew that it had become aware of his gaze. A fierce eager will was there. It leaped towards him; almost like a finger he felt it, searching for him. Very soon it would nail him down, know just exactly where he was. Amon Lhaw it touched. It glanced upon Tol Brandir — he threw himself from the seat, crouching, covering his head with his grey hood.

He heard himself crying out: *Never, never!* Or was it: *Verily I come, I come to you?* He could not tell. Then as a flash from some other point of power there came to his mind another thought: *Take it off! Take it off! Fool, take it off! Take off the Ring!*

The two powers strove in him. For a moment, perfectly balanced between their piercing points, he writhed, tormented.

Suddenly he was aware of himself again. Frodo, neither the Voice nor the Eye: free to choose, and with one remaining instant in which to do so. He took the Ring off his finger. He was kneeling in clear sunlight before the high seat. A black shadow seemed to pass like an arm above him; it missed Amon Hen and groped out west, and faded. Then all the sky was clean and blue and birds sang in every tree.

Frodo rose to his feet. A great weariness was on him, but his will was firm and his heart lighter. He spoke aloud to himself. "I will do now what I must," he said. "This at least is plain: the evil of the Ring is already at work even in the Company, and the Ring must leave them before it does more harm. I will go alone. Some I cannot trust, and those I can trust are too dear to me: poor old Sam, and Merry and Pippin. Strider, too: his heart yearns for Minas Tirith, and he will be needed there, now Boromir has fallen into evil. I will go alone. At once."

He went quickly down the path and came back to the lawn where Boromir had found him. Then he halted, listening. He thought he could hear cries and calls from the woods near the shore below.

"They'll be hunting for me," he said. "I wonder how long I have been away. Hours, I should think." He hesitated. "What can I do?" he muttered. "I must go now or I shall never go. I shan't get a chance again. I hate leaving them, and like this without any explanation. But surely they will understand. Sam will. And what else can I do?"

Slowly he drew out the Ring and put it on once more. He vanished and passed down the hill, less than a rustle of the wind.

The others remained long by the river-side. For some time they had been silent, moving restlessly about; but now they were sitting in a circle, and they were talking. Every now and again they made efforts to speak of other things, of their long road and many adventures; they questioned Aragorn concerning the realm of Gondor and its ancient history, and the remnants of its great works that could still be seen in this strange border-land of the Emyn Muil: the stone kings and the seats of Lhaw and Hen, and the great Stair beside the falls of Rauros. But always their thoughts and words strayed back to Frodo and the Ring. What would Frodo choose to do? Why was he hesitating?

"He is debating which course is the most desperate, I think," said Aragorn. "And well he may. It is now more hopeless than ever for the Company to go east, since we have been tracked by Gollum, and must fear that the secret of our journey is already betrayed. But Minas Tirith is no nearer to the Fire and the destruction of the Burden.

"We may remain there for a while and make a brave stand; but the Lord Denethor and all his men cannot hope to do what even Elrond said was beyond his power: either to keep the Burden secret, or to hold off the full might of the Enemy when he comes to take it. Which way would any of us choose in Frodo's place? I do not know. Now indeed we miss Gandalf most."

"Grievous is our loss," said Legolas. "Yet we must needs make up our minds without his aid. Why cannot we decide, and so help Frodo? Let us call him back and then vote! I should vote for Minas Tirith."

"And so should I," said Gimli. "We, of course, were only sent to help the Bearer along the road, to go no further than we wished; and none of us is under any oath or command to seek Mount Doom. Hard was my parting from Lothlórien. Yet I have come so far, and I say this: now we have reached the last choice, it is clear to me that I cannot leave Frodo. I would choose Minas Tirith, but if he does not, then I follow him."

"And I too will go with him," said Legolas. "It would be faithless now to say farewell."

"It would indeed be a betrayal, if we all left him," said Aragorn. "But if he goes east, then all need not go with him; nor do I think that all should. That venture is desperate: as much so for eight as for three or two, or one alone. If you would let me choose, then I should appoint three companions: Sam, who could not bear it otherwise; and Gimli; and myself. Boromir will return to his own city, where his father and his people need him; and with him the others should go, or at least Meriadoc and Peregrin, if Legolas is not willing to leave us."

"That won't do at all!" cried Merry. "We can't leave Frodo! Pippin and I always intended to go wherever he went, and we still do. But we did not realize what that would mean. It seemed different so far away, in the Shire or in Rivendell. It would be mad and cruel to let Frodo go to Mordor. Why can't we stop him?"

"We must stop him," said Pippin. "And that is what he is worrying about, I am sure. He knows we shan't agree to his going east. And he doesn't like to ask anyone to go with him, poor old fellow. Imagine it: going off to Mordor alone!" Pippin shuddered. "But the dear silly old hobbit, he ought to know that he hasn't got to ask. He ought to know that if we can't stop him, we shan't leave him."

"Begging your pardon," said Sam. "I don't think you understand my master at all. He isn't hesitating about which way to go. Of course not! What's the good of Minas Tirith anyway? To him, I mean, begging your pardon, Master Boromir," he added, and turned. It was then that they discovered that Boromir, who at first had been sitting silent on the outside of the circle, was no longer there.

"Now where's he got to?" cried Sam, looking worried. "He's been a bit queer lately, to my mind. But anyway he's not in this business. He's off to his home, as he always said; and no blame to him. But Mr. Frodo, he knows he's got to find the Cracks of Doom, if he But he's *afraid*. Now it's come to the point, he's just plain terrified. That's what his trouble is. Of course he's had a bit of schooling, so to speak — we all have — since we left home, or he'd be so terrified he'd just fling the Ring in the River and bolt. But he's still too frightened to start. And he isn't worrying about us either: whether we'll go along with him or no. He knows we mean to. That's another thing that's bothering him. If he screws himself up to go, he'll want to go alone. Mark my words! We're going to have trouble when he comes back. For he'll screw himself up all right, as sure as his name's Baggins."

"I believe you speak more wisely than any of us, Sam," said Aragorn. "And what shall we do, if you prove right?"

"Stop him! Don't let him go!" cried Pippin.

"I wonder?" said Aragorn. "He is the Bearer, and the fate of the Burden is on him. I do not think that it is our part to drive him one way or the other. Nor do I think that we should succeed, if we tried. There are other powers at work far stronger."

"Well, I wish Frodo would 'screw himself up' and come back, and let us get it over," said Pippin. "This waiting is horrible! Surely the time is up?"

"Yes," said Aragorn. "The hour is long passed. The morning is wearing away. We must call for him."

At that moment Boromir reappeared. He came out from the trees and walked towards them without speaking. His face looked grim and sad. He paused as if counting those that were present, and then sat down aloof, with his eyes on the ground.

"Where have you been, Boromir?" asked Aragorn. "Have you seen Frodo?"

Boromir hesitated for a second. "Yes, and no," he answered slowly. "Yes: I found him some way up the hill, and I spoke to him. I urged him to come to Minas Tirith and not to go east. I grew angry and he left me. He vanished. I have never seen such a thing happen before, though I have heard of it in tales. He must have put the Ring on. I could not find him again. I thought he would return to you."

"Is that all that you have to say?" said Aragorn, looking hard and not too kindly at Boromir.

"Yes," he answered. "I will say no more yet."

"This is bad!" cried Sam, jumping up. "I don't know what this Man has been up to. Why should Mr. Frodo put the thing on? He didn't ought to have; and if he has, goodness knows what may have happened!"

"But he wouldn't keep it on," said Merry. "Not when he had escaped the unwelcome visitor, like Bilbo used to."

"But where did he go? Where is he?" cried Pippin. "He's been away ages now."

"How long is it since you saw Frodo last, Boromir?" asked Aragornx

"Half an hour, maybe," he answered. "Or it might be an hour. I have wandered for some time since. I do not know! I do not know!" He put his head in his hands, and sat as if bowed with grief.

"An hour since he vanished!" shouted Sam. "We must try and find him at once. Come on!"

"Wait a moment!" cried Aragorn. "We must divide up into pairs, and arrange — here, hold on! Wait!"

It was no good. They took no notice of him. Sam had dashed off first. Merry and Pippin had followed, and were already disappearing westward into the trees by the shore, shouting: *Frodo! Frodo!* in their clear, high, hobbit-voices. Legolas and Gimli were running. A sudden panic or madness seemed to have fallen on the Company.

"We shall all be scattered and lost," groaned Aragorn. "Boromir! I do not know what part you have played in this mischief, but help now! Go after those two young hobbits, and guard them at the least, even if you cannot find Frodo. Come back to this spot, if you find him, or any traces of him. I shall return soon."

Aragorn sprang swiftly away and went in pursuit of Sam. Just as he reached the little lawn among the rowans he overtook him, toiling uphill, panting and calling, *Frodo!*

"Come with me, Sam!" he said. "None of us should be alone. There is mischief about. I feel it. I am going to the top, to the Seat of Amon Hen, to see what may be seen. And look! It is as my heart guessed, Frodo went this way. Follow me, and keep your eyes open!" He sped up the path.

Sam did his best, but he could not keep up with Strider the Ranger, and soon fell behind. He had not gone far before Aragorn was out of sight ahead. Sam stopped and puffed. Suddenly he clapped his hand to his head.

"Whoa, Sam Gamgee!" he said aloud. "Your legs are too short, so use your head! Let me see now! Boromir isn't lying, that's not his way; but he hasn't told us everything. Something scared Mr. Frodo badly. He screwed himself up to the point, sudden. He made up his mind at last — to go. Where to? Off East. Not without Sam? Yes, without even his Sam. That's hard, cruel hard."

Sam passed his hand over his eyes, brushing away the tears. "Steady, Gamgee!" he said. "Think, if you can! He can't fly across rivers, and he can't jump waterfalls. He's got no gear. So he's got to get back to the boats. Back to the boats! Back to the boats, Sam, like lightning!"

Sam turned and bolted back down the path. He fell and cut his knees. Up he got and ran on. He came to the edge of the lawn of Parth Galen by the shore, where the boats were drawn up out of the water. No one was there. There seemed to be cries in the woods behind, but he did not heed them. He stood gazing for a moment, stock-still, gaping. A boat was sliding down the bank all by itself With a shout Sam raced across the grass. The boat slipped into the water.

"Coming, Mr. Frodo! Coming!" called Sam, and flung himself from the bank, clutching at the departing boat. He missed it by a yard. With a cry and a splash he fell face downward into deep swift water. Gurgling he went under, and the River closed over his curly head.

An exclamation of dismay came from the empty boat. A paddle swirled and the boat put about. Frodo was just in time to grasp Sam by the hair as he came up, bubbling and struggling. Fear was staring in his round brown eyes.

"Up you come, Sam my lad!" said Frodo. "Now take my hand!"

"Save me, Mr. Frodo!" gasped Sam. "I'm drownded. I can't see your hand."

"Here it is. Don't pinch, lad! I won't let you go. Tread water and don't flounder, or you'll upset the boat. There now, get hold of the side, and let me use the paddle!"

With a few strokes Frodo brought the boat back to the bank, and Sam was able to scramble out, wet as a water-rat. Frodo took off the Ring and stepped ashore again.

"Of all the confounded nuisances you are the worst, Sam!" he said.

"Oh, Mr. Frodo, that's hard!" said Sam shivering. "That's hard, trying to go without me and all. If I hadn't a guessed right, where would you be now?"

"Safely on my way."

"Safely!" said Sam. "All alone and without me to help you? I couldn't have a borne it, it'd have been the death of me."

"It would be the death of you to come with me, Sam," said Frodo, "and I could not have borne that."

"Not as certain as being left behind," said Sam.

"But I am going to Mordor."

"I know that well enough, Mr. Frodo. Of course you are. And I'm coming with you."

"Now, Sam," said Frodo, "don't hinder me! The others will be coming back at any minute. If they catch me here, I shall have to argue and explain, and I shall never have the heart or the chance to get off. But I must go at once. It's the only way."

"Of course it is," answered Sam. "But not alone. I'm coming too, or neither of us isn't going. I'll knock holes in all the boats first."

Frodo actually laughed. A sudden warmth and gladness touched his heart. "Leave one!" he said. "We'll need it. But you can't come like this without your gear or food or anything."

"Just hold on a moment, and I'll get my stuff!" cried Sam eagerly. "It's all ready. I thought we should be off today." He rushed to the camping place, fished out his pack from the pile where Frodo had laid it when he emptied the boat of his companions' goods, grabbed a spare blanket, and some extra packages of food, and ran back.

"So all my plan is spoilt!" said Frodo. "It is no good trying to escape you. But I'm glad, Sam. I cannot tell you how glad. Come along! It is plain that we were meant to go together. We will go, and may the others find a safe road! Strider will look after them. I don't suppose we shall see them again."

"Yet we may, Mr. Frodo. We may," said Sam.

So Frodo and Sam set off on the last stage of the Quest together. Frodo paddled away from the shore, and the River bore them swiftly away, down the western arm, and past the frowning cliffs of Tol Brandir. The roar of the great falls drew nearer. Even with such help as Sam could give, it was hard work to pass across the current at the southward end of the island and drive the boat eastward towards the far shore.

At length they came to land again upon the southern slopes of Amon Lhaw. There they found a shelving shore, and they drew the boat out, high above the water, and hid it as well as they could behind a great boulder. Then shouldering their burdens, they set off, seeking a path that would bring them over the grey hills of the Emyn Muil, and down into the Land of Shadow.

Here ends the first part of the history of the War of the Ring.

The second part is called THE TWO TOWERS, *since the events recounted in it are dominated by* ORTHANC, *the citadel of Saruman, and the fortress of* MINAS MORGUL *that guards the secret entrance to Mordor; it tells of the deeds and perils of all the members of the now sundered fellowship, until the coming of the Great Darkness.*

The third part tells of the last defence against the Shadow, and the end of the mission of the Ring-bearer in THE RETURN OF THE KING.

Fiction

Joan Aiken	**Blackground** (A)
Kingsley Amis	**One Fat Englishman**
Julian Barnes	**A History of The World in 10 1/2 Chapters** (A)
Stan Barstow	**Joby**
Samuel Beckett	**More Pricks Than Kicks**
Heinrich Böll	**The Lost Honour of Katharina Blum**
Jorge Louis Borges	**The Book of Sand**
Vera Brittain	**Account Rendered**
Vera Brittain	**Born 1925**
Anita Brookner	**A Start in Life**
Anthony Burgess	**The Piano Players** (A)
Truman Capote	**Breakfast at Tiffany's**
Peter Carey	**Oscar and Lucinda** (A)
J L Carr	**A Month in the Country**
Bruce Chatwin	**Utz**
Susan Cheever	**Doctors and Women**
Tessa Dahl	**Working for Love**
Margaret Drabble	**The Millstone**
William Faulkner	**The Sound and the Fury**
Penelope Fitzgerald	**The Beginning of Spring**
Jock Gallagher	**To the Victor the Spoils**
Jane Gardam	**The Sidmouth Letters**
David Garnett	**Aspects of Love**
André Gide	**La Symphonie Pastorale**
Stella Gibbons	**Cold Comfort Farm**
B M Gill	**Time and Time Again**

(A) Large Print books available in Audio

Fiction

Nadine Gordimer	**A Sport of Nature**
George & Weedon Grossmith	**The Diary of a Nobody**
Doris Grumbach	**The Magician's Girl**
O Henry	**Gift of the Magi**
Christopher Isherwood	**Goodbye to Berlin**
Thomas Keneally	**Towards Asmara**
Margaret Kennedy	**The Constant Nymph**
Rudyard Kipling	**The Light That Failed**
Gaston Leroux	**The Phantom of the Opera**
Doris Lessing	**The Grass is Singing**
Doris Lessing	**The Fifth Child** (A)
Eric Linklater	**Sealskin Trousers**
Penelope Lively	**Passing On** (A)
David Lodge	**Nice Work** (A)
Jack London	**The Call of the Wild**
Carson McCullers	**The Heart is a Lonely Hunter**
Bernard Malamud	**The Fixer**
David Malouf	**Harland's Half Acre**
Robin Maugham	**The Servant**
Brian Moore	**The Lonely Passion of Judith Hearne**
W Somerset Maugham	**The Moon & Sixpence**
Katharine Moore	**Moving House**
Iris Murdoch	**Under the Net**
Edna O'Brien	**Girls in Their Married Bliss**
Edna O'Brien	**A Pagan Place**
Boris Pasternak	**The Last Summer**
Alan Paton	**Cry, The Beloved Country**

(A) Large Print books available in Audio

Fiction

Anthony Powell	**The Fisher King**
J B Priestley	**The Shapes of Sleep**
Mary Renault	**The Bull From the Sea**
Mary Shelley	**Frankenstein**
Alan Sillitoe	**Out of the Whirlpool**
Elizabeth Smart	**By Grand Central Station I Sat Down and Wept**
John Steinbeck	**Cannery Row** (A)
Jan Struther	**Mrs Miniver**
Sir Rabindranath Tagore	**Crescent Moon**
Angela Thirkell	**Wild Strawberries**
Colin Thubron	**Falling**
Alice Walker	**Meridian**
Marina Warner	**The Lost Father**
Evelyn Waugh	**Men at Arms**
Evelyn Waugh	**A Handful of Dust**
Fay Weldon	**The Wife's Revenge**
Rebecca West	**Sunflower**
Tennessee Williams	**The Roman Spring of Mrs Stone**
Edmund Wilson	**Memoirs of Hecate County**
Virginia Woolf	**Flush**

(A) Large Print books available in Audio

Short Stories

Angela Carter	**Fireworks**
Colette	**Gigi** and **The Cat**
A E Coppard	**The Higgler and Other Stories**
Roald Dahl	**Kiss Kiss**
Leon Garfield	**Shakespeare Stories**
Thomas Hardy	**Wessex Tales**
Nathaniel Hawthorne	**Tanglewood Tales**
Henry James	**Daisy Miller and other stories**
M R James	**A Warning to the Curious (A)**
D H Lawrence	**Love Among the Haystacks (A)**
Saki	**Beasts and Super-beasts**
Alan Sillitoe	**The Far Side of the Street**
Peter Ustinov	**The Disinformer**
Robert Westall	**Antique Dust**
Marguerite Yourcenar	**Oriental Tales**

(A) Large Print books available in Audio

Humour

Douglas Adams	**The Hitch Hiker's Guide to the Galaxy**
Mary Dunn	**Lady Addle Remembers**
	Echoes of Laughter
Giovanni Guareschi	**Don Camillo and the Devil**
Barry Pain	**The Eliza Stories**
Walter Carruthers Sellar & Robert Julian Yeatman	**1066 And All That**
Tom Sharpe	**Blott on the Landscape**
Tom Sharpe	**Porterhouse Blue**
Tom Sharpe	**Vintage Stuff** (A)
Tom Sharpe	**Wilt on High**
E OE Somerville & Martin Ross	**In Mr Knox's Country**
Sue Townsend	**True Confessions of Adrian Albert Mole, Margaret Hilda Roberts and Susan Lilian Townsend**

(A) Large Print books available in Audio

General Non-Fiction

Michael Bright	**The Living World**
Estelle Catlett	**Track Down Your Ancestors**
Bruce Chatwin	**What Am I Doing Here**
Phil Drabble	**One Man and His Dog**
Jonathan Goodman	**The Lady Killers**
Anita Guyton	**Healthy Houseplants A-Z**
Duff Hart-Davis	**Country Matters**
William R Hartson	**Teach Yourself Chess**
Stephen W Hawking	**A Brief History of Time**
Dr Richard Lacey	**Safe Shopping, Safe Cooking, Safe Eating**
Doris Lessing	**Particularly Cats and More Cats**
Vera Lynn	**We'll Meet Again**
Desmond Morris	**The Animals Roadshow**
Desmond Morris	**Dogwatching**
Desmond Morris	**Catlore**
Frank Muir & Denis Norden	**You Have My Word**
Shiva Naipaul	**An Unfinished Journey**
John Pilger	**A Secret Country**
R W F Poole	**A Backwoodsman's Year**
Valerie Porter	**Faithful Companions**
Beryl Reid	**Beryl, Food and Friends**
Sonia Roberts	**The Right Way to Keep Pet Birds**
Yvonne Roberts	**Animal Heroes**
June Whitfield	**Dogs' Tales**
Ian Wilson	**Undiscovered**
Andrew Young	**A Prospect of Flowers**

History, War and Reminiscences

Charles Allen	Plain Tales from the Raj
William Bligh	An Account of the
Robert Bowman (ed.)	Mutiny on HMS Bounty
John P Eaton &	
Charles Hass	Titanic: Destination Disaster
Richard Garrett	Great Escapes of World War II
John Harris	Dunkirk
Angela Lambert	1939: The Last Season of Peace
Frank Pearce	Sea War

Poetry and Drama

Lord Birkenhead	John Betjeman's Early Poems
Joan Duce	I Remember, I Remember...
Joan Duce	Remember, If You Will...
Dan Sutherland	Six Miniatures
Herbert W Wood	And All Shall Be Well

Cookery

Rabbi Lionel Blue	Kitchen Blues
Rose Elliot	Your Very Good Health
Grace Mulligan	Farmhouse Kitchen
Jennifer Davies	The Victorian Kitchen

Reference and Dictionaries

Moyra Bremner	Supertips to Make Life Easy
Margaret Ford	In Touch at Home
	The Lion Concise Bible Encyclopedia
	The Longman English Dictionary
	The Longman Medical Dictionary
	Longman Thesaurus